Benton Security Services Omnibus #1

By Christine D. Shuck

Includes Books 1-3:
Hired Gun
Smoke and Steel
Broken Code
and
two bonus short stories:
Better Choices
Learning to Speak

This is a work of fiction. Similarities to real people, places, or events are entirely coincidental.

BENTON SECURITY SERVICES OMNIBUS, BOOKS 1-3

First edition. September 24, 2023.

Copyright © 2023 Christine D. Shuck.

Hired Gun

Book 1

Blackmail Fail

Danny Witt loosened his tie, undid the top two buttons of his shirt, and let loose a victory whoop. He had done it, and now he was going to celebrate. His car, a beat-up hand-me-down, started up, the engine roaring loudly.

"This time next week it'll be a Lexus, by damn!" he said, his foot heavy on the accelerator as he pulled away from the curb and headed out of the city, west towards Denver.

Blackmail was a delicate thing, but Danny had handled it with a light touch, never giving an ultimatum, just reminding his boss of how much he had to lose if the information went public. Dirty deals and fraud. Danny had found the tip of the iceberg and dug in, discovering a laundry list of inflated real estate, payoffs, and irregular cost expenditures. Even a sorry tale of investors swindled out of their money. He had taken his time, realizing the gold mine at his fingertips. Right about now, Danny was sure that his boss was ruing the day Kurgen Real Estate had hired him for the accounting job.

And at a fire sale, by God. That measly $50k a year he made at Kurgen was barely enough to cover expenses, live a little, and pay the minimum on his student loans. Those damned student loans. The college tuition, books, and campus housing had taken up the bulk of the $167k. Sure, he had taken an extra year to finish college after spending most of his first-year guzzling beer at keggers and frat parties. *Hell, that's what college is for, right? Party all night, drink a couple of V8s and sit in the back of class and hope to God the professor doesn't pick on you.*

He had lived off that government-backed loan money. Now it had come due and it cost more than his basic living expenses combined. And that was just the minimum payment!

The briefcase on the front passenger seat included a banded stack of Benjamins that he was going to make use of, living it up while spending a weekend on the slopes with several of his buddies from his alma mater, Denver University.

As he settled in on I-70, he set the cruise control and turned up the volume on the aging radio. *Maybe a Beemer instead of a Lexus. I could handle making some payments, build up my credit.*

The road was clear; he'd gotten a late start, and most of the folks heading out of town for the weekend were well on their way. The cars left on the road were sparse and well-spaced, yet Danny didn't notice the white van following at a discreet distance. His mind was busy tallying the costs for a case of Grey Goose vodka and the huge bag of weed he was planning to splurge on. That would show his frat brothers that he wasn't such a loser after all.

His buddy Zach had started a business during college that mined data for the big-time online retailers and ended up selling the company for millions last year. He had lorded it over them, and given half a chance, he told them over and over how his new company was going to sell for quintuple his investment in a few years.

Jonesy wasn't financially well-off, but he had a goddamn alpaca farm and a baby on the way, way up in some Podunk town in the Colorado mountains. He grew some fine weed on the side since alpacas didn't pay squat. The weed was in better digs than Jonesy and his woman were in. They said they loved living in a yurt.

Yeah, sure they do.

Deep in a stand of trees, well covered and hidden from prying eyes, was a large barn, outfitted with the latest in lights. Jonesy had gotten off to a rocky start, but the week before had seen the biggest harvest yet, four friggin' pounds of Sour Diesel. That asshole was in fucking hippie heaven, a friggin' off-grid paradise on earth.

Then there was Mal. Mal hadn't ever graduated, disappearing halfway through their fourth year, dropping out to travel the world and write a bestseller, by God, that everyone was talking about and reading. Mal had described the book as the biggest pile of monumental horseshit he could have possibly written. But now he was a friggin' millionaire who lived out of hotels and couch-surfed his way through Europe. And, most recently, Australia and New Zealand, while writing about the folks he met and making an ass-ton of cash. And the load of pussy that dude got put them all to shame. It seemed that, short of being a brooding songwriter, writing a book and looking all melancholy and literate netted you more tail than you could shake a stick at.

Danny shook his head. Until the last few weeks, he had been in a depressive funk, alternating between hating his dad for insisting that he become an accountant *all because I was good at Monopoly at age fucking ten* and himself for letting the old bastard win. But following that trail of money, labyrinthine and hidden as it was, had been like winning the friggin' jackpot. He might be in a "stifling, boring job working for The Man" - as Jonesy had so aptly described it - but he was going to be fucking rich.

"Ten percent of the take, that's all I'm asking for," he said out loud to the empty car, the words lost in the roar as the car hurtled down the highway. His lips moved silently as he ran the numbers again. It would turn his salary into chump change in comparison. *Hell, I could get both a Mercedes* and *a Lexus. And fuck staying in that cruddy old apartment in Northeast; I'll move to a loft in downtown instead.*

He had copied all the data onto his laptop, and as a backup to the backup, he had also saved it to an SD card and his home computer. He had reassured his boss that the details of the corruption at Kurgen didn't need to be aired. Oh no, he was happy to be included in the Ponzi schemes and more; he even had suggestions on how they could better hide these corrupt transactions so that their financial misdeeds were not only nearly impossible to find, but they could be multiplied exponentially. More money for both of them. He had smiled, charmed his flustered and tense boss, and told him that this wasn't a *bad* thing, it was an *opportunity*.

Danny laughed out loud, the wind carrying it away. *Hell, I was born for this. Dear old Dad had no idea how perfect of a career this would be for me.* His dad had just wanted him out of the house. The teen years, followed by the endless college years of parties and smoking weed and playing video games had been a little too much for the old man. But he was from a different generation, after all, the generation that worked their fingers to the bone instead of making a few clicks on a computer and sitting back to rake in the dough. Dad wasn't a bad guy, he just wasn't very forward-thinking. *Ya gotta make the money work for you, Dad, not sweat all day for a dollar.*

As the hours passed and the radio stations faded into the distance, crackling with static and hiccups of voices, Danny shut the radio off, the mountains slowly rising around him, cutting off cell phone service completely until he reached a plateau of sorts. Ahead in the distance, in the thick darkness, he could see the lights from a car. It was pulled over on the side of the road.

Danny wasn't the type to stop and help. Hell, he couldn't even change a tire. But the sight of the scantily clad, hot-looking chick waving her arms at him had him hitting the brakes. He pulled over, his dented and worn Civic kicking up dust as he rolled to a stop. A friggin' IROC with a flat rear left tire was attractive enough, but the girl, with her skimpy skirt and skin-tight shimmering metallic top, barely left anything to the imagination. The Lycra hugged every tanned curve, and she bounced and smiled at him with kohl-rimmed blue eyes. Her legs were encased in boots with stiletto heels and her dark hair fell in cascades of curls past her shoulders. She walked over to his window.

"Oh my God, *thank you so much* for pulling over!" Her hair spilled over, brushing his side mirror, as a wash of Juicy Couture perfume filled his nose and he became eye-level with her tits. *Those cannot be real.* They were huge and stood out like two missiles. He leaned forward, trying to catch an eyeful of her round ass.

Danny smiled. "Hey there." *Let me just bend you over that hood there.* "Got a flat tire?"

She smiled at him, a pink tongue moistening her lips. "I do! I can't even get a tow truck to come fix it." She waved a cell phone in her left hand. "No service. I can't get a single bar up here! Could you help me?"

Danny nodded, "Uh, sure, let me see if my phone has any service. You never know, sometimes the different providers have a wider reach and all." He powered it on, checked the bars. "Well, shit."

"Maybe if you get out of the car the grade goes up a few feet." She suggested, wiggling her ass a little. Damn, but this girl was *smoking* hot. He stepped out of the car.

How hard could it be to change a tire? I'll bet if I did, she'd let me tap that sweet ass.

A few steps up didn't make a bit of difference. He tried his phone again, getting no love, not one bar of service. By then, bright beams from another vehicle lit the road up.

The headlights were set higher; perhaps it was a truck. He waved his arms and the vehicle slowed, pulling over next to them. Nope, it wasn't a truck, but a plain white van instead. The side door slid open and the dull dome light inside lit up two men, crouching on what looked like a plastic covered floor.

"Hey, would you guys be able to help change this tire?" he asked, walking towards them.

There were two loud pops like the sound of a backfiring car. Danny heard them, but didn't understand why his steps were slowing, faltering, as a bloom of red filled his shirt and searing pain obscured all rational thought. He looked down, his fingers shaking as he pulled them away from his shirt, covered in blood. He didn't understand. His legs buckled beneath him and he crumpled to the ground in a heap, legs twisting underneath, head slamming into the gravel.

He lay there, the sharp gravel digging into his back. He could see the hot chick approach, a dull gray handgun in one hand. She wasn't smiling anymore. She tilted her head, eyes assessing him, saying nothing.

Danny heard shoes crunching on gravel. "Shit, Zella, now there's blood on the ground. We needed this to be a clean hit. You couldn't wait for five more seconds, could you?" One of the men stood over him now, his eyes as cold as the woman's. "You saw the plastic was all laid out, for fuck's sake."

Above Danny, the night sky was filled with stars.

"I didn't like the way he looked at me," she said, her voice barely showing emotion.

One of them was red-hued and seemed bigger than the rest. That had to be Mars.

"Well, how did he look at you Zell?" the second man asked, appearing in Danny's line of sight.

He watched a flash of light fill the sky. He had never seen a shooting star before, but Danny was pretty sure he had just seen one now. He watched it light a path down, down, down before disappearing behind a mountain in the distance.

"Like he wanted to fuck me."

Maybe if he made a wish, it would be granted. And he would wake up and realize this was all a bad dream.

Both men laughed.

"What's so funny?" she asked, narrowing her gaze, her long, slender fingers tapping out a rhythm on the gun.

Coldness was spreading, radiating from his chest, to his arms, creeping up his fingers.

"Zella, everyone wants to fuck you," the other man said. "We just don't wanna get fuckin' murdered afterward." He turned back towards the other man. "What are those damned insects, the ones that bite off their mate's head during sex?"

"Praying mantis."

He snapped his fingers. "Yeah. That. You're a fucking praying mantis, Zella. Or a black widow. It's a wonder you ever get laid."

Zella stared at him impassively. "Whatever. He stared at my tits too long." She aimed the gun at Danny's head and pulled the trigger.

The stars turned to black.

"Damn it, Zella. You clean that shit up. Fuck if there aren't brains to clean up now. That's on you. We weren't supposed to leave any evidence. Hank and I will get the meat." He picked up Danny's legs and motioned for Hank to grab his arms. Together they hauled Danny Witt's corpse into the van and slammed the door shut.

"Heads up." the third man, still in the driver's seat of the van, said, as headlights flashed in the distance.

The first man turned to Hank. "You're up. Inflate the tire, take care of dumping the car, and then catch a ride with Zella."

"'Long as that crazy bitch don't try to waste me too," he muttered, grunting as he straightened up, checking for blood spatter on his clothes.

"I heard that." Zella was rinsing her fingers with some water from her Contigo, having tossed several handfuls of bloody gravel and a piece of skull over the edge of the precipice a few feet away. She smiled at him, her teeth gleaming in the gloom. It was a predatory and dangerous look. "Wanna see my tits?"

The man resisted a shudder even as his dick jumped in his pants at the thought of Zella's pair of perfect tits. If he ever did get to see them it would probably also be the last thing he saw before he died. Zella was like a black widow and far too crazy to mess with. "Nah, I'm good." He avoided looking in her eyes.

She grinned, baring her white teeth. Her incisors looked sharp in the moonlight.

The beams of light sliced through the night; the car was closer now. The van pulled away, a shower of gravel in its wake as it sped up, matching highway speed.

Hank turned to the business of re-inflating the IROC's tire as another car slowed down and stopped. Inside were a young couple, with two kids in the backseat. The wife rolled her window down, a bright smile on her face, "Hi there, need any help?"

"Nah, we got it handled." Hank could see Zella's hand twitching, her fingers busy caressing the handgun she held just behind her slim, muscled back.

The husband leaned forward, ogling the IROC, and Zella.

Hank closed his eyes, *oh buddy, you do not want to do that.*

"You sure?"

"Almost got it. No worries."

"Daddy, Daddy!" a small boy yelled from the back, "Deer's blood on the ground, Daddy! See all the red?"

Zella stepped closer to the car, a predatory smile painted on her face, her even white teeth gleaming. "There was a deer. It ran off."

"Oh Benny, don't look at that!" the kid's mom said. "Poor little deer."

The dad persisted, his eyes focused on Zella's tits. Her hand caressed the gun now tucked in her waistband. "I got a decent jack in the trunk."

Hank stepped forward. It was one thing to waste the target, but a whole family? Zella was itching for another round. "I got it," he said with a little more force. "Almost done."

"You heard the man, Patrick," the woman in the passenger seat said, her mouth pursed in disapproval at how her husband was staring at Zella. "He's got it. Let's go, or we won't get to my sister's until after midnight."

Hank breathed a sigh of relief when the small car, at the urging of the wife, finally pulled away.

Far from Colorado, a phone rang. The room was dark. "What is your status?"

"It's done. I got another guy taking care of the files at his apartment," Hank updated the voice on the other end.

"Excellent." The voice was smooth, emotionless. Hank could hear keys clicking in the background. "Your fee has been paid in full."

"I appreciate it." He listened as the phone line clicked. The boss didn't waste words. He nodded in Zella's direction. "Time to go."

She smiled at him. It made his skin crawl. "I'll drive."

Hank nodded and said nothing. *Next job, I'll be damned if I'm getting stuck with this crazy bitch.* He settled into the car and cinched his seatbelt into place as she accelerated, wheels spinning, engine screaming, onto the dark highway.

Slipshod

"Can I help you?" The pretty strawberry-blond girl at the reception desk was staring at him, a friendly, professional smile on her face.

Alex gulped, winded from his half-jog down the hallway outside. The ticket had specified that one of the techs needed to arrive by 10 a.m. Traffic, snarled and slow around highway construction and blocked lanes, and difficulty finding parking had meant that he was nearly forty-five minutes late.

He gaped at her; she was one of *those* kinds of girls. Her strawberry-blond hair and big blue eyes combined with a floral sheer top over a white cami and shiny gold earrings in her delicate ears. She was pretty. One of those girls who combined beauty with complete unattainability for someone like him. And he reacted to them much like Raj on *Big Bang Theory*, with a wide-eyed silence. Standing there in the office, with its high-end carpet and sleek, spotless furniture, he willed his tongue to work.

"I'm uh," he blinked, "Uh, I'm from…"

I can't even remember the name of the company. What kind of loser can't remember the name of the company they work for?

It was Alex's third week, the training was over, and now he was on his own. Thankfully, the young goddess who had robbed him so effectively of his words was also kind.

"Are you from Nerds R Us?" she asked, smiling brightly. "I've been expecting you. You must be new; where's Ernie?"

Alex stammered. "Uh, yeah, I'm uh, the nerd. I mean, I'm from the Nerds." He closed his eyes, winced, and started again, "Sorry. I'm Alex, from, uh, from Nerds R Us."

The girl smiled again, wider this time, and his pulse began to race.

"I'm Trish." She leaned back and to one side. "Here it is." She placed the machine on the desk and pushed it towards him.

"Oh, right, um, should I stay here or..."

"We have an open office just over there." Trish pointed to a small office within eyesight of the reception desk. "It's, um, not being used at the moment." A look of discomfort crossed her face. Just a flash, before being replaced with a smile again.

Alex picked up the laptop and nodded. "Okay, great, I'll get started on it. Should I just..." He pointed at the office and shrugged, his body language forming a question.

"Yep, just over there. Make yourself at home and let me know if you need anything," Trish chirped. Her phone began to ring and her attention shifted. "Kurgen Real Estate, how can I direct your call?"

The office she had directed him to was small, but it had a great view of the front desk and Trish's shapely legs peeking out of her conservative, yet short, skirt. He sat down, looked at her talking animatedly on the phone, and sighed.

If only the view could be like this every day.

He set the laptop onto the empty desk, plugged it in, and then opened his briefcase and reviewed the ticket.

He was supposed to re-image the drive and delete any business files from the laptop or the cloud. The sign-in screen appeared, the cursor blinking.

"Are you doing okay?" Trish was standing in the doorway, and Alex jumped, his heart hammering in his chest.

"What? Uh, yeah, I'm doing fine. Um, just running some diagnostics." He tried to play it cool, but his words came out fast and ran together.

Face it, dude, there is nothing cool about you. Chicks like this, they don't go out with geeks like you.

"Well, um, would you like the light on?"

Alex realized he was sitting in the dark. No wonder he couldn't find the power strip. He stared at the dark screen of the laptop, back up at Trish, and felt a warmth spread over his cheeks. "I, uh, I mean..."

"It's right here." She reached over and flipped on the light, flooding the room with a bright fluorescent glare.

Alex blinked and blushed even harder. "Uh, thanks."

Trish smiled, her lips curving up in delight. "No problem." She stood there for a moment and then spoke again. "It was so weird. The guy who had this laptop, Danny, he just stopped showing up for work one day." She shrugged. "I mean, this was his office here. The last day he worked, he was walking around like a cat who just ate the cream. Said he had found a 'lucrative opportunity' - whatever that meant - and asked me if I'd go out to dinner with him the next weekend."

Alex swallowed; his mouth was hanging open and he hoped she hadn't noticed. "So, uh, did you?"

"Did I what?"

"Go, uh, go out with him." He stumbled over the words. The sweat was so bad in his hands that they felt damp.

"Oh, gosh, no." She gave him a wide-eyed look. "He was a bit of a perv. He was always staring at me. I'd look over and he'd be staring, and then he would give me this smile that just creeped me out."

Alex nodded and made a mental note not to stare.

At least, don't stare a lot.

"I mean, I didn't tell him *no*, but I really didn't want to tell him *yes*, because, you know..." she said and shrugged again, "...perv vibes."

Alex looked over at a cardboard box filled with personal items and asked, "Is that his stuff?"

"Yeah, he never picked it up. They even tried contacting him and his landlord is looking for him too. He just dropped everything and *left*. It was crazy!" She paused for a moment, leaning out of the small office to look around. "I get so bored sitting at that desk all day. There's no one interesting to talk to."

Alex's face must have betrayed his concern over that.

"I mean," Trish said, looking embarrassed, "I'm sure *you* are interesting. I've just been talking away and not giving you a chance!" She leaned in closer and her perfume, full of floral notes, washed over him. "So, what did happen to Ernie?"

Ernie Ott had been caught in a blackmail scheme with a client and been fired three weeks ago, just as Alex was being hired. On his second day of work, instead of accompanying Ernie on his rounds, he had found himself with Bob, a portly tech with a receding hairline and persistent mournful expression. It had been the longest two weeks of his life working with Bob. By the end of it, Alex had dreaded going to work. It felt like Bob's gloom was infectious.

Meanwhile, the rumors in the small army of IT nerds had spread fast. The client in question had been a well-known call girl with a rather elite clientele. From the mayor, city leaders, and several well-placed businessmen, she had slowly built her clientele. At some point, she had struck up a relationship with Ernie. Whether it was Ernie's idea or hers, the webcam hidden in a potted plant over a period of three months had netted its fair share of indiscretions.

Ernie would then approach the target and give them a memory stick with the videos and stills taken in compromising positions and suggest a sum of money to keep quiet, and a bigger sum of money if they wanted the originals to go away forever. It had been quite effective for the first two, and rather disastrous with the third. Between the man beating Ernie within an inch of his life, placing his Smith & Wesson 9mm in the would-be blackmailer's mouth and suggesting he tell him where the duplicate memory stick was hidden, and then retrieving and destroying the evidence - the jig was up.

The fact that the third target was also a partner in Nerds R Us, silent yet influential due to his mob connections, meant that Ernie was out of a job as well as nursing two black eyes, a broken nose, and two fractured knees. Despite clear evidence to the contrary, he was surprisingly closemouthed to the police who questioned him at length after he was released from the hospital.

Alex couldn't tell Trish any of that. "He uh, I think he moved out of state."

It wasn't a lie. From what he had heard, Ernie hadn't bothered to move out of his ratty efficiency apartment near Twenty-Eighth Street. He had packed what he could carry, hobbled to his car, and left town.

Probably the smartest move he could have made.

"Oh." Trish peeked outside of the office, and then turned back, shrugged. "He was kind of, I don't know, kind of greasy. Like a used car salesman or something." Her intonation was unusual, not with the typical Midwestern twang.

Alex had stopped sweating as much. His pulse, though, showed no signs of slowing down. He was in the presence of something rare, a *nice* pretty girl. *It's like finding a unicorn in space.*

Trish, after another glance outside, walked closer and sat down on the corner of the desk. She was, Alex decided, absolutely perfect. A perfect pink tongue darted out between her lips and Alex's left knee began to jump uncontrollably, the sweaty palms returned and he felt a flush in his cheeks.

"So, tell me about you. How long have you been with Nerds R Us?"

Alex was doing his best to stammer out a response when the doorway was filled with a platinum blonde woman in her early 50s. Perhaps older, it was hard to tell. The woman appeared to be on good terms with plastic surgery. Anything that could be tucked and lifted, had been.

"There you are, Patricia!" Blanche stood there, her lips thin and curving into a false smile, her eyes cold.

Trish flinched at the sound of the woman's voice, and quickly stood. "Ms. Artinian! I'm sorry I left the desk, I was just making sure Alex has everything he needs."

"Alex, is it?" Blanche advanced into the tiny room and Trish skittered around her, heading back to her desk as the phone began to ring.

"Yes, ma'am." He felt a wave of dislike wash over him and tried his best to hide it.

"Well, good, I'm glad you decided to finally make it here." Blanche made a show of examining her watch, eyebrows raised. and face pinched in disapproval. "Standard terminated employee procedure. Wipe the hard drive, reformat it - or whatever it is that you do - and then return it to the front desk." She glanced at her watch again. "How long will it take?"

"Uh, if there aren't any problems, I should be done by noon." He thought of apologizing, but then remembered how Trish had snapped to. If he were a betting man, he would lay down money that Blanche was one of those closet dictators who ruled the office with a fake smile and venom. He had run into a few since starting with Nerds R Us, and they were difficult to deal with. Something in him bristled at the way Trish had jumped when she heard Blanche's voice.

"Excellent." She turned to go, looked around and then asked, "Where's Ernie?"

Alex shrugged and said, "I don't know, ma'am, sorry."

"Hm. Well, let me know if you have any questions." She walked away, towards the reception desk, as Trish hung up the phone. "I'll be out of the office for the rest of the day; forward my calls."

"Yes, Ms. Artinian!" Trish smiled brightly. Alex watched her as Trish's eyes tracked Blanche out of the main set of doors. The girl's shoulders slumped in relief as soon as the elevator doors in the hallway beyond slid shut. She turned, rolled her eyes, and then flashed a dazzling smile at him before walking back over.

"Whew!" She sat back down on the corner of his desk. Alex's pulse began to race again. "She is a beast, let me tell you. Once, I slipped off my heels for just a few minutes and was walking around in my stocking feet. She said it 'wasn't professional' and I swear she *intentionally* stood on my toes in the coffee room with one of those stiletto heels of hers. It *hurt*. I had a bruise for *weeks*."

Alex's cheeks flushed. "Man, that's just, that *sucks*." He bristled at the thought of Trish's tiny feet being crushed under the older woman's pricey pumps. A fantasy of stepping forward and forcing Trish's boss to back off ran pell-mell through his mind. It ended with the pretty girl giving him a kiss in return. The thought of it caused his entire body to react. He hunched over, desperate to hide his sudden erection.

I don't need her thinking I'm a perv.

Trish brightened. "You are so sweet!" She leaned in and tapped his nose with one pink fingernail. "I know some girls go for the bad boys, but

I like the sweet ones." She paused, glanced back at the empty office, and swiveled towards him with a smile that was both intimate and exciting. "So, what should we do?"

"Well, I, uh." Alex felt the flush creeping back into his face and the sweat gathering. "I need to work on this laptop here."

"Well, of course you do. But *later*. Everyone, except me of course, is at a team-building event." She pointed at the clock. "Yep, in about five minutes they are going to be locked inside of a room for four hours. It's a mega-event at Escape Room - unless someone drops dead of a heart attack or gets a serious case of claustrophobia, *none* of them will be back until nearly the end of the day, if at all. No one important is going to call, and I can forward the phones to the service and then just write down all the messages and distribute them on Monday like I normally would. I'm always the first one here anyway." She grinned mischievously, brushed her hair back and tucked it behind her ear. "So, what should we do?"

Attraction warred with a healthy dose of fear. He was the new guy, and he couldn't afford to lose this job. But one of the prettiest girls who had ever bothered to talk to him wanted to spend the day with him...how could he say "no" to that?

"Give me twenty minutes. I'll set the reformat to running and cut a couple of corners, but it will get the job done."

Trish clapped her hands together and wiggled with excitement. "Perfect!" She slid off the desk. "I'll go freshen up."

Alex began the process on the laptop, noting first that an SD card had been left in the machine. He popped it out and sat it on top of the open laptop bag. He needed to ask his boss what Kurgen typically did with SD cards; were they to be reviewed before disposal? One of the other techs, Ian, had told Alex about finding porn on an SD card once. He glanced out of the room, but Trish still wasn't back. Should he look at it? He began to reach for it, thought again of the story Ian had told, and decided against it.

It would be just my luck and have something over the top on it and she would walk in at just the wrong moment and think it was mine. No thanks!

He stared at it and said, "Fuck it, I'm not getting in trouble either way." He unzipped a deep pocket and let the small card slide into it. "SD card? What SD card?"

He watched the bar on the machine slowly crawl towards completion. He had already accessed the cloud and wiped the files off it. The notes on the work order had stated that everything important had already been backed up.

Freshening up took all the twenty minutes he had requested, plus some. She disappeared into the ladies' restroom and emerged dressed in tight, hip-hugging blue jeans and a knit top that conformed to her curvy breasts. Her lips were sporting a pale pink with a clear gloss, and her lashes were longer than humanly possible. She smelled divine, the scent of her perfume sliding off her in waves through the air. She walked around the desk and peeked over his shoulder, resting one hand lightly on his arm.

"You ready?"

Alex's leg jiggled under the desk. "Um, sure, where should we go?"

Her lips curved up, shining, pink, and perfect. "Anywhere. Everywhere. Take me somewhere weird and cool."

It was a beautiful Friday afternoon, after all, and Alex slipped his hand into hers and smiled at her. He searched his mind for the best place to take her. "Have you ever been to the hair museum in Independence?"

She blinked and then grinned. "Nope, but it definitely sounds weird and cool. Let's go!" Hand in hand, they exited the building, Trish giggling like a giddy schoolgirl.

The laptop sat on her desk - zipped up and neatly put away, reformatted and ready for the next user. A new employee was starting on Monday.

Anomaly

"Mr. Endon?" The voice at his door was tentative, and Morris tore his gaze away from the stack of contracts he was reviewing with some difficulty.

"Hm, yes?" The girl looked familiar. He'd seen her in the office kitchen the other day fiddling with the coffeemaker.

"I'm Lila, the new data analyst." Her long black hair was pulled back in a neat bun and she was dressed business conservative in a demure silk blouse and gray pencil skirt, something Morris appreciated more and more each day as the Millennials continued to make inroads into the workforce. They brought with them a measure of fashion that seemed completely inappropriate for the office - he still couldn't fathom how golf shirts were considered business casual. Business casual was not wearing a tie, for Christ sake!

"Right, Lila Bu...Ben..."

"Benoit, sir. Lila Benoit."

"Ah yes, Miss Benoit." Morris smiled at the girl and leaned back in his chair. "Please come in."

"I hope I'm not interrupting something important," Lila said as she entered the room, her eyes on the stack of papers on his desk. "I could come back later when you aren't so busy."

He rubbed his eyes. "Frankly, I could use a break. I've been at this for two hours straight. Sit down, sit down."

The girl sat, her long fingers fiddling with the printout in her hand. She nibbled on her lip, obviously ill at ease.

"You started last month, right?"

"Actually, it was in June, Mr. Endon, so almost four months now."

"Please, call me Morris." He smiled at her. "That's right, I was out of the country at the time. You have been reporting to Blanche, isn't that right?"

"Yes sir. And I'm sorry to bother you about this, but Blanche is out of the office and I found an anomaly that, well, it doesn't make sense." She leaned forward and slid the printout onto his desk.

Morris squinted at it; he had accidentally grabbed the wrong pair of glasses as he left the house, picking up his old prescription instead of his newer pair. The letters and numbers remained slightly blurry, but he could still suss out what it was saying.

"A sales report from six months ago?"

"It was in my laptop's files, but it doesn't match any sales report I have seen before. This one lists properties we don't have any record of owning through Kurgen Real Estate. It also shows transactions back and forth between an Oladni Investment Corp, but I don't find any records of such an organization."

Morris kept his reaction neutral. "How odd. I've never heard of this company either; perhaps it was some practice spreadsheet? Maybe something from a training exercise?"

Lila shrugged. "I thought that at first, but then the amounts and dates lined up exactly to a sales report from six months ago, just not the *names*. Everything else matched. And..."

Morris interrupted her, "Well it's obviously not something of ours. As you said, the names of the companies don't match. I fail to see why this is important."

Lila's face betrayed her nervousness. "I guess you're right, sir."

"Please, call me Morris." He tapped the page. "So, this was in your files?"

"Yes, on my laptop. I ran across it when I was preparing data for the upcoming quarterly report. It's just...*odd*."

Morris shrugged, trying his best to appear unconcerned. He could feel sweat beading on his forehead. *Had they turned on the heat?*

"Well, it isn't anything that I recognize. Hell, you could probably delete it and chalk it up as something the technician preparing your computer missed removing. I tell you what." He reached into his desk drawer and rummaged around. "Save it onto this flash drive and drop it on my desk. I'm heading out for lunch and meetings, but I'll look at it later." He handed her the flash drive.

"Thank you, sir, err...*Morris*, I'll do that." Lila looked relieved as she took the flash drive from his outstretched hand. "Sorry to bother you."

"Not at all, Lila, I have an open-door policy around here, and you are more than welcome to stop by if you have any questions or concerns."

He watched the girl leave and the broad smile on Morris's face dropped away.

How was this possible?

He picked up the phone. "Arlene? I need you to look into the records for Ms. Benoit's work laptop. Who had the machine before her?"

Dread formed in a pit in the center of his stomach at her answer. "Let's see, it looks like it was Danny Witt's machine. Wasn't that the accountant that quit and then his family came looking for him?"

Morris forced his voice to sound nonchalant. "Didn't he end up in Tahiti or climbing the Alps or some other ridiculous place?"

Arlene, who was prone to gossip, clucked her tongue and said, "His family insisted he hadn't contacted them, but who knows, you know my niece, well niece by marriage, did something similar. She vanished off the face of the earth for nearly three years before showing up in Detroit, married to some mafioso. It about broke my sister-in-law's heart. Between you and me, the girl always was a bit off. But now he's in prison and she lives in some mansion and is married to someone else with questionable business practices. You just never know."

"Indeed. Thank you, Arlene." He set down the phone and pressed his fingers to his temples, taking several deep breaths in and out. He got up and quietly shut the door to his office before returning to his desk. He picked up his phone and dialed, waited for the familiar voice to answer. "We have a problem but I think I've handled it."

"What kind of problem?" asked the voice on the other end.

"Danny Witt's computer still had one of the files on it. It must not have been reformatted completely. The new girl, the data analyst, found it and brought it into my office today."

"I see."

Morris felt sweat bead along his forehead yet again. "I told her to copy the file onto a flash drive and then delete it from her computer."

"It seems we have been in this place before," the voice said.

"I know, but she doesn't know anything, she just had questions." Morris could feel his anxiety rising.

"She's a data analyst," the voice said, hardening, "she can put two and two together."

"If she hands over the info and wipes it from her computer, it will all be a non-issue."

"We shall see. I'll have Lucifer go through the reports on Benoit's computer and make sure she has done as you asked. If not, then you know what will need to happen."

Morris felt a rivulet of sweat run down the back of his collar. "I'm sure it won't come to that."

God, he really hoped it wouldn't. Witt, he'd had it coming. He'd sauntered in as smug as he could be, looking like the cat that swallowed the canary. He hadn't been smiling in the end.

The line clicked and went dead, and Morris stared at it even as the dial tone sounded through the receiver.

Shit. Please don't let it come to that.

Lila had returned to her desk, a feeling of disquiet lodging lightly in the back of her brain. The document was odd, but Mr. Endon, *Morris, he said to call him Morris*, was undoubtedly right. It didn't match any of the companies and transactions they normally had, so this had to just be some anomaly, some practice spreadsheet from whoever had the laptop before her.

She stared at the document, open on her laptop. There was just something about it she couldn't place, something that bothered her. She stuck the memory stick into a free port and clicked File Save As. The file name, Jackpot, had been the thing that had caught her attention when she had first found the SD card.

God, why didn't I tell Mr. Endon it was on an SD card in the laptop bag? I could have just given that to him instead of the flash drive.

She left the SD card where it was, plugged into the laptop, and typed "odd file" into the file name field and hit Enter. Too late she realized she hadn't saved it to the E drive where the flash drive had appeared when she plugged it in.

"Damn it, where the hell did, I put it now?" she muttered, clicking File Save As again and making sure to choose the E drive this time.

"Talking to yourself again? A sure sign you need to stop working so hard and come have lunch with me at Nara." Kaylee's voice interrupted Lila from her plan to hunt down wherever she had saved the file.

"Oh, I don't know if I should, Kaylee." She stopped long enough to smile at her friend. Kaylee was decked out in a gorgeous pale gray linen suit with Jimmy Choo shoes elevating her diminutive frame by six inches or more.

"Should?" Kaylee shook her head and strode into Lila's office. "Lila, you don't have to work ten hours a day, seven days a week. You are doing fabulous here; Blanche was talking you up the other day and that woman isn't a fan of *anybody*. C'mon, last time you skipped out on lunch at Nara's you *promised* me you would come with me the next time. And that time is now."

"I just need to get this flash drive over to Mr. Endon and..."

Kaylee leaned over the laptop and pointed. "This one right here?"

"Yes, I..." Lila's voice trailed off as Kaylee slipped the flash drive out of the port and grinned at her.

"I'll be right back." Seconds later she reappeared. "It's delivered." She leaned over the desk and Lila was hit with a gentle breeze of Kaylee's perfume, Bulgari Jasmine Noir. "Lila, all work and no play makes for a dull friend. C'mon, their grilled salmon salad is to die for. And you haven't lived until you have tried the spicy coconut curry." She grinned mischievously and lowered her voice. "Blanche won't be in for the rest of the day and neither will Mr. Endon. We could grab a Pomo Cosmo and slip in a little late...no one would notice or care."

"I wish I could Kaylee, I just..."

"Build your own bento box."

"Have a ton of work left before..."

"Crispy smoky tofu roll!"

"Really need to..."

"Come with me to Nara's. I *know*. Now grab your jacket and let's get going before the noon rush hits!"

Lila laughed and acquiesced. When Kaylee set her sights on something, there was no stopping her. "Okay, okay, but I'm sticking to the Nara Cure; there's no alcohol in it."

"Well, I suppose that's acceptable, but only if we split the tempura rumchata cheesecake bites at the end. You have to start living a little, Lila; life is too short for such a Spartan existence!"

Lila rolled her eyes as she reached for her coat. "Right, because a new car and a new apartment isn't enough right now."

"It isn't. Girl, you are in your 20s, no kids, no husband, no commitments. Live a little, will you? We could go by the Plaza this evening and go shopping for shoes. You have to at least visit Aldo and see this gorgeous shipment of boots they just got in."

Lila shook her head. "Not a chance. I've got a one-on-one scheduled with my kickboxing instructor at six. Besides, my wallet couldn't handle a hit from a place on the Plaza, no way."

Kaylee sighed. "Fine. Nara for now, but I'll take you out shopping soon. You need to get out more. How are you ever going to meet anyone if you don't do anything but work and sleep?"

They left the office, bantering back and forth as they went.

That evening, long after the employees of Kurgen Real Estate had left the building, a young girl sporting a piercing in each eyebrow, her lip, nose, and more ran a report. It consolidated the data collected through the keylogger software into a series of data sets that showed her clearly every movement Lila Benoit had made that day. From a quick visit to the Prius dealership website to schedule regular maintenance on her new car, to a handful of Facebook Messenger exchanges with another office worker and obvious friend, Kaylee Stromm, Lucifer paged through every moment of Lila's work day.

She picked up the phone and pressed speed dial. The phone rang twice. "You have an update for me?"

"I do. It looks like she accessed the file in question from an SD card, saved it to her personal Dropbox account, and then placed it on the flash drive. She probably went to lunch then and at 1:52 p.m. she removed the SD card from the drive."

"I see."

"Do you need me to check anything else on this user?"

"No. Thank you, Lucifer." The line went dead.

The girl stared at the phone in her hand, "Okay then." She shrugged and closed the report, turning to the paused game on the other screen. "Let the Battle of Azeroth begin!"

Miles away, Dominic's phone buzzed in his pocket. He handed the waitress a crisp one-hundred-dollar bill, saying, "Keep the change," and slid the phone out of his pocket. "Riehl."

"I have a job for you. It's right up your alley."

Dominic smiled again, nodding to the waitress as he exited the building. He would be back; their saag paneer had been exceptional. "Go on." He reached his car, slid inside it, and closed the door.

"Kansas City, Friday evening, make it look like a burglary or assault turned deadly. Your choice. I'm sending over the basics now." The phone vibrated and he pulled it from his ear so that he could see the picture. He would print it out when he got home. The woman was smoking hot. Dominic grinned; he was going to enjoy this.

"Got it. My standard fee applies." His phone dinged again, this time showing a figure with five zeros behind it.

"I've sent over your retainer. The rest payable after the contract is complete," the voice on the other end of the line said.

"I'll update you then," Dominic answered and the line clicked as the other caller hung up. Dominic tossed his phone into the passenger seat and hummed to himself as he started the car and drove away. It had been more than a month since his last contract and he had been getting antsy.

This call had been the perfect end to his evening.

Hitman

Lila's heightened sense of smell may have eliminated the first half-second of surprise, and it certainly saved her life. Such a short amount of time, yet in retrospect, so vital to gaining the upper hand. Dominic Riehl sussed this out hours later, obsessing over how badly he had screwed up while nursing a set of swollen and painful testicles, along with bruised ribs. He would curse himself for a full three days, as he hobbled around the cramped apartment he had rented and listened to the squabbling voices of the tenants above, below, and on all sides through the thin, cheap walls.

If he hadn't indulged in that damned Indian buffet on 75th and Wornall, she wouldn't have turned at just the last millisecond, ensuring that his initial rush towards her was off by just enough. It had to have been the smell of curry that had given him away before he could grab her and stun her with a crack to the jaw. Just another half-second is all he would have needed as he swiftly emerged from the shadows in the poorly lit underground garage.

Lila had found the parking garage in her apartment building slightly creepy. Chalk it up to watching an unhealthy amount of horror movies in her teens, or the news of another body found in a vacant home in the Northland two nights previously, but her spider sense had tingled the second she stepped into the dimly lit expanse of concrete pillars and empty cars. A disastrous blind date set up by her boss Morris had ended in her waiting for some loser that never showed, before she gave up in disgust and ended the night at a late-night movie at the AMC Barrywoods. Just her and her delectable dates - twins by damn - a bag of popcorn and a large box of Junior Mints.

The movie had been creepy and sinister, which would have been great if she were hooked up with a special honey to cuddle up to during the worst scenes. Instead, she had seen the movie with a handful of other pathetic loners, each of them lounging or scrunched in their seats in turn among a sea of empty red leather recliners. She could have just waited for it to come to Redbox and rented it alone.

She pulled into her parking spot, gliding silently into position with her fuel-efficient wunderkind Prius. She noticed that the light near the stairwell door was out again. Why they couldn't use the LED lights, instead of those wattage-sucking losers, Lila couldn't understand. The cheap bulb hadn't lasted more than a month this time. It was dangerously dark in the underground garage and Lila felt a tingle of fear wash over her.

All those damned specters coming around corners. Get a hold of yourself, girl!

She slipped out of her seat, grabbed her purse in her right hand, and closed the door behind her. The remote locked and alarmed it with a quiet chirp. Her heels clicked on the cement floor and Lila felt annoyance all over again. She had dressed up, and for what? Some loser no-show. She hadn't been interested, but Morris had been so insistent. And really, how do you say "no" to your new boss? She was still worried about making a good impression; it had only been four months since she started there, after all.

As she neared the stairwell door, there was an odd odor, something she couldn't quite pinpoint, and then the shadows moved impossibly, coalescing into a man's shape closing in on her. She blinked, delayed for a moment over the impossibility of what she was seeing, a rush of darkness coming straight at her. In the last crucial millisecond, her body reacted and she turned and shifted to one side as a man smelling of curry attempted to tackle her. The mixed martial arts training she had been taking for the past four years came in handy, and so did those endless miles on the treadmill in her apartment building's exercise room, earphones in her ears, music turned up, as she did her best to avoid giving her neighbor in Apartment 1503 any opportunity to ask her out.

Her response, despite being slowed by the stiletto heels she had worn for her "didn't bother to show up or even call" failed date, probably saved her life. Instead of being thrown against the pillar, or being knocked unconscious and choked out from behind, she was now facing her attacker, hands at the ready as he course-corrected and came at her again. He moved fast and powered through her side kick to his groin with a pained grunt, before grabbing her leg and twisting it, pushing her off balance. Lila hit the pillar hard, her right shoulder popped, and the corresponding arm lit up in a bright wash of pain. It felt as if she had touched a live wire, her arm burning and tingling. When she tried to move it, it refused to respond, shocked by the violence done to it. Lila's brain was slow to catch up. Sparring with her instructor or with the other students was one thing, but this was completely different. Her opponent wasn't waiting for her to catch her breath or solicitously inquire as to her well-being.

Riehl's brain and body were still processing the groin hit Lila had scored. Beginner's luck with that kick of hers had cost him his first option on the hit, to make it look like rape. And she sure as hell had made it so he wouldn't get a chance to use the equipment he was so proud of. Having scoped out the patterns of the residents for the past few days, he had figured he had time, or time enough, to have a bit of fun before killing her, thus fulfilling the contract. Instead, his balls were informing his brain that the only thing he would be boning in the next couple of days was an ice pack. It took a conscious effort to ignore the rising tide of pain that was crawling its way up from his balls to his stomach. Hell, he felt the impact of her knee in his throat.

Slamming the woman against the pillar had knocked her breath out of her, and his hands closed on her neck before she could scream. The garage was far from any of the tenant apartments, many floors above, but Riehl wasn't taking any more chances. Lila's left arm slammed into his ribs with a surprising amount of force. There wasn't much to this woman - slender, small-boned - but she had obviously taken some kind of self-defense training. The heel now raking along his instep with brutal sharpness was painful, possibly bloody, but he would be damned if he was going to let his commission get away from him. He tightened his grip. She let out a choked squawk of pain, fingers digging at his, trying her best to break his grip.

One...

"Three seconds, Lila, that's all it takes for a person to lose consciousness when being choked out," Lila's coach had told her. *"If you are ever in a choke situation, get out of it... quick."* She crunched her knee into the man's groin with all her might. His body shuddered in response, but his grip didn't loosen.

Two...

Lila's vision was darkening at the edge, narrowing down to a tunnel...

"What the hell? Hey! You! Get the hell off her!" The voice belonged to a man, someone familiar, but she could see nothing. The hand at her throat shook, broke free at the force of impact, a new body in the mix. Lila flew backward, back against the pillar, cracking her head sharply, scraping skin as she sprawled on the hard cement floor. It was a maelstrom of arms and legs, on the ground, her attacker and someone familiar, someone she knew. It took a moment for her to regroup, and find the top of the pepper spray she kept on her key chain in her purse which lay within reach. Slamming her thumb down hard enough to bruise, the spray shot out, just at the moment her attacker had taken the advantage, and made the mistake of looking down at her.

Riehl snarled curses and fell back, temporarily blinded. So did George, her neighbor from down the hall in Apartment 1503, who had also received a fair share of the spray while being slammed on the rough concrete parking garage floor. George lay there and writhed, caterwauling in a high, shrill voice.

"Oh my God, my eyes, my *eyes*!"

Riehl, realizing his opportunity had elapsed and fighting to see from eyes that were now filled with liquid pulsing fire, had enough sense to get up, stumbling, running, and swearing as he peered, half-blind, out of one half-functional eye. The other felt fully on fire, enough that he was tempted to claw the damned thing out of its socket, if only to end the pain. He disappeared into the depths of the garage, becoming one with the shadows, his footsteps receding.

Lila's throat was constricted, and she could barely speak. Meanwhile, George was screaming loud enough to wake the dead, or at the very least, some of the nearer level of residents. A stream of words issuing from him as well, random thoughts, just... noise...

"Couldn't sleep, thought I heard something, my EYES, oh my God my EYES! Just thought I'd go for a walk, but no, oh God, what if I'm blind? The burning...Jesus..." His nose was bleeding freely as well, but George was too busy pressing his hands against his eyeballs to notice. The blood dribbled over his cream polyester shirt.

George continued to scream while Lila frantically pulled her phone from her purse and dialed 9-1-1. By the time the cars arrived, lights flashing like strobes and weapons at the ready, George had settled down to a pitiful sobbing, and Lila's attacker was long gone. The police had nearly arrested George, thinking *he* was the attacker. Lila had explained for the third time that he had come to her aid, not attacked her.

"Anyone with a beef? A jealous ex-boyfriend perhaps?" The officer asked, his gaze traveling down her long, shapely legs, lingering on the rip in her dress. "Were you on a date with the neighbor, perhaps?" Lila winced as the doctor tried to flex her arm. The shoulder felt as if it were full of hot knives and fire. She caught the cop eying her cleavage; the front of her dress had ripped and a delicate lace bra strap was showing. The sleeve of the dress slipped from her exposed, and rapidly darkening, bruised shoulder.

"George? No, I, no, we aren't dating, he's my neighbor," Lila answered, hissing in pain as the doctor tried again to manipulate her right shoulder.

"Okay, Ms. Benoit, this is going to be a little painful. Just try to relax."

Lila bit back a retort. Why did doctors tell you that and then tell you to relax? She bit back a yelp as the doctor first turned and then gave her arm a short, decisive yank. She felt it pop back into place and rode a red wave of pain. It still hurt like hell, but at least the shoulder was back in the socket where it belonged.

The doctor handed her a prescription bottle. "You are going to be sore for a few days. Especially with those bruised ribs. Make sure to take these with some food and try to avoid driving."

"Thanks, Doc."

The officer muttered something indistinct as the doctor left and asked, "And you don't know anyone who would want to harm you?"

"No."

"Alright then." The officer eased his large bulk up from the small chair at the end of the ER room bed and stood slowly. The woman was a looker and that was for sure. Straight black hair, piercing green eyes, a slim figure, and legs that just didn't stop. Pretty. Her pale skin was bruised, but that just gave her a vulnerable look. The radio on his shoulder squawked and he muttered into it. "Well ma'am, I've got all I need."

"You don't need to do a sketch of the guy or have me look at some photos?" Lila asked.

The officer laughed. When he did, his stomach jiggled. "For a snatch and grab? Sweetheart, you have been watching too much Law and Order. Nah, this guy got the crap kicked out of him and pepper sprayed to hell and back. My bet? He's back at home in the 'hood, washing out his eyes, cradlin' his balls and thinking that walkin' the straight and narrow would be a hell of a lot easier than dealing with another babe in high heels schooling him."

"You think it was just a robbery?" Lila felt a sense of unease rise up in her.

"Sure, seems like it. I mean, hell, he probably would have tried for a little more, if you know what I mean. A pretty girl like you, he woulda taken advantage of that." He paused, nonplussed at Lila's reaction. "Why, you got this all figured out as going some other way?" The cop asked, a smug, condescending smile on his face.

"No, I, well, I mean..." Lila's voice petered out. *The way he had grabbed her throat, the look on his face.* She shook her head, which made the room dance and her stomach clench. "I guess not."

The officer smiled. "You got someone to pick you up? Take you home?" His eyes traveled up and down her again, as if he were imagining her without her clothes on. Lila's mouth tasted sour... *ew*.

"Yeah, sure do. Thanks Officer."

"Officer Tom Collier. You can call me Tom." He winked at her and her stomach clenched again. "If you need a ride, you just give me a call."

He handed her a card. She took it and managed not to shudder until after he had turned his back. So *not* her type.

An hour later, her right arm in a sling, her other injuries reviewed and treated, and higher than a kite on pain meds, she slowly eased her way into her friend Kaylee's backseat.

"Oh my God, Lila! What happened?"

She fell asleep halfway through telling the story, slumping in the seat on the short ride back to her high-rise. She barely blinked when Kaylee and her roommate Andy half-walked, half-carried her to her apartment door. As she nodded off in her own bed, Lila was thankful that it was Friday.

She had two days to recover before returning to work. No rest for the wicked, or those saddled with student loans.

A Clue

Monday came too soon. Kaylee had called twice, once on Saturday and again on Sunday, to check on her. Lila had reassured her that she was fine and she didn't need anything. If she had relented, Kaylee would have been knocking on her door. All Lila wanted to do was sleep, and the pain meds kept her in a thick haze.

She had curled up in the thick feather-top bed, a new purchase that had arrived the month before, and watched endless episodes on Netflix and napped the entire weekend. It had been a luxury Lila rarely allowed herself - time to recover and rest from her injuries. Her throat, ribs, legs, and arms all had livid bruises from the struggle in the parking garage. She took stock on Sunday night after a long, hot shower, noting that several were turning from a deep black and blue to green and yellow. Her skin was fair, and easily bruised, but she was also fit and active and young. A few more days and they would fade out completely.

On Monday, however, she had to stop taking any pills. She wouldn't have been able to drive or work or even really think if she was all wonked-out on opioids.

Her body was stiff, and her ribs and shoulder hurt like hell. The bruises on her face and neck were still a little shocking, but Lila didn't want to stay in the apartment another day. It felt suffocating, the plain walls devoid of any pictures, a few of the boxes still unpacked.

Besides, she was new at her job. She had done her time straight out of college in a bottom of the barrel intro level marketing position that had made her question why she even bothered with college, especially with those hefty student loan payments. Working for wages barely above the poverty line, with a Bachelor's degree, had been a slap in the face. If it hadn't been for her friend Kaylee who she had run into at a First Friday's event in the Arts District, she would probably still be there.

"There's an opening at Kurgen for a Market Research Analyst," Kaylee had told her after commiserating with Lila's latest tale of woe, the two perched on stools inside of Christopher Elbow Chocolates, sipping coffee while nibbling on the decadent confections. "It's better pay, *and* you would be working with me, so we could lunch together!"

Kaylee was quite obviously making better money, if her Jimmy Choo shoes and handbags were any indication. Kaylee's address had also changed from a ratty apartment south of the city to an upscale loft in the Western Auto building. "They *say* that you need at least four years' experience and a Master's degree, but I've seen the sad line of applications coming through HR and they would snap you up in a heartbeat." She grinned, revealing perfect white teeth, and tapped her long, well-manicured nails on the counter. "Especially with me recommending you." She had leaned in close, washing Lila in the scent of bananas and rum from the Bananas Foster chocolate she had just finished. "Promise me you will go home tonight and email me your resume."

Lila had, of course, sending the resume to Kaylee that evening while the neighbors down the street blasted music that sounded more like a mariachi band and kegger party instead of the festivities for the toddler who was celebrating her second birthday. Lila had watched the older kids playing in the neighborhood from time to time but rarely interacted with them. The neighborhood was relatively quiet, a mix of young families, a couple of old codgers, and plenty of transitory residents, especially in her building. The tiny one-bedroom apartment, complete with shag carpet that had matted in spots into hard, intractable lumps, with windows that rattled and blew in ice-cold air in the winter, and the regular cockroach visitors, was all that she could afford after trying to pay down a hefty student loan balance each month. She poured the rest of her "disposable" income into a decaying Honda Civic and wondered if she would ever be able to afford a new car.

That had been her life four months ago. And now? A modern one-bedroom loft with a view to the west and tons of light that poured in through the tall windows in a secure building in midtown Kansas City, where the scent of the defunct Folgers Coffee plant still infused the air with ghostly whiffs of coffee. After nearly a century of roasting coffee beans before the company gave way and moved into a modern processing facility, the very bricks of the building held the rich scent of coffee.

The Honda Civic had expired, rattling its dying breath on I-70 as she returned from a trip to Lawrence and a show at the Granada two months ago. The payments on the Prius had simply replaced what she was paying to keep the Civic running. The loft space had an option to buy if she wanted it. She was giving it at least a year, and if things continued to go well at Kurgen, she had already decided she would go for it.

Each Saturday morning included a pilgrimage to the lively River Market for breakfast at Beignet's and then shopping for fresh spices and produce with the local market vendors.

Lila was living her dream, finally, and she wasn't about to endanger that by missing any days at work. She would feel better there anyway; there were several accounts that she was working on that were odd - properties that should have sold by now, but had instead lingered on the books for over nine months.

Kurgen Real Estate was a heavy hitter, aggressive, in control of a large part of the real estate market in the Kansas City Metropolitan area, and her job was to make sure that she gave her boss the advice he needed to eradicate dead properties that would glut their portfolio and reduce their profit margin. She had requested the entire files nearly two weeks ago and was still trying to open several puzzling encrypted files, as well as some kind of email correspondence. She would work on that, along with her regular work load, instead of sitting at home feeling sore and sorry for herself.

Morris Endon, her boss, nearly dropped his mug of coffee when he registered her arrival, his eyes widening in shock, his ruddy red face paling at the sight of her. "My God, Lila!" His exclamation brought several other gawkers into the hallway. "Kaylee mentioned you had been mugged. I thought you would still be at home!"

Lila gave a rueful smile, suddenly deeply aware of the dark marks on her face as well as the lurid yellow bruising on her neck. *Perhaps this was a mistake.* "I'm fine, Morris, just a little sore." She forced a light laugh.

"Really, there is so much work to do, and sitting at home seemed overkill for an overzealous purse snatcher."

If she hadn't been going stir-crazy at her house, there was also the pesky matter of her neighbor George, who, after returning from his own visit to the ER, had promptly begun haunting the hallway outside of her door. All she wanted was to be left alone, but instead George had come by her apartment no less than six times on Saturday for a variety of reasons. Lila had finally stopped answering the door. She wasn't interested in hearing again about George's insomnia, or how his mother still felt it necessary to buy him underwear and socks, or explain why she wasn't interested in dating despite being quite obviously single. Work was a respite from all of that.

Blanche, one of the high-powered sales reps, stared at her bruises in horror. In her early 50s, Blanche had managed to accrue more debt in Botox and plastic surgery than Lila did in student loans, despite making at least triple the earnings. As a result, Blanche looked as if she could be Lila's contemporary, instead of from her parents' generation. "Oh sweetie, you need Vitamin C and K for that bruising! I'll be right back." She zipped away, her diminutive five-foot frame augmented by five-inch stiletto heels. Lila watched her go, consistently amazed that the woman hadn't so much as stumbled wearing those instruments of evil. Lila wore heels, one had to, but she did her best to find the lowest heels possible. The stilettos on Friday had been an exception to the rule and one she would not be repeating any time soon.

She made her excuses, grabbed a cup of coffee from the break room, and escaped to her office in the far corner. It was one of the smaller offices, but it had a view of a corner of the Sprint Center. The walls were a uniform taupe, the same as the rest of the office. The exterior wall was floor to ceiling glass windows. She had opaque, solid walls on each side, and the door and wall to the hallway and cubicles outside were glassed-in as well. Her office had a sleek wood desk, a Herman Miller chair, and silk plant in the corner. She had tried to bring in live plants, but, despite regular watering, they had quickly died. Like her inability to cook, she also seemed to have a black thumb, and any unfortunate plants left in her care immediately returned her attention and love by dramatically wilting and dying.

The office had a couple of extra chairs, and a huge wall of files, but otherwise was rather spartan. Lila sat at her desk, relieved to be in her office away from all the looks of pity or horror. Blanche swished through the door and plunked down a large jar on the corner of the desk. "Here, honey, my plastic surgeon *swears* by this line of supplements. He says it cuts healing time in half and removes bruises overnight. You just help yourself; I'm not lined up for anything until next year, and he hands these things out gratis, so I don't even need them!"

Lila smiled at her co-worker. Blanche was a sweetheart. She had given Lila a welcome basket her first week at Kurgen and taken her out to lunch twice. "Thanks, Blanche, you are so good to me!" Blanche merely waved her fingertips, painted a blood red this week, and dashed out of Lila's office as her cell phone began to sound. She punched a button and Lila could hear her cooing to someone on the other end, probably her granddaughter, a tiny and adorable three-year-old that Blanche had brought by the office one day.

With her cup of coffee in hand, and her computer booting up, she pulled the sheet of paper she had found out of her purse and stared at it. It just didn't make any sense. She wasn't anyone; this had to be a joke. But a joke that just happened to line up with someone who tried to strangle her to death in her parking garage? That seemed a little too coincidental.

She mused, *Occam's Razor, the simplest explanation is often the correct one.* But why? Why would someone be trying to kill her?

"Lila... what the hell?!" A voice at her ear, Kaylee's, made her jump a mile. She had been so absorbed in the slip of paper in front of her that she hadn't even registered her friend's presence.

Kaylee jumped back as well. "Jesus, Lila! What are you doing here today? You had the crap beat out of you and here you are! And what the hell is that thing?" Kaylee grabbed the slip of paper and stared at it, her eyes widening.

"Where did you get this?"

Lila breathed deeply, trying her best to get her breathing under control, her heart pounding from the scare Kaylee had given her. Her friend was dressed to the nines in yet another new designer outfit, her blond hair perfectly coiffed in a haircut reminiscent of the 1920s. Kaylee had a talent for changing her look on a weekly basis. Last week she had looked like one of the actresses on Mad Men, right down to her manicured toes.

"I found it on the ground in my building's parking garage. I wasn't sure what to make of it." The paper was torn, but it had several color photos of her and a general body description, along with Lila's name. It also had something that looked like a price… $30,000…next to her photo, which must have been taken when Lila was just exiting her car. It was a candid shot, with Lila half-facing the camera, caught in the act of turning, her long black hair flying in the wind. For the life of her, Lila could not imagine when it could have been snapped. She certainly hadn't noticed anyone with a camera that close. Could they have used a telephoto lens?

Kaylee sucked in a breath. "Lila, this is bad. I don't care what that cop told you about it just being a snatch and grab. That's bullshit. This is something else, it has to be. Why would that guy have been waiting there for you in the garage? And why you?"

Lila just shrugged. When she had found the piece of paper on the ground, all her senses on high alert, she had grabbed it and then sprinted to her car. Coming here, where there were plenty of people, seemed far safer. "Don't tell anyone, Kaylee. It could just be a joke. It could be nothing. It probably is nothing." Saying it out loud didn't sound any more convincing than it had in her head.

Kaylee looked at Lila, her lips pursed, eyebrows raised, "Right." When Lila's eyes returned to the paper, Kaylee made up her mind. "I know someone and I'm going to give them a call."

"You *know* someone? What does that even mean, Kaylee?"

Kaylee stared at the paper, and a haunted look crossed her face in a brief flash. It was quickly covered up with a glare.

"Look, I'll call them. They are… discreet." She grabbed the crumpled paper and scooted away before Lila could stop her. "I'll be back in a flash."

Lila stared at her friend's retreating back and shook her head. None of this made sense. She was a nobody - she had no family, no money, nothing. She hadn't been the unwitting witness to a murder, and she didn't know anyone with ties to the criminal underground.

Just thinking those words sounds so ridiculously like an episode of Law and Order *gone wrong.* Lila winced at the memory of the police officer laughing at her.

Unless it was a case of mistaken identity. She laughed and shook her head. *Next it will be an alien conspiracy!* It was all crazy and ridiculous. Whoever that guy was, he was gone, run off, and that was that.

Forget It

Twenty minutes later, Kaylee was back in Lila's office.

"What's this?" Lila stared at the card Kaylee held out to her.

"You need to call them; they can help you."

"I don't need some damned rent-a-cop, Kaylee," Lila snapped, glaring at her friend, "And I certainly can't afford one."

Kaylee didn't bat an eye. "Good, because they don't do rent-a-cop. Benton Security Services is the real deal. They provide high security, protective detail, and they keep millionaires and witnesses alive while rent-a-cops are busy trying to figure out their asses from their front ends." She smiled at Lila, patted her friend's undamaged hand, and then squeezed it reassuringly. "Trust me on this."

Lila looked doubtful... the bruises on her neck ached and her right arm was in a sling. She had managed to fight off her attacker, but only just. All her years of martial arts training hadn't prepared her for a dark garage and one incredibly fast opponent. If it hadn't been for her neighbor George and his "damned insomnia," as he had put it, she was pretty sure she would have lost that fight, despite getting a handful of solid punches and kicks in, at least one of them to the man's groin. She really hoped he was sitting somewhere hurting like hell and having to ice his balls.

It all happened so damned fast.

"Just call them," Kaylee insisted, handing her the card.

Lila took it from her friend and examined it.

It was on plain white card-stock, with no-frills black type that read Benton Security Services. Lila stared at the card; the feel of the paper was thick, heavy, made for a firm that didn't need to advertise their services, because word of mouth did the job so much better.

"Kaylee, if these guys protect millionaires, they do it for some serious money. Maybe even tens of thousands of dollars. I'm just getting on my feet; I can't afford this."

"Lila, trust me, they can help you and they won't charge you anything. Jack takes on special cases. I've already talked to him and he is interested in yours."

"Jack? You know this guy by his first name? What the hell, Kaylee? How do you know these people?" Lila asked her friend, suddenly intensely curious. Kaylee was petite, with honey-blond hair and big brown eyes. She certainly wasn't the type to need the services of a bodyguard, unless it was to protect her collection of high heels and designer bags. *There is some serious cash going there. What did she know about all of this, anyway?*

Kaylee gave a small, tight smile. "Long story. Maybe I'll even get around to telling you sometime. Meanwhile, would you just call them? Just, call. Seriously, Lila. *Call.*" The look on her face was so full of worry that Lila found herself nodding.

"Okay, okay, I'll call the number."

"Today?"

"Yes, today. Right after I finish this report."

Kaylee gave her a look, one that conveyed her doubt that Lila would make the call. She shook her head and left, calling over her shoulder, "I'll hold you to that, Lila Benoit!"

But Lila couldn't seem to bring herself to call right away after Kaylee left her office. Instead, she placed the card on her desk and did a little research. There was a website listed on the back of the card, and Lila pulled it up on her computer. It was as basic and no frills as the business card. The owner, Jack Benton, was the only name listed on the website. His name seemed familiar and Lila clicked the About tab. There was little information - the company had been started over ten years ago by Benton and it showed a picture of him, well-dressed, professional, with a sprinkling of salt and pepper through his dark hair. He was handsome, *very* handsome.

Lila had seen his face before, but she could not remember where. His posture and demeanor spoke 'old money' to her - he obviously had tailored clothing on but wasn't wearing anything ostentatious - no large diamond cuff links or heavy rings. The watch, half-hidden by his sleeve, looked like a Rolex. Someone that rich didn't have a need to advertise their wealth.

Oh wait, there is his bio.

She clicked on the link and read through it.

There was the connection, and that was why his name seemed familiar. Lila smiled. He was a benefactor for her alma mater and had actually helped pay for most of two years at her college through a scholarship. Lila had run track and played the cello in high school and college. Both of these interests had netted her a respite from the high tuition costs. Jack Benton's name had been on the cello scholarship, as she recalled. The Allison Benton Scholarship, named after his sister, who had been a cello player. Yes, that was it.

It had meant the difference between eating ramen and being able to buy fresh produce and not worry about student loans racking up the equivalent of indentured servitude once she graduated.

Lila's mom hadn't been able to help much, and Lila's dad had died when she was sixteen. They had struggled ever since, so Lila hadn't wanted to ask her mom for help. Her mom had been so proud of her, but Lila had known that she was barely making ends meet, so helping Lila with tuition and expenses was simply not in the cards. As it was, Gina Benoit had been slowly dying for years from terminal cancer. By Lila's last year in college, Gina was in bad shape, and she insisted that Lila stay in school instead of caring for her. "Don't do what I did, Lila. Don't drop out; stay in and get your degree, make something of yourself, or you will spend the rest of your life pushing paper around in some office. It's a meaningless job; you deserve better."

Gina Benoit had even made her death convenient, passing away during the Christmas break. Lila had gone home to be by her mother's side as she took her final breaths. She had buried her, and returned to Georgia Tech in time to start the new semester. Only a few friends from Mom's work, along with their neighbor from across the hall, had attended the funeral with her. Her mother had kept to herself, worked hard, and then returned home to be a mom to Lila. She had been good at it, better than most.

She closed the website, pushed the thick card to one side, and dove into her work. She had three major projects to deal with, plus the odd one; it was time she stopped wasting Kurgen Real Estate's money and time and got to work. As a market research analyst for the firm, her job was to make the data talk - what materials would work best on a job site, how could Kurgen achieve the highest profit in the market, and how could they reduce expenses? She lost herself in the work, and all these questions kept Lila occupied the next few hours. She barely touched the clear clamshell that was delivered to her desk by the secretary, Trish. Even though it contained her favorite veggie sandwich with extra pickles, she kept her nose to the grindstone until well into the afternoon.

Finally, after two more check-ins from Kaylee, who voiced increasing concern, Lila could put it off no longer. She ate a few bites of the sandwich as she tried to figure out how to get out of making a pointless phone call. She couldn't afford their services. And no matter what Kaylee said, nothing came for free in this world. She nibbled her bottom lip and stared at the phone on her desk.

Ugh. Might as well get it over with.

Nervous, her lunch already doing the rumba in her stomach, Lila reached for the phone and dialed the number with her slim, manicured fingers. The phone rang once, twice, before a smooth, calm voice answered, "Benton Security Services, how may I direct your call?"

"I was given your firm's name, I'm... I'm not sure if I need your services or not, but..."

The voice on the other end was crisp and efficient. "Your name, please?"

"Lila Benoit."

"Yes, Ms. Benoit, we have been expecting your call. One moment, please..."

Lila was surprised. "You have? But I..."

There was a series of clicks then, "Hello?"

On the other end was pure Southern drawl, which brought up visions of pecan pie, vanilla ice cream, and a fantasy of all of it between twisted bedsheets. "Ms. Benoit?"

"You can call me Lila." His voice, ye gods, his voice was amazing. She could feel herself blushing; had she just told him he could call her Lila? Why not ask him to whisper some sweet nothings? Or, or, or...

"My name is Shane Ellis." She could hear him smile through the phone. He was probably a toad in real life no one could ever sound that good, that *yummy*... it wasn't possible. She found herself calculating how long it had been since she had broken it off with Todd. Two months? Three? He had been terrible in bed. He had actually asked her to *rate* him once and she had... "We need to meet."

Oh, hell yes! Meet a man that sounded like sex and food all rolled into one? She could see how it would go from there, she closed her eyes, imagining Mr. Sexy Pants Shane Ellis, muscled, molasses dribbled over bare skin, big strong hands, and...

"Ms. Benoit? Are you there?"

Not yet but give me a minute.

"Umm, yes, but..."

Reality interceded. What in the hell was she doing? She didn't have the money for this. Men were never as sexy as they sounded on the phone, and she didn't need this. She didn't need protection, she didn't need Sexy Pecan Pie Shane Ellis whispering sweet nothings in her ear. She needed, she needed, *I need to get laid so bad. Don't care if that is a bad girl thing to say or not, it's the truth.*

"I'm sorry, Mr. Ellis, I - I don't think I need a protective service after all."

"Ms. Benoit, Lila, based on the information given to me, I would suggest that we at least meet to discuss this." He was persistent, she had to give him that. "This hit that was ordered on you, believe me, it is real."

Oh, sure he would say that. In the end, everyone is trying for their piece of the pie, so why would he be any different?

But the reality was, Lila couldn't afford it. She was on track, making all her payments, she was working on reducing that hefty car loan balance by just a little more each month, and life was finally starting to look up.

But pay for a protective detail? Those things didn't come cheap. Kaylee had misunderstood, and the whole thing was absurd in any case. The officer's words came back to her; it had been a snatch and grab. Nothing more. She'd just pissed him off by fighting back. That's why he had gone after her throat.

And as for the paper she had found, well, okay, so that didn't jive. *But I'm a nobody. You don't put out a hit on a nobody.*

"Look, just, just, forget it. Really. I'll be fine. I promised my friend I would call, but really, I'm good. I'm sorry for taking up any of your time. You have a nice day." She stabbed her finger down onto the plastic button and hung up the phone.

Brushing her hair away from her bruised face, she straightened her shoulders, despite the pain in her arm. This was ridiculous. She didn't need a bodyguard, and she didn't need protection.

I need to focus on work and stop wasting company time.

Her computer chimed and she saw it was a message from Kaylee.

KayleeS: Did you call?

Lila sighed, and typed back an answer.

LilaBe: Yep, it's all taken care of.

KayleeS: Great! I've got a meeting for the next few hours, good to know you are in good hands!

Lila felt her stomach twist. She hated not telling her friend the entire truth, but honestly, she was too worn out to argue. She had a pile of work, two case studies she needed to dig deep into, and the last thing she needed was to argue with her best friend. Later she would put her foot down and explain that she was fine, and didn't need some overpaid bodyguard.

Shane held the phone to his ear until the dial tone sounded. Lila Benoit had sounded nervous, but not scared. She should have been terrified. The crumpled paper that Kaylee had faxed over was standard in the industry. It had several candid shots in color, along with Lila's basic information. Her address, basic schedule - it was enough for any professional to be able to find their quarry and eliminate the target. Someone had ordered a hit on the petite, raven-haired beauty. Shane didn't know *why* but he was certain of one thing - whether she thought she was in danger or not, Lila Benoit had a price on her head. Her chances of surviving another attack were small and there *would* be others.

He pulled up the sheet on Tor and stared at it. After the failed attempt on Friday, the price on Lila's head had jumped from thirty to fifty grand on the darknet. Whatever this woman had done, or whoever she had pissed off, she was in big trouble. He drummed his fingers on the table. *She's got no idea what is heading her way.* Frowning, he dialed Jack's number.

The phone rang once. "Benton speaking."

"Hey, Boss, Ellis here. She says she doesn't need protection."

There was a pause. "And?"

"I checked the site and the bounty just jumped to fifty."

"Round her up, use that Southern charm if you have to, and take her to the house on the hill. Handle her carefully, but don't take no for an answer."

"Roger that." A dial tone sounded in Shane's ear. Jack Benton didn't waste words or time. Shane stood up from his small yet tidy desk and slid two extra clips into his belt loops and headed out the door.

As the hours passed, and Lila followed up on several leads, her gaze was pulled back to the phone over and over. She would call up the police officer later, show him the paper she had found. There had to be a good explanation for it. And if it was something serious, the cops would do something, protect her, or... *I have work to do right now.*

She dove back into her work, losing herself in the Cahill file, and tried to forget the attack, Kaylee's occasional IMs, and the way Shane Ellis' voice had made her feel. Just thinking about his voice sent a thrill down her spine.

Pecan pie... molasses... mm.

Call Me Shane

Shane watched the woman work. Despite the bandaged arm, she typed at a furious pace, switching between open tabs on her computer, completely absorbed in her work to the exclusion of anything else. He had watched her for nearly an hour now, as the sun slipped slowly behind the horizon and darkness stole across the expanse of steel and glass, removing the harsh glare.

The office was large, meandering, with a mixture of both antique and modern influences - in its furnishings and knickknacks. Outside of Lila's office was a large Oriental wardrobe that was in pristine condition, its lacquer shining despite being hundreds of years old. The company was family-owned and family run. Shane had learned that Mrs. Kurgen spent several months each year traveling the world and collecting treasures. Never satisfied to limit herself to one culture or region, Mrs. Kurgen's collection spanned the world.

He had heard this from the receptionist, Trish, who practically trembled in her seat whenever he smiled at her. She had rattled on for a while about the 15th century artifacts in the west wing, which apparently included a full set of armor worn by a duke or European prince. He had just smiled and nodded as the girl stammered on.

He watched her body and mind struggle to maintain a professional appearance. A few well-placed inquiries and he learned that the real estate firm did not have an internal security system or guards specifically assigned to the floor. The only cameras were in the elevators and a single camera for each main hallway, something easily avoided or short-circuited. In short, the security here sucked.

He waited for most of the staff, including Trish, to leave the office. His questions and research into Lila Benoit had revealed very little about *why* she was being targeted, but volumes about her personality. He couldn't just march in there, sling her over his shoulder, and drive her to the safe house. This had to be finessed. So, he made as if he was leaving, waited out of sight in the men's room in the outer hall, and watched as Trish and the others slowly trickled out, leaving the office empty save for Lila.

"She shows up before everyone else and is still here when we leave," Trish had said. "She's the most dedicated worker here."

He had watched them all leave over the course of a few minutes before 5 p.m., moving with purpose towards the banks of elevators. Lila wasn't one of them. He gave her a full thirty minutes after the last one left before he walked into the office. It was empty, the maze of cubicles quiet, the front desk abandoned.

Shane had also learned from Trish that when Lila had a free moment, she would often walk this floor, gazing at the different pieces. He wondered if she imagined going to those faraway places someday. Shane stood there next to the intricate lacquered cabinet with its depictions of various nature scenes and watched Lila work. The scanned image that her friend Kaylee had sent to his boss - the crumpled and torn note that Lila had found in her parking garage - had given him few clues. Tor had yielded little more. Someone definitely wanted her dead, and they had been watching her for at least a few days. But why? Her record was clean, not even a speeding ticket or fender bender, and she was barely out of college. He shifted his position and continued to watch her.

The fact that she hadn't registered his presence told him a lot about her. She certainly wasn't like the rich bastards he was usually assigned to. He couldn't help but wonder what she had done, or possibly seen, that could have put her in this predicament.

The reality of providing security, especially a one-on-one detail, with high-level armed security, like the services provided at Benton Security Services, was that a solid percentage of clientele were shitty human beings. They weren't victims; they were rich, powerful people who had earned the enmity of others by doing something scurrilous, something that had truly welcomed the price they now found on their heads.

Most of them were folks that made the life he had lived before this look like a walk in the park. Sure, Shane had screwed people over, literally and figuratively, but the rich fucks he was tasked with guarding? They wrote the book on screwing people over.

Shane knew that Jack Benton preferred to avoid those clients and often turned down contracts for the worst of them. But business is business, and Shane had found himself assigned to plenty of cold-hearted, self-absorbed pricks or their spoiled, trust fund babies. After a while, he had gotten a knack for reading people. Hell, he had acquired that before he ever ran into Jack Benton. Watching Lila Benoit now, he could see she was a refreshing change from the usual clientele of half-criminal, egocentric pieces of crap he had been pulling in recently.

The last one he had worked with had been a mob informant that the police weren't sure they could protect, especially not with a mole in their ranks. He had spent three long weeks with the guy. The killing blow had been when the piece of shit broke the code, got online, and they both nearly died. The guy had gone straight to his favorite kiddie porn site, which his old cronies already knew him to frequent. It hadn't taken them long to track his online activity and then the general vicinity of the safe house. Shane had discovered it well before that and relocated him to a new safe house. But not before he punched the perv in the face, breaking his nose.

That was when Jack had stepped in and told him he was reassigned.

No real surprise there.

Less than ten feet away and she hadn't even noticed him. She was alone; the last two office workers had made a beeline for the elevators some twenty minutes ago. He had watched them go, checked in with the boss, and sent a text to Kaylee letting her know he was on location and that Lila was fine. Despite his stare, despite him moving well within her line of sight, still she remained there in her seat, fully absorbed in her work.

Shane shook his head. This woman was definitely different from his usual client. They were nervous as cats, and with good reason; they usually deserved the situation they found themselves in. But her? Not a chance. Still, a little more awareness of her surroundings would be preferable over this. This kind of behavior was what got most people killed.

Hours earlier, when the dial tone had signaled the end of their conversation before it had even truly begun, he had stood there listening to the low drone issue through the receiver. He had stared at it, thought of calling her back, and decided that meeting her in person made more sense. The arrangements had already been made, after all. His assignment had been formally issued from Jack, and Shane had been arranging for the safe house when her call came in.

He stared at her shapely legs, peeking out from the standard pencil skirt, her ankles crossed and tapping a silent beat on the floor, against one leg of her desk chair. She was wearing a charcoal silk blouse that scooped down, just low enough to show a hint of perky breasts. His gaze moved to her neck, which would have been flawless if it hadn't been for the mottling caused by strong, large fingers. The bruises were already fading, and he felt his jaw clench at the thought of her struggling to survive that attack. There was a bruise on her right cheekbone, along with a small cut, and her left arm remained in a sling. It hurt; she winced when she had to move it. And yet, here she was, working harder than anyone else in the office, alone on a Monday evening.

Lila's hair was black, straight, falling just past her shoulders. A few minutes ago, she had gingerly pulled it up in an impromptu bun, twirled it a few times and stuck a pencil in it, wincing in pain as she moved her right arm. She had high cheekbones and was athletic and slim. With her hair up, she reminded him of a librarian he once knew. His lips twitched at the memory of Liv Parker; she had made a difference when few others had.

Lila had been attacked three days ago. The attack had been interrupted by a neighbor within her building, giving her enough time to put some distance between her and her would-be killer. The attack had all the hallmarks of being a planned murder for hire, and the fact that the police hadn't bothered accessing Tor, asking Lila any questions, or even questioned the method of the attack, was puzzling. It hadn't been random.

Perhaps it is because her record is so clean that they didn't bother to investigate. Occam's Razor, and all that. With all things being equal, the simplest answer is usually the right one. A contract hit doesn't make sense.

According to her file, she was single, which Shane found surprising considering her looks. *Who knows,* he mused, *perhaps she's high maintenance. A beautiful woman knows how to twist a man around her little finger. Do they teach pretty girls that maneuver straight out of the cradle?*

Her delicate fingers moved like the wind on the keyboard, typing, pulling up charts and graphs that he could see dimly in the reflection of the glass window behind her now that the sun had slipped behind the buildings and held the world in an orange-hued glow. She was tiring. He could see it in the way her shoulders slumped. That wasn't surprising considering the beating she had taken. And it appeared that she had been hard at work all day. Shane checked his watch, it was almost 7 p.m. and she was still at it.

He didn't trust their isolation to continue. If he was watching, others could be as well. It was time they met.

He cleared his throat.

Lila heard the sound, looked up, and gave a small yip of fear. *Who was this man and how long had he been standing there?* She jumped to her feet, her eyes dark with fear. He watched as she reached into her desk and pulled out a letter opener with her left hand. Her fingers curled around it tightly, her body tense. The office chair drifted away from her, and Shane could see she was preparing to fight or flee.

Shane didn't advance. He didn't want to spook her any more than she already was. "Ms. Benoit? We spoke on the phone earlier today."

Lila took in the man standing in the doorway. He was tall, over six feet, with dark hair and brown, almost black, eyes. A five o'clock shadow covered a strong jaw and he wore a black button-down shirt, tucked into clean, well-fitted jeans, the shirt rolled to the elbows, giving her a tiny glimpse of a tattoo on his upper arm. At first, she was at a loss. Who had she spoken to? Distracted by a hunk appearing in her doorway, she had forgotten, if only for a moment, about that phone call. She stared at him, momentarily unable to speak.

"Ms. Benoit?" He took a step forward. "You called Benton Security Services and we spoke about a protective detail?"

Benton Security Services... he really did look as good in person as he sounded on the phone.

"Oh! You! Pecan pie..." She stopped, looked embarrassed, and shook her head at his puzzled expression. She couldn't seem to concentrate; all she could see was this extreme hotness standing before her. "I mean, I... you..." Trying to *un*-see hotness was apparently too hard for her sex-deprived brain.

And then it hit her.

"Wait a minute, how are you *here*? How did you find me?" And suddenly, she felt a cold wash of fear. She had made a call and now he was here, *here,* at her work. What was he doing here?

Shane, having already crossed the threshold into her office space, sat in the chair farthest from the door. She was nervous... he could see it in her eyes. Lila took a defensive stance, her body twisting and her hands raising into position, ready to strike out and defend herself. *Interesting,* he thought, *she had obviously had some training. Not enough to stop someone with a specific skillset, but still.* He put up his hands.

"I'm not here to hurt you. Your friend Kaylee, she gave us your basic information yesterday. And everything else is online; anyone can find it if they know where to look." He smiled wryly. "She said you would be difficult to convince, that you weren't sure you were in danger." His smile faded. "But you are, whether you are willing to admit it or not. And that is why I am here."

Lila's initial panic faded, and she relaxed slightly as she approached him. She reached out her left hand, which he took and clasped firmly with his. His skin was warm, slightly calloused.

"You can call me Shane."

Atomic Coffee

"You can call me Shane" was standing too close for comfort. *Hell, across the room would probably be too close for comfort,* Lila thought. This close to him, however, just an arm's length away, and she could smell him. He didn't smell of pecan pie and molasses, but he didn't smell bad. It was a clean scent, not cologne or deodorant, just a sexy man smell that reminded her yet again of how long it had been since she had been with someone.

The confining walls of the office galley made him seem even taller than he had in the doorway of her office a few moments ago. She hadn't even noticed the rest of her coworkers leaving the floor, she had been so lost in her work.

"Would you like some coffee?" Lila asked, nervous and hoping to look anywhere else than at his stubbled jaw, sexy lips, lean hips, and muscled forearms. *A man like this, well, he could pick her up, set her against a wall, and...*

"Sure."

His voice was liquid, warm, and she shivered a little in response as she turned away. The coffee maker's light was off, the pot empty and dry upside down in the drain tray. *Well of course it was. The last pot had been made, and consumed, hours ago. I'll have to make a new pot.*

For a moment she paused and considered telling him they were out of luck. But that would mean looking up at his sexy smile and those warm brown eyes and dark hair. She caught herself imagining him walking down the street, random women falling down in front of him, throwing their phone numbers at him, or simply humping his leg like sex-crazed dogs. She stifled a giggle at the last image. No, she couldn't look up, not yet.

The coffee packets were in here somewhere, or had they switched to bulk? Lila couldn't remember the last time she had made coffee. Anytime she offered to, or was even caught doing anything more complicated than operating the microwave, her co-workers looked terrified. Cooking was not her forte, and coffee wasn't either, according to her co-workers who, upon tasting her idea of coffee the first day she had worked there ordered her to never, ever touch the coffeemaker again. It didn't matter what they were doing during their day, if she uttered the words, "There's no coffee, shall I make some?" one of them would jump up and offer.

She sorted through the drawers, locating a bag of coffee, along with creamer and sugar packets.

Shane watched her closely. She appeared nervous, jumpy, but not necessarily as a result of the attack. She avoided looking at him, staring instead at the coffeepot as if it were a great mystery. Her body was stiff, and she maintained as large a distance as she could - a feat in the narrow galley-shaped kitchenette.

He could only deduce it had to do with *him*. He wasn't used to that. Women tended to like him - hell they damn near threw themselves at him - but Lila Benoit seemed to be doing everything she could to keep her distance. And the way she was opening all the drawers in the kitchen told him that she didn't normally make coffee. This suspicion was confirmed as he watched her add nearly triple the coffee he would have used for a full pot, and then overfilled the coffeemaker with water, sending a torrent of water spilling over the side.

"Oh... well, I..." She glanced up at him for a moment, stared at his mouth, paled slightly, and glanced away.

What a perplexing woman.

"I don't make coffee very often; perhaps we should go to Starbucks."

"No." He said it firmly, in a tone that brooked no argument. Lila's hackles raised and she was distracted from her nervous response.

Ugh, he's a chauvinist pig, I knew *he was too good to be true!* "I beg your pardon?"

"I said no. It isn't safe in public spaces."

Shane deftly reached past her, above her head, and pulled out two mugs from an open shelf. One was labeled "Cat Mom" and she could see the script on the other side: "The perfect child has four legs and a tail." He handed Lila a black and white one that read "I work hard so my cat can live a better life."

"Don't be ridiculous!" she sputtered. "I don't need someone to wrap me up in a cocoon and protect me from the world. I can take care of myself."

Shane leaned back, giving her a once-over, his eyes lingering on the bruises, her bandaged right arm. She bristled slightly. "No doubt you can dissuade the casual attacker, wannabe rapist, or garden variety lech."

His eyes moved down her body, cataloging her curves, the tone of her muscles, admiring the shape of her ass and how it fit so perfectly in her pencil skirt. She was fit, obviously kept in shape, and definitely had some basic self-defense moves. She wouldn't have lasted as long as she did down in that dark garage without them. But moves and athleticism notwithstanding, she wasn't going to stop a trained killer.

Lila straightened under his gaze, lifted her chin and eyed him defensively. "I managed pretty well the other day."

He nodded and smiled. "Yes, you did."

Then he moved closer, reached up, placed a warm hand on her neck. Lila shuddered at his touch and he felt himself growing hard in response. Instead of backing off, he used it, stepping even closer, invading her personal space, combining her fear and the desire he saw returned in her eyes to bring his point home.

"Until he had you here." He slid his hand to the same position her would-be killer had used. "You only had three seconds to get out of it. And did you? Or was that when the neighbor showed up?"

It wasn't the work of a trained killer, these bruises, but the man had definitely been hired. A scan of the note scrawled next to her photo flashed in his mind: "Make it look like a burglary or rape gone wrong."

"He would have choked you until you passed out, raped you, murdered you, and left your body there on the cold cement."

Shane had seen plenty of scumbag rap sheets. Rape would have been just one of the guy's list of talents. He'd dug into Tor further on his way here. The guy who had taken the assignment, Dominic Riehl, had done two years in Leavenworth for statutory rape, and another stretch of eight years after that at Farmington Correctional for forcible sodomy and attempted murder. He would have strangled the woman to death if a group of frat guys hadn't been on some bro camping trip and taken that particular trail. Dominic Riehl was bad news, and Shane didn't have to guess at how it was supposed to end; the note said it all. The only question was, why Lila Benoit?

Lila's breath caught at the feel of Shane's hands, however light the touch, on her throat. A hedonistic rush of desire and fear washed over her. *He was so damned strong...just imagining his hands sliding down her, brushing against her breasts, settling on her waist, cupping her ass in his hands, those lips on her mouth.*

His eyes locked onto hers. She was pretty. Usually he found himself attracted to more voluptuous women. A woman like this, with small breasts and a tight ass, were not his usual turn-ons. Despite this, he realized that the softness of her skin had sent all kinds of haywire messages to his libido, and another wave of desire crashed over him. He had thought he had control of this. He let go of her throat and backed up a step, embarrassed by his own response. He was a professional, and this was against The Code, *his* Code. *You don't fuck the clients Ellis. You keep them alive. You do your job.*

Shane forced his attention back to the job. The *job*, the *client*, whose perky breasts and tight ass notwithstanding, needed his protection. The scent of atomic, acrid coffee cut across his senses. "Coffee?"

Lila nodded, broke eye contact, and took a breath. Shane Ellis was a serious hottie, but obviously a misogynist. A well-intentioned, well-muscled, sexual god of a man with a hero complex. He had shown up here, without being asked or encouraged, and was busy telling her, Lila, how she couldn't take care of herself.

If he utters "little woman," I'm kneeing the son-of-a-bitch in the balls and leaving, Lila promised herself. She watched as he poured the acrid coffee into the two mugs. It smelled awful, far too strong, and she wondered if it was possible that the spoons would disintegrate in its intensity. She took the offered cup, topping it to the brim with tiny cups of cream and two packets of sugar. She set it on the counter, carefully stirred the mess, and then took a small sip. *Ugh.*

Shane watched her with something akin to amusement. He took a gulp of his own coffee and regretted it instantly. "This should come with a warning label," he said gruffly, pouring the contents down the drain. "Did all that milk and sugar crap you added make yours any more palatable?"

Lila choked down a second sip. "Um, it's, oh hell." She poured it down the drain, the swirl of creamer chasing the straight black, slipping out of sight into the darkness. "I'm, um, I'm not allowed to make coffee."

"I can't imagine why," Shane commented dryly.

She glanced up and saw him smile briefly. Her body sang in response. He had one of the sexiest smiles she had ever seen. *Hands, hips, right here on the counter. Just bend me over, hike up my skirt from behind, and oh sweet Jesus.* Lila bit down on her lower lip.

His smile dropped. "Ms. Benoit, we need to talk about your protection detail."

Her fantasy fled, and his mouth was all business and no sweet, sexy smile.

"I suppose we would, if I had hired you, Mr. Ellis, but..."

"Call me Shane."

"Shane, then. But I haven't hired you, I doubt I could afford your *services.*" She paused, her words dying on her lips at the look on his face.

Did that sound like she had just called him a prostitute? Oh God, not a prostitute, a gigolo. That's what they call the men. Strong hands, washboard abs, the sex would be... "Athletic." The word just popped out. "I mean..."

His left eyebrow quirked up, confused as she tried to get control of her mouth.

"Word salad, I've uh, got it. The scuffle the other night, I knocked my head, and..." she nodded, shrugging weakly and avoiding his penetrating gaze. "Sorry, word salad."

Oh my GOD, word salad? Really? The man is going to think I'm a complete lunatic!

"Ms. Benoit."

"Call me Lila."

"Lila."

"Word salad." Maybe if she just kept repeating that she would believe it herself.

"Right. Look, Lila, you need my protection. At least until this is looked into further."

"But as I said, I can't afford it, I'm sure I can't." Lila could feel the panic rising right alongside her libido. If this man came one step closer, she was pretty sure she would start humping his well-muscled leg like a dog. He was so hot, so amazingly sexy, and strong, and that voice, that voice. *Pecan pie and molasses, a spot of real whipped cream. Mm, yeah.*

"Lila, I don't handle the books. I don't do negotiations. My boss said this is on the house and I just read the folder, go where I'm told, and keep my clients alive." He eyed her sternly. "And I'm sticking by you until this mess gets sorted out. Understand?"

Lila nodded, managing a small squeak that she hoped sounded like a yes, but didn't.

More of a pathetic whine, really.

If she didn't get control of her response to his uncontrollable sexiness, she was pretty sure she was going to turn to jelly or tear her clothes off, possibly both.

He tilted his head, slightly bewildered, then smiled again, reassuring, almost paternal in nature. "Come on, we need to take you somewhere safe, and I'll explain it on the way to your apartment."

Her legs practically shook off of her body. "My apartment?"

Shane nodded and said, "Yes, your apartment. I'm assuming you will want clothes, toiletries."

Lila shook her head; that wasn't the answer she expected. Although if he had gripped her ass and lifted her up against the kitchen counter...

My mind is never leaving the gutter, is it?

"I need clothes?"

He arched an eyebrow, and she blushed. She could feel the red lighting up her cheeks, her neck, hell, even her ears. "I mean, *why* do I need clothes?"

Oh yeah, great, now I sound like a complete slut, or nudist, or, or...

At the other end of the floor, a muted click of a door closing caught Shane's attention and his mood changed immediately, switching from solicitous and mildly amused to another person entirely. It wasn't just that his entire demeanor changed, but also an almost physical metamorphosis seemed to occur. He felt changed into someone different, capable, and lethal in a period of mere seconds. Beneath his shirt, his muscles flexed as he assumed an alert position.

Lila stared at him and wondered if it were possible to be even more turned on by this handsome "call me Shane" stranger. He reached a hand to his belt, shifting his weight to the balls of feet, alert and listening. His free hand reached out, pulling her close to his side. His lips grazed her ear as he murmured, "Who works here late? Cleaning staff? Co-workers?"

His left hand eased a lethal, gray handgun from a holster she hadn't even noticed until now, his eyes searching for any movement in the corridor outside.

Her heart rate sped up. *Hot man. Danger. It's like something out of a movie. Come with me if you want to live.*

She whispered back, "The cleaning crew comes through later, eleven, maybe? And everyone else went home."

She clutched his arm, close enough to smell him. No cologne, oh no, not Shane Ellis. Instead a clean, almost woodsy scent came from him. He smelled amazing.

The footfalls, noticeable only if one concentrated, were heading past them, towards a bank of offices, Lila's included.

"*Stay here,*" he mouthed to her and her eyes widened. Suddenly it was all feeling very real and not so sexy, just terrifying.

She shook her head at him, but he had already turned away and began to move silently down the hall. In the distance, Lila heard the door to the office open and close again.

Does that mean someone left? Or someone else came in? Who were these guys? And what do they want with me?

Lila's heart began to race, her body shaking. She nearly screamed when Shane reappeared, his hand warm on her arm as he pulled her towards him, his mouth at her ear.

"A second one just came in. We have to go, *now*," he whispered. "Stay close. Follow my lead." And with her arm firmly in his grip, he moved out of the kitchen.

The Stairwell

Lila's breath came in short, panicked gasps.

The last few seconds, a run from the kitchen galley to the stairwell, had been terrifying. As soon as they had emerged from the relative safety of the kitchen walls, a shot had rung out, then another, and another. Shane had gripped her arm harder, painfully, as they dashed from one cubicle area to the next, and his gun firing so close that her ears felt stuffed with cotton, along with a distant ringing. She could hear nothing else, momentarily deafened by the shots.

As they had weaved out of one hallway and into the next, wood had splintered and flown from the lacquered 17th century cabinet outside of her office. The gunshots blasted simultaneously from the far end of the hall, and another shot ricocheted past her ear. The world had tilted on its side, tangling and rolling, as Shane pushed her down with his body and snapped off another burst of gunfire in the shooter's direction. He had dropped like a sack of potatoes. One minute a living, breathing human being, the next, a marionette without strings, limp on the floor, blank eyes staring. Lila swallowed a scream.

Shane had picked her up then. Just one quick yank and she was vertical. She might as well have been weightless.

"Stay with me," he hissed in her ear, a sound she could barely hear. "We need to head for the stairwell."

The second man could disguise his footfalls, but not when he was at a full run. The sound of his feet came at the same time as a flurry of shots, one of them shattering a tall enamel vase on a pedestal just inches from Lila's head. She screamed and hit the floor, the hard concrete below the thin industrial carpet jolting her injured arm painfully.

59

Shane turned, pivoting on his heel as he fired. Glass shattered, the wall of an office shredding into slivers. He reached down, picked her up by the waist and then shoved Lila into a corner. She winced as she felt a bruise begin to rise on her undamaged arm where her body slammed into the metal edge of a door. Her shoulder took the brunt of the impact and she huddled on the floor, staring at a carpet covered in enamel shards. Each day, on the way to her office in the morning, she would walk this hallway, just so she could enjoy the scenes depicted on the beautiful vase. It was 15th century, from the Ming dynasty, and priceless.

Well, it had *been priceless.*

The shots were deafening - her ears rang and her head ached. With each gunshot, her body jerked in terror, pulling away from the noise, although there was nowhere to go. She was trapped in a corner. She covered her face, curling into a ball, wondering if there was some way to make herself invisible.

Where is Harry Potter's invisibility cloak when it is needed most?

Suddenly, there was silence. Her ears were still ringing, and she felt more than she heard the thud of a second body hitting the floor. She was too frightened to look. If Shane was dead, then the killer was going to put a bullet in her head next. *Why bother looking up and seeing the gun pointed at me? Better to just close my eyes and...* A hand closed on her arm, yanking her upright again, eliciting a sob of terror.

Shane pulled her close and Lila opened her eyes to the view of a black shirt, tight over a muscled chest.

The assassin was on the floor, a spot of red blossoming on his chest. His eyes were open, staring, and Lila watched death take him. The eyes dulled and went blank. Shane had kicked his gun aside as a precaution, scanned for any other intruders, and then pulled her away from the body and on through two sets of doors to the safety of a quiet stairwell. His hand was tight on her wrist, bruising her skin, but Lila didn't complain.

"Oh my God, oh my God, what just happened back there?" She skidded to a stop, her high heels scraping and the sound reverberating off of the cement walls. The handrail dug into her back and the cement wall of the stairwell was ice cold against her. She shook in fear and shock and she barely noticed Shane's hands as he ran them down the front of her. He turned her around effortlessly, checking her back as well.

She gasped as his hands ran over her. "What are you..."

Nothing, no wounds. *Damn, but that had been close.* He breathed a sigh of relief. He'd let himself get distracted, and very nearly gotten them both killed.

"Are you hurt?"

"What?"

She couldn't think, the shock of what had just happened closing in, a dark hand of fear clutching at her heart and throat, squeezing them tight. She felt dizzy. *Can't catch my breath.* She wheezed, struggling to inhale and exhale. Lila closed her eyes. She tried to concentrate on relaxing her throat, her chest.

She hadn't had a panic attack in years. They had come in the aftermath of her father's death, in her mid-teens. It had taken years for her to learn to control them. She had learned guided meditation, was given a prescription for Xanax that she rarely used, and finally found a mixed martial arts instructor who was a firm believer in breath work.

Not even the fight in the garage on Friday had triggered one, but the past few seconds sure had.

His hands paused. "Lila, look at me." He tipped her head up and she opened her eyes reflexively. "Hey. It's okay, I've got you."

She nodded, her eyes wide with panic, her throat and lungs still fighting for air. *There wasn't enough air.*

He set her back against the cool concrete wall, his body close to hers, and he placed a warm hand on her chest. She could feel his warmth, his breath slowing.

"Look at me, Lila. There is only me and you here. Match my breath," he whispered in her ear, "just focus on the breath."

Shane's ears strained for any sounds. They didn't have time for this; there could be more of them out there. He recognized the signs of a panic attack - it wasn't so different from an asthma attack and he had certainly seen his fill of those. He needed her to be able to run, but she couldn't do that if she was in the throes of an attack and he sure couldn't carry her down thirty plus flights of stairs *and* fight any more would-be killers off.

Her body, shaking against his, was distracting him from the job at hand. He could smell a faint whiff of perfume, possibly jasmine, mixed with her natural scent. Desire, so akin to the adrenaline rushing through his body from the shootout, flooded through him again.

What was this woman doing to him?

His hand, resting on her chest between her breasts, itched to move to the left and encompass her breast. He wondered how her nipples looked. The vision of her body, stripped of everything but that black lace bra he had seen tantalizing hints of, and thigh-high stockings, leaned against the stairway railing flitted through his head. He imagined leaning in and slipping his tongue between those red lips, turning her gasps into moans of desire.

The smaller head hardened, straining against the durable denim, eager to turn that "fight or flight" response into a "fuck her senseless."

Damn it, this was his client.

"Just breathe." he whispered, trying to channel calm and ignore the attraction he felt. He willed his dick to go back to sleep and it gleefully ignored him.

The minutes ticked by and gradually her breaths slowed from the ragged gasps to even breaths in and out. The pounding of her heart was no longer a visible thing.

"I'm okay." Her voice was faint.

"You sure?"

"Yeah."

"Okay." He leaned down and pulled one of her shoes off, then the other. He stared up at her, and Lila flushed. It felt *intimate.* "This way you can run easier." He smiled at her. "And far quieter."

He grabbed her left hand. "Come on, we need to leave...*now.*"

"Wait!" She resisted as he pulled her down the stairs, hugging the wall. "Oh my God, we can't just leave them there!"

"Yes, we can. They are dead, both of them," Shane replied tersely. "We need to get out of here, now. Before any more come along and try and kill us."

"*More?!*" Lila squeaked. "But..."

He stopped, his body still close to hers, his breath warm. "Were either of those men the same guy that attacked you in the garage?" He was so close that she could feel him, hard against her. Her body quivered uncontrollably in response.

"No... he was shorter, heavier... but..."

"I don't know why someone wants you dead, Ms. Benoit, but I can guarantee you they are getting pretty insistent. If you want to live, you follow my lead, and do as I say." He was so close and scary with his intense stare, that Lila felt her heart rate speed up even further, jackhammering in her chest, so close. He had killed two men. Men who were trying to kill her, but still.

He began to pull her down the stairs and she resisted. "Wait, my purse, it has my keys and wallet in it. I can't leave it here."

"Shit." He paused, thinking. "Wait here." And with that he vanished through the door, as silently as the two men had. It closed with a soft click.

It couldn't have taken any more than a minute for Shane to return, but it had felt like forever. Lila trembled. She felt exposed, helpless, standing there in the stairwell alone. Every creak, or gust of air, and Lila was convinced someone would appear ready to finish the deed. She jumped when the door opened, biting down on her tongue with an aborted yelp of fear.

Shane smiled and held her purse out to her.

"Thank you." She took it from him and wrestled it onto her uninjured shoulder.

"Come on," he said, "we need to get out of here. Now. Stick to the wall side and avoid the inside railing."

Lila wondered if there were more lurking, just waiting for her or Shane to lean over and look down. A quick head shot, the roar it would make in this echo chamber of a stairwell. She nodded and slid along the wall, her heels tucked securely into her arm sling.

Kurgen Real Estate was located on the 39th floor of a building known as One Kansas City Place. It took a long time to get down thirty-nine flights of stairs. At the bottom of the stairs, Shane stopped abruptly and placed a hand on her shoulder, pushing her firmly against the stairwell wall, out of sight of the door and its sliver of a window. They were at P2, the second level of the parking garage, and had been no other people. No one with bad intentions, or good, had appeared, but it was clear that Shane wasn't taking any chances. He pressed her against the wall and quickly stole a glance through the window.

"Wait here."

He opened the door, the latch clicking quietly in his grasp and the door creaking just enough to start Lila's heart thumping. She couldn't help but imagine hearing the sound of a gunshot and watching Shane collapse to the ground. He peered out, and slowly edged his body out the door. A few seconds later he beckoned to her.

"It's clear. Follow me."

Seconds later they were in his car. He had opened the passenger's side and unceremoniously shoved her in.

"Stay down. Out of sight, until we get out of here." She didn't argue, simply folded her body into the tiny space, still out of breath from running down thirty-nine flights of stairs. He didn't tell her about the dead parking attendant sprawled in the booth, a single black hole between his eyes. A spray of the poor man's blood painted the glass on the far side of the toll booth. Shane drove out of the parking garage and onto the darkened city street outside.

The terrifying events of the past ten minutes, combined with the cold of the car, and of the outside, the temperatures having suddenly dipped into the 30s after sundown, brought on a fit of shivering that no amount of heat from the car vents could abate.

Once they had moved out of the city, and Shane was sure no one was following, he turned down the road, heading for the safe house, and reached over to help Lila out of her cramped position. She had a run in her stockings. He sucked in his breath; she was wearing garters and he caught a flash of them as she struggled out of the footwell and into her seat. She smoothed down her skirt, but not before he had seen a flash of black lace juxtaposed against a smooth white thigh. His dick hardened, then throbbed eagerly in his pants, as randy as a middle-school boy eyeing a cute girl in the seat in front of him. He let out a small groan of discomfort as he calculated how long it would be before he could get to the safe house, explain The Code and what would happen next, and then see her off to bed so he could go to his own and jerk one off.

Although I'd much rather fuck her senseless. Damn, but why didn't I get a fat asshole to protect?

Lila continued to tremble. She stared out at the dark night, "My apartment is off of Broadway, in the other direction." She said it without any real conviction, shell-shocked at the images the last few minutes had given her. She had seen the blood on the glassed-in wall of the parking attendant's booth after all.

Shane reached over, squeezed her left hand, and said, "I'm sorry, but those two guys showing up changes things. It wouldn't be a good idea to go to your apartment right now. I'm taking you somewhere safe." He used his most professional tone, the one he reserved for the rich fucks who paid a hell of a lot of money for him to keep them safe from all the people they had screwed over.

Lila couldn't have screwed anyone over. He didn't know what she had done, or seen, to deserve this, but he was going to protect her. His fingers strayed to the delicate bones in her wrist and he felt his pants tighten in response.

If only he could get back control of his body and do...his...job.

The Code

It didn't take long to reach the safe house, at least, not according to the clock on the dashboard. A mere twelve minutes, which felt more like an hour. The adrenaline rushing through her had slowed, but her mind just kept turning in circles.

Why would anyone want to kill me? I'm nobody!

The black Jeep exited the highway, slipping through the dark fall night, and eventually passing through the seedier part of town. Lila watched the wide streets turn to a narrow, winding road, occupied on both sides by aging, mid-century homes that grew smaller in size. The road dead-ended ahead - the locked gates of what looked to be an industrial plant of some kind looming tall on the horizon.

The Jeep slowed, stopping before it reached the plant, and turned left at a smaller set of locked gates near the bottom of the hill. Shane rolled his window down and keyed in a long code. There was a short pause, and then the gates slid open. Shane put the Jeep in gear and drove through. The gates slowly closed behind them.

Perhaps the dilapidated state of the other homes so nearby was why the house situated high above them at the top of the long, private drive struck Lila as so extraordinary. Built in the low-slung sprawling look of the late '60s, it commanded a view of rolling acres, fortified behind a solid fence, and with a million-dollar view of the Missouri River. Here on the hill, separated by a thick forest of trees from the string of simpler homes below, the views were extraordinary. They turned the corner and the garage door rumbled upwards. Shane eased the Jeep inside, his free hand still resting on the delicate bones of her hand. She hadn't stopped trembling once during the twenty-minute journey.

He pressed a button and the garage door closed, sealing them inside. A light on the door mechanism above shed a weak yellow light over the garage. It was spotless and uncluttered. When Lila didn't move, Shane reached over her, unlatching the door, savoring the feel of her body against his. He paused, his face inches from hers, and saw her pupils expand. Was she afraid? Turned on? Fight or flight response did odd things to a person, and after the experience they had both shared, the answer was probably yes to both questions. He stared at her and strongly considered kissing her. It wouldn't stop there, though, and he knew it.

What in the hell am I doing? She's a client.

It wasn't just him. Not that it made it any better, not that it made it *right*, but he could feel her body respond. The way she held her breath, bit her lip, tightened her fingers against his hand. He forced himself to break eye contact and pull away, to stop his lips from claiming hers and taking what he wanted.

Wordlessly, she exited the vehicle, her stockinged feet soundless on the cold cement floor. She stood there for a moment, the Jeep door open, staring at him as if unsure what would happen next. He shook off the vision of her spread against the warm hood gasping in pleasure and tilted his head towards the door.

"This way; let's get you warmed up."

Hours before he had logged in to the safe house via the secure link on his phone and set the thermostat to seventy-two degrees. With a few more swipes and push of the button, he had also ignited the gas log in the fireplace. He was glad he did. They were greeted with warmth and comfort, and an orange glow emanated from the sunken living room at the end of the hall.

Inside the house, the floors were lined with plush wall-to-wall carpet. Shane led the way down a short hallway, past a luxurious half bath that screamed "I'm from the seventies and proud of it!" It was paneled with a heavy, dark wood on the lower half of the walls and a dark red velvet flocked wallpaper on the upper half.

Shane paused briefly in the front entry, removed his shoes, and placed them neatly by the door before stepping down into the sunken living room and disappearing around the corner. Lila paused to take in the view of rough-hewn beams of the ceiling high above and a wide spiral iron and wood staircase that led to the floor above. A large wrought-iron chandelier also hung from the ceiling above. It was lined with at least thirty dim candelabra bulbs set in wide, faux pillar candles. Their combined glow, however, was bright.

Lila heard the clink of glass, ice, and the low, slow gurgle of liquid. By the time she stepped down into the living room and turned the corner, he was handing her a heavy glass of cut crystal, filled with ice cubes and an amber liquid.

"Here, you look like you need this."

Lila took the glass, her hands brushing his, hers still trembling. She lifted the glass to her lips, took a sip. The alcohol burned her throat, clawing its way down, deep inside her, and warmed her belly. She didn't look at him, but she could feel his gaze just as she had felt his hands glide over her in the stairwell, checking for injuries, for bullet holes. This chain of thought led to the image of the two men, crumpled on the ground, blood blooming from their chests.

Dead, Shane had said, *dead after trying to kill her.*

Shane watched her as she took a second sip, then a third, the trembling slowly fading as liquid courage took its place. He wanted to fuck her. And he struggled with it. This woman, she was doing something to him. He didn't know how or why - she wasn't his type. He loved the loud, brassy women with big tits and asses that could hold up a shelf.

He'd said it to his buddies in college, "More cushion for pushin', man, who wants a scrawny chick when you can go the mile with a real woman?"

But looking at her, he didn't see scrawny, he saw tight. He saw an athletic ride-you-all-night kind of woman. He threaded his fingers through his hair and looked away. He had to get his mind off fucking her.

She's a client, *asshole.*

He stepped away, crossing to the other side of the room, the entrance to the kitchen.

"You need something to eat, and we need to discuss what comes next."

He said it over his shoulder, walking away. She would follow, and she would listen to him now. They all did once the bullets started flying. He crossed the kitchen to the refrigerator and pulled out a package of cheese, some salami, and reached for the crackers in the cabinet next to the fridge.

"There's some fruit there on the table, and some grapes here in the fridge." He reached in and pulled them out.

He arranged it all on a plate, complete with a sharp knife, and then he carried the food over to the table, holding out a chair. She had followed him into the kitchen, her drink empty, save for the half-melted ice cubes. He didn't ask, simply filled the glass with more amber liquid from an expensive cut glass crystal carafe on the table.

"We are safe here, that's the biggest thing to remember." His eyes were dark, fierce, and quite intense.

Lila looked away, first staring at her plate, then out at the lights of the towns across the river. She could see the steady blinking lights of the planes flying in and out of an airport.

He continued, "I expect my clients to abide by The Code while they are under my protection. It's simple, and it will keep you alive."

He ticked off the items one by one on his fingers, watching her as he did.

"Number One, absolutely no contact with the outside. Not your friends, your family, your boss, no one."

He paused, momentarily distracted by the bruises on her throat. *I would happily kill the sonuvabitch who touched her.*

"Number Two, do not leave the safe house without me by your side."

She met his eyes and he was struck by the unusual shade of green. Not unlike jade, but with flecks of brown. He couldn't help wondering what her face would look like mid-orgasm, tilted back, eyes closed, gasping for air as he...

"Shane?" Her voice interrupted his fantasy. He realized he had been silent for far too long. She blinked at him, her mouth a moue of concern.

"Number Three, no unsecured phone calls or internet access. And, most important of all, Number Four, don't withhold information."

Lila stood up and looked away from him out the sliding glass doors to the river and the lights of a town in the distance. Miles away, they could see the planes circling in the sky, descending and ascending, their running lights slowly blinking in a steady, reassuring pattern. She stared out into the distance and drained her glass, nibbling at the tidbits of food on her plate. He refilled her glass.

"Do you have any questions?" His words hung in the air, the alcohol burned in her belly, and Lila shook her head silently. Several moments passed.

"Is this your house?"

"No, it belongs to Benton Security Services, well, to the owner Jack."

"It's huge," she said, her eyes finally moving from staring into the dark night sky, back to meet his. They were such a striking green. Her mouth, a tiny expanse of delicate pink lips, opened enough for the tip of her tongue to moisten them, before darting back to safety.

What he wanted to do to that mouth.

Shane ran his hand through his short-cropped hair. He had to stop thinking about her like that.

He stood up abruptly and turned away. "I'll show you where you will be sleeping." He left the room without a backward glance.

Lila watched him go. A small surge of resentment ran through her. She wasn't used to obedience being something that was expected or taken for granted.

What kind of sexy, pecan pie, sweet molasses misogynist is he, anyway?

Conflicting emotions warred within her. Part of her wanted to stay here, stare at the amazing view, and watch the planes continue to dance in the sky. Another part of her wanted him to walk back into the room, pull her against him, and kiss her ruthlessly. She'd seen the desire in his eyes; he wanted her as much as she wanted him.

I shouldn't follow him like some obedient dog. That will only encourage him to be more of a chauvinistic pig.

For a moment she hesitated and then she couldn't help but wonder.

What does it look like upstairs?

Curiosity won over making a stand. She rose from the table and followed anyway.

The thick pile of the carpet muffled all sound and gave off a feeling of sinking, similar to a sandy beach, with every step. It was everywhere, and Lila followed Shane up wide, circular stairs to the landing above. The wood was heavy and there were large beams of dark, rough-hewn timbers and heavy wrought iron. Shane waited for her to reach him, then turned and opened a door, bowing slightly and motioning for her to proceed him. The door led to a short hallway that opened into a large room with a vaulted ceiling. The dark heavy wood pillars were covered with iron work and it reminded Lila of the inside of a church.

A fireplace with a gas log glowed warm against the far wall. There was a dim lamp in one corner next to a massive four-poster bed. And around another corner, there was a large, pleasantly appointed bathroom complete with a claw foot bathtub. This seemed at odds with the '70s hunting lodge look, but Lila wasn't going to complain - she loved long soaks in a hot bath.

Lila's initial nervousness around Shane had been cured by the liquid courage she had tossed back with the light dinner. The drinks had lit a fire in her belly and loosened her tight, aching muscles. She was no longer shaking, no longer afraid. Instead she could feel all the experiences of the past few hours turning from terror into an intense, hot need.

She stared at the fire, her mind firmly on the man standing behind her.

Southern drawl, pecan pie, whatever, she couldn't help but picture him without his clothes. She would nibble that tattoo, lick her way down his chest, and explore the treasure hidden behind that jean zipper. *Mm...*

His voice brought her back to herself with a start, "I should let you have some time to settle in, update my boss on what happened tonight, and all that."

She turned to face him. He was standing close, too close, and she could feel the heat of his body hanging in the air, warming the layer, an almost visible current of it forming between them. His eyes moved over her, and she caught herself wondering what it would be like to have his hands moving there instead. She felt her breaths coming closer together, heavy, deep, and she took a step closer.

Shane could feel the pull of attraction between them. He stared into her eyes. The alcohol had calmed her, and he could see it in the way she held herself - less stiff and afraid, more languorous, sexy. All it would take was a touch. His hand sliding up her arm, his mouth on hers. He just had to reach out and...

Shane matched her step forward with his own step back, and then another, retreating towards the door. "If you need anything, I'm on the other side of the house, down the hall. In the morning we need to talk."

He put a hand on her uninjured shoulder, keeping her at arm's length. "Someone wants you dead. And we need to figure out why. Otherwise, they will *never* stop."

Lila blinked, the spell broken. Fear flooded her again. *Who was trying to kill her? And why?*

"It has to be a mistake," she said. "I'm no one."

He smiled, white teeth flashing and she melted all over again. "Everyone is someone, Lila." He squeezed her shoulder gently. "Take a bath, get some sleep. Help yourself to whatever clothing you can find in the closet. We will figure this out in the morning."

He turned away from her, walked down the short hall, and closed the door to the suite behind him. His thoughts were whirling in his head, the imperative to call his boss and report the situation warring with an overwhelming impulse to turn around, walk back through that door, and...

Fight or flight, he counseled himself, *she's reacting to everything that just happened to her. And no, it doesn't help that she is smoking hot.*

He had never slept with a client. Never even come close. Of course, it probably helped that most of his clients were pasty-faced white men who owned hedge funds or had seen something they shouldn't. Hell, most of them had done something they shouldn't, and were now running for their lives.

There had been the pair of girls, hollow-eyed, scared. They had also been traumatized, malnourished, and sporting bruises on their arms, necks, and faces. He had looked at them and felt a murderous rage towards whoever had mistreated them. Even when the youngest, a girl of seventeen, had tried to climb into his bed one night, he hadn't been the least interested. The girl needed counseling, patience, and safety - not another man taking advantage of her. He had gently led her back to her room, and the poor kid had looked confused, yet relieved. He had also made sure to lock his door for the next two nights until they were out of his care.

Shane shook his head, realized he had been standing, lost in thought at the top of the stairs, and quickly made his way down and then across to the west wing of the house.

He pulled his phone out of his pocket as it vibrated. "Hey, Boss, sorry I didn't call sooner. The scene was hot, so I had to get her out of there before anyone else showed up."

Jack didn't waste words. "Tell me everything."

Shane described the shootout and the dead guard. "She's not much help. She doesn't seem to know *why* anyone would want to hurt her. My gut says she's telling the truth."

"*Two* hit men?" Jack's voice held surprise. "What the hell has this girl gotten herself into?"

"She's pretty shook. I'll take her life apart piece by piece tomorrow and see if I can get some clarity."

"Yeah, do that. I'll talk to Azule, see if I can get her to dig into Tor further and find out who is sending these guys. Also, Teeny says the police scanner is reporting cops are already on scene. Someone called in hearing gunshots."

"Mine," Shane replied. "Those two men had silencers on their Sig Sauers."

There was a pause and a slow exhale on the other end. "Sig Sauers?"

"Yeah."

"Shit. That means…"

"I know."

"Update me in the morning, Ellis."

"Will do."

Shane's finger was hovering over the End Call button when Jack added, "And Shane?"

"Yeah, Boss?"

"Keep it professional."

"Always, sir." A dial tone sounded in his ear.

I'm always professional. Except for that asshole kiddie porn shithead that I decked. But he had it coming.

Shane stared at his phone, the screen dark and blank. Jack had gotten a look at Lila's file. He was well aware of how smoking hot she was. He sucked in a breath and tried not to think about those stockings and garters peeking out of her rumpled skirt.

No wonder Jack's warning me off her.

Shane tossed the phone onto the nightstand and stripped off his clothes before lying down on top of the covers. He stared at the dark ceiling, brooding, until sleep claimed him.

Crime Scene

Morris Endon stared at the body bag. A few feet away a small yellow photo evidence tag sat next to the shards of a priceless vase. The tall black letters read, "18." He flinched as a bright flash went off from across the room, temporarily blinding him. The detective holding the camera ignored him, focusing on a shell casing next to yet another yellow plastic sign. The flash came again, and then again, as the man took picture after picture, changing angle, moving to the left, kneeling and then standing.

He had been reading *Inman News* on his couch, listening to Tchaikovsky, and sipping from a whiskey highball with ice and ginger ale when the doorbell rang. The deep, rich tone of the Westminster chime had been jarring in the quiet night. The police officer stood at the door, with his cruiser and its indiscreet flashing lights in the driveway behind him. Already he could see his neighbors peeking out of their curtained windows. The HOA bi-annual meeting was next week, he was sure he would be the topic of plenty of idle gossip.

Standing there staring at the officer, Morris suddenly regretted the alcohol. The warm glow of it had spread through his body and engendered a lassitude he found difficult to fight, yet felt necessary to eradicate. Despite his meteoric advancement from the cheap inner-city apartment of his youth to a well-heeled existence in one of the wealthier parts of town, police officers still unnerved him.

It isn't as if he can arrest me for drinking in my own home after all. Or can they?

"Morris Endon?" The officer was young, late 20s at most, and his hand rested lightly on his utility belt, close to his service weapon.

"Yes, what can I do for you, Officer?"

"Sir, I need to ask you to come with me. There's been an incident at Kurgen Real Estate and your presence is required there."

"An *incident*? It's nearly ten o'clock. What sort of incident?"

"A shooting, sir. If you could please come with me."

"Of course." His mind whirling, he wondered if he should call someone. A lawyer? Mr. Kurgen?

What do they want with me? He could feel the panic rising. *I haven't done* anything.

He had slipped on shoes and a coat and locked the heavy, burled walnut front door behind him and followed the officer towards the flashing lights. Morris had contemplated telling the officer he would drive himself but sat in the back seat of the cruiser instead.

He can smell the alcohol on my breath, I'm sure of it.

The ride there had been silent, but quick. There was no traffic this late on a weeknight. Outside a sliver of a moon had risen. It played peek-a-boo in the sky as it repeatedly appeared and disappeared behind the abundant cloud cover. They arrived, and he was taken into the building through the front door, past a coroner's van and the media truck, both parked in the circle drive normally reserved for limousines and taxis.

Morris's eyes tracked back to the body bag. There was blood on the carpet, a deep, red stain that crept to the left and stopped by one corner of the antique lacquered Chinese cabinet. Calling it an incident had been such an understatement. How was he going to explain to Mrs. Kurgen that the irreplaceable antique vase had been shattered? Or the Chinese cabinet shot full of holes?

It wasn't supposed to happen like this. There are rules.

"Sir?" He flinched again. The officer who had escorted him here laid a reassuring hand on his sleeve. "Mr. Endon, if you could come this way, please."

He followed him, away from the body, past the cleaning crew and the detective interviewing them, and two men wearing jackets emblazoned with "CORONER" in yellow on the back.

My office. They are leading me into my *office.*

The detective was in plain clothes, a gold badge clipped to his belt. He stood up when Morris walked in.

"Mr. Endon, I'm Detective Rob Stone. Sorry to roust you out of bed and bring you in here so late." He clasped Morris's hand and gave it a quick, authoritative shake. "Please, sit down."

He sat back down in Morris's new desk chair, motioning for Morris to take a seat normally reserved for visitors. The seats were lower, something that had been quite intentional on Morris's part when setting up the office. It was easier to maintain a psychological advantage that way. He sat down, sinking into the cushioned seat. It was comfortable, but he was sitting lower than he was used to. A thread of resentment ran through him and he struggled to keep it from showing on his face.

"What the hell happened here?" Morris asked, trying to keep his voice even.

There are two god-damned body bags in the office. It wasn't supposed to happen like this.

"We are still trying to figure that out. We have two men dead here in the office, and the parking attendant who serves as security at night has also been killed."

"My God!" Morris didn't have to manufacture that response; he was horrified. How had things gone down like this? "Who would do something like this?"

"Well, like I said, we are working on it. If I were to guess, I'd say that one of these men shot the security guard and then headed up here."

"To what end?" Morris asked, "To steal the collection?"

Perhaps I can steer them in that direction.

The detective shook his head, dissolving Morris's hopes of diverting the police attention. "No, if they had intended theft they wouldn't have been armed with silencers."

Morris blinked at the detective, his face frozen.

Rob leaned back, the chair tilted without a creak of protest, despite the man's girth. "This chair is amazing. I really need to get me one of these."

Morris managed a weak smile, the resentment of being displaced slightly stronger now. "It's new."

"What brand is it?"

"Herman Miller."

"Oh yeah? I've heard about them, but this is real luxury here."

Morris fought to keep his emotions in check. "Yes, the Eames lounge chair is top of the line."

And at over four thousand dollars, it is completely out of your price range.

"Mmhm, I'll say it is," the detective sighed and stared out the window. "Quite the view as well."

Morris felt his face flush. "Detective, is there a reason you had your officer roust me out of my home? Perhaps we could talk furniture choices and skylines when it is daylight out."

The detective smiled and said, "My apologies. I was waiting for a list of office personnel. And we are dusting for fingerprints as well, but I'm sure you can imagine that is quite a task with this size office." He leaned forward, staring intensely into Morris's eyes. "What I'm hoping to understand from you is what two men armed with silencers would have been looking for in a real estate office, and who killed them."

Morris stammered, "I'm sure I don't know." His face flushed and the resentment transformed into fear. They actually considered him a suspect?

I'm not involved. Say it, over and over, until they listen. It wasn't supposed to happen like this.

"You deal in commercial real estate? Or is it residential?"

"It's a mix, actually. Commercial, high-end residential, and corporate clients mainly." Morris answered promptly, relieved that the detective had turned away again. The man stared out at the city's skyline; lights sprinkled the high rises and there were wide swaths of darkness, the closely spaced homes in the distance devoid of light. The city, and most of its inhabitants, peacefully snoozed away.

A silence fell, and the minutes seemed to tick by. His anxiety increased. "I am happy to help with the personnel list if you need any assistance. I don't know everyone; there are a few newer employees that have come on board recently that I am not familiar with..."

His voice petered out and died as Rob stared at him.

"Tell you what," said the detective as he leaned forward, "I'll get that list and talk to you in the morning." He stood up and reached into his back pocket, removing a business card and handing it to Morris. "You could come by the station if you prefer."

Morris was relieved. "Sure, I can do that. What time?"

"Give me a call in the morning when you are up. I imagine you will have a few things to deal with - getting a crime scene cleanup crew in if the techs are done working the scene, insurance claims, and I'll want you to double-check with all your employees. We will get to that last bit tomorrow."

Morris winced at the thought of the blood-soaked carpet. "Right. Will do."

The detective called past him, "Stevens, can you give Mr. Endon a ride back home?"

Morris shook his head as he pulled out his phone. "No need, I'll catch a cab home."

He then stepped gingerly around the crime scene tape and avoided looking at the body bags now being loaded onto gurneys.

It wasn't supposed to happen like this.

Morris did his best to not break into a trot as he reached the outer doors of Kurgen Real Estate and disappeared from the detective's view.

The ride down the elevator was silent as Morris searched on his smartphone for a local Uber to take him home. It was there in moments, and he spent the next ten minutes silently fuming until he found himself relaxing at the sight of his upscale neighborhood.

And really, all they wanted was information; he hadn't done anything wrong. I hadn't been in that office shooting it all to hell.

His heart gave a painful thump at the memory of the priceless vase and antique lacquered cabinet, both destroyed.

Whose bright idea had it been to send those assholes in?

He paid the driver and returned to the warm, welcoming wood tones of his house, relieved and angry at the same time. In his office, he unlocked a small drawer and took out another cell phone and pressed a button on speed dial. It rang twice and went to voice mail.

"I just got hauled down to my office. It looks like a battle zone. What the hell happened there? Call me when you get this; you have some serious fucking explaining to do."

He jabbed at the End Call button and tossed the phone onto the couch in his den. It bounced and then slipped behind a seat cushion. Morris let out a long, ragged breath. Everything had gone so well, for so long, and even the hiccup with Witt had been dealt with quickly and easily. The discrepancies had been fixed, the numbers changed and morphed and slipped into (and out of) different funds until the errors were erased to all but the most practiced eyes. And those eyes could be bribed. How, how in the hell, could this have happened? And how did he make sure it didn't happen again?

His eyes strayed to the cut crystal that housed the whiskey, and the glass, still with a finger of amber liquid waiting inside it, the ice long dissolved. His stomach flip-flopped with nerves. He stood to lose *everything*. The commission would come after him, the one standing in the light, not the others obscured by shadows.

He reached out, grabbed the glass, and swallowed it in one large gulp. It burned, but the alcohol barely touched the fear that was growing in his gut. Had he sold his soul?

Of course, I did. Long ago. There's no going back now.

The heavy gold ring on his right hand caught his attention. The intricately carved black stone on top absorbed the light and hid the small catch on one side. Morris set the glass down, and trailed his finger along the tiny depression on one side, pressing it, and watching as it slid to one side, revealing the primitive shape beneath. The place on his wrist where the tattoo went was smooth, just a slight gleam of white scar.

He had done better than his father. The old man had worn the tattoo proudly his entire life, convinced he had done well, that he was well-placed in the Indalo. He had never even known about the next step up. When they had come to Morris, told him things were about to change, his father had already been in a nursing home for a year, half gone with Alzheimer's. Morris had been eking along, performing infrequent favors, playing the family man, the doting father, and waiting for the chance to truly prove himself.

The degree had been dictated to him years before upon his induction. "You will obtain a degree in finance and apply at Kurgen Real Estate." It had been planned for him, and he had followed the edict, clawing his way to the top of his class, and applied to Kurgen as he was told to do. What followed was a steady climb to the top. The way, no doubt, greased by those in the shadows. They needed a high-level fixer and that is what he did for over fifteen years - through a divorce and an ex-wife who moved away to Oklahoma with his two boys.

In return, he had an enormous house, a discreet high-end call girl who visited once or twice a week, and the boys visited for a month in the summer and alternated Thanksgiving and Christmas. He had everything he could possibly need, and he vacationed in a different tropical destination each year, soaking in sun on pristine beaches and enjoying perfectly manicured golf courses in luxury resorts.

It was a good life. A comfortable one. And Morris Endon could not shake the foreboding certainty that it was all going to crumble down around his ears.

He tipped the carafe into the glass, amber liquid splashing his hand and the silver tray. He ignored it, sucked down the liquid and repeated, once, twice, and finally a third time. The carafe was empty, his glass was empty, and Morris felt the hot rush of it as it hit his bloodstream. He had done everything they asked of him. He was loyal. They would take his years of service into consideration.

Yeah, keep telling yourself that.

Morris sat down at his desk and waited for the sun to rise.

Ten Years

Back in the posh offices of Kurgen Real Estate, Rob had watched Morris leave. There was something the man was hiding. He wasn't sure yet whether it had anything to do with tonight's events, but it was there. He had been doing this job for long enough to have a knack for following his intuition.

He leaned back, the chair tilting without a single creak or groan. He turned to look out at the Kansas City skyline again, his thoughts on the tiny red tattoo he had glimpsed peeking out from under both of the dead men's wristwatches. Both men, both tattooed, the symbol of a man under the canopy of the heavens...

Ten years fell away, and he was plunged into the memories he had tried so hard to forget. The Indalo, whoever they were, had undoubtedly taken his wife from him, threatened to kill his child, and ended his career at the CIA.

Rob stared at the dark night skyline, but all he saw was a sunny playground in Virginia, less than a month after Claire's death. His memories of that day remained as sharp as if they had happened yesterday.

He had forced himself to get dressed and take their daughter to the playground near the house. It had been two weeks and he was due to return to work. He had made all the arrangements - found the perfect preschool, one that Claire had talked about sending her to, and they had agreed to take her mid-week instead of a Monday. He sat there, watching Maddy run and climb on the jungle gym, his mind still clouded with grief, his heart shattered.

A woman, clad in yoga pants, a T-shirt, and running shoes, the standard attire of a stay-at-home mom, had sat down on the bench next to him.

"They certainly are having fun, aren't they?" she had asked and smiled at him. The children shrieked and ran, several of them engaged in an elaborate game of tag.

"Yes, they sure are." He watched as Maddy's frizzy curls bounced as she slid down a bright blue slide. She was smiling, something that he hadn't seen her do in weeks.

"Let me guess which one is yours. Hmm. Is it that cute little one that's on the monkey bars?" She pointed and he saw a small tattoo peeking from her bangle bracelets. They slid away as she pointed, and he saw it, edged in black, on her right wrist.

"Um no, the one with all of the frizzy curls. I haven't figured out how to wash her hair right," he sighed. "Her mom always handled it." He watched Maddy climb into a tunnel.

"Don't brush it."

"What?"

"Curly hair, don't brush it, just finger comb it while it's wet. It will make all the difference in the world." She smiled.

"I'll try that. Thank you." She nodded, and they sat in silence for a moment. Maddy was still in the tunnel and he straightened, trying to see if she had come out the other end.

"Divorced?"

"What?"

"You said her mom always handled her hair," the woman asked, friendly, her tone relaxed, yet curious. "So, I'm guessing divorce, right? Or she's on a trip?"

Rob blinked and said, "Uh, divorce, yeah." He didn't want another word of condolence. They meant nothing. Just empty words in the face of howling grief.

"Recent?"

"Sure."

"I knew it," she said, her expression sympathetic, "You have that shell-shocked look I normally see on my girlfriends' faces after their husbands leave them for trophy wives."

He managed a weak smile and said nothing. Maddy's frizzy hair disappeared from view as she moved farther into the bright yellow tunnel.

"Kids are wonderful," the woman mused, "Really keep you going when nothing else will, don't you agree?"

Rob thought of the past week. He had spent most of it in pajamas and a bathrobe, the dishes piling up in the sink, staring numbly at the television, Maddy at his side.

"Um, yeah." He stood up. The tunnel had a fork in it. He could see that now, a second entrance and exit that was close to a man-made cave. Had she gone into that?

"I think of them as our little piece of immortality. If we didn't have that, what would we have to show that we were ever here at all?"

"Um, right. I, uh, I don't mean to be rude, but I need to go find where she has gone to. It was nice talking to you." She had murmured something in return, but he had been too far away, all of his alarm bells going off at once.

The first time I take her to a park since losing Claire and I manage to lose sight of her. Nominate me for Father of the Year award.

He had found Maddy sitting at the edge of the rubber matting, near the entrance to the faux cave, tears in her eyes.

"Daddy, I fell and hurt my knee on the rocks there." She pointed a tiny hand at a section of pea gravel.

"It's okay, Pumpkin, I've got you. Here, put your arms around me and I'll carry you." She reached out and encircled his neck with her small arms, leaning her head on his shoulder. He felt her tears wet his shirt and then there was the scrape of paper on the back of his neck.

"What do you have there, Pumpkin?"

"A picture of our house, Daddy; a nice lady gave it to me. She said it was a present for you!"

He took the photograph, staring at it, and Maddy shifted in his arms. "She said you would like it, Daddy."

It was a picture of their house. The car in the drive, and a bouquet of flowers that had been delivered yesterday from an associate who had just returned from vacation and learned of Claire's death. He flipped the photograph over. On the back were two words:

Stop Digging

Rob felt cold fear grip him, washing over him like in an icy wave. It was a hot summer day and a cold sweat formed on his brow, goosebumps on his skin.

"I think of them as our little piece of immortality. If we didn't have that, what would we have to show that we were ever here at all?"

He turned to look back at the bench. The woman was gone. His gaze traveled over the park as he mentally reviewed what she had looked like: brown hair pulled in a ponytail, brown eyes, yoga pants and a T-shirt, the typical look that most of the moms here shared. Skinny, lattes in hand, with their makeup and manicured nails. She had looked like any of them. Nothing stood out, nothing except for that tattoo.

"Daddy? Can we go home now?"

"Maddy, who gave this to you?"

"Some lady."

"What did this lady look like?"

The little girl shrugged. "I dunno. I guess like a mommy. She was in the tunnel. She said you would like it."

"Can you see this lady now?" He turned around slowly; the tunnel was filled with preschoolers. "Can you look, Maddy, and see if you see her?"

The little girl lifted her head up and stared at the children on the playground. Several groups were leaving, even as others settled down at picnic tables to dive into sandwiches and juice cartons.

If Claire had been here, she would have remembered to make a picnic lunch.

He noticed that many of the mothers had claimed the premium shaded spots, staking out their favorite lunch spots as early as possible.

Maddy stared at the playground, her eyes fixing on the kids at the picnic tables. "I'm hungry, Daddy."

"Just look a little bit more, Sweetheart."

A whine had escaped her, "I don't see her Daddy. And I really want some goldfish crackers."

"I know you do, Maddy, but this is important. Do you see the girl who gave you the picture?"

The little girl had begun to cry. "I don't see her. Daddy, I'm *hungry*!"

He had given up, leaving the park, eyes darting as he studied the women he passed intently. His direct gaze unnerved a couple of the mother hens. They had stared at him, and one put a protective hand on her daughter's shoulder, watching him as he broke into a jog. Maddy shrieked with excitement, her hunger forgotten for the moment.

That night, after dinner, she had drawn a picture. It was eerily similar to the mark on the woman's wrist.

"What's this, Sweetheart? Where did you see it?"

"It's pretty, isn't it, Daddy? It was on the lady's hand. The one who gave me the picture for you."

He leaned closer. "On her hand, Sweetheart? Or here, on her wrist?" He pointed to his wrist, and the little girl nodded.

"It was on her wrist." She pushed at his hand. "I need my other crayons, Daddy, I'm gonna make a rainbow now."

"Could I have this picture, Sweetheart?"

She smiled up at him, and his heart broke; she looked so much like Claire. Except for her eyes. Instead of Claire's pale blue, she had warm, chocolate brown ones like his own. "Sure, Daddy, will you put it up on the fridge?"

"I think I'll put it in my office, Pumpkin."

Later that night, Maddy sound asleep in her bedroom, he had stared at the picture.

Two different people, both with the same tattoo. The person who had given Maddy that photograph had done it while she was in the tunnel, nearly thirty feet away from where he was sitting with the woman. It was no coincidence. They were connected. He reached for the bookshelf that rested between his desk and Claire's. She had written fantasy stories for children, and she had been deep in the middle of one when she died. *The Element Encyclopedia of Secret Signs and Symbols* sat on the second shelf down, scraps of paper that marked Claire's research at intervals.

He paged through the book from the beginning, examining the symbols, finally locating the matching symbol a fraction of the way through the thick book.

"Indalo, huh?" His finger followed the text. "It serves as a reminder of the complex belief of man as the microcosm and the Universe as a macrocosm."

He had heard whispers, nothing more than rumors. Hell, that was what most of his existence at work was built on. Follow the whispers, listen, dig deeper. What if this symbol stood for far more than just an ideal? What if it had some very real, very dangerous people attached to it?

He sat back, staring at the image of the Indalo and the words scribbled on the back of the photograph.

Stop Digging

It was all related, he was sure of it. And he was also sure that the last thing he needed was to be involved. That woman had threatened him; more specifically, she had threatened Maddy. And the more he thought about it, the more it felt as if Claire's accident hadn't been an accident at all. Taking a turn too fast, that wasn't Claire's style, not even before Maddy was born. He had jokingly called her Grandma when she was behind the wheel, while she had called him Mario Andretti in return.

His parents were dead. His mom to leukemia when he was ten, his dad and his love of the bottle months before Rob turned twenty-two. Claire had lost her parents to a car crash a year after Rob and Claire's wedding, and both were only children. He was all that Maddy had, and she was the only thing he loved left in the world.

I can't do this job anymore. Not if it means losing Maddy.

The next day he had quit the CIA and put the house on the market. Two days after that, he and Maddy had boarded a plane for Kansas City, leaving Virginia, his life with Claire, and a career as an analyst with the CIA behind him forever. The file he had been compiling, the files and papers he had accumulated over nearly a year of digging, were returned to headquarters. Someone else could research the mysterious group he had found linked to shadowy financial dealings and hired hits across the globe. Someone who didn't have a child to protect. Someone who hadn't lost his wife.

Until tonight, that is. Ten years. It had been ten years since he had lost Claire. And he was as sure then as he was now, that it had been no accident. Someone had deliberately made him a widower, and his child a motherless orphan. Someone had threatened him, and promised to finish destroying what was left of his life if he kept prying. And with a tiny, innocent three-year-old child to protect, who was he to argue?

He had walked away. He had abandoned his investigation and chosen to live. He had fled with the only things that mattered - his life and Maddy's. And here, in the middle of flyover country, he had thought he was safe. Quietly, in a way that would not reveal his curiosity, he had looked up the symbol. The symbol, he learned, was the Indalo and depicted man under either a rainbow or the vault of heaven.

Such a tiny mark. The information he found on it was small. No hint of any shady criminal organization. Just the tattoos, and the warning.

A red Indalo. Just like the black Indalo tattooed on the woman's wrist. She had been part of it, something I had known all along. How do these two men fit into all of this?

And as Rob sat there in an overly expensive armchair, he wondered if he dared to dig deeper. Or should he walk away while he still could?

He reached into his pocket and hit speed dial. It rang twice and she answered.

"Hey, Dad."

"You should be asleep by now."

"Dad, you called me." Her voice held a slightly petulant tone. "What is that term for 'damned if you do, damned if you don't?'"

"An idiom."

"Right. An idiom. So, you call me at almost midnight. If I don't answer, you come home, wake me up, and demand to know why I didn't answer the phone. But if I answer the phone, you ask me why I'm not asleep." She sighed and yawned. "See the problem here?"

Rob chuckled. "I guess you have a point there. But you weren't asleep."

"Nope, I was finishing the book you gave me."

"*Voyage from Yesteryear*? What did you think of it?"

"It was good, but," she paused for a moment, "Do you ever think humans could ever truly get along in a society without government and laws? I mean, *really* get along?"

"You are far too young to be so cynical."

"Whatever, Dad."

"I'll be home soon."

"Okay. G'night." Her phone clicked as she ended the call. He stared at his for a moment. Whatever was going on here, whatever the Indalo were doing here, he was now tasked with finding it out.

How You Find Her

Riehl was fighting. His opponents were falling like dominoes, flying through the air in response to his fists in their abdomens. He snarled, grinning, reaching for a blade on the floor and burying it to the hilt in one man's guts. A quick wrench, left, then right, twisting as he went. Blood flew from his opponent's wounds as the man sagged to the floor, still alive, his arms flailing, a dead man going through the motions until blood loss and shock caught up to him. Riehl felt the bloodlust surge through him.

Only the woman remained. She was petite, slender, tied to the bed, her body writhing in fear. Her eyes pleaded with him, even as he tossed his weapon to one side, slid out of his bloodstained shirt and began to unbuckle his pants. His dick was stiff, throbbing with anticipation and he smiled at her, enjoying the fear that turned to panic as her struggles renewed. That vanilla musk smell he had detected, just before she brought a knee to his balls a few days earlier, made him harder than Chinese algebra. Finally, after tracking her down, after all the days spent cradling his balls and waiting for the pain to subside, he was going to finally get the chance to fuck her.

Everyone else in the building was dead. He had all the time in the world and he planned on making it last for days. The bitch deserved it after what she had done.

"We'll start nice and simple," Riehl said, pushing the zipper down and grinning as she whimpered in front of him. "No one will be here for days. You don't mind, do you?" His tone was conversational. It was a stark contrast to the look of horror in her eyes as he leaned over her, his favorite knife in his hand, slicing the buttons off of her silver-gray blouse, one button at a time. Each button flew in a lazy arc to the right, skittering to the floor and out of sight.

Within seconds her blouse lay open, a lacy bra underneath. He reached up under her skirt and ripped the panties off. This made her whimper in fear as she squirmed, desperate to avoid his touch. He spread her legs, his hands bruising her knees as she fought him every inch of the way and then he thrust into her, hard, and watched as the tears slid down her cheeks.

Just as he was hitting his stride, an insistent and familiar ringing needled into the back of his brain, breaking his concentration, and the world fell away.

Damn it, I was only dreaming.

Beside him, on the battered wood nightstand, his phone buzzed, the green backlit screen flashing as he felt the remnants of his dream scatter. His eyes struggled to focus in the darkened room. Leaning forward put pressure on his swollen balls and he winced in pain, cursing as he reached for the phone.

"What?"

There was a momentary pause on the other end, before the caller asked, "What happened last Friday?"

Fuck.

"I misjudged her." It was the truth.

"You wanted to fuck her. I'm guess it didn't quite go as planned?"

"You could say that."

"The higher-ups are impatient to get this thing squashed. They sent in the Derasmo brothers."

Riehl sucked in a breath. "So, it's been taken care of." The Derasmo brothers were bad news. If they had been sent in, then someone was desperate for resolution. Bringing in the brothers was akin to bringing a nuclear bomb to a knife fight. They didn't do stealthy in and out, with no collateral damage. They did heavy duty, level the building and kill all witnesses, kind of operations.

"The Derasmo brothers are in the morgue."

Against one tiny slip of a woman? "*What?*"

"There's another player in the game."

"Just one? Are you sure? Who is it?" Riehl sat up, biting back a curse; his balls still ached, and one remained swollen and discolored. He stood gingerly, pushed open a curtain, and let in a sliver of light.

"They haven't gotten back to me with that information."

"So, what do you want me to do?"

"Stay put and wait. Sooner or later she will pop up. When she does, track her down and finish the job."

"That's it? What about this other guy? I need intel. I'm not going in there blind, especially not after some asshole good enough to take out the Derasmo brothers."

"You'll get it. And one more thing."

"What?"

"Call the contractor back. He's in a panic after the police rousted him out of bed and took him to the crime scene last night."

Riehl growled, "I don't do customer service. I don't hold their hands and tell them what they want to hear."

"If you hadn't fucked it up in the first place, we wouldn't be having this conversation. The contract would have been completed. So, go kiss his ass. This one's on you."

Riehl cursed as the line clicked and was silent. He held himself back from flinging the phone across the room. "The fucker can wait until I've had something to eat."

It didn't hurt as much as it had yesterday to move. By tomorrow he should be back to normal. He flipped on a light and it blinked for a moment, a low glow, before slowly warming and brightening. The room had a tiny mini-fridge which was stuffed with five boxes of various leftovers. He grabbed one. The smell of curry and tandoori hit him as the box was shifted and opened a small crack.

If he hadn't had the Indian food that night, she would have not had that extra half second of warning. He ate a bite and then tossed it in the trash in disgust.

He dialed the number and let it ring. There was a short pause after the second ring and then, "Morris speaking."

"I was told you needed an update on the situation."

"An *update*? Christ on a crutch, I need more than an update. I need to figure out what to say to the detective in charge of the case. He hauled me in last night and it looked like a goddamn war had erupted. It's on the goddamn news right now!"

Riehl rolled his eyes up, staring at the crack on the wall near the ceiling that traveled the width of his rented room. He had spent three days cradling his balls staring at that crack. The Derasmo brothers worked as a team, and were lethal - Lila Benoit should have been no match for them. So, who the hell was this other player?

Morris was still nattering on, and his voice raised an octave as Dominic said nothing in return and let the man sit and spin himself up into a lather.

"They are asking for a personnel list. They're gonna go down the entire list and talk to her and find out about her being attacked the other night and put two and two together and..."

"Don't include her name on the list," Riehl interrupted.

"What?"

"Leave it off the list and let the police work their way through the office personnel. I'll see that she's taken care of before the police come back to you asking why you forgot her. And if they do, well, tell 'em she was new and you forgot to add her to the list."

There was silence on the other end. Riehl closed his eyes. If he concentrated, he was pretty sure he would hear the wheels of this simpleton's brain turning.

"Do you know where she is?"

"No, but you do."

Morris sputtered, "No, I don't!"

"She has a company phone, right?"

"Uh, well, yes, she should."

"It should have a tracking app in it. Find it and send it to me via the secure email I just texted to you. I'll take it from there and contact you when the job is done."

"Christ. Are you sure this isn't going to blow up in my face? What if she calls the police?"

"What if she does? It will give me her exact location and I'll move on it then."

"This better work. I don't want this blowing back on me. I've worked too hard to get caught up in this bullshit."

Riehl held his tongue. Obviously, Morris Endon had worked hard. He had worked very hard at lining his pockets. But he hadn't covered his tracks well enough, hence the issue at hand.

"I'll wait for the email." His hand pressed the End Call button.

He lay back down in bed, his balls still aching. It set a different tone to life than his dream had. He could only hope he would get a chance to take his time with Lila Benoit. He knew of a place where he wouldn't be disturbed. It wasn't near here, a solid three-hour drive away, in fact. But if he got the chance, he'd take her there. It was remote, at least three miles from the nearest house, and he could take his time, spend days with his prize before he took her on a drive into the canyons and let the animals have her.

It was a natural paradise with bobcat sightings as well as a local wolf population. Disposing of bodies

there had never been a problem.

Boxers or Briefs

Lila stared at the door Shane Ellis had closed behind him. The thick carpet had absorbed the sound of his departure, only a small creak on the stairs below betraying his progress away from her door. She stared at the door, willing him to come back and complicate her life further. If he would just pull her up against him, slip his hand up under her skirt, and…

"Oh girl, as if you don't have enough problems!" She shook her head, fighting to get her hormones under control.

She was wide awake and certainly not ready for bed. The bourbon had taken the edge off and her jumpiness had vanished. It had left her with this delicious fire in her belly, one that would easily have been ignited further if hunky "call me Shane" hadn't left so abruptly. How she wished he had stayed, even as she was relieved that he had not. Her bruises from last Friday were still livid and angry against her pale skin.

This summer I really must *get a decent tan. If my skin gets any whiter, I'll look more like a vampire than anything else.*

She stared around her, drinking in the details.

Her curiosity led her to explore the room further. Shane had described the property as a safe house, which brought images of crummy, low-rent motel rooms to mind. Lila may have watched a few too many crime shows; but this room with its plush carpets, heavy ornate furniture, and Victorian-era knickknacks sang a different tune. It was more like staying in a private home, more personal than a bed and breakfast or upper-end hotel room. This house had class.

The room hovered between two distinct eras, however. There was a strong '70s vibe in the rough brown-black timbers that cut across the ceiling. The heavy iron accents and glass sconces added to that. The windows were simple, a crank at each angled the glass outward instead of up, and the molding along the base of the walls was simple, spare. The stonework of the large fireplace, firmly centered on one wall, paired with the rough timbers, iron and glass, gave an almost a church-like feel to the room. She eyed it, and thought briefly of her grandmother, now long-gone, and her attempts to bring Lila with her to Sunday services. Perhaps it was the dour congregation, or the preacher who threatened hellfire and damnation if his parishioners were foolish enough to choose rock music, alcohol, or a host of other Satan-centric activities - after nearly two years of regular church attendance, Lila had begged off. Granny had been going through chemo by then and didn't pursue it. Thankfully, Mom had never been interested, or religiously inclined for that matter, and Lila had been happy to never return.

The other era was positively Victorian, with antiques like the four-poster bed, its headboard carved with cherubs, and delicate, spindle-legged tables scattered through the room among ferns, cloth-bound books, and other bric-a-brac.

There was a built-in dresser in one corner of the room, another sharp trip forward in time to the '70s, accompanied by a large plain mirror. Next to it was the open door to the bathroom. She explored it further, noticing that in addition to the clawfoot bathtub, there was an odd tiled open shower of sorts. It was enormous and large enough for two people, possibly more, as evidenced by the multiple shower heads.

She licked her lips, imagining sharing it with the hot pecan pie and molasses guy who had just left her room. She could still feel the heat of his touch.

"Hell, he's probably some misogynistic prick beneath all that hotness and muscles. No one can look that good and be a nice guy." Lila said out loud to the empty room.

The room didn't answer of course, and suddenly Shane's suggestion of a nice, hot bath, sounded more appealing than anything else she could think of.

She let the water run in the tub until it was hot and steaming. Just stepping into it and slipping underneath the hot water was heaven. The heat melted into the tight muscles of her damaged arm and shoulder and she slid deeper into the water, her entire body immersed up to her earlobes. She loved her modern flat but found herself wishing for a huge bathtub like this. As if she could fit one in the tiny bathroom. It would have been impossible. There was barely room for the tiny shower.

There were three small dark blue glass bottles on the tub tray. The labels were in French, and she smiled as she quickly recognized what each bottle was for. "Shampooing, conditionneur, well those are both obvious. And let's see, sels de bain." She tapped her lip for a moment. "Ah, yes, sels is salts and bain means bath, so that must be bath salts."

She took some time to add the bath salts and relaxed, her hair up and out of the water, her eyes closed as she breathed in the floral scents of raspberry and vanilla. "A safe house, huh? This feels more like a spa."

Steam billowed, creeping along the low ceiling, obscuring the long mirror above the double sink and the window on the opposite side with a thick opaque layer.

Her thoughts turned to Shane. The man was dead sexy. So much for caramel pecan pie being a toad in person. Instead he was ooh la la attractive, confident, and a man of action. If he hadn't been there when those two gunmen came through, she would have been... Lila shuddered.

She hated thinking of it. It was terrifying, and she felt a knot form in her guts. What did they want with her? And why? It had to be a mistake.

She sank lower in the water and willed her mind to think of anything other than the bullets and blood and the fear she had felt. She thought again of Shane, turning away from the fear to the memory of how he had looked at her there in the kitchen, or in the car, or the stairwell. His hands, warm against her, checking to be sure she hadn't been shot or hurt. He'd given her a look that, despite having only a few lovers - Lila could count the men she had gone to bed with on one hand and fingers to spare - she could read clearly. He had been attracted to her, *was* attracted to her.

It had been like some electric current running between them - the lightest touch of his fingertips touching hers when he handed her the glass - she had felt his and her desire meet and sizzle like fire in between them.

He didn't make a move, though. Why? It probably went against that Code of his.

Well, Code or not, it was a shame he hadn't stepped one foot closer. After all she had seen tonight, a man like Shane would have made her forget those terrifying moments in the office. Just the thought of him touching her, the heat of his body...

A sigh escaped her lips at the thought of what it would feel like.

The water rolled slowly through the bathtub, soothing, the heat digging as deep into her muscles as if she were under the competent hands of a masseuse. Lila sighed again, and her left hand slipped down between her legs, fingers stroking the nub of her clit, her mind imagining what it would feel like to have his mouth on her, his tongue licking and teasing her. She closed her eyes and imagined his strong hands sliding along the side of her body, his lips on her neck, seducing her, claiming her body beneath his. Just imagining what he looked like under that tight-fitting shirt was enough to send her over the edge. Lila propped one leg up out of the sudsy water, her finger sliding back and forth, her neck stretched back. The wave of sensation crashed over her, her mouth open in an 'o' of pleasure as her finger danced and wrung out wave after wave of pleasure.

After the waves had subsided and she had slipped into a somnolent state, edging closer and closer toward the dark yet welcoming blanket of sleep, she sat up. Lila poured a generous dollop of the shampoo into her hand, breathing in the heady, clean scent of lemongrass as she lathered her long hair, sliding under the water to rinse the shampoo away. She relaxed every part of her body, letting the hot water dig deep into her sore muscles. It was marvelous, this bath. She stayed, unwilling to leave until she could feel the water beginning to cool.

Lila pulled the plug then and reached for a soft, richly fluffy towel, and wrapped herself in it. Standing on the bathmat, water running in rivulets off her warm, relaxed body, she stared at the clouds of steam that floated through the air, turning, rolling. The heat of the water had turned her muscles to mush and her eyelids were heavy with exhaustion.

Padding out of the bathroom, she walked barefoot, her toes sinking into the plush carpet, and pulled the heavy down comforter back from the bed, then slipped in between the silky bedsheets. The bed was warm, luxurious, and she felt her body sink into it as if she had crawled into a pile of downy comfort. She didn't bother to turn off any of the small lights that dotted the room, her eyes already heavy and her mind slipping into sleep. The day had been full of stress, and within minutes, Lila had fallen deeply into a dream.

The house was silent.

On the opposite side of the house, in the west wing at just past 2 a.m., a red light flashing in the top left corner of his room went unnoticed. Shane was deeply asleep, but the sharp buzz of his cell phone woke him instantly. He sat up, his sight blurred and then cleared as he checked the status of the compound on the app.

A door was open on the property. All vestiges of sleep were gone and his 9mm Ruger was in his hand, his feet in motion the second they hit the thick carpet. No time for clothes; this was a breach, a sliding door off of the kitchen, according to the alert that scrolled on his phone.

He was on high alert, and the dream he had been enjoying mere seconds before was a distant memory as he ran down the dark hallway, down the half flight of stairs, and through the kitchen. The curtains billowed slightly, a cool evening breeze sucking them out to the deck outside the sliding glass door. The deck outside was partially lit by a bright moon playing hide and seek behind dark clouds that slowly rolled across the night sky.

He saw her feet bare on the deck before anything else and immediately lowered his weapon. Lila was clad in nothing but a blanket, her hair dark, and still slightly damp from her bath. She smiled at him, raising her eyebrows as she took in the handgun he held in his right hand. "Don't shoot, I'm unarmed."

"Silent alarm," he explained. "It went off the second you opened the door."

"Sorry about that." Lila pulled the blanket closer to her body. It was unseasonably warm for late fall, but nonetheless there was a nip to the air. "I looked out the window, saw the river and the lights, and just had to take in the view. Is that Parkville, over there?"

Shane stepped closer to her, followed her finger. "Yes, and that's Park University right there and over to the left, that's the airport." She smelled of lemons. It combined with her own unique, sweet vanilla musk scent, and he caught himself leaning closer and reaching for her with his other hand. The dream of her was still lingering in his animal hindbrain - and he suppressed a flash of desire. The things he wanted to do to her, *had* been doing to her in that dream that was so maddeningly interrupted. He placed his free hand on the railing and forced himself to look off into the night sky.

"The view is incredible!" she breathed, her attention absorbed by the stunning skyline. The lights shimmered off the water, the wide river undulating and twisting, the black water occasionally showing a frothy wake as it moved over sandbars, heading inevitably toward the Gulf of Mexico hundreds of miles away.

"When the judge bought it back in 1970, the total acreage was 20 acres, but he sold five of the acres to the city of Kansas City, Kansas so they could build a water treatment plant. It is remote, yet accessible, so it works quite well for our needs," Shane explained.

Lila's eyes were locked on the distant glow of lights from Parkville's pride and joy, Park University, which sat on a hilltop, a collection of turn-of-the-century brick buildings. Even in the middle of the night, the lights clearly lit up the main building.

"Jack Benton, a multi-millionaire who owns a private security firm," Lila said, shivering in her blanket. "There has to be a story behind that."

"Undoubtedly, but it isn't my story to tell."

"But you know it."

"Yes."

Lila laughed softly and said, "A circumspect bodyguard. How interesting."

Shane didn't respond. In his line of work there were many times when silence was the more prudent answer.

Silence followed, interrupted only by the steady low thrum of the plant in the near distance. Lights lit up the plant at intervals and Shane could see a lone security guard making the rounds before disappearing back inside through a side door. They watched a plane take off into the air, lights blinking steadily, as it slowly ascended into the night sky and disappeared into the clouds.

Lila shivered again.

"You're cold. Come on, let me get you inside and get you warmed up." Shane guided her back to the open door, acutely aware that he was rather under-dressed to be outside in late fall wearing only boxer briefs. Lila's eyes traveled over him and he could smell the lemongrass shampoo in her hair as she passed close to him, heading into the house.

"Can I get you a drink?" he asked once they had stepped through the door. It felt wonderful inside after the chilly breeze on the back deck. Shane slid the lock into place.

"Yes, please." Lila stared down the hall into the sunken living room.

"Sit down, I'll get you something."

Chesterfield and Bourbon

The living room Lila stepped into was actually more of a den, fully masculine, complete with hunting trophies. Three rather unfortunate deer heads adorned the dark wood-paneled walls, and an enormous, tufted black leather Chesterfield sofa and chair took up most of the space in front of the fireplace. The plush, high carpet had been abandoned here for a parquet floor and a fur rug in front of the hearth. The thick fur felt luxurious under her feet. Above, the open rafters were a chocolate brown, almost black, rough-hewn and large. The den held that odd mesh of styles - the '70s vibe cluttered with various groupings of Victorian antiques that included an Edison Victrola and large organ with mother-of-pearl buttons, tabs, and pulls. The fireplace emitted a fair amount of heat from the gas logs within, the flame slowly rippling in a lazy cascade of orange, yellow, and occasionally blue.

Lila chose a corner of the immense Chesterfield sofa. The buttons were buried deep in the black leather, and it had a high back and matching arms. It conveyed a feeling of wealth and intimidation all at once and she could clearly imagine men in coattails sitting and puffing on cigars while the delicate ladies of the manse tittered in some small dainty room on the opposite side of the house.

Shane placed a glass in her hand. "Is bourbon alright?" The glass was heavy, cut crystal, and the two ice cubes sloshed seductively in the amber liquid. "Or perhaps you would rather have wine? I could check and see if there is any downstairs."

There was a room below the den, lined in stone, with racks of wine. It was an extensive collection.

Shane had been surprised when Jack had told him to take Lila here. His boss still used this as his own private residence when he was in the area and there were other safe houses that were more modern, less filled with antiques and cut crystal. Nice, but not opulent.

Benton had kept all the odd furniture from the last tenants, two men with a love of everything Victorian who had somehow landed in a 1970s ranch house instead of where their hearts belonged, in Victorian England.

Benton had bought the house, all its contents, and changed little. He said once to Shane that he "liked the cacophony of it all." The wine cellar was one small improvement, and the security cameras and alarms were a big one. No one could come within one-quarter mile of the house without a bevy of alarms being sounded and a host of security cameras recording their every move.

Lila suppressed a shudder at Shane's inquiry. Wine gave her headaches, vodka gave her hangovers, but bourbon or whiskey, when used in moderation, seemed to have zero negative effects on her.

"Bourbon is just fine, thanks."

Shane sat down in the matching Chesterfield chair, swallowed up by the high back and sides. She raised the glass to her lips and let the strong liquor roll past her lips and over her tongue. She didn't drink often. And while she had created a tiny liquor cabinet in her apartment, she had rarely touched it. Only socially, when entertaining, and her social life had been rather hit or miss lately.

The kegger parties in college hadn't really appealed and she hadn't had much in the way of discretionary spending until the last few months, but she had on a few occasions been exposed to quality liquor. Mainly from tiny pilfering of her parents' liquor cabinet where her dad had only stored the really good stuff.

He had told her that there was no point buying cheap liquor. "Your mom is always reminding me that cheap liquor is like buying cheap shoes - neither of them is good for your body. Get the good stuff or don't bother getting anything at all. I guess that means we all need to go barefoot or something like that." Lila's dad had been funny and sweet. She missed him. He believed in quality everything. They didn't have to have the newest, or the most fashionable, but he did want them to have the best that they could afford. Those stolen nips of bourbon, whiskey and more had definitely taught her the difference in taste.

She savored the taste of the bourbon in her glass. This was excellent. It just added to the mystery of Benton Security Services. So far, this whole protection detail was nothing like what she had expected.

Where were the grimy, barren rooms with beige curtains and mustard-yellow walls? There wasn't a grim detective smoking a cigarette and warning her that the bad guys were just waiting for her to step out the door. And this also wasn't the Ritz, with its maddening fusion of '70s wood and beam, and Victorian froufrou.

She stared at Shane, who had settled into the chair, and Lila felt confused and turned on all over again. She tucked her feet deeper into the blanket and tried not to notice the large bulge in his boxer briefs. The rest of his body was bare, smooth skin, muscles prominent but not ridiculous.

Lila couldn't stand those men who spent hours lifting weights until their muscles bulged unnaturally, limiting their movement so that they just lumbered by like a proud stag, flexing their muscles. Who wanted that, really? A guy who couldn't even bend or flex normally? And if she was carrying the metaphor of the deer a little further - those stupid deer got shot. Shane was quick, strong when he needed to be strong, and sexy as hell. That five o'clock shadow, and the chiseled jaw. Her internal dialogue stopped dead as he quirked an eyebrow at her. She had been staring.

"Um, what?" He had spoken, but she hadn't even heard him.

"I talked to my boss," Shane said again. "The men I shot in the hallway there at Kurgen. They were contract killers, Lila." He paused, looked her over, and frowned. "Someone really wants you dead. Got any ideas why?"

"Unless it's for overdue library books, I've got nothing." She shrugged. "I'm nobody, Shane."

"Lila, everyone is..."

She blew out a breath, took a sip of bourbon, and leaned forward, preoccupied with the mystery. "I haven't witnessed a crime or found stolen merchandise, and I'm not into drugs or any illicit activity. I'm a data analyst."

"Okay, tell me more. What do you do for Kurgen in your role as a data analyst?"

"For the most part I simply analyze market trends and then make recommendations - when to buy, when to sell, what markets are up, which are down, that sort of thing."

"So, would you call it marketing?"

"Not really, although marketing is a component. Basically, I'm the translator of data. Information, numbers, statistics. By understanding the data and interpreting it, I help management make better business decisions moving forward."

"That sounds like quite a demanding position."

She shrugged. "I do end up working more hours than I initially thought I would, but it's interesting work and the best job I've ever had. I really enjoy it."

He leaned back, drained his glass, and set it down. "Somehow this has to do with your work."

Lila shook her head. "I just don't see how."

"Occam's Razor. It means..." She put up her hand.

"I know what Occam's Razor means."

"Of course, you do. Look, what else could it be? You're squeaky clean. Believe me, I can smell dirt a mile away and you haven't got any. You've seen something, heard something, maybe just read it. It might be sitting on your desk at this very moment, some piece of a puzzle you stumbled on and didn't even recognize, but it is there."

His words stirred a random memory in her mind.

It might be sitting on your desk at this very moment. It couldn't be that. Surely not.

Lila could feel his eyes on her, assessing her, observing her every reaction. She smiled wryly and took the last sip of bourbon. The fire of it slid down her throat and she could feel it working already, a layer of calm lassitude settling over her. Between that and the fire, her thoughts were slowing, and exhaustion from the past few days seeped into her. Being in pain took energy, fear did too, and her body and mind were conspiring to send her into a warm, fuzzy land surrounded with Egyptian cotton sheets and the slow warmth emanating from the fireplace.

Lila leaned her head back, the high back of the sofa swallowing her up.

"Another bourbon?" Shane's voice was low, and she closed her eyes and shook her head.

Why did he have to sound so damned sexy? Normally a man like that would have her as jumpy as a cat, but now, with the bourbon coursing through her bloodstream and her body and mind exhausted from her injuries, the fear and flight from the office, and the reassuring quiet and isolation of the house she was now in, all she wanted to do was sleep.

Shane watched her. The arch of her neck, her delicate skin still mottled with bruises. The way one delicate breast was half-exposed, peeking out of the blanket. Her legs were drawn up to her chest and angled to the right, exposing a toned, shapely thigh.

He let his gaze travel from her toes all the way to her sleep-tousled hair. He took his time, listening as her breathing slowed and deepened. Shane stood up and plucked the now-empty glass from her hand.

She snapped awake.

He reached out a hand to help her up. "You're done in. Get some rest. We will talk more in the morning."

Lila nodded and made her way up the stairs. Her steps were silent, swallowed up in the plush thickness of the carpet. So were Shane's. It gave her a jolt to realize he was directly behind her, towering over her as she placed her hand on the doorknob and it turned effortlessly. He looked down into her eyes, and reached behind her to push the door open.

He was close, and despite her exhaustion, her heartbeat increased, a sharp desire running through her. She sucked in a breath, and the gap between their two bodies closed as he moved closer, one hand straying to the small of her back.

He bent his head down, his mouth mere inches from hers. "And no more going outside of the house. At least, not without me."

His words were a dash of reality, a splash of ice on her libido. She stiffened and turned away from him, through the door, and closed it with a decisive kick of her foot.

Shane smiled as the door slammed, then shook his head. *Damned if she isn't sexy when she's pissed off.*

The bulge in his underwear hadn't lessened one iota. But he could hear Jack's words echoing in his head, "Keep it professional."

"I'm trying my best, Boss," he muttered under his breath as he descended the stairs and made his way towards the west wing of the house, "But damned if she doesn't have something about her that I can't stop thinking about."

Behind the closed door, Lila stomped to the bed, the sleepy lassitude she had felt in the den gone, replaced by indignation. She slid into the covers, fuming. "Stay in the house. Like I'm an errant child! As if I can't take care of myself!"

The bed, with its silky soft sheets and feather softness, slowly worked its magic. And despite herself, as she drifted off, she couldn't help imagining what it would have been like if instead of speaking, he had kissed her instead. He had wanted to, she was sure of it. She imagined him leaning in, his lips soft yet demanding, his tongue slipping past her teeth. She shivered at the thought of it. A full body-tingling shiver of desire. She closed her eyes and imagined him kissing her breasts, down her stomach, and a tongue touching in the most sensitive spot of all. The fantasy morphed into dreams of hot bodyguards and danger around every turn.

On the far side of the house, Shane sent a quick text to Jack, updating his boss on what little they had discussed. Then Shane lay down in his own bed and spent the rest of the night tossing and turning, his head filled with images of Lila's lithe body in this bed and how it would feel to touch her, kiss her, and slip his way between her legs. He saw the clock click to 2 a.m., 3 a.m., and even 4 a.m. before a deep sleep stole him away shortly before dawn.

Call in Sick

It was her first day of work all over again and Lila followed Blanche into a glassed-in office. It was empty, and she was shocked all over again to realize that it was meant for her, that she wasn't being shunted off to a gray cubicle the farthest from windows and natural light. Instead, the rays of the rising sun reflected off of the building on the opposite side of the street, turning the glass walls into a reflection of the fiery ball pushing its way up on the horizon, round, bulbous clouds slowly marching across the sky. The office was for her.

"Let Human Resources know if you have any specific needs," Blanche said, "And they should have your laptop delivered and up and running by the end of the day."

She had nodded wordlessly, overwhelmed at her change in fortune.

The young man from Nerds R Us had knocked on her door a few minutes later. She had passed him on the way in as he stood at the front desk to talk to the bright-eyed receptionist.

His black polo shirt sported a bright yellow splat on the front left breast, the words Nerds R Us filling it. Below his name badge read Alex M.

"Hi, Miz Benoit? I'm Alex and I'm here to get you up and running on your new computer."

The sun shining in her eyes was bright. It bleached out everything else.

The first bright rays of the sun crawled through the windows and across Lila's covers. She was awake, lying there in the bed, her mind racing. This is how it was for her in the mornings. Often before the sun rose, Lila's brain would turn on and she would know that sleeping in was simply not in the cards. Instead, she would plot out her day, review whatever duties or errands were necessary for the hours ahead, and jump into problem-solving while others were still blearily reaching for their coffee cups.

Today, despite her lack of sleep, was no exception.

The dream still hung in her mind, like gray smoke curling from a chimney... no substance, but still a reality.

Dreams are funny things and Lila usually took hers quite seriously. She had good reason to. A week before her dad had died in a car accident, she had woken up screaming, the image of a huge tractor/trailer bearing down on her as she straddled a bicycle in the middle of I-70. It had been less than a month after earning her driver's license and her mother had dismissed it with, "It is nothing but nerves, dear."

Lila had listened to her mother, smoothed over the image of that enormous tractor trailer, and intentionally changed it to a more positive mental image of her driving a convertible in the summer. On a sunny day in March, a long-haul driver had fallen asleep at the wheel, just long enough to cross the median and crush the compact Smart car Anthony Benoit had so proudly purchased the year before. He had died instantly.

Lila closed her eyes and willed the memories out of her mind. Those empty years after, first in their overly large, quiet house, watching her mother fade, losing her color, her laughter, her ambition. Later in the small apartment they had moved to when the mortgage payments had proved too much for a widowed, grieving mother. Mom had never recovered. They had been high school sweethearts, separated for a decade after high school before reuniting and marrying in a whirlwind romance. They had been inseparable all of Lila's life and losing Dad had hollowed them out, removed the heart and soul of their family.

She pushed the sadness away. She needed to focus on getting the laptop and taking another look at those files. Those files could explain everything. She stretched, pushed the covers aside, and caught a whiff of...bacon? Apparently, she wasn't the only early riser.

A quick review of the closets and built-in dresser revealed basic sweats and T-shirts, all sizes and colors. Lila found a pair of black yoga pants and a zip-front gray sweatshirt, both of which had plenty of room on her lean frame, and slipped them on. They would do for now, until she could get back to her apartment and change.

By now, the delectable smell of bacon and fresh coffee had drifted fully into her room and her stomach had responded, growling. Lila walked out onto the landing, then down the carpeted stairs barefoot, finding her way to the kitchen with ease, guided by her nose and grumbling stomach.

Shane was dressed in black jeans and a black T-shirt, his back to her as she entered the kitchen. His jaw was stubbled with a five o'clock shadow. She swallowed down a squirmy feeling of desire and nerves. He was good-looking, dead sexy, and she was all alone with him in this enormous house.

Beside him was a plate filled with bacon and he was apparently cooking the entire dozen eggs.

"Where is the army?" she asked, reaching for the bacon. He smacked her hand. "Hey!"

"Not yet," he said, "wait for the eggs. Have some coffee." He didn't even make eye contact and she was amused and annoyed at the same time.

"Good morning to you too!" she said, and poured the rich black coffee from the glass French press into a waiting coffee mug. A man who cooked, what a novel concept. Her dad had been completely hopeless, and Todd, the few times she had stayed over, was even worse. He had kept microwaveable bacon in his cupboards, rows of it. She shook her head, remembering it, *absolutely disgusting.*

"Cream? Sugar?" Shane asked, jolting her out of her memories of Todd, bad sex, and even worse eating experiences. He pointed to the small sugar dish. "There's creamer in the fridge."

Lila sat at the long dining room table, the mug steaming, warming her hands. The sun's rays lit up the eastern set of sliding glass doors and she would have been blinded in the bright light if it hadn't been for the thick curtains. Shane's work at the stove yielded two large plates, one of bacon and one of scrambled eggs, both heaped high. He handed her a plate and a fork, and then helped himself after she had taken what she wanted.

"So, where's everyone else?" Lila asked, gesturing towards the food left on the plate.

Shane quirked an eyebrow. "I have a high metabolism."

He wasn't kidding. He ate every scrap on his plate, before returning for more, stopping only once to offer one last chance at the food before he finished it off. Lila watched, fascinated, until the last bite was consumed. She had never seen anyone eat so much food in one sitting.

"I need to get to work," Lila said, breaking the silence that had gathered between them.

Shane shook his head. "No. You need to call in sick."

"What? I can't call in sick, I don't *want* to call in sick!"

Shane leaned back in his chair, tossed down the last of the coffee in his mug, and regarded her steadily. "Last night someone tried to kill you."

Lila snapped, "Yes, I do remember that, I was there."

Shane raised an eyebrow. "I can't protect you in a public place. You need to stay here until we can get to the bottom of things."

"I can't just stay home from work. I can't, I'm *new*. I *need* this job." Not just that, but she needed to look at her laptop. Somehow it was connected with her dream, she was sure of it.

"No can do. Besides, no one in your office will be at work today. I checked in and they still have it roped off while they process the scene. The only place you are going is to the police station to make a statement, and that's *when* they contact you."

Lila thought of the men dead on the floor. The priceless art, the possible finger of blame that might be directed at her. She had been there. They would dust the cups in the sink and find her fingerprints, and, and...

And what? Know you worked there? Big deal. They had bodies *to deal with.*

The eggs and bacon suddenly turned in her stomach. The memory of blood staining the carpet amid shards of the priceless vase was burned into her brain.

Can I even go back there after that?

Still, his attitude rankled at her. He wasn't asking her, he was *telling* her what she would do. And that didn't sit well with her, not at all.

She tried a different tack. "Look, I need to be at work, or at the very least *working*, and that requires my laptop."

"And your laptop is at the office."

"Yes, well..." She blinked, remembering suddenly. "Hold on, I've got one at home that has all of the same files and access to the rest on the cloud. Would that be easier to pick up?"

He nodded. "Yeah, that could work. Let me make a couple of calls and I'll see if I can't get it for you."

"And what am I supposed to do until then?" She sounded bitchy, she knew she did. She hated the feeling that the entire world was out doing something and she had to stay hidden. *I didn't do anything wrong, so why is this happening to me?*

He stood up, gathered her empty plate, and turned to the sink. "I'm sure you will think of something. Stay inside, though. I need to talk to my boss and get some updates and by noon we should have a plan of action."

Lila swallowed back a biting remark. Her life had been turned upside down in the past few days. The hearty breakfast she had eaten sat heavy in her stomach. A week ago, her life had been perfect. *Well, nearly perfect.* And now it felt like a train going off the tracks. She sighed and stood up.

"I'll wash, you dry." She shooed him away from the sink and plunged her hands into the soapy water. It was, after all, an excuse to do *something*.

She tried again after the dishes were done and the kitchen back to the way it had looked last night, neat as a pin, everything in its place. "Look, I just need to get there and pick up the laptop." She reached out and touched his hand. Men liked that, at least, that's what Kaylee said worked for her, and from what Lila could tell, Kaylee ruled half of the floor on just a smile and a light touch of her hand. She mustered a bright smile. "You could come with me."

He slowly looked at her hand resting on his and moved his eyes up. She forgot to breathe as they crept up her, a slow crawl of desire coupled with danger, a threat of the rules changing. She had changed them; she had crossed the line.

When he pulled his hand away, it didn't feel like rejection. She wasn't an overly sensitive girl who hung meaning on every word or movement from a man. She was, however, relieved. Once she had touched him, felt his heat, stepped into his personal space and broken that unspoken rule, she had been unable to let go. *Third rail.* Like the trains in the tunnels that flew along, electricity humming, hugging that third rail that enabled the connection and through which one could feel a raw, surging power. Touching him felt like it must feel to stand on the third rail and make a connection guaranteed to light your hair on fire and scorch your shoes. She stepped back as their connection broke, feeling the electricity between them snap and release.

"I'll go and you will stay. This isn't a negotiation." He said it in a cool way that dumped metaphorical ice all over her raging hormones.

Now *that* was rejection, or at the very least a smack-down that made her bristle with indignation before turning away. She hated that he was right. This man had saved her life, the least she could do would be to stay on the property for now. He would bring the laptop and then she could see if her dream had been the clue that she needed to solve this mystery. A cold wave washed over her, dampening her indignation further as she remembered the night before.

After all, he's right, someone is trying to kill me.

Shane strode away from her, trying desperately to ignore the growing bulge in his jeans. As he headed down the hall, phone in hand, he shook his head, trying to desperately to rip the fantasy of what he wanted to do to her from his mind. *Fucking the client is not allowed, Ellis. Yeah? Tell your dick that.*

He jabbed at the phone in his hand and Jack answered a few seconds later. "Talk to me."

"She's gung-ho about going to work. More specifically, she needs her laptop. She mentioned she also has data backups at home, on her home laptop." Shane answered.

"I'll have Lou retrieve the laptop from her apartment. If we go directly to the company and someone is dirty, they will know she has help. I'd like to keep her invisible and them in the dark for as long as possible," Jack said. "Meet me at the usual place at 10 a.m. sharp."

"Will do." Shane snapped the phone shut and checked his watch. It was nearly nine. He had time for a shower and a quick shave.

Suspicions

Rob sipped the coffee, curling his lip at the saccharine sweet aftertaste. "Ugh."

"Buck up, Dad, it's better for you than sugar." Madeleine slid past him and reached into the fridge.

"A couple of teaspoons of sugar can't hurt," he answered. "And what's with this inky black color? Are we out of creamer already? I thought I got some last Friday."

She shuffled containers around. "I threw it out."

"Why would you do that, Squirt?"

She emerged, a small stack of containers balanced in her hands as she toed the door closed. "Do you realize we never eat leftovers? And then they fill up the fridge and block the yogurt and produce bins."

"It's still good."

"Yeah? This one has green fur growing on top."

She deposited the containers into the sink and he could see a green creeping mass on top of the white rice in one, the other streaked with orange was a mystery he wasn't interested in solving.

"And that 'couple of teaspoons per cup' adds up to a lot when you drink twelve cups in a day. Ms. Watts says you need to watch your triglycerides as well, so I tossed the creamer and we are both going to get used to drinking it black."

"Oh, for crying out loud, that health teacher is out of her mind." Rob glared at his daughter. "I'll eat what I want."

She stared at him, her eyes big, looking just like Claire would when she was determined to win an argument through whatever means necessary. Rob had to wonder if it was something Maddy remembered or if it was just ingrained in her feminine psyche.

"Dad, all I have is you. If you drop dead of a heart attack, what happens to *me*?" She looked vulnerable and scared, and even though he knew she was manipulating him as only one possessing such formidable feminine wiles could, his resistance melted.

"Fine," Rob mumbled, and sipped his stevia-laced coffee, his shoulders sagging in defeat. He never could muster a defense to that kind of argument. It was pointless to try. Maddy smiled and kissed him on the cheek.

"I have to leave early. I'm meeting Julia at her house; she needs help with her spelling practice. We're entering the spelling bee and I promised her we would practice before school."

"I should drive you."

Maddy rolled her eyes. "Dad, she's at the corner. You can watch me walk there, okay?"

"You have the pepper spray, right? And your phone?"

"Yes, Dad, of course I do." She rolled her eyes, reached up and hugged him. The past year had seen a growth spurt and his daughter had shot up two, maybe three inches. The top of her head reached his shoulder. She had nearly passed her mother's height and she still had a few years of growing left to go. Her strawberry-blond hair had darkened to a fiery red and it was shoulder length and a mass of ringlets.

He hugged her back.

Maddy was a beauty. Rob sighed. *Just like her mother.*

"Did you sign up yet, Dad?"

"Sign up for what?"

"The link I sent you, Meet Your Match."

Rob groaned.

"Dad, you *promised*."

"I promised I'd think about it. And I did."

"And?"

"And I have time before you go off to college. Plenty of time. Five years' worth of time, girl. Stop playing matchmaker."

"Look, Dad, you need to find someone before you get any older."

He choked on his coffee, liquid spraying from his lips. "Christ."

"See what I mean, Dad? Hand-eye coordination is one of the first things to go." She grinned. "Besides, I'm seeing some white hairs in that goatee."

"Believe me, girl, they are all thanks to you," he growled, dabbing at the coffee that had dribbled onto his shirt.

Her lips tickled his cheek. "Gotta go. Love you!" She was out the door, the storm door banging closed behind her.

He really needed to fix that door spring so that it didn't make such a racket. He took another gulp of coffee, his lip curling in disgust. Its saccharine-sweet taste was disgusting. He stood up and poured the rest down the sink.

His spine popped and his left side spasmed. He'd pulled his back out last year while clearing some brush in the yard and it hadn't felt right since. *Christ, I am getting old.* He shook his head and headed to the bathroom. As he brushed his teeth and ran a comb through his hair, he remembered Claire plucking at a white hair that had sprung out of his chest.

"Can't have you turning into a silverback quite yet, now can I?" She had pulled it out, root and all. It had hurt like hell. In the decade since, that one silver hair had been joined by a sprinkling, and in the past year, a cascade of others.

"Time and tide wait for no man." He leaned in closer, peering at the streak of white among the still mostly dark hairs. He kept it trimmed neatly; Claire had liked it that way.

Rob sighed, staring at his reflection. If he could ask her, he knew what she would say. Hell, she *had* said it.

"Life is too short. Grieve, but get over it. Face it, my love, we humans are better suited to relationships than not."

But meeting someone else, all the delicate dances that come from learning how to live with someone else, to anticipate their moods, their needs, and finding a way to balance being a father to Maddie while sharing time with someone new?

He had gone to the site and been run through its paces. Answering the questions on the personality quiz had been challenging and frustrating. Was this really how people did it these days? Answer some quasi-scientific questions and get connected with your future mate? It had to be bullshit. A computer algorithm couldn't tell him who he was supposed to love. Yet he had kept returning to it.

I'll try it out and do a test run. Hell, it could be fun.

He left the bathroom and headed down to the basement where he had built a small office and kept everything under lock and key. He was a homicide investigator, after all, and Maddie didn't need to see how base and cruel humans could be with each other.

Rob sat down at his desk and opened an email from work and stared at the tattooed image of the Indalo on each of the dead men's wrists. There was no mistaking it, the symbol was simple, rudimentary, and exactly like the tattoo he had seen ten years ago. He reached into a box, rifled through its contents until he found Maddie's crude drawing, now a decade old. A memory flashed through his mind of the day before their trip to the playground, when he had called Milo and Steve at the CIA. The case they had been working on, spearheaded by Rob, had languished in the weeks after Claire's death. He had conferenced them in, told him he would be returning to work in two days. It was time to take the bull by the horns and get back to work, he had told them.

The next day had been their trip to the playground and the run-in with that woman, the not-so-veiled threat of the two women with the photograph and the note. Was it the phone call to his co-workers that had triggered the message to be sent? Had they bugged his house there in Virginia? Had he gotten too close to figuring out who they were? Rob searched decade-old memories, trying to remember details of the case he had investigated.

He hadn't called Steve or Milo again, just left them to be targeted in his stead. He took a deep breath in and released it slowly. *I'm no fucking hero, am I? I just took care of me and mine and said fuck off to the rest.*

But now, here in Kansas City, in flyover country, where politics, shady financial deals, and hired hits were unheard of - here is where the Indalo had popped back up.

"Indalo."

Just saying the word gave it substance. This wasn't something he could run from. If they were here, then they were everywhere, or damn near. He shook his head and stifled a rueful smile at the thought of running away with Maddie to some lone mountaintop with sheep and mountain goats. She would *not* be down for that. The girl was connected at the hip to her iPhone. So much so that he had banned devices at the dinner table and at the movies. How could she watch a movie while texting on the phone, anyway?

His hand reached for his phone and then stopped. *Could they still be listening?* The question sent his mind spinning. He wouldn't have been hard to track, after all. He stood up from his desk. For the first time in nearly ten years he felt afraid, unsafe even, in his own house.

His cell phone buzzed. Maddie's face flashed on the screen, red hair, curls, and her beautiful brown eyes.

"Everything okay, Sweetheart?"

"Everything's great, Dad. I forgot to tell you it was a half day and it turns out that Julia's mom is taking her to Coco Key after school today and they invited me. Can I go?"

"Sure. Do you want to come back here and get your swimsuit?"

"Nah, mine's here from the last time we went swimming. We were planning on dinner and a movie after, is that okay too?" He smiled, even if she couldn't see it.

"Sure. Be home by ten?"

"Will do. Thanks, Dad. I love you!"

"Love you too, Maddie."

His shift didn't start until 6 p.m. tonight, so he would have the house to himself for a few hours. And that was convenient; he didn't need an excuse to get Maddie out of the house while he swept for bugs. But first, he needed some supplies and to visit someone he knew could help. He grabbed his keys and headed out the door.

A short drive to Historic Northeast and Rob parked his car in front of a nondescript brick building and got out, locking the door.

"Hey there, handsome, looking for a date?" The voice was effeminate, and a prominent set of breasts protruded from the top of a skintight dress, but the Adam's apple was a dead giveaway that not all was as it appeared.

Rob said nothing, just flashed his badge as he walked on past. The effect on the male prostitute was immediate. He said nothing, just spun on his high heels and disappeared around the corner in two seconds flat. Rob suppressed a smile and entered the building, a small buzzer sounding as he walked through the doorway into the brightly lit shop.

"Robbie!" The grizzled older man stood up and walked over, clapping him on the shoulder, "I haven't seen you in nine tomorrows, where have you been? And how is that beautiful little girl of yours doing?"

"Hi, Ben, good to see you." He hugged the older man. "You've lost weight, old man."

"Eh, the fuckin' cancer came back." He shrugged. "They keep tellin' me I got six months, tops. Hell, I've been hearing that for four years now, but the last few weeks have been vexing."

Rob stared at him, a long look that took in the dark circles under his eyes, the pale, unhealthy sheen to Ben's complexion, and the way his clothes hung from him.

"Shit, Ben, I'm so sorry."

Ben shrugged. "Eh, c'est la vie. I've lived a great life, Robbie, traveled the world and loved a woman long after she left me for greener pastures. I've seen plenty and lived more than most. Sometimes it's just your time, y'know?"

Rob nodded. "Yeah, I do."

Ben clapped him on the shoulder again and grinned at him. "How old is Maddie now?"

Rob shook his head and groaned. "Thirteen going on twenty-one. The girl is starting to turn heads."

"Time to get that shotgun primed with rock salt, Robbie. Put the fear of God in any of those hormonal teenage boys that come sniffing around."

Rob laughed and said, "I'm working on it. Believe me, I'm working on it!"

"So, what brought you my way today? I can see you have something on your mind." Ben might be dying, but he was as astute as ever.

"Let's say I think that someone's listening in."

"House or work?"

"My home."

Ben nodded and was still, his face thoughtful. "That would be odd, considering you are a homicide detective. Unless you are thinking it's mafia-level."

"I wasn't always a homicide detective, Ben."

"I'm aware. Hell, you still carry yourself like a company man. It's spooked some of my customers over the years."

Rob and Ben had met over eight years ago after a spike of murders in Historic Northeast had played out along Independence Avenue. The older man's background with the police, he was once a homicide investigator like Rob, and his keen eye for noticing when things were off, had helped collar a man targeting prostitutes on the Avenue.

The older man didn't play games, he didn't ask questions he had no place asking, but he also saw far more than he let on. He'd known what Rob was, and said nothing.

"I need to find out if someone is watching or listening."

Ben nodded. "I've got what you need, but it would be a good idea for you to bring any laptops or other devices in and have my techie look at them. Be able to tell if there is any keylogging software installed."

"I'll bring mine in on Saturday if that's okay. As for that kiddo of mine, I'm pretty sure she's attached at the hip to it. It might require surgery. If the operation is a success, I'll bring hers in as well."

Ben snorted, "Tell me about it. That's the way all the kids are these days. Give me a couple of minutes and I'll get you set up."

Rob nodded and examined the wares in a new glass case Ben had installed since the last time he had visited the shop. "Hey Ben, add one of those onto my order, please." He pointed to an object in the case. "You never know when that might come in handy."

"Sure thing, Robbie."

A few minutes later, his purchases bagged and paid for, he hugged the older man. "Let me know if you need anything, Ben, anything at all."

"Hug that beautiful girl of yours, Robbie. And stay safe."
Rob nodded. "See you on Saturday."

Re-Open the Case

Rob walked into the house. It was time to get answers, one way or the other. He pulled out the detector and began moving through each room of the house. By the time he had reached the third room, he was so angry he couldn't trust himself to speak. His home, his sanctuary, had been defiled. And for how long?

Had they listened to every conversation he and Maddie had ever had in this house? Listened as she grew from a tiny little girl missing her mom to the teenager with a full bevy of friends and middle school crushes?

The times he had spoken to Claire, out loud, missing her so bad it took his breath away, telling her about their child, how Maddie had learned to ride a bike, how she had read from her first book one night, just days before starting kindergarten. And all the moments in between.

He had thought it was all private, that he and Maddie were safe here, but he had been wrong. So wrong. There was nothing safe or private about this place.

Rob felt lightheaded, his heart rate skyrocketing as he stared at the red x's he had drawn on the walls. He dug into the sheetrock with his knife, feeling the difference when the tip of it found the bug. He pulled it out of the wall, seething, and carried it into the garage. He ground it into a mass of plastic shards under his foot on the bare cement floor and returned to the house. One by one, he dug them out of walls, found them in light fixtures, and the undersides of furniture. One by one, he carried them to the garage and ground them under his shoe. In all, he found fifteen, two in Maddie's room. The fury he felt at that, at his child being watched by these bastards, ran through him, a river of ice and fear.

And who could he trust? Was there anyone he could go to, talk to, and be sure of?

What did these people, this shadow organization, want? They had taken Claire from him, he was sure of it. They had threatened him, threatened to hurt his little girl, and that was more than he could bear. Maddie was all that he had left. Finding the bugs had proven to him one thing; they had *not* gone away and they never would. No more running. It was time for him to become the hunter instead of the prey.

But first he had some spackling to do. Maddie didn't need to know about this and he would do whatever he had to do to keep her safe.

Later that afternoon, Milo Barnaby picked up the phone and answered it, distracted, his attention on the report in front of him.

"Milo Barnaby."

"Milo, Rob Stone here."

"Stone? Rob *Stone*? Damn man, it's been years! How are you?"

"I'm doing well enough. And you? How's Diana?"

"We split three years ago," Milo sighed. "She traded up for silver hair, a Porsche, and a house in the Hamptons. I get a visit with Gus when they go out of town and a month in the summer. She told me her mother always said she had married beneath her. So much for happily ever after, right?"

Rob whistled, "Damn. I'm sorry to hear that."

"Hell, that's all right. I'm dating a twenty-something intern now. She's a knockout. Natural tits that defy gravity with nipples that'll put your eye out. It's a hell of a way to go blind, but still."

Rob laughed.

Milo dropped his voice, "Now what's going on with you, man? If you are calling me, something has gotta be up. All I get is some goddamn Christmas card every year. You never call and I'm thinking there's a real good reason for that. You got my spider senses a'tingling."

Rob smiled. Milo had always been good at reading people and he still was.

"I tried Steve first, but couldn't find him in the directory. Has he moved on to greener pastures?"

"Shit. No." Milo paused and he closed his office door. "You hadn't heard? He died maybe six months after you left. Lung cancer, extremely aggressive. It was a few weeks between diagnosis and then hospice. A few weeks after that and he was gone."

"Lung cancer? Steve never smoked a day in his life."

"Eh, it's like breast cancer in men. No one ever thinks a man can get breast cancer, but goddamn, they sure as hell can."

"He wasn't exposed to anything?" Rob asked, rocked at the thought of a world without Steve in it. How had he not heard? And then he remembered that his cards never had a return address. A small idiosyncrasy, one that made no sense since he was easily tracked here to Kansas City if anyone had been so inclined.

Milo practically guffawed, "Seriously? We're *analysts*, Rob."

"Milo, I've got to ask about the investigation we were working on, the one right before I left."

Milo's easygoing demeanor changed, and his tone became guarded. "Stone, you know the rules. You aren't with the agency and we *cannot* discuss this."

"Hear me out, Milo. The file I had been compiling, the files and papers I had accumulated over nearly a year of digging, were returned to the agency. They threatened me, Milo. They probably killed Claire and then they threatened to do the same to Maddie. When they sent me a photo of our house from the day before, sent it *using my child* with a note to stop digging, I did what I had to do."

Rob sighed and leaned back against the park bench. The air had a nip to it and his knees were aching. An early snow was in the forecast. Home wasn't an option right now, not until he was sure he had found all the bugs.

"I did what I had to do to protect her, and myself. I thought it would be over if I walked away, if I cut all ties. But I just did a sweep of my home and found monitoring devices - in my office, the kitchen, my bedroom, even my kid's bedroom, for fuck's sake. If you closed the case, re-open it, because after a decade, these bastards are not only watching me, but *they are here*."

"Jesus, Rob." Milo fell silent, but Rob could hear a drawer opening and papers rustling. "Fuck this smoke-free workplace bullshit." The click of a lighter and the steady drag of a cigarette came over the line faintly. "Are you sure it isn't something from your line of work now?"

"I'm a homicide detective, Milo, I don't work for the Company anymore. I deal with shootings and assaults and burglaries gone wrong, nothing more."

"Shit, Rob, I wish I knew what to tell you." Milo sighed. "You aren't missing a thing not being here; even the higher-ups are pussy-whipped and I've been handed bullshit assignments while the real issues get locked down. That's what Steve would have told you before he died. The higher-ups shut the investigation down. No reason given. Steve was all set to fight it and then his health took a swan dive. And we all know you two were the smart ones. I wasn't gonna rock the fucking boat, not with Gus going into that nice private school in Avalon. I had bills to pay and a marriage on the rocks."

"I hear you, man. But, Milo, do you have anything, anything at all that could help? Any of your files, or even Steve's, that I could..."

"Jesus, Stone! No! I got nothing. And even if I did, I would *not* give it to you. Not for love, or money, or a night with the woman of my dreams. Gus is lined up with an early acceptance to Georgetown and I just passed the twenty-year mark here. Don't try and take back channels or this shit will blow up in your face harder than Tailhook did for the Navy back in ninety-one."

A cold drizzle was beginning to fall. Rob felt a hot anger swell up inside him. Milo wouldn't, hell, he *couldn't* help him.

How long had those bastards been listening?

He had become complacent, let his guard down, and allowed himself to be frightened off in the first place. More than ever, he was convinced. The Indalo, for lack of a better name and description, were the bogeyman under the bed. Claire's death, that note telling him to abandon his investigation, and now even Milo and Steve had been pulled into this. Rob didn't buy lung cancer, not for a minute. Inhalation of enough polonium 210 would certainly manifest as a particularly aggressive lung cancer. Steve had led too healthy a life to explain this away so easily.

"Stone? You still there?" Milo's voice crackled in his ear.

"Yeah, yeah. Look, I'm sorry, man. You are absolutely right and I shouldn't have pushed you. I gotta go, so..."

"Don't worry about it." Milo's voice had returned to its natural friendly tone. "I'll just pretend this never happened. Try not to let ten years go by before you call again. Y'hear me?"

"Will do. Thanks, Milo, you take care."

"You too, buddy."

One thousand miles away in his small office in Virginia, Milo set the phone back in its cradle and stared at it. "Shit." He lit another cigarette; fairly certain he wouldn't have anyone poking their head in through the door. He needed to get one of those ionizers and stick it under his desk. His hands shook until the nicotine mellow hit. He chain-smoked three cigarettes in a row before getting up the nerve to pick up the phone again. This time it was a small flip phone hidden in an inner suit pocket. He pressed a button and waited until he heard a voice on the other line.

"I just heard from Rob Stone. He was asking me to re-open the investigation."

He ground out the last of the cigarette butt into an old takeout box and then stuffed the box into the trash. "Yeah, I know. I told him I couldn't help him. But Stone does what he thinks is right and to hell with the consequences."

He listened and nodded. "Yeah, he knows about those too. Look, I want out. I don't know anything, and I'm not interested in pointing any fingers, I just want *out*, got it?"

He waited, listening to the voice on the other end. "Yeah, you do that."

Milo ended the call and stared at the phone in his hand.

He'd damn near sold his soul - all so that his life would go on as usual. In return, his marriage had failed and his son barely spoke to him. And the twenty-something tail he'd been chasing had been quickly losing interest after realizing he was up to his eyeballs in debt.

A sick feeling of dread began to form in his stomach. They would never let him walk away. Folks like this, they never did.

Fuck it.

He stood up and strode over to the bookshelf where Diana's last gift to him resided. A soldered, heavy Steampunk masterpiece of gears and cast-iron parts from long-demolished engines. It was heavy in his hand. He returned to the desk and brought it down hard on the burner phone, a grim smile on his lips as the plastic crunched.

No more. To hell with the consequences.

Signal Lost

"Indalo." The word, spoken aloud in the target's house, had triggered a report, and the report had pinged Lucifer's email with a red flag alert. A moment later, her phone buzzed and played the first notes from The Imperial March.

It woke her up and she lay there in the half light of morning, the heavy blanket of sleep still fogging her mind and wondered why the hell she was awake. She had been online until 3 a.m., her armies victorious, surrounded by a sea of dead trolls before she lay down her flaming sword and retreated to the comfort of her bed. It was far too early to be woken by anything, much less an alert. *God, I have to work. And at this ungodly hour of the morning?*

She groaned and blearily reached for the phone among a menagerie of objects that crowded the bedside table. Annabelle flopped over and groaned, stretching in the bed beside her.

The lip balm skittered off the table and rolled across the cement floor. The bottle of aspirin made more of a clatter and Annabelle whoofed in alarm, rolled to a standing position, and shook. Her collar and tags jingled. She jumped off the bed and walked, her toenails clicking on the floor, to stand by the back door.

"So much for sleeping," Lucifer muttered in disgust, still unable to find the phone in the gloom. Annabelle whined quietly at the door. "Yeah, yeah, I'm coming." The dog, once wakened, would not stop until she was let out to do her business.

She stumbled out of bed and let the dog out. The sun was bright and she retreated from it, shutting the door firmly behind Annabelle, and cursed as the door caught and dragged across the top of her bare foot.

"Shit! Ow!" Lucifer limped back to her bed and cradled her foot while Annabelle barked outside, intent on chasing squirrels, no doubt.

"It is too early for this crap," she growled and lifted the covers, searching for her phone. It clattered to the floor; she reached for it and banged her half-shaven scalp into the sharp metal corner of the bed frame. "Fuck!" She rocked on her heels, clutching her head, and then lurched to the other side of the room where a bank of computers and monitors hummed. As she sat in her chair, the movement jarred the desk and the hum changed, monitors blinked on, and the room brightened, lit by the multiple screens before her.

She set her phone down and ran her fingers along the keys, reaching over to click the mouse. *It's easier to read on a screen anyway.*

Her fingers flew over the keyboard and she sucked in a breath as her eyes took in the information on the screen. "Shit, that is not possible." She whistled, "Shit, shit, *shit.*"

She grabbed her phone and rapidly typed a message.

RE: Subject RS

The lights are out but the power is still on. Call me.

-L-

She checked the connections, made sure there weren't any power outages reported, and double-checked her reports. Then, with nothing left to do but wait for a call, she opened up World of Warcraft and plunged in. Two hours later, surrounded on all sides by trolls, she groaned when the phone rang. Her hand hovered over it.

It rang twice, then a third, before she answered, "This had better be the six-foot-tall, hung like Michael Fassbender cabana boy I ordered from Guilty Pleasures."

"Sorry to disappoint."

"I'm guessing you want an update."

"Yes."

Lucifer leaned back in her chair and rubbed at her scalp. It still hurt where she had banged it against the bed. "All of them are offline."

"Offline as in...?"

"From the little information I have, I would say that he found them and disabled them. They didn't go off all at the same time. That would have been a power or connectivity issue since they piggy-back on his Wi-Fi signal. Instead, they went off at irregular intervals over a space of two hours. I'd say he used a locator and then dug 'em out one by one. No matter how it happened, he got them all. We no longer have eyes or ears in the house."

"I see." There was a small pause. "I want you to look through the past two weeks of data and see if you see any patterns."

"Already on it. Also, he used a trigger word, about an hour before the first device was deactivated."

"A trigger word?"

"Yeah, the voice recognition software notifies us if certain words are used. And he used one. *The* trigger word." Her voice dropped to a whisper, "*Indalo.*"

The voice on the other end said nothing, just a hiss of displeasure.

Lucifer gulped and continued, "Anyway, I'll keep you updated if anything comes up. So far, nothing much out of the ordinary. Just the typical tween bullshit coming from the daughter and all the old man does is go to work, come home, and Netflix binges in between tailgating from his home all the Chiefs games. Oh yeah, and two more things."

"Go on."

"He joined a dating website last week."

"Very interesting." There was a short pause. "A dating site, you say?"

"Yeah, Meet Your Match; it's a local company."

"What was the other thing?"

"He tried calling a Steve Hardison in Yorktown, Virginia. But there wasn't anyone by that name listed in the directory."

The caller's voice changed, sounded almost concerned, "I see." There was a long pause. "You still can monitor the website searches and log keystrokes, right?"

Lucifer allowed herself a smug smile. "Yep, there's no way they find that; I buried it with a rootkit virus. It sends me hourly updates and then scrubs the evidence of the updates."

"Keep me updated on any internet searches as well."

"Parameters?"

"You'll know. He's looking into *us*."

"Got it."

"Thank you, Lucifer. Your hard work continues to be a boon to all of us." And with that the line went dead.

Lucifer grinned like a Cheshire cat. The boss didn't hand out compliments very often and that made them like gold, especially to the likes of her. She understood better than many just how low she was in the organization, and how inconsequential. Her Indalo tat was red, the color of blood, and if she got out more, she would have had to fend off curious looky-loo's who usually wanted to know why a sweet little girl like her had marked her skin with some heathen-looking icon.

That would be especially true at home in Highfill, Arkansas, where everyone not only knew everyone else, but were related somehow. Returning last year after five years away in glitzy L.A. had been a shock to Lucy's system, and to the gentler denizens of Highfill. Her once luxurious shoulder-length locks of blond hair had been transformed into a jet black, ragged, chopped rat's nest, with one side buzzcut so short she could see her scalp had pimples. Well, at least no one would be calling her that "cute little Eastman girl" anymore.

She clicked on the feed one more time looking for cameras and bugs. Nothing. She went down the list. Damned if he hadn't gotten every single one of them. The Indalo had been watching Rob Stone long before Lucy Lucifer Eastman was recruited five years ago. So, what had tripped the mark up? What made him suspect he was being watched? And how the hell did a Podunk cop in flyover country know how to find not one, but *all* of the bugs in the house? Those were questions Lucifer would have asked, if there was anyone who would have told her. But the nature of what she did, and the people she did it for, did not encourage those lines of questions.

"Well, at least I've got the keystroke and activity tracking," she mused. "That should yield something." She would dig in and see what she could find. The customized virus she had created for the Android phones Stone and his daughter carried, similar to Ghost Ctrl but better, continued to provide her with a stream of useful information.

A whine and a short bark at the door informed her that Annabelle wanted back in. To hell with the World of Warcraft, she had work to do.

Broken Code

The property was massive, some fifteen acres in total. The trees that lined its borders were in the height of their fall colors - the leaves alternating between yellow, orange, and a fiery sunset-red. The day was clear and sunny, but there was a cold chill that the sun had not yet chased away. On the ground lay a fine layer of fallen leaves.

Lila walked through the open field, noting a pair of horses in the distance. The smell of woodsmoke was heavy in the air. Despite the faint sounds of the highway in the distance, it felt as if she was alone in the middle of nowhere. From the north along the border of the property farthest from her, hidden by the trees and skirting the edge of the river, she could hear the steady clickety-clack of a train. The air was crisp, clean, and she stopped by the small orchard at the edge of the field and selected two rust-red and yellow-striped apples from one of the trees. The branches were heavy with them and she could see from the high grass that it had been a long time since the orchard was tended.

Two horses now hung their heads over a fence, their eyes on her and the apples in her hands and nickered. Lila grinned. Her mom and dad had taken her to a farm when she was small, visiting a distant cousin, and there had been two horses there in a corral attached to a barn. She had fed them apples and even gotten a chance to ride one, her legs stretched over the wide body, her feet dangling miles away from the stirrups. The horse had been old, gentle, and slow. She remembered how the coarse hairs of its mane had felt, that and the velvet smoothness of its nose as it had taken the apple from her outstretched hand with such delicate care.

Shane had left an hour or more ago, saying little, except to remind her to not leave the house. But it was such a beautiful sunny day, and winter was just around the corner. To stay inside would be such a waste. She was safe here and no one knew where they were, so what could a short little walk hurt? She would stay on the property, which seemed rather vast, and keep to the grounds.

She headed across the field towards the horses and they tossed their heads and nickered louder as she approached, their eyes firmly on the treats she held in her hand.

"Hello, you gorgeous beasts. Would you each like an apple?" One horse was a soft brown, with white on its lower legs that reminded her of lace, the other was mottled with tan and white patches all over. They nudged her hands with their velvet noses, snuffling softly, clearly interested in the apples inside. She smiled and held her hands open. The fruit disappeared in seconds, velvety lips and strong teeth gently removing them from her hands and crunching down on the sweet treats.

Lila ran her fingers lightly over their soft muzzles, sighing at the velvety richness. The tan horse snorted and pulled away, her hooves dancing on the ground, but the brown one held still, light chuffing noises issuing from his throat. He leaned further over his side of the fence, his nostrils flaring as he sniffed her, looking for more apples.

She loved the feel of his soft hide and the earthy smell he gave off. It brought to mind one of her earliest dreams as a girl. She trailed her fingers along the side of his face and leaned closer. "Do you know what I dreamed about when I was little? Having a horse just like you. I wanted to live on a farm, raise chickens, and sheep and ride horses all day." She laughed. "So how in the hell did I end up in an office job, anyway?"

Lila sighed and leaned against the horse. He chuffed again, his massive flank expanding with each breath. She shuddered as memories of the night before suddenly shot to the surface. Blood pooling on the carpet, eyes wide, staring at her vacantly from the floor. Why was this happening to her? What had she done to deserve it?

The horse tossed his head then, stomping his hooves, and Lila pulled back from him. "Done with me now that the treats are all gone, eh? Well, okay then, I think I'll check out the pond while you go hang out with your friend. I'll bring you more apples later if I can!"

The horse wheeled around, tossing his mane, and took off at a trot. Lila watched him go and then turned to the east where a creek and small pond cut through the property. It was mostly hidden by the trees, but now that the leaves were falling it was easier to see. The pond was not very large, but apparently it was deep enough for a boat. A small aluminum one was out of the water and leaning against a tree. She made her way down the path. Frost glistened here and there in the thick shade untouched by the sun. It was strange to stand out here and realize that, just a few miles away, there was a city filled with people, sirens, and traffic. Here it seemed impossible, an oasis of nature flanked on all sides by trees. The clickety-clack of the train faded into the distance. Even the water treatment plant was silent and, except for a sprinkling of cars, deserted.

She heard the crunch of gravel before she saw the car. Shane was back. She waved and his expression suddenly changed. The car stopped abruptly at the base of the drive and he emerged striding towards her.

Uh oh, he looks pissed.

"Miss Benoit, *what* are you doing out here?"

Ooh boy, he really was *pissed.*

"I was just..."

His anger seemed to stretch his legs and he closed the distance between them in two more strides. He reached for her wrist, his hand hot against her skin. "Get in the car now, please, Miss Benoit."

He had an iron grip and she fought the urge to rip her hand from his. "Let go of me this instant."

He was standing inches from her and she could feel his anger. *All because I went for a walk?* She stared up at him, her eyes snapping, angry enough to match his sharp edges and roughness. *I'll be damned if he's going to manhandle me!*

His nostrils flared, his jaw was set, but his hands released her wrist gently, taking a deep breath before he spoke again, "My apologies, Miss Benoit. It is not safe outside of the house. I need for you to please get in the car and accompany me inside."

His measured tones were contradicted by the pulse jumping at his neck. *How very interesting.* She nodded, tried to calm herself as well, and led the way to the car, which was still idling at the foot of the drive.

Sitting next to him in the Jeep brought back memories of the evening before. And the anger left her, replaced by the ever-present question. *Why would anyone want to kill me?* Which immediately caused her to blurt, "My laptop? Did you get it?"

A quick shake of the head shot down all of her hopes of understanding *why* this was happening. "Your apartment had been tossed. The laptop was missing."

"Tossed? Oh God, I need to go there, who knows what else might be missing!"

"It wasn't a robbery, Lila, although they certainly wanted to leave that impression. All of your electronics, iPad, Kindle, and laptop - everything that might have the information on it was missing." He shifted out of park and drove up the hill, pressing the button to open the garage door.

"If we can get my laptop from work..."

They drove into the garage and Shane killed the engine and pressed the garage door button again. It slid down, quietly plunging them into darkness. "We can't get to it right now."

Jack had reached out to Kaylee Stromm, Lila's friend who worked in the office, and asked her to try to retrieve it, but the office was closed for the day. The host of insurance inspectors and a cleanup crew would need to fix the place up first. There was plenty of work to be done spackling over the bullet holes in the walls and replacing the bloodstained carpet. Whether the laptop was in the hands of the police or the company, no one knew for sure.

"Damn it!" Lila felt like screaming or hitting something. "I hate this!" Her fingers curled into hard fists. "Someone is trying really hard to kill me and for what, and why? And I'm stuck here, where I can't even go outside without you turning into some damn knuckle-dragging caveman and yanking me back inside by my hair."

Shane felt a smile tugging at the corners of his mouth. "I didn't touch your hair. I'm far more circumspect than that."

"Circumspect? What kind of bodyguard are you, Shane Ellis?" She laughed ruefully. "I'm sorry, the knuckle-dragging comment was rude and inaccurate."

Shane laughed in return and held his knuckles up as if examining them closely. "I dunno, there might be some callouses from dragging them while I chase around angry women." He paused. "Look, I can't get you your laptop, but I can help you deal with it in a constructive way."

"How's that?" she asked, her curiosity piqued, and that familiar surge of attraction she felt when she was near him quietly began to build.

"Well, first, how do you feel about guns?"

"How do I *feel* about them?" She arched a delicate eyebrow at him.

"Have you ever handled one?"

"Are we speaking in metaphors here?"

He laughed then. "C'mon, let me show you the basement." He slid out of the driver's seat, tilted his head at her, and smiled. Lila felt her insides heat up. *Does this man have any idea how sexy he is?*

She slipped out of the passenger seat and followed him out of the garage, inside and past the half bath, and down a set of stairs she had seen him use the night before. A half flight down and there was a door directly on the right. A long hallway stretched in front of them.

"Right down here," he said, "and watch your head on the last step." She passed under it easily and turned in time to see him duck. "I guess you aren't six foot two."

"Try five foot one." she shrugged. "It has its advantages, but it sucks when I need to change a lightbulb." She turned away from him and assessed the room, "So definitely not metaphorically speaking."

He admired her chutzpah. She had held her own against an attacker in an underground garage, then been shot at by two highly paid assassins. Many would have lost it, hell, he'd seen grown men shivering and crying under similar circumstances, but Lila had spunk. Spunk would only get her so far, however.

"No matter how you feel about firearms, knowing how to use one, and how one can be used against you, is important." He walked over to the area Benton had set up as a firing range and unlocked the cabinet door. "Have you ever held a pistol?"

"No, my parents were both children of hippies. I'd probably have to dig into a third, possibly fourth generation before I found anyone in my family tree who was familiar with any weaponry." She smiled at him and he felt a surge of attraction in response. "I'm not anti-gun, I've just never had the opportunity."

"I'll give you a rundown of the different parts, and then we will fire off some test rounds and let you have a little practice on a target." He leaned towards her and placed large noise-canceling protective gear over her ears.

She nodded and moved closer to him, too close, as he detailed the different parts of the weapon, disassembled and reassembled it in front of her, and reviewed the basics. "Never aim it at anything you don't intend to shoot," he cautioned. "Slide this back to load a round in the chamber, keep your knees and elbows slightly bent, and line the sights up."

His lips brushed her hair and Shane felt the slightest quiver in response, her musky vanilla scent intoxicating in his nose. His voice dropped lower, quieter, and he hovered behind her, trying to focus on the task at hand.

"When you are ready, pull the trigger back gently."

She stood still, her knees slightly bent, her elbows as well, and she stared down the sights, aiming for the center of a simple black outline on white paper at the far end of the firing range. She tried to focus on the target, and not on the man so close to her that she could feel his body heat. The target hung there, waiting for her. There was an explosive bang and concussive recoil of the gun in her hand as she pulled the trigger. The target fluttered slightly.

Nothing.

"You missed, but that's okay. Try again."

Her hands shook a little as she raised the weapon up and squinted down the sight line. She squeezed the trigger again.

A hole appeared in the target. "Nice shot. Center mass. You did good, Miss Benoit."

"Lila."

"I'm sorry?"

"Call me Lila. Every time you call me Miss Benoit, I imagine a seventy-five-year-old librarian with a bad attitude and intolerance for noisy patrons."

He laughed. "I've known some pretty sexy librarians."

"Were they seventy-five?"

He grinned and stepped closer, his hand on her waist. "No, a fair sight younger."

"And here I was imagining you with a cougar." His eyebrow quirked up and he smiled, slow and sexy, and her insides turned to jelly. He was close, too close, and she resisted the urge to grab his shirt in her fist, wrap her legs around him, and kiss him in a dirty, uninhibited way. He looked at her, standing that close, and studied her face, a half-smile on his lips.

He nodded at the gun still in her hands. "Go ahead and empty the magazine. Keep aiming for the center of the chest and take the shots nice and slow."

Two shots went wild, but the rest remained tightly packed center mass on the target.

"Excellent, you're a natural."

"So, I shouldn't aim for the head?"

"No, a shot to the chest is both easier since you have more to aim at, and just as deadly."

"Got it."

His hand slid over hers, warm, hot even, and plucked the weapon from her hand. "How did it feel?" He was standing so close. Her fingers tingled where he had touched them.

"To shoot a gun?" She shrugged. "It's heavier than I thought it would be. It's quite a bit of recoil for something so small. Loud as well." She paused, her green eyes assessing him. "I guess, when it comes down to it, I'd use one if I had to, but I don't particularly feel comfortable with it."

"You have a healthy amount of respect for a deadly weapon. There's nothing wrong with that." He disassembled the weapon with ease and efficiency and began cleaning it. "I figured you wouldn't mind killing time and learning something new. You never know when knowing your way around a firearm could save your life. Even if you never have to pull the trigger."

"I didn't mind at all. Thank you for that." All the hairs on her arm felt as if they were filled with electricity. He was so close that she could feel his body heat. His gaze dropped to her lips, and Lila leaned closer, just as her stomach took that moment to complain, loudly, about its lack of food. Lila felt her skin heat up, her face blushing in embarrassment.

Shane chuckled, "I think we had better rustle something up in the kitchen."

"Indeed."

Reaching Out

Rob scratched his head and looked at the list of employees that Morris Endon had sent over yesterday morning. "Someone's missing."

"Talking to yourself again, Stone?" Max asked, two coffees and a small bag from Donut King clutched in his hands. "Christ, take this damned thing. They made 'em nuclear today. I think the coffee is eating through the Styrofoam. I'm pretty sure my fingerprints have been melted off."

Rob reached up and took one of the cups. "Piping hot, just the way God intended." He waved the printout at Max. "You're late, Peisker, I've handled all of the paperwork."

"Huh, sounds like I was right on time."

They both laughed and Max pointed to the printout. "Whatcha got there?"

"A list of employees at Kurgen Real Estate. There were a total of twelve offices and work stations, but there's only ten names on this list," Rob answered, staring at the list again.

"So, they have a couple of extra workstations for visitors or they're down a couple of staff members."

Rob shook his head. "Nah, I did a schematic of the office, based on my memory of the layout and the crime scene photos." He pointed to the board. "This office here, it had personal belongings, a couple of pictures of family, and also one of what looks like Kaylee Stromm, who *is* listed on the personnel list but works in this office right here." He pointed to the far side of the diagram. "So possibly a friend?"

"So why isn't this person on the list?" Max asked, leaning back in his chair and taking a large bite of an enormous glazed donut. He leaned forward again and shoved the bag in Rob's direction.

"Perhaps their new, perhaps Morris Endon left this person off the list on purpose. I asked him to come in to the station, but he put me off, said he's got his hands full with dealing with the mess at the office."

"You think he might be hiding something?"

Rob reached into the bag and pulled out a twin to the giant donut Max was quickly making disappear. "He seemed nervous, had a hard time maintaining eye contact, definitely set off my bullshit meter when he asked if the art collection was intact. It might have made sense, but I kind of got the feeling he didn't give a shit about the collection. Nothing concrete, but yeah, something about him was fishy."

"Sounds like it's time to pay him a visit." Max tried sipping at his coffee and jerked it away just as quickly, wincing. "I'll leave my coffee here; it's still too damned hot to drink."

The drive to the exclusive enclave of upscale homes was a short one. Tucked into a hill off Highway 169, close to the shopping center at Briarcliff, which housed the well-stocked, if more expensive Green Acres Market, was a small, exclusive housing development.

The lawns were neat, perfectly manicured, and the cars, when visible, cost more than either detective made in a year.

"Damn, what the missus wouldn't give to live in a place like this," Max commented from the passenger seat. "She's been on me to put the house up for sale and move to one of those goddamn HOA communities. I keep telling her horror stories and she tells me crap like that doesn't happen to police officers." He groaned, "All those ticky-tacky boxes that all look alike, nothing out of place, the same beige fucking paint in each one. Who the hell *wants* that?"

Rob snorted, "Good luck with that, Peisker, that woman has got your balls in a vise grip. You'll be living in HOA land in two shakes of a lamb's tail." He slowed the car, "And here we are. Shit, all he's missing is a moat and guard dogs."

The house was impressive, stone walls and large leaded glass windows gave off an old-world vibe on a house that couldn't be more than five years old. The copper guttering had already aged into a soft rich green patina and the large, over-sized front door was made of a thick, hand-hewn dark wood that looked one of a kind.

Real estate really pays well.

They parked in the large circle drive and walked to the front door. It had a large wrought-iron knocker which seemed connected to a doorbell system. The solid thunk of the knocker was followed by a loud gong that echoed inside of the house.

Morris Endon opened the door a few seconds later and Rob caught a look of dismay on his face at the sight of the two detectives, one that vanished almost instantaneously and was replaced with a look of pleasant surprise. "Detective Stone, I didn't expect a visit this morning; I'm actually running a bit behind."

He made a show of staring at his watch, a platinum and gold Rolex if Rob didn't miss a guess. "Perhaps I can spare a few minutes. Please come in, come in." He ushered them inside and gestured towards the living room. It was austere, filled with tasteful white couches and chairs. "Please, have a seat."

"Nice place you have here," Max commented, his eyes on a large painting on the west wall.

"What? Oh, thank you, yes, I love the community, I really do. Very peaceful." He checked his watch again. "So, what can I do for you, Detectives?"

"Well, we wanted to give you an update on the investigation and double check the personnel list you provided us with," Rob replied. He leaned forward and passed the printout to Morris. "We've contacted everyone on that list and interviewed them, and no one seems to know anything about a reason why those men would be there in the office at that time or who might have killed them."

Morris gave a smug smile. "Well, obviously it was a robbery then. Perhaps they shot each other squabbling over the priceless artifacts."

"Perhaps, but the angles are all wrong. That, and the men had silencers. Robbers often carry weapons, but silencers?" Rob pointed to the printout and continued, "Could you look again at that list and tell me if you might have missed anyone, left them off of it by accident? Possibly someone new to the department?"

Morris looked disgruntled. "Well, sure, but then I really need to go. I'm meeting with the owners of the company to brief them on the current status of re-opening the office on Monday." He stared at the list, then frowned slightly. "I think there might be a new girl. She's in the southwest office. A Lila-something. I'm sorry, she's new and I must have forgotten her entirely."

Max spoke up, "That would make sense. A Kaylee Stromm, one of the sales managers, mentioned her friend Lila. I thought you had interviewed her, Stone."

"Nope, sure didn't." Rob stared at Morris as he said that, watching the man's face intently.

"Say, does this community have an HOA?" Max asked, standing up and looking out of the massive picture window that gave a stunning view of the golf course behind the house.

"Uh, yes, of course," Morris stammered, frowning at the change in questions. His eyes slid away from Rob's.

"My wife keeps on me to find us a house in an HOA community," Max mused, staring out of the window. "She says the houses don't just keep their value but appreciate over time."

"Most HOA communities hold that as a core value," Morris said, warming to the topic. "It is a significant factor for people who see their home as an investment." He glanced at his watch. "I hate to cut this short, Detectives, but I really must be leaving."

Rob stood up, held out his hand. "Thank you, Mr. Endon, we will be in touch if we have any other questions."

The man gave him a limp, rather sweaty, hurried squeeze back. "Of course, Detective, any time, any time at all."

The door closed behind them, then opened just as quickly. "I remembered the girl's name. Lila Benoit," Morris said. "She's our new data analyst. Market trends, property values, that kind of thing."

Rob jotted the name down in his notebook. "Benoit, got it. Thanks again, Mr. Endon."

As they drove away, Rob gnawed on his lip.

"What's your read on Morris Endon, Stone?"

"He's lying. He left Lila Benoit's name off that list on purpose."

Max nodded, staring at the upscale homes they passed. "Yeah. But why?"

"I'm not sure. To buy time, maybe?"

"You think he's the one pulling the strings here?"

"I'm not sure, but I want to talk to Lila Benoit. Now. See if you can pull up her info."

Max nodded and pulled the laptop open, typing the data into the police computer. "Got her. She lives off Broadway Street, in the old Folgers Coffee building."

"Hell, that's just a few minutes south of here. Let's go check it out."

They headed down Highway 169, passing the Downtown Airport and crossing the Broadway Bridge. The old brick building was one of a string of historic buildings in the area, their all-brick or stone exteriors holding their turn-of-the-century age well.

"Looks like the parking is for passholders only. No guard. We'll have to park on the street." Rob pulled over a block later and parked. They caught a break; there was no front lobby and the doors were well-secured, but a resident leaving held the door for them to enter when Rob flashed his badge.

"She's on the third floor, number thirty-eight," Max commented as they entered the elevator.

The door, when they reached it, was ajar. "Shit," Rob said, drawing his Glock. He entered slowly, Max close behind.

The main room was a fair size, with tall ceilings. The door to the bedroom and the one bathroom beyond that was also open. It was clear that the loft had been trashed. Someone had emptied every drawer, every cabinet, and gone through Lila Benoit's life with a fine-toothed comb. A desk near the tall windows overlooking Broadway Street below had drawers open or on the floor. The top of it, slightly dusty, showed a clear rectangular laptop-shaped space where there was no dust.

"Clear. And cleared out. Looks like her laptop is gone. And whoever went through this place was clearly looking for something." Rob holstered his weapon and Max followed suit.

"Whatcha thinking now?" Max asked as he slowly evaluated the scene.

"I'm thinking Morris Endon ordered a hit on Lila Benoit. I'm thinking those men were there for her. And wherever she is, if she is still alive, she's being hunted."

"Jesus, Stone. This isn't the CIA. We live in flyover country." Max shook his head.

"Yeah? Got something better for me?"

"Not really. But *damn*." Max stepped to avoid a pile of papers strewn across the hardwood floor. "So, you think they tossed the place looking for something. Not just her, but something she has?"

"Yeah. And then there's the..." Rob stopped; he wasn't ready to explain the Indalo to Peisker. If his partner thought he was paranoid now, wait until he told him about the mysterious shadow organization, he suspected was following him.

"The what?" Max asked.

"Nothing. Half-assed thought that just vanished clear out of my head." Rob stared at the scene before him. "We need to talk to Kaylee Stromm and find out what she knows. Also, we need to dig into this Lila Benoit. Who is she and why is she being hunted?"

Kaylee Stromm lived in a cute little house in Brookside. She ushered them into a tiny living room filled with warm colors and tasteful furniture. "Can I get you anything? Coffee, tea, or water?"

"I'll take water, that would be great," Max answered, smiling at her.

Rob shook his head. "Nothing for me, thanks, though."

A moment later, she sat down on the gray modern couch. "How can I help you, Detectives?"

"You are friends with Lila Benoit, is that correct?" Rob asked.

The girl's warm brown eyes showed concern. "Yes, I am, we were in college together, and I helped get her the job there at Kurgen this past summer."

Rob scribbled in his notepad. "We didn't have her on our initial list of employees."

Kaylee frowned. "Well, that's strange."

"Perhaps it was just a mistake. But we went by her apartment and it looks like someone has trashed it. Have you seen or talked to Miss Benoit since work on Monday?"

The girl looked apprehensive. "No, I haven't."

"That seems odd considering the circumstances."

"She's safe." The girl looked down at her hands. "And that's all I can really say about it."

Both detectives stared at her. Rob spoke first, "Do you know where your friend is, Miss Stromm?"

"I do not." She said it firmly, looking up, her eyes showing firm resolve. "You will need to speak with Jack Benton, of Benton Security Services, for further information on that."

"Miss Stromm, what are you saying?"

"I'm saying that someone tried to kill Lila. Not once, but twice. First last Friday, in her parking garage, and again on Monday at Kurgen."

"And why would someone try to kill your friend, Miss Stromm?" Rob asked, his heart rate increasing.

"I have no idea, Detective. But she found something, in her parking garage a few days after the attack. A piece of paper that indicated that someone had put out a hit on her. I told her to call Benton Security Services."

"And how do you know about Benton Security Services, Miss Stromm? What is it they do?"

"Jack Benton is a personal friend. And they do what you think they do; they keep people alive."

Rob sat back. His mind was spinning. None of this made sense. Paid assassins, a data analyst barely out of college and now under protection of some bodyguard service, and a well-known real estate firm. Not to mention the assassins were Indalo. *Here.* The name Benton was familiar as well. A street in the area was named Benton, but there was something else, something in the back of his brain. *Benton. Benton. Jack Benton.*

"We need to speak to Lila, Miss Stromm."

Kaylee nodded. "Yes, I'm sure you do. She stood up. "One moment." She walked out of the room and Rob turned to Max.

The other detective's mouth was hanging open. "What the hell kind of crazy case have we got here, Stone?" He shook his head. "This just keeps getting bigger and bigger. I feel like I've stepped into the Twilight Zone."

Kaylee returned and handed a card to Rob. "Here is Jack's direct line."

"Thank you, Miss Stromm." Rob took the card from her and paused. "How is it that you are friends with Mr. Benton?"

She smiled. "Please don't take this the wrong way, but, that's really none of your business, Detective."

They left the tiny house silently, the door closing firmly behind them.

Max whistled. "Two dead assassins, pretty girl in Gucci with a secret past, hits ordered on a data analyst still wet behind the ears from college, a lying manager, and a tossed apartment. This feels like the beginning of a damned action movie. Next thing you know there will be missing nuclear launch codes and the missing data analyst will have to save the world."

"We need to call this Jack Benton character and get access to Lila Benoit. Maybe then things will be a little clearer."

Closer

The mood between them kept changing, and Lila wasn't sure how to feel about it. She had been so mad at him earlier, indignant at the way he manhandled her outside on the grounds. And then he showed her how to handle a weapon and she had felt everything from scared to thrilled as she aimed it at the target and pulled the trigger.

There had been a moment between them when she was sure he was attracted to her. A moment ruined by her traitorous stomach as it growled like it hadn't been fed in weeks. Her cheeks flushed, embarrassed, and she took the steps up to the main level at a jog, the thick carpet swallowing up any sound.

"Do you like Vietnamese food?" Lila asked as Shane headed for the kitchen. "There's the Vietnam Cafe, and we could get it delivered through Uber Eats."

"No deliveries, no leaving the property."

Lila bristled. He was so annoying when he said it like that and she remembered how he had marched her back to the car and insisted she stay inside.

"Oh, is that against The Code?" she asked, her voice betraying her irritation.

Shane had his head deep in the refrigerator. He took it out, met her eyes, and smiled. "Exactly."

Smug jerk.

The man was infuriating. He was also extremely good-looking.

He continued to paw through the fridge, pulling out produce and setting it on the counter.

"What are you doing?" Lila asked, her curiosity outweighing her irritation.

He closed the fridge and pulled the elastic off the broccoli. "I'm going to cook dinner." He reached into a drawer on the left and took out a chef's knife, deftly slicing one end off of an onion from the basket on the counter, peeling the skin off, and beginning to dice away.

Lila blinked. "A bodyguard who also cooks?"

He shrugged. "It comes in handy. Everyone needs to eat." He set a pan on the stove and turned on the burner underneath it, drizzling oil into the pan before returning to chopping vegetables. He pointed to a cabinet behind Lila and said, "Grab me the pressure cooker in that cabinet there, will you?"

"This one here?" She reached inside, pulling out a large, heavy contraption. A cord dangled from it.

"Yeah, there's a plug on the wall next to the cabinet. Just plug it in there."

Lila followed his directions, adding rice and water into the pot and seating the lid in place before pressing the Start button. "So, it just cooks the rice in there, without you having to do anything?" she asked, staring at the pressure cooker as it began to steam, building up pressure.

"Yup. It'll be done in around ten minutes. Just in time." He added the diced onions to the pan and they sizzled. "We have some chicken I can slice up and add to the stir fry if you like."

"Sure." Lila stared, entranced by his efficiency. Stir fry was something she had only had in restaurants. Her mother had managed basic foods, and Lila never really learned much past reheat and toast.

Shane looked up at one point, tilted his head at her. "What?"

"Nothing."

He shrugged and continued to add ingredients. Carrots came next, followed by celery and seasonings. A small bottle of sesame oil yielded a rich smell that permeated the kitchen and Lila's stomach rumbled again, reminding her that she hadn't eaten since early that morning.

He pointed with his free hand. "Could you hand me the fish sauce? You'll find it in that cabinet up there."

"Fish... sauce..." That sounded horrific, but the smell of the food cooking was making her salivate and her stomach rumble fiercely. She would leave it in his capable hands. She retrieved the bottle and handed it to him.

"Thanks." He uncapped it and poured it deftly onto the browning pieces of chicken.

Behind her, the pressure cooker beeped, indicating it was done. "Could you press Cancel?"

She pressed the button and turned back. "What now?"

He mixed the vegetables and the meat together, drizzling another thick brown sauce onto them. Steam billowed from the pressure cooker and the smell of rice joined with the stir fry.

"The dishes are in the cabinet closest to the table," he replied.

Lila retrieved two plates and searched until she found the silverware drawer, retrieving two forks.

Seconds later, they sat at the table, plates of steaming stir fry and rice in front of them. Shane's plate was heaped with twice as much as hers. As it was, she wasn't sure she would be able to eat all of her plate, despite her hunger. She dug in, closing her eyes at the tang of the ginger, the sweet, salty taste of the teriyaki, and the crisp vegetables.

Cooking had always felt a little bit magic to her. How did a person manage to add a little of this, a little of that, and come up with complex flavors that worked? Every time she tried to be adventurous it ended in unpalatable, over-seasoned, salty disasters. She couldn't even brew a pot of coffee without turning it into nuclear waste.

There was a piece of chicken in the next bite and she closed her eyes, a wash of culinary bliss flowing from her mouth down to her stomach.

"Oh, my word, this is *so* good. Seriously, how did you learn to cook like this?" she asked, rolling her eyes, taking another bite. It was a huge mound of food. But it was amazing, so full of flavor, that she was determined to eat every single bite. She scooted her chair in closer, digging into the food.

Shane shrugged. "It was just my mom and me growing up. She taught me to cook and when she got too sick to take care of herself, it came in handy."

"Is she still...?"

"Alive? No. She passed away when I was 21, almost ten years ago now, of congestive heart failure." He shoveled a forkful into his mouth.

"I lost my mom too," Lila said. "Well, both my parents. My dad in a car accident right after I turned sixteen and my mom one semester before graduation. She had breast cancer. I was closer to my dad, but we grew really close after he died. I really miss her."

"It never goes away," Shane said, "Missing them, that is. My mom was great, a real rock, she kept me in line and didn't let me get away with any of the typical teenage bullshit. I got into some trouble after she was gone, but if it hadn't been for her, I think I would be a very different person."

"How long have you done this bodyguard thing? What were you in school for?" Lila asked, as she slipped another bite of the stir fry into her mouth. Shane could see a small smear of sauce on her chin.

"Nearly six years now. And I had wanted to be a doctor at one point."

She raised her eyebrows. "A *doctor*? Seriously?"

Shane grinned. "Hey, don't sound so shocked." He shrugged and said, "When my mom got sick, I dropped out to take care of her and lived on the student loans. Fell behind, couldn't go back, and then I met Jack."

She leaned back and regarded him. "The way you said that, that you 'met Jack'... there's something more to that, isn't there?"

She was intuitive, he had to give her that. No one had ever asked him these questions before and he hesitated, unsure of how to answer.

"Isn't there always?"

"Does that mean you aren't going to tell me?" she asked. She pushed aside her plate, decimated, with only a few bites of food remaining.

"Quid pro quo. What do you need the laptop for?"

Lila smiled at Shane's parry, and then the smile dropped away. "I think I found a file I shouldn't have. It's the only thing that makes sense."

"Tell me about the file."

"Uh-uh, you first. Tell me about meeting your boss."

"I broke into his house and was planning on stealing from him."

"*What*?!"

He smiled. "So, tell me about the file."

"It's a list of transactions with a company I've never heard of Ol...Olad...something," She answered. "Did he catch you in the act?"

"Yes, but I also saved his life. My partner was going to shoot him and I stopped him."

Lila's eyes were round in shock. "Oh my God. Did you go to jail?"

Shane gave her a slight shake of the head. "Why do you think this file is out of the ordinary?"

"Fine, fine. Because it was identical to another sales report, same dates and amounts, but with companies we have done business with."

"So, what, fraud?"

"Oh no, you don't. Tell me what happened next."

"I disabled my partner, restrained him, and then ran like hell. Tried to disappear." He had finished his plate as well and pushed it away, sliding his chair out from the table. "So... fraud?"

"Fraud, or something else. I didn't look at the whole document. It was large and on this SD card in a pocket of the bag that came with my work laptop." She leaned forward. "So... what happened next?

"Benton found me. And against all good advice to the contrary, he offered me a job." Shane stared back at her. "Who else knows about this file?"

And that is when it hit her. "Oh shit." She closed her eyes, remembering Morris Endon's face, the odd way he had reacted when she first came into his office over a week ago. "Only one person," she whispered. "My boss, Morris Endon."

He set it up. He ignored me completely until I showed him that file and then I would see him every day. He was watching me, watching my every movement, and he's the one who set up the blind date with the guy who never showed up.

"Except he *did* show up. In my parking garage three hours later." She stood up abruptly. "I think I need a drink."

Shane followed her. "I think I missed something there. Did you say your boss was in the parking garage?"

She made a beeline for the liquor cabinet, locating the scotch easily in its cut crystal flask. She poured two fingers into a glass and sucked it down. Poured another two fingers and swallowed it as well and reached for the bottle, exhaling, her heart racing.

"Woah there, tell me what you are thinking." Shane plucked the bottle out of her hand, set a second glass down, and deftly poured more of the scotch into her glass and his.

"Morris Endon, my boss and the president of Kurgen Real Estate, he set me up on a blind date last Friday. Except the guy never showed up," she practically spat. "Because it was all bullshit; he had a guy waiting there in my parking garage. He was there to kill me." She shuddered. "Mr. Endon was the only one who knew anything about the file, the only one I had shown it to. I didn't even *know* anything and he wanted me dead." She put the glass to her lips and swallowed it in one gulp, giving another small shudder as she did.

Lila reached for the bottle, intercepting Shane's hand, her fingers shaking. He caught her hand, held it, and she felt a surge of desire run through her body. He was warm, hot even, standing so close. He smelled good, no cologne, just a down-to-earth manly smell that made her insides twist and turn. He was attracted to her, she was sure of it, and at the moment, the scotch was turning fear into a loose, swirling pool of want. How she wanted to feel safe, cared for... wanted.

Shane breathed in her scent, a musky vanilla, the scotch on her breath. She was upset, scared, and he wanted to pull her against him, tell her it was going to be alright, and slide his hands underneath her shirt, touch her bare skin, taste that sweet spot behind the ear, and...

They stood there for a minute. It might have been an hour, a day, a lifetime. Neither of them moving, neither of them breathing, both fighting to find a space to exist, to separate themselves from desire and fear and attraction. Shane was the one who broke the spell, lifting the bottle out of her hands.

"Take it easy on the scotch; it bites back."

Right on cue, the alcohol hit her bloodstream and she swayed, suddenly enveloped in its influence, the euphoria hitting and pushing her in a haze to turn away and sit down heavily in the embrace of the tall Chesterfield armchair. It swallowed her up and she looked like a small child as she tucked her legs up underneath her and stared off into the distance.

Shane poured more scotch into the two glasses, set the bottle down and brought Lila's glass to her, settling himself on the couch. "It's a lot to take in," he said, gazing at her steadily. "You are safe here, and once we get access to the laptop, we can take a look at the file and turn it in to the police. It will all work out."

She shivered, not from the cold - it was toasty warm in the den, and a fire crackled merrily in the hearth - but from fear. *How had her dream job turned into a nightmare? And was the file truly responsible? Was Morris Endon really a bad guy, someone who had ordered her murder? It didn't seem possible.*

"He looks like a nice guy, I mean, he was *nice* to me."

"Looks, and actions, can be deceiving." Shane sipped at the scotch and watched Lila closely.

She tipped the glass back and drained it, swallowing the scotch in a gulp, her eyes troubled. "So, it would seem."

"Perhaps we have it all wrong. We might be linking two separate events that have nothing to do with each other." He leaned forward. "Let's look at this another way. Was the laptop new or did someone else have it before you did?"

Lila shrugged. "I'm pretty sure it was someone else's, but who I don't know. I'm sure there are records there in the office. Perhaps Kaylee, no, never mind. I don't want Kaylee involved in this. I would never forgive myself if anyone else got hurt, especially Kaylee."

"Have you known her long?" Shane asked.

"We were roommates in college together. We've been close friends ever since. She helped get me the job at Kurgen." She shook her head, sat up abruptly. "Look, can we, I don't know, can we not talk about this anymore? Could we just do something? Turn on some music, maybe. I saw there was a pool table in the other room."

Shane watched her steadily. She was struggling with it all, and really who could blame her? There wasn't much that could be accomplished at this point. Jack would call with an update and to check in later, and it would do her good to take her mind off things.

He stood up, offered her a hand, and smiled. "I should warn you, I play a mean game of pool."

Stay

It had been a while since he played pool regularly. Years, in fact. And Shane was dismayed to realize he had lost his knack for it.

They had taken their glasses with them into the large game room where a competition-length table sat. Perhaps that was the problem, he was used to playing on bar-length tables. And Lila played better than any woman he had ever played against. He had just four shots to get it right before she took control of the table and ran it, dropping balls into the pockets with precision.

"I think I'm being played," he said dryly and shook his head.

She laughed. "Beginner's luck."

He could see she was teasing him. "Right. Or you hustle pool at night as a side gig."

Lila giggled. "Hardly. But Kaylee and I did get pretty good. It was how we blew off steam during finals. The studying would get to be too much and we would go down to the student commons. I had to be good at it; I only had a couple of dollars to spend and it had to last me all night."

"Necessity is the mother of invention. Another game, then. And take it easier on me; I don't know if I can afford this."

That earned him another laugh and he racked the balls and let her break. That game was better, or at least less of an annihilation. It ended with just one of his balls on the table, instead of four. "Believe it or not, I used to play pool for extra side money."

"I believe it, you are good. I'm just better." She grinned at his indignant look. "Another game?"

"Of course, but hold on." He walked over to the stereo in the corner and selected songs from the display. Benton had a significant collection of music. "We have everything from classical to hip-hop, heavy metal to elevator music." He gave Lila a once-over. "I'm going to take a guess and say that you might enjoy Marian Hill, and some Phantogram, along with some other alternative rock."

He pressed a button and the first notes of "Blackout Days" started playing. Lila stared at him. "How did you do that?"

He shrugged. "Actually, I had no idea what you would like. I was just hoping we liked the same music."

For the next two hours they played pool, listened to music, and laughed. It was what Lila needed. Her fear slid away and she found herself flirting with Shane as they danced, played pool, and raided the freezer for ice cream. Outside, a light rain began to fall, the darkness around the isolated house nearly complete. Only the lights from Parkville, miles away across the river, shone blearily through the drops of rain pelting against the windows.

It was almost ten when Lila yawned. Her jaw popped and she grinned sheepishly at Shane. The effects of the scotch had worn off and now she was tired, worn out from worry and uncertainty through and through.

Shane lifted an eyebrow and she shrugged as she said, "My dad used to tease me when I was a kid that, as soon as the sun went down, I started yawning and was ready for bed. He said that I had to have been a chicken in my former life."

"Do chickens go to bed when the sun goes down?" he asked, an amused look on his face.

"They sure do. My dad said that they were the only creature with any common sense. I don't know if I would take it that far - chickens are pretty stupid - but as soon as the sun goes down, so do they. And me too, apparently!"

"Well, you've had a rough couple of days, it's understandable."

"Is it?" She looked embarrassed, self-conscious.

"Of course. Take a hot bath, relax, and I'll talk to Jack about contacting the police in the morning and seeing what we can find with that SD card."

Lila nodded, paused, and then reached out to Shane, her hand on his shoulder. "Thank you," she said softly. She looked as if she wanted to say more, but instead she turned away and walked up the stairs silently without looking back.

He could still feel the warmth of her hand on his shoulder, a memory of her touch lingering there. He was relieved when she walked away. The swirl of attraction he felt towards her had intensified with her touch. He wanted to slide his hand around her waist, to the small of her back, run his mouth along her neck, and...

Get a hold of yourself, Ellis. She's a client.

He watched her walk away, disappearing up the stairs, a tantalizing fantasy and someone he had no business getting close to. Shane gathered the dishes and walked into the kitchen. A few dishes to wash and then he would call Jack and update him. He stared at the dishwasher, shrugged, and turned the water on. *It's easier to wash them up right now.* He wiped down the countertops while waiting for the water to heat and was just about to begin when he heard Lila scream.

Adrenaline fueled his dash up the stairs as he took them two at a time, his Glock unholstered and a round in the chamber, safety off. He burst through the door and nearly knocked Lila to the ground as they intersected in the small hallway that opened into the large bedroom.

"It's a bat. It scared the hell out of me when it swooped through the room." Her face was bright red. "I didn't mean to scream, it just flew past me and I couldn't help myself!" Behind her, Shane could see the bat zip from one side of the room to the other and back again, even more frightened than Lila had been by the presence of two humans.

Shane realized he had Lila folded in his arms, smashed against his chest and that their lips were inches apart. He tried not to laugh, but he couldn't help it. A small chuckle escaped and Lila, looking first embarrassed and then amused as well, laughed right alongside him. The bat continued to swoop back and forth in the room.

"We can't hurt it," Lila said, "we just need to find a way to get it out of the house." He stared at her. Most of the women he knew were terrified of all manner of creatures.

"What?" she said defensively, "It just... *startled* me, that's all. I'm not scared of it and I don't want to see it hurt. I just want it to leave."

Shane couldn't help but admire her. Lila had spunk, and a kind heart. "I'll open a window and see if we can convince our little friend to leave." He opened the window, slipped an unused towel off the towel bar in the bathroom, and slowly moved towards the bat. It had stopped wheeling about back and forth and settled in a corner of the room, probably hoping they would forget it was there, hiding its face against the wall. When in flight, its wingspan was nearly two feet in width. On the wall, however, crouched there, its wings folded in tight, it was scarcely bigger than a large mouse. Shane closed in, the towel bunched in his hands.

"Careful! Don't hurt it, it's so beautiful and the poor thing is probably terrified!" Lila cautioned, her eyes fixed on the tiny creature.

"I'm doing my best," Shane murmured and gently wrapped the creature in the towel. A low buzz came from it, a sound that they could both feel in their bones, off the auditory register for humans, only slightly within their range. He felt the tiny body within the folds of the towel and gently maneuvered it so that it came away from the wall and was wrapped in the towel, unable to move, but also unhurt. The buzzing increased.

He turned it back towards them and Lila gasped and leaned in close. "Oh, hello you! You poor dear, I hope we haven't frightened you too much." Her hand rested on Shane's arm, and her face was less than a foot away from the creature. There was no fear on her face, only fascination. Shane watched her, his attraction to her growing.

Beautiful. Sexy. Smart. Strong. Likes animals. He ticked off Lila's good qualities in his mind, running through scenarios that were completely inappropriate. *She's a* client, *damn it.*

"We had better let this little guy go. The rain has stopped and he should be able to find a better place to hang out than in here."

"You're right. I love seeing wildlife. Especially in the city." Lila shrugged. "Even though it is certainly more like the country out here."

She followed closely as Shane walked towards the open window, reached both hands outside, and gently released the bat from its bonds. It sat there for a moment, sure that its freedom was a mistake, an impossibility, and when Lila shifted at Shane's side it darted away, disappearing into the darkness.

Shane stared out into the night, a small smile on his face. "That was amazing." He closed the window and turned towards Lila. They were inches apart.

This woman is a client. Jack will have my ass.

She smiled at him. A small, sexy smile that turned him on and made his jeans uncomfortably tight.

Her hand on his arm. "Stay."

Heat and desire swirled between them. He stepped closer and she closed the gap between them, her left hand setting his hand on her hip, leaning up to run her soft lips against the stubble that lined his face and neck. He smelled *divine*. She had read once that individuals who smell good to the opposite sex are the best possible breeding partner - the best genetic choice one can make. Her mind registered this analytically, but her mouth was too busy reaching up to take the tip of his earlobe in her mouth. "Stay... with... me." She breathed softly in his ear. She felt him shudder in response. *Now look who is trembling...*

His reaction was instant. She felt his hands reach around to encircle her waist, closing the few inches between them as he pulled her up, her feet leaving the plush carpet below. Her legs wrapped around him and he held her tight against him. She could already feel his erection pressing into her lower belly. Desire danced through her, knowing he was turned on, feeling the heat of him so close to her.

Shane growled, a small rumble of lust crawling up from the back of his throat. He leaned down and claimed her mouth with his own and moved his fingers down under her waistband, hooking into her panties, then sliding in from one side, dipping into her depths.

Her neck arched back, breaking from his hot lips and gasping sharply as his fingers slid into her, forcing a low moan from her throat.

Lila's left hand moved feverishly over his body, kneading his shirt, resting on his neck, sliding her fingers into his hair. He liked the feel of it. She wasn't tentative, girlish or shy. Instead, she was woman who knew what she wanted, and didn't play mind games. Shane dealt in facts, actionable movements and in real life and death.

His mouth moved over hers again. Shane felt her moan into his mouth as his hands probed, rubbing, teasing. His erection increased, throbbing now in his jeans, feeling how hot and wet she was for him. She gasped as his tongue slipped into her open mouth, his thumb moving against her clitoris, his tongue thrusting deep, tasting its sweet freshness, and behind it, the heat of the bourbon. Who needed a bed? He was ready to fuck her here, in the middle of the room.

At that moment, just as his fingers were easing open his fly, his other arm encircling her and having settled for the moment on pressing her lithe, hot body against a nearby pillar with enough force to make the wrought iron and glass sconces rattle, his back pocket began to vibrate. The boss was calling.

"Fuck..."

Ignore That

"Ignore that." Lila's voice was husky, wanton, and a delicate hand pulled on his shirtsleeve.

Shane groaned, pulling away from her as he reached into his back pocket. "I wish I could, darlin'...but..." The phone pulsed, his dick was pulsing as well, but only one was going to get any satisfaction. "I've got to answer this."

He pressed Accept on the phone, sliding away from Lila, turning towards the door, his voice professional, clipped. "Ellis here." A small pause then, "Hey boss... yeah... okay... yeah... will do." He pressed End and slipped the phone back in his jeans.

He stared at her.

Lila was leaning against the pillar, clothing askew, a black lace bra exposed. His gaze traveled down to that warm, hot center of temptation. She was returning his gaze, and her hot sexy tongue dipped out and licked a corner of her lips.

Shit.

He should have walked away.

He should have told her that a police detective wanted to talk to her like Jack had asked him to do. So, they could get to the bottom of this mystery and stop whoever wanted Lila Benoit dead.

He should never have touched her in the first place.

She wasn't his kind of woman.

Two steps, that was all it took for Shane to return to her. She had a smile on her lips until he growled, pressing her against the pillar, rattling the iron and glass sconces as he matched his mouth to hers, seeking that quick, delectable tongue with his own. His hands roamed over her, pulling at her shirt, demanding all of her, in motion, prowling over her body.

She wrapped her long, athletic legs around his waist, her left hand fighting with the buttons on his shirt, eager to see the skin and muscle hidden beneath. Her injured right arm was tucked against her and nearly forgotten except for an occasional twinge of pain when his body connected with hers. The pain was almost pleasurable, and she was lost in a heady swirl of lust. One of his hands was neatly cupping her left buttock, the thumb traveling between her legs, straining to reach her hot, wet clit. His tongue was assaulting her mouth, sending waves of passion through her.

Pulling her tight against him, he could feel her heat as she squirmed deliciously against him, and he thought briefly of the bed in the opposite corner. *Later.* Her hand was moving frantically now, dipping down to his belly, pulling insistently at his jeans, fucking his mouth with her sexy pink tongue. Here was a woman who knew what she wanted and didn't hold back.

Shane unbuttoned his jeans, slid the zipper down, and eased the denim away from his almost painful erection. They slid down to pool at his ankles. He kicked them off, continuing to unbutton the last buttons on her blouse as he did so, determined to view the hot, hard nubs he could feel straining against the t-shirt.

Lila had unbuttoned his shirt, and was pushing it off his shoulders with her uninjured hand, while grinding her pelvis against his. Her panties, a ridiculous and insubstantial little strip of lace firmly clasped between two fingers, barely made a sound as he tore them from her body. Lila let out a lustful moan as Shane's kisses moved off her mouth, trailing a tongue along the curve of her jaw, then down her long, thin neck, stopping for a moment to savor the hint of salt on her skin. He lowered her gently to the ground, her bare feet digging into the rich carpet pile, as his mouth moved over her. The stubble on his chin, and his teeth gently nipping, set her skin on fire.

Lila weaved her fingers through his hair and sucked in a breath of pleasure as his mouth continued to travel down her body, zeroing in on her breasts. He pulled the shirt off of her, tossing it on the floor before circling back to hook one of the delicate lace bra straps off of her shoulder roughly, exposing a small, pert breast. He cupped her breasts, teasing them with a rough, calloused hand, then leaning in for a taste. They tasted amazing. He had been with his fair share of women, and the tits were always his weakness, the more the merrier. Lila's were small, perky little things. He doubted she had more than a B cup, but they tasted like nothing he had ever experienced with any other woman. There was this delicate vanilla musk scent and taste to them, and he took one small, taut nipple in his mouth, and sucked hard enough for her to tighten her fingers in his hair, pulling hard in response to his attentions, moaning. His dick throbbed as he fastened his mouth on the other breast, rolling the nipple with his tongue before lightly nibbling it with his teeth. Lila clenched her left fist in his hair, pressing her body against his.

Outside the wind had picked up, and regular pings on the window indicated that rain was moving in. The windows rattled, as did the iron and glass sconces on the pillar, as Shane and Lila moved, shifted, and twisted, their bodies hot with passion.

His hands slid back down her body, returning to swirl and probe between her legs, into her slick folds, moving in, out, and around. Shane used two fingers to enter her, thrusting up to his knuckles into her as she moaned, her hips gyrating in time with his thrusting fingers.

Lila's body felt as if it had been torn open and filled with liquid fire, full of lust and wantonness. It had been months, *months*, and this man obviously knew how to give pleasure to a woman. Shane was such a far cry from her last boyfriend, who at the moment she was having a ridiculously hard time remembering the name of, especially now that Shane had slipped most of his hand into her, while biting her nipple lightly. Lila felt as if it was all one-way; she wasn't even sure what to do with her left hand, and the injured right hand was desperate to join the fray, wrenched shoulder or not. His mouth on her nipple, hot, alternately flicking it with his tongue and then nibbling it with his teeth, was threatening to bring her to orgasm there and then. His hand worked between her thighs, a finger now probing her ass, adding a new dimension to her desire.

Just as she was about to beg him to fuck her, he moved again, sliding further down her body. He looked up at her then, seeing her half-lidded eyes, heavy with desire, her lace bra askew, with the straps off her shoulders. He lifted her then, pushing her hard against the pillar, spreading her legs and pushing his mouth deep between her legs, licking her, nibbling, his tongue pressing in until it felt the hard, erect nub of her clitoris. He began with the letter "A."

Lila's hips bucked as his tongue found home. What man had ever done this to her? None, not a one. From the fumbled backseat adventures of her first boyfriend in high school, to a handful of men in between, Lila was unused to this level of attention. She fell into it, felt every thrust of his tongue against her clit and his hands on her skin, honey and gold and pecan pie all rolled into these moments of ecstasy. Shane reached "H" when Lila shuddered, crying out wordlessly, her hips rocking back and forth, hot slickness spreading. He didn't stop.

Lila couldn't help but wonder if it was possible to pass out from such an intense orgasm. She was seeing stars, and even after she came, he kept going. Like some goddamn Energizer bunny. She wanted to argue with him, or do something in return, but feeling his hands roaming over her, his mouth and tongue flicking against her most sensitive parts, it was addictive.

Ecstasy, like liquid gold, flowed through her. She was close to a second orgasm, her entire body pliant under his capable hands, his mouth. But she wanted more than that, she wanted to feel him inside her, feel and hear his own pleasure as he fucked her. She tugged on him, pulling him back up her body. He moved up, his hands cupping her breasts, thumbs stroking the tips, his breath hot on her neck. His dick pressed against her belly, and she reached down to stroke it, feeling its velvety smoothness. It throbbed in her hand as she continued to stroke it, gently squeezing, rubbing, and her mouth moved to his neck, to his ear, "I want to feel you inside me...*now*."

He growled, low in his throat, thick with lust and heat. It took only a second for him to guide his dick to her wet, hot opening and thrust into her willing folds. Lila gasped with pleasure. The second thrust took him balls-deep, filling her depths, causing her to cry out a single wordless scream of abandon as he followed it with thrust after thrust. Her slender back dug into the pillar, the metal and glass rattled emphatically, his mouth sucked and pulled on a tender earlobe and she tensed her long, slim legs around him as he fucked her. His hands cupped her buttocks, lifting her off the carpet, thrusting into her body with a quick intensity, slowly building in speed. Her moans increased with each thrust, both of them building in anticipation, thrusting again and again.

The sensation of heat, her moans of ecstasy, and finally the rush of the orgasm sent fireworks rocketing behind his closed eyes. Lila tightened her legs, her legs rubbing against his hips, and exploded, a star on

fire, right along with him.

Butt Dial

They rocked there in place. She had closed her eyes, her mouth open, riding the wave. He had never seen a woman come like she had. Such abandon. Just feeling her body shudder made him hard all over again and her eyes shot open in surprise, meeting his. This time, this time he would take his time. He could feel his erection swelling, responding to the waves of orgasm that continued to shake her lithe frame. He shifted his hands, taking her uninjured hand and pinning it to the pillar and reaching the other up to rub her nipple.

Sweat beaded both of their bodies, and he could feel the lust building inside of him again. He thrust once, deep inside of her, before a voice stopped him in his tracks.

The owner of the voice spoke... from the vicinity of Shane's jeans just a foot away. "I believe that is one of the more innovative questioning tactics I have heard of, Ellis," Jack Benton, Shane's employer and the owner of Benton Security Services remarked dryly. "Give me a call back when you have... well, when you have a moment." There was a click and a beep as the call ended.

Lila gasped, her eyes widening, and Shane slid out of her hot body, cursing quietly.

"Do you think he..." Lila asked, pulling her bra back in place, self-conscious.

"Oh yeah," Shane answered, tight-lipped. "I, uh, I need to talk to my boss. And you should probably get some sleep."

"Sleep?" Lila stared at him, unsure of what came next, but she was certain that sleep was not on the list. She watched Shane gather his clothes, dressing hurriedly.

"Yeah, we will talk more in the morning." He didn't look at her as he left, and Shane could feel her stare hot on his back as he slipped out the door. The door clicked closed behind him and he dressed in the hallway, his fingers and lips still holding her musky vanilla scent. He dug the phone out of his jeans and stared at it for a moment, wishing he didn't have to call Jack Benton back, and split between the desire to go back inside the bedroom and fuck Lila Benoit late into the night, or somehow completely undo the last half hour of his life.

Shane had never, *ever* slept with a client before. *Technically speaking, you haven't* slept *with her, just fucked her senseless,* he couldn't help thinking. It helped that most of his clients were fat, rich assholes. There had been a small handful of female clients, even a couple that he had found quite appealing, but that wasn't the job. The job was to keep the client alive, not put his dick in her. What the hell had he been thinking? What was wrong with him? Just thinking of her sexy body against his woke his dick up again. It jerked in his pants, hopeful as only a penis or a five-year-old with an entire bag of candy hidden in his room can be. He growled in frustration and dialed Jack's number, walking down the steps to the main floor of the rambling house, up another half flight and down the hall to the security office.

Shane sat down in front of the array of monitors that showed real-time views of all angles of the rambling property and waited for his boss to answer. Jack Benton answered on the second ring. "I trust you are in a less compromising position, Ellis?"

Shane could feel his face flush red. "Sorry about that, sir, it won't happen again."

Jack chuckled. "No, it won't; your next client will weigh 300 pounds and be on the outs with organized crime. He will also have a wife and kids, all of which will hate him and you in turn. And just to really make your day, I'm planning on sticking you in butt-fuck nowhere with spotty cell service and no internet or cable TV."

Shane winced. "Understood, sir."

"Can I trust that your attention is fully on the job at hand?" Jack asked.

Shane's spine straightened instinctively. Jack Benton couldn't see him, but that didn't matter. "You can, sir," he responded decisively.

There was a moment's silence and Shane felt a cold sweat building. This wasn't just any job. This was a good job, and a fucking great boss, and he had just fucked it up completely by boning a smoking hot client. A *client.* Jesus Christ, he had fucked a client. *You don't fuck the clients, Shane, you keep them alive.* The silence was killing him. Just as he was sure Jack would fire his sorry ass and worse, Jack broke his silence.

"So, the dead men. Definitely both contract killers."

Shane shook his head; no matter that Jack Benton couldn't see him. "It makes zero sense. She's young, no ties to organized crime, an orphan with no drama."

"Something she might have seen?" Benton asked.

"Nothing she can think of. There is a file on her laptop at work that she mentioned. Something she thinks might be important. She mentioned an SD card as well," Shane answered.

"I'll see if I can get access to the laptop."

Shane could hear the pipes running. "She's in the shower now; I can talk to her afterwards."

"Give her the night to rest up. Tackle this in the morning and report to me then."

"Will do, sir." Shane sat back in his chair. It made no sense. Lila wasn't a criminal, and she hadn't been at the real estate firm for more than a few months. Before that, she had worked a series of dead-end jobs to get through college and beyond. Her last digs had been in an aging apartment building in a high-crime section of the city. Perhaps she had seen something there? He would ask her in the morning.

The monitors showed an ever-changing array of images of the grounds and house. Most of them focused on the border of the property and the outside of the house, but every room was monitored as well. Shane watched as, after nearly half an hour of water running through the pipes, Lila emerged from the bathroom, naked, hair dripping, tendrils of water still making their way down her slender back. She had removed her shoulder sling and her right shoulder and arm were a series of livid, dark bruises. The cameras were in black and white, but there was no mistaking the bruising. It was a wonder she could even use the arm.

Seeing her there, naked, her long, shapely legs and perky nipples, as she made her way to the bed, made him hard all over again. He reached into his pants, adjusting everything in what were suddenly rather tight quarters. His dick pulsed, calming only when she slipped under the covers, her body hidden from his sight.

He closed his eyes, shook his head, her scent in his nose, on his lips. He would be damned lucky if Jack Benton ever trusted him with a client again. His dick calmed, relaxing, and Shane yawned. It had been a long day, an eventful evening, and it was high time he got some shut-eye.

Date Night

"Dad, for crying out loud, you cannot wear that on your date."

Rob tugged at the collar of his shirt and then glanced at Maddie perched on the side of his bed. "Why not, kiddo? This is one of my nicer golf shirts."

"Because, it practically screams *cop*." Maddie slid off the bed and threw open his closet door. "You need one that isn't so in your face. Something that doesn't promise to arrest her if she has more than one drink and doesn't call a cab to take her home." She pulled out a short-sleeved Hawaiian print shirt and said, "How about this one?"

He stared at it. It had been a gag gift from the department head two Christmases ago. It was a bright, flamboyant red and had a large gold-colored tiki on the front guzzling an enormous drink.

"Seriously?"

"What?" Her mouth was twitching as she tried to suppress a smile and failed. "It's cute and you look good in red."

"I'm not wearing that."

"Okay, fine. Wear the black shirt and don't forget to show her your taser."

Rob sighed. "You're killing me, kid."

"Just try it on."

"Not a chance."

"You are being incredibly recalcitrant, Dad."

"Recalcitrant, eh?" He grinned at her.

"And that's not a good thing."

Rob suppressed a snort at the serious look on Maddie's face. "All right, I'll try the shirt on, but I think it looks ridiculous." He slipped off the golf shirt and Maddie bounced up and down as she handed him the red shirt. It was silky, and the fabric felt cool against his skin.

"Huh," he said, cocking his head to one side as he contemplated his reflection, "That isn't half bad."

"Told you!" Maddie crowed, giggling. It was moments like this Rob wished would last forever. Maddie was growing up so fast, but at the moment, she was as excited for him as she would have been to go to the movies or miniature golf just a few short years ago, before her friends had taken priority in her day-to-day existence.

Not that I have anything to complain about with Maddie's friends. She had good friends, kids who were respectful and kind. Her friend Amanda down the street was one of the best. Her parents had instilled in her early a need for service and she had quickly roped Maddie into it as well. The girls volunteered at a soup kitchen twice a week and also helped an elderly neighbor by walking her dog.

"Aren't you going over to Amanda's tonight?"

"Yes, but I wanted to make sure you were ready for your date first, Dad. I mean, obviously, you *needed* me!" She bounced once more on his bed and then headed back to the closet.

"What now?"

"Shoes," Maddie answered, her voice muffled as she rummaged inside of the space.

"I was just going to..."

"Uh, uh, Dad, those are cop shoes." She emerged with cowboy boots in her hands.

"Oh hell no."

"Dad." Maddie's face had taken on a long-suffering expression, "You will look great in these. This patch of gold here, it matches your shirt."

"I'm not sure what look you are going for Mad, but I doubt that me looking like a cowboy visiting Hawaii is in the date night playbook."

"Dad, trust me. You don't want to look like..."

"Like a cop. Right. Got it." He sighed. "Fine, give me the boots. What the hell, the first date is usually awkward and uncomfortable anyway. I might as well send her as many mixed messages as possible. I'm a cowboy. I'm not a cop. I'm a devout worshipper of an angry Hawaiian tiki god." He pulled the boots on, one at a time and stared at his reflection in the mirror. A relic of Claire's, he had hauled it halfway across the country when they moved from Virginia. Eventually, it would go to Maddie. It had been in Claire's family for generations and the glass was old, wavy, and the paint that covered the ornate carved wood, was chipped. Claire had painted it white, but, beneath, it had once been a particularly awful shade of pink.

"I look stupid."

"You look retro with a flair of je ne sais quoi."

"Jenny say who?"

Maddie giggled. "Je ne sais quoi. It means that which cannot be understood or explained."

"That doesn't sound good at all."

"Dad, it means you are mysterious, perhaps even Avant Garde, which is a lot better than your clothes screaming *cop* when you walk in the door."

"Says you." He turned and peered at himself sideways. At least he didn't have a gut like most of the men in his department.

"Says me." She gave him a bear hug. "You look great. Any woman who can't see that doesn't deserve to date you."

He hugged her in return. "If she's mean to me, I'll call you and you can come beat her up for me." Maddie giggled and snuggled against him. He glanced over at the clock on the wall. "Oh hell, I've got to get our laptops over to Ben for updates before I meet my date. I need to hit the road, or else I'll get caught in traffic and be late."

"And I need a ride to the soup kitchen on Paseo. I'm meeting Amanda and her mom there. Do you mind if I sleep over at Amanda's tonight?"

"If it's okay with her mom, sure. But make sure first."

"Thanks, Dad, I'll call her now." She jumped off the bed and was dialing the phone before she ever left the room.

Rob suppressed a grimace as he watched her disappear down the hall. He had checked the house every morning and every night of the last three days for additional listening devices. Tonight, was the first time they would both be out of the house and he had to wonder if anyone would try and access the house and reinstall any bugs while he was gone. Probably not. They knew he knew. The question was, what would the Indalo do about it?

He had agreed to this date only because he wanted more than anything to maintain the facade of normalcy for Maddie. The move halfway across the country, that had been for her. Claire had loved visiting Kansas City when they were first together, childless, and fancy free. She had especially loved the Nelson-Atkins and burgeoning arts scene in the Crossroads.

Here, in flyover country, Maddie could have a normal childhood and grow up in a safe neighborhood. At least, that was what he had thought it was. He hadn't imagined they were watching. In the past few days, one question kept rolling through his head; *When had the bugs been planted*? He was working on getting those answers, but meanwhile it had to be business as usual.

Ben had promised to help make sure that Rob and Maddie's laptops were not being monitored. Rob had simply told Maddie that the bios needed updating. She hadn't questioned it, but of course, if it had been her phone, she would have questioned it more. She knew how those updates worked.

The traffic on I-70 heading into the city was congested. Plenty of people heading to the stadium for a Chiefs game and the rest heading for dinner or the bars in Power & Light. It slowed to a crawl before the stadium exit and then picked back up again. The Chiefs had begun the season strong, and plenty of folks were hoping for a Super Bowl win this year.

Independence Avenue was crowded as well, although with a far different crowd. Sure, some were hitting the various restaurants, grocery stores, and the Dollar General. Others were shopping for drugs or sex. The sun's rays had disappeared behind the skyline, and the rapidly darkening sky was alight with the deep pinks, reds, and oranges of the sunset.

"Shall we play 'I Spy,' Dad?" Maddie joked. An inside, rather off-color joke to be sure. He had taught her how to spot prostitutes and drug dealers last summer and they had made a game of it.

"I'd say 'yes' but there are far too many of them," Rob commented dryly as they passed what had to be the fourth prostitute in as many blocks.

A handful of blocks were passed in silence before he slowed and pulled the car over in front of Ben's shop. "Come in with me; I don't want you waiting out here alone."

She nodded. "Fine with me."

The front light was off, and the door was locked, but Rob could see Ben inside along with a young man. He knocked on the glass and Ben smiled and unlocked the door for them. "Madeline! You have sprouted on us, I see. How are you?"

Maddie grinned. "Hi, Uncle Ben!" She wrapped her arms around him and gave him an exuberant hug. "Dad said he needed to come by and have you handle some updates on the computer, and I am volunteering at a soup kitchen on Paseo so I came with." She drew back and looked at him, her face worried. "You are super-skinny, Uncle Ben. Why don't you come by for dinner at the kitchen? We are making a beef stew!"

Ben laughed, pulling back and patting her hand. "I might just do that."

The young man studied them; his thin, angular frame remained hunched over a computer and his dark eyes looked over Rob with suspicion. Ben motioned to him. "Liam, come here and meet Rob Stone and his daughter Maddie. Two of the best people you could ever know."

Liam unfolded himself from his seat and Rob realized he was looking *up* at the boy. He didn't look much older than Maddie, but he was over six foot in height.

"Hi," the boy said, obviously uncomfortable. Rob nodded and Maddie smiled at him, an open sunny smile that made the boy's mouth twitch up in return.

"Son, could you go downstairs and get that bag of software we talked about?" Ben asked Liam and the boy nodded and slunk away silently. Ben waited until he had disappeared through the door that led to the back room and down into the basement. "He's been staying with me for the past six months. His father's in prison, his mother's a drug addict, and

I found him sleeping in the basement in late spring. He'd been there for months, going in and out through a window."

"I see," Rob said. "I could make some calls for you, see about getting Family Services to help him out."

Ben scoffed. "Family Services? Hell, might as well send him to Juvie right now with first-class tickets to prison after. He's better off here with me. I got him enrolled at Northeast High School and they didn't even bat an eye when I said he was my nephew. He's been getting straight As and working for me here in the shop. Besides, it's nice having someone around."

Rob knew how much Ben had lost - not just a wife, but also his young daughter, victims of a hit and run nearly twenty years earlier. He had worked for a time as a consultant for the CIA specializing in spy hardware and software before moving to Kansas City and opening his own store.

Rob nodded. "Say no more, my friend. And let me know if you need my help, for anything; you know you just have to ask."

Ben clapped Rob on the arm. "You know I will, Stone."

"I brought in the laptops so you could, um, update the BIOS for me," Rob said, stealing a glance at Maddie. She had wandered over to one of the display cases.

Ben followed his gaze and slowly nodded. "Right. I can have them back in your hands by Saturday, if that works for you."

"That'll be great. Thanks, Ben." He set down his card on top of the laptops. "Here, give me a call when you know more."

The boy returned, a stack of CDs in his hands. His eyes were glued to Maddie and he set down the software and walked over to her, murmuring something Rob couldn't hear but it made Maddie giggle. She whispered something back and Rob's hackles rose. He didn't know this boy and Maddie was thirteen, for Christ sake. *Time to start cleaning that shotgun and priming it with rock salt.*

He cleared his throat and the boy flinched away from Maddie, his flirtatious grin disappearing from his face. Rob tried to not bristle as the boy slunk past and back to his work station behind the main counter, astutely avoiding eye contact with Rob.

"Time to go, Maddie. I'm sure Amanda and her mom will be wondering where we are by now."

"Okay, Dad. Bye, Uncle Ben. Bye, Liam!" she chirped and headed for the door.

Liam managed a half-audible "Bye!" before glancing at Rob and then ducking his head down to his work. Rob could feel the boy's eyes follow him and Maddie out the door.

The drive back down Independence yielded less than half of the prostitutes. They had been replaced by lean, twitchy men on various street corners. The sunset was gone and the dark had descended fully, broken only by the streetlamps and headlights of passing cars. "I hate how early it gets dark," Maddie sighed. "It makes it feel so late. But it isn't even five thirty yet."

The parking lot was well-lit, and Rob insisted on going inside with Maddie. The neighborhood could be rough, but he knew that the people who ran the soup kitchen and Maddie and her friend were in good hands. He walked her to the door, verified that she would be spending the night at Amanda's, and hugged and kissed his daughter.

"Remember to smile, okay, Dad?"

"Will do, kiddo, will do."

"Have fun, Dad, and use protection!"

"Christ, Maddie." Rob shook his head, feeling his ears heat up with embarrassment. He couldn't meet Amanda's mother's eyes. "I'll see you tomorrow."

It was a short drive to the Power & Light district and barely a hop and a skip away from the grisly crime scene he had dealt with on Monday night. He looked up at One Kansas City Place, noting that the floor was dark. It had taken them most of Tuesday to process the crime scene. After that, it was held unchanged for the insurance adjuster and then a specialized crime scene cleanup crew would go through. One last run-through with new carpet, and the office would be back in business and open by next Monday. He had finished interviewing the last of the employees on the list that Morris Endon had provided and none of them had been in the office that evening. He needed to compare notes with his partner Max, who had handled several of the interviews, because something didn't add up. A shootout with two dead assassins and no one from Kurgen Real Estate in the office? It didn't make sense. Why there? The last person on the list, that Lila Benoit, once he talked to her, perhaps things would be clearer.

Those questions occupied Rob's thoughts as he slid into a parking spot in a nearby garage. It was half a block to the Bristol Seafood Grill; time to get his head out of murder and into smiling and being debonair. He sighed and reminded himself that dating after ten years alone was more than okay; in fact, it was necessary. He plastered a smile on his face and walked into the restaurant.

Early Morning Call

It wasn't quite six in the morning when the phone rang. Rob had been up for an hour, gone for a run, and eaten a small breakfast. He stared at the number. It was an unfamiliar one, a 518 area code. He answered, "Stone."

"Rob? It's Diana, Milo's ex-wife. Do you remember me?" A familiar voice asked, sounding muted, weary.

"Why, of course I do, Diana. How are you?" The fried egg and half a grapefruit had turned to an unmovable stone in his stomach. Diana calling him could not be good, not at all.

"I'm not good," Diana sighed, a sob escaping. "I'm calling with really bad news, Rob. Milo died two days ago. I know you two must have stayed in contact after you moved; I found Christmas cards from you in Milo's possessions and I just wanted to tell you the news personally."

"God, Diana, what happened?"

"The police said it was a mugging. He was in the wrong place at the wrong time and," she stopped, sniffled, "he fought so hard. There were two attackers and it looks like they were interrupted by a man walking by and they ran off. The good Samaritan got him to a nearby hospital and they life-flighted him to Inova. I thought he would make it. I'm still listed as his emergency contact now that his parents are both gone, and I flew down there the next morning with Gus." She took in a breath and let it out slowly. "He made it out of surgery. He was talking, even joking. But the next day they detected internal bleeding and took him back to surgery. They said he had a bad reaction to the anesthesia and he died on the table." She let out a long breath. "Gus is devastated. They weren't getting along so well. He's fifteen, after all, and he doesn't get along with any adult well right now. But now, he's really hurting, you know?"

Rob felt ill. Had this happened because of his call? Had the Indalo been watching Milo too? Were they making sure there weren't any more loose ends?

"I'm so very sorry, Diana. I just spoke with Milo earlier this week. I'm just... I can't believe he's gone."

"I know, me either. It was so sudden."

"Is there," Rob struggled to find the words, "Is there anything I can do for you, or for Gus?"

Diana sniffled, excused herself, and blew her nose in the background. "No. Jonathon, my husband, he's helping with everything. The funeral arrangements and all the decisions, I just... I just wanted to let you know, Rob. And give you the basic info in case you could make the funeral next Sunday." She rattled off the information, sniffling again. "No matter what happened between Milo and me, I just, God, I'm reeling. He was a good man, and a good father to Gus. Don't be a stranger, Rob. If you are ever in town, look me up, okay?"

"Of course. Thank you, Diana, and thank you for letting me know. I am so sorry." The phone clicked and Rob stood there, in shocked silence.

A mugging. I don't buy it for an instant.

Milo was dead. Steve too. He sat there in the dark, watched the clock slowly click over to 6 a.m. The house was silent; Maddie was still asleep, her plans to stay at Amanda's that night had been changed after Amanda's mother called him in the middle of his date to let him know there had been a family emergency. Maddie had been sound asleep by the time he made it back home.

Outside, he could hear a siren in the distance. Would they come for him next? Would they hurt Maddie? And what would happen to her if he was gone?

His phone chimed, showing there were messages. Rob sighed in frustration; the phone had been acting up, not ringing at times, not showing messages until hours later. He needed to get a new one. It was old, far older than anyone else's. He fought technology, and its built-in obsolescence, obstinately. He had been the last one in his circle of co-workers and friends to get a smartphone, and it had been a used one at that. Now it was outdated and occasionally malfunctioning. A small smile quirked at the edges of his mouth.

Maddie will be overjoyed when I tell her I'm upgrading. She's been at me for months. Hell, maybe I'll spring for a nice one this time, top of the line; it will only be obsolete in a few months.

He reviewed his messages. One from his date from the other night...

Hey, handsome, I had a wonderful time the other day. How about dinner at my place tomorrow night?

Maddie had already added an overnight at her friend Megan's. He would have the evening free.

Who knows, I might even get lucky.

He typed a response back and hit Send. His phone made a whooshing noise.

The other message was from Jack Benton, and it had come in even earlier, around three in the afternoon yesterday.

Jack Benton here. Would like to connect you on a secure line with Lila Benoit. Miss Benoit is currently in a safe location and has engaged the services of Benton Security Services after two attempts on her life.

Two attempts on her life? He had convinced himself that Benoit's friend and co-worker, Kaylee Stromm, was being paranoid, but now this Jack Benton was saying the same thing. *Benton, Benton, where do I know that name from?* He opened up the internet and searched for the name Jack Benton.

His thoughts drifted back to Milo.

Maybe I'm being paranoid. Muggings happen every day. He tried to swallow the paranoia and the fear. He tried to explain it away. But no matter how he tried, he couldn't shake a sense of foreboding.

The search for Jack Benton yielded pages of info, mostly salacious gossip. Rob knew he had recognized the name and now, looking at the first page of results, he knew why. "Jack Benton, playboy billionaire," he read out loud, "Orphaned at age 22, he and his young sister were sole survivors of a plane crash that killed their parents and two other siblings nearly twenty years ago. And the sister was kidnapped and murdered just days after her sixteenth birthday two years later. Huh." He paged through photos of Jack - at his parents' funeral, his young sister at his side. By all accounts, they had been extremely close and Jack had been devastated by her death, even more so than losing his parents. Rob continued to browse the pages, running across a news headline from three years after Allison Benton's death covering the founding of Benton Security Services. Jack Benton was just a decade younger than he was and recent pictures showed gray hairs creeping into the jet black. He had never married and showed no signs of it, although he was one of the more eligible bachelors who wasn't a celebrity.

"According to Celebrity Buzz, you split your time between your California estate and a place in the Hamptons. But I'm guessing you have properties throughout the United States, don't you, Mr. Benton?"

Outside, the sun was beginning to peek above the horizon, the sky a brilliant pink. He stood up from his seat at the kitchen island and walked over to the cabinet and pulled out the herbal tea that Maddie had recently taken a shine to. He smiled at the thought of it, she had wanted him to switch from coffee to herbal tea, citing all kinds of evidence that indicated caffeine at his age was not advisable, and he flatly refused. After nearly three decades of daily, multi-cup infusions of the bitter black brew, he had zero intentions of switching to some hippie-dippy herb-infused cranberry water. It was simply not happening. Maddie, just as obstinate as he was, had continued to drink the herbal frou-frou ever since.

He slid a mug of water into the microwave and pressed the Start button, unwrapping the tea bag from its glossy envelope and setting it on the countertop next to the honey. There was a yawn and creak of the stairs. "Morning, Dad." She rested her head against his shoulder briefly before leaning over and turning on the kitchen light. "Why are you sitting here in the dark?"

"Just thinking." The microwave beeped as it finished. "The water for your tea is hot."

"Thanks, Dad." She yawned again, and Rob heard her jaw pop, "Ugh, I wish I hadn't let Megan rope me into meeting her early to cram for the chemistry test. I really could have used a couple more hours of sleep."

Rob's phone lit up briefly, but when he picked it up and logged in, nothing showed in the messages. "Damn this thing, I swear it is eating my messages. I won't get them right away, sometimes not for hours, I just read two from yesterday afternoon. It's damned annoying." He paged through the list of text messages. "I'll bet I've got another one in the queue, *somewhere*, but where is it?"

He looked over at his daughter, "Well, it's good news for you. I give up, it's time for two new phones."

Her eyes widened, her drowsy demeanor vanishing. "Seriously? Oh, my God, we might actually join this decade?"

"Well, I don't know if I would take it that far." he said, teasing her. "I mean, they still sell flip phones, don't they?" He laughed at her horrified expression. "Don't worry, I wouldn't do that to you. I'm thinking of getting the new Voyage they released last month; how would that be?"

She bounced, her teenage cool shed and the young child she had been trying so hard to eradicate from her demeanor suddenly front and center. "Oh Daddy, that would be so amazing!"

He chuckled as she jumped around the kitchen and then hugged him exuberantly. "I can't wait to tell my friends! When can we go shopping? How about tomorrow after school? Please? Pretty please?"

"Okay, okay, it's a date then."

She twirled, squealing with joy. "I'm so excited!" Maddie stopped suddenly, a serious expression on her face. "But we need to donate the old phones to this guy at the soup kitchen, okay? He collects them and re-distributes them to the women's shelter that helps battered women get back on their feet."

"We will definitely do that, Mads."

She squealed and wiggled. "I have to go tell Megan and everyone else right away! Love you, Daddy!" She kissed him on the cheek and rushed off, leaving her tea steeping on the counter.

Rob had a half-smile on his face as he watched his daughter disappear upstairs. "You would be proud of her, Claire. I know I certainly am."

At the thought of his wife, his smile faded. Ten years of her gone, longer now than the time they were actually together, and he felt as if he was betraying her memory, turning his back on what they had together. Perhaps this whole dating thing was a mistake. What if there had only been one woman for him? One and done, and no one else could come close? Sure, he had enjoyed last night. His date had been beautiful, funny, and they had certainly clicked. But she wasn't Claire. No one had ever touched him like Claire, not before her, and certainly not after. Sure, there had been fleeting attractions, the flush of desire, but a woman who he wanted to spend his life with? Only Claire had inspired those dreams, and those dreams had died with her, alone, in a car on an icy road.

His thoughts switched to Maddie. She was becoming a young woman. She needed an older woman to guide her, to help her with all the feminine details that left him bewildered and uncertain. Was that why she had been so insistent that he begin to date? Was there some part of her that unconsciously sought that, *needed* that which had been denied her for the past decade? Claire's death hadn't just left a gaping chasm in his life... their daughter had suffered too. He had seen it over the years, in nightmares, her artwork even, and the close relationship that they had. She and Claire had been two peas in a pod, a connection that had seemed magical to him at the time, but one that he had only been a third wheel in. Maddie had been inconsolable when she died, refusing to sleep in her own bed for months, plagued with nightmares, and waking fears of losing him. Their relationship had changed, become closer, and she had clung to him at every leave-taking, terrified that he would not return. But perhaps now she was ready and needed a female influence. He knew that her friends' mothers paid extra attention to her. They had always been quite kind, reaching out to him directly when necessary, but it wasn't the same. They were someone else's mother. Maddie needed someone who would fill Claire's role, at least as much as anyone else *could* fill that role.

It was that realization that made up his mind. "It's time I moved on, Claire." He said it in the silent kitchen, his coffee mug empty, cool in his hand. Maddie needed this, and perhaps he did as well.

Miles away, Lucifer sat red-eyed and sleep-deprived in front of the bank of computer screens, the cell phone clamped in her hand. The phone rang once, twice, and a voice answered, "What is it, Lucifer?"

"We've been shut down on the computers."

"Explain."

"Someone has disabled and removed the keylogger I installed on both of the computers. Well, not *someone*, I know exactly who it was because he sent a text last night and again this morning to Stone."

"I see." That voice, never sounding angry, never changing tone, was far more frightening to Lucifer than anyone else she had ever dealt with in the organization. "And who is it?"

Lucifer fought to keep her voice even, "A Benjamin Carlson; he runs a small spyware store on Independence Avenue. From the text I intercepted, it looks like they have known each other for a number of years. I took the liberty of digging further, and Carlson did some consulting work for the CIA fifteen years ago. I think they met then."

"You said you intercepted a text?"

"Yes, Carlson was alerting Stone of the spyware and then following up with the same message this morning."

"Thank you, Lucifer. I'll handle it from here." The phone clicked and Lucifer sat there, phone in hand, staring at the now-dark screen. Part of her was relieved. She couldn't help wondering what "handling it" meant for this Benjamin Carlson.

She put the phone down. "Really, Luce, I don't think I need to know what that means." There were Indalo, and then there were *Indalo*. Lucifer pulled up World of Warcraft and watched as the game began. She was deep in the Wrath of the Lich King, hanging on by a thread, but still making progress. *That* was what she could lose herself in, not what was going to happen to Ben Carlson. Frankly, it was none of her business.

Riehl answered his phone on the first ring. "Riehl."

"I have another job for you."

"Go ahead."

"A Benjamin Carlson. He runs a spyware store on Independence Avenue. I need you to eliminate him. Burn the building down while you're at it. I don't want a single shred of evidence left. I've texted you the address." The phone chimed in his hand.

"Consider it done." He paused. "Any updates on the woman?"

"We are still trying to track her down. I'll have Lucifer call you when we know more."

Riehl smiled. His balls still hurt, but he was looking forward to dealing with Lila Benoit.

No More Loose Ends

Ben squinted at the business card in his hand and beckoned to Liam. "Take a look at this, will you? Is that number there an eight?"

Liam slid off his seat, walked over, and leaned close. "Which one?"

"That one there." Ben stabbed at the card.

Liam snorted. "You're going blind, old man. That's the fax number; you want this one here." He pointed at the line above it and Ben squinted, moving the card away, trying in vain to focus his eyes.

"Where are your glasses?"

"If I knew that, I wouldn't be asking for your help," Ben replied, exasperated. "Read this damn thing to me, will you?"

"Want me to dial the phone too? I think you might be having a senior moment," Liam teased the older man.

"Why I oughta." Ben swung at the boy, low and slow, and Liam danced out of the way, a grin on his face. "You kids, you just wait until your eyes start failing you."

"I'm pretty sure all of the polar ice caps will have melted by then, don't you think?"

"C 'mere boy, I'll show you polar ice caps!"

Liam laughed, swooped in, and grabbed the phone from Ben. "It's okay, old man, I got your back." He dialed the number while Ben grumbled and tried to hide the smile behind more bluster.

The truth of the matter was that he got as much out of caring for Liam as the boy did, possibly more. Before the kid had showed up in his basement, wet, cold, and scared, Ben had been lonely, depressed, and generally miserable. The kid had filled an emptiness, the chasm of grief that had opened at the loss of Angie and little Charlotte in the car crash nearly two decades ago. Now in his late fifties, Ben had lost his parents ten years ago and his only sibling, Frank Jr., two years later of a massive heart attack. He was all alone in the world, until Liam had shown up.

He snatched the phone from the boy after Liam dialed the number and listened, "Oh hell, it's going to voicemail *again*."

Liam grabbed it back out of his hands. "Here, it's quicker to send a text message. What do you want it to say?" His fingers flew as he typed Ben's words and then pressed the button to send it. The phone produced a "whoosh" and Ben stared at it, frowning.

"What the hell was that sound?"

"Just the phone saying the text has been sent," Liam answered, trying to hide a grin and failing.

"Alright then. I hope he gets back to me soon."

"Me too. Both of the computers had keylogger software on them. And it wasn't any I've seen before," Liam said. "This was rather elegant, hidden in lines of code, and it took some work to find it."

"And you're sure that's what it is?" Ben asked, his face showing concern.

"Yeah. Absolutely." Liam's dad was in prison for his hacking skills, many of which he had passed on to his young son.

"Well, Stone will want to know about it. Were you able to get it out?"

"I think so, but there's a couple more tests I want to do. And also, there's the new release, League of Angels III, that I found a copy of that I need to check out down in the basement." The basement was where the internet router was and it had the best reception in the building.

"*Found* it, did you?" Ben gave Liam a sideways stare.

"Don't worry, it won't come back on you. I piggybacked on the porn store's Wi-Fi." Liam replied, grinning.

"It's locked down with a password." Ben stared at the boy. "How the hell did you get around that?"

"Easy, the owner is really into dogs."

"What?"

Liam grinned. "The password is Hundeficker, which means dog fucker."

"Oh Christ, how the hell you find this kind of stuff is beyond me." Ben shook his head. "Well, I'm heading upstairs to fix dinner. I'm guessing you will be running late with this, so I'll just put it in the fridge, and you can heat it up when you come upstairs."

"Will do."

Ben began to walk away, then stopped and turned around. "Homework?"

"Did it in study hall in last period."

"Alright then." He walked a few more feet and stopped again. "Be in bed by ten. I read an article the other day that says teens need at least ten hours of sleep."

"Aye aye, cap'n."

Liam headed down the stairs to the basement. He made his way by feel because the lone lightbulb in the ceiling had burned out last week and finding the ladder and getting it changed out was a hassle. Besides, he would see fine once he booted up his desktop in the far corner. He had lived down here for weeks before Ben had caught him flat-footed one night in early February. It had been colder than a witch's tit, but the dank basement was better than the crack house his mom was staying in and no one tried to jack his stuff here. He had made a nice little nest for himself in a far corner, behind a couple of old doors. It was when he had lit a small fire in the camp stove that the old man had sniffed him out.

Liam made his way to the desk - his feet knew the way - and he felt for the tower and pressed the power button. When the screen came to life, he saw that Ben had added a brand-new space heater, unpacked it and everything, and a note was attached to it. Liam leaned over and read it in the dim light.

"So, you don't get cold while you're killing trolls." The boy smiled. Ben was alright. Hell, the old man was more than alright. He had insisted Liam take a room upstairs on the second floor, even let Liam put a lock on it, and he'd never tried to cross any lines with him, unlike some of the losers his mom had shacked up with since his dad went to prison. Hell, he'd even marched down to the local high school and enrolled him in classes. Just eyeballed the office staff and damned if he wasn't enrolled and attending classes for the first time since last year.

He sat down in the office chair and it creaked in protest. He logged in and pulled up League of Angels, flexing his fingers until they cracked. He checked the time and the clock read 6:26. He had just under four hours; he could complete at least one quest in that time with the cheat codes he'd dug up.

The speakers were set to low volume. Old habits die hard, after all. *People can't sneak up behind you if you got the sound down low.* Besides, there was only so much singing swords and battle cries that one could take. It was the thumps that caught his attention. An out of place sound, completely different from the sounds Ben made as he walked across the floors, or even of something falling. Something hitting the floor, *hard*, and a muffled shout. The building was old, turn of the century brick, two stories high, three if you counted the basement. Ben had owned the building since he moved to Kansas City some twelve years ago, moving into it when the neighborhood was even uglier and more dangerous than it was now. With the shop closed since six, there should be no one in the building except the two of them.

Liam turned the volume to zero and listened longer. Another thump, the sounds of feet on stairs, walking across the shop floor, and the chime of the back door. Liam stood up. What or who had that been? He thought of calling out to Ben and stopped before his mouth could produce sound. Something was wrong. Every instinct in him told him to be silent. He shut off the monitor, removing all light except for the weak light filtering in through one barred window from the street lamp outside.

The building was silent. He moved as quietly as possible to the stairs and walked up them, the occasional creak of a loose riser betraying his presence. He moved silently up the stairs, smelling an odd, nasty smell. It was not unlike the smells from the copper thieves, the ones who burned the plastic off of the copper wires in large barrels, filling the neighborhood with a stench that twisted at your guts and made you breathe shallow, hoping not to suck in the nasty chemicals that hung in the air. *Carcinogens.* That's what Ben had said about them. The smell was stronger on the main floor and he could see little; the security lights were outside and the thick glass blocks that let in light but stopped folks from breaking in allowed only a filtered light inside. There was no one there. Had Ben gone outside? Liam turned to the left as he reached the top step, stopping only at the glint of something dark on the floor to the right. The door to the upstairs, the one that they kept closed when the shop was open, was slightly ajar and there was some dark liquid on the floor.

Liam squatted down, alarm bells ringing in the back of his head. He could hear a strange sound coming from upstairs and this odd liquid on the floor; something was terribly wrong. Behind the door he heard a small sound, almost a gasp, and he slowly pulled the door open, falling backward in shock as he did. It was Ben. A tangle of limbs, blood on the older man's face, from his mouth, his head, and his eyes stared straight at Liam, unblinking.

"Ben!" Liam's voice was hushed, almost a whisper. An overwhelming feeling of fear washed over him. There was no way Ben had fallen down the stairs, no way he had been alone on the second floor. He had heard someone else, he knew he had, and now that the door was open, he could see a glow from above. Fire. Flames spreading fast from the direction of the kitchen.

He reached out and touched the older man, fingers shaking. Ben was warm still, but from the amount of blood, the unseeing eyes, Liam knew what he was looking at. A junkie in one of the crack houses he had lived in with his mom had died one day last year. The same, wide-eyed vacant expression on his face. A mixture of horror and longing, as if he had seen death coming and almost welcomed it. Liam couldn't tell if Ben's face held that same expression, but he knew death when he saw it. Above, the flames crackled and began to build. He could see the century-old wood frame catching fire, the paint smoking, peeling, and blistering.

He had to get out. Before someone saw the fire and called it in. Before they blamed him. Which they would.

Good Samaritan takes in kid off the streets. A kid who broke into his building and squatted in the basement. Good Samaritan ends up dead at the bottom of his stairs and the building on fire.

He was sixteen. Old enough to be tried as an adult if they had a mind to. And with that kind of story, damned if they wouldn't. He had to go.

He had to leave Ben behind, possibly to be consumed by the fire. The old man deserved better. He'd told Liam about his wife, his daughter, both killed in a hit and run. The driver had never been found. Ben hadn't deserved that. And he sure as hell didn't deserve this.

Liam steeled himself, reached out, and shut the old man's eyelids. "I'm so sorry, Ben. If I can, I'll find out who did this. I promise you that."

The fire was spreading. He could hear it beginning to roar. There was no time to get any of his belongings, no chance to save the extra clothes Ben had bought him or the Kindle sitting by his bedside. He had to go. *Now.*

Liam stood up, his heart racing, and the noxious fumes drifting down the stairs almost knocked him back down. He coughed, pulled his shirt over his face, and ran not for the back door, but back to the basement stairs. The back exit was well lit, but the street was dark on the east side of the building and there was a window there he could get out of. It was, after all, how he had first entered Ben's building eight months earlier. Down the basement stairs, out through the basement window, and onto the dark street. He could hear sirens now. The second-story windows shone with flames and he could hear the glass popping, exploding. He ran, fast and far, towards the train yard and disappeared into the poorly lit streets beyond it, leaving behind the one person who had given a damn about him since his dad ended up in prison.

It took two fire trucks to put out the fire. Hours later, within the smoldering timbers dripping with water, the firefighters discovered Ben's body at the bottom of the remains of the stairs. "Damn, it looks like the fire started in the kitchen upstairs and the old man tried to run down and out of the building. Probably overcome with smoke and fell down the stairs." They loaded the body up and into the coroner's van.

"Hey, Robbie, did you see this other bedroom here? Looks like it was occupied. We got what looks like high school textbooks, clothes, maybe a teenager?"

"Just the one body. Maybe the kid was out." Robbie shrugged. "Or maybe he started the fire. Tell the captain and I'm guessing the police will want to look into it. It looks like either a grease fire or electrical short, but you never know."

Dominic Riehl stood in the crowd, listening. He tuned out the rant from a slipper and robe-clad overweight neighbor with rollers in her hair who was convinced it had been a clandestine meth lab on the second floor.

"All of the fires around here are from those illegal drug-cooking operations," she announced loudly to anyone who would listen.

A second person living in the building? Why wasn't I told that the old man had someone living there with him? He glanced around at the crowd. There were a handful of kids nearby and he moved slowly towards them.

One of them, a girl, had tears in her eyes. "The skinny kid, Liam, in Miss Forbes class, he was staying here with Ben," Riehl heard her say to the other girl.

"Oh my God, Laney, do you think he's still in there?" the second girl asked.

"I hope not. He was really nice. He helped me prep for the bio quiz last week. He's super smart."

The second girl saw Riehl and tugged at Sarah's elbow, backing away and giving him a sideways look. "C'mon, let's get out of here. That guy is creeping me out."

Riehl didn't follow. He was busy trying to figure out how to deal with the situation. Should he tell his employer? *After fucking up the hit on the woman, and now missing someone who lived in the building? Hell no.* He would deal with this himself. He'd track down this Liam kid and put him in the ground right next to the old man.

He smiled and whistled a cheery little tune as he walked away from the crowd and the smoldering building. All in a day's work.

Alone

Liam watched the eastern sky lighten from black to gray, staring bleakly at the skyline as the sun's rays warmed the horizon. It didn't seem fair, it sure as hell didn't seem right that the sun could rise today. Surely, for just one day, the sun should sit still, the earth should cease to turn, in mourning for a man who had made a difference, and who hadn't deserved to die.

He had cried, sitting there on the roof of the decrepit warehouse near the train tracks, thinking of Ben being consumed by the fire. Had he been dead? For sure? What if he had left him there, conscious, unable to escape the flames?

"Stop it, stop it, you know he was gone." Liam's voice was raspy, damaged from the smoke and the tears. His cheeks were wet again. As much as it felt selfish and self-centered, his thoughts went to the question.

What the hell am I going to do now? Do I find Mom? What do I do?

His books, his homework, it was all back at Ben's and ashes now. Along with his clothes, his computer, everything. He had less than nothing now. He had no home, no belongings, and no one who gave a damn. Except Dad. And Dad was in prison and would be for at least the next five years, maybe longer.

Probably longer. Dad doesn't play well with others.

He shifted, shivering, and noticed the first movements of the city around him. It was coming to life, the traffic beginning to hum along the highway to the south. Headlights still on, the cars coming thicker, slowing and braking. He could see headlights pulling into the parking lot below, the first employees in the metal fabrication company next door arriving for their day's work. He didn't even have a cell phone. The one that Ben had given him had been charging next to his bed and was now nothing more than melted plastic and silicone.

Liam stood up, his legs aching from the cold, and dug into his pockets. A coupon for a free Egg McMuffin and drink from Mickey D's that he had won in English class for having the highest score on the test.

Well, I've got breakfast.

And the rough edge of a card. He dug it out of his right pocket and peered at it. It was the cop's card. The one with the cute daughter, Maddie. Liam smiled, a brief one, immediately feeling guilty at thinking of a girl when Ben was... Ben was...

"Ben's dead. And you aren't. And it fucking sucks." His breath fogged in the cool morning air.

He stared at the card. It listed not only the cell phone number, but also an office phone number. Perhaps that was the number he needed to call. Ben had left messages on the cell phone, but had he tried the office number? His stomach rumbled. He needed to get some food and find a phone to call the cop. Ben deserved that much.

An hour later, the inside of the McDonald's on Independence was almost empty, compared to the long line of cars that snaked around the building, impatiently waiting their turn for coffee and something that could be called food, but was highly suspect. Liam swallowed the last of the greasy breakfast sandwich. The sausage was dry and the eggs rather tasteless, but he choked it down to shut his stomach up. He winced at the bitter, hot coffee and wished he had chosen an orange juice instead.

"Liam? Oh my God, are you okay?" He looked up into a familiar face. Laney, the girl he had helped with a bio test the other day, was standing there, a small gaggle of girls behind her. They stared, one of the shorter ones nudging the other.

"Huh? Oh yeah, I, uh, I was out last night. I got back and uh, well." His voice petered out and he stared down at the remains of his coffee.

Laney set her tray down and slid into the seat across from him, her eyes focused on his. "Where did you go? Do you have somewhere to stay?" She reached out and put a hand on his.

"I, uh." He stopped and looked up at the other girls, before looking away again. "Could I, uh, could I borrow your cell phone? I need to make a call." The other girls tittered and whispered among themselves.

"Um, sure, okay." She pulled a pink phone out of her purse. The case was covered in pink and silver jewels. She slid it over to him.

"I, uh," he stammered and looked back at the girls, "I'm gonna just take this in, uh, the bathroom and make a quick call. It'll be really quick, I promise."

Laney nodded and smiled at him, frowning as her friends continued to whisper and giggle. "Sure, Liam, go ahead."

He slid out of the booth. "Excuse me," he muttered as the other girls parted, moving away from him as if he had a contagious disease.

He walked away, but not before he heard one of them whisper loudly, "Oh my God, Laney. He's probably the one who *set* the fire."

By the time he returned from the bathroom, Laney was sitting alone, her cheeks crimson, her mouth set in an angry, flat line. Her friends were gone, and she was angrily shoving a breakfast sandwich into her mouth.

He slid the phone back towards her. "Thanks."

She managed a small smile. "No problem." The smile slipped away. "I'm really sorry about Tanya. She's a bitch. I know you didn't set the fire." She hesitated, looking at him, at the smudges on his face. "What *did* happen, Liam?"

He shook his head. "He was... Ben was..." Words seemed insufficient. What had the old man been to him? A friend? A mentor? A parent? He'd stepped up, opened up his life, and welcomed Liam into it, with no expectations, no demands, just...

He gave a damn about me. More than anyone in a long time had. He didn't get anything out of it, he was just...

The look on his face must have betrayed his misery. Laney reached out, squeezed his hand. "Liam, it's okay. You don't have to talk about it. I, I understand. Hey, listen, my uncle keeps an old Airstream on our property. It's out of sight of the house. I could give you the keys, and you could stay there for a couple of days. You'd be roughing it a bit, but it's something. At least until you work things out."

"Yeah?"

"Yeah." She pulled her hand back, checked her phone. "Shit, we've got less than ten minutes until the first bell. C'mon."

She stood up, gathering her trash and his, and looked at him expectantly. He shook his head. "I don't think I can."

"Of course, you can. Besides, who did you call? Are you waiting for a call back?"

Shit. I didn't think that one through.

"Uh, well, yeah."

"So, they'll call back this phone number, right?" She wiggled her phone back and forth and he nodded.

She shrugged. "We share the first three periods. If you get a call back before lunch, I'll be able to tell you right away." She said it so confidently, that Liam felt a little less lost. He found himself standing up and following her out of the McDonald's, down the street and into the high school just as the first bell sounded.

Rob Stone walked into the station balancing the coffees. It was his turn to get the jolt of java to keep him and Max going every day. His partner looked up. "Well, look who finally decided to show up. I was about to cave and go get the damn nuclear waste that's eating a hole in the coffeepot down the hall."

"Careful, they made it hot enough to melt the Styrofoam again," Rob warned and Max winced as he took one of the cups.

"Christ, I got no idea how the cups aren't melting into slag." He deposited the cup onto his desk and shoved two Post-its towards Rob. "I pulled two messages off our voicemail. Some kid, name of Lee, Leem..."

"Liam?"

"Yeah, that's it. Also, that Jack Benton guy finally called us back. I was just about to call him, or do you wanna?"

"I'll call Liam, you give Benton a call."

Max saluted him and picked up his desk phone. Rob stared at the message Max had scribbled. He didn't recognize the number, but the only Liam he could think of was the boy from Ben's shop. The one who had stared at Maddie with moon eyes and looked distinctly uncomfortable when he learned that Rob was a cop.

What's he doing calling me?

He picked up his desk phone and dialed the number. It rang three times before a girl answered with a whisper, "Yeah?"

"This is Detective Rob Stone with the KCPD. I'm returning a call from a Liam?"

The girl gave a small gasp. "Um, yeah, hold on." Rob could hear a voice steadily droning in the background, along with a frantic shuffling and incomprehensible whisper of the girl before Liam's voice answered the call.

"Uh, hello?" He was also whispering.

"Liam? This is Detective Rob Stone."

"Uh, yes sir, I..." The boy was interrupted and there was more rustling before a louder, authoritative female voice came on the line.

"I'm sorry, but Mr. Sorenson is in class right now."

"Yes, I imagine he is," Rob said dryly, smothering a smile. "This is Detective Rob Stone of the KCPD and I was returning Mr. Sorenson's call."

"I, uh, one moment." There was a brief pause as the phone was handed back to Liam. "Take that out into the hall, Mr. Sorenson. You too, Laney Miller. I know Mr. Sorenson doesn't own a jewel-bedecked iPhone. Take it to the principal's office and return with an appropriate explanation, if you please." The woman enunciated the last three words in a huff.

A few seconds later and the laughter from the classroom faded with the click of a door and an echoing hallway. "Um, Mr. Stone? I'm back."

"What can I do for you, Liam?"

"Do you know about the fire, sir? The one last night?"

Rob frowned. "No, what fire?"

Max, already off the phone, put his head up. "Oh man, I forgot to tell you. The spy shop burned last night. The one on Independence Blvd in Northeast. They said the owner died in it."

Rob felt ill. "What? What happened, Liam?"

"I was down in the basement. I heard something. Someone. I went upstairs and he was dead. Someone killed him, Mr. Stone. Set the fire."

"Where are you, Liam? What school?" He knew the answer, even as he stood up, the receiver in his hand, reaching for his coat.

"Uh, Northeast, sir."

"You go to the office, wait there for me. I'll be there in five minutes." He slammed the phone down without waiting for an answer.

Liam stared at the now-dark phone and turned to Laney. Her eyes were huge. "You called the cops?" Her face held a mixture of surprise and awe.

"Ben said he was a friend."

"A *cop*?" she asked it again, the look changing to doubt.

"Yeah."

"Okay, look." She slipped the phone into her back pocket and pulled out a pen and her notebook and scribbled onto the notepaper. "This is my address. If you need a place to crash, go in around the back, from the alleyway. It's supposed to be locked, but my uncle lost the padlock, so you can get in through the gate. After school, I'll be home. But don't come to the door." She rolled her eyes. "My mom's weird, y'know? Anyway, just hang out on the back side of the Airstream. I'll unlock it when I get home."

"Thanks, Laney."

"Yeah, no problem." She grinned. "It's all kind of exciting." Her eyes went wide and she covered her mouth in horror. "Oh God, Liam. I'm sorry. I shouldn't have said that. I didn't mean it like that."

"I know. Don't worry about it."

"I'm going back to class. Mrs. Henderson can bitch at me if she wants, but next to you, I'm her best student, so..." She backed away. "I hope I see you soon."

"Yeah. See you, Laney."

Half an hour later, Liam was sitting in a cracked plastic bucket seat at the East Patrol station. It was busy, and Detective Stone hadn't said much in the school office, just flashed his badge and intimidated the hell out of a new secretary and then hustled Liam out of the school and into his car. It hadn't been a patrol car. The detective had gruffly motioned to him to sit in the front seat of the Acura and then instructed Liam to buckle up.

The drive to the station had been a silent affair. That had changed after they arrived at the station. After the second repeat of the events of the night Rob had stepped away to confer with his partner Max. Liam sat there, staring at Rob's desk. There was a note with his name and Laney's phone number on it. There was also a note from a Jack Benton from Benton Security Services. Liam stared at it, wondering what the company did. He pulled the notepaper with Laney's address on it and borrowed a pen to scribble down the name on the other side of the paper.

He listened too. Even as he leaned back and pretended to have dozed off, he listened to the two men talk. They weren't just talking about him, and about Ben. They also talked about this Jack Benton guy who was apparently holding on to someone they wanted to question. Some woman who was under his protection.

The detective had seemed to believe Liam. That had been somewhat of a load off his mind because he had been scared. Scared they would think he had hurt Ben and set the fire. You never knew with cops. They fucked with your head. Liam had seen it plenty of times before. They would pretend to be your buddy, someone you could trust, and then they would haul your ass off to Juvie or jail all the same. They had promised Dad a deal, but then they had taken it away, left him holding the bag and looking at twenty years behind bars all because he didn't finger any of the hackers that they had really wanted. It was such bullshit. So, he listened, because the way it was looking, Detective Stone would probably be talking about handing him over to Social Services next.

Liam knew where that would lead. Nowhere good. He'd been in foster care twice. Once when his dad was arrested five years ago, and again a year later when they realized what a fuck-up his mom was. Apparently, they objected to crack whores and impressionable teenagers growing up in crack houses and getting busted lips from mom's pimp. Hell, it was a toss-up as to which was worse, the shitty digs they had him in where he shared a room with six other boys and ate mac and cheese every day or the rundown, crumbling apartment with peeling lead paint and junkies shooting up in the hallway. Nobody stepped forward and asked for a sixteen-year-old to take care of and love forever. They wanted the cute little babies, the sweet, loving little toddlers.

Ben had been his one shot at a decent life and that had ended with the old man dead at the bottom of the stairs, his body burned to a crisp in the fire. Liam's mind raced. Why had he contacted the detective?

Sure, whoever had killed Ben, it was probably connected to Stone. Who the hell else could it be? Ben didn't make enemies; he was a great guy. The only thing that had come down the pike, the only thing out of the ordinary, had been the keylogger software Liam had found. After the second round of the same damn questions, he had gotten frustrated, tired of being asked the same damn things.

"Look, Detective. You aren't asking the right questions."

Rob had looked at him. "Oh, and what should I be asking?"

"You should be asking where those two voicemails Ben left for you on your cell phone went."

The detective had cocked his head, dug into his shirt pocket, and pulled out the phone, searching it thoroughly before answering, "I don't have any messages from Ben."

"But he left them. *Two* of them. A hacker can break an Android phone like yours, easy." Liam snapped his fingers. "You need to be asking yourself who took those messages. Just like you should be asking *who* put the keylogger software on your laptops. Because when you find that person, you will find out who killed Ben."

"My phone has been malfunctioning."

Liam shook his head. "Nope. Whoever's hacked it is getting it to work just fine."

He had folded his arms over his chest and stopped talking.

That had been nearly an hour ago. He practiced breathing deeply and regularly, his eyes closed, his ears straining to hear their muttered conversation. Finally, he heard it, the words he was afraid he would hear...

"I guess we need to make the call to Social Services."

It was definitely time to get the hell out of here. He stretched, yawned, and slowly stood up. "Is there a bathroom around here?"

The partner, Max, nodded and pointed. "Just down the hallway, then turn right and it's the second door on the left."

"Great. I'll be right back. Y'think I could get a sandwich or something soon? I'm getting kind of hungry."

The two men nodded at him, still intent on their conversation. Liam headed down the hallway and turned right. Up ahead he could see the front counter and an exit sign. He kept walking, no hurry, no nervousness.

Just nod and smile if they look at you.

Minutes later he was outside of the station and disappearing into the surrounding streets. He had already memorized Laney's address, but he pulled out the note and double-checked the address. It was written in her flowing, looping script. He cut through an open backyard, past barking dogs and a homeless encampment in an abandoned lot, and skirted the railroad tracks. There was no way he was going back in the system. And no way he was going back to his mom's, even if he could find whatever flophouse she was crashing at now. Somehow, he had to come up with a plan. Because if it was like he thought, if someone had gone out of their way to murder Ben just because of that keylogger software and the bugs Ben said that the detective had found in his house, then they would be looking for him too.

Whoever it was who had set the fire, who had killed Ben, they had been upstairs, and it wouldn't take much to put it together that there had been someone else living there with Ben. And if and when they did figure that out, and that he had hacking skills like his dad, then they would come for *him* next.

Quid Pro Quo

Liam slipped in through the back gate. It creaked loudly and he listened for any noise, any indication that he had been heard, before he settled onto a chaise lounge behind the Airstream, out of sight of the house.

The day was warm now that the clouds had cleared. The sleepless night, the grief over losing Ben and the best home he had ever had, it caused his eyes to droop, and he could feel the exhaustion like a weight, carrying him down.

The creak of the Airstream door opening a few feet away was enough to jar him from his dreamless sleep. He sat up abruptly, and the chaise lounge scraped on the wood deck, complaining at his sudden movement. Liam struggled to focus his eyes.

"Sorry, I meant to let you sleep for a little while. You looked like you needed it." Laney's face swam into focus and he relaxed, leaning back and rubbing his eyes.

"S'okay." He yawned then, his jaw cracking. "What time is it?"

"After three, almost four."

He sat up again. "Woah, I slept for three hours?"

Laney grinned at him and shrugged. "I guess. I've only been here for an hour."

"Watching me sleep?" He stared at her. "Creeper much?"

She laughed. "Whatever! Besides, it takes one to know one!" She nodded towards the door. "C'mon, I got the key and opened it up. Come see."

She disappeared inside and Liam followed her, taking in the '50s decor, the cherry red and soft cream paint colors.

"This is really cool," he said as he slowly looked around.

"The stove, refrigerator, and microwave all work. And there's water and gas so you can take a shower." She stared at him, her nose wrinkled. "Believe me, you need it. You smell like burned popcorn."

Liam picked at his shirt, sniffed it, and grimaced. "Yeah, you got a point."

"I think that my uncle left some clothes here." Laney opened a small drawer and pulled out sweat pants and a T-shirt. "My mom's shift started an hour ago, so I could do your clothes in the washer after you take a shower and you can wear these until everything's dry. There's a towel and all that in the bathroom."

"Thanks, Laney." He swallowed past a lump in his throat. "I, um, I really appreciate this."

Laney just nodded and turned towards the door. "You hungry? I'm gonna make a sandwich. I didn't eat lunch and I'm starving."

"Yeah, that would be great." He turned away, pulled off his shirt, and stopped, remembering the name Benton Security Services scribbled on the note in his pants pocket. "Oh hey, Laney? Could you bring your laptop out here too? I gotta try and find someone."

She nodded and shut the door firmly behind her.

A wave of grief came over him as he turned the water on. He had no one now. Dad couldn't help, not from a prison cell, and Mom was too jacked up to help herself, much less anyone else. He couldn't stay here. Laney was cool, and she was risking her mom's wrath to help him, but he couldn't risk her getting hurt. Whoever had killed Ben and set fire to the building, they weren't the kind of people to leave witnesses.

The water poured over him and he closed his eyes, felt the tears slip out and mix with the water. Ben had died because of what they found, he was sure of it. Could he trust the detective? Ben had. But Ben was also dead, thanks to whatever the detective had on his trail. It felt like nowhere was safe. Nowhere and no one.

He finished soaping and rinsing, and his skin no longer smelled of smoke and loss. Instead it held the faint scent of lavender. He reached for a towel and dried off quickly, pulling on the clean clothes Laney had set out for him. Her uncle was shorter than he was, and the pants ended at mid-calf, but the T-shirt fit fine, even a little loose.

He was drying his hair when Laney returned, her laptop slung in a bag over her shoulder and two enormous sandwiches on a plate in her hands. Two soda cans bulged in each of her front pockets.

He opened the door for her and she slid inside, handing him a soda and one of the sandwiches and turning to set her laptop up on the small table before sliding into the one side.

His stomach growled loudly at the sight of food. Liam lifted the sandwich to his mouth and bit down, closing his eyes in relief.

"I kind of included everything because I didn't know what you would like," Laney said, around a mouthful of sandwich. A piece of lettuce fell onto the plate, followed by half of an olive. "I hope it's okay."

"Mmhm, yeah it's..." He stuffed another enormous bite into his mouth and sighed, "the best sandwich I've ever had."

The girl grinned at him, and they said nothing more until every last bite was consumed and their soda cans were empty.

"So, who do you need to look up?" Laney asked as Liam reached for the laptop.

"Benton Security Services," he answered, fingers tapping. "I saw the guy's card in the police station and I'm just hoping, I don't know, I guess I'm hoping they might help me."

"Not the police?"

He snorted. "The detective didn't believe me. I told him his phone had been jacked and he just wanted to call Social Services on me."

Laney frowned, nibbling on her fingernail as she stared at the screen, leaning forward so she could read it at the same time. "Huh, says they provide personal security. So, what, the guy is a bodyguard?"

"His name sounds familiar. Hold on..." Liam tapped at the keys, opening multiple windows. "He's a billionaire... he founded Benton Security Services a few years after his baby sister Allison Benton was kidnapped and murdered. Huh."

"A billionaire who runs a bodyguard company?" Laney asked, intrigued. "So, what are you going to do?"

Liam opened up a web-based email program that Laney had never seen before and typed a short message, pressing Send before Laney could finish reading it.

"I'm sending Jack Benton a message. If anyone can help me, he can."

"What? Like for protection?"

"Sort of," Liam said, glancing up at his friend. "More like, 'Hey, do you want to hire me?'"

Laney gaped at him. "Seriously?"

Liam shrugged. "I'm really good with computers."

"You mean you're good at hacking."

His mouth twitched. "You say toe-may-toe, I say toe-mah-toe."

She giggled. "You're pretty cool, Liam."

"Um, thanks, I think." He felt self-conscious around her, and plenty nervous. Girls felt like an unknown, and unknowable species. Even Laney, who had helped him with a place to stay, food, and clean clothes. What did she want with him?

"Why..." his mouth closed, and he fell silent.

"Why what?" Laney's eyes were locked on his.

"Why are you helping me?"

She shrugged. "You need help. And my friend Tanya was talking trash, saying you started the fire, and that's bullshit. I know you didn't, Liam. I don't care what Tanya says, or anyone else, for that matter; you're a nice guy. My dad, he used to tell me, 'Those who can, should.' And I guess I try to remember that. I knew we had this trailer out here, you needed a place to stay, so I offered."

"Where's your dad now?" he couldn't help but ask.

She hitched her shoulders, looked away. "Car accident. He lived, but he's in a residential care facility now. He doesn't really remember me or mom. Brain damage and all that."

"I'm sorry." The words felt empty, useless.

"What about your mom and dad?"

"My dad's doing a stretch for hacking. He'll be out in five or six years. Mom's high as a kite most days and meaner than hell in between. I haven't seen her since early summer." He looked at her, "But you know most of that."

Laney nodded. "Tanya and some of the others."

"Figures. Why do you hang around girls like that?"

The email program on the computer beeped and Liam's attention was pulled away from Laney.

He pumped his fist in the air and then grabbed the pen and notepad tucked into the lazy Susan on the table and scribbled down an address before returning to the computer and zipping off an email reply.

"What did it say?" Laney asked.

"Quid pro quo."

"What?"

He grinned. "He said 'quid pro quo' - it means a favor in return for something."

"How do you know this guy will even help you? I mean, seriously, how can you trust *anyone* after what has happened?"

"I keep my eyes open and trust my instincts." Liam shrugged, "What choice do I have?"

"You could, I don't know, I mean, you *could* go into foster care. There are good foster families out there, you know."

"I'm not a cute and cuddly little kid, Laney. No one wants a six-foot-tall kid with fucked-up parents." Liam stared out of the window, avoiding her eyes. "Ben was a lightning strike, like winning the friggin' lottery. He woulda..." he stopped, unable to keep his voice even, felt his throat thickening. "It doesn't matter. He's gone. All the wouldas and couldas and shouldas don't matter now. I'm not going into the foster system. I'd rather live on the streets. I'd rather work and just earn my way, y'know?"

Her hand on his shoulder was comforting and kind. "Okay." She ignored the tears that had formed, the ones he brushed away as he stared out of the round streamlined window. "You can trust me, Liam. I'll help you any way I can."

He nodded, sure his voice would break if he said anything more.

As the sun slipped below the horizon, she brought him his clothes, fresh-smelling and warm from the dryer. "Keep the lights off. My mom comes home late at night and she would notice if there was a light on in here and call the cops."

"Got it."

She stood at the door, uncertain, then leaned over and gave him a quick kiss on the cheek before fleeing out the door. Liam thought about the kiss for a long time as he lay in the dark and listened to raccoons fight somewhere nearby.

Ben would have liked her.

Finish the Job

In the end, it was Lila's fault that Riehl found them. Just two minutes was all it took for Lila to break The Code for the second time and for the GPS tracking to turn on.

Two minutes.

The last thirty-six hours had been anything but fun. Shane had barely spoken to her, hell he wouldn't even *look* at her, which made her embarrassed, pissed, and indignant all at once. He had left twice, saying only that he needed to meet with his boss, or run an errand. To his credit, he *had* brought her pho from the Vietnam Cafe, along with an order of spring rolls and crab Rangoon.

Despite the offering of tasty food from her favorite restaurant, she noticed that Shane Ellis could not, or would not, meet her eyes. They had engaged in mind-blowing sex less than forty-eight ago and ever since he had avoided her as if she carried a contagious disease. Lila gritted her teeth; she knew he had probably gotten his balls busted by his boss thanks to the butt dial, but still, she couldn't help but feel like it was some tawdry experience Ellis would prefer to sweep under the carpet.

Perhaps he got his rocks off like that every day and she was just a cheap thrill. Lila, on the other hand, could close her eyes and still feel his hands on her, the way his tongue felt against her...she gave a small shiver. What she would give for another night like that!

She had even tried to talk to him about it. After eating breakfast alone in the kitchen, she had crossed into his territory, walking down the long hallway to the first bedroom on the left, significantly smaller than her room, and knocked on the door. A small rustle and he had opened the door, pulling a Bluetooth from his ear. He had *not* invited her inside.

"Yes?" He said it while staring slightly to her left, as if addressing a ghost behind her.

"Could we talk about the other night?" Lila asked, a tentative smile on her face.

"I, uh," he said, his mouth closed in a hard line, "That was a mistake and it won't happen again. I took advantage of the situation and forgot my place."

The smile slipped from her lips. "I just, um, I know it wasn't exactly the best situation, especially with the butt dial, but..."

His expression was closed, unreadable. It showed nothing of the passion and attraction they had shared on Wednesday evening. Had she been wrong about him? Had the attraction she felt all been on her end?

"Miss Benoit..."

"I think that now that we've had mind-blowing sex you can call me Lila," she snapped in annoyance.

"Actually, Miss Benoit, I can't," he said, a note of steel creeping into his voice. "I made a mistake and I apologize. Now, if there isn't anything else, I need to call my boss back. He said that a police detective is asking to speak with you, and..."

Lila could feel the hot flush of anger and shame flood up through her pale cheeks. She spun on her heel and marched away from the door. "Right. I'll let you get back to work, then."

I've been a complete idiot. How do I always manage to pick the jerks? Well, at least he didn't ask me to rate his sexual prowess. Although, she thought, wincing, *I went ahead and told him what I thought of it. Mental note for future lovers, never let on that you loved it. If I hear a dull thud it will be that guy's ego exploding!*

She marched to the other side of the house, restlessly pacing through the front entry, the den, kitchen, and formal living room before returning and repeating it. At one point, she unlocked a side door and walked out onto a small balcony off the living room. The wind had picked up, and the temperature had dropped precipitously. It might only be mid-October, but the weather was already clearly heading into colder temperatures. She shut the door and resumed pacing. It was on the third time through, her face still red and flushed, that she noticed the closed door to the office.

Books, it had books in there.

Books, they smoothed out the rough edges of life. Lila turned the knob and opened the heavy wood door. Inside the room were floor to ceiling bookshelves crammed with all manner of reading material. In the center of the room was a large ornate executive's desk, as well as a loveseat that was an obvious match to the massive, button-tufted Chesterfield sofa and armchair in the living room. The books were organized by genre, which wiped the anger off Lila's face and made her smile.

Whoever organized these books is a person after my own heart.

Several shelves held thrillers, another shelf was dedicated to self-help topics, another on DIY topics like gardening and home remedies. There were three shelves dedicated to romance books, another to mystery, and several more for just sci-fi and fantasy.

Lila settled on a book from the last category, a thick paperback written by Charles deLint. She had read several of his earlier books in high school. She settled into the loveseat, placing some of the pillows behind her and draping a fur-covered blanket over her. The temperatures had plunged the night before and Lila had woken up to frost on the windows and a nip in the air. She lost herself in the book, walking into a world where the real world found itself slipping into fairy realms, where magic and cars co-existed. An hour slipped by, then two.

When she uncurled herself from the loveseat, she noticed her phone sitting on the far corner of the desk. She hadn't thought of it in days and immediately Lila's thoughts went to Kaylee. She stood up, walked over to the desk and picked it up. It was new, just under three months, a perk of working for Kurgen Real Estate, and the battery life was phenomenal. When her old phone had crapped out days after her 90-day evaluation period, Blanche had handed her a brand-new phone with a happy smile, reminding Lila that her work in the past three months had been exemplary. And because Lila wasn't one of those people glued to her phone 24/7, the battery usually lasted all week before needing to be recharged. It must have been sitting here since Monday night. She remembered Shane asking for it. She picked it up, and then froze, her finger hovering over the button, an inch from turning it on.

What was it that Shane had said? It was one of the items of that blasted Code he talked about. Let's see, no contact with friends, family, boss. No phone calls or internet access.

She turned the phone on.

I'll just look at the texts and emails. That's it.

There was a long list of texts. One from Kaylee on Monday around seven in the evening, a ton from Blanche pleading for Lila to contact her and tell her she was alright, and two from a Detective Stone asking her to call him. There were also ten texts, growing progressively frantic, from her neighbor George. Lila sighed, regretting ever having given George her phone number.

She turned off the phone and set it down in the middle of the desk. All this waiting, just sitting around and doing nothing, it was maddening. She held herself back from picking up the phone and calling the detective back. She frowned, imagining how Shane would react if she did.

He'd probably go overboard, just like he did when I went for that walk.

From here she could just barely see the horse paddock on the other side of the property. No horses in sight, not that it would matter if there were, because one hundred yards outside of the house was as unacceptable as standing on the back deck was. "Don't go anywhere without me," she said, her voice cranky and petulant even to her own ears. She set the book down on the desk and went to raid the kitchen for cheese and crackers.

Miles away, in her basement studio with blacked-out windows and the bank of computer monitors, a quiet warning beep sounded. Lucifer almost didn't hear it - she had the speaker volume up as she fought an epic battle, the sound of the trolls grunting and the blades singing made her grin as her fingers danced across the keyboard. But the beep was out of place, and seconds later, the game paused, she checked to see what had caused it.

"Yes! I've got you!" Her fingers moved rapidly over the keys, pulling up a map and reaching for her cell phone to press speed dial at the same time.

The phone rang once. "I hope this is good news, Lucifer." No hello, just straight to business.

Lucifer grinned, even though the person on the other end couldn't see. "She just turned on her phone."

The voice's tone changed, sounding pleased, even excited. "When?"

"Just now. It shut back down after two minutes, five seconds, but it doesn't matter. The GPS locater logged the location; I've got the address here for you."

"Excellent work, Lucifer. Go ahead with the address."

Lucifer rattled off the address, a large house surrounded by land on all sides from the looks of it, close to a water treatment plant and the Missouri River in Kansas City, Kansas.

Within seconds, Riehl's phone began to buzz. He had just walked away from the front door of a post-World War II starter home that this area was filled with. The woman who answered the door had been suspicious and threatened to call the police after he asked if she had seen a young teenage boy in the neighborhood. He had posed as a detective before, but this woman wasn't buying it and shooed him away from her door before he could ask to see if the kid was hanging out in the Airstream trailer out back. He was sure he had seen the kid slip in through a gate off the alley as he drove slowly through the neighborhood.

His stop at Northeast High School had been fruitful. He now knew not only Liam's last name, but what the kid looked like, thanks to the rattled young secretary in the front office. The kid being hauled out of there by a KCPD detective had certainly made an impression.

"Riehl here."

"We found her," the caller said, a note of smugness creeping in. "I've texted you the address. She activated her phone a few minutes ago."

"I can be there in a couple of hours, when it's dark," Riehl answered, staring at the small house with the Airstream poking out behind it.

"You'll go *now*. She turned the phone back off. She might be moving to a different location. I want this dealt with. No more screw-ups." The phone beeped and went black. Riehl swore and stuffed the phone in his pocket, then pulled it out again as he walked to his car. Sure enough, there was the address, a good twenty minutes away if he didn't run into traffic. The sun was already sinking into the west. There would be traffic, but it would mean that by the time he got there the sun would have set. That way he could approach under cover of darkness. He reached under his seat and caressed the handgun and extra clip that were attached with Velcro to the underside of the bucket seat.

Time to finish this.

Shane had watched Lila walk away and fantasized about going after her. She was angry, he could see that, but it didn't take away from the lust raging through him.

Angry sex can be fun.

His hand flexed open and closed as he watched her march out of sight down the hallway and around the corner.

If things were different, I'd go find out just how fun it could be.

Shane blew out a breath of frustration. He had never been attracted to a client before, not like he was to Lila. The past two days had been difficult, to say the least. All he wanted to do was reach out, touch her, smell her, and make those lovely sounds come out of her again. She had been so responsive, so hot and wet. Being in the same house, especially the same room, was becoming agonizing. He wanted her, in a way he couldn't remember wanting any woman.

I have a job to do and it doesn't involve fucking the client. And she is a client, damn it.

The look on Jack's face had spoken volumes. He wasn't pleased, and who could blame him? It wasn't done.

He took a chance on me. One hell of a chance. And I've let him down.

Shane closed his eyes and tried not to think of the feel of her bare skin, the musky vanilla scent of her, and the memory of her moans of pleasure as she had climaxed not once, but twice. If his phone hadn't butt dialed his boss, would he have stopped? Shame flooded him.

Not likely.

She was angry. At least he had that. After she had tried to talk to him, touched him, and smiled at him with that sexy little smile.

Christ, I wanted to pick her up, wrap her legs around me and have her right there against the kitchen cabinet.

He had pushed her away. Put distance between them, forced a coldness into his voice. A woman like that deserved better than a man like him anyway. She needed someone who would wine, dine, and romance her, someone who could fly her off to the Bahamas for a mini-vacation on a whim. Shane wasn't that guy. Sure, he made a pretty penny working for Benton. Jack paid his men well. But being gone for days, weeks, and even months at a time? Traveling constantly? He didn't live a life that encouraged something more than a casual affair. And he sure as hell had no place going near a woman like Lila.

Don't shit in your own nest, Ellis.

He needed a shower. Somehow, he had to find a way to put a lid on his desires and focus on the job. He closed his door, stripped off his shirt and pants, and turned on the hot water. It poured out of the showerhead but remained ice cold. "Shit." The water heater was on the fritz, *again.* He pulled his jeans back on. "Maybe it's the pilot light."

In the kitchen, Lila ran the hot water, waiting for it to warm up so she could wash the handful of dishes that sat in the sink. After all, Shane did all the cooking, unless he brought takeout, so the least she could do was wash the dishes. She watched it run and put a finger in it.

Nope. Still cold.

She groaned quietly. That meant she would have to talk to him. Which was like talking to a stone, really. She turned off the water and headed for the opposite side of the house. The door to the basement on the right stood open and the light was on. She paused at the top of the stairs and made her way down the steps, following the muffled sounds at the far end of the basement. There in a dim corner she could see Shane crouching at the base of the water heater, clad only in a pair of black jeans.

Why does he have to looks so damn perfect? Every muscle, not a single ounce of body fat.

Desire warred with resentment. Shane jerked towards her, finally hearing her approach. She could see not just a six-pack, but an eight-pack, the muscles coiled tight, skin smooth on his bare chest, just a thin treasure trail disappearing down into his jeans. Her breath hitched in her throat.

"I came to tell you the hot water wasn't working," she said, struggling to not stare at his chest, "But I'm guessing you already figured that out."

"Yeah, I went to take a shower and it was nothing but cold, so..." He took in the hip-hugging capris and scoop neck tee she had found in the closet that morning, his eyes traveling over her before he shook his head and forced his attention back to the malfunctioning water heater. Her heart fluttered in her chest.

So, he does *still find me attractive.*

A smile lifted the corners of her mouth and she squatted down next to him, one thigh touching his. "How can I help?"

He smacked the side of the machine and it made a dull thump. "The pilot light won't stay lit, so I'll have to give the boss a call." He stood up and extended his hand. "C'mon."

As she slipped her hand into his, Shane pulled her up, his free hand settling on her waist, his mouth inches from hers. This time Lila wasn't taking "no" for an answer. Her soft lips fastened against his mouth, one hand resting on his chest. His desire for her, which had never gone away and had seethed and boiled away inside as he struggled to be professional, pushed its way to the surface and he pulled her close, running his hand along the small of her back, lips parting, tongue darting, drinking each other in. He could feel his jeans tightening, and he drew his left thumb over the firm nub of her breast, felt it respond and harden. Lila gasped as he lifted her against him and walked with her to the far wall. A pile of targets fluttered to the ground as he lifted her onto the countertop of the indoor firing range and buried his face in between her breasts, his mouth searching, nipping, sucking at her nipples through the thin fabric.

The tiny, soft moans she was making were driving him nuts. How could something so wrong feel so good? He slipped a hand up her shirt, gently pinching her nipple until she cried out, and then smothered the cry with his tongue as they locked lips. Her hands caressed him, running along his bare skin, sliding down his back and into his jeans as she wrapped her shapely legs around him. He pulled away, just for a moment, to stare into her eyes.

Her pupils were dilated, black disks with a sliver of green surrounding them. Her skin was moist, a sheen of sweat that smelled of her unique musk and vanilla scent. He wanted her and he didn't give a damn about the consequences.

That is, until he heard the footsteps above.

Walk into My Parlor

It didn't hurt, not at first. More of an ache, maybe a bee sting magnified. But Rob knew it was something far more. Still, he couldn't help but feel confused - was this a dream? He could see the gun in her hand now. Small, innocuous, really. He looked down at the hole in his abdomen, a spot of red blossoming like a rose, petals unfolding, away from the wound, staining his shirt.

That will be a hard stain to get out, he thought as his legs folded, crumpling beneath him, boneless. Hitting the ground hurt worse than the bullet had.

Will you walk into my parlour, said a Spider to a Fly;
'Tis the prettiest little parlor that ever you did spy.
The way into my parlour is up a winding stair,
And I have many pretty things to shew when you get there.

The ground was hard, cold, and his hip ached from a sharp tip of rock or root sticking in it.

"Why did you..." Rob struggled to find the words, his tongue heavy and thick in his mouth, his words slurring. "Why did you do that?"

The evening hadn't started out like this. He didn't normally work late on Fridays if he could help it, and it had been a close one. He had driven with Peisker searching for Liam for nearly two hours before giving up. The kid had vanished on them, said he was going to the bathroom and then rabbited before Social Services had arrived. A bored social worker had shrugged, handed Rob her card and told them to call her if they caught up with him.

"Good luck, Detective. Kids that are Liam's age don't fare well in the system. But if you find him, I can squeeze in a bunk for him at Crittenton or a group home."

As they drove down one street after another, Rob had cursed his luck. Liam was the only link he had to the Indalo, and from what Ben had told him, the kid had talents for hacking that the Indalo would not want him sharing, especially when it concerned their activities. He couldn't help but wonder if the kid had been right. What if his phone had been hacked? He checked it again for messages from Ben. Nothing.

"Oh, no, no! Said the little Fly; to ask me is in vain:
For who goes up that winding stair shall ne'er come down again.
Said the cunning Spider to the Fly, Dear friend, what can I do
To prove the warm affection, I have ever felt tor you?

Breathing was difficult, as if the ground were taking his oxygen and sucking it away into the dirt. His fingers scrabbled, inching towards his belt, his holster, but nothing was there. He lay there and remembered two hours before, Maddie sitting on the side of his bed, watching as he examined his ties and held one after the other against the new shirt, he had bought on the way home.

"No tie, Dad, seriously. She'll think you are old enough to be her dad and not want to go out with you again. And you sure won't get to third base with her either."

"What do you know about getting to third base, young lady? Is it time I started cleaning my shotgun?" he asked her, arching an eyebrow.

Maddie rolled her eyes, "Give me a break, Dad. That joke is so old! You have been saying it since I asked for my first bra!"

"Yes," he said drolly, "Because a lot can change in eighteen months."

"Whatever, Dad."

He reached for his shoulder holster.

"You are not actually going to wear that, are you?"

"What? She knows I'm a cop."

Maddie lay back on the bed and sighed dramatically. "Dad, knowing you are a cop and having it in her face are two different things. Unless you are planning on arresting or shooting her, leave it at home for once.

Seriously, Dad, if you don't get with the program, you are going to be old and lonely and probably fat."

Rob laughed. "Thanks for nothing, kid." He set the holster down. "Fine, you win."

I have within my parlour great store of all that's nice:
I'm sure you're very welcome; will you please to take a slice!
Oh, no, no! Said the little Fly; kind sir that cannot be;
For I know what's in your pantry, and I do not wish to see.

Linda's face appeared above him, intersecting his view of the leaves in the trees. The sun was setting, but there was still enough light in the sky to illuminate the rich fall colors of yellow, gold, pink, and red.

She had suggested this park. "A nice walk through the forest after dinner, what do you say?" Her face held no trace of the friendly, happy woman he had spent the past hour with. She was a good cook; she had cooked dinner there in her spacious kitchen, a mix of spicy pepper steak and the sweet freshness of bell peppers, onions and broccoli on a bed of basmati rice. She had winked at him. "Then back here for dessert?"

The way she had said dessert, with a smile and a wink.

Where was that smile now?

Sweet creature, said the Spider, you're witty and you're wise;
How handsome are your gaudy wings, how brilliant are your eyes!
Oh, thank you, gentle sir, she said, for what you're pleased to say,
And wishing you good morning now, I'll call another day.

"Look, the kid will turn up sooner or later," Peisker had said, tired of driving around in circles. "I'll call the school and see if I can get a list of all of his friends, classmates."

"It's three, school's closed and I doubt we will find anyone interested in even answering the office phone this late on a Friday," Rob replied, checking his phone for messages from Ben for the umpteenth time. "Forget it, I'll deal with the kid on Monday."

Max nodded and turned the car around, heading back to the station. "Sounds good, man. Besides, you got a hot date tonight, don't you?" He grinned, wiggling his eyebrows. "Maybe you'll get lucky. If you still remember how to get it up, that is. How long's it been, Stone? You sure that thing still works?"

"Shit, Peisker, just because you want to screw anything that smiles at you." He shut his phone off; it was running low on batteries anyway. "You know, I saw a tranny the other day on Independence that was asking after you."

"Ha, ha, asshole. My wife would cut my balls off if I so much as looked at another woman." They pulled into the station and Rob's phone dinged. Rob squinted at the screen.

"Finally. That Jack Benton guy is getting in touch to set up a meeting with me and that Lila Benoit. Looks like I'll see her tomorrow. You gonna be there?"

"Hell no, I got Simon this weekend. We're gonna drive up to Saint Joe and see my dad."

"Right, I had forgotten about that. Well fine, I'll do all the work myself."

The Spider turn'd him round again, and went into his den,
For well he knew that silly Fly would soon come back again.
And then he wore a tiny web, in a little corner sly,
And set his table ready for to dine upon the Fly;

The life of a CIA analyst is pretty tame, nothing like what others saw on television. Jennifer Garner's character in the television show *Alias* was bullshit, didn't exist, and Rob lay on the ground still trying to process the fact that he had been shot. The why, that was something too. A ball of confusion, mixed with a dull roar in his ears. His blood, pumping out of him, spreading over his hands, his shirt, running in a thick, slow drip down one side, escaping to the ground below.

She hadn't said anything, hadn't answered him, just stood there over him, head cocked to one side, watching him.

This wasn't how it was supposed to go; this can't be happening.

But it was happening. Blindsided, dirt mixing with blood, he could feel his heart slowing, giving irregular thumps every now and then. Cops get shot every day, but he wasn't a beat cop, he never had been. He'd gone straight to detective, and although he carried a service revolver while on duty, he had rarely even taken it out of its holster. And he certainly didn't have it now.

Hell, I spent more time shooting at targets on the range with it than in the line of duty.

He cast around, looking for something, anything, a way to defend himself. But there was nothing. Less than nothing, especially against the tiny, snub-nosed revolver in her hand that had already drilled a hole into him.

And went out to his door again, and merrily did sing,
Come hither, pretty little Fly, with the gold and silver wing.
Alas, alas! how very soon this silly little Fly,
Hearing his wily flattering words, came slowly fluttering by.

Maddie's phone had chimed and she grabbed it, read the message, and quickly typed a response. "Amanda can't wait to see my new phone. I'm going to walk down the block and show her."

"You're abandoning me?" Rob fiddled with one of his buttons. "What if I make a fashion faux pas? Wear leather instead of denim, or vice versa? Do you think she would be offended by a feather boa?"

Maddie giggled. "You are such a dork, Dad, seriously. But brownie point for using 'faux pas' in a sentence. I'm impressed."

"Ah teenagers, start out as whiny brats and turn into snobs." He swung a tie at her and missed as she dodged and giggled.

"You know you love me."

"To the moon..."

"And back. Yeah, I know. I am pretty lovable, after all. So are you." She lay on the bed, silent.

"I thought you were abandoning me for your friend."

"She can wait." She was silent again, then asked, "So what is she like?"

"Who, Linda?"

"No, the desk sergeant." Maddie rolled her eyes and Rob couldn't help wondering if they would get stuck that way. "Yes, Linda."

"She's attractive, successful. She said she's an investment banker."

"Did you do a background check on her?" Maddie asked, rolling onto her belly, her chin cupped in one hand.

"What? No, of course not!"

"Well, you can never be too sure, you know."

Rob stifled a snort of amusement, imagining Maddie in ten years, fresh out of police academy and doing background checks on potential boyfriends. *Huh, that doesn't sound like too bad of an idea, after all.*

"When do I get to meet her?" Maddie's voice held a mixture of anticipation and concern.

"Give it a couple of dates, Mads, before I inundate her with teenage girl hormones."

With humming wings, she hung aloft, then nearer and nearer drew.
Thinking only of her crested head and gold and purple hue:
Thinking only of her brilliant wings, poor silly thing! at last,
Up jump'd the cruel Spider, and firmly held her fast!

Rob felt colder, weaker. His thoughts strayed to Maddie. She had nearly left without kissing him goodbye. He had called her back and she had tossed her head impatiently, reminding him of a young colt full of life and potential. The future was there, his little piece of immortality, and it was ready to run off without a proper kiss and hug. He pulled her close and she snuggled against him, hugged him tightly and said, "Love you, Dad."

Lying there on the ground, the edges of his vision began to tunnel, blackness creeping in, his sight winnowing to tiny faraway points of light at the end of an impossibly long tunnel. "Love you Maddie," he said, his tongue thick and unwieldy in his mouth, "to the moon and..." He felt his heart stop, the blackness close in completely, and then there were no more breaths. He lay still on the ground, his soul and consciousness racing into the void.

"Back," the woman standing above him said, her voice flat, emotionless. She wiped the gun with her blouse and then tossed it from her. It flew in a slow arc before falling with a solid plunk in the lake several yards away. "Love you to the moon and back, Detective."

She turned and walked away.

He dragg'd her up his winding stair, into his dismal den,
Within his little parlour; but she ne'er came down again.
And now, my pretty maidens, who may this story hear,
To silly, idle, flattering words, I pray you ne'er give ear;

Lucifer's phone rang. She stared at the caller ID and clicked the Pause button on the game, muting the growls of the Orcs. "Yeah, boss?"

"It's done. Wipe all records of my presence from Meet Your Match and anything else you need to do - GPS tracking on his phone, whatever, leave nothing."

"I'm on it. I already set up a program to handle it." Lucifer grabbed her mouse, pulled up the tab on her work machine, and clicked a button. "Everything's wiped."

"Excellent. Thank you, Lucifer." The phone clicked and Lucifer stared at the dark screen and the red Indalo etched into the skin on her wrist.

She just killed a cop. And I just helped her cover it up.

Lucifer stood up and Annabelle gave a soft *whoof* from the bed that she was sprawled across. Her huge head lifted to watch her mistress, her tail thumping out a rhythm on the bed.

There was no getting out now. She reached out and gave her dog a scratch behind the ears. Annabelle closed her eyes, stretching and groaning with pleasure. "In for a penny, in for a pound, right, Annabelle?" The dog said nothing, just tilted her head back and forth under Lucifer's fingers. She looked again at her tattoo. She had signed on for this the minute she had let the needle touch her skin; there was no getting out of it now.

Unto an evil counsellor close heart, and ear, and eye,
And learn a lesson from this tale of the Spider and the Fly.

When Seconds Count

The sun had slipped behind a dark, cloudy sky moments before Riehl had arrived at the location his boss had texted him. As he looked around on the road, which dead-ended at the gates of a power plant, he evaluated the possibilities. There were several properties here, nondescript houses of smaller size, and two larger homes set back away from the road. He could see no cameras on the east drive, but the west drive had several, well-hidden, but visible to the discerning eye. The house on the west was up on the hill, perched at the top of a very long drive.

If he wanted privacy and security, he would choose that house. It had a view of anyone coming from any direction, a high fence, security cameras, and isolation. That was the house where he would find Lila Benoit. He was sure of it.

He took his time moving in. Circling along the boundary of the property, in the dark, was not an easy feat. It took time, patience, and he watched the windows of the house for movement as he skirted the perimeter, keeping to the trees. He was dressed in black pants, a black shirt and shoes - perfect for blending into darkness. As he slipped from the tree line to the north of the house, he listened for sound, but the occupants inside were silent. He smiled; that would change when he got his hands on the lovely Lila Benoit. He would take his time and listen to her scream before he killed her. He was looking forward to it.

He circled the house and found a door to a small deck off the living room near the kitchen. He listened for a long while before slipping a thin plastic card in between the frame and the doorknob. He found it fascinating that people forgot the side doors or put less security into them, focusing only on front or back doors while leaving access to a home possible through a flimsy, hollow-core door with a simple lock that a credit card could unlock in seconds. As if because they were so used to coming and going through the front door, so would everyone else. Much of the time, that easily overlooked side door didn't even have a sensor tied into the burglar alarm, *if* a house had a security system at all, which most did not. This side door had a deadbolt, but it hadn't been secured. Within seconds he was inside and had fastened the door behind him, a tiny click as he turned the lock in place.

Riehl moved with silent precision, taking in every detail of the house that he could. He didn't see any signs of life, but it was a large, sprawling structure, and the woman and whoever was protecting her were sure to be nearby. As he stepped out of the sunken den, standing in front of an office filled from floor to ceiling with books on three walls, the floorboard creaked in protest. Riehl's lip curled, and he froze, ears and eyes alert for any sound or sight that would give his prey away. They were here, he was sure of it.

Lila felt Shane stiffen. She opened her eyes. His mouth and tongue, which had been busy sending waves of shudders down her body as he ran them along her neck, was now closed, his eyes fixed on the ceiling above. She nearly asked what was wrong, then the floorboard directly above them creaked.

What room was that? She ran through her mental map of the house above. The office, right next to the den, where the books were and *her phone*.

Oh God. I turned on the phone. I'm a complete idiot!

She locked eyes with Shane, opened her mouth to speak, and he shook his head, a finger to his lips. Then he put his lips to her ear, whispering urgently. He didn't have his handgun in the holster on his jeans, nor his cell phone. Both sat on the dresser upstairs. The basement itself was an armory, so lacking a weapon was not an issue. Not having a phone *was*.

Lila couldn't help but remember the saying, "When seconds count, the police are minutes away." How soon did they have before whoever was upstairs found the open door and decided to come downstairs? They were trapped.

Shane's lips next to Lila's ear explained what she would have to do. She nodded and he opened a closet door near the firing range and guided her inside the dark space. Reaching past her, he pushed a button and a tiny click brought a cool breeze from inside of the closet to ruffle her hair. There was no time; they could hear the creak of the top stair. Whoever was in the house had found the open basement door.

A closet close to the firing range was actually not a closet at all, but a tunnel that led under the front drive and away from the house. He slipped a small, yet surprisingly heavy handgun into one of her hands and handed her a Maglite for the other. "Go to the end of the tunnel, out through the door and wait for me there by the pond." He whispered and gave her a small push into the inky dark of the tunnel, walked out of the closet, and shut the door firmly behind him, sealing her into darkness.

She nearly turned around twice. The ground beneath her sock-clad feet turned from concrete into gravel and then dirt. It was cold and uncomfortable. Behind her she could hear something; she stopped, listening, and heard a tremendous crash, then another, and what sounded like gunshots. She was frozen to the ground in fear... should she listen to Shane and get to the end of the tunnel? Or should she see if she could help him?

I'm armed, after all. What if he needs help? What if he's hurt?

And against her better judgment, against the keen monkey-brained part of her that told her to run away, fast, Lila pivoted and began running back down the tunnel, back to the basement, towards gunshots and danger.

No Proof

Maybe all the hype of "weighted blankets" actually wasn't *all* hype, thought Lila randomly, as she answered the paramedics' questions. The blanket they had draped over her wasn't just warm, it was heavy as well. Perhaps it was one of those tools that remained on the down low, a way to calm the recently traumatized enough to make them easier to handle. If so, it was certainly working. As was the attractive EMT who was asking her questions while a second, equally attractive EMT bandaged her leg.

Why are paramedics and firefighters so damned good-looking?

Despite the heavy blanket and the fact that the assassin sent to kill her was dead on the ground only thirty yards away, shock eventually did set in. Lila began to shiver uncontrollably, even after they added another blanket and closed the door to the ambulance to ward off the blasts of chilled air coming from the river. She had tried to insist on riding with Shane to the hospital, where they would treat his head wound and the arm where the bullet had ricocheted off of the wood and grazed his flesh. Not even the arrival of the silver-haired fox, Shane's boss and her benefactor, Jack Benton, would dissuade her to leave Shane's side.

"You told me never to leave your side. It's part of The Code."

He had stared at her and then guffawed, startling the nurse bandaging his arm. "*Now* you are following The Code?"

"Better late than never." That made him laugh even harder. She laughed too, if only to forget, just for a moment, that she had taken a life tonight.

He must have seen it in her eyes. He reached out with his undamaged hand and took hers, glancing at his boss as he did. Jack Benton watched them both but said nothing.

Shane's boss was older than Shane, possibly by a decade or more, and his jet-black hair was liberally streaked with silver gray. He was handsome and had the look of wealth. Not new wealth either, but lifelong. Jack Benton had never known lack or wondered where his next meal would come from. Despite this, he didn't have the snobbishness or built-in expectations she expected him to have. And he had instantly come to her aid in regard to the police, insisting that any questioning wait for Rob Stone, the detective on the case who they were tracking down now.

It was crowded in the ambulance, but the paramedics allowed Lila and Jack to both accompany Shane. The police officer followed behind in a patrol car. When they arrived at the hospital, however, Jack stepped forward, placing a warm hand on Lila's shoulder.

"Miss Benoit, if you please, they will get Mr. Ellis cleaned up with stitches, and you and I need to speak with the detective when he arrives."

Lila found herself looking at Shane, who nodded at her. She turned back to Jack Benton and walked away from Shane, listening as they wheeled him away to one of the glass-walled rooms in the back of the ER. Jack looked around the large waiting area and found a corner that was empty of others and steered her towards it. The police officer followed, sitting across from them, his eyes watchful as he surveyed the room. His phone rang then, and he stood up and walked away to answer it.

Lila sat, shivering again. "Can I get you some coffee or tea, Miss Benoit?" Jack asked, a small smile on his face.

She shook her head, "I'm not cold... it's nerves, I guess."

"Perfectly understandable." He regarded her for a moment, saying nothing.

The silence was uncomfortable. Lila couldn't stand it any longer. "So, you know Kaylee?"

"I do."

"How?"

He smiled. "That's not my story to tell, Miss Benoit."

Lila grimaced. "Right."

She was saved from having to say anything more to this enigmatic, good-looking man by the police officer who returned from his phone call. "Miss Benoit, I'm going to have to ask you to return with me to the station. You will be speaking with Detective Peisker and he will also take your statement on tonight's events."

"I thought I was going to be speaking to Detective Stone," she said and turned to Jack. "Isn't that the detective that was assigned to the shooting at Kurgen?"

Jack frowned, but before he could speak, the officer answered. "Yes, ma'am, he was, but Detective Peisker is also working that case."

Jack stood up. "Did you say *was,* Officer, as in, no longer *is*?"

The officer looked grim. "I'm really not at liberty to say, Mr. Benton, but I must insist that we go to the station directly. If you wish to accompany Miss Benoit, that is fine, but Peisker will be questioning her at the station."

It was a tense yet short ride to the station, which was just a handful of miles from the hospital. The wait in the interrogation room felt interminable. At one point, Jack Benton turned to Lila and asked, "Miss Benoit, would you by any chance have a dollar that I might have?"

A billionaire was asking her for a dollar?

Lila blinked and handed him the only bill she had on hand, a ten-dollar bill.

"Thank you, Miss Benoit." Jack Benton smiled at her, neatly folded up the bill, and placed it in the breast pocket of his designer jacket just as a tall, heavyset man entered and closed the door. His eyes were red-rimmed, and he tried and failed to smile at Lila. "Miss Benoit, my apologies for keeping you waiting. I'm Detective Peisker."

Jack, who the detective had nodded to but mostly ignored, asked, "Where is Detective Stone?"

Peisker sighed. "Rob Stone has just been found murdered."

Lila gasped, her hand going to her mouth. "Oh, my God."

Jack asked, "Is it possible this is related to your current case?"

"I have no idea, Mr. Benton, but we will be exploring all leads." He rubbed his eyes. "Rob and I worked together for nearly a decade. He was a fine man, a great partner, and a devoted father. Don't worry, the

KCPD will not rest until we find out what happened to one of our own. Meanwhile, ma'am, I would like to question you about the events that occurred on Monday night as well as tonight."

"Before I say anything, do you know if Detective Stone was able to find the SD card?" Lila asked, her hands twisting. "The file that I saw, it was on an SD card and it was there in my laptop. I also copied it onto a flash drive for my boss, Mr. Endon."

Max shook his head. "I'm sorry, Miss Benoit, but there wasn't any SD card in your laptop."

"But..."

"And Mr. Endon handed over the flash drive. It was empty."

"That's," Lila blinked and stammered, "that's not possible." She raised a delicate finger to her mouth, nibbling on an already ragged edge of nail.

"Mr. Endon stated that the flash drive was blank and he had no knowledge of an SD card. I'm sorry, Miss Benoit, but we can't find any trace of these suspicious files you believe you may have found." He stared at her. "So, is there anything you aren't telling me? Anyone you might owe money to? Any crime you may have seen committed or," he paused before continuing, "possibly had a part of committing?"

Lila jumped to her feet. "*What*? You cannot seriously be blaming *me* for this! I've been attacked, not once but three times! I've been shot at! That man I killed tonight, he was the one in the parking garage!" A vein in her neck twitched and Lila could feel heated blood rushing to her cheeks. She began to shake again. Jack Benton reached out and gently put a hand on her shoulder.

Max gave a tired, half smile. "My apologies, Miss Benoit. These are questions I would ask of anyone in your situation. Now, if you could sit down..."

Lila glared at the man and sat down slowly. She closed her eyes and took two deep, slow breaths in and out, remembering the breathing exercises her judo instructor ran his students through each Monday and Wednesday evening at the beginning of class. She needed to calm down and not let this man rile her.

She felt Jack Benton's hand lightly squeeze her shoulder. "Miss Benoit has had some terrifying experiences this past week, Detective."

Max turned to the billionaire and frowned, his mouth settling into a disapproving line. "It is highly irregular to have you here, Mr. Benton. I understand you were communicating with my partner, Detective Stone, but I think it would be advisable for you to wait outside until I have had a chance to speak with Miss Benoit for a few minutes alone."

Jack nodded. "I understand how you might feel that way, but I'm afraid that you misunderstand the situation here. Miss Benoit is a client."

Max snapped. "Yes, Mr. Benton, I'm aware that she has retained Benton Security Services for personal protection, although that worked so well that she had to kill the attacker herself."

Jack smiled. "Actually, Detective, she did not retain my security company's services, those were provided to her at no cost." He reached inside his coat pocket and set down a simple, yet elegant card onto the metal table. "I happen to be an attorney and Lila is my client."

Lila gaped at him and just as quickly shut her mouth before the detective turned her way. *So that was why he had asked for the money!*

Max Peisker did not look pleased. "I see," he said, tapping his fingers on the table. "Miss Benoit, do you wish for your legal counsel to stay here with you while we talk?"

"Yes, thank you."

The detective grimaced, having expected the answer, and began to question her. Some of the more outrageous questions he asked were immediately shot down by Jack, while others he allowed Lila to answer. The hours ticked by as she recounted the incidents of the past week that had led to her shooting the dark-haired assassin that evening. By the second repetition, Lila was having difficulty stringing her words together. It was past midnight and the detective had asked her the same questions worded differently so many times she found herself hunched over, holding her head in her hands. She was exhausted, terrified, and numb.

"Detective, I must insist that we continue this line of questioning after my client has had a chance to rest," Jack said, his hand once again upon her shoulder. "I am assuming she is free to go?"

The detective looked exhausted as well, gray circles beneath his eyes. "At this time, we have no proof of the existence of these suspicious files that Miss Benoit claims to have found, but I think that, until we have discussed this in its entirety, it would be best for her to remain in protective custody. *Not* in a jail cell," he clarified as he saw the look on Jack's face, "but under police protection."

"Fine," Jack said, "But I would like one of my men to be there as well."

"I'm afraid that won't be possible, Mr. Benton," Peisker said, shaking his head. "No civilians."

"Jesse Bardin is one of your own, Detective, a member of the KCPD who has worked part-time for me for the past two years."

Max gritted his teeth. "Fine, Mr. Benton, have it your way." He stood up. "I'll make the necessary arrangements and we will pick this up again in the morning."

"Afternoon."

"What?"

Jack smiled. "I think one in the afternoon will be early enough considering it is *already* morning."

Detective Peisker glared at him and walked out of the room.

Jack gave a low, soft laugh.

"Thank you, Mr. Benton," Lila said as she stood up, weaving slightly from exhaustion. "Have you had any word on Shane?"

"Yes, he's fine and has been released from the hospital. I received a text from him an hour ago. And now, if you will excuse me, I need to contact Jesse and arrange for him to stay with you at the safe house. Frankly, he's the only member of the KCPD I trust with this right now. We will get you some-place safe, Miss Benoit. After you have had some time to rest, we will discuss what happens next. Sound good?"

Lila nodded, weary. More than anything, she just wanted to curl up and go to sleep. She watched Jack knock on the door and wait until they opened it. She sat back down and settled against the cold wall and closed her eyes.

As the door opened, she could hear a young woman's voice clearly. "You aren't listening to me! He was on a date. He met her through Meet Your Match, and..."

"We don't show any matches for your father, Maddie; he didn't meet anyone through the dating service." It was Peisker's voice.

"Yes, he did! Her name was Linda, and..." The door closed, cutting off the voice, sealing Lila into silence with nothing but indeterminate sounds in the distance.

It felt like forever before the door opened again and a man who looked like he was in his late twenties walked in. "Miss Benoit? I'm Jesse Bardin, and I'll be providing protective detail for you."

An hour later, their arrival at the safe house was uneventful. It was a small, decrepit-looking house with a cinder block exterior and bars on all of the windows, a far cry from the sprawling, opulent house where she had spent the last few days. It had a slightly sour smell, one that brought feelings of fear and doubt, but Lila was far too exhausted to care. She said little as Jesse, her new bodyguard, showed her one of the small bedrooms. The door clicked shut behind her and she stepped out of the thin shoes they had found for her and fell into the bed too tired to bother undressing, even if she had felt so inclined.

She pulled a thin blanket over her, wrapping it around her like a cocoon, and pulled the cord on the lamp by the bed. Through the thin walls she could hear Jesse speaking quietly to the other guard, a police officer in uniform, before the overriding need for sleep carried her away into oblivion.

Jackpot

Liam stared at Jack Benton. Beside him, Laney folded and re-folded the paper that had encased her straw. She had insisted on accompanying him despite his objections, and he was glad she was there. Her fingernails were bitten to the quick, and her long, thin fingers smoothed the paper out and started again, perfecting each fold with precision before rotating the wrapper and folding it again.

The man sitting across from them was older than he had expected, his hair heavily threaded with gray. His clothes were quality, the kind that spoke wealth in a subtle way.

"I know some good people who could help you; Liam, the foster care system isn't all bad."

Liam shook his head, beginning to wonder if he had made a mistake in contacting Benton. "I want a job, that's all."

"In what capacity?" the older man asked, a half smile on his face.

"Cyber security, for one; your website could use work as well. And..." Liam paused.

"And?"

"Other things."

"The kind of things that landed your old man in prison?"

Liam hid his surprise in a nonchalant shrug of the shoulders. *So, he's researched me like I researched him.* There was more to Jack Benton than met the eye.

Jack leaned back and studied him. Liam felt his stomach clench in a nervous twinge.

"Where are you staying?"

Liam shrugged. "Around."

Jack looked at Laney, "He's staying at your house?"

"No!" She said it quickly, reflexively, then added, "My mom wouldn't be okay with that. He's staying in the RV, in our backyard."

Liam shrugged again. If this guy had looked him up and knew about Dad, he also knew about Liam's mom, and probably Ben and the fire as well. It wouldn't be a difficult thing to look up the IP address and track his email back to Laney's. *Hell, he probably just knew from looking at us.*

Liam picked at a divot in the Formica tabletop, scraping it with his thumbnail.

"I talked to the police, to a Detective Peisker, about you, Liam. He really wants to talk to you."

Liam rolled his eyes. "Peisker's a tool. Detective Stone's almost as bad."

"Detective Stone is dead, Liam."

Liam shook his head and looked sick. "No, that's not possible. I talked to him *yesterday.*"

"As did I." Jack tapped his fingers on his coffee cup. It had a chip, near the handle, and Liam stared at the crack that ran down one side of the cup and struggled to understand how a man he had just seen living and breathing could be dead. And then he thought of the detective's pretty daughter, Maddie.

I can only imagine how she feels. Losing Ben has been awful, but I knew him less than a year. Maddie has just lost her dad.

All he could see was her face now and he was startled by Laney's hand on his. She squeezed his fingers in hers.

"What happened to the detective, Mr. Benton?"

"It's being investigated as a homicide."

A cold wave of ice washed through Liam. "This is all connected. I'm sure of it."

Jack nodded, his eyes showing admiration. "Yes, I'm beginning to suspect that might be the case. If so, it puts you in the crosshairs as well."

"Me?"

"You said yourself that you found evidence of keylogger software and other tampering. You mentioned that Detective Stone was former CIA, a fact I had my people corroborate. Your guardian died before the fire consumed the building, a fire that is being ruled arson by the way, and now Detective Stone is dead." Jack stared at Liam. "I'm a pretty good judge of character, Liam. Either you are guilty of killing the only man who ever helped you and setting fire to the first decent home you have had in years, or you are in a great deal of danger. At some point they are going to figure out where to find you. Are you willing to let your young friend Laney be hurt like Ben was?"

Liam stole a glance at Laney's face; she looked pale, her mouth a small "oh" of surprise.

"What? No, of course not!"

"Then quid pro quo does seem the best course of action. You come work for me *part-time* and I will make sure you are safe and have a chance to finish your education."

"Finish my education, um, how exactly are we going to do that?"

Benton shrugged. "How do you feel about moving to California? I have a house outside of L.A., a full staff, and you could attend school or take classes online, whichever you prefer."

"I'd prefer not to go to school at all."

"That's not one of the options, Liam," Jack said firmly.

"Take the deal, Liam," Laney whispered. "Seriously."

"How do I know you're on the up and up, huh?" Liam suddenly challenged, trying to shake the older man, "What if you are some perv trying to get me out of state? Away from anyone who could help me?"

Jack smiled. "Look, I know you've done your homework. You researched me before you contacted me. And I'm happy to give you a job, but *on my terms*. You are only sixteen..."

"I'll be seventeen in two weeks," Liam bluffed.

"I can do research too, Liam. You will be *sixteen* in two weeks. You need an education, you need job skills, and you need a place to stay. You will have all of those things here or in California, but I think you would be safer there." He tapped his finger on the chipped Formica, emphasizing each point. Then he reached down and pulled out a laptop from his bag. "I think you're good, really good, so let's say this is a test. Pass it, and you get the job. I'll put 60k a year into a savings fund with your name on it, accessible at age eighteen, give you a stipend of one thousand a month, and you'll have the guest cottage with food and utilities paid, as well as access to a private high school education. That's mandatory, by the way, as is maintaining passing grades." He smiled. "Which shouldn't be a problem, since you are a straight A student."

Liam sat there, reeling as he tried to absorb what was being offered to him. Sixty thousand dollars a year? *I'll be rich!* No more scrabbling to survive, living on the streets or those damn crack houses he and his mom had...*Mom...shit...*

"Get my mom into rehab." he said, "That's part of the deal. And a place to stay when she's better. Take it out of my earnings. A decent apartment and a chance at a job." He stared up at Jack. "You can do that, right?"

Jack nodded, his voice softer. "Yes, Liam, I can do that." He nudged the laptop across the table and Liam opened it and let it boot up. The splash screen showed One Kansas City Place, with Kurgen Real Estate emblazoned across the top of the screen.

"This is someone's work computer," Liam said, and he began to click at the file folders, rummaging through recent documents and file history. "Real estate holding, sales information, et cetera."

"I want you to look for this file and tell me what you see." Jack pushed a business card forward with a file name written on it.

Laney sipped her coffee and watched as Liam's fingers flew over the keys, accessing the file history. "It looks like the file was opened from a different source, possibly a memory stick or SD card, and then copied."

"Copied where?"

"Um, possibly another flash drive? Also, the Cloud."

"Anywhere else?"

"Yeah, a Dropbox folder, a personal one." He looked up. "If the flash drive can't be found, I'd look there."

"Thank you, Liam, that helps." He reached for his wallet, laid a $100 bill on the table, and stood up. "Eat some breakfast. I'll send a car for you at your friend Laney's this afternoon." He turned to go, then stopped. "I'll also get one of my people to work locating your mom today."

Laney whistled long and slow as they watched Jack Benton drive away in a dark green Jaguar. "Holy shit, Liam!"

Liam nodded and said nothing. *Holy shit, indeed.*

Lila had emerged from the bedroom, out of sorts and starving for food. The seductive smell of coffee brewing had crept under the bedroom door and wooed her from sleep. Once she opened the bedroom door, the delicious aroma hit her in a wave, along with something that smelled a lot like eggs and bacon. The man from last night, well, early that morning, really, was at work in the kitchen, his back to her as he stood in front of the stove, the coffeepot steaming next to his right elbow.

What was his name? Justin? No, Jesse.

He looked over before she could open her mouth and nodded, "Good morning, Miss Benoit. Help yourself to some coffee... there is cream in the fridge." He slid half of an omelet onto a plate and placed it at the breakfast bar before handing her an empty mug. "Sugar is there on the table as well."

"Thank you." The words came out as a whisper. She still felt exhausted. "What time is it?"

"Half past ten," came his reply. "Mr. Benton is heading over. He said he had something for you to look at."

"Where's Shane?"

"Ellis?" Jesse shrugged and gave her a smile. "I haven't been read in on that."

Lila blushed then, and Jesse saw it and shook his head. "The boss runs a tight ship, Miss Benoit. I imagine he's been re-assigned."

Lila's face burned even hotter and she looked away, focused on her omelet, and took a bite. She closed her eyes and sighed with pleasure. *Bodyguards who can cook. I've actually died and gone to heaven; there can be no other explanation.*

She opened her eyes to find Jesse staring at her, his eyebrows raised in concern. "Is this like part of Bodyguard 101? You all learn how to cook gourmet meals?"

He laughed and ate a bite. "It's survival; there's only so much microwaveable meals a person can eat."

Outside, the sound of a car pulling into the drive and a door opening and closing had Jesse on his feet. He quickly peered out of the window and strode to the front door to let Jack Benton in. "Hey, Boss. You want some breakfast?"

Jack smiled. "No, but a mug of that fine-smelling coffee would be great. Thanks, Jesse." He clapped the younger man on the shoulder and nodded to Lila. "Miss Benoit, I trust you slept well?"

Lila was suddenly very aware she had not brushed her hair. "Um, yes, like a stone, in fact." Her eyes drifted to the laptop slung over Jack's shoulder. "Is that my..."

"Yes, I managed to get the laptop from the office. Kaylee was kind enough to help me retrieve it."

"I thought you said it didn't have the file on it."

"It doesn't," Jack answered, pulling out the laptop and setting it next to her on the bar. Jesse reached over and retrieved his plate, giving his space to his employer and sliding a cup of coffee in his direction. "But you can access it all the same."

"I don't understand."

"Think back to the day you found the file." Jack said as he opened the laptop. "You said you found it on an SD card, right?"

"Right. And the SD card was in the laptop bag, but it's not there now."

"And you said Morris Endon asked you to save it on a flash drive and give it to him. Is that correct?"

"Yes." Lila looked frustrated. "And he told the police the flash drive was empty, but I'm sure it wasn't."

"Do me a favor. Open up an Excel file, type a line or two, and then save it to this flash drive." He held out a flash drive to her.

Lila suppressed the urge to snap at the man. "Okay, but I really don't see how this is going to help." She pulled the laptop closer, opened the program, typed a few numbers in, and began to do as Jack asked, sliding the flash drive into the port. "Okay, now what?"

"Is the file saved on the flash drive?" he asked, the traces of a smug smile on his face.

"Of course, it is!" She looked back at the directory, stared, and looked away in embarrassment. "I forgot to select the correct drive."

She clicked the file again and this time saved it correctly, the flash drive lighting up as the data moved over.

"That happened last time as well, didn't it?" Jack asked softly.

"Yes, yes it did!" Suddenly she remembered. She had been looking at a loan amortization file moments before, one from her Dropbox account. "I had my student loan file open, one that's on my personal Dropbox account. I had been playing with it to see how much interest I could save if I paid an extra one hundred dollars each month on top of my regular loan payment. And then I saw the SD card, put it in, and it saved it to the same folder!"

She turned back to the laptop, searched for the Dropbox folder, and seconds later they were looking at the missing file.

"Jackpot," Jack said, grinning.

Lila felt a sense of vindication surge through her. "Now the police can't say it doesn't exist! Here it is!"

Jack peered at the file, pulling the laptop closer and then clicking on the tabs. His eyes focused on something and he pointed at the screen. "What is that symbol there?"

Lila looked at where Jack's finger rested. It didn't look like any account symbol she had ever seen, more of an ancient pictogram, or rune. "That's weird." It was a simple stick figure with the arms sticking straight out at each side and a half circle above them joining the two ends.

She brought the mouse over the image and it changed from an arrow to a hand with one finger pointed. "It's a link of some kind." She clicked it and the screen flashed as the laptop began to cycle, struggling to open something massive in size.

Five minutes later, Jack let out a low whistle. "This is big, Lila. You realize that, right?"

She nodded mutely, unable to form words. The spreadsheet she had seen, that she had asked Morris Endon about, it had been the tip of the iceberg. The icon that she had clicked on, that was the real key, the real jackpot. The rabbit hole went deep, far deeper than she could have ever imagined. Her omelet cooled, forgotten at her side, as her eyes raced over the data.

"This is, this is..."

"Corruption. Payoffs," Jack added, "Kurgen Real Estate is a front. A massive, well-engineered front, but a front nonetheless. This is a record of decades of dirty deals, corruption on a level I haven't seen before."

Lila shook her head; everything felt numb, unreal. She took a bite of the omelet, now cold, chewed it mechanically and swallowed. It stuck in her throat.

"This is bigger than what the local police can handle, Lila. These transactions, many of them are across state lines, which makes this a federal issue. We have to take this to the FBI." She stared at him, mouth dry. Her mind raced as she took it all in.

Jack could see it in her eyes, that deer in the headlights look, and the realization that the life she had been living just days ago, was over. There was no going back to normal. Never again.

Witness Protection

The next three weeks moved both quickly and slowly for Lila. There were moments when it felt as if she were on a speeding train, hurtling towards a dark abyss. Meetings with investigators, questions, and moves from one safe house to another.

At other times, there was nothing to do, no one to talk to. She couldn't call Kaylee, or anyone else, and after spending two days being questioned by the FBI, she had been relegated to a small apartment in Chicago, where beefy, grim-faced strangers had guarded her 24 hours a day. They were nothing like Shane, or even Jesse. No shred of humor, for one.

They were polite, but there was no conversation. They didn't even reveal their full names, just last ones, Jenkins this, and Beech that. At one point, desperate for the sound of another person's voice, she had asked Beech about his background. She didn't understand military rank, so it had sounded like a litany of Marine this, that, and the other thing before joining the FBI. She didn't bother asking Jenkins about his background.

Most of the time she spent staring at the television in the hotel room, an endless loop of daytime soaps and reruns from the '70s that had her bored to tears, before finally breaking down and asking for a list of books to keep her occupied. After that, she kept to her room, emerging only to eat meals.

The meals were a depressing array of fried foods served in takeout and fast food bags.

Her guards didn't cook, not at all. Each meal came in a sack or a Styrofoam container and she was pretty sure she was gaining weight from all of the extra calories and lack of exercise.

At least she had her books. A wide variety at that. She had handed Jenkins the list last week and he had blinked at it. "I don't care who you have to ask, or where you have to go, but bring me a stack. If I have to watch anymore daytime TV, Judge Judy or that damned Springer Show, I'll lose my mind."

A smile had ghosted past his lips. "I'll see what I can do, Miss Benoit."

The next morning two stacks of books had been sitting next to her bedroom door in a large plastic bag. The bag was labeled Myopic Books, that listed an address on Milwaukee Avenue. That was the street they were on as well. She wasn't sure of the exact address, and the only stores in view were the UPS Store and a tanning salon across the street, but Lila figured it had to be close. Her two guards stayed in the apartment, leaving only when it was time to fetch meals or run an errand.

It was an eclectic mix of new and used books, which Lila didn't mind at all. One of her joys had been to drift through the stacks at Prospero's on 39th Street. Especially during the last year of school when she desperately needed a break from school and couldn't afford to see a movie or really go out, a trip to the bookstore and a few dollars had given her an escape and entertainment for hours and hours.

She had already read two of the books, but she smiled when she saw them, more than happy to re-visit the stories as one would re-connect with an old friend.

"Thank you, Jenkins, for the books."

He shook his head. "Wasn't me, Miss Benoit. I just passed on the message."

"Oh, well, thank you anyway. And do pass on my thanks to whoever did get them; they found some great titles. A couple I have read, but don't mind reading again, and several I have been meaning to buy and not gotten around to."

He nodded and said nothing, and Lila felt a surge of loneliness return. She missed Kaylee. She missed her life at Kurgen. From what little she had been told, the entire office was closed down and each of the employees questioned. She couldn't help but worry about Kaylee, as well as a handful of the others she had been friends with - Blanche, even if no one else had liked her, Trish at the front desk, and several of the others in the office. Morris Endon had been arrested, but he had refused to talk with the investigators or cooperate in any way. She hadn't seen Shane since that fateful night. Jack Benton had said that he had been re-assigned, his tone had not invited additional inquiries, and it had been several weeks since she had seen the billionaire. These days it was nothing but federal agents, lawyers, and prosecutors.

She sat on her bed, the paperback in her hands forgotten as she stared at the thin folder sitting next to the bed. She hadn't filled out all the paperwork, not yet, and they would be asking for it this afternoon. She had already put them off twice.

It seemed so final - the death of her old world, the start of another. She was free in many ways, no more student loans for one, a whole new identity for another. The locale and background had been crafted for her. She wouldn't even be a data analyst any longer, and she was being sent to an area of the country that was completely unknown to her, a small town in Maine where she would be managing a bookstore. She had even helped choose it, but still, despite this, she delayed signing the agreement, filling out the last of the paperwork - avoiding, if only for a day or two, her new reality. It would be a year at least until there was any trial. The FBI continued to sift through the data they had found, and her part in it was small and insignificant when compared to the massive trail of corruption and dirty deals they had found. Nevertheless, she was in danger from the Indalo. They now had a name for the organization, having found a wealth of information in Detective Stone's home office in the wake of his murder.

"You will be safe in the Witness Protection Program. Frankly, Ms. Benoit, we keep finding more and more levels to this, and you were the one to find it in the first place." One of the agents, a woman with a beak nose and perpetually grim expression, had told her. "That they attempted to murder you, not once but *three* times, it indicates just how vital your part in our case is. I promise you that we will do the best that we can to help you settle into your new life."

Lila had been the one to suggest that she manage a bookstore. If she couldn't dig into data and research market trends, then she could do the thing she loved just as much, if not more: live surrounded by books.

The Bookstore

He shouldn't be here and he knew it. Two girls in their late teens passed by, ogling him, and he could hear them whisper and giggle as soon as they passed by.

The new kid, Liam, had helped, of course. He had struggled to get used to living in the guest cottage there at Benton's home in the hills. Mostly it seemed that he was lonely and missed his life in Kansas City. When Jack had asked Shane to drive Liam out to Los Angeles, they had had a couple of days of driving to bond. The kid had never been out of Kansas City and it had been fun to take a few side trips to see the Grand Canyon as well as a sprawling mountain town, Flagstaff, that Shane had spent a few months in a few years earlier. When he had learned of Liam's serious hacking skills, Shane had sworn the boy to silence and slipped him some cold hard cash, which had quickly disappeared into a pocket.

It had taken him a couple of days, and Shane could only imagine what Jack would say if he knew what the two of them were up to, hacking into the FBI database to find Lila. But here he was, a week and more than three thousand miles later, standing on Pleasant Street in Brunswick, Maine, outside of the bookstore. *Her* bookstore. It was a two-story affair, a creamy-yellow and white turn-of-the-century building with wood floors and red shelves filled with books. On the side of the building was a hand-painted mural, a street scene filled with people, art, even a turquoise Buick on the left. The town was clean, small, and the tourist season was just around the corner. Shane could feel Jack Benton's touch on this. Whether he had funded the purchase of the bookstore, or just known what strings to pull, he had made sure that Lila would be somewhere she could be happy.

He stood back, across the street, half-hidden by a tree, eyes on the building. The wide windows let in plenty of natural light, and the dark green doors were welcoming. For the past two hours he had watched people go in and leave half an hour later with bulging bags of books. Finally, as the sun slipped below the horizon, the foot traffic dwindled and then stopped altogether. The streetlamps flickered on, and the smell of the sea washed through. In the distance he could hear the clickety-clack of a train moving past the railyard and away from the sleepy town.

Would she even want to see him? It had been more than six months after all. Lila Benoit was now Annie Brewer, a bookstore manager who rented a room just blocks away, kept to herself, and led an unexceptional, and rather bookish life. Ever since Morris Endon, Lila's former boss and the president of Kurgen Real Estate had been found hanging in his jail cell, things had been quiet. It had been ruled a suicide, at least by the local papers. There would be no trial, but with Jack's help, the Witness Protection Program still applied. He had pointed out, rather astutely, that they weren't able to prove that Morris had acted alone. In fact, the chances of it were unlikely, especially when you figured in Detective Stone's murder, which was still unsolved.

Jack had made good on his promise. Shane's last assignment had weighed close to four hundred pounds, had two teenagers and a wife that hated him, and guarding the family had meant holing up in a cabin in the desert with majestic views of sagebrush and a sagging wire fence that disappeared into the distance. It was the closest to nature any of them had been in years and had involved endless sniping. Shane was tapped to eradicate the invading vermin, sixteen rats, four scorpions, and too many spiders to count. By the end of it, he had been close to doing for free the job the crime boss in New York was willing to pay seven figures for.

He waited until he saw her approach the front doors, before he crossed the now-deserted street. She froze, in the middle of flipping the sign from Open to Closed, and locked eyes with Shane, a look of shocked surprise filling her face. She smiled then, a slow, sexy smile, and his doubts disappeared. She opened the door and he walked inside, following her as she drew him inside, out of view of the front door and windows. The building didn't have an old-book smell, not at all. Instead, his nose detected citrus, a hint of summer just a couple of months away, a heady, bright smell that promised sunny days and sparkling sandy beaches.

He looked around. The ceiling was high, maybe twelve feet, and there was an airy open feel, despite the number of books crammed onto bookshelves. Half of the bookstore was already in darkness. Lila followed his gaze, a look of pride on her face. "The first thing I did was paint the walls a light color and add more lights. It's slow right now, but the summer draws a lot of crowds and the cafe in the back courtyard will be a great draw. It will serve breakfast and lunch and coffee, of course." She frowned. "I've been forbidden to touch the coffeemaker."

He snorted. "Probably for the best. You nearly killed me with that nuclear waste you made that first night."

Lila laughed. A full-throated, peal of laughter. Shane couldn't help but laugh too. She looked great. Her demeanor was relaxed, not surprising now that she was safe from men trying to kill her. She had shed the smooth, professional look and swapped it out for a more down-to-earth, relaxed look. Her hair was cut short, in a bob, and she was dressed in a jean skirt and a scooped T-shirt that read, "Careful, or you'll end up in my novel."

She noticed his glance and grinned. "I'm writing an erotic thriller."

He stepped closer. "Does it have a good-looking bodyguard in it?"

Her lips curved into a sexy, wicked smile. "Sexy, bad boy, a bit of a controlling jerk at times, but really great in bed."

"As I recall, we never actually made it to a bed."

She laughed, and she looked happy, capable, and sexier than he could have imagined. She grabbed his belt buckle and pulled him against her, "Why start now?"

Her lips met his with a hungry abandon, without hesitation, her delicate fingers warm through his shirt, sliding around his waist, wandering up his spine. She tasted sweet and he breathed in a rush of her musky vanilla scent, and reached out to steady himself, one hand at the small of her back, the other against a pillar. He reached down further, cupped her tight, firm ass in his hand and lifted her up, pinning her between his body and the pillar. She gave a breathless moan, one that grew louder as he broke away from her mouth and moved to her left ear and began to work his way down her neck. Her nipples pushed against the thin fabric of the T-shirt, and he took hold first of one, then the other, leaving the T-shirt wet, his teeth nipping, his tongue licking.

Her legs wrapped around him and she pulled her shirt off, leaving only a lacy bra between them, and slid her hands under his shirt, tugging it out from his waistband, desperate to remove all obstacles between them.

"I was going to ask you out to dinner," he said, pulling back for a moment.

Lila ignored him and slid his shirt off his head. "Dinner sounds wonderful. I know this fantastic Thai restaurant." Her hands were unbuckling his belt and tossing it aside before focusing on his fly. She grinned at him lasciviously. "Help me work up an appetite."

A woman after his own heart. He chuckled, then leaned down to kiss her deeply, tongues entwined, slipping her skirt off, and hooking her panties with one finger. He pushed her against the pillar, his breath warm on her neck, one hand cupping her ass, the thumb of the other hand exploring her wet slickness. She gasped and moaned again. He moved his fingers into her, slipping past the damp panties, teeth nipping at the soft flesh of her earlobe, feeling her body tremble in his hands.

"Come for me."

She shook her head, her breaths coming in gasps. "Not until you are inside of me."

Shane didn't have to be told twice. He let her guide his way, her hands warm, urgent, as they stroked up and down his shaft, pushing, pulling, and then wrapping her legs around him as he thrust into her. She arched her back, one hand on his chest, the other on the pillar behind her holding on, alternately tightening and relaxing the muscles, until he was sure he would go insane. He thrust, again and again and again, and her cries of pleasure as she met each thrust were intoxicating. He could feel the waves of orgasm coming towards them, a tsunami of impulses and bliss rushing his way. Lila moaned louder, faster, and he slid in and out, desperate to bring her with him.

The bra straps had slid down, as had the fabric, and he leaned in, taking her left nipple in his mouth, thrusting as he sucked, nipping with the next thrust, staving off the rush of orgasm, waiting for her moans to come closer together.

Seconds and centuries, there was no difference. Not in the moment that the wave came crashing down and the multicolored bombs exploded behind his eyelids. A rush of orgasm unlike anything he had ever experienced scorched his neurons and Shane felt it through every inch of his body. A second later, Lila let out a cry, shuddering in his arms, her eyes closed and mouth open in ecstasy.

They slid to the floor, still entwined, a slow descent to the wood floor and the clothes they had scattered there. She lay against his bare chest, skin moist, a strand of her hair tickling his lips.

Shane groaned. "Oh, my God."

Her soft, breathless giggle tickled the skin on his chest. "I'm strongly considering chaining you up in my office in the back. I could visit you every day, multiple times in a day if you like."

He snorted. "Chain me up? Hell, if it is like that every time, you couldn't get rid of me if you tried."

She sat up, straddling him; one small breast had escaped from the bra and he found himself staring at it, mesmerized. And despite having had the most satisfying orgasm ever just moments before, his dick was waking up, hardening again, eager for an encore.

Lila leaned closer, smiled, her lips slowly curving up. "I'm ready for you to take me out for dinner." On cue her stomach rumbled and they both laughed. "After that," she said as she reached down and caressed his chest, "I expect dessert."

Hours later, after dinner and a walk back through the quiet town, they finally used a bed. As Shane lay there, sweat beading his skin from an encore that proved even better than sex in a bookstore, Lila laughed quietly.

"I actually had a dream about you last night. The first in months that didn't include being shot at by assassins. I can't help but think that some part of me knew you were coming." Her finger drew lazy circles on his chest.

Shane couldn't help but notice how well she fit against him, as if she were made for him. The curve of her hips, her body molded to his.

"You're going to give me a swelled head."

"Really?" She reached down and stroked him. "And here I was worrying that it might be all worn out."

A laugh rumbled from his chest. "Give me a minute to recover and I'll show you different."

"I don't doubt you would." Lila propped herself up on her elbow and stared at him. The lightning lit up her face and he could see she looked serious. "I have a good life here, Shane. It's simple, no frills, but I love it, even more than I thought I would."

"I can tell." Shane waited for her to say it, knew it was coming.

"I guess that, in a way, this life is better than my old one. I miss Kaylee, and a few friends from my old life, but I love this town and running the bookstore. After six months, I feel at home, more than I ever did in Kansas City. At least, not since I lost my mom." She paused, broke eye contact, stared at her fingers. "Thank you for coming to see me," she said, grinning, "and for some mind-blowing sex, but..."

Shane reached up, tucked her tousled black hair behind one ear, and finished it for her, "But where is this going?"

One tear glistened in her eye. "Yeah. Just so I know where I stand with you."

Shane kissed her softly on the lips, "I'd like to stay, if you'll have me. Fair warning, though, Jack will call, probably sooner than we are both ready for, and I'll be off on assignment."

"Protecting some other sexy woman in a rambling safe house? Lila asked, a touch of jealousy in her voice.

Shane laughed, "Are you kidding me? Jack has made it his mission to give me all of the assignments involving three hundred pound ex-gangsters with bitter wives and entitled offspring. It's been hell."

Lila giggled, "I like Jack more and more every day."

Shane heard the low buzz of his cell phone and sighed. He had hoped for a longer break than this. He had to wonder if Jack knew exactly where he was.

He pulled out his phone, thumbed it off silent, and logged in. There was a text from Jack.

Maine is stormy this time of year. Your next assignment is waiting.

"Shit." At this rate he was going to be on the top of Benton's shit list for the next decade. It was worth it, though. *She* was worth it. He typed a reply to Jack.

I'll be in L.A. tomorrow on a red-eye.

The response was immediate. *Nope. Tonight. Private jet waiting at airport. Sending Uber now.*

"Shit."

Lila's smile dropped. "You have to go."

"Yeah. But, I'll be back. That is, if you want me to."

She nodded, "You'd better." She kissed him deeply, hungry for more time and they sat there in the darkness until he heard a car pull up in the drive and a moment later a door slam. It was time to go.

Headlights lit up the front door as he opened it. "Hey, did you call for an Uber?" The kid was young, acne covering his face. He stood there impatiently on the doorstep.

"Yeah, that's me." He turned back to Lila who had followed him, wrapped in a white robe. "I'll see you soon."

She stood up on her tiptoes and kissed him deeply as the teenager gawked at them. "You will come back, Shane Ellis, or else I'll have to come and find you and drag you back."

Shane didn't want to walk away. In that moment, all he wanted to do was stay, right here, with this mesmerizing woman. Lila made up his mind for him. She gave him a push, "Go on. Off with you. I have to work in the morning."

He walked away, conflicted, and got into the Uber. It was time to go to work, but all he could think of was Lila. He groaned as he thought about Lila, alone in the bed, waiting. He only hoped that this assignment would go by quickly. He would count the days until he returned.

Smoke and Steel
Book 2

A Voice from the Past

Present Day...

"**I** love you, Jack." The feel of her body nestled in the crook of his arm; her soft lips captured in his was so real. Then the ratchet of a nail gun in the distance jarred him from his sleep. His dream evaporated, leaving behind an emptiness that compressed his heart. It had been five years, plenty of time to get over her, but the dream brought her back as if it were yesterday.

The sun barely lit the horizon, creating a hazy, indistinct glow through the large picture window on the far side of the room. The latest wildfire, now contained, had trapped pockets of haze in the valley. A decent wind and heavy rain would deal with that, but Mother Nature seemed loathe to cooperate. The air quality remained poor, and it had forced Jack to take his daily run on the treadmill inside of the house, where the air filters cleaned the quality of the air and smoke didn't burn his throat or redden his eyes.

He sighed, stretched, and glanced over at the other side of the bed. He didn't miss Tiana, and he certainly wasn't dreaming about her. A few months of fun, but not worth the pettiness or bullshit mind games. He wanted something more than just a pretty body by his side. He rubbed his hand through his hair, thinking of Kaylee. The softness of her skin, how she had felt in his arms; it hung in the air, an echo maybe of what he had, what he still wanted.

Maybe I want too much.

In all of his life, only one woman had captured his heart. And she was half a continent away and likely had forgotten all about him.

Jack sat up, tossed the covers off, and stood. The haze was driving him nuts, the traffic and plastic people in L.A. were driving him even more so. He wanted to leave, escape somewhere, anywhere, and get away for a while. This was a thought that was quickly discarded as more basic needs made themselves known.

In the opulent marble bathroom filled with stark colors of black, white, and gray, he stood in front of the mirror, inspecting his reflection. His hair was no longer black, streaked with just a little gray. It was now predominantly gray, with only a few jet-black strands remaining. His father had been the same. The color gone by the age of forty, even if his face had remained youthful. He wondered briefly how Dad would have looked today, would the gray have turned white?

Jack ran his hand over his stubble and then slipped on his running shorts. He'd get in a run, then shower and shave before Azule showed up. He shook his head thinking about his assistant; she had been worrying over some investments that had tanked and wanted to talk to him first thing about Benton Security Services. Azule's mind was a formidable weapon, one she wielded daily. He wasn't sure what she was going to say, but he knew something was bothering her. It had been for weeks, and he dreaded the conversation they would have in a few hours.

He left his suite and made his way down the curving staircase to the main level. He pressed a panel in the wall and walked through it to another set of stairs leading down to the basement. The door closed, soft and silent behind him. The basement comprised a completely self-sufficient living space which included three bedrooms, each with their own bathroom, that shared a kitchenette, and a large living area. They had converted one bedroom into a workout room, moving it from its original location in the living area. There were no windows, nothing to even show that the house above had a basement. And it had served its purpose well a time or two in the past. It was literally a panic *suite*, rather than a panic room.

Malcolm was still asleep, not that he expected anything different. His baby brother rarely varied from his routine, and that meant that he had at least an hour before Malcolm would emerge from the furthest bedroom and head upstairs. Plenty of time for him to get a workout in.

Jack stretched first. He could feel the muscles tighten around the scar that ran along his abdomen, a curve of silvery scar tissue that wrapped around from the left of his belly button into a long, upward curve towards his back. No matter how many years had passed, or how much he had continued to work his muscles or tone his body, the scar tissue still gave him twinges. It was a permanent reminder of his failure to keep the woman he loved safe.

As he reached for the weights and ran through his reps, toning each muscle, slow and steady, he could think of nothing else. It was the dream that had started it. It had certainly set the tone for his morning.

Jack shook his head, wishing he could shake out his thoughts of her. It did no good to think about it, no good to miss her.

He stepped onto one of the two treadmills and pressed the preset for a punishing five-mile trek, his feet stretching as the treadmill rose in height. It wasn't the same as being outdoors, pounding down a trail outside, but he also wouldn't be gasping like an asthmatic in less than ten minutes. The air quality remained poor, thanks to the wildfires and haze that filled the air.

Two hours later, Jack sat in his office across from Azule and wished he had followed that brief, waking desire to flee Los Angeles.

"Benton Security Services is over budget by nearly one hundred thousand dollars in the past six months," the large, buxom woman declared, her full lips pressed tight, disapproval written all over her smooth brown face. "It doesn't make good business sense."

Jack leaned back and folded his arms against his chest, unconsciously mimicking the woman across from him. "I understand that, Az, but..."

"But nothing, Boss. You can't run things at a loss, not in this economy, and not if you want to stay rich. Benton Security Services is hemorrhaging money and your other investments aren't keeping up."

Jack hid a smile. Azule was a financial wizard, among other business-centric talents, but she was rather one-minded. To her, if the money wasn't growing, then it was in danger of heading the other way. As it was, he could overspend twice as much as he had, twice a year for the rest of his life and still never see a significant decrease in his overall worth. No one, not even Azule, was privy to all of his financial dealings.

That it bothered her, however, was exactly the reason he kept her on. Azule looked after his interests and he paid her 50% above the average salary for the area.

"This is a project I'm willing to take a loss on."

Azule scowled at him, her rich dark skin showing frown lines around the eyes as she contemplated what to say next, whether to argue further, before shaking her head and rolling her eyes. Was she appealing to the heavens to save her from the clutches of a mad white man with far too much money and not enough sense? Jack wasn't sure, but he couldn't help but grin when she threw her hands up in disgust.

"Have it your way, Jack." Her eyes narrowed. "Where's the mantiquer? I haven't seen her in days."

"Mantiquer?" Jack asked, laughing.

"You know who I'm talking about."

"Tiana?"

"Right, her."

Jack couldn't stop laughing. "Why did you call her a mantiquer?"

Azule sighed, rolling her eyes so hard he saw the color disappear into white. "Women like that don't want you, they just want your bank account. Guaranteed she was with a couple more on the side. Hope you wore your pelvic poncho when you tapped that."

Jack threw back his head and guffawed. The sound filled the room as he rolled the words around in his head.

Guaranteed, "pelvic poncho" is a term I won't be forgetting soon.

The phone rang then. Not the one on the desk that Azule insisted on answering, but his private cell, which only a handful of people knew of. Jack reached into his pocket and pulled it out, his eyebrows rising as he saw the 816 area code. He didn't recognize the number, but there was only one person he could think of who lived in flyover country, and he was the one who had helped get her there.

He pictured her face as he stared at the phone. It rang again, insistent.

Azule looked at him curiously, but said nothing, her eyebrows raised.

How long had it been? Four years? Going on five? Not a single call, no emails, nothing. The silence had been complete. It had felt like a death. It still did.

The phone rang a third time, and he pressed the green button, bringing it up to his ear. "Jack speaking."

"Hi, Jack." Her voice was the same, unmistakable, and one that he couldn't forget. His heart beat faster, and he could feel a warmth spreading through him. It was as if she were here, standing next to him, and her unique scent of honey and vanilla filled his nose.

"Kaylee." He breathed her name out, his mind a whirlwind of emotion, and Azule's eyes crinkled around a smile, one that looked almost victorious. She nodded at Jack, and then stood, stepping out of the room and closing the door firmly behind her.

"I'm sorry to call you like this, but..." There was silence and he could picture her nibbling on her lower lip, a habit she had tried hard to eradicate but one that was intrinsic to who she was. "I need your help, Jack. It's for a friend."

"Five years." The words escaped his lips. "It's been five years."

"I know." She sighed then. He could see her face, imagine just how she looked. Eyes closed, her face a mixture of sadness and regret. "I thought it would be best. For both of us. For Malcolm. I just wanted to forget my life from before and concentrate on starting over again."

Jack wanted to be angry. He had been. But now? He knew how afraid she had been, that the shadow of her family's deaths, and of the darker force of the people behind those killings, two forces that seemed too large, were too overwhelming for them to fight. It was why she had been in danger. The people who had killed her family had taken everything from her, had broken her, and she watched everyone she loved die. She had left in order to protect him, even if he hadn't needed protection. If he didn't handle it right, she would rabbit again, and Jack wasn't ready for that.

"I understand." Saying those words felt like he was chewing on sharp glass. It was a lie. He didn't understand, couldn't.

"I'm calling for a friend," she continued. "Someone in need of protection. I think her life is in danger."

How long had he hoped for her call? And even if it wasn't to have her return to him, he couldn't help but take this small opportunity and run with it.

"Tell me more," he said, his voice all business. "I'll be happy to help."

Jack listened as she described the situation. Her voice sounded stronger, more self-assured, and he had so many questions. But they would wait. He listed off the main phone number, the one that would route through Azule and set a bodyguard detail into motion. The property there in Kansas City, Kansas, would do as a safe house. It was well-stocked and prepared. He had made sure of that when he knew Kaylee would end up living in the area. From the sound of it, Kaylee's friend direly needed it.

"Don't worry, I'll make sure she's safe," he promised.

The relief in her voice was unmistakable. "Thank you, Jack." She paused, then whispered, "For everything."

There was a click, the rapid triple pulse that showed the caller had hung up on the other end, then nothing. Jack stared at the dark screen. That was it?

Azule was waiting for him to reemerge, her long, ornate fingernails tapping away at the computer. She looked up, gave him an assessing stare, and stopped typing.

"Well?"

"Benton Security Services will receive a call from a Lila Benoit in Kansas City," he said. "Put Jesse on it. He just moved to the area last month to work for the KCPD, but he might have time."

Azule shook her head, "He's out until the end of the week. He had that family emergency, a sick sister."

Jack groaned, "Shoot, I forgot all about that." He thought for a moment, "What about Ellis?"

Azule nodded, "I'll call him and arrange for the flight," she said, scribbling the details onto a notepad. Then she stared back at him expectantly.

He shrugged, turned on his heel, and returned to his office. As the door closed behind him, his steps slowed and he stared out at the thicket of trees outside his window. Like the rest of the L.A. hills, they looked dry, desiccated. There had been too much heat and not enough rain. El Niño was in full force.

Five years.

Just hearing her voice had brought it all back. His entire body was reacting. Even after all of this time, all that Jack wanted was to wrap his arms around her, press his nose into her hair, and feel her body against his. His reaction shocked him, but the thrill of connecting with her again helped him realize that there was a reason no other woman had stayed in his life longer than a few months. This time, he was going to do something about it.

This time? I'm not going to just stand there and watch her walk away.

Nowhere to Hide

Five years earlier...

There was no use fighting the restraints. She couldn't get out of them. Sure, she had tried at first, and realized that she would be better off trying to bend steel bars. She was lucky the older man hadn't tied them tighter and cut off the blood flow. Perhaps he had done that on purpose. Perhaps it would make it easier to administer the drugs.

Adrienne watched as the older man slid out of his coat, the blue shirt underneath clearly displaying an LAPD badge. Him not caring that she knew he was a police officer was terrifying. It meant that, whenever they decided she had no more useful information, that would be it, lights out. She thought of Rainier, Lincoln, and the blood that had pooled beneath their bodies. These men didn't care if she knew they were cops because the only way this would end was with her buried in a shallow ditch.

The tray had a bottle on it, but she couldn't read the label. It was too small, too far away, despite her excellent eyesight. Her stomach plummeted as she watched the man insert a needle into the tiny bottle and fill the slender syringe with the colorless liquid.

"Tie off her arm...I don't want to miss the vein," he said, and the younger man wrapped a length of tubing around her arm, snugging it tight.

Adrienne could feel her heart pounding, her entire body shaking with fear. The gag in her mouth prevented her from speaking, arguing, even pleading with them. She could feel beads of sweat forming on her forehead, despite the cool dampness of the warehouse. One foot twisted against its bindings.

It didn't matter what she did. She was tied tight, completely at these two men's mercy, and mercy wasn't something either seemed capable of.

She tried to catch the younger man's eyes, to plead her case, desperate to find some way to stop them from injecting her with that needle. Whatever was in it, it would either kill her or subdue her.

The older man removed the needle from the bottle and gave a tiny squeeze. The arc of tiny droplets spun through the air, vanishing. He looked up at her impassively and she shook her head slowly, wishing she had the power to stop him, to talk him out of what came next. The corners of his mouth quirked up in a small smile as he closed the distance between the tray and Adrienne's chair.

She moaned in fear, the sound low, primal. The younger man turned away.

"Please hold still," the man said, his tone indifferent. "This won't kill you, simply loosen your tongue, but if I waste the injection and miss the vein, the second dose almost certainly will do damage. An overdose could stop your heart. So be a good girl and hold still."

It took seconds for the needle to slide into place, yet it felt like forever as she watched him slowly press the plunger down. She could feel the coldness spreading, mingling with her blood, then racing through her body with each beat of her heart.

He spoke again, but this time he directed it towards the younger man.

"Remove her gag and leave it off unless she does something stupid like scream. The drug can cause nausea and I wouldn't want her choking on her own vomit." He had turned away from Adrienne and set the syringe down on the small tray before reaching for his coat that hung a few feet away on a nail.

"I've been up thirty-two hours straight and I need caffeine. You?"

The younger man nodded. "Uh yeah, grab me a Red Bull, would you? There was a convenience store about two miles down the outer road."

The older man nodded, and to Adrienne he suddenly looked hazy, almost blurry. "Perfect. It'll take a few minutes for the drugs to take effect and then we'll get started."

He slid his coat on, reached in a pocket, and jingled his keys in his hand. It seemed like such a normal gesture. Like something Rainier would do before heading out to meet his friends. But there was nothing normal about this. Adrienne could feel tears tracking down her cheeks. Rainier was dead. Lincoln was dead. Her father was dead. There was no one left to trust, and nowhere that she was safe anymore.

My fault, my fault, my fault.

She watched as the older man walked away, out the far door, into the rain and wind. A few seconds later, she heard a familiar car engine start up and gravel spit under the tires. She had spent most of a day locked in the trunk of that car; she was overly familiar with the sound of its engine.

The young man had turned back towards her when the other man put the needle down. He didn't like needles, and that was the only thing she had learned so far.

Then again, he looked at my breasts a little longer than a second. Which is far better than how the older man had stared at me like I was already dead. I might as well be a piece of furniture as far as that guy is concerned.

He leaned over and removed her gag, fishing the rough cloth out of her mouth before setting it on the rough-hewn table next to the tray. She coughed a little, and licked her dry, cracked lips.

"Please," she asked, "a little water?" She could feel the beginning of a headache, one that thudded in time with her heart. She felt nauseated, as well. Whether it was from the drugs or the constant state of fear she had found herself in for the past twenty-four hours, she wasn't sure, but it felt as if it were increasing by the minute.

The younger man mumbled something and walked away. A moment later, he returned with a cup and placed it roughly against her lips. His eyes slid away from hers.

He doesn't like this. He doesn't want to hurt me. I can work with that. I just need to get him to let me go.

"Thank you for the water."

He didn't respond.

"My name is Adrienne."

No response.

Adrienne searched for what to say next. Every word mattered. She remembered the instructor telling her to choose her words carefully.

Keep it simple. Have your captor connect with you as a person. Tell them your name. They might already know it, but that doesn't matter. What matters is that you establish a connection, one in which they see you as more than a dollar sign or something to abuse and kill.

The instructor's words had stayed with her, even though over three years had passed since taking the training.

Somehow, she had to get him to look at her differently.

"Please, I..." Adrienne did her best to look embarrassed. "I need to pee something awful."

"Hold it." He said it and stared away from her towards the far end of the warehouse. Adrienne wondered how long she had before the older man would be back.

"I have been holding it since I was in the trunk. I'm going to burst. Please." Her voice dropped to a whisper. "I don't want to go in this chair but if I don't go soon, I..." She let her voice trail off and she looked down, hoping her expression matched her words, and that it would convince him enough to release her bonds.

She could feel him staring at her. A moment ticked by. How much time did she have left? The younger guy had said the convenience store was two miles away on an outer road. Two miles, at forty miles per hour, plus at least three to five minutes in the store itself, meant, what, seven, maybe eight minutes at a minimum. At least two had passed since then. She had to get out of her restraints, disable her captor, find keys, and escape before the older man returned.

"Oh God," she sobbed, "please don't make me soil myself, please. I just, of all the..." Real tears ran down her cheeks and she clenched her legs together. "Please."

"Fuck. Okay, fine. But don't you try anything. I swear, if you do, I'll fucking kill you myself."

He reached for the first restraint and she curved her body inwards, cowering, hoping against hope that all he saw was weakness and fear. The drug, whatever it was, made everything feel weird, hazy. She waited until he removed each of the restraints, eyes down, shoulders slumped. He stood back.

"Get up, then," he said, gesturing at her, confused. "The bathroom is behind you."

"I, I can't. I'm dizzy and nauseous, and I don't know if I can stand on my own."

She needed him close. Really close.

"Christ." He threw up his hands. "Just don't throw up on me, or piss right here. Damn it. I should wait for Ro…" He stopped before he said the man's full name. "Never mind, just, here, lean against me."

Adrienne let him slide his arm around her and lift her from the chair. She was shaking, whether from nerves or the drugs or the actual fear she would fail and die here, she wasn't sure. But she used it, turned the shaking to her advantage just like she had learned in the class with Rainier and two others, twins, whose family had owned a lion's share of stock in Berkshire Hathaway. All of them rich, all vulnerable to kidnapping.

She placed her left hand on the side of his jacket. She had inches to go. Did he remember what was there? Had he ever even used one?

He didn't respond, and she moved slowly, shakily, as if on uncertain, half-numbed legs, and calculated how long she had until he remembered or she lost the chance.

No time like the present.

She jerked, as if stumbling, and his hands briefly were off of her, long enough for her to reach for it, and twist away, her instructor's words ingrained in her memory just as the movements themselves were.

Step, rake your heel down along the instep, then twist away from them.

It was a textbook move, and as he reacted, she stepped away from him and jabbed the taser in her hand into his side, pressing down hard on the side buttons. The taser leads imbedded into his chest and he stiffened, hands falling from her, a stuttering howl erupting from his mouth. She pressed the buttons again, holding her fingers in place.

He screamed and flailed his limbs, pinwheeling as if they had a mind of their own. It nearly knocked the taser out of her hand. He fell to the floor, his head smacking hard against the concrete.

Adrienne knew better than to stop. How many times had she forgotten and been dragged back by the instructor? Too many to count until she had learned her lesson. She pulled her leg back, then swung it as ferociously as possible into his groin. His body shuddered and lay still. Whether it was from the force of his head hitting the concrete or her testicle-destroying kick, Adrienne wasn't sure, but she was sure he was unconscious.

She reached for the bulge of keys in his front pocket, fingers shaking, heart racing. He had to have driven here separately, because he had been here, outside next to the car when it had rolled to a stop on the gravel. She had heard him walk over to the vehicle before the older man had even gotten out of the car.

She ran for the door, her stomach heaving, the headache having wrapped its tentacles around her brain and squeezed, sweat trickling down her forehead and in the small of her back. She had no time, no time to get out of here, but she was going to try.

It had been near dusk when she first arrived, trussed up like a Christmas turkey, ready for slaughter. A light rain had been falling then, but now it was a downpour, heavy, relentless, and she could barely make out the outline of a beaten-down Civic. She stared at the keys in her hand. Did they belong to the Civic? Adrienne wasn't sure. She ran for the vehicle and the door opened at her touch, unlocked. She scanned the horizon. There was nothing in sight past this long, low-slung warehouse. No lights, no trees, no buildings, and just one road in and out. Her one shot to get out. Here it was.

Adrienne slid into the seat, closed the door, and jammed the larger key into the ignition. It fit. She was about to turn it when she saw a set of lights flicker on the horizon. The road here had felt like a series of low hills, the car tilting up and down with each hill they crossed. Adrienne watched as the headlights disappeared and the incoming vehicle dipped down out of sight.

Adrienne turned the key in the ignition, which was rewarded with a slow rumble. She pulled her seatbelt on, fingers shaking, and glanced over to see if the door to the warehouse was closed. It was. Time to go. If she dared to drive past the oncoming car, it was still a distance away. She could see the headlights come into view and then disappear again.

It's now or never.

She put the car in gear and pressed down on the accelerator, a shower of gravel spewing as the tires spun and then caught and the vehicle careened out of the small parking area and towards the road, towards the oncoming car.

In seconds, she could see it flying towards her, and then she was past it and moving past, accelerating as much as she could without the risk of going airborne, as she navigated the wet macadam in the dark. Occasionally she glanced behind her. Sure, the car would have turned around, recognizing her. But it didn't.

And just when she was sure she had escaped, she saw the railroad crossing ahead. The arms were down, the train already blocking the road, and nowhere to go. Nothing to do but to stop and wait. Moments ticked by. The train rumbled, the rain pounded, and Adrienne's fear ratcheted up by the second. She had to get out of there before the older man got to the warehouse, realized she had fled, and caught up to her.

Her eyes continued to dart from the train to her rearview mirror. Were those headlights she just saw? She turned to look through the rapidly fogging back window and sucked in a sharp breath when a brief flash of headlights appeared, then disappeared down the hill. They were three, maybe four hills away.

Adrienne turned back to the train. She could see it now, the end of it was in view, a short caboose on the back in the distance, coming closer.

Her stomach roiled again, and she felt the burn of stomach acid in her throat. She stared back at the rearview mirror. The headlights were closer. Once again, they disappeared from view.

"Come on, come on, come on!"

The train rumbled on, oblivious, set in its ways and indifferent to the danger. The caboose was closer, nearly there.

The headlights flashed again. One, maybe two hills away.

The caboose clacked by but the crossing arms didn't move, wouldn't move, not until the train was thoroughly past and long gone.

Adrienne yanked the wheel to the left and stomped on the gas. The Civic jumped forward, narrowly missing one arm, and snapping the end off of the second as she floored the pedal and sped through the train crossing. The ground was more level here, and her eyes flicked to the rearview mirror and saw the headlights appear and disappear one last time.

Heart racing, mouth dry, she drove faster than was safe. In the distance, she saw the headlights crest the last hill and now hold steady in her rearview mirror.

The miles flew by and she finally saw the signs for Highway 101, turned onto it, and increased her speed until the aged Civic shuddered in protest. She raced past cars, some honked at her, but the highway was clear, thanks to the downpour.

Once, twice, she felt the little car hydroplane, and she slowed enough to regain control before accelerating again. As the lights of Los Angeles appeared in the distance, she knew she had to get off of the highway. It wasn't safe to stay on it, not with traffic ahead slowing and knotting, as she drew closer to the city.

I need to ditch this car, find another.

The thought of trusting the police again made her shudder. The police had taken the lives of her brother and his friend. She could never trust them again.

The drugs the man had injected her with, combined with sleep-deprivation, wore at the edges of her consciousness. Adrienne yanked on the wheel, taking the next exit without reading the sign. She needed to get somewhere safe.

There's nowhere that's safe. There's nowhere to hide.

The car was shaking now, a yellow warning symbol flashing, and Adrienne slowed the car. The rain had slackened somewhat, and the road she had chosen was dark, empty. A two-lane road stretched and wiggled before her, lined by trees, nothing else. She drove down it, noticing a slight rise in elevation, and driveways at long intervals, curving away from the road and out of sight, likely large, private estates.

If I drive down any of these and ask for help, they will just call the police. And the police are in these guys' pockets. Come on, Adrienne, think!

Thinking, however, was something better done with a well-rested and drug-free mind, neither of which she possessed.

Driveway after driveway passed, and occasionally a flash of lightning lit up the sky above, which was mostly hidden by the thick overgrowth of trees. Once, an oncoming set of headlights had her holding her breath, her heart rate once again ratcheting up, until Adrienne reminded herself that they would come from behind, not ahead. Behind her, the road remained empty of everything except rain and leaves.

It was one of those moments of staring into the rearview mirror, terrified of what might come for her, that took her attention away at a crucial moment. Just a half second, really, and that was all that was necessary. In the dark of night, the denizens of the forest traveled, whether it was raining or not. And the family of raccoons, a group of perhaps three adults and half a dozen juveniles, were lit up in the Civic's headlights, a wash of yellow that caused them to stop in their tracks in the middle of the road.

Adrienne stomped on the brakes and felt them lock up as the steering wheel went rigid in her hands. The car fishtailed back and forth, enough to break the raccoons loose from their headlight-induced trance. They scurried out of the way, as Adrienne fought to regain control. The car spun, out of control, and she felt the tires bite into the edge of the tarmac, then slide over the edge, down the embankment, in free fall.

The last thing that Adrienne saw before everything went dark was an enormous boulder caught in the headlights.

It was the rain pelting her that woke her first, wet and cold, falling through the shattered remains of the driver's side window. Adrienne lifted her head and instantly regretted it. Her neck and back were in agony, and her face ached where it had slammed into the airbag, the remnants of which surrounded her. She reached with her right hand and felt for the seatbelt latch. The car was silent. Adrienne looked around in the dim interior.

How long was I out?

There was no clock to inform her, and her captors had taken her cell phone. The dash of the Civic was dark, unresponsive, and she slowly looked over the car, her head muddled. Whether it was from the drugs or the impact, she did not know. She felt, rather than saw, the dried, crusted blood on her mouth. A tooth felt loose. After a moment of fumbling, she finally found the button for the seatbelt and unlatched herself, thankful she had been wearing it on impact. The car was on a steep incline and her body fell forward without the belt holding her in place. Everything hurt and Adrienne groaned.

Her hair was soaked. Her dress was as well.

How long was I sitting here?

She walked the fingers of her left hand over to the door, finally finding the latch. She pulled it, but the door didn't move. No amount of yanking made the difference, and moving hurt. There were no broken bones, but she still could feel a dozen different pain points.

If I get out of this, I'm going to be all kinds of colors.

There was no other option. She was going to have to climb out of the window. She moved slowly, hurting, thoughts muddied, and slowly levered her way out of the crumpled car. The boulder was within arm's reach, dark and gray, lined with lichen and moss. The window's safety glass had already shattered into hundreds, no, thousands, of square pieces that poked at her uncomfortably as she half crawled, half slid out of the car.

She could hear the rushing of water nearby, a low roar that distinguished itself from the downpour of rain.

There was little in the way of light, the distant glow of the vast city the only aid to her making her way through the darkness. If it hadn't been raining, she would have been able to see enough to walk, but the rain and the cloud cover combined to consume the forest and trees into a thick gloom that had her stumbling as she tried to make her way towards the sound of the water.

A few minutes later, now scratched and bleeding from falling, one ankle aching after she slid a few feet in the mud, Adrienne had found the source of the water. On a normal day, it was likely nothing more than a gurgling creek with plenty of boulders to balance on when crossing.

Now, however, it was a raging torrent of ice-cold water, tumbling and roaring along. There was no crossing it. Not unless she wanted to drown.

Adrienne tried making her way first upstream, then doubled back and heading downstream. It made no difference; it was completely impassible. At the furthest point downstream, she had discovered a wooden footbridge, the ends of which were poking out by less than a foot. The rest of it disappeared beneath the torrent of tumbling, frothing, growling water.

She had no choice; she would have to climb up the hill, back towards the road. The idea of it frightened her. What if they were there, searching for her? What if she couldn't find a place to shelter?

Adrienne could feel the difference between the rain and her tears. Her tears were warm, and they quickly washed away in the cold. Her teeth chattered, and she was so tired. She thought briefly of returning to the car, taking shelter in its battered remains, and then shook her head.

That's the first place they would look if they found the tracks off of the road.

She had to keep moving. Slowly, exhaustion seeping into her tired and aching body, she slogged her way up the steep embankment, towards the road, towards civilization or shelter.

All You Have is Each Other

It felt like forever. Adrienne's limbs moved slower and slower, and dragging herself up the steep embankment took forever. The car had come a long way before stopping at the bottom. Her eyelids were heavy, the adrenaline that had served her so well to escape her captors now wearing off. Whatever was in the needle the older man had injected into her, combined with a lack of sleep over the past three days, it wore at her. She clawed her way up the hill, inching her way toward the same road she had come from. She had to find help, or a place to shelter. Every piece of her ached.

Near a tree, she stopped, her foot tangled in the roots that protruded from the ground. It stood at a slant, desperate to keep its place despite the sharp angle of ground, determined to survive. That wasn't so different from what she felt like. Adrienne stopped then and rested, her heart hammering in her chest. She was cold, her fingers stiff, coated with mud and leaves, her dress torn. She leaned against the base of the tree, her eyelids drooping. The rain slackened and Adrienne caved to the exhaustion clawing at her.

Her eyes closed, and she fell into a memory of childhood, of her mother. The rain and dark replaced with the memory of warmth on a humid New Orleans summer morning.

Adrienne stood by the side of her mother's bed and waited for her to open her eyes. It didn't take long...it rarely did. Mom always seemed to know when her daughter needed her.

Colette's eyes flew open, and a smile appeared seconds later. Her skin was ashen, and the only spots of color were the dark gray shadows under her eyes.

"Good morning, Bumblebee," she whispered.

When Adrienne didn't smile, a look of concern appeared. "What's wrong?"

"Rainier told me to go away. He says I'm a pest."

"Oh dear, what made him say that?"

"I wanted to play Mario Kart with him, but he won't let me. He only has one friend visiting, and there's four controllers, so he should let me play too!"

"Rainier has a friend over, darling. You remember how it feels when you have Sydney over. All you want to do is spend time with her. Not us, not Rainier or his friends."

"But..." Adrienne stopped, frowned, and stared at the ground. She knew Mom was right, and she couldn't come up with any good argument. Sydney was away at camp, and every day since she left Adrienne had been bored to tears. Normally Rainier would have let her play with him and his friend, but since last year, when he turned thirteen, her brother was different, less kind, more impatient with her. He no longer wanted to spend time with his nine-year-old sister.

Colette sighed. "Bumblebee, you and your brother need to work this out. Sometimes, Rainier needs to be by himself and other times it is important for him to spend time with you. There needs to be a balance, my love."

Adrienne's bottom lip pushed out. "There's no balance. None!" She would have run out of the room if it hadn't had been for her mother's hand on her sleeve.

"Adrienne, my love, all you have is each other." Her mother's eyes glistened with unshed tears. "How I wish I had had more children so that you had others to play with. But we live with the life we have been dealt, my darling."

Adrienne had snuggled up to her mother in bed and watched cartoons for hours until Mom was strong enough to get up, the dark circles under her eyes just one of the many signs that Mom wasn't okay. Adrienne watched as her mother slowly slid clothes on, her body pale, thin.

"Mom?"

"Yes, Bumblebee?"

"Will the surgery make you better?"

Her mother smiled at her, bright white, a stark contrast to the weary lines on her face. "Oh yes, I hope it will."

"And you are going to have a hyster...hyster..."

"Hysterectomy."

"Right." Adrienne slipped into the bunny slippers she had left by the side of the bed. "Rainier says that it means you won't be able to have babies anymore."

"No, I mean, yes, that is what that means. No more babies." Adrienne could hear the sadness in her mother's voice.

Colette sat down on the edge of the bed. "There are other ways to have children, Bumblebee. And once I have the surgery, and have time to recover, I'll feel better, stronger, not so tired all the time." She ran a hand through Adrienne's hair, kissed her forehead, and smiled. "We can go to Disney World, visit New York for New Year's Eve, or so many other places, once I am better. Would you like that?"

"What other ways, Mom?" Adrienne's curiosity whetted.

"Well, there's fostering, adoption." Colette's smile broadened. "Why? Would you like another brother or sister?"

"A sister, but not a brother. I think brothers are too much of a pain," Adrienne answered, her eyes shining with excitement.

Colette laughed. "Well, it's a long way off. And your father and I haven't even discussed it, but I'll keep your request in mind." She stood up, reaching for the bedpost to steady herself as she swayed in place. "Now for some very important decisions, Bumblebee." The edges of her mouth quirked up in a conspiratorial grin. "Crepes at Muriel's or Eggs Hussarde at Brennan's?"

Adrienne jumped up and down. "Just the two of us?"

"Of course, Bumblebee. Besides, Rainier and Jesse have eaten a metric ton of Eggo waffles by now, if I know those two. Just you and me."

"Crepes! Crepes!" Adrienne jumped up and down in excitement, and her mother laughed. "Can we go to the park afterwards and feed the ravens?" Adrienne loved the ravens who flocked to Louis Armstrong Park, a few blocks away from the restaurant. She had sat patiently, a seed in her hand, until one had approached her and took it from her fingers. After that, it had become something they just did each time they visited the restaurant.

Mom smiled at her. "We might need to drive to the park instead of walking."

Adrienne whooped in happiness. "I'll go get my shoes on now!"

Her mother laughed and called to Adrienne as she ran out of the bedroom, "Change out of your pajamas as well!"

The brunch had been marvelous, but they cut their adventure short as they left the restaurant, Colette shaky, her skin pale and clammy to the touch.

"Bumblebee, I'm sorry, but I just don't feel well enough to go to the park," she had said as she grasped the wall of the building and leaned against it. "I promise you, we will go next time, alright?" Mom had managed a small, tired smile, and Adrienne had wrapped an arm around her, trying to provide the support her mother needed to make it to the car which was parked nearby.

"It's okay, Mom. I had a wonderful time with you today." Adrienne had blinked away tears, sad to see her mother so weak, so fragile. "Crepes with you are better than playing Mario Kart with Rainier any old day."

Colette had chuckled then and threaded her fingers through Adrienne's hair. "My sweet girl. What would I do without you? I promise we will go to the park soon. Cross my heart!"

But there had been no more parks. No more brunches at Muriel's. Mom had gone in for the surgery just two weeks later. A simple thing, they had all said, and Adrienne had kissed Mom on the cheek and ran off to the car where her best friend Sydney and her mother were waiting, turning her back on Mom without realizing it would be the last time she ever saw her.

"These things sometimes happen," her father said, his face drawn, his eyes red and recessed in his face. "The doctors tried everything, but she just fell asleep and never woke up."

No more Mom. And with her had gone any talk of fostering or adopting. No more siblings. And if she were honest, it was the beginning of losing Dad as well. He had already worked long days and spent months out of the year traveling around the world, managing the shipping business, before Mom had died. Now he buried himself in his work, shutting himself away from his children, from their home.

Rainier, four years older than Adrienne, had abruptly changed as well. He stopped going to friends' houses for sleepovers and limited the ones there at the house, even though there was no one to stop him. Instead, every night, weeknight or weekend, he made time to play Mario Kart with Adrienne. It was the only light in their new darkness. After Mario Kart came checkers, chess, cards, and Scrabble. In the months following their mother's death, during which Gerard Cenac was conspicuously absent from the family home most evenings, Rainier filled the role of a parent to Adrienne. He would help her with her homework, order food or make something simple, and then the siblings would play games until it was time for bed. And thus, their lives had gone on, until everything turned on its ear once more, less than a year after Colette Cenac died.

Adrienne opened her eyes with a start. How long had she been sitting here, leaning against the tree? Long enough that her body felt stiff, her joints popping in protest as she shifted in place. She had to get up the embankment, back to the road, and find shelter, find somewhere safe.

She moved her legs, which felt numb, and pushed off from the tree. It exhausted her, through and through, but she had to keep going. Lightning cracked overhead, and she could see she still had a long way to go. One hundred feet, maybe more, to get up to the roadway above. She sighed and climbed. It was painful, slow, and she shuffled along, grasping at tree roots, limbs, and boulders as she fought for every step up the hill.

Her breath soon came in ragged gasps and, once again, consciousness became a flighty creature, ready to escape at any moment. The lightning flashed in a quick burst, jagged strips of light that hurt her eyes and simultaneously lit her way. Twenty more feet. It felt like forever. A sharp branch dug into her leg, drawing a fiery burn as it cut her skin. She kept going. Climbing. Hands grasped for roots, trees, whatever looked stable enough to hold her weight as she fought her way up the hill. It had taken seconds to fly down it, but now? Now, every foot gained was a struggle.

The rain continued. At one point, Adrienne looked up and saw the drops falling from the sky like a shower of jewels rushing towards her. A beautiful moment, just a second of beauty before reality interceded. She was cold, sopping wet through and through. Her body ached from the accident and the myriad of abuses it had seen over the past few days.

Her skin burned from the cold. She stopped, her breaths coming in sharp rasps, the mud and rocks and plants digging into her knees, her hands. She couldn't go on much longer. All she wanted to do was curl up in a ball and close her eyes.

Instead, she looked up and saw it. The edge of the road. Just a few feet now, just a couple more. She surged forward, pushing all of her energy into making her body move forward. Fingers abraded, knees sore, shoe missing, dress torn. Gasping breaths of cold, wet air into her lungs until, finally, she felt the rough macadam under her fingertips. One last handful of gnarled tree root and she was up, onto the road itself, where she collapsed on the ground. No matter the cold or the rough ground under her body, her grip on consciousness slipped away yet again and Adrienne knew no more.

The Lady in Blue

Jack strained to see the road. The wind lashed the trees, and the darkness was nearly absolute, the rain pouring in great sheets from the sky. The only sources of light were his headlights and the occasional crack of lightning illuminating the sky in bright flashes. He had slowed the sports car to a tame thirty miles per hour. It still felt too fast in the inky black of the night, and the engine surged irritably, fighting the weight of his foot on the brake pedal. If it were a living thing, it would growl with impatience at the sedate pace he was setting, but at the moment he was far more afraid of running off the edge of the road. On one side was a tall cliff, with the occasional tree fighting for purchase along the dark rock wall. On the other, a thick forest and steep embankment away from the road. Except for branches and leaves, there was nothing but a dark abyss.

The party had been the typical Hollywood scene, plenty of high-end booze and vacant-eyed women who were afraid to eat from the buffet and talked about their modeling careers like it was an art form. It had bored him in minutes, and he had stayed for as short a time as possible and then made his escape. It had been tricky; some women could sniff out money as if it were made from chocolate. One had attached herself to his arm like a lamprey eel and refused to let go. Eventually she had grown bored, however, and wandered off "to the little girl's room," which was code for getting high on the complimentary trays of cocaine in the overly gilded bathrooms.

He had watched her go and made his escape seconds later.

The lightning flashed, slamming into a tree up ahead. The light was intense, blinding, the earsplitting crack and boom of the thunder simultaneous. Jack felt the sound pass through the vehicle and he slowed the car even further. This act saved his life, and the car's, as three deer, a doe and two fawns, came barreling across the road. He slammed on the brakes and fishtailed slightly before coming to an abrupt stop in the dark, rain-soaked road.

He rocked with the car, his body pushing against the tightened seatbelt. "Jesus H.," Jack swore, his heart hammering in his chest. That had been close.

He sat there as the deer disappeared from view, leaping from the roadway into the dark abyss and passing by something crumpled by the side of the road. "What the...?"

He put the car in park and unbuckled his seatbelt, grabbing a small Maglite from the center panel. The rain instantly soaked his hair as the downpour continued. He pressed the button and turned the Maglite on, playing it across the edge of the road. Rocks, tree branches, ferns, and a body. *A body.* "Oh shit."

He ran over to it, this crumpled lump of blue on the ground. Pale white legs, bruises, one shoe on, the other missing. She had scratches on her legs, filthy and bloody. The bruises weren't recent. At least, not from a car crash. His eyes caught on the abrasions and dark bruises at her ankles, her wrists. She wore a blue dress that was torn, bloodied, and the rain had plastered her hair to her skull. Twigs and leaves snarled in her long, honey blond hair. Her eyes were closed, her lips a bluish gray. His phone was back in the car and Jack felt torn. Did he dare touch her and see if she was alive or simply run back to the car and call the police?

"Miss?" he asked. He touched a hand to her shoulder. Her skin was cold, but he could see the rise and fall of her chest now. She was alive. He had to get her off of the hard ground and out of the rain.

Was it safe to pick her up?

Jack looked around. There were tire tracks, furrows, cut deep in the mud at the edge of the road. Far below, he could see the glint of metal, deformed, and bent. If she had come from there, she had climbed a steep embankment to get up and out.

I doubt I'll hurt her by picking her up then.

"Miss, I'm going to need to pick you up and get you out of the rain, okay?"

He gently slid his arms underneath her and stood up easily; he dead-lifted weights heavier than her four days a week. Her head lolled back over his right arm and she moaned slightly. He had to get her out of the deluge. That was the first order of business. He was thankful there was no one else on the road. They were in a blind curve and any oncoming vehicle would have seconds to react. Those gouges in the mud on the side of the road showed how it had gone for her. A car accident for sure. Could there be anyone else still down there? He tried to stare down through the trees and see if he could glimpse the car somewhere below but, despite the bright light show in the sky, he couldn't see anyone else.

He shook his head, spun around, and walked to his car, gently balancing the woman's unconscious body against his as he fumbled with the passenger-side door open and gently settled her inside. Her eyelids fluttered, but she didn't move.

Jack ran around to his side of the car and slid inside, wiping the water from his eyes. The heavy rain soaked him through. The windows fogged up. Her eyelashes fluttered again, and she opened her eyes a crack, shivering from the cold. Jack damned himself for not having put the emergency kit in his car.

She flinched as Jack spoke. "Miss? I need to get us off the road and out of the way of oncoming traffic. Were you in a car? Was there anyone with you? Anyone we need to go back for?"

She shook her head and whispered, "No" before closing her eyes again.

"Okay, my house is just up ahead. Hang in there. I'll turn on the heat until I can get you inside and warm." He reached out and flipped the heat to max, started the engine, and clicked his seatbelt into place before straightening the car out and continuing down the road. The rain had slackened somewhat, for which Jack was very thankful. He could drive faster, and within minutes he was turning onto the long private drive and passing through the gates. The water dripping from both of them had soaked the seats and he could hear a steady drip from her dress onto the floor of the car. Her eyes were closed again, her skin pale, her lips blue from the cold. He probably needed to call the police, but at the moment all he could think to do was to set her in front of the large hearth in the great room and warm her up.

The garage door closed silently behind them and the Ferrari purred to a stop, the heat from the vents ceasing the second the engine stopped. The girl still didn't move. In the bright, harsh light of the garage, it was clear how young she was. Perhaps twenty, possibly younger. Jack slipped open her door and leaned in, murmuring gently to her as he lifted her out of the car. A few quick strides took them from the spacious six-car garage, through the mudroom and into the back hall. It was a few more seconds' walk to the great room, where a fire burned merrily in the hand-cut, imported marble fireplace. The warmth of the fire enveloped them, and Jack set the girl gently in a chair near the fire.

"I'll be right back," he said, covering her with a thick, luxuriously soft blanket.

The half bath yielded a first aid kit nearly obscured at the back of the sink cabinet. Jack grabbed it, along with a handful of towels, and glimpsed his reflection in the mirror. His shirt, a black silk Versace tee, was muddy and soaked. His pants weren't much better. Water still dripped from his hair down the back of his neck. He grabbed a fluffy robe with his free hand.

He turned and walked back into the great room. The young woman was still there, staring at the fire, shivering uncontrollably.

"I've got a first aid kit and some towels. And a robe if you would like to get out of those wet clothes." She shook her head, and he wasn't sure if it was her shivering or telling him "no."

He knelt at her feet and gently slid off the remaining shoe, lightly wiping at the sticks and leaves that covered her pale skin. She flinched, and he looked up at her, realizing with a start that she was stiff with fear.

She's terrified of me.

Her pupils were enormous.

Is she on drugs? Afraid the police will catch her driving under the influence?

"I won't hurt you. You're safe here," Jack said softly, gently. She reminded him of a cheetah, and he half-expected her to spring away from him and streak away into the stormy night. "I should call the police, they could help..."

"No, please, no police." Her voice was soft, almost pleading. "It's not what you think."

"Honestly, I don't know what to think," Jack replied, focusing once again on her legs. The left knee was a snarl of mud, blood, and chewed-up flesh. "If it hadn't been for the deer running across the road, I never would have seen you. You could have died out there."

He felt rather than saw her nod, and her knee jerked back at his touch. She sucked a breath in, wincing as he gently cleaned the wound. Her legs held bruises, the ankles a mess of abrasions. The bruising didn't look as if it had come from a car crash, but as if someone had restrained her.

A shudder went through him. And Allie's face flashed before him. Her eyes were different, and of course Allie had been younger, just sixteen, but still.

This, whatever it is, is more than just a car crash.

"My name is Jack, Jack Benton." He waited for her to recognize it, but she didn't respond, just stared at him. A surge of relief went through him. She didn't know who he was. There had been no look of recognition, no change to a coquettish flirtation, like the girls at the party he had just come from, the look that betrayed their glee at meeting a billionaire, and a single one at that.

This girl, whoever she was, turned away instead, saying nothing, biting her lip. He waited, but she didn't speak.

And then it hit him. "You're scared, aren't you?"

The gentleness of his tone had an effect. When she looked up again, her eyes were full of tears. They spilled down, even as she tried to brush them away, to wrest back control of her emotions. She nodded, still shivering in the blanket.

"I can help you. No strings. No expectations," Jack said, turning away from her tears, focusing instead on the knee. "I guess you could say I've made a career out of it."

She had likely fallen on the hillside on the long climb up. There were pebbles and dirt in the torn flesh. He stole another glance at the abrasions on her ankles, took in the other bruises. They were recent, but different. Someone had hurt this girl, terrified her, abused her, and restrained her. And somehow, she had gotten away, possibly been in a car crash, run through the night and the rain, and collapsed on the side of that lonely road.

"Look, let me get this knee cleaned up, and there is a large guest suite upstairs that you can use. The door locks from the inside. You can take a shower, change out of your wet clothes. I'll fix you some tea or coffee; perhaps you would like something to eat? And then we could talk, or not, about your options. How would that be?" He looked back up at her face, so pale, so frightened, and she nodded, a small jerk of her head.

What or who was she so frightened of?

"Okay. I'll clean this up and bandage it, and don't worry if it loosens up in the shower; I have plenty more and we can just re-apply it. I've got the dirt out and this might sting a little." She winced as he sprayed on the Bactine. "I know, they always said it's not supposed to hurt. Ouch-less spray and all that B.S. Or perhaps I was just overly sensitive as a kid, but this stuff always hurt like hell." Jack caught the small smile that ghosted across her lips and just as quickly vanished.

Their trip upstairs was slow. She moved slowly, gingerly, her feet likely bruised and swollen. At the top of the stairs was a long hallway on the right, which took them past several doors. "I'm that first door on the left, at the top of the stairs, and I'm going to put you over here, in the guest suite," he said, his arm gently supporting her as she hobbled on the thick, plush carpet. "It has a full en suite and there are some clothes in the closet that will probably fit you. You are welcome to use them." They stopped at the doorway and he opened the door, revealing a spacious suite with a high ceiling, modern fixtures, and a small sitting room off the bedroom. "Let me know if you need anything. I'm going to go change and then I'll be downstairs. Okay?"

She nodded and walked inside. As Jack turned and made his way toward his room, he heard the door gently close and the lock engage.

Fair enough. She doesn't know me.

He walked into his room, an extensive suite that included his office, a library, a smaller workout room, and a spacious bedroom and bathroom.

Except for food, he could spend most of his days in here and never need to leave. He didn't, but living here in this giant house felt rather lonely, even with Malcolm's silent presence. When Allie had been here, it hadn't felt like it did now. Allie had been full of life, and it had been impossible not to notice how she filled everything she touched with energy and light. Of all the properties he owned, it was here, deep in the Los Angeles hills, where he felt her absence the strongest. She had loved the house, loved the remote feel of the place with the nearest neighbors a good half mile away.

He pulled off his shirt and tossed it into the hamper in the corner of his walk-in closet, reaching for a charcoal silk T-shirt, and looked down at his pants in surprise. Burrs ran down the length of one leg. Off they went as well, and he slipped into a pair of Rag and Bone denim jeans, kicking off his shoes and leaving his feet bare. He took a moment to towel out the last of the rain from his hair.

As he walked downstairs, he could hear the water in the guest suite running.

The kitchen was large and rustic. The heavy wood beams met the sleek matte black of the appliances. Jack reached into the Sub-Zero fridge and pulled out a carton of eggs, a haunch of prosciutto, mushrooms, and cheese. He set the heavy cast-iron pan to heat on the range and set to slicing the mushrooms. Jack had just finished slicing the ham off in paper-thin slices and had a pile of mushrooms and a small diced onion already sautéing to a golden brown when he heard the water shut off. He added a dollop of butter to the pan and it sizzled as it melted. Jack whipped the eggs into a froth and poured them into the buttered pan, adding the cooked mushrooms and onions and the shredded cheese, and flipped the omelet over with a practiced hand as he heard the door open from the guest suite above.

"Do you prefer coffee or tea?" he called, glancing over at her. She was wearing a pair of yoga pants and a T-shirt that disappeared into a zip-up sweatshirt. A pang of sadness hit him. Allie had loved that outfit.

"Coffee," she answered, paused, and then added, "Please."

"Help yourself," Jack said, and nodded at the coffee station. "There's cream and sugar if you want it. And I've made an omelet. I figure it's after midnight, which makes it morning, so it's breakfast time, right?"

A tiny smile. "Thank you."

He slid the omelet out of the pan and cut it in half, slipping one half onto her plate and the other onto his. He ate his slowly, fascinated as he watched the girl tuck into hers with an appetite he had not expected. Moments later, the plate was clean. Half of his food remained. He slid the plate over, smiling, and received an actual smile in return as she demolished it in a handful of bites.

Her hair was quickly drying into a mass of blond and honey-brown ringlets. Some color had returned to her cheeks. She sipped her coffee and his eyes fell on the bruises on her hands, the red chafe marks on her wrists.

She noticed his gaze and pulled the cuff of the sweatshirt down, trying to hide the marks. "Thank you for the food. I can't remember when I ate anything that good." It was by far the most words in a row she had said aloud since he had found her.

"So, shall we start with your name?" he asked, hoping she was ready to talk.

"The less you know about me, the better. Especially my name."

"I see." He sipped his coffee and thought on that. "Well, I have to call you something."

The girl was silent for a moment.

"Call me Kaylee. I've always liked that name."

Jack smiled. "Ah, it brings back memories of *Firefly*. I met Nathan Fillion at a party a few months ago. He's a nice guy."

The girl blinked at him, and Jack thought he saw the ghost of a smile cross her lips and then disappear.

"So, Kaylee, what can you tell me about yourself?"

"Nothing."

"Nothing?"

She reached up and rubbed her temples. She looked exhausted. "Honestly? You seem nice. Really nice, and I don't want anyone else to die because of me."

Search Party

"**I**s it possible she came this way?" Stephan asked.

Rohan shifted his attention from peering through the rapidly fogging windshield and heavy rain, to trying to see where his partner was pointing. He slowed to a crawl.

"I see nothing." He reached his hand out and jabbed at the defrost button.

Is this thing even working?

Stephan batted his hand away. "You just turned the damn thing off."

Rohan growled at his partner, "Then fix it so I can fucking well see. Because right now, it looks like we're in a goddamn fogbank from 'Cisco instead of L.A."

Stephan's mouth twitched, and Rohan could see the kid grit his teeth. He suppressed a smirk of satisfaction. Stephan was born and raised in San Francisco. Rohan knew city natives hated their beloved city being called 'Cisco. The kid was snarky, pretentious, and Rohan took no small joy out of digging at his junior partner's professional façade. This was especially true tonight when it was all Stephan's fault the girl was loose. His head, at least the larger one, had not been in the game. *Think with your dick and you'll end up losing both heads, you stupid little shit.*

He dug his lens cloth out of his pocket and wiped at the windshield; the car slipping to the edge of the road and the built-in edge alert sent a deep thrum through the vehicle. Rohan edged it back into the lane, wishing he could see the middle line better. Not that it mattered, there wasn't a car in sight. Goddamn rain. The view of trees and winding road was picturesque during the day. Who wouldn't love a sun-dappled, tree-lined drive through southern California? At regular intervals were nondescript private drives that led to some of the richest celebrity homes in the area. Right now, however, at just past midnight, it was a nightmare to navigate. The rain was heavy, so much so that there would surely be reports of mudslides somewhere in this mass of twisting, narrow roads by morning. The trees bent down, leaves ripped from them by the force of the rain, a mass of green and wet that reduced the unwieldy town car to a slow crawl. She had gotten Stephan's keys to his piece of shit beater car. If she had stolen the town car, they would have been able to track it through OnStar, but as luck would have it, she had given the kid a set of aching balls and wrestled the keys from him. Pretty slick, considering the trust fund bitch had been restrained when Rohan left for a coffee run. If they didn't find her, though, it would be both of their heads on a platter, no matter that the kid had been the one to try to get some in the space of time Rohan had taken to go get them some coffee and a couple of half-stale donuts that had to be nearly a day old. The same coffee that was sitting back at the facility, likely stone cold by now. They had to find her, and soon. How far could she have gotten, anyway?

Who am I kidding? We might have passed right by her standing on the side of the road and not seen a thing.

"How are your balls?" he snarled at the kid. Stephan mumbled something indistinct, which sounded suspiciously like fuck off. "Yeah? Well, guess what? We don't find her and I gotta call this in, I'm tossing your stupid ass under the bus. I'll be goddamned if I'm going to get sanctioned just because you can't keep your small head in line."

Stephan muttered something else, his head turned away.

"What's that?" Rohan asked as he yanked hard on the steering wheel to avoid a fairly large branch in the road.

"She said she needed to pee."

Rohan barked out a short laugh. "And you fell for that? Damn, how stupid are you?" He laughed again. "And here I thought it was all about you getting your dick wet."

"She was all of a hundred pounds soaking wet," Stephan protested.

"Yeah, so? Those trust fund babies get specially trained on how to get out of dangerous situations. Her family is worth tens of millions. Hell, maybe more. You think they don't teach 'em young how to get out of an unpleasant situation? That they don't know what to say, or hell, how to say it, and then fight dirty the minute they get an opportunity?" Rohan shook his head and let the car drift into the other lane to avoid what appeared to be the top half of a tree covering their side of the road. "Were you born yesterday?"

Stephan said nothing, just stared out of his window into the darkness.

Rohan returned his attention to navigating the road. The rain wasn't relenting, and the windows continued to fog, despite the air pumping away full-blast on defrost. "Shit, we're never going to find her. That girl is likely miles from here, we just need to..."

Stephan interrupted him with a shout. "Stop the car!"

The town car skidded on the tarmac before lurching to a stop. Stephan threw open the door, his feet sliding in the thick mud and leaves as he fought to maintain his balance. A moment later he had nearly disappeared from sight, and Rohan could only see the weak light of the young man's flashlight bouncing along some ten yards behind the car. It slowed, then stopped, as Rohan threw the car in park and got out, swearing under his breath as his shirt absorbed the torrent of rain falling from the sky, blinding him. He had the sense to close his door, unlike his young, impetuous partner. He slipped twice on the leaves coating the tarmac, wishing he had a ball cap to stop the fire hose from the sky from damn near drowning him in water to where he couldn't even see where the tarmac ended and the forest began.

Stephan's flashlight bounced impatiently and then left the side of the road. Rohan couldn't really see more than the outline of him as he tried to negotiate a descent. The incline was steep but littered with smaller trees to hold on to.

"I got tire tracks going down the side. I'm going to go check it out," Stephan called out, his voice already fading as he slipped and slid down through the mud.

Rohan spat out the water dribbling down into his mouth, bent forward, and struggled to stay upright in the slick mud. "Yeah, you do that."

Stephan's light quickly faded from view, popping up occasionally as he moved from tree to tree, slipping and sliding down the steep embankment. Finally, the kid must have entered a far thicker canopy of trees, because the light disappeared entirely, leaving Rohan blanketed in darkness and wondering if he should return to the vehicle. He couldn't see a damn thing, and he was soaked to the bone and cold. It wasn't adding to his positivity, not at all.

The minutes ticked by and his eyes ached from straining to see any light at all in the forest below. Had the kid actually seen anything? Or was he just full of hope that somehow that crazy little trust fund bitch had slid off the road and removed herself from the equation? The boss wouldn't care if the girl ended up dead. In the end, that was her fate, anyway, once they had made sure she hadn't spoken to anyone else past her brother and the journalist. And a few more well-placed questions after the drugs had taken effect would've done the trick. He'd just needed a jolt of energy. A simple cup of coffee, maybe a doughnut, and the coffee shop was just five minutes away, for Christ's sake. Ten, fifteen minutes tops, and it had been long enough for her to sucker Stephan into loosening her bonds to where she could fell the kid with a solid kick to the balls. By the time Rohan had returned, coffee in hand, and saw the car gone, he knew it had been Stephan's car that had passed him on the road. But Rohan had to make sure. So he had run inside, only to find Stephan, still in a haze of pain, moving slower than an octogenarian, a small trail of puke wetting his shirt. She'd nailed him dead center in the 'nads. The kid could barely walk. From what little he had said, she had knocked him out. Then she'd grabbed his keys and hung the lock on the outside of the storage container door, preventing him from following. Not that he'd tried. When Rohan arrived, he was still on the ground, next to a pile of puke. That girl was a hellion.

"Anything?" Rohan called out into the void. There was no response. Or if there was, he couldn't hear past the downpour. He was just about to head back to the car when he saw Stephan's flashlight bobbing in and out of the trees. It took longer for Stephan to make it back up the hill. By the time he did, he was covered in mud, a steady stream of curse words tied together as he slipped, crawled, and wrestled his way up the hill. When he made it to the top, the kid stopped, his sides heaving, then pointed to the car.

They squelched back to it, and Rohan realized as he slipped into the cool interior, that it really didn't matter that he had closed his side. The wind and rain had been fierce enough that everything inside of the vehicle was as soaked as the outside. He reached over and turned the dial to the hottest possible setting, not giving a damn if the inside fogged up.

"Well?"

Stephan sat there, his jaw set, a steady drip issuing from his hair onto the upholstery. "She drove it off the road, ran it into a tree. Airbag deployed. No blood that I could see. But she wasn't anywhere in sight. I couldn't tell for sure, but it looks like she might have come up the embankment onto the road. Fucking rain took out any sign of footprints, so for all I know she's in the forest somewhere. Don't know."

"We've got to call this in," Rohan growled. "She's going to be pissed."

"How pissed?" Stephan asked, not even trying to hide the look of concern on his face.

"Let's just hope we catch her in a good mood."

"Shit." Rohan watched as Stephan clenched and unclenched his hands. The kid hadn't been in this line of work for long, and if their boss was in a foul mood, he wouldn't have time to make another mistake. How many had "reported to the office in person," never to be seen again? Damned if he was keeping count, but if she ever told him she wanted a face-to-face, he would ditch everything—car, phone, hell, even his clothing and identification—burn or cut the damned tattoo off his wrist, and disappear. He'd seen enough to know that you didn't get fired or written up, not in this business, and not working for these people. You disappeared. He was just damned and determined that it would be him doing the disappearing with no help from Management. It was every man for himself, though, and Stephan had brought this on his own head.

Rohan clipped on his seatbelt and put the town car in gear. He was cold, soaked to the bone, and the girl was in the wind. He'd make the call when they got back to a motel and toss the kid under the bus. Hell, he'd probably end up under there with him, but his track record was far better than the kid's. It would likely save his ass from the grinder. If he was lucky, they wouldn't stick him with someone so green again. He needed to work with someone far more competent, who didn't get sucked in by a set of big brown eyes and the promise to be good. The kid had it coming, and Rohan knew better than to feel sorry for him. In this business, you did the job, or else.

They drove in silence. The rain continued to pummel the windshield, and he drove slowly, rounding each curve carefully, the tires occasionally slipping on the thick coating of leaves on the road. She was here, somewhere. Perhaps she had slogged her way towards one of the houses tucked into the cliffs and valleys. Stephan's car was toast, but it also meant she hadn't made it out to the highway. She was still here. And even if it meant waking up the boss, it could also mean that he didn't go down in flames with the kid. He could help figure out where the girl had gone. He had to update her...now.

"What are you doing?" Stephan asked, as Rohan pulled out his phone and pressed a few buttons on the shiny new Samsung Galaxy that Management had issued him last week. He didn't bother responding. It was enough to drive through the maelstrom and hold the phone to his ear. She answered on the third ring.

"It's late," she said, her voice gruff. "I trust this is important."

"Yes, ma'am. We have lost the package you were expecting us to open."

"I see." He could feel a thread of frost emanating through the connection. "And who is responsible for this...loss?"

He didn't answer her immediately, and she sighed. "Was it the newbie?"

"Yes, ma'am." Project Throw Partner Under the Bus was officially in motion. "But the package is definitely in the area. Requesting additional feet on the ground to help locate it."

"You'll have them in one hour." He had his finger hovering on the End Call button when she spoke again. "I'll expect a full explanation when this is complete."

"Yes, ma'am." He pressed the button and slid the phone into his pocket.

"Is she pissed?" Stephan asked. "What happens next?"

Rohan jerked the wheel to the left to avoid a large branch. "What happens next is that we find the girl. Now shut up and watch for her. You never know, she might have headed back towards the road."

The kid heaved a sigh of relief. Rohan kept a pleasant expression on his face. The kid was a fool. Hell, he was a walking, talking dead man. But that was fine. It wasn't his ass that was going to burn. He'd damn well find the girl, torture the information out of her, and bury her with the others. And he'd keep doing the job he was paid so damned well to do, keep himself out of trouble, and run like hell if Management called him in for a face-to-face.

Rohan was in it to survive.

I Can't Sleep

He had gotten nowhere with his questions. Kaylee, or whatever her actual name was, had proved quite reticent. And really, could he blame her? Whatever had happened to her, she was scared.

Instead, he had handed her a small brandy after the meal and changed the subject. Instead of focusing on her, he had told her about the house after seeing her gaze travel over the walls, studying it with an intensity that betrayed her interest in architecture.

"Frank Lloyd Wright." Jack said, anticipating her next question.

"Excuse me?"

"He was a famous architect," Jack explained.

"Yes, I'm familiar with who he is," Kaylee said, a small smile on her lips, "And I certainly can recognize his work. This house has many elements of Falling Water, but the upstairs is different."

Jack nodded, a little chagrined. He hadn't meant to talk down to her, and of course she would know who Frank Lloyd Wright was...who didn't?

"It's reminiscent of John Henry Howe's style," she added. "I studied Wright last summer as part of my application to Cornell. John Henry was his chief drafter and occasionally made changes like the ones on the second floor. It was not without controversy, however, even if Wright usually allowed the alterations."

Jack blinked; this girl knew her architecture. "That's impressive. You obviously have studied it because this building was designed almost exclusively by John Henry Howe. He was a friend of my grandfather's. They went to school together. Most people have never heard of him, so it is easier to just attribute Wright to this house." He cocked his head and stared at her. "Cornell is a long way from California."

She shrugged. "I never got to go. My dad nixed the idea. My brother went off the reservation, took a gap year, and found himself—so I got tapped to carry on the family business." She downed the brandy and stared off into space. "So much for doing what you love." She ran her fingers lightly around the raw skin around her wrists. "In reality, I would have sucked as an architect."

"Why is that?"

"I am obsessed with Victorian architecture," she admitted, pursing her lips. "Nothing else fits." She gave a small shrug. "I mean, I tried to study other architecture, I really did. I focused on Wright as part of my application, and said all the right things, but in my heart of hearts, what I really want is to do nothing but reproduce and live in ridiculously ornate, over-the-top Victorian homes. There is neither the market, nor an affordable way to do so in this day and age." She held out the glass, her other hand showing she wanted a small amount more. "I would have been miserable."

Jack refilled her glass and nodded thoughtfully. She seemed grounded, not moody or flighty, not like the actresses and Hollywood debutantes he encountered every day. It was surprising for someone as young as she obviously was, but he could see why her father had chosen her to carry on the family business.

"I can relate," he said, tipping the decanter and adding a splash more brandy to his own glass. "My parents really pushed for me to get a juris doctorate, which I did, and it has come in handy over the years, but I couldn't do it full-time. I can't stand the immorality of it all, so I have found other ways to thrive. My family already had a variety of holdings, and I've started one or two myself. It doesn't bring in the almighty dollar, but I enjoy it."

Jack looked at his watch and realized it was after four. "You should get some sleep, Kaylee. Tomorrow, well, later today, I'll be happy to take you anywhere you want to go, and you are also more than welcome to stay here."

He took a chance and reached out, taking her hand in his. It was warm now, a stark departure from the icy, damp hand he had first grasped just hours before when searching for a pulse. He could see the angry, raw ligature marks where she had been restrained. "You are safe here, Kaylee. I promise you."

She had stiffened in the first seconds that he took her hand. She took a deep breath, and let it out, visibly trying to relax. "I can't sleep. I just, I just can't."

Jack could see the exhaustion in her eyes. Whether she realized it, she was inches away from collapsing. Sleep was precisely what she needed.

Her hand was still in his and he rubbed his thumb near the edge of her raw flesh, avoiding the bruised and torn skin. "I understand, I do. How long has it been since you've had a decent six hours or more?"

Her eyes welled up again, and she paused for a moment before replying, "I can't even remember. Maybe," her forehead wrinkled as she concentrated, "What day is it?"

Jack glanced at the clock. "Now? It's Sunday."

"Sunday?!" She pulled her hand away and rubbed her eyes. "I think I last slept on Friday. On a plane."

So, she had flown here from somewhere else.

Jack gave a low whistle. "I could give you something to help you sleep."

She snatched her hand back. "No drugs, nothing that will incapacitate me. No. I'll be... I'll be fine."

He raised an eyebrow. "I was going to suggest chamomile tea."

Kaylee blushed, obviously embarrassed. "I'm sorry, I didn't mean..."

Jack recaptured her hand. He knew he probably should give her space, but something just felt right about holding her small, fine-boned hand in his. "It's okay, really. Chamomile and a bedtime story, what do you think?"

Her expression changed from embarrassed to confused. "Um, a bedtime story?"

He grinned. "Well, actually, at the moment I'm making my way through poetry...Keats, to be more specific. I read it aloud, so if you would prefer the couch here, you are welcome to it, and I could fix you a cup of chamomile tea and read from Keats. I'm up to *Ode to a Nightingale*, which is one of his more well-regarded poems."

The girl blinked at him and he watched as a smile slowly lit up her face. "You are a very interesting person, Jack Benton."

"I'll take that as a yes," he said, letting go of her hand reluctantly. The warmth of her hand in his gave him a sense of peace. "Give me just a moment."

Moments later, he had brought her a soft blanket and pillow and a cup of chamomile tea. He had lightly sweetened it with the honey he had purchased last weekend at the farmer's market a few miles away, and a dollop of cream to cool it.

"I hope you like it with honey and cream," he said as he placed it on the glass and steel table next to her, then sat in the seat next to her and opened a weathered book.

Jack watched her as she sipped from the chamomile tea and closed her eyes, a look of contentment spreading across her face. Her honey-brown hair was still damp in spots. Her hazel eyes looked enormous in her pale, expressive face. It struck him hard in that moment, an overwhelming feeling that he was in the presence of someone very special, beautiful, and kind. How he wanted to ask her what had happened, and who had hurt her. He wanted to reach out and take her into his arms and keep her safe from the world. And as these thoughts raced through him, her eyes opened to meet his gaze.

"What?"

He shook his head. "Nothing, it's nothing." He focused on the page in front of him and read the words slowly, deliberately.

"My heart aches, and a drowsy numbness pains
My sense, as though of hemlock I had drunk,
Or emptied some dull opiate to the drains
One minute past, and Lethe-wards had sunk:
'Tis not through envy of thy happy lot,
But being too happy in thine happiness,—
That thou, light-winged Dryad of the trees
In some melodious plot
Of beechen green, and shadows numberless,

Singest of summer in full-throated ease."

Jack looked up. Kaylee had set the empty cup down on the tray and relaxed her body against the chaise lounge. Her eyes had been slipping closed, and she gave a small smile. "Please, continue. I'm enjoying it."

Jack looked back at the page and continued reading.

"O, for a draught of vintage! that hath been
Cool'd a long age in the deep-delved earth,
Tasting of Flora and the country green,
Dance, and Provençal song, and sunburnt mirth!
O for a beaker full of the warm South,
Full of the true, the blushful Hippocrene,
With beaded bubbles winking at the brim,
And purple-stained mouth;
That I might drink, and leave the world unseen,
And with thee fade away into the forest dim:"

He looked up. Kaylee's eyes were closed, her long eyelashes a dark fan against her pale skin. Her breathing was regular, deep. She looked so fragile, so small and delicate, lying there in Allie's clothes, the blanket tucked around her tightly.

Jack felt his heart contract. At first glance, in those clothes, he could only think of Allie. But having spoken to her, having watched her for this handful of hours, he could see how different she was from his sister. Whatever was making his heart do somersaults like this, it felt different, intoxicating.

"Don't stop reading," Kaylee said, breaking him out of his reverie. Jack started in surprise. He had thought she was asleep, but a small smile told him differently. He returned to the poem in front of him. Losing himself in the reading, he plunged into the images wrought by words written over two hundred years ago.

He read it without pausing, the rest of the words falling from his lips until the last line...

Fled is that music:—Do I wake or sleep?

He whispered it, his eyes on the girl curled up in his dead sister's clothes.

Kaylee was truly asleep this time, and Jack debated whether he should risk waking her by picking her up and carrying her to her room. He settled instead for making a nest for himself on the other couch a handful of feet away.

Rebound

Adrienne felt as if she were sinking into a soft, warm cushion of comfort. She could hear Jack's voice reciting the poem, and the words were reassuring, regular, punctuated with inflection. She descended into the depths of unconsciousness, deep into memories of another voice gently reading to her, a voice she knew she would never hear again.

Rainier had just turned the page, pausing as he did so, and Adrienne hunched on the couch, eyes large, shaking with anticipation as she waited for Rainier to resume, when their father walked in. For Rainier, whose mouth turned down in a frown, Gerard's appearance was an unwelcome distraction. He had just gotten to the most intense part of *The Order of the Phoenix*, something he had been looking forward to reading to his sister, and now, here was their father, standing there, expecting them to drop everything. He frowned and set the book down as Adrienne jumped up to hug her father.

Gerard smiled at her indulgently and nodded to the book. "I remember your mother reading you the entire series, Rainier, I'm happy to see you keeping the tradition."

Adrienne watched as Rainier nodded woodenly but said nothing. She missed her mother terribly, and Gerard's absence had felt like abandonment, but she hugged him anyway, frowning at her brother's reaction.

"It's good to have you back, Father. We missed you!" Gerard hugged her in return, lifting her off of her feet.

"I missed you as well, Bumblebee. And I have a bit of a surprise."

"Turkish Delight? Rosewater?" Adrienne asked, her eyes sparkling. Gerard had been on a business trip in the Middle East for two weeks. He usually brought back something unique and glittering for Mom, and a regional confectionary for Adrienne. She bounced a little on her heels, wondering if she might now get a glittering piece of jewelry.

"Well, yes, but... I, uh, I met someone and, well, I know it has been difficult for all of us with your mother gone." Gerard looked at his feet, and he shuffled them awkwardly before continuing. "And Julianna will never replace your mother, but, well..."

Adrienne looked over her shoulder at Rainier, who was scowling now, shooting daggers first at their father and then toward the front door. There stood an elegant woman. In several long strides of her stiletto heels, she was standing at Gerard's side, an overly bright smile plastered on her face.

She glanced quickly at the scowl on Rainier's face before focusing on Adrienne. She reached out and took Adrienne's small hands in her own. "You are every bit as beautiful and sweet as Gerard described you to be. I'm so pleased to meet you."

"I'm, uh," Adrienne turned to look at Rainier, who was shaking now, his eyes filling with unshed tears. "I'm uh, pleased to meet you too." She looked at the beautiful woman, her father, and then back at Rainier. "I don't... I don't understand."

"She's our new stepmother," Rainier ground out, a single tear tracking down his cheek, his face twisting into a snarl. "Father missed Mom so much that he went and got married again." Her brother spit the words out and Adrienne struggled to understand them. Rainier sounded bitter.

"Rainier!" Father began, but Rainier was on his feet and running out of the room. And in his wake, Adrienne followed. She wrenched her hands from Julianna's and ran after Rainier, partly out of fealty, partly out of fear of this strange woman in their home. Who was she? And why had their father married her? Her brother's door slammed seconds before she arrived and Adrienne stopped, unsure whether to go back or to hide out in her own room. She decided on her own room, closing the door behind her quietly. Rainier had never acted like this, and Adrienne felt lost. What should she do? What could she say? She sat down on her bed, trying to understand how her father could have gotten over Mom so quickly.

She heard a creak outside of her door, then a quiet knock, before the door opened a crack. "Adrienne? May I come in?"

Adrienne couldn't trust her voice, so she simply nodded and Julianna slipped in, closing the door behind her. She was tall, taller than Mom had been, and dressed in a cream silk pantsuit. Her lips wore a bright red lipstick and her skin was flawless, her body toned. She was beautiful and Adrienne felt a flash of guilt for even thinking that. How could her father have married so soon? Hadn't he loved Mom?

Julianna smiled at her. "Can I sit next to you?" Adrienne nodded and she sat down, inches away, and her gaze swept the room. "You have a lovely room, Adrienne. Did your mother decorate it for you? I hear she was very talented at interior décor, and painting, and from what I've seen so far of the house, and especially your room, I can see she had impeccable taste."

Adrienne shrugged, unsure of how to respond. She had a few memories of Mom redoing her room when she was younger, perhaps five, and Sydney always told her how she wished she had a swing in hers just like Adrienne did. The egg-shaped wicker swing sat in a corner, filled with cushions and a large stuffed dog. In the days after Mom had died, she had slept in it each night, nestled against the big stuffed animal, the swing gently swaying. She stared at it now and wondered what she was supposed to say to this woman who was here to replace her mother.

"I told your father that we should have given you both some warning, and eased into this," Julianna said, her hands twisting in her lap. "I know how hard this must be for you."

Adrienne said nothing.

"Adrienne, I am so sorry for this surprise. I know you want nothing more than to have your mother back, and I am a poor substitute. But I hope you will let me try." She reached out a hand and gently took Adrienne's hand in her own. Adrienne marveled at Julianna's elegant nails painted the same blood red as her lips. A delicate gold bracelet with a single charm dangling from it encircled Julianna's wrist. "I think you should call me Julianna, not Mother, if that's alright with you." She smiled at Adrienne, and Adrienne did her best to smile back and manage a small nod.

Their father must have been having a similar conversation with Rainier, although from the raised voices, it wasn't going so well. There were plenty of raised voices in the weeks to follow, and Rainier and Julianna's relationship remained strained. Adrienne, perhaps because she was younger, found Julianna to be kind and patient. She acted more like a big sister, and they bonded over a myriad of home-baked delicacies that were mouth-watering and plentiful enough for Adrienne to share with her friends. Just as Adrienne and her mother had gone to Muriel's, or to the park to feed the crows, now Adrienne would spend an afternoon or two each week baking scones or whipping up delectable, melt-in-your-mouth beignets filled with creams and jellies. Rainier stayed in his room or spent more and more time with his friends at their houses, avoiding interacting with Julianna at all costs.

Their father was busier than ever. With their marriage had come an influx of new business and Gerard was busy with it, returning home late at night, long after Adrienne was in bed. One night, raised voices woke Adrienne, and she left her nest in the swing to get some water. The drinking glass from her bathroom was missing. She would have to go downstairs. As Adrienne opened the door, she was suddenly aware of the anger in her father's voice. Rainier was sitting at the top of the stairs listening, and he raised his finger to his lips in warning. Adrienne sat down next to him, curious and unwilling to walk down there when her father sounded so angry.

"Who is this Oladni Corporation, Jules?" Their father sounded upset, angry.

The siblings could barely make out Julianna's quieter reply. "Gerard, my brother's done business with them for years."

"Really? Because I can't find anything older than two years back on them and, frankly, Tom's concerned about what's in the containers we are shipping."

"Darling, stop being so paranoid! They changed names a few years back. I told you that."

"Cenac Shipping has always maintained a high reputation, Jules, and of all of those who have risen and fallen, we have proven ourselves reliable for transporting legal merchandise at all times."

"Of course you have, Gerard! And that will always be the case. The Oladni Corporation also values privacy, because of the cargo it ships around the world for its clientele. There's nothing to be concerned about, Darling. I promise!"

Her words were soothing, but their father's voice remained raised.

"I don't care whose toes I step on, Jules, the next shipment will go through Customs and be thoroughly vetted, just like any other shipments on board Cenac's cargo ships. Is that understood?" Adrienne gave a small shudder at the steel she heard in his voice.

"Of course. Now please, let's have a drink and stop worrying about things that aren't an issue. I'll give my brother a call and ask him to clarify things with Oladni so that this doesn't happen again."

Their voices faded as they moved into the den, and a heavy door closed behind them.

"What was that all about?" Adrienne asked, yawning.

"Something that was shipped didn't go through Customs," Rainier answered, frowning.

"Is that bad?"

"Well, usually if they somehow make it so that the cargo doesn't go through Customs, it could be because there is something illegal inside that they don't want anyone to see." Her brother looked troubled. "Father would never let that happen, though. He says Cenac Shipping is the best because we turn away dirty business and focus on the good."

Adrienne yawned again and turned back toward her room. She would just drink from the tap. She didn't want to go downstairs after all of that.

"She's bad news, Adrienne, and she isn't someone you should trust," Rainier said under his breath.

She turned around to say something back and somehow defend Julianna. But her brother had already disappeared into his room and shut the door. Adrienne returned to her room. Sleep eluded her. She tossed and turned, Rainier's words echoing in her head. Julianna was nice to her. She'd spent time with Adrienne, taught her how to make delectable desserts, painted her nails, and wasn't trying to take Mom's place, or force Adrienne to call her Mother. But something undefinable niggled at her, keeping her from sleep until finally, exhausted, Adrienne finally succumbed to sleep.

She would have overslept the next morning if it hadn't been for Julianna waking her up. As it was, she could barely keep her eyes open in History, one of her favorite subjects. Later, in P.E., she lagged behind the others, her body slow, her brain sluggish. It took the teacher calling her name twice before she looked up, blinking in surprise to see Julianna standing at the door of the gym, her eyes red and swollen. Mrs. Walker, the vice-principal, flanked her.

Mr. Jenkins laid a hand on her shoulder. "Adrienne, your moth-...er, um, your stepmother is here to pick you up. There's been an accident."

Adrienne's brain spun as she gaped first at her gym teacher and then over at Julianna, now advancing across the gym floor. She reached Adrienne, took her hand, and leaned down to hug her. It wasn't as if Julianna hadn't hugged her before. She did it often, really. And Adrienne had liked it, felt soothed by it, even.

This hug was different. Julianna was shaking. "Darling, we have to go to the hospital. Your father, and Rainier, well, there was an accident."

"An... accident?" Adrienne could barely make words move past her lips. The last time she had been to the hospital, Mom had died. She didn't resist as Julianna released her from the hug and pulled her along after her. She could feel her classmates' eyes on her, silent as she was swept from the echoing gymnasium, out to the car, and on to the hospital.

Julianna filled the journey with a nervous monologue. They had scheduled Rainier for an exam, a follow-up visit after pulling a ligament a month ago during soccer practice. "And, well, I would have taken him, but you know how your brother is, and so Gerard took him and the police said the car just went straight off the road down an embankment. And I'm sure they'll be fine, Adrienne, I'm sure they will, but they said something about Gerard needing surgery and I..." Her perfectly manicured nails clasped the steering wheel and turned it hard to the right, going slightly up on the curb as she screeched to a stop in the parking lot and heaved a big sigh. "I just thought you should be here with me."

"Thank you." Adrienne forced the words out of her mouth. Her stomach roiled. Her exhaustion evaporated, replaced with a painful ache of fear creeping up the back of her neck.

Her throat had closed up as they jogged through the hospital doors and into the large front entrance. The smell wasn't unpleasant, only a hint of antiseptic, but enough that it reminded her of returning to the waiting room with Rainier. She could still see her father's tall frame bowing in despair at the news that his wife's routine surgery had turned into tragedy.

Hours later, the sun had set outside, pinks and reds and golds giving way to the blackness of night, interrupted only by the glow of the city and the parking lot lights. Adrienne sat on the hard plastic seat in the waiting room, her stomach growling for food, but the muffin Julianna had bought in the gift shop remained untouched by her side. She stared out into the darkness. Beside her, Julianna had wedged herself into a reclining position and her breaths came regular, deep, spaced.

"Mrs. Cenac?" A doctor in blue scrubs stood near the entrance to the room, his eyes tracking around it. The others in the waiting room had stirred when he made his appearance, but dropped their heads at the unfamiliar name. It wasn't their loved one he was here about. Julianna responded to Adrienne's hand, shaking her, and the doctor advanced.

"Mrs. Cenac, I'm Doctor Watanabe. I just wrapped up the surgery on Mr. Cenac and young Rainier."

Julianne stood, smoothing her clothes free of wrinkles. "How are they, doctor?"

Dr. Watanabe nodded and smiled. It was a brief thing. It appeared and then disappeared again. "Your son Rainier will make a full recovery. His leg had multiple fractures which require immobilization. It will be a few months of healing, followed by physical therapy. Your husband, however, received extensive injuries to his spine, Mrs. Cenac. Myself and Dr. Batanides, who specializes in spinal cord injuries, did everything we could, but the damage is extensive and, unfortunately, looks as if it is permanent."

"Spinal injuries?" Julianna responded, her fingers covering her mouth.

"Yes, I am very sorry to report that Mr. Cenac has suffered a permanent paralysis. It looks as if he severed his spinal cord at the same time as he crushed the T4 vertebrae in the accident. If Mr. Cenac had been wearing a seatbelt, like young Rainier was, he likely would have been fine." The doctor winced at his own choice of words. "That is, he wouldn't have sustained such permanent injuries."

Julianna wiped away tears, asked to see both Rainier and Gerard, and then turned to get her coat and purse.

The doctor walked away, then stopped in the doorway and turned back to them. "Mrs. Cenac, I know this is difficult, but your husband and your stepson are alive. And after a one hundred and fifty foot fall off of the embankment, that's quite a miracle."

"Indeed, it is, Doctor Watanabe. Indeed, it is. I am so happy they both have their lives." As she swung her purse over her shoulder, Adrienne glimpsed an expression on her stepmother's face that looked anything but happy. It was there and gone in mere seconds, replaced with a look of grateful hope that had Adrienne instantly doubting what she had just seen. Julianna was kind to her, after all. She was even kind to Rainier, who was rude and standoffish. They were all lucky to have her.

She's just worried about Father and Rainier.

Julianna strode from the waiting room, and Adrienne scuttled after her.

Rough Night

Jack lay there on the couch and listened to Kaylee's slow, rhythmic breathing. He would be a fool not to admit that he liked her; more than that, he felt drawn to her, an attraction that had nothing to do with protecting her slowly building.

She wasn't like the women he dated. Where they were hard, she was vulnerable. Where they were devious, Kaylee struck him as intelligent and troubled, but determined. He had quickly eliminated any concerns of her being involved in drugs or really anything illegal. Despite looking as if she were under the influence when she first came to in his car, he was just as sure that she was the injured, and innocent, party.

Her lips were parted slightly, and he could see her eyes moving in the quick back-and-forth movements of REM sleep. Her eyelashes, thick and dark, fanned out over the dark shadows under her eyes. He wondered what she was dreaming about as her face twitched and she huddled deeper underneath the blanket.

The skin on her left cheek was abraded. Had she fallen? Had they abused her? Anger rose in him at the thought of whoever it was who had hurt her.

Every part of him wanted to hunt them down and make sure they never had the chance to hurt her again. And his last thought as he fell into sleep, and into the dream, was how it would feel to run his lips along her jaw and capture her lips with his own.

The dream, more like a memory, really, was the same. It never varied. Despite knowing exactly how it would end, Jack could not wake from it, or escape it. He had to let it play out, just as he had for the past ten years, each misstep a reminder that his choices and mistakes had led to the life he had now.

It started, as it always did, with the day before it all came apart...

Jack kissed his mother on the cheek. "I'm heading out now."

"Darling, please be safe. And try not to stay out too late," she said, hugging him. "Your father wants to get an early start."

Jack rolled his eyes. "I know, I know. Although really, Mom, I'm not much for skiing."

"But you love it! We haven't missed our annual trip to Tahoe since you came down with strep at age six. It's a family tradition."

Jack laughed. "I loved snowboarding until I ran into the tree and broke my clavicle. Now I far prefer drinking at the chalet, finding some cute snow bunnies, and shooting pool. But don't worry, I'll be home by two, maybe three at the latest. I can sleep on the plane."

Renae Benton smiled up at her son. "Don't forget you promised your sister you would spend some time snowboarding with her. It will ease my mind to know you are with her on the slopes."

"Crap. Yeah, okay. A promise is a promise. Gotta go!"

He slipped out the front door and was nearly to the car when William Benton's voice floated out over the courtyard. "Where are you off to?" Jack turned to see his father close the door to the office and head his way.

"Just going out for a few games of pool with some friends, Dad. I'll be home soon."

The elder Benton scowled. "You aren't planning on drinking all night, are you? And it's your friends, not Jerry, right?"

Jerry Banks, who he had known since high school, was two years older and served as their pilot. William had hired him soon after they opened a branch of the investment firm on the East Coast and another in Canada. Most weeks, the elder Benton was traveling from one destination to another and not here to judge Jack's party-going enthusiasm. Today, however, was different.

"Nah, just meeting up with a couple of friends, nothing crazy."

His reassurance did nothing to change the grim look on William's face. "Mahoney called me this afternoon. You're failing one of your classes."

Jack kept his face calm with difficulty. If it wasn't bad enough having Dad insist that he pursue a law degree, William Benton had also made sure it was a college he chose, not Jack's first choice of UC Santa Cruz. He had scoffed at Jack's suggestion, called it a place where you went to get a doctorate in partying. He wasn't wrong, but it had stung. Instead, Jack's dad had pushed Jack towards Stanford, where his friend was Dean. Considering Jack's lackadaisical approach to his schooling in high school, he was lucky to get in there. He certainly hadn't earned it, but money and connections made all the difference in the world. They couldn't, however, magically convert him into a straight-A student.

"I've brought home my books; I'll get it up to snuff in no time."

The look on his father's face betrayed his lack of confidence in Jack's smooth answer.

"I'll be back soon, couple of hours, and I'll be sure and take Allie out on the slopes, and keep an eye on her."

Mom was protective, but Dad? He wrote the book on overprotectiveness when it came to his only daughter.

"See that you do." William turned away from him and, with it, dismissed Jack without another word.

Hours later, creeping home in the car at the lowest rate of speed possible so that his alcohol-soaked brain kept the bright red sports car on the road, Jack could feel the hangover headache snaking its tendrils into him. How many shots had he done? How many had Banks had? He'd lost count between the shots, dancing with twin redheads. They were identical and with piercing green eyes, by God. A fight in the bar between two short, dark-haired men had broken the dancing up and he had lost track of the girls and Jerry Banks and realized it was three in the morning. He'd spent an hour, possibly longer, weaving among neighborhoods, avoiding sobriety checkpoints and getting lost. Now, as he slipped off his shoes and made his way into the house, the dark black of night was turning to gray.

Christ, my head is killing me!

The house would soon be waking. The parents were both early risers, as was his sister. Jack was the black sheep. Given the chance, he would sleep all day and rise as the sun set. It had made his morning classes especially difficult, hence the failing grade.

"Dad's pissed." Allison's voice from the darkness nearly had him shooting out of his skin. "I just heard him talking to Mom."

"Christ, you scared the crap out of me!" Jack could just make out her form, stretched out on the couch. "Wait. He's up already?"

"Uh, yeah," Allison said, in a derisive tone she had cultivated over the past year as she moved into her mid-teens. "It's after five."

"No, the clock in the car said it was four." Then he smacked his head. "Time change. Crap, I keep meaning to fix that."

Allison laughed. "It's two weeks until we fall back. Might as well keep it where it is."

"Yeah, yeah." Jack moved towards the panel door that led to his basement bedroom. There would be no time for sleeping now. Plus, he hadn't packed. Who would have thought that the first snow of the season would come so early? Normally it wasn't until Christmas break, or later, that they flew up for their annual trip to Tahoe. This year, however, snow had come early. The Halloween decorations were still up, but they would be gone by the time they returned. A bunch of servants would pack them up and put them away in storage, then lay out the autumn colors for a month before moving on to Christmas.

A half-dozen staff ran the Benton estate with precision and a quiet efficiency.

An hour later, Jack slid into the back seat next to Allie and wished he had taken a second aspirin. His head was in agony, his heartbeat like pulsing fire in his forehead. He was tired, hung over, and had already gotten a reaming from the elder Benton. Mom said nothing, but that was typical. She let her husband handle the uncomfortable discussions, and that left her to the gentler pursuits and kind reminders. He had never seen her lose her cool, except maybe over Malcolm. His lips thinned at the thought of his baby brother stuck in some damned institution. Just because he was different, just because he didn't live up to their father's expectations of what was acceptable or not.

They had stopped without him even noticing, and Jack's father was already out of the car and snarling at anyone who came near him. Jack's mother leaned over and placed several pills in his hand, saying,

"Sweetheart, take another of these; you'll feel better. Vitamin C, multivitamin, and another aspirin. You'll be right as rain in no time."

A gray drizzle was falling, and the temperature was plummeting. Jerry reached for Jack's bag and winced, then grinned. "Where the hell did you go? The twins took the party back to their place. We looked for you, you know; Izzie really had the hots for you, but Lizzie was more my type." He stopped, frowning. "Or was it Izzie who was hot for me? Well, hell, I've got their number for next time you want to hit the town."

Jack slapped his friend on the back. "You're going to have to give me the details later, man. Damn! I'm sorry to have missed that!"

Later, far later, he would remember their conversation. And for years after, he would try in vain to remember just how many shots he had bought for Jerry, and which one of them had been the one that pushed it too far. Maybe all of it. Maybe none, if Jerry had continued to drink with the twins, Izzie and Lizzie, in the hours after. No matter, the guilt remained heavy, constant. It was borne in the screams of his mother and his sister, as the plane, coated with ice and piloted by a man who was sleep-deprived and hungover, dove toward the deep lake. The same guilt sunk as deeply in his psyche as Jerry, his parents, and the plane did when it sunk into the icy waters. It was laden deep in the questions from the investigators afterward.

The guilt festered as he sat by Allison's side in the ICU as he waited for his little sister to wake up. She looked so small, so vulnerable there in the bed. Allison didn't look fifteen in those moments. She looked as she had at ten. The makeup had long washed from her face, which was battered and bruised from the impact with the water. She had been closest to him, with his window already shattered on impact. It had been all he could do to get her seatbelt and his off, to drag her out of the window and kick, kick, kick his way through the icy water to the life-giving oxygen above.

The guilt had exploded inside him weeks later as he watched her face crumple at the news that she had lost her beloved mother and father.

The counselor was mandatory, and Children's Division was steadfast. "If you wish to take your sister home and have custody of her, we need to know you are fit to care for her."

For once, his family's money held no sway. Not in the face of a nosy, bureaucratic machine.

He had submitted to their demands. He sat in an exceedingly plain office across from a man who spent an entire year earning what Jack's family investments made in a day. The hospital psychologist was middle-aged, balding, and his cheap tweed jacket frayed.

"I see here that you have refused pain meds for your fractured humerus." The psychologist looked up from his notes. "My father-in-law had a fractured humerus. It was exceedingly painful."

Jack said nothing, just shrugged his uninjured arm. The pain from his arm throbbed through the thick haze of his grief. He had difficulty thinking through the pain, yet somehow it was easier to feel the pain than to be numb. He didn't deserve the numbing gift of the painkillers. This was on him, his fault, his guilt, his mistake.

Jack and the psychologist sat in silence for a moment, then another, each staring at the other. "This will go better, quicker, if you could tell me what you are thinking about. How you feel right now, sitting here in my office."

Jack had sighed, the air rushing out of him, a great exodus of despair. "How do I feel? I let them down. My parents, Allie. Hell, even Malcolm."

"This is your..." the psychologist consulted his notes, "...younger brother, is that correct?"

"He's a non-verbal autistic. My dad had him put in an institution two years ago, when he was ten. I haven't seen him since."

"Would you like to?" the man asked, his pen held at the ready. "How did it make you feel to see him taken away?"

The questions had gone on, seemingly endless. All Jack wanted to do was return to Allison's side, where he had stayed, day in, day out, as she slowly recovered. Besides a serious head injury, she had suffered two broken ribs and a bruised spleen. The doctors had also diagnosed her with a heart arrhythmia, the first either of them had heard of this, and Jack hated to leave her side, even for an hour at a time.

After two meetings filled with invasive questions, the man had finally relented and written a letter of recommendation to Children's Division to release Allison into Jack's care.

The next month had passed quickly. Dean Mahoney had reached out to Jack and offered him access to a sped-up online course instead of in-person learning. Jack, suddenly juggling caring for Allison, and now Malcolm, marveled at his newfound focus and completed the course early, despite the heavier study schedule.

"You aren't off partying all the time," Allie said, her face nearly healed, and the last of the bruises hidden under a careful application of makeup. "If you count up the hours spent doing that, and especially the time recovering from it, you can see how much of a difference it is." She hadn't been wrong. As it was, he was on track to take the bar exam in six more months at this rate. It wasn't his dream job, but he could see that it was something that would move him forward with building his own legacy in the Benton clan's fortune.

The social worker still came by monthly, but Jack could see a change in attitude from the woman. Any day she would sign off on Jack, and Children's Division would step away and leave the Benton family alone. Allie had recovered some of her exuberant self once her ribs had healed, and having Mal back had been a huge, yet welcome change. Nadine Roberts had asked Jack to consider giving her daughter Azule a position in the office now that she had graduated, and he hired her immediately. He had known Az since they were both small, and she was practically family. When she had seen Malcolm struggling in those first few days, it had been her suggestion to give the boy some magnetic words and see what happened. The results had been instantaneous. Jack couldn't help wondering how long his brother had been waiting to talk, to communicate. He certainly had it now. The simple box of magnetic words had quickly expanded to a folder. And their lives, these three siblings together in the house their grandfather had built, with the billions in wealth from three generations of savvy business dealings, slowly found a pattern and pace. It had been a good time, despite the terrible loss; if only they had stayed together.

Jack shifted, the dream ending, consciousness slowly returning. He was on the couch, and Kaylee's form, her back to him now, was visible in the dim morning light. The memories of his behavior, of the plane crash, and of the cruel turns that life still had yet to deal out, haunted him. He wondered if they always would, if he even had the right to want more, or better, from his life.

I Should Go

Kaylee shifted, one foot slipping out of the warmth of the blanket. Her eyes flew open, her body reacting in a moment of panic, disorientation. "Rain!"

Whatever dream she had been having seemed to scatter in fragments. She sat up, gingerly, and winced, no doubt from the myriad of scratches and bruises that covered her body.

Jack, stretched out on the couch just feet away from her, sat up as well. "Good morning. How are you feeling?"

She gaped at him.

"I, uh." She paused, took in a deep breath. "I'm fine. Um, better. Bad dream." Her eyes drifted to his bare chest, stuck there for a moment, and then looked away.

Jack moved slowly, first stretching, then slipping on the discarded T-shirt he had left on the couch. Kaylee reminded him of a frightened bird, one he was hoping would not fly off. She looked nervous, like she knew or at least suspected that he had been watching her sleep. Jack hoped he hadn't creeped her out too much. She'd looked so peaceful lying there, her lips parted, her breaths slow and regular.

It was daylight outside, and from the angle of the sun, it was quickly on its way to mid-morning. It surprised Jack that he had stayed on the couch as long as he had, watching her sleep, but it had been mesmerizing. He had so many questions, and perhaps today she would talk, and perhaps share her story. He wanted to know why she was so frightened, who had hurt her, and why she was unwilling to speak to the authorities.

Kaylee tried to stand up and hissed in pain. Her left ankle, which had been puffy and bruised a few hours earlier, was mottled dark with bruises and it had swollen significantly. It didn't look broken, but a sprain was possible.

"Here," Jack said, slipping an arm around her, "Let me help you."

"I'm fine, really I..." She hissed again as she tried to put her weight on her left foot.

"Let me help you, Kaylee."

She smiled then and nodded gratefully as he helped her navigate her way to a chair at the breakfast bar. There was a small click from the far wall and Kaylee gasped as she looked over Jack's shoulder, her body tensing.

Jack's brother Malcolm stood there, his lanky, long hair covering his eyes.

Jack smiled. "I'm sorry, I didn't mention my brother Malcolm."

Malcolm stood there, saying nothing. He had a thick binder tucked under one arm.

"Morning, Mal, you hungry?"

Malcolm nodded slightly, then shifted the binder so the front of it showed. It had a word on it. The young man tapped it, but said nothing.

avocado

"Avocado and cheese omelet it is."

Kaylee stared at him and tilted her head in confusion.

Jack shrugged. "Mal communicates using magnetic letters and words." He said it in a matter-of-fact way, as if he was used to explaining it to others. "The therapist suggested it as a communication tool early on. Avocados are one of his favorite foods. I usually make him a cheese and avocado omelet for breakfast. Would you like one?"

She nodded, her eyes fixed on Malcolm and full of questions.

"Where did he come from? It was like he appeared out of nowhere!"

Jack chuckled quietly and pointed to a long expanse of wood-paneled wall. "Press gently on the third panel from the left."

He turned away and opened the refrigerator while she slowly limped over to the wall.

The wood panels were a rich blend of gold and brown wood, and one could see the craftsmanship in each of the inlaid pieces. The wall was a work of art. It was only when she was a foot away that she leaned forward, spying the hairline crack on the right side of the third panel. Jack watched as she pressed it. The wall swung open silently. Inside there was a small landing, an enormous expanse of wall covered in beautiful paintings, and a set of circular stairs leading down to the basement below.

"My parents loved secret doorways and passages. Every house we own has them, either from them commissioning their installation or me keeping up the tradition. Mal lives down in the basement in one bedroom."

"Wow," Kaylee said, gently closing the door. The wall resumed its proper shape with only a ghost of a click. "That's amazing."

Malcolm had slid into one of the tall seats at the breakfast bar, his binder open. Kaylee limped back, and then slid into her own seat, leaving a chair in between for Jack. She could see what appeared to be hundreds of words, all black on white background, arranged neatly on magnetic sheets.

Malcolm flipped the sheets, returning AVOCADO to its open spot. He arranged it precisely on its black box, neatly edging it until it was straight, then returned to the back of the binder for another word. Kaylee watched in fascination. Before long, the boy pushed the binder toward Jack. There were two words on the front...

who she

Jack read it and said, "She's a friend, Mal, someone who needs our help."

Malcolm tilted his head and gave a quick nod. His hands moved words around and he slid the board back to Mal.

not bitch

Kaylee stared up at Jack, eyebrows furrowing in concern.

Jack grimaced. "No Mal, she's not." He turned to Kaylee. "I'm sorry. I had a... well, there was this woman and she..." He paused, gathered his thoughts, and said, "I was with someone and it didn't work out. She wasn't comfortable with Mal, and he wasn't comfortable with her."

Mal said nothing, just tapped the words with his finger twice and tilted his head so that he could give each of them a sideways glance. Jack watched his brother's eyes slide over her quickly. He was curious about her, and that was a good sign. Mal rarely liked visitors enough to ask about them.

"Do you have other siblings?" Kaylee asked, staring at Malcolm.

Jack's smile disappeared. "I did, but now it is just Mal and me." He turned away and focused on the omelets.

He could hear Mal shuffle through his binder of magnetic words, flipping pages upon pages. With a tiny sideways glance at Kaylee, Mal cupped his hand, blocking her view as he slid it forward.

Jack turned back, a perfect omelet on the plate with a row of neatly sliced avocado to one side, and placed the plate next to Mal's cupped hand. His eyes took in the words, flashed an apologetic look in Kaylee's direction, and then pushed the board aside.

"Enough questions, Mal. And you know it is impolite to not show the words. Eat up."

Mal's impassive face held a flicker of a frown, and he nodded slightly. His baby brother dug into the omelet and seconds later, Jack pushed another perfectly cooked omelet in front of Kaylee.

"Salsa? Sour cream? Hot sauce?" he asked as she took a bite and closed her eyes in contentment.

"Hot sauce, if you have it. This is fantastic, by the way." She managed a smile. Jack pushed down the sudden flush of attraction he felt seeing it. She was beautiful. He had sat there watching her sleep and trying to steer his thoughts away from dwelling on what it would be like to kiss her.

He slipped into the seat in between Kaylee and Mal with his own omelet a moment later and dug in. He looked up and caught Kaylee watching him in the wavy reflection created by the kitchen's backsplash of expensive, shiny tiles.

Who is this girl? Why is she so afraid of the police or hospital?

Mal finished first. No words, magnetic or otherwise, before he slipped out of the tall seat and walked his plate and fork over to the sink and hand-washed it. He disappeared just as quickly, heading back to his lair, most likely to read. Jack had brought him a stack of science fiction novels by Greg Bear and Mal appeared to be tearing through them, judging by the small stack of finished books he had left near the front door.

As soon as his brother disappeared through the secret door in the wall, Kaylee turned to Jack. "Your brother, he's autistic?"

"Yes. It's classified as non-verbal autism. However, as you saw, he has plenty to say." He shrugged. "How he learned to read is beyond me, but he just knows."

"My best friend growing up, Sydney, she had a cousin who was autistic. He spoke, but he really struggled." Kaylee sighed. "He would come for a week every summer to Sydney's house. He was excellent at checkers and chess, beat us soundly. Then his mother died, and they put him in a group home."

"My parents did that to Mal. He was eight. I brought him home after they passed away four years later. He belongs here; this is his home as much as it is mine."

Kaylee smiled and opened her mouth to say something more, when a soft chime sounded.

"There is a vehicle at the gate," intoned the security system.

Jack grabbed his phone and opened up the app. The wait icon blinked for a second before showing the vehicle, a town car with two men inside.

There was a small gasp from Kaylee as she saw the men and jerked away from the image on the phone. "Is this two-way?"

"No."

"Can they hear us?"

"No," Jack repeated.

Kaylee's skin had paled, her lips set in a thin line, her shoulders curved in, and she backed away from him and stared out of the windows. She looked like a wild animal desperate to escape.

The chime sounded again. "There is a vehicle at the gate."

"Kaylee, tell me what's wrong."

She shook her head, tears forming. "I should go. Please, don't tell them I was here."

She limped to the base of the stairs, casting about for the nearest escape as Jack said, "I won't let them in or tell them anything. Just...stay here. Don't run. I promise, you are safe here."

He pressed a button on the phone, holding a finger to his lips before he did. "Yes?"

The driver held a card up to the camera. "I'm Detective Daniels of the Los Angeles Police Department."

"Okay," Jack responded and waited.

"We're investigating a crash and missing woman. We found her car off the side of the road, about a mile from here, and we were just wondering if you have seen anything."

"Sorry, but no," Jack answered.

The driver showed a photograph next, one that was certainly Kaylee. "She's wanted in connection with a string of robberies, so if you see her..."

"I'll make sure and contact the LAPD right away, Detective," Jack answered.

A few more pleasantries later and the car backed up, maneuvered into the turnout, flipped around, and headed back towards the main road.

Jack watched the town car disappear from view and then shut the app down. He looked up at Kaylee. She was shaking her head.

"They're lying. I've never even shoplifted mascara!"

Jack blinked. He wasn't sure shoplifting mascara was a thing, but she looked absolutely scandalized at the idea that she was a burglar. "Look, I believe you."

He raised his hands. She still looked ready to flee. "Kaylee, sit down before you fall down. Please."

She nodded and rubbed her arm before sinking down onto the bottom step. "Was that live or recorded video?"

"Recorded. You want to see it again?" She nodded, and Jack said, "Okay. Hang on. I can put it up on the big screen."

It took a moment for him to pull it up and Kaylee limped slowly over to the couch, sitting down on the edge of one cushion. Jack watched her look repeatedly out the large windows of the house.

"We lock the gate, Kaylee. It's a six-foot-high fence all around." He pressed a button. "Here we go."

Kaylee's eyes locked on the enormous television screen and she grew pale as she stared at the images. Jack zoomed in, selecting and cropping the pictures.

"What are you doing?" she asked, glancing back at him.

"I'm going to find out who these men are," Jack said, as he pulled up his email and sent a message to Teeny.

"Who is Teeny?" Kaylee asked.

"He would say that he drinks and knows things," Jack answered as he shut down the email client and went back to the full image of the two men.

Kaylee pulled her feet up onto the couch and rested her chin on her knees. Jack glanced over and saw the corners of her mouth twitch.

"So, *Game of Thrones*?" she asked, color returning to her cheeks.

"Indeed. He's a midget, so the name isn't a play on words; he truly is tiny." He sat down in the chair to her right and stared at the screen. "Were these the same men who did that to you?" He pointed at her bruised wrists and she pulled them closer, out of sight, before returning her gaze to the screen and giving him nothing but silence.

"Well, just for the record, Kaylee, I'm not in the habit of handing women over to their abusers, in case you were wondering."

He waited for her gaze to return to his. After a moment of silence between them, she tore her gaze away from the screen and met his eyes. "Thank you for not telling them anything," she said.

"That's it?" Jack asked, raising an eyebrow.

Kaylee's face looked conflicted, and he could see she was struggling with what to say. Finally, she spoke, "They would have killed us all. They still might, if they think I'm here. I should go."

Jack nodded, keeping his voice calm. "Where would you go, Kaylee? Where would be safe?"

Her face dipped down behind the safety of her knees and her hair, which slipped down over her eyes. She sat there silently for a moment, and when she looked up, her eyes were brimming with tears. "I don't know, I don't think anywhere is safe. And I, I just don't want anyone else hurt."

Jack nodded again. "And they hurt others?"

"The others are dead, Jack." It burst out of her, a desperate whimper of fear, followed by more tears.

A crying woman had never been a turn-on for Jack. But in that moment, all he wanted to do was scoop her up in his arms, silence her tears, and then wrap his body around hers. He was falling for a girl he had met less than twelve hours ago, in the worst of situations, and all Jack knew was that he couldn't let her go.

He knelt in front of her and gently tugged on her hands until she unwrapped herself from her hunched position. "I promise you, Kaylee, I'm here to help. And I'm far better prepared to defend myself, Malcolm, and you than you might realize. I need you to trust me. I've sent the images off to Teeny. Let him do his magic, and while he does, you and I will watch a movie. How do you feel about Thai for lunch later? I'll have it delivered at the gate."

Kaylee's hands trembled in his own. She nodded wordlessly, and he released her hands and reached for the remote.

As the movie began, Julie Andrews' voice rang out from the meadow and Kaylee gave him a sideways glance. "You like this movie?"

"It's one of my favorites," he said, and grinned at her.

Take the Day Off

Sunday had slipped by with several movies, takeout from Ayara delivered to the gate as promised, and Kaylee falling asleep in the middle of the third movie, the remains of her Pad See Ew still clutched in her hand. Monday morning had been pleasant, but Kaylee had barely touched her breakfast. Now she was staring out of the window towards the front drive, her eyes round.

Jack followed her gaze out of the window, confused by Kaylee's panicked expression.

"Don't worry, that's Azule. She works for me."

His employee's car was making its way down the long, twisting drive. He glanced at the clock in the kitchen. Right on time. Every weekday morning at five minutes before nine, Azule's car would appear, regardless of traffic jams or road closures. He wasn't sure how she did it, but her ability to arrive at exactly five minutes before the hour was a talent he had seen day in and day out for over ten years. Traffic jams, tremors, not even the wildfires knocked her off her schedule. He couldn't believe he had forgotten she was coming. The weekend with Kaylee and Malcolm had blasted past far too quickly.

His words, meant to reassure her, only panicked her more.

"No, no one can know I'm here."

She stood up, wincing as her injured feet hit the ground, but just as determined to escape before anyone else knew of her presence in the house.

"Okay, okay, hold on. I'll just go out and ask her to work from home today." He held out a hand. "Just stay here, okay?"

Kaylee nodded silently; her expression tight, fearful.

He could feel Kaylee's eyes on him as he walked outside, barefoot. The cement was cool under his feet and Azule braked as he held a hand up.

Her window rolled down.

"Morning, Boss." Her round, brown-skinned face frowned for a moment. "What's wrong?"

Jack struggled to think of an excuse. "Hey, Az, listen, I uh, I've had a tough weekend with Mal. I uh, I hate to ask you this, but do you think you can work from home today?"

"Work from *home*?" Azule's face held a mixture of suspicion and shock. "You feeling okay, Jack?"

"Yeah, Az, I'm great, it's just..." he stumbled over his words. "I need a day. Alone. Here with Mal." He hated having to lie to Azule, but he had promised Kaylee he wouldn't say anything. He'd given her his word.

Azule's eyes narrowed. They strayed to the house as if she were trying to see into the windows, determined to discover what he was hiding. "What about the shareholder information you wanted me to work on? I need to have file access, which is here."

"I need you to postpone that meeting until next week."

"But, Boss..."

"Please? Azule, I promise I'll explain everything later. Just, right now, I need you to work from home today. Can you do that?"

Azule frowned further and then nodded slowly, her eyes troubled. "This isn't some dolphin in the jacuzzi bit, is this?"

Jack stifled a laugh. Azule's mind was like a steel trap. She forgot nothing. Years ago, when she had first started working for him, he had told her there were certain key phrases he needed her to memorize, for her protection and for his. You didn't get to be a multi-billionaire without having safety measures in place. He picked different catch phrases for different things, but the phrase, "The dolphin is in the jacuzzi" was code for "Call the police."

"No, Az. No dolphins in jacuzzis around here. Promise. It's all good. Take a day on my dime, Az. Relax. I'll explain everything when I can."

Azule chewed on his words for a moment. "All right, Boss. I'll go home. But you need me, you call."

"Will do, Az." He backed away from the car and Azule rolled the window up, still frowning. He had twenty-four hours, tops, to figure out what had happened to Kaylee, and how to help her, before Azule would be back.

He watched her pull away, waving at her as he did. Azule wouldn't rest until she had her answers. It was something that he depended on most of the time, but right now, it was a real pain in his side.

As she drove away, Azule Roberts could not think of a single day she had missed work. Nor could she think of a single instance, except for a 4.2 quake two years past, when Jack had told her to stay home. There had been a good reason for that edict. The road outside of her house in Compton had dropped five feet, crumbling into an impassable sinkhole. Every weekday for three months after, Jack had sent a car to pick her up just past the blocked street. He'd even arranged for grocery delivery.

She saw him wave and then turn away and walk back into the house. Then she turned onto the curvy road and quickly lost sight of the house in the trees. It was a long trip back into the city, and Azule felt a minor annoyance flash through her. Why hadn't he called and told her not to come? He had looked distracted, not upset. And wouldn't he be upset if Malcolm was having a hard time?

I can't say I've ever seen the boy have a tough time, what with Jack caring for him like he does.

Azule knew that, before Jack had taken over the family business, and before his parents had died in a plane crash, Jack's parents had seen fit to have Malcolm institutionalized. It had seemed an extreme reaction to the boy being diagnosed with non-verbal autism, something her uncle's youngest son had. Isaac was difficult, far more so than Azule's near-daily interactions with Mal, and he had been violent. But Mal was mild in comparison. She tried to imagine the boy striking out or being destructive and simply couldn't.

She had often wondered why Jack's parents had felt it necessary to send their youngest child away, even if it was a far better place than most folks in the same position would ever see. Money bought things, and that was for sure.

Azule had started working for Jack shortly after the plane crash. She'd been there when he first brought his brother back and watched him interact with Mal. The boy had been a mess. On the edge of turning thirteen, he was uncommunicative and withdrawn.

Jack had pulled him out of that. So had she, for that matter. She had come up with the idea of the binder and magnetic letters, and Jack had acted on it immediately.

Watching Malcolm come out of the dark place he had been in had been as good for the boy as it had been for Jack.

And that is why none of this made sense. It raised her hackles. Even if Jack had laughed off the dolphin phrase. Could he still be in trouble?

The trees thinned and the narrow, two-lane road appeared. She slowed and waited for a town car with two men to drive slowly by. They stared at her, brazen, curious, and Azule felt another twinge of concern. Their car looked out of place and so did they.

Might be casing the area, looking to burglarize some homes.

Azule watched as they eased by and made a mental note of their license plate. She would ask Teeny to run it later, just as a precaution. She frowned as she maneuvered her car onto the busy, congested highway and headed for home.

"Auntie, I'm home!" Azule called, dropping her keys in the drawer near the front door before locking it behind her. It had been unlocked, which was odd, since she distinctly remembered locking it when she left. "You left the..." She stopped in mid-sentence as her cousin Marley came into view.

"Hey, Az." He grinned at her; his two front teeth yellowed but edged with gold.

"What are you doing here, Marley?" Azule ground out. Her cousin was trouble, no denying it, and from the look on his face, he sure hadn't expected her to come walking in right then.

"I just come to see Mama, that's all." He gave her a shit-eating grin she didn't return.

"Yeah? How much you borrowing from her this time?"

Marley rolled his eyes. "Now, Az, I don't see as how you need to worry yourself over..."

Lorna appeared behind him, a vacant smile on her face. "Hi, Azule, honey. Is it already time for dinner?"

"No, Auntie, it's still morning. I had a short day today." She didn't want to get into it, not with Marley standing right there.

"Still working for that rich white dude?" Marley asked. "You know I got this investment opportunity that…"

"Save it, Marley. He ain't interested and neither am I," Azule gritted out. "Auntie, I need to have a word with Marley in private." She gestured towards the door. He grinned at her and stood his ground.

"Now."

He made a show of playing the dutiful son with Azule's aunt as he hugged the older woman. "Mama, I'll come again real soon and see you. Play canasta with you, okay?"

"Alright, son, you do that. And you bring me those clothes you need fixin', I ain't too old to take care a'you, y'know," she called out as Azule unlocked the front door and hustled Marley out of the house.

Azule shut the door firmly behind her and spun around, hands on hips. "So how much you hustle from her this time?"

Marley raised his hands in front of him. "Honestly, cousin, I don't know why you think…"

"Save it, Marley. Don't you dare bullshit me. I asked you how much."

"Just three hundred." He looked off in the distance, avoiding her eyes.

"And how much do you owe?"

"C'mon, Az, I tole you, I'm looking for…"

"How much?" she barked at him.

Marley stole a glance at her, then stared at the ground, silent. He scuffed the broken concrete with his foot. "A hell of a lot more than three hunnert."

"She can't help you, Marley." Azule folded her arms over her chest. "And I'm not going to either."

"Az!"

"Don't you 'Az' me, Marley Remus Black." He backed away from her as she lashed out his full name. "We've had this discussion. You know we have. Last year I went and pulled out the last of Auntie's money, and paid off that damn bookie after you went and fucked up. I take care of Auntie, and I send Jamal enough in prison to keep him from bein' the bottom of the damn pile in there. And that's it, Marley. You gotta help yourself and figure out a way out of this. I'm done fixing your mistakes."

Marley's mouth moved the way it had when they were kids and he was trying to come up with something to say, some way to change her mind or convince her to give him the last of her pocket change. They'd grown up together. He'd been a baby when Azule's grandparents had died and Azule's mother had moved in with Aunt Lorna. Decades later, when Lorna needed help, Azule's mother Nadine had insisted she come and live with them. Marley had been a few years older than her. Back then, he had been a lot more effective at getting what he wanted. She'd learned a lot in the decades since. If she didn't stand up to Marley, no one would, and he'd run amok on her savings enough as it was.

"Don't bother arguing with me, Marley. I'm done. And I'm done with you takin' what little your mama has."

"And how you gonna stop that?" he snapped at her. "I'll just come back tomorrow, or the next day. You ain't gonna be here to stop me."

Azule smiled then. "She won't have any more cash on hand, Marley. Unlike you, I keep my money in bank accounts, CDs, and an investment portfolio. When Aunt Lorna asked for that three hundred, it was me who went to the bank and got it out."

The smug smile slipped from Marley's face.

"Because it was my money, not hers. You drained her dry two years ago, and I have been taking care of her ever since. And that's fine. I'll keep taking care of her. I promised Mama I would. But I'm telling you now, cousin, that this here well has run dry."

And with that, she walked back into the house and then turned and slammed the door in her cousin's face.

"Azule, honey, is everything okay?" Aunt Lorna was sitting in her rocking chair, a pile of knitting in her lap. Her face was smooth, only a few wrinkles, but her mind had begun to slip nearly a decade back. It was one reason Aunt Lorna could no longer care for herself. Marley, and Jamal before him, had rummaged through their mother's meager savings until there was nothing left.

"Everything's fine, Auntie," Azule answered, her insides roiling. That no-good Marley. He was just as bad as Jamal, worse. He was the youngest of three, and Lorna doted on Marley. At least he hadn't ended up a gangbanger like his two older brothers. Terrell, Lorna's oldest, had died in a shootout when Marley was barely ten years old. Jamal had been in prison for the past ten years, caught selling drugs and unwilling to rat anyone out for a reduced sentence. Azule figured he'd be there for another fifteen at this rate.

"Is Marley coming back?" her aunt asked, a small frown on her face. "He said he needed a little more for that stock he's a'gonna buy. I told him that was all I had, but..."

"Don't worry about it, Auntie. He said he had someplace he had to be." Azule knew she would need to talk to her aunt soon about not giving Marley any more money, but that was something she didn't look forward to. Lorna's mind came and went like the tide. No matter what she remembered about her finances, which wasn't much, she always had an excuse for her youngest child. Just as she had had for her husband, who would have gambled away every penny of their life savings if he hadn't died in the middle of a card game shortly before Marley was born. He hadn't even known his dad, so how had Marley followed in his father's footsteps so well?

Azule shook her head. That was irrelevant, really.

If Marley can't get his shit in order, that's his problem.

She hadn't even brought up Demetrius, Marley's four-year-old son. At least the boy had a wonderful mom. Nia struggled, but she managed three square meals a day, kept the boy clean, and put a roof over his head. Nia had kicked Marley to the curb when Demetrius was just three, and it had been a sound move, if not long overdue. Azule sent them two hundred dollars every other week to help them out. Nia thought it came from Lorna, and Azule preferred it that way.

"It wasn't enough, was it?" Lorna asked, her fingers working away, needles clacking. "The way he asked if he could get more, that boy has gone and gotten himself in deep, hasn't he?"

"Marley is a grown man, Auntie. One who has got no place coming to his mama begging for money," Azule answered.

The older woman nodded and said nothing, the needles clicking rhythmically. It was a soothing sound.

"I could take on some work."

"Auntie, he'll be fine," Azule said, although she wasn't entirely sure of that.

"Why are you back so early?" Lorna switched colors, and the needles resumed their steady clickety-clack.

"Jack said for me to take the day off or work from home."

"Huh."

"I'll be back tomorrow. Meanwhile, why don't I call and see if ShayTwin Hair has an opening for one of us to get our hair done and then I take you out for lunch? It's been a minute since we had a meal we didn't cook," Azule suggested. "Would you like some Chinese at Sunny's?"

Lorna smiled, setting her knitting down and standing slowly. "I been hearing of this soul food place called Not Your Mama's. Janine's baby daddy works there as a line cook. She says the mac and cheese there is better than mine."

Azule whistled. "Well, that's gotta be wrong. But sure, we'll go give 'em a try. Now that you mention it, I heard something about peach cobbler, and you know how I feel about cobbler."

The day passed swiftly, and it wore Lorna out by the time they returned, the sun already low in the sky. The older woman had sat and knitted while Azule had her hair done in braids and swept up onto her head. They had eaten at Not Your Mama's and, while good, the mac and cheese fell short of Lorna's. The cobbler, however, had been exceptional.

As she locked the heavy security door behind them, Azule's thoughts fell once more on Jack Benton.

What was going on up there? Tomorrow morning, come hell or high water, she was going to find out.

Fever Bright

Jack walked back inside and waited by the window, watching as Azule drove away.

I've got twenty-four hours to get some answers before Azule comes in and wrests them out of this girl.

He turned and gave Kaylee a smile. "She's gone. I imagine she'll be back tomorrow with a thousand questions for me. Az is one of the best, and you will see what I mean if, well, *when*, you meet her."

Kaylee had settled back into her seat at the table and she poked at her breakfast half-heartedly.

"Tired of my cooking already?" he asked.

"Sorry, I'm not hungry right now." She pushed the plate away from her. "And you are an amazing cook. Could I have some more water?"

He took the glass from her, his fingers brushing hers. Her hand was warm to the touch, and he was suddenly aware of how flushed her cheeks looked.

"Are you running a fever?" He reached over, ignoring her flinch, and touched her forehead. It was burning up. "You are! No wonder you don't feel like eating. We need to get you back to bed."

"Jack, I can't stay here. I..." She swayed slightly in place, her skin paling. "I need to..."

"You need to rest, Kaylee." He strode over to her side and slipped a protective arm around her.

Malcolm, whose plate was empty of food, held up the binder. It read...

juice

water

331

sleep

"See? Even Mal agrees. C'mon. I'm going to make sure you make it all the way up those stairs."

The heat rolling off of her was fever bright, and Jack wondered if he should call a doctor. All of those hours out in the chilly rain had done it, he was sure of it.

She leaned on him, despite her objections that she was fine, and stumbled slightly, clearly unsteady on her feet. By the time they made it up the stairs, he was practically carrying her. How had he not seen how sick she was this morning? How had he missed the red cheeks and clammy, sweating skin?

She felt so small in his arms at the top of the landing when he lifted her up, off of her feet. Kaylee didn't even protest, her eyes fluttering and then shutting as he carried her the last few feet to her room and gently placed her on the bed. She showed some signs of life when he tried to cover her with a blanket, shoving it off as she turned on her side with one feverish kick.

He turned away from her and nearly slammed into Malcolm. His brother stood there silently, eyes on the floor, two pills outstretched in one hand and a glass of juice in the other.

"Thanks, Mal." He took the pills and juice from him and flashed back to Azule. From the look on her face when he had talked to her and given her such a flimsy excuse, she had seen through it. Azule knew Malcolm nearly as well as Jack did. It had taken time, but Malcolm was far better now than that shell of a boy Jack had found locked away in the institution. Why Dad had found it necessary, he would never understand, just as he couldn't stomach why Mom hadn't objected to it. Mal would never live what others would consider a normal life—there were no kids or a career in his future—but he didn't deserve to be locked away like some animal. Mal was all Jack had, just as Jack was all Mal had. That's just the way it was. Azule got that. So really, it wasn't any surprise that she didn't buy his flimsy excuse to send her home. He was half-shocked that she had actually left when he asked her to, instead of digging her heels in and insisting on the real reason for him sending her away.

He grabbed a pillow and seated it under Kaylee's head, gently raising her shoulders and then extending his palm with the Tylenol towards her.

"I need you to take these. They'll lower your fever. Mal brought you the last of the fresh-squeezed juice."

Kaylee's eyes flickered open. She shakily took the pills from Jack's hand and put them in her mouth before reaching for the juice. Her entire body was shaking now.

"Mal, do you remember where the thermometer is?" Jack asked, as he steadied the glass in her hand. Seconds later, Mal pressed the thermometer into Jack's hand.

Jack activated it and held it against Kaylee's forehead. Her fever seemed to have grown in just the few minutes. The thermometer flashed twice and then gave a discordant beep. The number 102.9 glowed, back-lit in red.

"Christ."

Kaylee's eyes fluttered closed as she sank back on the bed. "I should, I should go."

"Kaylee, you are running a high fever. You need to rest." He touched her shoulder, felt the heat of the fever on her skin, and damned himself for not having realized she was sick earlier. "You are safe here. Now get some rest."

Jack left the room, closing the door gently behind him. Malcolm waited outside, binder in hand.

Jack read the list of words his brother was holding out.

food

quiet

I watch

He nodded, surprised at the last line. Mal kept to himself. Anytime there were others in the house, he slipped away, down into the basement, hunkered down in his room, and avoided the others.

"I'll place a grocery order for delivery later this afternoon," Jack said in response. "Are you sure you are okay with keeping an eye on her?"

Mal nodded. It was nearly imperceptible, but Jack was used to Mal. His brother communicated volumes, if you only knew how to see the signs.

"Okay, well, I need to check in with the team and a few other tasks. I'm going to go over to the office. You let me know if I'm needed here, okay?"

Another small jerk of Mal's head and Jack left him there. When he reached the bottom of the stairs, he looked up and saw Mal seat himself in a comfortable chair on the landing a few feet from the door, his binder in his lap, his hands busy flipping the pages.

I've never seen Mal react like this to anyone except Az and me. Well, possibly Luke, as well. But never protective or concerned.

It was a first.

Jack walked briskly towards the far end of the house, then outside, to the building at the far end of the garden. Here the architecture remained the same, but they'd designed the building with business in mind. It blended in perfectly with the clean lines of the house, but inside there was a distinct business-like feel.

There were four offices, a galley kitchenette with coffee station, two bathrooms, and a spacious conference room. It wasn't often that they needed the conference room, only a handful of times in the year, but it came in handy when meeting clients. Jack had added onto the back part of the building nearly a decade ago, eradicating his father's putting green and instead installing an atrium with several small fruit trees that reached up to the tall, glassed-in ceiling. The center of the atrium held a pond that burbled and gushed. It held a cluster of fish and there were seats, several bistro tables, and chair sets scattered about. Jack often ate lunch here with Az on the weekdays.

Az will be back tomorrow with a barrage of questions for me, guaranteed.

He needed to check in with Jesse and Shane, who were both on separate jobs. Shane was busy with a minor mob boss turned informant out of Atlanta, along with the guy's hyena of a wife. Jack suppressed a grin at Shane's description of the woman. Apparently, his charges had been fighting like cats and dogs since they arrived at the safe house and showed no signs of calling a truce. The client was due in court to testify in another month, and Shane was as unhappy as they were.

Protecting the seedier characters like this minor mob boss paid for the other work, and the clients who didn't have money. And since Allie, well, Jack knew he was filling a need. Battered wives, abused teens, and dozens of innocents with no money or options, they got the help they desperately needed. If his guys had to babysit some shittier players in order to provide the seed money for making a difference in the lives of innocents, then that is what they would do.

Jack varied the clientele among his guys. Right now, he had Jesse protecting a battered wife and her two small children in Mississippi while they waited for the divorce and custody hearings. The court had released the husband from jail with no monitoring two days after he had put his estranged wife in the hospital and broke his six-year-old son's arm when the boy tried to protect his mother. The bastard was still walking free while the prosecutor's office took its time trying to decide whether they had enough to charge him.

Jack shook his head, his lips a thin line of disgust as he read his emails. Jesse had moved the woman and her two kids to a secure location, and things were quiet for now. There was a message from Shane informing him that the ex-mob boss and his wife had actually gotten into a fistfight. The other two men on assignment had checked in as well, with nothing to report, and a third was on vacation. He'd sent a photo of a giant catfish he'd caught on Lake Powell in Arizona where Jack had a houseboat.

He believed in paying his men well, contributing to their retirement funds, and letting them make use of the properties he had scattered all over the United States and the rest of the world.

Hell, why not? The houses were just sitting there, after all.

Jack pulled up the Bristol Farms website and began preparing an order. It was something that Az typically handled, a task which always looked effortless when she did it, but took him nearly an hour. He ordered the basics, along with some specialty cheeses and meats, and sent the order in. Seconds later, his email chimed, informing him they would deliver it after two. He set an alarm on his phone. Mal refused to answer the gate notifications, and the delivery guy always needed a signature.

With the general housekeeping duties and email checked, Jack could now dig into Kaylee, if he could find anything at all.

False name, for sure, and likely there won't be anything on the police scanner, but I should check.

He dug in. Jack wasn't half as efficient as Azule would have been, but he managed. He responded to three new inquiries for Benton Security Services. One was for rich kid bodyguard detail for three months. He could put Aidan on it since the detail he was on was ending soon. He refused the second one out of principle. A protection detail for a well-known pedophile? No way in hell. The third was a general inquiry, and after a fair amount of searching through the files, he found the standard fee list and attached it to a form reply and sent it.

In between emails, Jack called Teeny and asked him to keep an ear out for any missing woman cases, car accidents in the area, and recent murders.

"Where's Az?" Teeny asked, sounding surprised when he heard Jack's voice.

"Out today."

"She's okay, though, not sick or nothing?" Teeny persisted.

Jack's eyebrows raised. "Uh, no. She's fine, Teeny." He listed out his requests and Teeny promised to message Jack's phone with the lists in an hour.

Jack grinned to himself. Teeny sounded a bit lovestruck over Azule.

Just as he set the phone down, an instant message popped up.

come back

"Shit." If Malcolm was asking for him to come back this soon, something had happened. He jumped up and headed for the house, taking the long, low steps two at a time.

"Mal? What's wrong?" Jack called as he loped into the house, the door shutting behind him with a slam. He saw instantly what the problem was. Kaylee was standing in the doorway of her room, clutching at the door frame for support, a jacket in one hand. Mal stood next to her, his eyebrows furrowed, silent, clutching the cell phone in one hand while steadying Kaylee with the other.

Jack ran up the stairs, reaching out for the girl just as she collapsed.

"I'm sorry," she said weakly. "I thought, I thought I was feeling better."

He pressed his hand against her forehead. Her fever was down, but she was still warm to the touch.

"I need to go," she whispered.

"Kaylee, I promise you, I will take you anywhere you want to go." Jack leaned down and scooped one arm under her trembling knees. The heat rolling off of her was concerning, and he was beginning to second-guess keeping her here. Perhaps she needed a doctor. He wasn't looking forward to explaining to hospital staff the marks on her ankles and wrists. They were livid bruises now, a deep purple and black in some areas, fading to a sickly yellow in others. "But please let me help you right now. I promise you; you are safe with me."

She weighed nothing. At least, nothing compared to what he dead-lifted three times a week with his trainer. Jack carried Kaylee easily back to her bed and set her gently down on the soft mattress. As he did, his nose grazed the side of her neck and he breathed in the faint scent of lavender and sandalwood.

"It's not safe for me to stay here," she whispered. "You aren't safe. He's not safe." Her eyes darted to Malcolm before returning to his. "I can't let them hurt anyone else." Tears pooled in her eyes.

Jack brushed a stray tear away with his thumb.

She's worried about me. About Malcolm. Not herself. What happened to this girl? Who has she lost?

"Kaylee, listen to me, please. You are safe here. I am safe, and so is Malcolm. I promise you that. But if you don't take care of yourself, if we can't get this fever down, then I will have to take you to the hospital."

"No hospitals."

"No hospital, no police, Kaylee..." He stopped, took a deep breath. Close behind he heard Malcolm shuffle through his binder and then it appeared next to him.

tell her

Kaylee read the words as well. A look of fear crossed her face. "What does Mal mean? Tell me what?"

Kaylee certainly fell under that category. Whoever she was, wherever she had come from, and whatever she had been through—it was all still unknown. But nothing about this girl struck him as being anything other than a victim here.

"Tell me what?" she repeated.

"I run a security service, one that protects those who need it most."

"A security guard business?" The look on her face made it clear she was unimpressed.

He fought down a laugh. "No, the people I protect are usually running for their lives, Kaylee. Like you. Women who are looking to escape abusive husbands. Witnesses of crimes who the police can't or won't protect." He reached for her hand, turned it gently, and traced the bruises on her wrist. "Someone hurt you, Kaylee. I can also see from your wrists that this same person restrained you for hours, possibly days. You don't trust the police, and you don't trust anyone, really. Considering what you have been through, that's completely understandable. But you need to trust me. I can help you, Kaylee, so please, rest. Please trust me to keep you safe. And when you are feeling better, I'd like to know what happened."

Kaylee nodded slowly. "Okay."

Jack smiled, relieved that she wasn't jumping out of the bed and running for the door. She needed to rest. Mal rattled the bottle of pills in his hand and bumped it against Jack's arm. "And that's Mal reminding me you are due for more Tylenol. That and a large glass of water," he added as Mal shoved two pills and a glass into his hand. "Apparently he is worried you are dehydrated."

Kaylee smiled at Jack's brother, her eyes warm. "Thank you, Mal." She didn't act concerned when Mal turned around and walked out of the room. Mal's silence, a hallmark of his autism, typically unnerved people, but Kaylee wasn't like the others. And somehow, that made Jack even more curious. What was her background? Who was she?

The questions kept piling up. Eventually, she was going to have to trust him enough to answer some of them.

No Recovery

She took the Tylenol, drank the water. Despite everything that had happened to her in the last week, Kaylee felt relatively safe here. More than anything, she was afraid of bringing down danger on more innocent people. Hadn't there been enough of that already? Learning that Jack dealt with dangerous situations, and could protect others, had eased many of her concerns. He had steered those two men away yesterday, and they hadn't returned. And then his employee this morning, which showed he could be circumspect, but battered wives were a far cry from international trade deals and multi-million-dollar illegal activities.

Whoever the Oladni Corporation really was, and what part Julianna might have had in it, was still unknowable. It made her question everything she thought she had known about her stepmother. Not to mention what role Cenac Shipping had in it all. The company was hers, her family's, and she was supposed to be running it just as her father did before her.

The heat from her body faded, the Tylenol taking effect, and as she slipped into sleep, there were two very different thoughts in her mind. One, what part did Julianna have in all of this. Two, what kind of man was Jack Benton and why, oh why, did she find him so attractive?

Memories of the days after the accident interceded, and Kaylee fell into a memory-filled dream...

Adrienne was relieved when they finally allowed her into Rainier's room. Father was in the ICU and the doctor had glanced at her before shaking his head at Julianna, explaining that his condition was still critical and that they allowed no minors on that floor. Her brother was on the floor below, recovering, and still woozy from the surgery that had been necessary to reset the bones in his legs. The nurse on duty seemed to take pity on Adrienne who, according to hospital policy, should have stayed in the waiting room.

"Just a few minutes, mind you." She leaned close and whispered, "If you see a doctor walk by, duck. You can't be in here without a parent."

Adrienne whispered an equally quiet thank you back, but the nurse had already disappeared down the hall. The room was quiet and empty except for Rainier's bed. She sat down in a chair on the far side, out of sight. She was small for her age, and with the hospital bed in the raised position that it was, the top of her head wasn't even visible. Rainier looked so pale, lying there in the bed, and Adrienne held her breath until she saw the steady rise and fall of his chest. They had immobilized both of his legs in bright, lime-green casts that ran from his ankles to his hips. There was a line of neat stitches along the side of his face, and she wondered how he had gotten it. The doctor had said Rainier had stayed in the car, thanks to his seatbelt, but that Father was thrown from the vehicle.

The embankment had been steep, some hundred feet or more of a descent before trees had stopped them. Adrienne had heard paramedics talking about it as they had walked by. They had needed the Jaws of Life to cut Rainier out.

No wonder his legs had been broken.

His eyelashes fluttered and Adrienne felt her tears spill over onto her cheeks, a relieved gush of them, as he opened his eyes and stared at her there next to him.

"Hey," he croaked and tried to shift in the bed. His lips thinned, and he winced.

"Hey," she said back and cried harder.

"Is Dad..." Rainier stopped, winced, his face twisting with pain. "Is he...is he okay?"

"He's in the I..." Adrienne hiccupped and sniffled, reaching for a tissue box, "...the ICU. He's hurt bad. They won't let me see, but they told Julianna that he was going to make it." She wiped her tears away, but they kept on coming, falling faster. "I was so scared, Rainier, and the doctor says Father might never walk again. And you," she said as she pointed at his casts, "Are you going to walk again?"

"Yeah. I'll be okay. It just really hurts right now." Adrienne could see that Rainier was crying too. Just a single tear tracing its way down his cheek, but definitely a tear. She had seen Rainier cry only one other time before. Last year, when Mom had died.

"What happened?" she asked, struggling to understand how they had ended up in such an awful accident.

Rainier shrugged and shook his head. "I don't know. One minute Dad was driving me to the orthopedist in Ponchatoula because she had screwed up and scheduled me for there instead of New Orleans like I normally do. Dad said he had a meeting out that way and so he would take me. The next thing I knew, the brakes stopped working. We were on Route 22, near that spot where it gets all twisty, and Dad just kept pushing down on the pedal and swearing. We couldn't slow down. And then the road took a real sharp twist, and we just weren't on the road anymore."

Another pair of tears leaked from his eyes and he brushed at them furiously, as if their existence on his cheeks was simply unacceptable.

Rainier stared at the empty room in silence before adding, "I bet she did something to the brakes. I bet she wanted us dead."

"Rainier! That's not fair. Julianna is nice," Adrienne protested, feeling defensive of her stepmother. "If you weren't so mean to her, you would see for yourself."

Her brother bit his lip. "You're just a kid. You just don't get it."

It hadn't been long before the kind nurse had returned. And with Adrienne now standing, hands on hips and looking ready to do battle, she was ushered back to the waiting room where Julianna, pinch-faced and looking angry, had appeared moments later. With a swoosh of her arm, she had grasped Adrienne's hand and pulled her towards the parking lot, Adrienne struggling to keep up with her stepmother's long stride.

"Julianna?"

"Put your seatbelt on, Adrienne."

Adrienne did as Julianna directed, the seatbelt barely in place before Julianna reversed out of the parking slot, tires screeching a complaint.

"Julianna?" she asked again. "Is Father going to be okay?"

Her stepmother yanked on the wheel and zoomed out of the parking lot, the car bucking over the speed bumps, waving a free hand dismissively at a security guard signaling at her to slow down. She didn't respond for a long time. By then they were on the freeway, heading home, and Julianna had cut off several other motorists, causing a cacophony of car horns in the process before she slipped past, moving over into the fast lane, and pushed the speedometer past 75 and kept speeding up, weaving among cars as she did so.

"Your father will need to be cared for, Adrienne. He'll need nursing care, now, and likely for the rest of his life." She passed another car, missing clipping its bumper by inches, and Adrienne flinched as the driver rolled down his window and screamed at the pretty red sports car that had nearly run him off the road. "The doctor is sure he will never walk again. There will be pain as well. Likely severe, and for the rest of his life. Thanks to the severe nerve damage." She sighed. "It looks as if I'll need to step up and take care of most of his business dealings. Thank goodness my family business runs itself."

As if she suddenly realized she was speaking to a nine-year-old traumatized by the events of the day, she looked over at Adrienne. "Oh, my dear, I am so sorry. I didn't even check on Rainier." She slowed the car. "Should we go back?"

"I saw him," Adrienne said, releasing the death grip she had on the side of her seat. "He's in two leg casts."

"Well, it's past dinnertime and I doubt you have eaten anything, have you?" Julianna nodded at the exit. "We'll stop and eat. Go back to the house and see if you can't get something to keep Rainier occupied for a while. He's going to be laid up in bed for weeks. And I'll need to contact a contractor to handle the renovations."

"Renovations?" Adrienne asked, faintly.

"Yes, the large room on the east side of the main floor. I'll convert it into a suite for your father. He won't be able to make it up the stairs, after all." She continued to talk, but for Adrienne it was all static. The room that Julianna was talking about had been her mother's art studio. It still was. The sun had filled the room with a natural light in the mornings, and Mom had spent hours painting and sketching. When they had come back from the hospital without her, it had been the one room Adrienne would spend hours in, just sitting, sketching buildings and columns, recording the details of the

ornate wood carvings above the mantel, like she had when Mom was alive. Nothing had changed in that room since Mom had died.

The antebellum mansion had been in the family for nearly half a century, and extended family for a century before that. Adrienne felt a little ill at the thought of what Julianna could mean by the term "renovations." What would happen to her mother's artwork and her supplies?

"A suite?" she asked, trying to visualize what Julianna could mean to do with the enormous room. The wood inside of the room was all original, the floor planks Cyprus and oak. Her mother had taken such care, laying down thick oilcloth to protect the floors, her paints, brushes, and more neatly placed in cabinets.

"Yes. It will need a bathroom installed that is fully wheelchair compliant. I hope we don't need to take out any of the wall on the north side to handle the pipes and wiring." Julianna turned abruptly into a parking lot in front of a greasy spoon diner. "They'll likely need to remove that monstrous fireplace and mantel as well." The tires spit gravel before coming to a stop. She pawed through her purse, then looked up to see Adrienne's look of horror.

"But you, you can't, Julianna."

A shadow crossed Julianna's face. She stared at Adrienne, tilting her head to one side, and the look on her perfect face chilled Adrienne. "I beg your pardon?"

"The, the, the room." She tried to stutter out an explanation. "Mom told me that the fireplace is original and the wood has never been painted, not in over 150 years. It's, it's, it's our heritage," she finished in a whisper. Bad enough that they would clear the room. In Mom's absence, just as it had been when she was alive, the room was a refuge, a place of peace. A place she could step inside and walk quietly through, touching the things that Mom had touched, breathe in the smell of paint and mineral spirits, note the paint that had flown down to the oilcloth below and tacked it in a spray of aubergine, of salmon pink, and a serene cottage blue.

Where would she remember Mom? Where would she go when the world outside became too complicated and loud and she felt as if she would lose her place in it? And to paint it. That would be a cardinal sin. Even Father would never agree if he knew.

From the moment that she had first met her stepmother, Julianna had been kind. Adrienne had never seen her grow angry, or frustrated, not even in the face of Rainier's obvious dislike of her intrusion into their family unit. The look on her face earlier in the day, when the doctor had told her how lucky it was that neither Rainier nor Father had died, Adrienne had already convinced herself that she hadn't really seen it. It disappeared just as quickly, and it could have meant anything, really. Father wouldn't have married just anyone. Not so soon after losing Mom. Julianna had her own business, her own wealth, she didn't need Cenac Shipping; she had her own business too.

But now, in the car's quiet, Adrienne saw someone different. This was not the woman who had laughed and rolled the dough out on the long marble countertop in the kitchen. She wasn't the one who had shared her lipstick one night after giving Adrienne a manicure, despite her ragged, bitten stubs of nails.

And then, just as before, the look vanished, replaced with concern. Adrienne could hear a burst of noise erupt from the greasy spoon diner as the door swung open, and a family breezed down the steps, laughing and talking, a bag of leftovers held in one of the teenager's hands.

Julianna reached out and took Adrienne's hand in her own. "Forgive me, Adrienne, I didn't think. Your mother's art, her supplies, and..." she said as she closed her eyes, rubbing her forehead with her free hand, "...today has been overwhelming. Of course, you are right, we will figure something out, so that your father will have a place that can accommodate him and we won't be changing the property. I'm just panicking a bit." She opened her eyes and smiled warmly at Adrienne, giving her fingers a warm squeeze. "I'm hungry and trying to problem solve. It's never a good mix. We will eat and I'll pack a bag for Rainier, all the pieces for him to futz about with his video games while he's laid up in the hospital, and we will talk to someone about getting a chair lift installed. How does that sound?"

Adrienne managed a smile in return. This was a side of Julianna she had never seen. Then again, her father and brother had nearly died today.

Julianna is just upset, like me. Except she doesn't get to cry or panic, because everyone is depending on her.

Still, the look on Julianna's face continued to haunt her long after they finished eating crawdads, etouffee, and gumbo at Big Sal's and headed home. A few weeks later, and both Rainier and Father were home. It felt weird. Rainier lay in his room, housebound, with only visits by the physical therapist for company for twelve long weeks as the bones slowly knitted themselves together.

Father was a changed man. The active, always on the go businessman replaced with a broken shell of a man. He rarely used the chair lift, preferring to stay upstairs in the suite of rooms he shared with Julianna. Adrienne would pass by his door on the way to her own room at the end of the hall. Usually, she would find him staring out of the window, his face slack and expressionless.

Rainier transitioned from the bed to a wheelchair and eventually to crutches. Spring gave way to summer, and summer moved into fall. It was nearly time to return to school, and Julianna had promised Adrienne she would take her shopping for a fall wardrobe in Baton Rouge. She skipped upstairs to grab her purse and slowed to a stop outside of Father's bedroom. Rainier was there in the doorway, watching, his eyes troubled.

"He takes too many pills," he mumbled. Father sat, unmoving, slack-jawed and staring.

"Julianna says they will help him feel better," Adrienne protested.

"Sure, if you want to be a zombie." He scowled. "She gives him too many pills."

Adrienne stayed silent. Part of her thought Rainier was wrong, but the person her father had become frightened her. It was as if that sharp business executive was gone, replaced by a ghost of a man who only looked like her father.

In the end, Julianna's voice had floated up the stairs and Adrienne had run away, relieved to leave the ghosts behind.

Move Aside

Jack checked on Kaylee every few hours throughout the afternoon and into the night. Her fever shot back up, barely responding to the over-the-counter medications.

Malcolm, who was dependable down to the hour and minute, maintained a vigil in the chair outside of Kaylee's door, waking Jack whenever the girl's temperature climbed past 102. Jack had seen nothing like it. Ever since Jack had brought his brother home ten years ago from the institution his parents had put their youngest child in, Mal had been a silent fixture in the rambling house. Jack had questioned whether Mal would be better in a group home, around others like him. He had even asked Malcolm if he wanted something different, and his baby brother had produced the same answer each time.

no

happy here

What was happiness for Mal? Jack couldn't detect a single iota of it on his brother's face. The only communication, the only sign, came from the binder of magnetic words. Over the years, the smallest of changes in Mal's pattern showed the most.

When Alexandra, his latest short-term dalliance, had invited herself over, and done her best to move in, Malcolm had made his displeasure known by slipping the following words to the front.

she go home now

He hadn't even bothered to cover them. Every morning, without fail, Malcolm had shown the words to Jack until, six long weeks later, Alexandra had set her sights on an easier, and far older, target. It had been a relief for all involved.

Mal liked Kaylee and showed concern for her welfare. Well now, that was something more than unusual. It was a good sign, really. And Jack nodded to his brother as the last of the night gave way to the bright morning sun. Kaylee's temperature was still over 102 degrees, and she was slow to respond to his efforts to have her drink more water, turning away before finishing the glass.

Azule's car turning into the drive at a quarter past eight was a surprise. Normally she arrived at a few minutes before nine, and Jack was sure it had to do with his assistant's curiosity. She cared little for being kept in the dark about anything.

Jack walked down the stairs and met her at the front door.

"Move aside, Jack." He suppressed a smile. Azule had a forceful personality. If he had ever wondered who the real boss was, he recognized the truth then: she was.

"Morning, Az."

"Well," Azule said as she turned to face him, hands on hips, "Who is it and where are you keeping them?"

"Her name is Kaylee, and she's upstairs in Allie's old room."

Azule nodded and headed for the stairs. Jack followed. In some ways, it relieved him Azule was here. She would know how to get the girl's fever down or likely die trying.

As Azule stared down at Kaylee, who slept on, unaware of the attention she was receiving, the older woman noted the thermometer and half-full glass of orange juice. Malcolm walked in, board in hand, and nudged Azule with it.

fever high all night

on the run

no hospital

Jack blinked. It was the most he had seen his brother communicate in a long while. And it showed he'd been keeping up as well.

Azule read the words and met Jack's eyes. "On the..." She shook her head. "And a high fever all night? Are you two trying to kill her?" She dug into her purse and pulled out her cell phone.

"Who are you calling?" Jack asked, and she gave him a frosty look, raised her palm towards him, and walked away to the far end of the room.

"Marley? I need Diamond at Jack's house. Tell him to rattle his dags too." She stabbed the End Call button with a fingernail and her eyes swept the room. "He'll be here in an hour."

"Who?" Jack asked, mystified.

"The doctor, of course." Azule walked away. "I told him to hurry, but there's traffic."

The short black man clad in ragged jeans and a T-shirt with Snoop Dogg emblazoned on the front with the words "Paid the Cos' to be the Boss" did not look like a doctor. Despite this, he set up an IV, complete with a collapsible IV stand, with a few quick, efficient movements.

"Um..." Jack stepped forward as the smaller man wrapped rubber tubing around Kaylee's arm.

"Don't worry, she'll be fine. I'm starting with a cocktail of antibiotic fluids on her," Doctor Diamond said, his voice cultured and reassuring. "Once she is awake, have her take these twice daily for five days and call me if you don't see improvement by tonight. She's receiving the first round via the IV." He set the bottle of pills down on the nightstand. Jack could see from the label that it was a common antibiotic. The doctor closed up his satchel. "That'll be one gee for the house call and antibiotics. I left my card there in case you need me again. Just return the stand when you get a chance, Az, I've got spares."

Azule slid past Jack and handed him a small stack of hundred-dollar bills. "Thanks for getting here, D, give my regards to your mama."

The man nodded and said, "Will do, Az. Hey, her birthday is on Saturday if you can make it. I know it would really make her day if you came by. I'm pretty sure she likes you better than any of us, anyway." He turned his gaze to Jack and offered a hand. "Pleasure doing business with you, Mr. Benton."

Jack shook the man's hand. "Thank you, Doctor." He watched as the man left the house, got into a van that had seen better days, and drove away.

"Who the hell was that, Az?"

"I grew up with him," Azule answered. "I've known him my entire life. His mama's house is just down the block." She shook her head. "Diamond there, he got out, was on track to be a bigshot neurosurgeon until his cousin went and borrowed his car. A week later, Diamond gets pulled over. The police want to search his car."

"Why did they want to search his car?" Jack asked, interrupting.

Azule gave him a look. "Because he was black, Jack. Why else? He was black, driving a nice Mercedes in a nicer part of town. So of course, they wanted to search the car. And he didn't think he had anything to hide, so..."

"So, he let them search it, and..."

Azule snorted. "It wasn't really a choice for him; he said yes so they wouldn't break a taillight or something worse." She stared at him with a look that spoke volumes and then shook her head. "Anyway, his cousin had neglected to remove all the cocaine, or had tried to skim it off of the top of the shipment. We never learned the entire story because the fool died of an overdose the week after they arrested Diamond."

Jack blinked. "So he has a drug conviction?"

Azule nodded. "Served five years, lost his license, and now he handles medical care for folks who can't go to a hospital without raising suspicion or causing the authorities to get involved."

"I'm guessing he does business with gangs?"

Azule gave him another withering stare. "And playboy billionaires who hide pretty girls away in their luxury homes. Diamond doesn't ask questions; he just takes care of his patients. He does what they trained him to do: be a doctor."

Jack nodded. "Fair enough, Az." She gave a harrumph and slung her purse over her shoulder.

"I took it out of petty cash, just so you know. I'm going to see what else you messed up in the office while I was out. You know where to find me." She headed out of the house without a backward glance, and he watched her make a beeline for the office.

He glanced over at Mal. His brother's fingers were busy with his board and folder full of words.

K better soon

tired

bed

Jack nodded. He slept poorly as well, but Mal had stayed in that chair all night. "You want any breakfast first?"

There was no answer, not so much as a head shake. Instead, Malcolm walked downstairs, pressed the panel, and disappeared inside with a quiet click.

Jack looked back at Kaylee, asleep in the bed, the IV dripping into her arm, the antibiotics on the nightstand.

You aren't doing her any good standing here staring at her like some damned pervert. Get to work, Benton. Find out who those guys were the other day, track down the lead, keep Kaylee safe, and stop thinking about her. She's a client.

That's what he kept telling himself, even if she hadn't agreed to it. She needed help, and that's what he did. Kaylee wasn't one of those models or wannabe actresses who could smell money a mile away. She was hurt, traumatized, and now ill. Once she recovered, he'd get her to tell him why she was running and who she was truly running from. And he could help her then.

He shut the door to the guest suite gently. She had slept through Doctor Diamond's visit, hadn't even twitched at the needle piercing her skin, and he could only hope that this would be what she needed.

He walked downstairs, stopping at the kitchen long enough to grab an apple to take the edge off of his hunger, and headed for the office.

Azule was waiting for him to arrive. She looked pissed. Her hands were on her hips and one foot was tapping in time as she barked out her questions. They were the same questions he had been asking for the past two days.

Who was she?

How did she get those marks on her wrists?

Where did she come from?

Why no police or no hospital?

Jack held up a hand, his lack of sleep catching up with him.

"Az, please, I don't have any answers yet."

The black woman's foot tapped faster until she was practically stomping. "Well, what do you know?"

Jack sighed and sat down in an armchair, relinquishing the power of the room to Azule, whose fiery eyes showed she was questioning everything, including what part he had played in the whole debacle.

"I found her on the side of the road, about a mile from the house. She had those bruises, scratches, and injuries from a car wreck."

"A car wreck!" Azule barked. "She could have internal injuries!"

"Az, please, hear me out. I checked for injuries. She's fine."

"She sure as hell doesn't look fine, Jack." She parsed her words, pausing between each for emphasis. Jack couldn't remember the last time she'd looked this angry.

"The rain soaked her to the bone. It stormed Saturday, do you remember?" Azule arched an eyebrow at him and said nothing. "Look, she likely caught a cold from the exposure. I don't know how long she was out there, but she had climbed out of the wreckage, up the embankment, and was there by the side of the road when I came along at what, one or two in the morning?"

Azule gestured for him to continue and Jack did, explaining the first few hours, her panic at the thought of involving the police, and the two men who had come by the house looking for her.

"Why didn't you tell me all of this yesterday?"

"She was so panicked every time, I just needed to gain her trust more than anything." Jack shrugged. "It seemed the best course of action."

"Well, it wasn't," Azule said, her eyes still angry, a flash of hurt seeping through.

And suddenly, Jack understood. She was worried about him, not just Kaylee.

I upset Az when I excluded her and sent her away. Shit.

"Az, I'm sorry. I should have told you. I should have trusted you and told Kaylee that as well."

Azule raised her chin, nodded, and said, "Apology accepted."

She sat down in his office chair with a sigh, "I worried about this all damn day and night, wondering what was going on that you wouldn't let me in. Well, what's done is done. Now we have to get those answers, find out who that girl is, where she's from, and what the hell happened to her, before someone else comes sniffing around looking for her." She tapped her long nails, painted a deep, metallic green, on the rich wood of the desk. "You think she's on the up and up?"

Jack nodded, relieved that Az was focusing on Kaylee and not him. "I do. She's young, maybe twenty, or twenty-two?"

Azule snorted. "That girl isn't a day over nineteen."

Jack sat back. "What else did you notice?"

"Manicured nails, eyebrows been shaped, and her hair might have been colored. She's got dark eyebrows, but brown hair with blond streaks. I'd have to hear her talk, but I'd guess she comes from money, like you."

Jack gaped at her. "Damn, Az, that's a lot of noticing for just a few minutes with her."

"What was she wearing when you found her?" Azule asked, a flicker of a smile on her lips.

"A dress. Blue. It was pretty torn up; I tossed it in the trash."

Azule stood up and walked out of the office without a word. Moments later, she was back. "Gucci."

Jack shrugged; he never looked at labels, or price tags. "And that means?"

Azule gave him another one of her looks. "The girl is a trust fund baby, just like you, Jack Benton."

"So, a kidnap victim?" he mused.

Azule shook her head. "Not if she was afraid of the police."

Jack rubbed his forehead. A headache was forming, and it exhausted him. "I don't know what it could be then. She's too young to be a battered wife. A kidnap victim wouldn't be afraid of the police. And she's too scared to be playing games and be the one up to no good here."

"And she won't tell you anything?" Azule asked, frowning.

"No, nothing. Other than she doesn't want me to get hurt." He paused. "Her words were, 'I don't want anyone else to die because of me.'"

Azule folded her arms over her ample chest and stared off into the distance. "We need answers."

Jack nodded. "We certainly do."

Wrong Place, Right Time

The room was quiet, the voices who had filled it, gone. Kaylee opened her eyes. The door was closed, the curtains drawn. She wasn't sure if it was day or night. They'd secured the tubing that ran from the IV bag to her arm, and the bag was nearly empty. She contemplated taking it out. Her fingers moved to the spot, ready to peel away the adhesive, but then she stopped. If there was something inside meant to keep her unconscious, well then, she wouldn't be awake. Perhaps it was to help, not hurt.

Her eyes focused on the bottle next to the bed and squinted at the label. Something ending in "cillin"—which meant an antibiotic. She must have been sicker than she realized.

She remembered Mal's steadfast presence in the armchair outside of her door. How long had he stayed there? It had felt like forever. Jack had been in and out as well, talking to her, reassuring her. Kaylee squirmed with discomfort at that memory. She smelled, she was sure she did, and that was not attractive at all. She wanted to get up, take a shower, feel clean again.

He was hot. Several of her dreams had included him, and man, had they been X-rated.

Am I truly safe here?

The men had come, and he had headed them off. But they might come back. She shivered at the thought. It was an impossible situation, one that she couldn't seem to figure a way out of. If only she had known to hide, or stay silent. She wished she hadn't overheard what she did, or gotten Rainier involved. If only she had understood the depths of danger that one overheard conversation would put her, and the only family in the world she had left, in. If only she had understood how much was at stake.

She closed her eyes as the memory of that moment came flooding back. It began, of course, nearly two months before, with Father's funeral.

Julianna's hand was warm compared to Adrienne's. The rain hadn't been unusual, but the temperatures, normally warm by early May, had been unusually cold. It seemed appropriate for where they were, and Adrienne shivered under the black tent, shifting on the hardness of the wood chair. Rainier was on her left, and Julianna on her right, the rest of the mourners scattered behind them, the chairs half-empty. The rain fell steadily on the tent, and Adrienne could see that the back of the minister's coat was becoming soaked as he stood, his back to the rain, and extolled the virtues of a man who had once headed a shipping empire. Julianna squeezed Adrienne's hand as the man, a stranger who knew nothing of the past decade's slow and inevitable descent into addiction and despair, continued to speak of "dedication to his family" and "forward-thinking" and all the rest.

"Garbage, all of it. Who is this guy?" Rainier grumbled next to her. He said it low, but it was loud enough for Julianna to hear, apparently. Her grip on Adrienne tightened.

Moments later, the minister led them in a prayer and Adrienne wiped her eyes and did her best to smile graciously as the mourners filed past, offering their condolences. What did it matter, really? Father had been as good as dead the moment his car went off the cliff nearly ten years ago. As they lowered the casket into the ground, she could feel the tears wash down her cheeks. For the death of their family unit, the happiness that had once filled their home, and the loss now of both of her parents. She was an orphan.

Julianna handed her a tissue and rubbed her shoulder. Rainier cast a dark look at the woman and Adrienne felt ill. Even here, even now, his antagonism towards their stepmother was so obvious. To her credit, Julianna never responded or grew angry, and that somehow made it all the worse in Adrienne's eyes. She loved her brother, but would it kill him to be kind? To be polite?

She shot Rainier a look, and he looked away. The mourners had dispersed and now the gravediggers waited, likely hoping that the rain would abate long enough for them to do their job.

"Come, they are waiting for us to leave. There's a reception back at the house and the others will be waiting." Julianna tugged at Adrienne's lapel, pulling the black coat closed around her. "This weather, it will make us all ill if we stay out here much longer."

Adrienne stood and walked with Julianna, only to realize that Rainier was not next to her. She turned back, and he shook his head. "I'm not going. None of those people care. They barely knew Father."

It was her look of anguish that seemed to change his mind. "Okay, but I've a flight out this evening."

"Rainier, there are financial matters to discuss. Your father's will, and his wishes," Julianna interjected.

"Father's wishes were that I run the business after he passed. But you seem to handle that well on your own, Julianna." He waved his hand when she protested. "Please, we all know who has been in charge of Cenac Industries since the accident, and likely even before that. I want no part of it. Besides, I have finals next week."

Adrienne suppressed her tears. She had missed him, dreadfully, in the past two years. The day he turned eighteen, just two days after graduation, had been the day he moved out. He had enrolled in a college on the west coast, chose a major of marine biology, and had avoided visiting home for the holidays two years in a row.

She told herself it was for the best. He had been miserable since Father married Julianna, even more so after the accident. And while she hadn't believed their stepmother had had anything to do with the accident, Rainier had held onto it, even tried to have it investigated, which had of course come to nothing.

He had been closest to Father. And as their sole remaining parent had slowly faded away in front of their eyes, lost in a sea of pain and addiction to the pain medication and his now severely limited life, Rainier too had pulled away. He would escape each weekend to his friends' houses and no longer wanted to have them come to his. It was hard for both of them, but far harder for Rainier.

"Rainier, please stay the night," Adrienne asked, her voice hitching with emotion. "For me?"

Her brother looked at the ground. "I'll see if they can reschedule the flight to tomorrow morning. But I am not staying for the reading of the will." He shot a glare at Julianna. They were now at the parking lot, and he stood still for a moment before looking up at Adrienne. "I'll drive you home, Sis." He had rented a car and it sat a short distance from Julianna's sleek forest-green Jaguar.

Julianna said nothing. She squeezed Adrienne's shoulder and nodded, turning away. Moments later, they followed her car in silence, the rain still falling, and the windshield wipers steadily clicking away.

"How is school?" Adrienne finally asked.

Rainier sighed. "It's great, actually. I love it there. You should come and visit this summer."

"I'd like that. A lot."

"Where are you planning to go in the fall?" Rainier asked, his fingers tapping out a rhythm on the steering wheel in time to the windshield wipers. "Did you settle on Cornell?"

Adrienne gulped past the tears that were threatening again. "No. Father said I should study business instead. I'll intern at Cenac this summer and enter Harvard in the fall."

Rainier frowned. "And Father suggested this? Or was it Julianna?"

"Well, of course it was Father, Rainier. I mean, Julianna told me, but she was just repeating what he had said."

"And when was that, Adrienne?" her brother pressed, his fingers tightening down on the wheel until his knuckles turned white.

"I don't know. Months ago, I guess. I mean, come on, Rainier, you know all I want to create is the Victorian era in buildings. I would have been hopeless as an architect." She shrugged. "Father is just looking out for me."

"And Julianna gets just what she wanted," Rainier hissed. "She's getting you out of the way, just as she did Father. You'll spend the next six years in college and come back to a business you don't even recognize."

"At least I'm coming back to it, Rainier! Father wanted you, not me. As if I had a choice. As if you even cared!" The last words flew out of her mouth and she dissolved into tears again. The last thing she wanted was to fight with him. Rainier was the only family she had left. As kind as Julianna was, she wasn't Mom.

They pulled into the driveway in silence, and Adrienne dried her tears. As she slid out of the seat, Rainier said quietly, "Don't trust her, Adrienne. She does not have your best interests at heart. She doesn't care about either of us."

One month later, she had walked into Cenac, her stepmother by her side, for the first time in years. Adrienne had dressed in a slim pantsuit, one of a new wardrobe full. Julianna had taken her shopping days after Rainier had left without another word early in the morning.

"Now, we are starting you out on the ground floor, Adrienne. A simple girl Friday kind of position. This is only for a short time, but you need to understand how this company works, from the ground up," Julianna said, beaming. "That pantsuit looks absolutely lovely on you! I'm so glad we went to White House Black Market; their line fits you well."

Adrienne smiled in return. It felt awkward, strange. There had been little to smile about. Graduation from high school was supposed to be the beginning of it all, but it had felt so anti-climactic instead. Her friends were going to far-off places, but none to Harvard, and certainly no one was working this summer as she was.

An hour later, she filed thick folders, all alphanumerically, then assisted the mail clerk in delivering the interoffice envelopes. She had even taken notes at a meeting. In some ways, it was just what she needed. She remembered with great fondness when she would visit Cenac with her mother for lunch with Father. Some faces were familiar, but much had changed in the years. The support staff, the guards, the mail clerks, and the receptionist in the front all smiled and told her how much she had grown, but the secretaries and many of the managers and other higher-ups were unfamiliar, different.

"How was your first day, Adrienne?" Julianna smiled at her from across the table. It was a small bistro, one that she had never visited before. Julianna had ordered a watercress salad and roast duck. Adrienne had settled on a seared salmon over wild rice.

"It was strange to be back there. I used to go often with Mom and we would make a day of it after taking lunch with Father," Adrienne answered, picking at her salmon. "It was familiar, and yet not, at the same time. So many unfamiliar faces."

"The nature of business, dear. People come, they move up, they move on," Julianna said and slipped a bite of her salad in her mouth.

"Father used to say that he didn't believe there should ever be turnover. It showed the company was unwilling to grow with their employees, or vice versa."

Julianna blinked, and for a moment Adrienne saw a flicker of something move across her face. It disappeared the next second as her stepmother smiled and said, "My goodness, I did not know he had talked about the business with you. I'm happy that you remembered such a conversation. It bodes well for the future of Cenac in your hands, Adrienne. Once you have finished your studies, of course."

Adrienne smiled back at her stepmother, Rainier's words from the day of the funeral bouncing about in her thoughts. She focused on her food and tried not to think any more about it. After all, Rainier had never given Julianna a chance, never warmed to her, and certainly spent no more time in her presence than he had to. He had to be wrong. He just had to be.

The next week, however, changed everything.

Adrienne had moved from one department to another, receiving brief overviews of how each interacted with the other. The thrill of it coursed through her. This would be her company one day. Her employees. Overall, everyone was friendly and took the time to answer her questions, of which she had many. The unfamiliar faces were predominantly in power positions, and when she would ask about their predecessors, there were few answers. It was as if they had simply disappeared. She brought it up again with Julianna, only to receive a dismissive wave of the hand and an offhand comment about how many had reached retirement age. It made little sense. Most of them had been Father's age, and certainly not ready for retirement. And their replacements were in their late forties to early sixties, so it just didn't add up. And if that had been the only thing different, Adrienne wouldn't have given it another thought. But the atmosphere in the company had changed, drastically. She questioned her memories over and over, comparing them to the daily reality as she walked the halls. The managers were polite, willing to answer her questions, but she could feel a reticence, an almost invisible wall, one that stood between her and the others. It was unnerving, and she wondered why Father had truly wanted her to take her place here.

It was a Thursday, in mid-June, when everything came crashing down. She was working in a small office outside of a conference room, filing documents, when she heard the voices. She recognized them instantly—they were both high in the ranks—and Julianna had introduced them as her "right-hand men because in a world like this, you need two!"

"Hastings bungled it big time, and if we don't get on top of this, we are toast," Tom Denkins said, his voice cracking.

"Well, Julianna already knows we didn't fuck it up, so there's hope." The second voice was gravelly and belonged to Jerry Einsdale, the VP her stepmother had said she hired personally shortly after Father's accident.

Tom swore. "She rushed it. She ordered it dumped, and soon, and Hastings did as she asked, and now we've got three hundred dead or dying villagers to deal with. They'll track it back."

"Not to us. To Cenac," Jerry replied with a short, barking laugh. "That was the plan all along. Lay it all at the feet of Gerard, then Julianna and the rest of us walk away scot-free as long as we get rid of the evidence."

"Yeah? And how the hell are we going to do that?" Tom asked, his voice rising. "The village is steeped in toxic waste and the deaths are increasing."

"We burn it to the ground," Jerry responded calmly, and Adrienne felt the hairs on the back of her neck rise. "Tactical strike. Say they were hiding insurgents, and that backwater country's military will take care of the rest. Why do you think she donated millions to Cruzar's campaign?"

Adrienne could not believe what she was hearing. Part of her quivered in fear as well. If they were willing to kill hundreds of people to cover up something, what would they do if they found her?

"So, burn it to the ground and kill the trail back to us, and Cenac, and it buys us time?" Tom's voice had leveled out. "Damn, that's brilliant."

Jerry laughed. "Don't mess with the best. I'll propose the strike, in case she hasn't already thought of it, and the rest will just go away. No one's going to build a new village on the bones of the dead. No one will discover the toxic waste's source, and it will dissipate in the Pacific quick enough. Then it's back to status quo for another six years, or longer if that girl is slow at her studies."

Adrienne sucked in a breath. She felt cold seeping into her bones. They were talking about her. She had to get out of here. Now. She looked around the room wildly. There was only one way in or out of it, through the conference room that was currently occupied by the two men. There was also nowhere to hide. She reached for her purse, for the phone inside. Perhaps she could call the police, or Rainier, or... The change she had received for the soda sitting on the filing cabinet jangled. Not a loud sound, and nothing that should have been noticeable above the two voices...if they had still been talking. Instead, the noise had come at a lull in the conversation.

"What was that?" Tom asked, suddenly alert to her presence. The door to the room was open a crack. And Adrienne did the only thing she could think of at the moment.

She slipped her earbuds into her ear, turned away from the door, and faced the filing cabinet and hummed as if in tune to the music. In the seconds before the door was flung open, Adrienne quickly hit Play on her music and shoved the phone into her pocket, gyrating her hips. She slid the folder into its alphanumerical slot and, pulse pounding, turned to pick up the next. Tom Denkins stood there staring at her and she jumped slightly, then pulled the blaring earbud out of her ear.

"Oh, hi!"

He stared at her, and Jerry appeared behind him, a pleasant grin plastered to his face. It didn't reach his eyes.

Tom had paled slightly, and now he reddened. "What are you doing here?"

Adrienne forced a vapid, half-bored look on her face. "More of this boring filing stuff. It's, like...endless." She paused and did her best to morph into a confused, somewhat put-out look. "Was, like, the room scheduled or something? Do I need to come back later?"

Jerry smiled wider, showing his teeth. "No, no, not at all. Carry on."

"Okay. Whatever." Adrienne shrugged, her heart hammering in her chest, and turned away, slipping the earbud into her ear and surreptitiously turning down the volume to zero. A moment later, she heard them leave. She stood there for seconds, maybe minutes, trying to calm her heart rate, to stop the shaking that had overcome her.

The façade of working for her family's company, the dream of becoming their future CEO evaporated, and suddenly all Adrienne wanted was to run away. She slid her phone out of her pocket and dialed the number. It rang three times before the voicemail engaged. She waited for the beep and said, voice shaking, "Rain. You were right. Call me back right away." She paused for a moment, then added, "I'm scared, Rain, I need you."

I Dreamed of You

His lips grazed hers, and she wrapped her arms around his neck. She had to stand on her tiptoes to do it, but the heat of him and his musky scent were intoxicating. The kiss deepened, and he groaned, his tongue entwining with hers, his hands roaming down her sides to grab hold of her ass and pull her up, suspended from the ground, pushed against the cool, hard wall, her body touching his. She could feel him throbbing against her lower belly.

"Adrienne," he breathed, pulling back to meet her eyes, "I want you."

His hands moved back to her hips, the left one sliding its way along the edge of her panties, the fingers working their way to her clit even as his mouth broke away from kissing her, headed towards that sensitive spot behind the ear. Bursts of sensation blew through her every time his fingers moved and she moaned, digging her fingernails into his back as he continued to stroke her, teasing each new spark of sensation until she couldn't think of anything past this moment, this man.

The feel of his strong, muscled back under her fingers, not an ounce of fat, just pure muscle was intoxicating. It put the boys she had dallied with in high school to shame. They didn't hold a candle to Jack. Adrienne gasped as his fingers continued on their quest, pushing her closer and closer to ecstasy.

The bird fluttering its wings and squawking loudly nearby shattered the dream into pieces.

Kaylee blinked, stretched, and felt a tug on her arm. The room was dimly lit; it was sunrise or sunset by her glance out of the part in the curtain, and the gloom spread long shadows in the room. The door was closed, and she noticed with some alarm that there was an IV bag, empty now, hanging from a pole next to her bed and a tube trailed from it to a neatly wrapped bandage on her arm.

Did he drug me? Wait, this was here when I woke before, wasn't it?

Her panic subsided as she read the side of the bag and surveyed the bottle of pills. Antibiotics, a saline drip, not drugs. Well, at least, not any bad ones, from the looks of it. She wanted the IV out of her arm. Her fingers gently pulled the IV out, then tossed it aside. It hurt more to pull the bandages off as they caught at the fine hairs on her arm.

She felt...better. Less groggy, less hot. The fever seemed to have passed. Had they called a doctor? They must have.

I need to get out of here. A doctor will talk.

She swung her legs off of the bed and stood up. A wave of dizziness hit her and she sat down again.

Okay, so not completely better yet.

The dizziness eased and instead was replaced by two things: body odor and a growling stomach, neither of which she could fix by sitting on the side of the bed. She stood up, swaying a little, but feeling less dizzy. She needed a shower. Thankfully, there was one just fifteen feet away.

Kaylee looked down at her clothes. She was still wearing the borrowed pants and shirt. She hoped it was okay to borrow something else. Moments later, clothing discarded in a hamper, she leaned against the cool tile of the shower and let the water cascade over her. The heat of the water was invigorating, and she felt better than ever. Stronger. It was as close to ecstasy as she was going to get. Outside of the dream that still lingered in her mind, that is. She could still feel Jack's mouth on hers. His fingers, his... Kaylee shivered with desire. The man was undeniably hot. In another place or time, would she act on her desires? Most definitely.

Kaylee chewed on her lower lip, closed her eyes, and her fingers traveled down to that sensitive nub, her own finger tracing it gently, imagining it was Jack here in the shower with her. She rubbed harder, faster, and the water continued to cascade down her neck, tenting over her hand, swirling around the drain. She watched the fireworks explode behind her eyes as she came and opened them, only to find Jack standing there, mouth open, his eyes traveling up and down her body for a brief second before he wheeled around and put his back to her.

Kaylee gasped, reaching for the tiny washcloth on the handle, as if that was enough to hide her body from him.

"I apologize," he said, his hand raised in defense. "I just woke up, heard the water running, and wasn't thinking. I'll, um, just go downstairs now."

Kaylee's face felt flushed and hot. He had walked in on her in the shower. That was bad enough. But to catch her masturbating? And oh my God, masturbating to her dream of him!

She shut the water off, exited the shower, and grabbed a towel before peeking through the open door. The bedroom was empty, the door to the hall firmly closed. She toweled herself off and picked an outfit out of the closet. Whoever had occupied this room before her, they had been the same size, even down to shoe size. Her mind briefly flashed on a sudden paranoid thought.

Did he have all of this ready for me? Is this all an elaborate ruse of Julianna's to discover what I know or what evidence I might possess?

And just as quickly, she realized she was truly being paranoid.

Complete with an autistic brother and a house that was obviously owned by someone with considerable wealth? Right.

It was far more likely that Jack was just who he said he was. That he was wealthy was obvious. He talked and walked and acted like everyone else she had ever grown up with. As she pulled on the yoga pants, crop top, and a light sweater, she wondered if this is what he meant when he said he "used to" have other siblings besides Malcolm but didn't any longer. Was she wearing a dead girl's clothes? She had a quiver of discomfort with the thought, but then instead her thoughts flashed back to him coming into the bathroom, seeing her naked, her fingers between her...

He was staring at me. I should be creeped out by that, but I'm not.

Instead, it left her embarrassed and weirdly turned on. Her fingers slowed and paused as she bent to tie the shoelaces of the shoes she had found neatly arranged on the bottom shelves of the closet. She felt horribly self-conscious. Could she actually go down there and look him in the eyes? Perhaps she could just make a run for the door.

Right. Run out of the man's house. After all, this is probably the only safe place in the world for you right now. After all, they can track you with the first swipe of a credit card. The police seem to be in on this, and every person you love is dead.

She finished tying the shoes and then stood up. The truth of the matter was she didn't know how far Julianna's reach extended. And she wasn't willing to risk her new friends' lives finding out.

Face it, girl. You can't even tell him your actual name. That's how scared you are.

She stood up and straightened her clothes, ran her fingers through her damp hair, and let out a long sigh.

The person you were. She's dead. Adrienne Cenac is dead, or as good as.

All that mattered now was survival. Somehow, she had to disappear. Completely. How did one do that without access to her family's money?

Kaylee realized she had been standing there, immobile for several minutes. Her stomach growled, and she shrugged.

Time to feed the beast and figure a way out of this.

She walked to the door, flung it open, and walked down the hallway before she lost her nerve. Jack was in the kitchen, vegetables sizzling in one pan, bacon in another. She felt the flush creep back up her neck and face. She paused on the stairs, then squared her shoulders, walked down them, and slipped into a seat at the breakfast bar. Jack turned towards her. "Kaylee, I am so..."

She held up her hand to stop him, her eyes avoiding his. "Please, it's fine, really." She could feel her own blush start up again. "Let's just forget it ever happened, okay?"

"Right, okay." He turned away, back towards the stove. "I'm fixing omelets again. Honestly, it's the only meal I'm good at."

Kaylee smiled at his back. "You make an excellent omelet."

The smile he flashed her before turning back to his work made her weak in the knees. It was devilish and sweet, all rolled into one. Was it any wonder she'd had such an X-rated dream of him?

"I'm uh, glad to see you are feeling better," he said, glancing back at her. Her cheeks burned. He was playing it straight, except for a twist of the lips, and she giggled first, her face in her hand. When she looked up, he was smiling in a way that turned her insides to jelly.

Before she could stop herself, the words fell out of her mouth. "I had a dream and you were in it."

He turned off the burners and slowly turned towards her. His hands held his weight as he leaned across the countertop, drawing closer to her than he had been since that first night when he carried her inside of his house. This close she could see the shadow of hairs on his cheek, neck, and chin. His lips looked as kissable as they had in her dream, with a rakish tilt at one corner of his mouth. His smile had vanished, replaced by an intense gaze that turned her insides to jelly.

"Was I?"

It suddenly felt like there wasn't enough air in the room. Her body thrummed as she watched his gaze slide from her face down to her crop top, before stopping at her belly-button piercing. The one she and Sydney had gotten on the same day last summer right before their senior year began.

She didn't trust herself to speak. Couldn't speak, actually. His eyes, dark brown with flecks of gold, sparked a sexy smile sliding across his lips.

Kaylee wondered if he was going to ask her if that was what she had been thinking of when he caught her there in the shower, but he didn't. Instead, he let the moment between them stretch, elongate, and heighten. Suddenly, Kaylee didn't give a damn who was chasing her, or what the days before they had met had been like. Their eyes locked.

He'd seen her naked. And not just naked but... touching herself. He moved closer, inches away now, and his lips parted slightly, betraying a set of perfect, white teeth.

"What if I told you I had a dream about you as well?"

Kaylee's body reacted, the thrum inside of her increasing, searching her mind for something witty or sexy to say. She felt, no, she *knew* she was out of her league. He had at least ten, maybe even fifteen years on her, and she knew countless women had likely warmed his bed. In comparison? She had gotten hot and heavy with all of two boys. And they had been boys, not men.

If the moment had not been interrupted by two very anti-climactic reasons, Kaylee knew that other far more deliciously sinful, pursuits would have been engaged in. But just as their lips hovered millimeters apart, her stomach ruined the moment by growling loudly. Malcolm's sudden appearance sealed the deal when he chose that moment to slip out of his basement lair with a tiny creak and click of the door.

If Jack's brother noticed how quickly Jack and Kaylee jerked away from each other, or how red Kaylee's cheeks became, his face did not show it. His binder under one arm, Malcolm slid into his customary seat, set the binder on the breakfast bar, and began plucking words out to add to the magnetic front. He slid it towards her and flashed her a sideways glance.

K better

yes

Kaylee smiled, trying to cool her burning cheeks down with her fingers. "Yes, Mal. I am feeling better. Thank you for asking."

Jack, who had returned to cooking, turned to give her an appreciative smile, nodding slightly, as if in approval.

Malcolm's hands were busy plucking words out once he put the first ones away.

K like word game

"Word game?" Kaylee turned to Jack, questioning, eyebrows raised.

"Mal wants to know if you like playing Scrabble. He's mad for it. It's okay if you don't; he takes rejection well," Jack explained as he cracked eggs and whisked them together.

Kaylee grinned and clapped her hands, turning to Malcolm. "I happen to *adore* Scrabble, Mal. I used to play it with my mom and my brother. I would love to play a game with you later."

She was picking up on Mal's tells. It wasn't easy. For most people, it might appear as if he had no expression on his face, but the tiniest flash of emotion showed, if only one paid attention. A tiny flicker of a smile appeared and then disappeared just as quickly, along with an almost imperceptible nod of the head.

Kaylee knew she should think about leaving here. She needed a plan. She needed to find a place to hide, to start over, if possible. Somewhere no one would think of her, no one would know who she was. But the thought of it, it was so overwhelming, frightening, really. She had played Scrabble with Mom, and later, with Rainier. It was a series of happy memories, one that meant far more to her than she could put into words. She should think about leaving here, before she brought danger crashing down on all of their heads, but in a few minutes, all Kaylee could think of alternated between kissing Jack and playing a game of Scrabble with Mal.

Jack slid a plate with a perfect omelet on it in front of her. He met her eyes when he did it, and her stomach flipped at the intensity of his stare. She had almost kissed him. And right now, if Mal hadn't been there, she would have grabbed ahold of his black silk tee and gone for it. Kaylee shelved that desire with an effort and looked away from Jack, down at the food. Her stomach rumbled again.

"This looks divine. Thank you, Jack." She dug in her fork and tried not to react when he walked around and slid into the seat next to her, his fingers brushing her shoulder as he did. She trembled slightly in response; her nerves alight, sensitive to the slightest touch.

"Azule will be here soon," he said, and cut a piece off with his fork. "We have an early meeting. A conference call with one of our offices on the East Coast."

Kaylee grew rigid, anxiety filling her again. She set her fork down.

Jack put a hand over hers reassuringly. "You may not remember, but Az arranged for the doctor. She will say nothing, and neither will the doctor. I promise you."

"She already knows about me?" Kaylee asked, the past forty-eight hours mostly a blur from the fever.

Jack smiled, his hand still over hers, warm, strong. "Yes, she saw you, actually. It rather annoyed her that I sent her home on Monday instead of 'fessing up." He grimaced. "There isn't much of my life that she doesn't know about. Her family has worked for mine for the past four decades, possibly longer, and I trust her implicitly."

Sitting there, her hand enveloped in his, Kaylee felt torn between wanting him to hold her and keep her safe, or kiss her and do far more than that. Her stomach growled again, and her cheeks flared red.

"Oh my God, seriously." She glared at her belly and Jack laughed and released her hand.

"It's a good sign," he said, eyes twinkling, "that you have your appetite back. Eat up."

Kaylee picked her fork up and closed her eyes as the first bite of omelet slipped into her mouth. She couldn't help wondering what else he could do besides serve up luscious, mouth-watering, perfect omelets.

Those hands, for example. Such long, dexterous fingers.

The Walls Have Ears

Rainier didn't call her back that day.

Adrienne pled a migraine the next morning, complete with a cool cloth over her eyes. When Julianna knocked on her door, her keys jingling in her hand, Adrienne felt every bit of the part she was playing. She hadn't slept, not at all. Her head was pounding and her stomach roiled as the door creaked open.

"Oh honey, you look miserable," Julianna said, her voice oily with concern. Adrienne wondered if her stepmother had always sounded that fake and that she just hadn't noticed, hadn't wanted to believe it.

That Rainier was right all along. That she's a liar, that she doesn't care about me or Rainier, or even Father.

Her mind had taken her all kinds of dark places last night.

"Perhaps I should stay. Maybe take you to the doctor?"

That was the last thing Adrienne wanted. "No, I'll, I'll be fine. I just need to rest." She could feel nausea rising in her as Julianna drew closer. "I was reading some early syllabi for my classes in the fall and I guess I shouldn't have read in the dark. It's just a nasty headache. I took two aspirin a few minutes ago. I, I'll be fine in a few hours."

She couldn't see Julianna's face, what with hers being covered with the damp cloth, but her stepmother seemed convinced. She retreated to the door.

"I'll bring you a cup of tea. It always helps me with my headaches. I'll be right back." Adrienne could hear Julianna's steps, purposeful, quick, as she strode away before Adrienne could object. A few minutes later, she could hear her stepmother climb the steps, pause for a moment, and then stroll the rest of the way down the hallway.

"Come on now, Darling, sit up and drink this. I guarantee it will help."

Adrienne hated the thought of Julianna in her room, but it was quite clear her stepmother was going to insist, so she sat up and squinted, the headache intensifying in the dim light. Julianna had dressed in red from head to toe. Adrienne remembered she had an important set of meetings today. She had mentioned it over dinner, going on and on about global positioning and new contracts. She stood there, a smile on her lips, the lipstick blood red to match her suit, stiletto heels to finish it all off.

No wonder Father fell for her. On his arm, they made the quintessential power couple.

Julianna handed her the cup of tea. "I added a touch of milk. It's a special blend and I promise you, drink this and in a couple of hours you will feel as right as rain." She smiled widely, her perfect, white teeth dazzling.

Was she really involved? Directing this? Did she really want all of those villagers dead? It seemed impossible.

Adrienne took the cup from her and sipped. The floral notes tasted odd with the milk, and there was a bitter aftertaste. She wrinkled up her nose and Julianna laughed.

"It isn't that bad, Adrienne. All Chinese herbs and flowers. Very good for you. Drink up."

She sat down on the side of the bed and Adrienne forced another gulp down. It tasted less nasty than the first sip. She wanted Julianna to leave, so she could try to call Rainier again. And it was obvious her stepmother would not leave until she finished the whole thing. Three more large gulps and she finished, a fine sediment of white coating the bottom. Adrienne poked at it with the spoon and shook her head.

Julianna laughed again and patted her shoulder. "Good enough. You will feel fine. I'll come back home at noon and check on you."

The warmth of the tea was settling her belly and spreading out through the rest of her body in a soft glow. Adrienne lay back on the pillows, her head feeling muddy, slow. Her eyes drifted shut, and she opened them to see Julianna watching her, the corners of her mouth curled up, satisfied.

"Get some rest," she said and gently lay the damp cloth over Adrienne's eyes. Adrienne yawned and heard her stepmother's steps as she closed the bedroom door behind her gently and then began walking down the hall.

Her eyes felt heavy. All of her felt slow, muddled, and as Adrienne's eyes slipped closed, she could hear Julianna speaking. It wasn't to her and there was no one else in the house. She tried to focus on the words, tried in vain to open her eyes, to sit up, but she couldn't. Long before the sound of Julianna's Jaguar roared to life and drove away, Adrienne had already sunk into unconsciousness.

She was ripped from sleep by Rainier's voice and his hands on her shoulders shaking her. "Adrienne! Adrienne, wake up!" Sunlight poured into her windows, and Adrienne blinked groggily, confused.

"Rainier? What are you doing here?" She tried to sit up and listed to one side, her limbs loose, uncooperative. Her brother steadied her.

"You called me. Yesterday."

"Yeah." She nodded slowly. Why had she called him? Why did she feel so tired? "I, um, I overhead this conversation, and..." Why did she feel so groggy? And confused? "What time is it?"

"Nearly noon. I've been calling and calling ever since the plane touched down."

"Oh. I didn't know you were coming to visit," Adrienne said, feeling thick and stupid. She could hardly think and it was impossible to concentrate. "Julianna will be home for lunch." She was waking up more now, and her words sounded slurred, slow.

Rainier leaned away from her, picked up the empty mug of tea, and stared into it. "What did she give you?"

"Tea."

"Yeah. Tea and something else. Damn it. We gotta go. Now." He stood up and walked over to her closet and opened the doors.

Adrienne pushed herself up. She had listed over the moment he let her go, dizzy and tired. Everything felt awkward. "What are you doing?"

"Trying to find something for you to wear. You need to get dressed. Now, Adrienne. We need to leave."

She wished he would slow down. He was so impatient, and he was moving way too fast. He yanked a handful of clothes off the hangers and tossed them towards her. Adrienne tried to catch them, but they fell flat, inches from her fingers.

"Would you just wait a minute? I can't, I can't think."

"No surprise there," Rainier said, and shoved her covers off her and pulled her to her feet, reaching down and tucking her clothing in a wad underneath his arm. "She's got you drugged to the gills. Just like she did Father." He took her hand and pulled her after him. "Come on, you can get dressed in the car."

"What? Wait. At least let me get some clean underwear." Adrienne could hear her voice now, her brain waking up faster than her body or her mouth. She was definitely slurring her words, and she was so tired, it was hard to keep her eyes open. She pulled away from him and lurched towards the dresser to retrieve a bra and panties. When she turned around, Rainier was standing, her clothes under one arm, her purse clutched in his left hand.

"Geez, okay, I'll change in the car." She rolled her eyes. It all felt rather dramatic. Even if what Rainier said was true, whatever was coursing through her bloodstream felt nice. She allowed her brother to hustle her along the long hallway, down the stairs, and out to his waiting rental car. The sun was high overhead, and the air was hot and muggy. Her headache had vanished. At least Julianna had been right about that. She didn't resist when Rainier bundled her into the passenger seat and shut the door. His haste to get away from the house was obvious as the car lurched forward and the wheels spun momentarily on the blacktop. They careened out of the drive, Adrienne snugly belted in, feeling rather exposed with only her crop top and pajama shorts covering her.

"I won't look." Rainier pointed to the pile of her clothes between them. "Just get dressed. I'll get you to a Starbucks, get some coffee in your system, flush the meds out."

"At least slow down first!" she protested, and immediately the car slowed as her brother released his lead foot from the accelerator. "Where are we going, anyway? And why did we have to leave the house?"

"Because the walls have ears, Sis. And you aren't safe there, not anymore. Hell, maybe we never really were." He kept the wheel steady as she shimmied out of her pajamas and into the clothing he had grabbed from her closet. As soon as her seatbelt was back on, he sped up. "I don't want to pass her on the road."

"Where are you taking me, Rainier?" Adrienne demanded, feeling more wakeful by the moment. Her body felt strange, numb, and kind of...floaty. What the hell had Julianna given her? She wondered if it had been some of Father's pain meds. There was an enormous bottle of them still sitting there in Gerard and Julianna's bedroom suite. She remembered how Julianna's steps had paused for a moment and then restarted down the hallway, moving slower than normal. Or had she imagined it?

"To the airport," he answered.

"What?"

"What did you find out? Was it about Dad?" he asked, pulling off the highway onto a side road that led to the nearest Starbucks. Adrienne looked down and realized she didn't have shoes.

"About Dad? No." She looked down at her feet. "We need to go back to the house. I don't have any shoes."

Rainier glanced down at her bare feet and swore as he wrenched the wheel hard into the parking lot. The car tires came up on the curb and the car lurched. "I'll buy you shoes on the way to the airport." They pulled into the drive-thru and he glanced at her. "Your usual?"

"Make it a venti instead of a grande."

He grinned and placed orders for both of them and then drove forward to the window.

"So, this isn't about Dad?" he pressed, looking confused.

"No. Why would it be about Dad?" Adrienne frowned as she waited for Rainier to pay for the coffees and hand over her cup. She sipped at it gently as he pulled away from the window, his own cup set precariously between his legs.

"Because I know Julianna killed him. I just can't prove it," he said, piloting the car out of the parking lot and waiting for an opportunity to merge onto the main road.

"Rainier, that's insane!" She took a sip. It was hot, but the coffee washed away the fuzziness she still felt. Her limbs and the rest of her body were coming out of it, but she still felt loosy goosy, high even. Like the time she had smoked weed with Sydney at the back of the bleachers after school. She had hated the feeling of it, her body suddenly uncoordinated, her mind fuzzy and slow.

Rainier shot her a glance that screamed "stupid little girl" and pulled out into an open spot neatly. "Okay, so what did you uncover?"

Adrienne told him about the overheard conversation and how she had played it off with the earbuds and pretended to listen to loud music.

"Huh." Rainier appeared to mull it over in his mind. "This makes sense, really. I thought she married Father for his money, but now I'm wondering if it wasn't something else."

Adrienne took another sip of the hot coffee and willed the fogginess to clear. "Control of the company?"

"Yeah. And the ability to make Cenac a legitimate cover for some far darker dealings." Rainier nodded, thoughtfully. "We need to get to California and talk to Lincoln."

"Lincoln? Who is Lincoln?" Adrienne felt out of touch. There had been a time when she knew every single one of Rainier's friends. Often, his friend's younger sisters or brothers had been her friends as well. She had never heard of a Lincoln.

"He's a friend. A couple of years ahead of me. He just graduated with a degree in Journalism," Rainier explained, as the car edged onto the on-ramp that would lead to the airport. "He's been helping me look into Father's death."

"But Father died from complications from the car accident, Rain." Adrienne was feeling as if she had ventured into the Twilight Zone. Sure, Julianna was up to no good at Cenac, she could see that, but kill someone? That was extreme.

Rainier gritted his teeth. "Sis, I love you, I really do. But you really are annoyingly optimistic. Before I got your call, Lincoln had just scored records showing that Julianna had two separate doctors prescribing medications to Father that could be deadly when mixed. We have the prescription bottles, I just needed those records, and Lincoln found them. But this, what you overheard yesterday, this takes it to a whole new level."

Adrienne rubbed her eyes. "But, Rain, murder?"

Rainier reached over and grabbed her hand. "Come with me to California. I'll show you everything Lincoln and I have cobbled together. See it with your own eyes."

He pulled into a parking lot next to a low-slung building with a large, red Avis sign on the front of it.

"I need shoes, Rain."

"The airport terminal will have some, don't worry." He squeezed her hand and parked the car.

Julianna was sitting in her office when her cell phone rang. She stared at it for a moment, then answered on the third ring. "Yes?"

"The house is empty. There's no one here." The man's voice was professional, no pleasantries given or expected.

"She should be dead to the world in her bed," Julianna barked. "I gave her enough to knock out a man twice her size."

The voice on the other end was unmoved. "All I can tell you is that she isn't here. I checked everywhere."

Julianna felt a surge of fury rush through her as she pressed the End Call button. Where the hell had Adrienne gone? And how? She had watched the girl drink every drop of the tea. She had laced it with two of Gerard's pills. There was no way that girl should be conscious, much less gone. And where could she have gone? She scrolled through her contacts, looking for Adrienne's friends' names. She would have to call each one. Her fingers were shaky. She would call them all before calling her back with an update.

And if you can't find her, you know who you will have to talk to next. You'll have to call her; *you know you will.*

Julianna felt a thick wedge of anxiety form in her chest. Of all the people she didn't want to call with failure, she was the one. Her stomach flipped, and she crossed her fingers for a moment before locating Adrienne's friend Sydney in her phone and pressing the Call button. She would find Adrienne, get her back to the house, take care of this. She wouldn't have to call her with an admission of failure. Anything but that.

Scrabble Me This

Jack tapped his foot, irritable, eager for the phone conference to end.

Azule had shown up a few minutes before seven and given Kaylee the once-over before chivvying Jack off to the office. As they walked, she kept smiling, but said nothing, just kept eyeing him with sidelong glances and that infuriating smile.

"What?" he finally broke, "It's obvious you have something to say, so, say it."

"I don't know what you are talking about, Mr. Benton," Azule responded with a smirk.

She never called him that.

"Damn it, Az!" he growled, and she laughed, a deep belly laugh that bent her over at the waist.

"She's a beautiful girl," she noted, once she had stopped laughing.

"I hadn't noticed," Jack responded, deadpan.

"No, of course you didn't." Azule took her customary seat in the conference room and leaned back. "Well? What have you learned about her so far?"

Jack sprawled in the chair at the end of the table. "That she likes my omelets and seems willing to play Scrabble with Mal."

"Wait." Az tilted her head. "Mal likes her?"

"Yeah, I think he really does." Jack threw his hands up. "Mal doesn't like anyone but you. He barely tolerates me."

"You know it's true," he insisted, as Az rolled her eyes. "It's the damnedest thing, really. He actually asked her to play Scrabble with him. And she didn't bat an eye. Truth is, she looked excited about it. I can't think of any woman under forty who likes Scrabble."

Azule fixed him with a hostile glare, her head bobbing on her neck. "Oh, you did not say that to me!"

Jack suddenly remembered that it had been Azule who had first introduced Mal to Scrabble. It was what had led to the magnetic letters, which had been a breakthrough that had rocked their world.

"Except for you, Az, of course." He tried to recover from the faux pas while Azule's head bobbed like an angry chicken, her neck gyrating back and forth. "When does that conference begin?"

She glared at him and wrenched the intercom/phone combination over and stabbed at the buttons with a sharp, long, perfectly manicured nail.

"It starts in one minute," she snapped.

Jack winced and hoped it wouldn't take her long to forgive him.

He leaned back in his seat, his thoughts focusing on his brother. Mal was like a puzzle box. It took the right person, with the right combination of inspiration and intuition, to understand the labyrinthine twists and turns of his brother's mind. Mal remained locked inside of his own head, thanks to the autism. In some ways, that had given him a bit of an advantage. Because he didn't talk, or even react, in a way that others would consider normal, often people's reactions were to ignore Malcolm, as if he were a piece of furniture or something incapable of feelings. Just by existing, Mal was a great barometer for measuring the worth of a person as well. Every single woman he had dated, even considered living with, or brought home, had failed that test. Until now.

Jack sat back in his chair as the call connected and wished he could go back to the house. He would even be fine with a game of Scrabble, especially if he got to go toe-to-toe with a beautiful girl.

He flashed back to this morning, both embarrassed and turned on by what he had seen. What in the hell had possessed him to walk into that bathroom? Sure, he hadn't had his morning coffee, but what did he expect to find? Had there been any thought in his head at all?

At least, not a single thought in the *larger* head.

And the sight of it, Kaylee standing there, the water pouring over her, eyes closed, her fingers between her legs, pleasuring herself. He hadn't stood there one or two seconds; he had stood there for at least two minutes, frozen in place, his dick harder than Chinese algebra, eyes locked on her.

What kind of pervert am I, anyway?

He tried to shift his attention to the phone conference. It was impossible. He simply could not concentrate. For each number or percentage rattled off, his monkey brain injected "naked thigh" or "suds rolling off her breasts" pictures, overwhelming any of the more mundane, practical affairs of running a billion-dollar business.

Luckily, he had Azule, along with a host of smart, thoughtful managers on the other end. Az had picked them personally, winnowing out the old-school, predominantly stodgy white men for young, forward-thinking, hard-working men and women. They crossed ethnicities and cut the median age by nearly half. Some of them didn't look old enough to drink, but they sure as hell knew how to double, triple, and even quadruple the business since coming on board. As it was, he didn't really need to be here. The meeting practically ran itself.

Jack sat up straighter and Azule looked confused for a moment, then outraged as Jack stopped the head finance gal in the middle of her report.

"My apologies, all, but I, uh, I have an important meeting I forgot all about."

He ignored Azule's hissed, "What are you doing?" and stood up.

"I'll leave you to it then. Az will give me the highlights." He practically ran out of the door, holding in a laugh until he was out the front door of the office and halfway to the house.

The scene that greeted him looked normal and odd at the same time. If anyone else had happened upon the two of them, it would have looked like Kaylee and Malcolm were engaging in a perfectly normal game of Scrabble.

If anyone who willingly *plays Scrabble could be considered normal.*

For Jack, however, the scene was at the very least odd, if not downright surreal. He stood there watching them, and neither had noticed his return. Kaylee was sitting on the couch, leaning forward to stare at the board and then back at her letters, and Mal also studied the board quietly, without a hint of emotion.

She lay down a short word, just four letters, and Mal made his move seconds later, expanding on her own word and hitting a triple word score.

"Participate? Ugh, Mal, were you lying in wait with that one? Can you see my letters? I swear, I think you can read minds as well!" She said it all with a grin on her face and it was clear she was enjoying herself. As for Malcolm, it was obvious to Jack that his baby brother was happier than he had been in a long time. Happier than he had been since they lost Allie.

Jack's heart panged with loss. It had been over eight years now and it made no difference. The memory of her loss was as painful today as it had been then.

Kaylee looked up with a start and spied him watching them. She blushed again, and Jack suppressed the urge to walk over, swing her up over his shoulder, and march her off to his bedroom.

Suds. Steam. Hands between her...

"I didn't hear you come in, Jack." She smiled and pointed to the board. "Mal is handing me my ass in this game. I think he is up to 230 points to my 98."

Jack smiled back and sat down on the couch next to her. He could tell from the way she shivered that he was affecting her just as much as she was affecting him.

I sure would like to know about that dream she had with me in it. I don't think I would mind reenacting it.

"He got me last week with perambulate. I'm convinced he is psychic or a cheat, likely both."

Mal opened his binder and laid out words in the middle of the magnetic front.

no just better

Jack and Kaylee laughed as Kaylee pointed to the board. "He's right. I'd say he could win at competitions." She turned to Mal and asked, "What about it, Mal? Would you ever like to play in a Scrabble championship?"

She watched as he assembled the words.

too many people
shake hands no

Kaylee tilted her head in confusion for a moment. "Oh, they ask you to shake hands at the beginning and end of a game? I understand. That would be difficult." She said nothing for a moment, thinking, and then said thoughtfully, "It is something you could learn to do, Mal. Just like anything, it takes practice. You could practice with Jack, or me while I'm here, or possibly Azule." Her lips curved up into a kind smile. "I think that if you wanted it bad enough, you could whomp a Grandmaster, show them who is the real boss at Scrabble. If I can help, you just let me know, okay?"

Jack saw Mal's head nod. A quick jerk, really, but far more than he usually did to acknowledge another in conversation. And as impossible as it might have been, it also looked as if a ghost of a smile had just run across his baby brother's face.

"Ooh, it's my turn, isn't it?" Kaylee busied herself with plucking out tiles from the velvet bag before handing it forthrightly to Malcolm. Jack's jaw dropped to see Mal reach for it, brushing his knuckles against Kaylee's. Malcolm normally could not stand another person's touch at all. He had been that way since he was a toddler. Jack hadn't forgotten the earsplitting shrieks from a far younger Malcolm that had sent his parents scrambling to a developmental psychologist. The diagnosis had been swift, brutal, and had set Jack's parents on the path that led them to institutionalize Mal when he was eight.

Jack's hands clenched at the memory. Allison had cried herself to sleep for days. She had been closest to him. It seemed incomprehensible that Malcolm's absence could fracture the family to such a degree, but it had. Jack had never forgiven his father for it. Instead, he had escaped into parties and fast cars and more. Anything but return to a home devoid of his silent youngest sibling.

"Jack? Is everything okay?" Kaylee's voice interrupted his dark memories.

"Hm? Sorry. My mind was miles away." He realized the board was now empty and Kaylee was handing a tile rack to him.

"I was asking if you would play as well. A third player can make the game even more fun. I used to play with my mom and brother all the time when I was a kid." Her smile clouded momentarily as she mentioned her mother and brother, and Jack wondered if she would ever be willing to share her story with him. He could feel her moving closer to that point, though, and moments of normalcy, like this one, could only help.

"Absolutely," he said, taking the tile rack from her. He winked. "If we cheat, I think we could beat him together."

Kaylee laughed and shook her head. "No way, I'm going to beat the two of you fair and square!"

What followed was a marathon of Scrabble games, broken up by a quick lunch, before they all dove back in for another, and another, and finally Jack stood up, stretched, and felt his back crack.

"I'm done for. If I lose another game to you or Mal, I'll be plagued with insecurity for the rest of my life." He shifted his gaze to Kaylee. All morning, through their early lunch and now mid-afternoon, he had felt their connection building, growing, tightening. His hand had grazed hers multiple times and she hadn't flinched when he hugged her the one and only time he hit a Triple Word score.

It was time to act on it. Time to take a moment away from all of this and be alone with her. Maybe he could get the answers he was hoping for. Maybe not. But he knew one thing for sure, if he didn't find a way to be alone with this woman, he might lose the opportunity altogether.

Practice Makes Perfect

"Shift your body to the left, lean back on the ball of your foot, and maintain your center of gravity," Nyra barked at her sister. The girl glared, but obeyed.

"And again," Nyra ordered, and attacked, swinging her staff at Zella, and Zella met it with solid resistance. Nyra feinted right and cracked the girl on the knuckles. Zella yelped in pain and attacked her staff, blurring as she swung it toward Nyra's skull, murder in her eyes.

Nyra stepped to the left and felt the breeze as it missed her head and grazed her shoulder. She grinned sadistically. "Better." Then she grasped her own with one hand and jabbed hard into Zella's gut, knocking the wind out of her. The girl fell on her butt with a small "oof" of pain, followed by a hiss of anger, and her staff whistled along the ground, slamming into Nyra's shin.

Nyra found herself on the ground, looking up as Zella, now on her feet. Zella copied the move Nyra had done earlier, jabbing downwards toward Nyra's guts, her eyes black with rage.

Nyra whacked the girl in the side of the head, knocking her off-balance, and as the stunning blow superseded Zella's bloodlust, the younger girl slumped to the ground. Nyra wrenched her sister's staff out of her hand, climbed to her feet, and stood over her.

"You'll never win if you let your anger take over, Zella Dean." She smirked at the girl lying on the ground holding her skull. "And you sure as hell will never win over me."

Zella mumbled something and spit bright red blood into the dirt. She got up slower than normal, but Nyra could see the girl wasn't done yet. Nyra grinned at her and tossed the two staffs off into the brush and crooked a finger at her sister. Zella charged at her, a wordless scream on her lips. It ended, as it typically did, with Zella on the ground. She was unconscious this time, however, and Nyra laughed and walked away. The girl would learn, just as Nyra had, and a few minutes on the ground in the scorching sun would serve her right.

She left Zella on the ground, and jogged the half mile back to the cabin. She had eaten a sandwich and was reading when Zella finally made it back. Zella's right eye was swelling and her lower lip split, the blood dried and black. She was also sporting a mild sunburn, which would quickly fade and turn her skin an even deeper olive tone.

Zella said nothing, walking past Nyra as she lay in the hammock. Nyra heard her curse again, and walk out of the cabin, practically stomping as she drew to within two feet of the hammock. Nyra didn't look up. Instead, she kept her focus firmly on the words on the page.

"You made lunch and didn't bother to make me any?" Zella growled.

"Losers fix their own meals," Nyra said, and continued to read.

Zella stomped away, back inside, and the pots and pans clattered loudly as the girl made her own meal. Once silence ensued, Nyra sat up and walked back into the cabin. Zella stared up at her moodily from her space at the table, then returned her gaze to her meal. Nyra settled into the chair on the opposite side of the table. She didn't enjoy sitting with her back to the door, no matter how isolated they were from others. She rubbed the tattoo on her wrist, remembering the day she had received it. It had been a day much like this one, only she had been the one lying in the dirt after.

Zella eyed the tattoo and took another bite of goulash, her split lip bleeding. She winced in discomfort but said nothing. "When will I get the tattoo?"

"When I think you are ready."

Nyra's sister grunted in anger. "Well, that'll be never then."

"You need to be more patient. You can't just act like a berserker; there are situations that will require finesse."

Zella rolled her eyes. "Next you'll have me reading that stupid book."

"You would do well to study *The Art of War*, little sister."

"This hand-to-hand combat is bullshit, anyway," Zella grumbled. "Give me a Glock any day of the week."

Nyra shook her head. "There are plenty of times when you will need a quieter alternative. A Glock is loud and draws attention when we need quiet. We kill and we vanish, that's our job."

"I still prefer my Glock. And a silencer works wonders." She scraped the bowl clean, stood up. and took it to the sink.

Nyra watched her move. She wasn't the jumpy, traumatized child she had been a year ago. But the trauma had transformed into a black, roiling anger, and a fury towards men the likes of which would cause waves if their employer caught wind of it. The anger worked for now. It had turned Zella into a thing of deadly beauty as her body, once bruised, underfed, and violated - had toned, strengthened, and grown over two inches since they had come to this desolate place. There had only been one incident, and Nyra had dealt with that. It's easy to make a body disappear in the desert. No one had even come round looking for him. Not that they would have known where to look.

Cut in under an outcrop of rock, the cabin was a perfect hideaway. It was here that Nyra had insisted on coming when she learned of the fire. She had taken a leave of three months to ensure her sister recovered from the abuse she had endured in their parents' home.

When Nyra had left home at fifteen, Zella had been nine, and their father hadn't looked at her twice, not with his sights set on Nyra. That had apparently changed when Nyra left.

Zella had been a shadow of the sister she had left behind. If it hadn't been for the anger she had seen in the girl's eyes, she might well have left her there, standing by the smoking remains of their childhood home. But Zella had set the fire, of that Nyra was certain. And could she even blame Zella? Their father had been a monster, their mother too weak to stop the atrocities from occurring, and Nyra had been too young, too desperate to escape herself to take her sister with her when Zen she ran away.

Her years with the Indalo had shaped her into a killing machine, one that had a pretty face, perfect body, and was just as perfectly lethal. And soon, the Indalo would have two perfectly trained killers. Another year, possibly two, and Zella would be ready, if Nyra could teach her sister to transform her fury into precision and stealth.

"Delta wants you cross-trained," Nyra said, wishing she had a way to take the patience she had learned and shove it into Zella. Her sister's endless capacity for anger and violence was exhausting.

Perhaps if I had gotten her out of there sooner.

But she hadn't. It had taken Delta's voice on the phone to send her scrambling to get back to the backwater hole of a town in the middle of Oklahoma. "Your sister set fire to your family home, Nyra." Delta had sounded calm, unruffled. "Assess the situation and if she is trainable, bring her back." How Delta had known this, when the local law enforcement seemed oblivious, Nyra was unsure.

A town that small didn't have any children's division or social workers—those were all in the next town over. The next-door neighbor, saddled with Zella until they had found suitable placement, didn't argue when Nyra had shown up at their door—especially when Nyra handed the thin-faced, twitchy husband a roll of crisp hundred-dollar bills with the advice to report Zella as a runaway. They looked positively relieved to have the girl out of their house, especially the mother, who held her young daughter close to her the entire time Nyra stood in their living room.

It occurred to Nyra that if Delta had seen Zella first, she would have likely left her there. She would have seen the maelstrom of dark fury the girl held inside of her far more clearly than Nyra had. Instead of assessing, Nyra had reacted on a gut level, powered by fear and guilt. She had gotten Zella out of there and realized later just how damaged she was.

Just as Nyra was about to speak to Zella, the phone, plugged into a solar charger that hung on the outside wall, its cord snaking inside through a rough hole in the wall, rang. The sound of it nearly made her jump in surprise. It had been silent for so long, months upon months.

She had asked for three months, which had turned into six, then nine, and now a year. In all of that time, the phone that only Delta ever called Nyra on had remained silent. It wasn't silent now, however, and both Nyra and Zella turned to stare at it. Zella picked it up and was about to hit the Accept Call button when Nyra warned her off. "Don't. This isn't for you. Not yet."

She took the phone from her sister and answered it. "Yes?"

Delta didn't waste words. She didn't ask how Nyra was, or even Zella. "I have an assignment for you. Details are at the drop site." There was a click, and the phone went dead.

Nyra nodded and set the phone back in its spot, connecting the charging cable once again. She looked at Zella. "Right. We have two weeks of food left, more if I'm not back soon."

"Where are you going?" Zella asked, her eyebrows furrowed. "And when will you be back?"

"I don't know. I'll know more once I get to the drop site."

"I'll come with you," Zella insisted, and Nyra could see the curiosity oozing out of her.

"No." Nyra shook her head. "Until you are one of us, you aren't, and you aren't involved. Delta was clear on this." She spun on her heel, walking out of the cabin with nothing other than the water bottle in her hand.

The drop site was two miles to the north, on the far side of the low hills they sheltered within. Another two miles beyond that was a private airfield. The Indalo kept the utmost secrecy, using dead drops that detailed the target, along with a need to know basis among a select few at the airfield. And assassins like her were nameless and unknown, just as Delta and the other high-ranking Indalo preferred. Nyra picked up the package. It included plane tickets, an ID identifying her as Nancy Smith, and a stack of cash tucked into the pockets of her nondescript outfit. As the tiny plane taxied down the runway, with Nyra as its sole passenger, she read over the dossier for Adrienne Cenac.

They had already dealt with one of the two Indalo who had failed to secure the target. Nyra had met him briefly while on an assignment outside of Los Angeles. The dossier detailed the girl's escape from two Indalo agents whose cover with the LAPD kept them in the know. And thanks to patchy surveillance of the surrounding area, all that the dossier could tell her was that Adrienne Cenac, age eighteen, was likely still in the area where her car, or the car of one of the Indalo agents she had escaped from, had been found.

Nyra leaned back and closed her eyes, aware that the pilot was watching her with open curiosity. She had at least two hours until they arrived in Las Vegas. There she would walk onto a flight to Los Angeles, dressed conservatively and armed with a boring name and an unremarkable identity.

I'll dress as a survey worker and get into each of the properties of at least one mile in each direction of where they found the crashed car. A survey for women only. Yes, that will do nicely. Something to do with makeup.

She typed a text message on the new burner phone and requested a MAC makeup samples case sent to the hotel room reserved for her in Los Angeles. Time for a nap. It would give her a chance to think over her approach if the survey taker angle didn't pan out.

A Walk in the Woods

"Take a walk with me," Jack said, and Kaylee sensed an undercurrent of intensity in his words. The spark between them was growing, feeding on the connection between them. Part of her wanted to stay where it was safe, here in the house. Perhaps challenge Mal to another game that she knew she would lose.

That would have been the safe way out.

Instead, she rose from the couch and slipped on the shoes she had found earlier in the day in a closet near the front door. A glance back at Mal before the door closed behind them and she could see him putting the pieces of the Scrabble game back in the same precise manner he had unpacked them with.

Jack was close, his lips brushing her ear as he spoke, "I want to take you to my favorite place in the entire world."

Kaylee shivered. Since the moment they had nearly kissed, heck, before that, Jack's presence was causing a low hum of anticipation to flow through her body. Despite the complications it created, on top of all the other complications and tragedies of the past two weeks, all she could think about was the way her body had reacted to him earlier.

The attraction between them was undeniable. And of all the men to fall for, someone with his background, his abilities, well, she knew she wouldn't get him killed. She had enough death on her conscience as it was. Rainier, Lincoln, their deaths kept running through her dreams, and they haunted her in the day as well.

"Where are you?" Jack's voice interrupted her thoughts. "You suddenly went a million miles away."

She hadn't paid attention to where she was walking, only to the fact that Jack's hand was in hers. The house was behind them now, most of it obscured in the thick line of trees and shrubs. He paused, squeezed her hand gently, and Kaylee's thoughts of others, anyone but Jack, fled. She stared up at him, mesmerized. He was older than anyone she had ever dated or flirted with. His dark hair was threaded with silvery gray, but his body was fit, lean, and he towered over her by at least six inches, likely more. His dark brown eyes were gazing steadily into hers. The look in his eyes turned up the hum in her body another notch and part of her wanted him to kiss her, now.

"Sorry."

"Don't be. You just looked like you had the weight of the world on your shoulders." He reached up with his free hand, traced the line of her jaw gently, then pulled away. "I promised to show you my favorite place, but it is a bit of a hike. Are you up to it?"

The body aches were still there, but not as bad as they had been in the first few days. Kaylee knew she would be fine, and being outside in the fresh air, away from the others, just her and Jack, well, that was well worth a little discomfort.

"Absolutely."

He grinned, his teeth white and perfect, and he tugged at her hand gently. "It's this way."

The path was well-worn, not just by human feet, but by deer and what appeared to be an enormous dog. Jack pointed at one particular track, deeply embedded in the thick mud that had now dried, hard as concrete.

"Mountain lion," Jack said, and placed his hand next to it for comparison. The track was slightly smaller than his hand, and Kaylee gasped. The pad of the track had three distinct lobes and she could see the hint of claw marks above each of the four toes. "Likely running," Jack said, "normally you can't see the claws otherwise."

He grinned up at her and winked. "Don't worry, she's likely long gone by now."

Kaylee still jumped a moment later at an unexpected screech. "What was that?" She closed the short distance between them, and Jack's arm slipped protectively around her.

Jack laughed. "Likely a parrot; they infest Pasadena, but I keep seeing them here as well."

Kaylee felt embarrassed. "Oh." His arm slid slowly off of her and she stared at the ground, trying to ignore the hum of attraction she felt towards him that had ratcheted up yet again with such near proximity.

"It isn't much further," he said, his stride lengthening, and Kaylee quickened her pace to match.

She looked back over her shoulder, but the house had long disappeared. The forest wasn't quiet, but she couldn't hear a single sound from the city, which she knew was quite near. It felt as if she had stepped into the middle of an untamed wilderness, one that contained just her and Jack, with the sounds of the parrots screeching, the gentle breeze making the trees creak gently, and the leaves fluttering. Kaylee could just barely make out the sounds of their feet scuffing the now-hardened mud.

It smelled different here. The Louisiana bayou had a swampy, almost pungent odor, but these woods smelled of dirt and pine. Kaylee was so caught up in the smells and looking off into the distance that she was unaware of the enormous tree until they stopped at the base.

She gasped with surprise. They had stepped into an opening in the forest, one enforced by the gigantic tree with roots that curled up out of the ground at least twenty feet in each direction, supporting a trunk that split into several smaller trunks, which in turn each climbed towards the sky. Interwoven through the tree was a structure of sorts, more than one, all connected by swaying bridges. The posts that supported it all were at regular intervals along the ground, gently woven among the tree roots in a way that would not harm the tree or disfigure it.

"It's a fig tree, native to Australia, and they planted it in the mid-1880s, according to family lore." Jack's mouth hovered at her ear, sending a shiver down Kaylee's spine. "It's approximately ten feet taller than Big Tree, in Glendora, and stands at over one hundred feet tall. My great-great-great-grandfather planted it. They had sentenced him to the penal colony in Australia. He worked off his sentence and ended up owning a fleet of sailing ships back in the day. He ended up marrying a woman from the Serrano tribe who saved his life. Beginning with my grandfather, a series of treehouses were built with each new generation. We have taken care not to damage the tree, and the tree is still growing. My design is near the top. Are you up for a climb?"

The dirty part of Kaylee's mind visualized their two bodies entwined far above in the branches of the tree.

The way he said it was intentionally seductive, thrilling, and the thrum increased, suffusing her body with desire. Kaylee shivered again, and nodded, not trusting her voice to stay even. They had been teasing, sparring, and dancing around this since she first opened her eyes in his car that first night. She could see that now.

There was a short run of steps up to the first platform, but after that Kaylee could see that it would take some work to get to their goal, the tallest part of the structure obscured by the tree and the network of rope and wood bridges and other small platforms and treehouses that wrapped around the tree.

Jack stepped forward, his long legs carrying him up the steps and onto a small platform. He turned and held out his hand, a devilish grin on his lips. His button-down shirt and linen trousers weren't intended for climbing trees, yet somehow, they looked perfect on him. He was handsome and sexy as hell, and Kaylee felt a flush of desire course through her. What would he be like as a lover?

Climb the tree and find out, girl.

She ignored his outstretched hand and reached for the first handhold, a rope looped gently around a thick branch, and climbed.

Jack followed, and when she looked back, his eyes were on her butt, right where she wanted them. She wasn't a fainting lily, she could take care of herself, and now that her bruises were fading and her body had recovered from the fever, he needed to know that she wasn't just some damsel in distress. She wanted to meet him on a level playing field, not have him think she was weak and in need of protecting. That kind of thing was only interesting for so long, usually until the next damsel in distress came along.

She stretched and pushed herself, despite the healing bruises and sore joints. She slipped then, one foot loose from the rope net, her arm jerking as she felt the other foot slip.

"Careful." His arm was around her waist, his lips hovering near her neck. A wave of desire crashed through her. If it hadn't been that they were at least thirty feet in the air and not in a safe position, she might have acted on that desire. As it was, she placed her feet in the net and continued to climb. Two nets, a well-constructed rope and wood bridge, a quick peek inside of one treehouse, and several moments for them to both catch their breaths, and they finally made it to Jack's treehouse.

Whatever Kaylee had expected, it wasn't this. It was small, perhaps five feet by eight, but not childish, not at all. The roof was clear, and she was thankful the sun wasn't overhead any longer, otherwise it would have been stifling inside. The walls were wood, sitting on what appeared to be a steel beam. A window on either side, once opened, provided a gentle breeze. In the center of the floor was a thick carpet and a dozen or more soft, thick pillows. A telescope sat nestled in one corner; in another, there was a stack of water bottles.

"No secret password?" Kaylee asked, taking in the clean lines. This was no child's playhouse. "Or marauder's map?"

Jack laughed. "No, not anymore." He handed her a water bottle and a towel from a neat bookshelf. "I'll admit, it looked different when I was younger. There may have been an, um, pirate phase. I flew the skull and crossbones; I even had the most enormous antique padlock you have ever seen on the door. I lost the key and our groundskeeper was not happy about the climb to go about cutting his way back in." He picked up another towel, wiped the sweat from his brow, and unbuttoned his shirt. Beneath the open shirt, Kaylee could see his smooth chest and toned six-pack.

He met her eyes and smiled. "A few years back, I had the roof replaced with glass. Every year, a powerful storm knocks out some panes of glass. I'm kind of surprised it's intact after last weekend's storm."

He slipped off his shoes, setting them in the corner, and Kaylee followed suit. When she had set them next to Jack's, she turned back to him and realized he was inches away.

They had been edging towards this, playing a complicated dance, and now, here they were, high above the ground, deep in a forest, yet minutes away from one of the largest cities in America.

Kaylee's breaths were uneven, more so now that she was this close to him. He reached out one hand, tucked a lock of hair behind her ear, and brushed the side of her face. He trailed his long fingers down her neck as he stepped closer, into her personal space, his eyes never leaving hers.

"I can't stop thinking about you, Kaylee. It's driving me nuts." His gaze dropped, and he reached for her wrist. "Whoever did this to you, I want to..." His teeth ground together, and his hand tightened briefly on her wrist as he visibly fought with his emotions. "I'd finish them if I could."

Kaylee felt the pulse of desire flare, the thrum of her body reacting to his, and she closed the distance, just a few inches, between them and placed her hands on his chest. His cologne, musky and rich, filled her senses. She stood on her tiptoes in order to reach his lips.

Jack leaned down to meet her, his lips gentle, sweet. Their first kiss almost chaste. He encircled her with powerful arms that lifted her up, cupped one hand on the small of her back, the other under her ass, and their kiss deepened in intensity.

Kaylee could feel her desire build, her body responding to his touch. There had been the occasional make-out session, the hurried and self-conscious groping at parties and behind the bleachers, but nothing prepared her for this. His hands roamed over her slowly, taking his time. No half-measures, no fumbling with clothing. Here was experience, and the promise of pleasure that wouldn't end in a few hasty, awkward moments.

He walked backwards, gently guiding him with her, and down to the softly cushioned floor. The sun was already low in the sky, and it warmed one window and set the rest of the inside in a light shadow. The kiss had intensified, transforming from the gentle kiss, to something far more primal, demanding. It promised more, tantalized, and teased. Jack slid one hand to her shirt, pausing at the first button.

"Are you okay with this?"

Was she *okay* with this?

God, yes, I'm okay with it.

The swirl of attraction and desire was in her blood now, flowing through every part of her body. His lips had moved to her neck, and they paused now, waiting for her response.

"Yes," Kaylee breathed out, reaching for him in return, wanting him closer. Her hand danced over his smooth chest. His shirt had vanished, tossed aside, out of sight. She could feel the hard ridges of muscle, the six-pack of abs covered in velvety-smooth skin.

He pulled back, undid the buttons of her shirt, and pulled it off of her before claiming her left earlobe, gently sucking the skin into his mouth.

Kaylee moaned as he nibbled the lobe, his hands busy as he removed her bra. No fumbling, no half measures. He reached up to the base of her skull, weaving his hands into her hair, and gently tugged her backwards down to the cushions as his mouth inched away from her ear, to her neck, and down to one erect nub of breast. He paused again, his hand warm against her hip, a finger notching at the waistband of her shorts.

"And this?"

Was he asking permission? To take what she was so willing to give him?

"Oh," she gasped as his teeth gently nibbled her breast. "Oh yes."

He pulled away from her, sitting up, and met her eyes as the fingers of both of his hands reached out and slid her shorts down and off of her body. Kaylee felt a moment of self-consciousness that vanished as she saw the look in his eyes. The gulf in age between them didn't matter to him, and it certainly didn't matter to her.

"You are beautiful," he said, his voice husky with desire. He reached down, slowly, and lifted the edge of her panties with one finger, slipping it underneath, taking his time as he slid it between her folds, smiling at her damp heat, and rubbing it against her clit.

Kaylee sucked in a gasp of air, her body humming. The waves of pleasure moved over her. It felt so good. Nothing she had ever done had felt that good. She closed her eyes and Jack reached out, stroked her cheek, and said, "Open your eyes. Look at me."

Kaylee obeyed, and he held her gaze, his finger circling and circling, until it was too much for her to bear any longer. Her breath caught, a cry issuing from her lips as she orgasmed, writhing against his hand, reaching for the other, fitting her fingers between it as she came.

"But you..." Kaylee couldn't say more. She shuddered again, and Jack smiled.

"We have time."

He pulled her against him and lay back on the cushions. Kaylee could still feel the pulses of pleasure rolling through her. His left arm was around her, threaded through her hair, and his other hand was now roaming, gently trailing his fingers along her skin, deftly avoiding her healing cuts and bruises and setting her skin alight with desire.

Kaylee realized he was still half-dressed, although from the bulge tenting the fabric of his pants, at least one part of him longed to be free. She moved her hand down his chest, discovering an almost delicate treasure trail of hairs that disappeared into his pants. Kaylee brushed her fingers along his groin and felt his dick strain against the fabric. She rubbed harder, reaching down to cup his balls in her fingers, her mouth on his pecs, kissing, licking. He groaned and shifted. She reached down and tugged on his pants, and Jack sat up, freed himself from the fine linen pants, and turned back towards her, a growl of desire escaping his lips.

He buried his face in her breasts, moving from one to the other, claiming them as his own, licking, nipping, until both were standing at attention and Kaylee ached for more.

"Jack, please, I want..." What she wanted was something she had never had. Part of her was afraid of that, the other desperate for it to happen.

His hand stopped at her groin and he tugged at the piece of fabric, pulling it off with one swift yank, before divesting himself of the last article of clothing on his body, silky black boxers.

He moved between her legs, spreading her wide, and thrust into her.

There was only a little pain. It faded with the next thrust, and the next, the slickness of her arousal, and of his easing the way. It was primal, and intoxicating, and her hips rose to meet his every thrust as she moaned in time. When he stopped, her eyes flew open, confused. He turned her, flipping her onto her knees, his mouth moving over her buttocks, then licking a line up her spine before he entered her again, hard and deep, his cock thrusting into her wet recesses, faster, harder, until there was nothing left to do but explode.

At What Cost?

The sun had slipped behind the horizon, the light fading quickly, and the first stars were peeking out. Sounds of their lovemaking from inside of the treehouse had finally faded, and the squirrels returned to their nests in the tree branches, settling in for the night along with the birds.

Now the creatures of the night emerged. The hoot of a barn owl, followed by a tiny scream of its prey, sounded through the night. Despite their proximity to Los Angeles, the night was reasonably quiet. Kaylee could hear the faint sounds of a guitar and in the very far distance the monotonous grind of traffic. This near a city center, traffic was unceasing, no matter the time of day.

She lay wrapped in a soft, fuzzy blanket, her head on Jack's chest.

"The stars will be out soon," he said, "but I have flashlights for our descent, and the way is lit with solar lights as well for safety."

"I like it right here," Kaylee said, her finger drawing a circle on his belly.

They lay there in silence. She was grateful for it. It allowed her to gather her thoughts. She needed to tell him the truth, about the past week, about her life, about all of it. It felt like he was waiting, patiently, for her to speak.

"My real name is Adrienne. Adrienne Cenac. My family has owned Cenac Shipping for five, no, six generations, if you count me," she began.

Last Friday

Rainier had handled purchasing the tickets, and Adrienne had looked at him in confusion when he asked for two first-class tickets to Los Angeles.

"I thought we would fly into San Jose...isn't that the closest airport to Santa Cruz?"

Rainier shook his head. "I've been staying in L.A. for the summer, with my friend Lincoln."

"Oh." Adrienne still felt foggy from the laced tea. "Okay." How little she knew of her brother's life since he had left home two years earlier. It suddenly made her feel sad at the thought. He had made a life for himself, and not only did she know nothing about it, but she didn't even know if he had a girlfriend or where he was living. She stared down at her bare feet and Rainier followed her gaze.

"Let's get you some shoes, Addy." He pointed down the long expanse of hall with stores on both sides. "I know I saw someplace that sells footwear."

Rainier using his pet name for her buoyed her spirits, and she slung her purse over her shoulder after the ticket agent returned her identification. It felt strange for the woman to not question her. The last time she had flown had been three years ago, for a trip to New York with Sydney and her parents. That had been like watching the Inquisition. A minor traveling with people who weren't her parents? It had been a big deal and Sydney's mom had brought along a letter signed in Father's shaky hand, allowing the trip. Now? The ticket agent had simply handed over the tickets. No questions, nothing. Eighteen really was the magic age.

A few minutes later, she had found some horrid slip-on shoes she would never have considered but found ridiculously comfortable. Together, she and Rainier made their way through security and to the gate without incident. Part of her wondered if Julianna would suddenly appear and she looked for her face, scanning the crowds, before Rainier put his hand on her arm.

"I'm keeping an eye out for her too, Sis, but don't worry, even if she found you here, she couldn't stop you from leaving. You are eighteen, an adult, and she does not have any power over either of us any longer." He said it with no small amount of bitterness.

"Did she try to stop you?" she asked, the thought occurring to her he hadn't come back for visits, not once, except for Father's funeral.

"Oh yeah. Well, not so much stop me as to make it really hard for me. She controlled the purse strings until Father died. And from what I learned from the reading of the will, that's still the case. At least until we are both twenty-one." He shook his head and grimaced. "I've got nine months to go, but you, well, yours is a ways away."

Rainier's eyes focused on the display screen for their flight. "We can pre-board now; our tickets are next to each other in Row Two." He stood up and handed her a large satchel he had purchased for her at the same place as the shoes. She had slid her spare outfit, a blue summer dress, into it and joined her brother in the line for first-class ticketholders.

Hours later, they stepped off the plane and out of the terminal into the hot California sun. They hadn't spoken on the plane much. Rainier had tried to ask her questions, but Adrienne had simply shaken her head. She didn't want others to overhear. She was still processing the thought of it herself. It left a sour taste in her mouth and an uneasy knot in her stomach. Julianna had used her family's business, one that was decades old, as a cover for nefarious activities. It sickened her. What was their family legacy in the face of this? She had finally slept a bit, despite having already slept most of the morning away. By the time she had woken as the plane was making its descent, the drugs seemed to have finally left her system. She awoke sharp and focused.

Rainier shouted and waved at a car driving past slowly. It swerved in front of a taxi and halted. The cab driver engaged in a frenzy of shouts and arm-waving as the man inside ignored the driver and waved back at Rainier. Rainier's friend was cute, dark-haired, and tall with warm, brown eyes. As they hustled over to him, the taxi behind honked impatiently and Rainier opened the two passenger doors and ushered Adrienne into the back seat before jumping into the front passenger seat.

Lincoln gunned it. "No-parking zone, sorry about that," he said, a friendly grin on his face, as he turned and flashed Adrienne a quick glance. It was hot outside the car and in, and Adrienne rolled down her window to at least catch a breeze. As it was, she just breathed in more fumes, and traffic moved at a snail's pace. The sun slipped low in the sky, a ball of fire that lit up the smoggy air in a riot of oranges and pinks. By the time Lincoln parked his car in a narrow alley behind a

Chinese restaurant, the sun had completely disappeared and night had descended. The smell of garlic and soy sauce hit her as she followed Lincoln and Rainier through a door, up a long flight of steep and narrow stairs, to a dingy apartment above the restaurant.

"This is where you have been staying?" Adrienne looked around. It was small, Spartan as only a bachelor's pad can be, and dimly lit. The canned music from the restaurant below wafted up, along with the tantalizing odors of stir-fry.

Lincoln laughed good-naturedly and patted her on her arm. "I like your sister. She has taste, something you are distinctly lacking, Rainier."

"Don't put this on me, Sorenson, it's your apartment!" Rainier turned to Adrienne. "I'll go get us some dinner and then I want to hear what you overheard, and I'll show you what Lincoln and I have put together." He didn't wait for her to answer, just disappeared through the door and back down the stairs.

"You want a beer?" Lincoln asked. "Or um, let's see, I've got some rum here and cola in the fridge. Would you like a rum and Coke?"

Adrienne blinked at his offer. He was offering her hard alcohol? Perhaps this was how early twenty-somethings lived, on alcohol and takeout. "Um, a rum and Coke would be great, thanks."

He grinned at her and turned away, searching, it seemed, for a clean glass in the small, dirty kitchenette that had a sink filled with dishes. He found one finally and pulled a cold soda can out of the fridge and appeared to pour the rum and soda in equal measures before handing it to her and pointing to one clear spot on the couch.

"Jeez, I uh, sorry about the mess. I've been ass-deep in financial records and more." He grabbed a mass of papers and books and moved them into a larger pile, which threatened to capsize. "I'm investigating a couple of anomalies with a recent election, digging into a recent sudden death in the ranks of the Hollywood elite, and helping Rainier with, well, with your dad and all. I guess I need to do some organizing."

Adrienne sipped the drink, wincing at the amount of rum in it. It was far stronger than what she had tried at the high school parties, which had mainly been composed of cheap beer and the occasional spate of Jell-O shots. She could hear Rainier coming up the steep stairs outside of the apartment seconds before he stepped inside, bags of food held in his hands.

The rum was already spreading its warmth through her body as she dug into the Mu Shu Pork and Chow Mein heaped on her plate. Rainier and Lincoln shoveled the food in, and no one spoke for a few moments, choosing instead to focus on the food in front of them. Rainier finished his meal first and reached for Adrienne's glass, taking a large gulp of it before glaring at Lincoln.

"Jesus, Link, she's eighteen!" he sputtered. "Did you add any soda to that rum?"

Lincoln shrugged and grinned. "Sorry, man. She looked like she needed it." He looked quite unrepentant. He winked at Adrienne.

Rainier frowned at his friend, grabbed the half-empty can of cola, and dumped it into Adrienne's glass.

"Julianna drugged her this morning. If I hadn't gotten there when I did..." He didn't finish his sentence, just stared at Adrienne, the edges of his scowl deepening. "One funeral is enough."

"It isn't as bad as you think, Rain, I just heard something about some illegal dumping and..." Adrienne's voice petered out as all the events of the past ten years, and especially the last year, came together. What she had overheard, all of Rainier's accusations, and the newspaper articles and specs she saw lying on the table when she had entered the apartment. Rainier had been investigating the accident from ten years ago, the one that had nearly killed him and Father. He had suspected Julianna from the very beginning.

"Oh, God."

Lincoln spoke, "Perhaps we should start with what we have learned and give you a chance to see all the evidence we have assembled. Then you can add what you know into it." He stood up, walked over to the table, and gathered the stacks of reports. Rainier cleared a space on the coffee table and took the empty food containers to the tiny kitchenette, pushing stacks of empty takeout boxes over, adding to the heap.

"Let's begin with the accident that nearly killed Rainier and your dad." He dug into the pile of papers and found a folder with several crisp photos inside of it. "The accident investigator took these. He died suddenly, less than one month after the accident."

The photos zeroed in on a cable. Rainier stabbed at it with one finger. "That cable was cut, not torn up in the accident."

"What is it? What does it do?" Adrienne asked and took another sip of the rum and Coke. It was easier to drink now with the addition of the cola.

"It is the line that delivers brake fluid from the reserves to the brakes, keeping them lubricated. Without it, the brakes burn up and stop functioning," Rainier answered, his eyes intense. "Someone cut those lines before Father and I got on the road. We had stopped for breakfast because we had been out of cereal that morning. Do you remember?"

Adrienne thought back to that morning. "Yes! And no eggs, either."

Rainier nodded grimly. "The one morning when we were out of everything, and Julianna had some unexpected appointment and couldn't take me to the doctor. Not just that, but she had scheduled us for the other office location, the one that took Father out of his way on a poorly maintained road that had plenty of twists and turns."

"A perfect storm of coincidences," Adrienne protested half-heartedly.

"Or the perfect storm of planned, intentional murder," Lincoln commented dryly. "Occam's Razor."

"Do you remember they had an argument a few days before?" Rainier asked. "One around some irregularities there at Cenac Shipping?"

"Yes," Adrienne answered with hesitancy, "Sort of."

"Well, I remember it well." Rainier's hand curled into a fist. "Father had questions and Julianna seemed intent on explaining it all away. Father worried about the legalities, concerned there was something being covered up, and then three days later, we both nearly died."

Adrienne took another sip of her drink. Despite the food, it was giving her a warm glow and the same half-numb feeling she had after drinking the tea Julianna had given her. "This accident investigator, how did you find out about him? How do we know he took pictures of Father's car?"

Lincoln tapped his chest. "I'm an investigative reporter. I have connections, and my connections have connections. It took some digging, and an impassioned plea from Rainier to the man's widow, to get these documents. The originals had disappeared from the police files, but he had stored the photos on a memory stick, and she gave it to us. These images, and the notes on the incident report, were all on the memory stick."

"This is evidence that she tried to kill you both. Why haven't you gone to the police with this?" Adrienne asked.

"We have proof that someone cut that brake line, but not the how or the why. Considering the short distance the car would have been able to travel with the brake line cut like that, it would have had to have been done while we were inside the restaurant, not at home," Rainier answered.

"So, you couldn't prove it was her?" she asked.

"Even if we know it was," Rainier answered grimly.

"We also have the quarterly blood draws," added Lincoln, "from the past few years of your father's health records. We just received them. But they aren't for your father, at least not all of them. They can't be."

Adrienne stared at him; her brow furrowed. "How do you know?"

"These reports should show opioids, painkillers," Lincoln explained. "Your father suffered from considerable nerve pain and from everything we know, he should have had high levels of those opiates in his bloodwork." He sifted through the stack of papers and pulled out several sheets, pointing to a circled number. "Here, this is from over a year ago. You can see this is a high reading, that's why it appears in red. Someone got concerned about the high dosages. Maybe Julianna received a call from a doctor expressing that concern." He shifted to the next page. "This was from a month later. No reading at all. As in, no more opioids in his system. At all."

Adrienne frowned and drank a large gulp from the glass, draining it. "And there's no chance she had his medications switched or actually took him off of them?"

Lincoln smiled. "You would make an excellent investigator; you have a questioning mind. And that was the first question I asked, and then I pulled the pharmacy reports. The drug in question is oxycodone. I show a continuing prescription for it over the past three years." He slapped down a readout of dates that occurred monthly and stretched to several pages. "But I also found this record, the same medication, the same dosage, and issued by a Dr. A. Smith and filled at another pharmacy for almost the same time period." He slid the other report towards her and she held it in her hands, staring at the circled data.

"Twice as much medication?" Her voice wobbled a bit, an image clear in her mind of Father seated in his wheelchair facing the large picture window, his gaze clouded, his reactions slow and often nonexistent.

"Yes. And in those doses, enough to kill him. It's likely why she pushed to have him cremated." He snarled, "I knew it was weird, having him cremated and then put into a casket. It made no sense at all."

Rainier met Adrienne's eyes and his voice grew soft, kind. "Julianna kept you distracted. I think she liked the idea of you enough to spend the time, the effort, to keep you in the dark. Especially once I left, and she knew she would need a figurehead to run the company if Father were to die." He sniffed, his lips twisting into a snarl. "Father had put the protections in place, even before he married her. And after, he had amended the will to include a stipend for her, but he locked her out of any power position in the company if either of us stepped forward to run it."

"Why wouldn't she just dissuade me from taking control of it after I returned from college, then?" Adrienne asked, desperate to find a place where Julianna wasn't guilty of murder and more.

"The will stated that if neither of us took control of the company by our twenty-fifth birthday, then it was to be sold," Rainier answered.

"And if I took control of it?" Adrienne asked. "What then?"

"You would have been a figurehead. If you actually paid attention, perhaps noticed the irregularities, well then, maybe you would end up like Father." Rainier shook his head at Adrienne's shocked expression. "She did it once, why not again?"

"Adrienne." Lincoln handed her another glass full of the rum and Coke. "Why don't you tell us what you overheard?"

Adrienne took a sip of the drink. It was less strong this time. She took a deep breath, then told them exactly what she had heard and how she had escaped from the situation.

"I thought I pulled it off," she said, taking another sip, "I thought I fooled them. But maybe they said something to her. And that's why Julianna drugged me with that tea. I mean, we don't know for sure if she drugged the tea. I was awake most of the night, trying to figure out what I overheard, but I've done all-nighters before and never fell asleep like that before."

"Oh, you were drugged, Sis. I was calling your name and trying to shake you awake for damn near five minutes. You don't sleep that deep." Rainier turned towards his friend. "What do you think of all this?"

Lincoln leaned back against the couch. "I think Julianna was going with Plan B. Plan A was to install Adrienne as the figurehead there at Cenac and be the perfect fall guy along with your dead father if the illegal dumping and fire-bombing became known. But Plan B was simply to keep what she had built within the organization protected, and if that meant offing Adrienne, then so be it."

Adrienne shuddered and drained the second glass of rum and Coke. She tried standing up, and the room swam around her.

"Easy there, Sis."

"I gotta pee."

"Yep." Rainier slipped a hand around her waist and walked her towards one of the half-open doors. "Right here." He steadied her until she could turn on the light and then released her so she could close the door. "Christ, Link, you got her drunk."

"She looked like she needed it," Lincoln responded, laughing.

Adrienne closed her eyes as the world tilted and swam. The bathroom was filthy. It was very much a bachelor pad, and a poorly maintained one at that. She finished the roll of toilet paper and levered herself upright, listening to her brother and his friend's voices murmuring. She flushed the toilet and stared into the cracked and smudged mirror. It had been twenty-four hours at most, and they had turned her life upside-down. Had Julianna truly murdered their father?

What had her stepmother planned to do with her once she had drugged her? She had so many questions and yet, she feared the answers.

Present Day

Kaylee stopped, her mouth suddenly dry, her stomach churning.

Jack's hands held hers. "The men who were looking for you, they killed them, didn't they?"

Kaylee nodded, wordless, tears falling against his smooth skin. She sat up, reached for a water bottle nearby and took a sip, wiping at the tears, her shoulders shaking.

"It all happened so fast. I was asleep on the couch. I think it was around midnight, maybe later. They shot Lincoln and Rainier. Just a couple of small pops, though, not loud. I would have thought it was a pop gun, not real, but then Rainier was on the ground and there was so much blood.

Before I could scream, before I could do much of anything except try to fight them off, they tied me up, drugged me. Then the big one slung me over his shoulders. I think the other one stayed behind long enough to set the fire." Her tears fell harder. "They were going to kill me too. I'm sure of it, once they were sure that the evidence burned up in the apartment and that I hadn't talked to anyone else."

Jack's hand was on her back, warm, soothing.

"They will kill anyone they think knows anything. I'm sure of that now. If they find me, they will kill you, Malcolm, and even Azule. You aren't safe around me. That's what you need to know, Jack. You aren't safe. No one is."

Survey for Prey

Jack soothed Kaylee as best he could. He held her in his arms and felt more helpless than he had in a long time. There was no way to take the experiences she had suffered from her mind, or go back in time and stop the murder of her brother and her brother's friend. Jack couldn't restore her parents to her, any more than he could his own. He felt as helpless as he had when he held Allie that one last time, knowing that she was gone and that he was powerless to bring her back. Allie, who had her entire life in front of her. Allie, who he had promised to protect and failed utterly at.

Kaylee, or Adrienne, he couldn't help but think of her as Kaylee. She also had her entire life in front of her as well. And Jack swore silently that he would do everything in his power to protect her, to make sure she had that life to live where others had not.

The stars filled the sky, even with the light from Los Angeles masking many of them. Here on this night, he could see so many. It was the planets that caught his eye tonight, however. He pointed to Mars, midway up in the southwest, and Saturn, its yellow hue clear in the south-southwest, only 30 degrees from the orange blob that was the Red Planet. He could just barely make out Mercury west-northwest. The waxing crescent moon hung just above it.

He whispered all of this in Kaylee's ear and gradually her sobs ceased, and she asked after the brightest of Virgo's stars so close to Saturn. "That's Spica, one of the twenty brightest stars in the sky," Jack said, his lips buried in Kaylee's hair. "It is actually two stars so close together that we cannot tell them apart through a telescope." His hand, restless, moved along the length of her, trailing his fingertips over the contours of her body, desiring more of her, but also wanting the simple connection that the feel of her skin against his made.

They lay there, staring at the stars, without words. Jack tried to think of the words to say to her, to reassure her, to encourage her to stay. Not just here, in this moment, but for longer. She was so young, younger than Malcolm, and yet, her presence here felt good and right. As if she had always belonged here with him.

Kaylee turned towards him and he could barely make out her features in the dark.

"Jack, I..." He stopped her from saying anything more with a deep, intense kiss. He didn't want her to tell him she had to leave. He didn't want to hear it, and he didn't want her to remind him of the danger of her presence in his life, or Mal's. Instead, he wanted to make love to her. The whole damn night, if that was what it took to take her fears away, or at least silence them until he could prove to her that she was safe here.

She returned his kiss, matching him in enthusiasm and attraction, her body moving under his in just the right way. Above them, the night sky blinked, the space station passed overhead in a slow, lazy arc, and the other denizens of the enormous tree listened, or slept, as the two made love in the treehouse, repeatedly.

There was no sense of time, up in the branches, far from any clocks. They slept, limbs intertwined, bodies sated, until the birds woke them at dawn.

Jack groaned. Cushioned or not, the treehouse was not half as comfortable as his bed, and his body ached. One arm had gone numb where he had wrapped it around Kaylee. She sat up slowly, stretching, her breasts perky. She covered them, a small blush blooming on her cheeks as she caught his gaze.

Jack protested, pulling her hand away from the left breast and sitting up to capture it in his mouth, feeling himself harden. He pulled her onto his lap, his tongue making its way up her chest to her neck and ear, before capturing her mouth again.

Kaylee groaned and then squirmed away. "There is one thing missing from this treehouse," she said, reaching for her clothes.

"A proper bed?" he asked, wincing as his back reminded him he was no longer ten and able to sleep on whatever surface he chose.

"Okay, two things then. A feather bed and a toilet!"

Jack laughed and turned to find his own clothes. They were mixed with hers, and they bumped heads twice trying to hurry into their discarded outfits.

The way down the tree was difficult in places, but Kaylee stepped confidently. She was a natural and not fearful of heights. If it was possible for him to like her even more than he already did, it was her ease in descending that impressed him the most.

"You aren't afraid of heights at all, are you?" he asked as she took a series of twisting steps in a rope ladder without complaint.

"Oh no, I'm terrified," she answered promptly, "but I'm more worried about peeing my pants right now to care about how high up we are, as long as we get down to the ground now."

Jack threw back his head and laughed. "We're almost there. You could go in the woods if it gets too bad."

"What, and wipe myself with poison ivy? No thanks." The ground grew closer.

"It's more poison oak rather than ivy around here, but I get your point."

The moment her feet were on the ground, Kaylee scampered down the trail and Jack was laughing so hard he couldn't keep up.

Jack watched as Kaylee zipped inside of the house and felt his stomach growl. They hadn't eaten dinner last night. He had been too busy to notice until now. He felt a twinge of guilt at the thought of Malcolm. His baby brother wasn't helpless, though. There were plenty of prepackaged meals downstairs in the second kitchen, and Mal could cook in a pinch. Jack usually gave him some kind of notice, though, instead of just disappearing. He'd have to fix something besides omelets. After four days in a row, he needed to make something else; all he'd done was feed her omelets and takeout. As he climbed the stairs to his own room, he could hear the water pipes. She was showering, and he paused, remembering how he had walked in on her showering. Had it only been two days? Covered in suds, steam billowing up over the clear glass walls of the shower. Eyes closed, her fingers...

"Hey." Jack's eyes flew open and he saw Kaylee standing in there in a fluffy robe, a half-smile on her face. She tilted her head towards the bathroom. "Join me?"

He didn't need coaxing. His shirt was already off, along with his shoes, and she laughed, shedding her robe inside of the door. A wash of wet heat greeted him inside of the bathroom and he stepped out of the last of his clothes and joined her inside.

When Kaylee reached for the shampoo, he reached out his hand. "Here, let me." He poured a generous amount into his hand and turned her so that her back was to him. She shivered as he worked the shampoo into her hair, digging his nails into her scalp slowly. "Are you cold?"

Kaylee sighed. "No, it just...it feels so good."

He pulled her closer to the water, the spray from the multiple jets sending the suds and shampoo spinning away into a vortex. His fingers made sure every bit of suds rinsed out, before his mouth worked its way along her slender neck, eyes closed in the downpour. Kaylee arched her back, fitting herself against him, her hips swaying as if to a silent beat. Jack could feel his cock swelling, his smaller head quite unconcerned with the lack of sleep or a sore back. He turned her around, so that she faced him, and pressed her against the cool tiles that lined the far wall of the shower, ignoring the water, capturing her mouth with his. She gasped as he lifted her up and then thrust inside of her, burying himself to the hilt in her silky depths. He stood like that for a moment, reveling in the warmth, the rush of sensation, and when he couldn't stand it anymore, he thrust in and out, harder, faster. Kaylee clung to him, her fingers digging into his shoulders. Jack's hands cupped her perfect round buttocks, his eyes watched as her mouth formed a perfect 'o' of ecstasy. She moaned with each new thrust and then, as the orgasm approached, her eyes flew open.

"Oh, Jack!" A rush of warmth, her hips bucking, and with one last thrust he came so hard he saw stars.

They stood there for what felt like moments, his heart hammering in his chest, and his face nestled in her shoulder, the water coursing over them. He let her go gently, her body sliding down the tiles until they reached the floor.

When his heart rate had returned to normal, he captured one last kiss from her and then pulled away. "I should see about breakfast."

"I could make us something, if you like," Kaylee said, reaching for her towel as steamy clouds billowed past them both. "Jul... well, my stepmother, she taught me a lot. We would bake something special each weekend." She wrapped the towel around herself and grinned. "It's not a breakfast food, per se, but I can make us some beignets, or even sweet potato ham hash if you prefer a healthier choice."

They settled on beignets, if only because he didn't have any sweet potato in the kitchen. Malcolm had a serious sweet tooth, and Jack figured that would trump his usual avocado omelet request. He headed to his own room, a spare towel wrapped around his waist, and dressed quickly.

Mal was sitting in his usual spot when Jack arrived. He had been waiting for Jack and his magnetic board read:

woman here yesterday

asked questions

looking for K

talk to A Z

Jack read the words and stared at his baby brother. "You're sure she was looking for Kaylee?" Mal gave a tiny nod and tapped the last line. "Did Az talk to her?" There was another small nod.

Jack felt a tight knot in his gut form, and it wasn't his hunger. Something felt off about this. He looked around the room.

The entire first floor was an open layout with high ceilings and tall picture windows. If this woman had gotten past the front gate, what would she have seen if she were standing right outside of the house?

Jack's eyes landed on the light jacket Kaylee had been wearing yesterday afternoon. It lay on the back of the couch, a delicate pink and blue.

Shit.

He strode around the kitchen island and reached for his Samsung Galaxy, which sat charging on the counter. He picked it up, tapped a few keys, and found a text from Azule.

Azule R: A woman was here. Said she was a survey taker. Black hair, lean, muscled. Her smile didn't reach her eyes. Mid 20s at most. Was asking after women between ages of 15-25. Raised my hackles. Looked around a lot. Said gate was open. CALL ME.

Double shit.

Jack turned to see Kaylee's face pale at the words on Mal's board.

"Could it be your stepmother? Julie..."

"Julianna?" She frowned. "I can't see her doing something like that, but I didn't suspect her of killing my dad and I'm pretty sure she did." She peered over his shoulder at the text. "Black hair? Lean muscles? No, definitely not."

Jack read the text to her, and Kaylee shook her head again. "No, that's not her."

He pressed the Call button, and the phone rang once before Azule answered. "You left your phone on the damn counter again, didn't you?" She didn't wait for an answer. "I've been thinking about it all night. And I don't like it. She set off my shit detectors."

Jack would have laughed except that right now all of his own alerts were going off. If Azule felt like something was off, then he trusted it. Az was a woman with excellent intuition. He cast an eye around, surveying the open floor plan with the large windows and semi-privacy with a fresh eye. Kaylee was not safe here. None of them were.

"Right. Az, here's what I need for you to do..." Before he could continue, he felt rather than heard the rush of air first and the crack of glass sounded immediately afterwards. The bullet sliced the air between them, shattering the glass tiles of the kitchen behind them. Jack circled a hand around Kaylee's waist and pulled her to the floor, yelling at his brother to take cover as the second, third, and fourth bullets hit the refrigerator, exploded the coffeemaker, and grazed the countertop as Jack pushed Kaylee against the dishwasher, hoping it would protect her even further from the gunfire. He then dove sideways and grabbed Malcolm by the back of his shirt and pulled him close. Malcolm struggled. Even now, faced with danger, his brother could not stand another's touch. He fought to get away from Jack, screaming wordlessly. Jack winced as Mal's free hand formed into a fist and delivered a glancing blow to the side of Jack's head.

Kaylee looked pale, terrified, her eyes wide.

"The basement is a safe room. We have to get to it." His gaze traveled from what little he could see over the kitchen island to the door set in the wall just fifteen feet away. "Mal, stop fighting me! I'll let you go, but you have to go with Kaylee." He released his hold on Malcolm and his brother ceased his struggles, scooting as far from Jack as possible while remaining down on the floor. He was out of range of the bullets for now. They had stopped, and Jack knew it was only a matter of time before whoever was firing got closer. A few feet away he could hear Azule's voice calling out over the phone, but there was no time, she couldn't help them.

When seconds count, the police are minutes away.

Jack reached into a cabinet, past the rolls of aluminum foil, and his fingers closed on the handle of the Smith & Wesson. He racked the slide back and slipped the safety off. Kaylee's eyes widened even more.

"What are you doing?" she whispered.

"Buying you time. You and Mal need to get to the basement. Get ready to run."

"What about you?"

"I'll be right behind you." He peeked over the kitchen island and saw a lithe figure running towards the house. "Go now."

Kaylee stood up and ran with Malcolm behind her, his binder in his arms. As they ran, Jack shot towards the window at their attacker. The picture window disintegrated in a crash of broken glass, the additional weapons fire overwhelming the expanse already damaged by the intruder's bullets.

The figure dove to one side and he could tell it was a woman now, her dark, long hair neatly braided in a long line down her back. She wouldn't go down for long, and he wasn't ready to hide in the basement below and hope that the police got here in time. The screen on his phone had gone dark, and he knew Azule was already on the phone with the police. He held no hope that they would get here in time to save them. Jack would have to stop her.

He glanced over. Kaylee and Malcolm had made it to the door and slipped inside. Malcolm had pulled it closed until only a sliver of his face was visible. Jack met his brother's eyes and said, "Lock it." He turned away even as he heard Kaylee object and the door snick closed, the bolts sliding into place. No one could get in there. Not without heavy explosives.

She was moving again. He could see her leap through the open wound that was the picture window, firing as she entered his home.

Time to Die

The afternoon before…

Nyra easily climbed over the gate and headed down the long, winding drive towards the house. She plastered her most winning smile on as she approached the main entrance. A voluptuous black woman was standing in the drive, her eyes narrowed in suspicion.

"Hi there! I'm conducting a survey on name-brand makeup choices, and I have free samples for anyone who matches my demographic!" Nyra called out, forcing perkiness into every inch of her voice.

"How did you get in here?" The woman had her hands on her hips and her eyebrows arched.

"I, uh." Nyra looked down at the ground. "Okay, look, I'm new and they assigned me all of this quadrant and *every single driveway* is gated and locked. If I don't come back with something, they'll fire me!" She gave the woman an anguished look. "I know I jumped the fence, but seriously, I'm just trying to keep my job."

The woman gave her a measuring look, and Nyra could see she wasn't convinced. "What age group do you need?"

"Ages fifteen to twenty-five females. Transgender and nonbinary are welcome as well," she reeled off glibly. "I have some lovely MAC eye shadow and blush, full-size samples!"

She had maneuvered her approach so she could see both the woman and as much of the inside of the house as possible. No one was in sight, nothing out of place, except…

"There's no one here in that demographic, miss."

Nyra noticed a spot of color on the white sofa. A pale pink and blue sweater, definitely female. She frowned, pouting a little in mock disappointment. "Are you sure?"

The woman's eyebrows raised even further, and her mouth compressed into a single, disapproving line. "Quite sure. Let me walk you to the gate. You may have better luck if you head to the north."

Nyra had no choice but to walk with the woman back to the gate. It didn't matter. She would scout the rest of the area out in the last two hours of daylight, just to be sure, but she had a strong feeling about this house. No matter, she could sneak back in later to find out more. She gushed her thanks and walked away, down the winding drive. Once she was out of sight of the gate, she pulled out her phone, located the right number, and pressed Call.

"Lucif...I mean, this is Luce..." the girl on the other end stammered.

Nyra grinned. "Lucifer, it's Nyra."

"Oh, hey Nyra, what's up?" The girl's voice on the other end perked up.

"Can you run a license number for me? And also an address?"

"Sure, uh, hang on a sec." There was a brief scrabbling in the background and then Lucifer returned. "Hit me."

Nyra gave her both numbers. "I need ownership on both."

"I'll work on those right now. Hey, how's your sister?" Nyra could hear Lucifer clicking away at her computer, already on task.

"She's doing good. A couple more weeks and she'll get her tat, become one of us."

"That's awesome! I can't wait to meet her!" Nyra smiled at that response; it was classic Lucifer. The girl looked terrifying with her goth makeup, piercings, and tattoos. Nyra knew better. She had met Lucifer when she first joined up, a little over a year ago, still big-eyed and green, a small-town girl in a big city. Nyra had been tasked with showing Lucifer some basic hand-to-hand combat, the standard stuff. None of the advanced "five-finger-death-punch stuff" as Lucifer had called it.

They had struck up a friendship of sorts. At least, as much of one as any of them could have when you worked for the Indalo. Fraternization was not particularly encouraged.

The reality of it was that Lucifer and Zella would likely never meet. Lucifer didn't really understand that yet. She didn't give a single thought to why Nyra needed the information or what she would do with it. And depending on how well she did, she might never know. Lucifer was good, though, very good at hacking, and therefore quite valuable at her job. That she didn't question was even better, because the deeper you went with the Indalo, the less you wanted to question.

"Okay, I've got a hit on the address," Lucifer said. "It belongs to a Jack Benton. Ooh la la! He's rolling in it. I'm getting society pages, a plane crash that killed his parents ten years ago, and, huh, he started Benton Security Services around eight years ago. Looks like they offer protection, high-end bodyguard detail, that kind of thing."

Bingo.

"Thanks, Lucifer, that's all I need."

"Oh well hey, what about the license plate?"

"Unnecessary. I've got what I need. Thanks, Luce."

"Alright, then. But hey, call me back sometime. They keep me in the dark and feed me shit like I'm a mushroom. I think I might get a dog to keep me company. A big one, like a Great Dane...got any good ideas for names?"

"Call her Annabelle," Nyra said, the name popping out of her brain with little thought. It had been the name of her first target, Annabelle Bouchard.

You never forget the name of your first kill.

"I like that."

Nyra didn't say goodbye, just stabbed the End Call button as she reached the end of the drive and turned left towards the north. She'd put on a show, kept the older black woman guessing, and hopefully convinced her she was who she said she was. Once she made her way to two other houses, she would double back and scope out the property.

She handed out samples to two girls, one eleven-year-old who glibly lied and said she was sixteen. Nyra had hidden her amusement and written useless bullshit on the checklist she had created to go with the survey-taker outfit before making the kid's day by giving her the entire bag of makeup. The sun disappeared behind the trees, but Nyra waited for nightfall to once again climb the fence.

There was the main house and then another building that was nearly as large as the main house. She kept to the shadows and investigated it. The door was locked, but that was easy enough to circumvent. Nyra's training hadn't been restricted to combat techniques and inventive ways to murder someone; she'd also learned how to pick most locks. The door to this building had taken nothing more than a credit card to open. It had contained offices, a conference room, and she had enjoyed watching the fish in the arboretum. She cased the house and debated whether to break in and wait inside for this Jack Benton to come back. It was easy enough to find a comfortable spot in the shrubbery that lined the glass house and wait for the billionaire to return from wherever he had gone to.

Nyra positioned herself so that she would be completely invisible to anyone inside of the compound or anyone driving in from the outer road. She crossed her legs, centered her mind, and thought of Zella. Her sister's anger ran deep. For Nyra, the distance of several years away had meant she had time to process the abuse her father had practiced upon her body. Zella had done what Nyra could not—kill him—and Nyra's thoughts flitted to their mother briefly. She had done nothing to stop Jeffery Dean from abusing and raping her daughters. She'd laid in her bed and not lifted a finger, not even acknowledged what was happening in her own house.

And for that, she deserved what she got.

What surprised Nyra was that Zella didn't hate her for leaving. She could have, and rightfully so, but she hadn't. Zella's black hatred of men hadn't faded in the past year, and it was for that reason that Nyra had delayed telling Delta that her sister was ready to join the Indalo. Her anger caused her to act with careless disregard for her safety or others. And while Nyra was sure that Zella could easily kill her marks, she seemed to kill indiscriminately and with no concern for the repercussions. Most of Nyra's assignments had carried with them the expectation of finesse. If Zella couldn't get her emotions under control, she would quickly put a target on her own back, and Nyra's. They were all expendable, after all.

The night was clear for Los Angeles. The smog was absent, and the stars had appeared in the sky, glowing jewels that appeared to wink, even move, across a velvet backdrop.

Her legs ached after several hours of maintaining the same position. Her ankle, the one Zella had hit with such accuracy, felt especially tender.

It was in quiet moments such as these that she wondered what a person had done to get on the Indalo's shit list. This Adrienne Cenac was barely out of high school, and a prestigious one at that. She didn't seem worldly, and Nyra closed her eyes for a moment and visualized the girl's face. They had taken the photo from her school yearbook, from the looks of it. She had a fresh, cheerful smile that reached all the way to her eyes.

Whatever had happened in Adrienne Cenac's life, it couldn't have been too bad. She was rich, pretty, and had her life in front of her. Or at least she had until they handed Nyra her file. Now she was dead, or as good as. Never mind the fact that she had gotten away from Stephan and Rohan. They were cops, after all. In the pockets of the Indalo, for sure, but cops.

As the hours passed, the sliver of moon worked its way across the sky and out of sight, and the horizon glowed as the sun rose behind it. Nyra heard voices coming from behind the house and within seconds, a girl appeared, sprinting for the door. She ran inside and up the stairs.

Honey-blond hair, with only the side of her face visible as she ran by. It had looked like a match to the yearbook photo. But Nyra wanted to be sure. Delta frowned heavily on collateral damage. Besides, she had time, even with the sun up. The black woman was obviously an employee. She had been leaving at five the evening before and would likely return by nine today. Nyra had over three hours to accomplish her mission and disappear into the woods that surrounded the estate. By the time law enforcement processed the scene, she would be back with Zella in their desert hideaway.

She stood, stretched her legs, and fitted the silencer on her pistol. Nyra marveled at the idiocy of the rich. What good was a tall fence without sensor alarms? And to have shrubbery so that they would feel like they were away from prying eyes just gave an intruder somewhere to hide.

Less than a minute after the girl ran inside, a good-looking guy in his mid-thirties came around the back of the building and walked inside. That was obviously Jack Benton. Lucifer had sent Nyra several photos of him with varying numbers of exclamation points after each picture, apparently showing levels of hotness. And he was good-looking, to be sure. Not Nyra's type. Her interests lay in women. She had enough of her fill of men before she ever left home. Nyra watched as he made his way up the stairs. She could just barely catch a second set of feet before the large window gave way to wall. She watched an interplay of feet and then Jack's following the girl out of sight.

They were lovers, then. Interesting. She had escaped Stephan and Rohan on Saturday night and likely found her way here sometime late Saturday or early Sunday. And was in the man's bed by Wednesday morning? She shook her head.

Men are nothing but walking hard-ons.

The minutes ticked by, and finally she saw Jack's feet head to a room at the far end of the upstairs hallway and disappear for a few minutes before reappearing and walking downstairs. As he did, it surprised Nyra to see a younger copy of Jack Benton sitting at the breakfast bar with a large binder open in front of him. His hair was dark, long, and rather shaggy. Where had this younger man come from? Her surveillance last night had shown only bedrooms on the upper level, and she saw nothing indicating there was a basement or lower level past the main floor. She peered through her monocular. Too old to be Jack's child, possibly a brother? Lucifer's info had included no info on a sibling, but Nyra hadn't asked her for a family history, just the standard property records. No matter. They were talking now, or at least Jack was speaking. The younger man had his back to the window and was as still as a stone. It looked as though Jack was frowning and she watched as he reached for his phone, read something on the screen, and then looked up and out. Nyra felt a thread of anxiety pulse in her.

Perhaps I have less time than I originally thought.

Had the employee she ran into said something to him? Nyra watched as he dialed the phone, put it up to his ear, and waited for an answer. She was so intent on watching his face, on trying to read his lips, that she didn't notice the girl's approach at first. Nyra examined her through the monocular in her hand. Her hair was damp from a shower, but the girl's face was a match. Adrienne Cenac was here. Exposed in this house of glass, she was hiding from the Indalo less than two miles from where the car had been found.

You should have run, Adrienne. Now it's time to die.

Nyra aimed her weapon carefully. Adrienne had moved closer to Jack, a slender hand on his sleeve, her face tight with concern.

Nyra fired and felt a poorly-time breeze at exactly the same moment and the bullet left the chamber. The shot, lined up perfectly accounting for distance, went wide, slamming into the tile between Adrienne and Jack. She fired again as they disappeared from sight. First Adrienne and Jack, and then the younger man, his binder still clutched in his hands as he disappeared from view. Nyra could see his legs kicking to one side, as if he were fighting the older man. She followed the first bullet with three more. They left holes with a starburst pattern around each, but the window held. She had to get closer.

She stood and ran, firing as she did. Nyra saw the small, dark muzzle of a handgun appear and fire, shattering the window entirely. She dodged from side to side, closing the distance, and firing back as she saw the girl and the younger man run for a distance before disappearing into what looked like a wall. Nyra swore silently.

A safe room, possibly. That's where the younger man came from. Damn it!

A bullet whizzed past her ear as she approached what was now an open wound into the house and Nyra dodged to the left at just the wrong moment, another bullet entering her chest, tearing through her like a hot skewer. It took her breath away, and she half slid into the house, gasping for air as she flopped over the edge of the open window and against a white couch.

That the bullet had hit her was shocking. In the past three years, she hadn't been so much as nicked by a knife, much less shot. Nyra lay against the couch, chest on fire, and breath bubbling in her chest. She spit a glob of blood out of her mouth and searched for a solution. None of them were good, none of them ended well. No matter what happened next, whether she was successful in her mission, her future, her life, was something she could measure in seconds and minutes.

Should have worn the body armor. Stupid.

Jack Benton was standing over her now. He reached down and wrenched the gun away from Nyra's hand and then set his own down, his right hand on her neck, checking her pulse.

Nyra whispered the words. It wasn't hard to pretend she was dying, because she knew she was. She gathered her energy as he drew closer. Her knife was in her boot, her leg folded up underneath her on the floor.

Come closer. I'll give you something to remember me by.

He shifted closer, and she struck, slicing with the last of her energy at his belly. It wasn't her mark; he wasn't her mission. But that was okay.

One less rich asshole who can't think past his dick.

And as Jack fell away from her, clutching his side, his blood joining hers, Nyra slipped away into the abyss.

The Price You Pay

Jack struggled to his feet, his left hand pressed hard against the gaping wound, blood leaking everywhere. His head swam. He had to get help. He had to protect Kaylee. These two priorities warred in his mind and worse, the world would not hold still. It kept tilting sideways. He shook his head, which didn't help, not at all.

He could hear a car screech to a halt outside and he turned, his body moving as if through waist-high mud. He couldn't get his feet to work right and he cast about for the gun he had set down on a nearby chair. If it was another like this one, he had seconds, perhaps minutes before the blood loss incapacitated him. He could see a figure running towards the house, but everything was blurry.

"Jack! Jack!" Azule's voice. She was closer now, choosing to cross through into the house the same way the dead woman on the floor had, through the remains of the picture window.

"Oh no, Jack, hold on. The police are right behind me. Ambulance too, by the sound of it."

"Keep her safe, Az." Even his lips felt numb, his tongue heavy. "Don't let the police see her. Don't let them know she's...here."

His feet weren't working, and the ground was moving again. Jack hit the carpet, his eyes closing as he heard Kaylee screaming.

Later, much later, Azule would question her life choices, extensively and with plenty of swearing about rich, white people and their messes. For now, she was hell-bent on doing exactly what Jack had requested. Blood everywhere, as pale as if he had lost half of the blood inside of him, Azule turned her attention to Kaylee, who had burst through the safe room door and was running towards them.

"Girl! If you know what is good for you, which you obviously do not, you will go back there right now. Jack doesn't want you seen, and you will damn well listen."

Kaylee gasped, stopping short of the mess, her mouth agape, her hands clutched to her mouth.

Little girl like this bringing disaster down on us.

"Go back to the safe room. Now. 'Afore the police get here." She gave the girl a stern look. The sirens were close. "I'm putting pressure on the wound. There's nothing for you to do here, 'cept get yourself killed. Jack's already paying the price, now go."

Malcolm appeared at the door as well. He managed a dozen steps into the room before his gaze slid over the blood that stained the couch and floor and two bodies on the floor. He opened his mouth and screamed wordlessly. It was a high, keening wail. He just stood there and screamed as Kaylee ran back towards him and tried to take him by the arm. The sirens were on the private drive; they were running out of time.

"Leave, Mal, I'll take care of him. Go, Kaylee! Now!" Azule bellowed, and Jack groaned as she pressed harder on his wound.

Mal continued his terrible keen as the police arrived, weapons drawn, and Azule did her best to stay calm.

"On the ground, now!"

"If I release pressure, he bleeds out. The screamer over there is his brother, he's autistic, he's non-verbal and harmless. I'm Azule Roberts, Mr. Benton's personal assistant, and I called this in."

The taller cop was a brother, something that gave Azule some hope that they would listen. He was the first to holster his weapon and held up a hand to the other, a nervous, skinny white boy who still had acne. Seconds later, the drive filled with medical personnel as the ambulance and fire department arrived.

Before Azule could stop them, they tranked Mal, and Jack's brother dropped like a stone. The EMTs swarmed the room, and Azule could stand again and stumble to the sink to wash some of Jack's blood off of her. She looked down at her jacket and felt ill. There was so much of it, she didn't know how he could stand to lose so much and be okay.

They were bundling him up on the stretcher, an IV in his arm. "We're taking him to Sinai," one man said. "Should I call an ambulance for psych transport for the brother?" he asked the police officer, who immediately looked over at Azule.

"No, that won't be necessary. Malcolm will be fine here. I'll get this cleaned up before the sedatives wear off."

"We will need to take your statement first, ma'am," the officer said as he watched the ambulance careen back down the drive, its sirens wailing.

"Of course. If I could make a few calls first. It will take just a moment."

She had to call one of the security team and the cleaners. Azule searched her memories. Luke had met Malcolm and been patient, plus he was between assignments. He'd have to do. As the phone rang, she pantomimed to the officer that she was going to step into the bathroom for privacy. There she avoided looking at the bloody mess on the front of her clothes in the mirror and focused instead on explaining to Luke that he needed to come over immediately. The second call was to a crime scene cleaning firm that promised one-hour metro-wide service. She had to get the place cleaned up before Malcolm saw it.

And the third call was to Nia, Marley's ex. "Nia, I know it's your day off, but I need you to do me a solid and bring a clean outfit up to my work. I'll text you the address."

With all of that out of the way, and praying that Kaylee would stay where she was, Azule left the bathroom and returned to the waiting officer. She was on her second repetition of the sequence of events when the driveway filled with vehicles, the crime scene cleanup crew, Luke and Nia, all arriving at the same time.

Nia had Demetrius in the back seat and she didn't want the boy alarmed. "Please," she said, turning to the officer, "could you ask my cousin in that little blue Civic to just come inside and leave her son out in the car for a moment?"

He smiled and nodded. "Sure."

He was good-looking, and Azule watched as he smiled at Nia. The girl was pretty, with her light-cocoa skin and hair perfectly coiffed. He opened the car door for her and she stepped out, giving a long stare at the broken window, before striding into the house, the officer strolling along behind her, getting a magnificent view, no doubt.

"Az, what in the..." Nia stopped in her tracks, her mouth dropping open as she stared at the white couch and chairs speckled with blood and the body lying underneath a sheet. "Is that your boss?" Nia's eyes widened as she took in Azule's blood-soaked clothes. "Oh my God, Az!"

"It's all right, everything will be fine. It's not my blood. And no, that's not my boss." She held her hands out for the large bag Nia was holding. "Please don't say anything to Auntie L., I don't want her getting all in a fuss."

"But, Az..."

Azule pressed a hundred-dollar bill in Nia's hand. "Go on, Nia, go get Demetrius and you somethin' to eat."

Nia shut her mouth, nodded, and with a weak, half-flirtatious smile for the officer, headed for her car. Which was just as well, since Demetrius was pitching a fit, madder than hell that he hadn't been able to follow Nia inside. She watched them drive away, the sounds of the boy's enraged screams floating through the air.

Luke scanned the grounds. His muscle-bound arms looked handsome in a plaid check shirt and jeans. He looked out of place here, as usual. Luke was a man who was at home in a wood cabin, wearing flannel and chopping firewood. Azule was thankful he had left his handgun out of sight. The hunting knife on his hip had already raised the white cop's eyebrows.

"How can I help?"

"Just keep an eye on Malcolm for now. They tranked him. Couldn't handle seeing all the blood."

Luke nodded and pointed a finger upstairs, silently asking permission. When Azule nodded, he hoisted Malcolm over his shoulder and carried his still unconscious body upstairs to Jack's room.

Azule directed the crime scene cleanup team to do what they could about the bloodstains on the couch and carpet and slipped into the bathroom to change. By the time she emerged, the handsome brother of an officer was wrapping up his notes.

"I think that about covers it, ma'am. We have your information if we have any further questions. I just heard from Sinai as well, and they have taken Mr. Benton into surgery. He's had a transfusion and was stable prior to surgery." He flipped his notepad closed. "The rest of our questions will have to wait for him."

He turned to his partner. "Go ahead, I'll be there in a minute." The skinny white cop shrugged and nodded at Azule before heading out the door.

"I live in the neighborhood," the tall brother said, pressing a card into Azule's hand. "I went to school with Nia, feels like a thousand years ago. Ask her to call me, would you?" He smiled then; his teeth white against his dark brown skin.

"Mm-huh, I'll let Nia know." The corner of Azule's mouth twitched.

"Thank you, Ms. Roberts." Another dazzling smile and the door clicked shut behind him.

Azule turned the card over in her hand. Officer Tyrone Hendricks' name was neatly printed next to the LAPD crest. She knew plenty of Hendricks in Compton. There was a whole extended clan of them two streets over. Tyrone. Huh, Janae had a boy named Ty who had joined the force.

She smiled at the thought of Nia hooking up with a cop. Marley wouldn't come skulking around too often if that was the case. He had a rap sheet a mile long. Just seeing a cop made him twitchy and nervous. And Little Demetrius needed a positive male role model in his life.

God knows he ain't getting it with Marley as his daddy.

Azule glanced at the wall that hid the safe room. It wouldn't do to open it while the cleaners were here. Kaylee would just have to wait a little longer.

It felt like forever, but the cleaning team filed out at a few minutes before noon, just as Luke signaled Malcolm was waking up. Azule signed the paperwork and shooed the last one out the door. The groundskeeper covered the gaping hole big enough to drive a car through where the glass window had been. He updated Azule with an estimate on how long it would take until the glass would be replaced and then turned on his heel and power-walked out to the driveway to order the news van off of the property. Azule watched him intimidate the driver until the van sped away, having snapped a couple of pictures of the broken window. She was sure they would camp out outside of Sinai and wait for someone to give them a scoop on the billionaire being treated inside.

Vultures.

Azule waited until the last of them had vanished down the drive, the gates locking behind them, before she turned to the safe room door. The door was unlocked and opened silently; the heavy door perfectly weighted, effortless to open. Two dozen steps down into the suite and Kaylee was waiting, her eyes red, face splotched with red.

White girls look a sorry sight when they been crying.

"Az, do we know anything? Is Mal okay? How did you get him calm? Please tell me Jack is okay. Is he?"

Azule held her hand up. "Girl, you need to stop and just breathe for a moment. Sit down and I'll tell you what I know."

Kaylee gulped, nodded, and sat down on a nearby chair. Around them were bookshelves crammed full of science fiction books.

There was also a small table and chairs along with a kitchenette. A long hallway with several doors stretched away in the opposite direction. Malcolm slept in one room and Azule knew there was at least one other guest bedroom down here, along with a workout room and another that held enough weapons to stop an army of invaders. She shook her head and wondered why in the hell Jack hadn't run inside of the panic suite behind Mal and Kaylee. It was just like him to play the hero and damn near get himself killed.

Azule grabbed another chair and sat down facing Kaylee, opening her mouth to speak just as her cell phone rang.

There was a smile on her face as she ended the call. "He's out of surgery and the doctors expect him to make a full recovery."

Kaylee burst into a set of fresh tears and buried her face in her hands. "This is all my fault."

"Funny, I thought the dead bitch knifed our boy, not you," Azule said dryly. "You order the hit on yourself?" Kaylee looked up at her in surprise. "Girl, he didn't have to tell me you were in trouble, you got the look. It says you got a lot of running left to do if you don't get help."

"Jack tried to help and look where it got him," Kaylee protested.

"Jack slipped up," Azule barked at the girl, her lips flattening in displeasure. "That's the price you pay for thinking a player's out of the game when they aren't. He let his guard down, and that's on him, Kaylee, not you." She examined her left ring finger. She'd chipped the nail in her rush to get here. Azule had been halfway to the house on the 101, nearly two hours early for work, when Jack'd answered. Hearing the shots and the screams, it had her hammering at the keys hard enough to damn near snap it off. "Besides, if that white boy ends up dead, I'll have to go down there and double-kill him. I'll never find a job as good as this one."

She heard something that sounded suspiciously close to a snort from Kaylee and turned to catch the girl's half-smile.

"Do you really think he's going to be okay?"

"Yes, I do," Azule answered steadily, her brown eyes connecting with Kaylee's.

The girl's lower lip quivered, the tears gathering again, and Azule reached out and gave Kaylee's shoulders a small shake. "Get it together, Girl, Malcolm needs you calm. I can already see what a difference you are making. That boy couldn't stand any of the women Jack has brought home, but you? He needs you even-keeled and level-headed."

"Where is he?"

"Upstairs." The voice came from Luke, who was now standing halfway down the stairs and leaning over enough to show his face. "He's asking for a 'K.'"

"That's me, um, Kaylee." She looked back at Azule with a panicked expression, as if suddenly concerned she had said too much.

Azule nodded. "That's Luke. He works for Benton Security Services." She flapped her hand at Kaylee. "Go ask him to play Scrabble. Something, anything, to bring him back to center. I'll go to the hospital. They said he would be awake soon."

She turned to Luke. "I'll be adding extra security, but once you both get Mal back to calm, get them down here. I know that's what Jack will want. There're meals down here, everything they could need."

Azule took a deep breath as she watched them both disappear upstairs. She had weathered the shit storm. She wasn't sure how, but she had done it.

I'm billing him for my outfit. It was my favorite.

Rabbit Hole

Kaylee nicknamed the basement suite the Rabbit Hole and did her best to stay occupied for the twelve long days it took for Jack to return from the hospital.

The suite held three large bedrooms; one was Malcolm's, the other a spare bedroom intended for guests, and the third had been turned into a workout room. Luke brought a pile of clothes down from the upstairs room where she had been staying and filled the closet with them. He slept on the couch and insisted they bolt themselves in whenever he needed to leave, which was often, as he was apparently overseeing the installation of the new security system.

If Kaylee had been more of the outdoorsy type, she would have fallen for this tall, blond Adonis in flannel. As it was, he was easy on the eyes, and Malcolm apparently enjoyed how Luke cooked steaks because he requested them for dinner each evening as he and Kaylee hunkered over the Scrabble board. Other times she read from *Voyage from Yesteryear* and *Podkayne From Mars*, both science fiction books of Rainier's she remembered him reading. It got to where Scrabble tiles and science fiction had entered her dreams at night, but Kaylee stuck with it. At the beginning and end of each Scrabble game, she convinced Malcolm to practice shaking hands.

"You'll need to know, Mal. It's expected."

In between games, Mal watched the YouTube videos of the World Scrabble Championships obsessively. It had progressed to where even Kaylee had memorized play-by-play the last two annual championship winning games.

The first time she had convinced him to shake her hand, Mal had groaned, as if the touch of another actually hurt him. It had taken him nearly a week to perfect a solid grip and another to manage brief direct eye contact. It lasted for less than two seconds, but Mal was improving, and Kaylee felt a sense of pride flood through her. He might be older than her, older even than Rainier had been, but he felt like a younger brother.

Luke watched the exchange and said nothing, a small smile often flitted across his lips. He had little to say, and Kaylee felt as if she was going stir-crazy. She'd been in the rabbit hole for nearly two weeks and, except for Azule, any conversation she had with Luke or Mal felt one-sided, even with Luke.

When a knock on the door came, Kaylee didn't even look up. She was biting her lip and staring at the Scrabble board, doing her best to figure out how to outsmart Mal's latest move. It was impossible, though. His skills had skyrocketed past hers with his constant study of the championship videos.

"Hey there," Jack's voice intruded on her thoughts.

Kaylee jumped, her eyes focusing on Jack's, and she leaped to her feet. "Oh my God, Jack! I thought they weren't releasing you until tomorrow!" She ran over and hugged him, burying her face in his shoulder.

Jack gave a small "oof" of discomfort and she immediately released him. He smiled down at her. "I got early release for exemplary behavior."

"Don't believe him for a second." Azule's voice floated down the stairs. "He was a terrible patient. If it wasn't for him being rich and good-looking, the nurses would have suffocated him in his sleep rather than spend another day listening to him."

"Now, Az, why do you have to ruin my image?" Jack called over his shoulder.

Azule snorted. "Seems to me the girl needs to know what she's getting into."

Kaylee laughed and, standing this close to him, remembered how he had looked lying there on the floor, his blood staining the carpet. Tears welled up in her eyes.

"Oh, Jack."

"Shh, I'm fine. A little sore, but nothing I won't recover from. I came down to see if you are ready to come out of your rabbit hole."

Kaylee snorted. "Ready? Um, yes, very much so."

Stepping back onto the main floor for the first time in nearly two weeks brought back every searing memory of that day. They had replaced the broken glass windows and the furniture and carpet. She had heard them working away upstairs over the past two weeks, distant thumps and bumps and the whine of machinery. From what Azule had told her, they had amped up security to where, as Azule wryly put it, "A mouse wouldn't be able to fart within a hundred yards without SWAT descending upon the house in under three minutes flat."

Kaylee stared at the large picture window and Jack followed her glance, saying, "They have replaced it with bulletproof glass."

"I'm so sorry, Jack. This is my fault."

"Kaylee, I promised you would be safe here, and I was wrong. This is my fault. I'm in the security and protection business and I never took the proper precautions with my house."

"Especially after that Shane character showed you how poor it was, too," Azule commented dryly.

Kaylee wasn't sure who Shane was, or what incident she was referring to, but the look on Azule's face told her that this had been something Azule had pushed for with Jack for some time now.

Kaylee looked over at Azule, who was wearing a gorgeous blue pantsuit. "That looks beautiful, Az, is it new?"

Azule beamed. "It is. New from Eloquii, courtesy of Jack, who ruined my favorite dress and matching jacket with all that madness the other day. Dry cleaners said I'd never get the blood out."

Jack arched his eyebrows at her and said nothing.

Malcolm slid past the group and sat down in the living room, turning on the television. Kaylee realized it was time for *Jeopardy*. And the creature of habit that Malcolm was, he wasn't about to miss it. The TV was not on its usual station, however, and instead, a news headline flashed across the screen at that very moment.

Kaylee gasped audibly; her eyes glued on the screen.

"What is it?" Jack turned to see, but Mal had already pressed the button and changed the channel. Alex Trebek was on the screen. He turned back to Kaylee. "What's wrong?"

She felt lightheaded, ill. "It's...it was...Julianna." She knew better than to ask Malcolm to change it back; *Jeopardy* had already begun and interfering with his routine caused a negative reaction, no matter how much he seemed to enjoy having her around. She had learned to work within his world, and gently draw him out of his own in increments. Changing the channel would likely cause him to howl in dismay. "I need to see the news, especially out of Louisiana."

A few moments later, after a quick search on Jack's laptop, she gasped and stabbed at the screen with her finger. "There, read that!"

Jack read the article and then glanced up at Kaylee. "That's your stepmother?"

"Yes," she whispered, eyes filling. "I know what Rainier thought of her, but she was kind to me."

"Except for drugging you," Jack pointed out, frowning.

"Well, yes, except for that. But Jack, they think I had something to do with it."

"Yes, I saw that towards the bottom of the article." He pointed to a link. "And it looks as if Rainier and Lincoln's deaths were ruled homicides and..." he clicked on the article, "...you are listed as a person of interest in that as well."

Kaylee's eyes grew wide in shock. "Do they really think I killed my brother and his friend? And my stepmother?"

Jack didn't look up, his lips moving as he read another article link. "Over $100 million in funds were transferred out of Cenac Shipping to an offshore account with your, well, Adrienne Cenac's, name on it." He looked up. "Neatly framed. You would spend years trying to prove your innocence in the courts."

"If she lived that long," Azule spoke up, sitting in front of her own laptop at the kitchen counter, her eyes fixed on the screen.

"Az, mind your bedside manners there," Jack replied, his forehead wrinkling. "It will be alright, Kaylee, I promise."

"No," Kaylee said, her heart plummeting. "It won't." She ran her fingers through her hair, felt them shake. "They, whoever they are, will not let this go. Not until I'm dead. And everyone protecting me is at risk as well."

"We will figure it out, Kaylee," Jack promised her, obviously worried, and yet so certain he could help her.

"No, no, we won't," Kaylee said, equally certain. She looked at him. "I need to disappear. Help me disappear, Jack."

Azule added her opinion to the mix. "She's right, Jack. The girl needs to disappear, not hang out front and center with you."

Kaylee watched as Jack's jaw dropped, and a look of betrayal suffused his face.

Azule persisted. "She can never be safe here. You live in the limelight. What are you going to do, hide out in that there rabbit hole until the bad guys just magically shrug their shoulders and give up? Girl needs an ID, a new look, and then she'll blend in on any college campus. Safe as a bug in a rug."

Kaylee met Jack's eyes and could see an internal war was being waged. He wanted her, and God, she wanted him, but seeing him there on the ground, blood everywhere, nearly dying because of her... She couldn't stand it, not if it meant risking his life and...

"You can't be by my side, Jack. There's Mal to consider. He needs you. You know he does." She looked away, her heart breaking. She had lost everyone she ever loved. Mom, Father, Rainier, and hell, even Julianna. No matter if she was behind most of this or not, Julianna had been kind to her. And now, on top of all of that, all the horror of the past few weeks, she had to say goodbye to both Jack and even Mal, both of whom she loved. Mal, who was well on his way to shaking people's hands and being able to calm himself enough that he could actually take part in a Scrabble championship in the future. She wanted that for him, wanted to be standing there in the audience when he won.

Kaylee didn't dare look at Jack. It was all she could do to not think of him holding her in his arms, making love to her in the shower, or high in his treehouse underneath the stars. She felt safe in his arms; she felt loved and desired. Kaylee uttered the words, quickly, cleanly, before she let the truth stop her and bid her stay.

"I want to leave, Jack, and I need to live my life as Kaylee. I need to be that person inside and out. Somewhere far from here, to college. You know I can't be with you." She met his eyes then. "Help me become someone else and then let me go to live my life."

Her stomach twisted even as she kept her face emotionless. He stared back at her, devastated by her words, before he nodded and turned on his heel, disappearing out the front door, and on out of her sight.

Your New Life

The hotel room had a view of the tallest, sleek downtown skyscrapers in Atlanta, but at the moment, neither of them had any interest. The moment the door had clicked shut, Kaylee had pressed her body against his, on her tiptoes, capturing his mouth in hers. Jack had barely had time to set the bag down. Her lips opened to his, their tongues intertwining. He backed up towards the bed, her body in lockstep with his, until he felt the end of the bed meet the backs of his legs. He fell backward, his feet on the floor, his back sinking into the soft mattress.

They had held off for weeks, Kaylee worried any strenuous activity would injure the stab wound. And he had wanted her, been starved for her, even as they lay spooned in bed together each night.

But today, well, today was different. Today was their last day together.

He had agreed to her wishes, even as every part of him fought the reality. He had gotten a new identity, one that would hold up to just about any scrutiny. She had cut her hair, and Azule had taken her to have it styled, permed, and colored. The colored eye contacts made her eyes a forest green. It was a stunning change, the green eyes and a curly mop of red. She had looked different enough that he had done a double-take, shocked at the transformation. He could still see the girl he had fallen for, especially when she smiled at him, and for a desperate moment hoped that her new look would be enough, even as he knew it wouldn't. He didn't want to lose her, but they were all in danger if she stayed.

She straddled him on the bed, pulling her blouse off in one swift motion and tossing it aside. She leaned down and kissed him again, her fingers busy on the buttons of his shirt, her nails brushing against his now-bare skin as she pushed aside the fabric and skimmed them gently over the scar on his abdomen. It twinged slightly. Another few weeks' recovery and he would be fine, but the scar was still angry and red. It would fade in time. He wasn't so sure if the scar forming on his heart would fade at all.

"Kaylee..."

"Shh, no talking." She unbuckled his belt, and in a few efficient movements had his pants down at his ankles. He kicked them off, along with his linen and leather boat shoes, and groaned as she settled down between his legs and took him in her mouth, her mouth and tongue working up and down his shaft, licking, sucking. Her breath was warm, and it tickled his hairs. He closed his eyes, overwhelmed by the sensation of her touch, awash in a sea of sensation as Kaylee took more of him into her mouth, enveloping him in ecstasy.

When she released him, and wiggled out of her skirt and panties, he was half out of his mind. He tried to sit up, but Kaylee pushed him back on the bed. "Uh uh, you are staying put." Instead, she straddled his waist once more while he rubbed the tip of one nipple until it was hard and tight. She slowly lowered herself onto him and closed her eyes in pleasure as she slid up and down, pulling him deep into her silken depths, then nearly releasing him, before doing it again, and again, and again.

Jack wanted to lose himself in her. He wanted the moment to last for a decade, a century, and for this to not be the last time, but the first. He groaned in pleasure as she slid up and down, the tempo increasing gently, his hands coming to rest on her hips as he drew her up and then back down, burying himself deep inside of her only to come away again, and then return.

He didn't want to be here. Jack wished he could disappear with her. He wanted to take her to Lake Tahoe, to his family's villa in the south of France. He wanted to fuck her in the moonlight high in the treehouse and never think of the people who had tried to kill her, or him, again.

Instead, he let the momentum build. Guiding her hips up and down, his fingers digging into her buttocks as they both drew close, a crescendo of heat, sensation, and light exploded as first Kaylee, and then he exploded into orgasm. They fell together, Jack still inside her, and rolled to their sides as the last shudders racked them both.

Jack wrapped his arms around her. Perhaps if he held her, just like this, she would see how much he needed her to stay, how much she needed him. Their breaths still came fast, and Jack could feel his heart ache in his chest. It wasn't just the lovemaking; it was the dread of having to say goodbye.

She had stayed with him for all of July and most of August. No one had bothered them, no other assassins had attempted to finish what the lone woman had started, and Jack had felt hope. Irrational and hopeless as it was, he had hoped that whoever was trying to kill her had finally given up. That they had a future together.

She was everything he wanted, everything he never knew he needed, and his heart ached at the thought of losing her even as he struggled to convince her to stay.

They had spent the last six weeks working out the details of her new identity. She was an orphan, raised in foster care after her parents died in a car crash when she was fifteen. With no family, she had qualified for a program that would pay for her room, board, and tuition entirely. In reality, the funds had come from Jack, an insignificant amount of funds to him, one that Kaylee had accepted gratefully.

Heir to a multi-million-dollar company. If she showed her face, she risked being arrested, charged, and then held in custody until her trial. The chances of her surviving jail and the murderous reach of the Indalo was small, as Azule had so astutely pointed out.

Which put them here, in this hotel room, the day before Orientation at Georgia Tech.

They lay there in silence, eyes closed, and Jack could hear the sounds of the city in the streets below them.

It was now or never.

"Kaylee," Jack breathed, his heart feeling as if it was breaking apart in his chest, "Please stay."

She sighed, long, sad. "I can't, Jack. I just, I *can't*." She couldn't look at him, or wouldn't. The end was the same.

He tried again. "Adrienne..."

Tears gathered in her eyes. "No. Adrienne is dead. She died with her mom, with her dad and Rainier and Lincoln. Everything she had, everything she was, she's gone." She looked down at her hands captured in his. "Besides, I'll always be Kaylee to you. I like Kaylee."

She changed the subject. "Mal's ready for his first tournament. I know he can beat some top Scrabble players; he's that good."

Jack wanted to argue with her, tell her that Mal would suffer with her gone, but he couldn't summon the words. They had hashed it out, over and over, in the past five weeks until there had been no more arguments he could use, nothing more he could say.

"Will you promise to sign him up for the tournament in Mendocino? Please?"

Jack nodded, not trusting his voice.

"Good." Kaylee rested her head on his chest, the red curls sprawled along her cheek. It was a good look, to be sure. No one would look twice at her. Well, they'd look twice, she was drop-dead gorgeous, but they wouldn't see Adrienne Cenac. They would see Kaylee. She would be safe, and she would remain that way if he kept his distance. But God, how he hated the idea. She belonged in his arms, in his life, and in his bed.

"Jack?"

"Yes?"

"I'm going to miss you. More than you know."

"You better." She gave a soft laugh in response and nestled closer.

The night before had been nothing but tossing and turning all night. And now, in the warmth of the late morning, with the sun's rays stealing in and warming the bed, Jack felt his eyes slip closed. He had everything he needed in his arms and he fell into a deep, untroubled sleep.

Kaylee's kiss woke him with a start. The light in the room had changed, moved, and he could see that the sun was lower in the sky than it had been. Her curls framed her face and, in the shadows, he could see the glimmer of tears in her eyes.

Jack realized she was dressed. Her blouse done up, her flared short skirt in place, and from the dampness of her curls, he would guess she had showered as well. All while he had slept like a stone, squandering these last precious hours.

"You looked so peaceful," she said, brushing her hand gently along his cheek. "I didn't want to wake you."

He hadn't slept well for days, weeks, really. The thought of her leaving had put everything he had dreamed of doing with her on hold. Barcelona, the apartment in New York, so many things. Instead, they had hunkered down, guards at the gates, and she had practiced shaking hands with Mal each morning, afternoon, and evening among endless games of Scrabble. In between those activities had been the selecting of the perfect college, his calling in a favor through his father's friend, Dean Mahoney, to get her a placement at Georgia Tech when their roster was already at capacity. Kaylee had chosen a major in business management and a minor in architecture.

The change in her appearance had been relatively simple. The haircut, perm, and color had changed the whole look of her face, as had the contacts. She wasn't Adrienne Cenac. Not any longer. And as Kaylee said, that girl was dead, along with the rest of her family. The birth certificate of a stillborn baby girl by the last name of Stromm and born just three months after Kaylee was, that had been the last piece of her new identity.

It was Azule's and Teeny's connections that had made it happen, the combined efforts of artistry and fraud that would hold up to most inspections, especially once she had her degrees to back her up.

"Come on, get dressed. I found a place that reminds me of home. They have a fusion of Louisiana, Central Mexico, and Belize cuisine. I haven't had red snapper in months." Her smile faltered for a moment, and Jack wondered if she was remembering a meal out with her family or friends. Just a few months ago, her life had been relatively simple, pleasant, and then everything had come apart.

"You want to go out?" He sat up and reached for his shirt and slowly drew it onto his body. "I'd love to eat in."

"It's on the way to the airport. You have that meeting tomorrow. Az mentioned it as we were leaving."

He didn't give a damn about the meeting, not if it meant he had to leave tonight.

I don't want to leave her here. Not for a minute, not for a day, and sure as hell not forever.

He dressed in silence and they stepped out into the fading light of the day. They ate dinner at Lemon Butter Seafood, which sound more like a menu item than the name of a restaurant. It was surprisingly good.

"I'll definitely need to come back here," Kaylee said, devouring her red snapper as Jack picked at his whiting fillet. She kept up a cheery patter of commentary, partly out of nervousness, partly out of an attempt to sound happy. Having spent the last two months in her company, he knew her better than that. She was miserable and anxious, just as much as he was.

The cab waited behind them as they said their goodbyes. The tears pooled in her eyes, then slid down her cheeks. "I'll miss you, Jack, more than I can say."

"If you need anything," he said in return, and she nodded. "And I promise to take Mal to the Scrabble tournament."

She smiled through her tears. "I'll hold you to that, Jack Benton. I expect to see Malcolm Benton in a YouTube video by the end of the year."

They both laughed then, and she stood on her tiptoes to kiss him once more. The softness of her lips against his made his body flutter with desire and ache with loneliness, even with her standing there before him.

She walked away then and did not look back. Jack stood and watched her go, ignoring the pilot until the cab had disappeared into the evening traffic, its headlights one of dozens of sets in the dark evening.

Jack sat down on the plane and reached into his bag for his phone. He had kept it shut off all day. Jack didn't want to talk to anyone, to worry about any problems or issues. He just wanted to spend the little time he had left with Kaylee. He noticed several pages folded neatly sitting next to it in the deep pocket. As he drew it out of the bag, he caught a whiff of Kaylee's perfume. A rich scent of Hermes Jour d'Hermes suffused the papers. He unfolded them and saw that they were from the hotel, the Crowne Plaza emblazoned along the top of each page, covered in Kaylee's looping script.

The pretty flight attendant brought him a scotch on the rocks and the small, private jet took off, pointing back west towards home. He wouldn't arrive home until past midnight. He paused, thought of how her skin had felt in his hands, her soft heat, how he had felt her come seconds before his own orgasm.

I could tell the pilot to turn around right now. I don't want to read this goodbye letter she has written. I don't want this to be a goodbye.

He willed the urge away and read.

Dearest Jack-

You look so peaceful there on the bed, as if all of your cares have slipped away. I've watched you sleep before; you know. Don't tell me I'm creepy, please, because I couldn't help it. You sleep HARD as if it is painful. Perhaps it is. Perhaps, like me, you think of everyone you have lost and they haunt your dreams like they do mine. But today, lying there, you are different, contented, peaceful.

I wish we could have that. But right now, we can't. We honestly cannot.

God, that hurts to even write that. Because, even though we have known each other such a short time, I am in love with you. I dare not say it out loud, or to your face, so instead, I put it here on paper, where you will find it later after we have said our goodbyes.

Thank you for all that you have done for me. I have a chance at a normal life. It isn't one I planned for, and it isn't one I expected or was raised for, but I can see it, just over the horizon, waiting for me. I want to lose myself in a lecture hall, go to parties, maybe join a sorority. I want to be normal, if only for just a little while.

I think you can understand that, or at least accept it.

I think too that you and me, we aren't over. For now, we go our separate ways and I hope that the time will come when it is safe for us to be together again. Jack, I want so much for my life, for yours, even for Mal's. I want to see his name up there in the rolls of champions, and I hope to see us all happy and safe and someday...someday...I want to kiss you again.

I love you, Jack. No matter what comes to pass in the years to come, I hope you remember that.

-K.-

The Situation at Hand

Five years later...

It had been five days of sheer hell since Kaylee's phone call. Whatever he had hoped to accomplish that week, it was derailed by thoughts of Kaylee. Her voice, her face, the memory of her skin against his – it consumed his waking hours and filled his dreams at night.

The updates from Shane had done little to distract him, and the situation had quickly unfolded there in Kansas City—paid assassins with an all too familiar tattoo had raised his hackles. Kaylee had gone radio silent as well, and he couldn't help wondering if she was okay.

It was mid-morning on Friday when he marched into Azule's office.

"Az, I need a flight to Kansas City, please."

Azule lifted one eyebrow and set her coffee down slowly. "I'm guessing you need it for today?"

"Yes."

A smile escaped her then. "Give me a few minutes and I'll get the private jet." She turned away, phone at her ear, long fingernails tapping away at her computer. Jack walked into the atrium, hoping the sounds of the waterfall would ease his angst. He had felt on edge since Kaylee's phone call on Monday, and getting an earful of one of his best employees boning a client, no matter how hot she was, had not helped. Whatever was going on with Shane, Jack was better off dealing with it in person.

He stared at the koi as they moved about, their round mouths sucking at the surface, searching for treats. Every night since her phone call, he had dreamed of her. They had been increasingly upsetting. First her kissing another man as he walked in, another of her telling him they couldn't be together, and the most recent ones had included her running, shot and hurt.

I should have flown out on Monday. I could have dealt with this business with her friend myself, or gotten Jesse involved.

Jesse had been on vacation through Wednesday, though, and Jack had been sure Shane could handle it. Shane had never gotten involved with a client. And Jack was mad as hell at this turn of events. But then again, he'd seen a picture of the young woman, Lila. An attractive girl. But Jack's mind was filled with thoughts of Kaylee. Her soft, Southern drawl, her honey-brown hair, and...

"I have you leaving on a flight at one, Jack." Azule's voice behind him broke his reverie, and he turned to face her. His assistant was grinning smugly at him.

"You look like a cat that just ate the canary, Az," he commented as he took the Post-it note she held out to him.

"I've been waiting all week to book that flight for you, Boss."

"Have you now?" Damn Az and her Cheshire cat smile.

Azule snorted. "Hell, yes. I saw it in your face the minute you heard her voice. Give her a hug from me, will you?" She winked then, a playful smile appearing on her face. "Or bring her back so I can hug her myself."

Jack had been telling himself all morning that he needed to go to Kansas City to deal with the debacle of the shootout at One Kansas City Place and the shortcomings of his employee, but it had been a lie. He could see that now, staring at Azule's smug, pleased look. He was going there for Kaylee. And if he had any sense at all, hell, if she still loved him, then he wouldn't come back until he had her in his arms. He went inside to pack a bag and left a note for Malcolm.

The plane landed after sundown near downtown Kansas City. As it did, his phone vibrated, and he saw he had a message. He read it and then placed a call to Azule as the plane taxied over to the low-slung building next to a busy freeway. "Az, could you please look up a Liam Sorenson? Looks like he might be here in KC." He waited patiently for her response before he thanked her and ended the call. It looked as if he would need to meet this kid while he was here. As the plane stopped and the outer door opened, his fingers flew across the tiny screen and he heard the email swoosh away.

Hours later, however, Jack faced a small army of police officers swarming the house on the hill. His client, Lila, was shivering under a blanket in the back of the ambulance. Ellis was now standing outside with the paramedics as they bandaged his arm.

"We will need to treat this at the hospital," the taller, heavier paramedic stated. "And we should probably get you checked out as well, Miss," he said, looking at Lila. "Your feet really took a beating."

Lila tucked her filthy, scratched feet under the blanket and replied, "I'm fine, really I am, but I'm not leaving Shane."

Shane stared at her and then laughed, startling the paramedic bandaging his arm. "Now you are following The Code?"

"Better late than never." That made him laugh even harder. She laughed too. Jack, however, did not.

Jack shot Shane a look. Between the butt dial that had caught Ellis in a more than compromising position with his client, and a shootout that had ended with a dead body in the basement of his property, Jack was less than pleased.

In the past six years, Shane Ellis had proven himself to be one of Jack's best bodyguards, despite his origins. Jack had worried that his lack of military training would be a problem, but Shane had handled himself well and become a valued member of Benton Security Services. At least, until he met Lila Benoit.

Shane reacted to Jack's look of disapproval, shook his head at the paramedic, and pulled away. "I'm fine, really. The bullet only grazed me."

A police officer walked over. "After they check you out at the hospital, Miss Benoit, we will need to speak to you down at the station."

Shane reached out with his undamaged hand and took hers, glancing at Jack as he did.

Jack interceded, "I understand that Rob Stone is heading the investigation into the shooting at Kurgen Real Estate. I believe the events of tonight are connected to that. I would request that you contact the detective and we will be happy to answer his questions after my employee and client are checked out at the hospital."

The ambulance was crowded, but the paramedics allowed Jack to accompany Shane and Lila to the hospital. The police officer followed behind in a patrol car. When they arrived at the hospital, however, Jack stepped forward and placed a hand on Lila's shoulder.

"Miss Benoit, if you please, they will get Mr. Ellis cleaned up with stitches, and you and I need to speak with the detective when he arrives." The sooner he spoke with the client, the sooner he could track down Kaylee. Jack looked around the large waiting area and found a corner that was empty of others and steered her towards it. The police officer followed, sitting across from them, his eyes watchful as he surveyed the room. His phone rang then, and he stood up and walked away to answer it.

"Can I get you some coffee or tea, Miss Benoit?" Jack asked. Lila was still shivering. The hospital staff had found her a pair of warm hospital socks once they had checked out her feet and pronounced them bruised but otherwise undamaged.

She shook her head. "I'm not cold...it's nerves, I guess."

"Perfectly understandable." He regarded her for a moment, saying nothing.

The silence stretched before them.

Lila finally asked, "So, you know Kaylee?"

"I do."

"How?"

He smiled. "That's not my story to tell, Miss Benoit."

Lila grimaced. "Right."

The police officer returned from his phone call. "Miss Benoit, I'm going to have to ask you to return with me to the station. You will speak with Detective Peisker, and he will take your statement on tonight's events."

"I thought I was going to be speaking to Detective Stone," she said and turned to Jack. "Isn't that the detective who was assigned to the shooting at Kurgen?"

Jack frowned, but before he could speak, the officer answered. "Yes, ma'am, he was, but Detective Peisker is also working that case."

Jack stood up. "Did you say was, Officer, as in, no longer is?"

The officer looked grim. "I'm really not at liberty to say, Mr. Benton, but I must insist that we go to the station directly. If you wish to accompany Miss Benoit, that is fine, but Peisker will question her at the station."

It was a brief ride to the station, and the officer ushered them both into the interrogation room.

Jack had a bad feeling about all of this. Lila Benoit not only needed his protection; she might need his legal services as well. He turned to Lila. "Miss Benoit, would you have a dollar that I might have?"

Lila blinked in surprise, then dug into her purse and handed him the only bill in her wallet, a ten-dollar bill.

"Thank you, Miss Benoit." Jack Benton smiled at her, neatly folded up the bill, and placed it in the breast pocket of his designer jacket just as a tall, heavyset man entered and closed the door.

"Miss Benoit, my apologies for keeping you waiting. I'm Detective Peisker."

Jack asked, "Where is Detective Stone?"

Peisker sighed. "Rob Stone has been murdered."

Lila gasped, her hand going to her mouth. "Oh my God."

Jack asked, "Is it possible it relates to your current case?"

"I do not know, Mr. Benton, but we are exploring all leads." He rubbed his eyes. "Rob and I worked together for nearly a decade. He was a fine man, a good partner, and a devoted father. The KCPD will not rest until we find out what happened to one of our own. Meanwhile, Miss Benoit, I would like to question you about the events that occurred this past Monday and tonight."

"Before I say anything, do you know if Detective Stone found the SD card?" Lila asked, her hands twisting. "The file that I saw, it was on an SD card and it was there in my laptop. I also copied it onto a flash drive for my boss, Mr. Endon."

Max shook his head. "I'm sorry, Miss Benoit, but there wasn't any SD card in your laptop."

"But..."

"And Mr. Endon handed over the flash drive. It was empty."

"That's," Lila said, "that's not possible."

"Mr. Endon stated that the flash drive was blank, and he did not know of any SD card. I'm sorry, Miss Benoit, but we can't find any trace of these suspicious files you believe you may have found."

Detective Peisker stared at Lila. "So, is there anything you aren't telling me? Anyone you might owe money to? Any crime you may have seen committed or," he paused before continuing, "possibly had a part in committing?"

Lila jumped to her feet. "What? You cannot seriously be blaming me for this! I was attacked, not once but three times! They have shot at me! That man I killed tonight; he was the one from the parking garage!" Lila shook, afraid.

Jack reached out and touched her shoulder gently.

Max gave a tired, half smile. "My apologies, Miss Benoit. These are questions I would ask of anyone in your situation. Now, if you could sit down..."

Lila did as the detective asked. Jack watched her as she closed her eyes and took two deep, slow breaths in and out.

Jack spoke up. "Miss Benoit has had some terrifying experiences this past week, Detective."

Max turned to him and frowned. "It is highly irregular to have you here, Mr. Benton. I understand you were communicating with my partner, Detective Stone, but I think it would be advisable for you to wait outside until I have spoken with Miss Benoit for a few minutes alone."

Jack nodded. "I understand how you might feel that way, but I'm afraid that you misunderstand the situation here. Miss Benoit is a client."

Max snapped. "Yes, Mr. Benton, I know she retained Benton Security Services for personal protection, although that worked so well that she had to kill the attacker herself."

Jack smiled. "Actually, Detective, she did not retain my security company's services; I provided those to her at no cost." He reached inside his coat pocket and set down a simple, yet elegant card onto the metal table. "I am an attorney. Lila is my client."

Lila's jaw dropped.

Max Peisker did not look pleased. "I see. Miss Benoit, do you wish for your legal counsel to stay here with you while we talk?"

Lila responded quickly, "Yes, thank you."

The detective grimaced and began his questioning. Jack shot down some of the more outrageous questions Peisker asked, while others he allowed Lila to answer. The hours ticked by as she recounted the incidents of the past week that had led to her shooting the dark-haired assassin that evening. By the second repetition, Lila appeared to be having difficulty stringing her words together. It was past midnight, and she hunched over, holding her head in her hands. Her skin was pale, and she looked exhausted.

"Detective, I must insist that we continue this line of questioning after my client has rested," Jack said, putting his hand once again upon her shoulder. "I am assuming she is free to go?"

"We have no proof of the existence of these suspicious files that Miss Benoit claims to have found, but I think that, until we have discussed this in its entirety, it would be best for her to remain in protective custody. Not in a jail cell," he clarified as he saw the look on Jack's face, "but under police protection."

"Fine," Jack said, "But I would like one of my men to be there as well."

"I'm afraid that won't be possible, Mr. Benton," Peisker said, shaking his head. "No civilians."

"Jesse Bardin is one of your own, Detective, a member of the KCPD who has worked part-time for me for the past two years."

Max gritted his teeth. "Fine, Mr. Benton, have it your way." He stood up. "I'll make the arrangements and we will pick this up again in the morning."

"Afternoon."

"What?"

Jack smiled. "I think that one in the afternoon will be early enough, considering it is already morning."

Detective Peisker glared at him and walked out of the room.

Jack chuckled to himself.

"Thank you, Mr. Benton," Lila said, standing up. "Have you had any word on Shane?"

"Yes, he's fine, and they released him from the hospital. I received a text from him an hour ago. And now, if you will excuse me, I need to contact Jesse and arrange for him to stay with you at the safe house. Frankly, he's the only member of the KCPD I trust with this right now. We will get you someplace safe, Miss Benoit. After you have had some time to rest, we will discuss what happens next. Sound good?"

Lila nodded, and Jack knocked on the door and waited until they opened it. It was late, far too late to see Kaylee now, but he had phone calls to make. Jesse, for one. And Azule, who had insisted on being updated as soon as possible. Despite the late hour, he knew she would wait to hear from him. He pulled out his phone and dialed.

There was no time for sleep. He had some research to do before meeting this Liam Sorenson later in the morning.

Where You Go, I Go

Jack's meeting with Liam, and subsequent discovery of the mistakenly saved file to Lila's personal Dropbox, had been the evidence they needed to hit the Indalo where it hurt. He stepped lighter, knowing that someone would pay for the attempt on Lila's life. With that business behind him, and the FBI taking Lila into witness protection, Jack was free to walk away, knowing that Kaylee's friend was safe.

He parked in front of the house on the narrow street. How often had he looked at this address on Google and thought of walking up and knocking on the door? More times than he cared to count.

There was a nip in the air, the temperature already plunging, the skies gray overhead. A winter storm was on the way, and Jack thought of his home in Lake Tahoe. How long had it been since he visited there? Too long. It had snowed there a few days ago, early for the season. He could picture it in his mind, though. The angular wood and glass house on the hill, framed by pine and aspen trees, the enormous fireplace glowing and warm. Every winter of his youth had been spent there—first frolicking in the snow building snowmen and sledding, then skiing, and finally snowboarding. The plane crash had ended that annual tradition. He wondered what Malcolm would think of the snow. Would he like it or stay curled up indoors playing Scrabble with anyone who was amenable?

She had said she wanted to live her life without fear. An impossibility, given what she knew, what she had learned. But he had honored it. He had paid for the best new identity money could buy. He had made sure she had a full ride at Georgia Tech, and not called her, not once, just as she had asked.

But was she safe? Really? The Indalo weren't small. If they were, someone at Kurgen, which was clearly Indalo-controlled, would have recognized her as the heir to Cenac Shipping. That didn't mean she was safe here, though, even if Kurgen was shut down. And that file that Lila Benoit had found, and nearly paid for with her life, it had more than just real estate holdings. He would leave it to Liam and Teeny to dig deep into that file and find out more.

The thought of her living here, in this house, with no one to protect her, no one to keep her safe—it was one reason he was here, now. Jack rubbed his hand over his face. But the real reason was far simpler. He hadn't gotten over her. It had been over five years since he found her, soaking wet, half-conscious, on the side of the road. Women had come and gone since, and none of them had held a candle to her. Not a one of them had even come close.

He watched a pickup truck rattle down the road and stop late, nearly getting hit by oncoming traffic. A chorus of honks back and forth between the truck and a small commuter car issued forth.

What am I doing out here, anyway? Go knock on the damn door or drive back to the airport. One choice or the other, Benton.

He cracked the door open and slid out of his seat, his mind finally decided. The house was a unique mix of wood and limestone that was quite prevalent to the area. The yard was stark now, the green fading to brown, but he had seen it full of flowers in the Google photos, carefully tended and full of blooming bushes and flowers. The door was a heavy wood, studded with metal. It had a tiny glass window inset high up. He could imagine her on her tiptoes as she peered out. Below the window was an old-fashioned metal knocker, which he reached for now, letting it hit the strike plate twice before he released it. The house was well-built. He couldn't hear anything from inside, not even a whisper of a footstep, before the door opened.

She smiled up at him, and his heart thudded in his chest.

"Hi, Jack. I was wondering when you would get here." She opened the door further, and he stepped inside, casting a glance around. He had looked up pictures of the house on Trulia when it was first listed for sale. She had made some changes. The furniture, for one. A mix of antique and mid-century pieces that blended in perfectly with the warm hues of paint that she had chosen for the walls. Where the previous owners had painted everything, including the woodwork, a stark white, Kaylee had returned the house to its original wood tones and then combined it with soft greens and blues and blush reds, saving the more vibrant colors for the fabrics on the furniture.

The door closed softly behind him, along with several locks.

He turned to face her. She had cut her hair in a cute pixie cut. It was still red, although she had stopped using a perm and it was now straight. The contacts still made her eyes the same forest green. Other than that, she looked much the same as she had five years before. Just as beautiful as he remembered her.

"I wasn't sure if you would want to see me." The words practically stuck in his throat. What if he had made a mistake coming here? What if she was just being kind?

Her expression changed, softened, and she reached out a hand to touch his face. "I can't think of anyone I would rather see right now."

"Mal misses you."

The corners of her mouth quirked up. "I told you he was a champion. I watched the competition live; his letter combination of prurient was devastating with the triple word score...he was amazing!"

Jack grinned. "He was. The first thing he asked after he won was if you had seen it. I told him I was sure you had." His stomach was doing flips just standing in her house, staring down at her. "I missed you more than I can say."

Two steps. That was all it took. His arms slid around her, lifting her up, his mouth on hers. They didn't bother with words or explanations or questions. It was need, and desire, and love, and a wanting that had waited five years to be acknowledged. He kissed her, deep and hungry. She matched him in urgency. Her fingers busy at the buttons of his shirt, his hand cupping her luscious, toned rear in his hands, her legs wrapping around his waist as they toppled onto a long, velvet-covered tufted couch, his body sinking into the cushions as she straddled him. His shirt gaped open half out of his pants and he slid his hand up underneath her soft sweater to her soft, warm skin underneath.

She pulled her mouth from his and ran kisses along his jaw, to his ear, and then pulled his earlobe in her mouth and nibbled it gently. His hands slipped down, grabbed the bottom edges of her sweater, and slipped it off of her, capturing her lips with his again, his tongue probing, teasing.

He slipped the yoga pants off of her ass and edged them down off one leg, then the other as Kaylee pulled the tails of his shirt out of his pants and undid the last two buttons. Her hands didn't stop there. They glided over his bulging cock and made quick work of his belt and the button and zipper on his pants. He pulled away, stood up, and slipped out of his loafers and pants. Her gaze traveled down to his socks and giggled as he struggled to yank them off. He stared at her lying there, wearing only a silky bra and panties, hair mussed and arrayed on the velvet cushions, waiting for him to return to her. Her eyes had returned to his boxer briefs and the beast that had woken inside. She wasn't an inexperienced teenaged girl any longer, barely eighteen and a virgin. It relieved him. In the months and years after she had left, he had wondered if sleeping with her had been a mistake. If she had regretted having him as her first.

His dick throbbed, almost questioning, as he stood there, watching her, watching him. She smiled then and ran her hands down her sides slowly. One stopped at a breast, the other made its way to between her legs. Her eyes closed for a moment; a delicate tongue licked at the corner of her lips. His dick throbbed again, no longer questioning. He hooked the edges of his briefs, slid them down, and released it.

Kaylee smiled, her eyes half-lidded with pleasure as he bent down and slid the satin and lace aside, settling his mouth on her breast, feeling it harden in his mouth as he sucked, licked, and nibbled it. Each time he did, she gasped in delight. One delicate hand stroked him, keeping him hard as she writhed on the sofa beneath him. He tugged at the panties, pulling them down her legs and tossing them away before he parted her legs and pushed his way into her.

Kaylee moaned his name as he pulled out and thrust in again, his mouth on her left nipple. She felt so good, he was seeing stars. She grabbed his arm, sat up, and twisted her body until he was off balance and collapsed on the couch. Kaylee straddled him then, lifting herself up and onto him, rocking as she worked her way up and down, up and down. The sight of her, her hair falling forward, her bra straps having slid down on her arms and her nipples erect, hard where they had escaped the thin, silky fabric, her mouth open in a round 'o' of ecstasy as he watched her climax. Felt her climax. He bucked his hips, driving deeper into her, and came inside of her, shouting her name.

Her breaths were coming in soft pants, her hands on each side of his face, fingers stroking, and she pulled away long enough to whisper, "I never should have left you."

He answered in a matching whisper, "I never should have let you go."

Later, hours after the sun had slipped out of sight and they had moved up to her bedroom, tastefully decorated with rich colors, he lay in her bed and looked around. It occurred to him only then that she might be involved with someone. Maybe even dating, getting serious, and here he had just waltzed back into her life.

Kaylee caught his gaze. "There's been no one, really. A couple of flings, here and there, guys who wanted to stick around, take it further, but I..." She spread her hands; her eyes focused on his. "I guess it always came back to you."

He gritted his teeth at the thought of any other man getting close, kissing her, maybe even fucking her in this very bed. Without realizing he was doing it, he growled, and she laughed and kissed him.

"Don't be jealous, Jack. You'll get wrinkles if you keep frowning like that."

He kissed her back, harder than he intended, and she responded, her mouth hungry against his. But the nasty business at hand, the reason he was here in the first place, brought him back to the present.

"They call themselves the Indalo," he said, pulling back from her and reaching for his pants pocket, where a card with the image of a stick man with the heavens above was hand-drawn.

"I've had Teeny working on it, and I just hired a kid whose hacking skills are going to get us deep into the heart of this. They are everywhere. They use large firms, like Kurgen Real Estate, to engage in money laundering, or Cenac Shipping for their illegal dumping and government-level bribery schemes."

Kaylee sucked in a breath, her body tensing.

"They are here in Kansas City, Louisiana, Central America, Los Angeles, key locations throughout the world. Nowhere is safe, and that's why we need to stick together." He threaded his fingers through her hair. "You will be safe by my side. One way or the other, we can bring them down, but if you stay here, then so will I. Because the thought of you alone...it would kill me if something happened to you, Kaylee."

He reached into his other pants pocket and pulled out the ragged remains of her note, the one she had written in Atlanta and secreted into his bag to read after they parted ways.

"If you still feel this way about me, Kaylee, then come with me, or let me stay here with you. I've been in love with you since the moment I found you there on the side of the road in the rain and no one, *no one*, has ever come close to possessing my heart the way you do."

Her eyes glistened with unshed tears and she nodded before her mouth met his and she pulled him over her. Kaylee's legs wrapped around him and he slid inside of her, marveling at how her body and his felt so right together. Her hips rose to meet his as he slid in and out of her warm depths, her moans coming quicker while her body writhed beneath his. He wanted all of her, every bit of her body, her heart, her mind. As he came inside of her, her name a shout, he knew he would never leave her side again.

Calling All Hunters

Zella Dean's phone rang. She stared at the caller ID. She was busy. It could go to voicemail. After four rings it stopped, then began again. *Damn it.*

She wiped the blood off of her hands and stabbed the green button. "What?"

"Am I interrupting?" Delta's voice always made her think of velvet wrapped in steel.

"I was just finishing up," Zella answered. She looked around. With this amount of blood, she'd be here for hours cleaning it all up. Her orders were to make him disappear, but the stupid fuck had looked at her tits, and really, that was all it took.

"I wanted you to know that the mark who killed Nyra has resurfaced."

Zella stilled, her skin tightening, her teeth gritting together.

"Would you like for me to send you that information?" Delta asked after a moment of silence. "Or, I could..."

"I'll take it," Zella answered, her words clipped, fury surging through her. Finally, she would learn who had dared to kill her sister.

"Excellent. I'll have it sent to the usual drop site." Delta sounded pleased. "Oh, and Zella? Make them suffer. Your sister was unique, talented, and, well, we miss her. Even now."

Zella ended the call. Triumph at finally being allowed her revenge flowed through her. She smiled, then got back to work on the body on the floor in front of her. She was going to make them pay in ways they couldn't imagine, not in their worst nightmares.

Broken Code
Book 3

Jack Benton Can Kiss My...

The bell over the front door jangled in time with the ice-cold blast of wind and Angela, wrapped head to toe, snow dusting her knit cap.

Lila shivered and pulled her cardigan closer. The wind raced along the street, and at the height of winter, it was especially frigid. Angela was late, as usual. Even in winter, the girl couldn't make it to work on time.

"Oh my God, the weather is really taking a turn for the worse." Angela said, shivering and stomping her feet to avoid tracking it across the front of the store.

Margery, who had been waiting impatiently for Angela to arrive, levered herself out of a nearby chair. "You're late. Again."

Angela peered at her through a static-filled billow of hair that stuck out and waved wildly now that she released it from the knit cap. "Um... sorry?" She replied. Her tone sounded put-upon, more than truly sorry, and Lila hid a smirk as Margery rolled her eyes in Lila's direction.

"Right, well, I'm off to lunch and my appointment. See you tomorrow... oh wait, are you leaving tonight?" She waggled her eyebrows. "With Hubba Hubba hot guy?"

Lila grinned. "He's flying in tonight. We'll leave the day after tomorrow. Are you sure you'll be okay to open tomorrow? If not, I can swing by and do it."

Margery waved her fingers dismissively at Lila. "Don't you dare. Take the time, relax, for once! This baby has another month to go before he's due to make an appearance. I can use all the hours you'll give me until then." She ran a hand along her rounded belly and sighed. "I can open tomorrow and through the rest of the week. I just hope that Angela here will be on time every day."

"Oh, absolutely. Not a problem." Angela answered, unwinding a scarf that had to be six feet long. Her blond hair was dancing in a halo around her head and Lila could see the snaps of electricity arc. It was dry, far drier than she had thought it would be this close to the ocean.

Margery met Lila's eyes and shook her head. It was quite clear she had no faith in the younger woman's ability to make it to her shift on time. Which was no surprise, really, since if Angela showed up at the appointed time, it would be the first time. Lila wasn't sure what she was going to do when Margery had her baby next month. She'd been advertising for weeks and no one seemed interested. She could handle running the store on her own, with Angela's infrequent and unreliable appearances, but with the first book done and published, she was eager to start on the second book in the series. It was easier with another body in the store. Even during winter, which was the slowest season, she barely had enough time to handle the unboxing of deliveries, running the cash register, and all the other sundry details that it took to keep the store running. As it was, even now she handled the financial aspects at home, a time she preferred to be writing or spending time with Shane when he was in between assignments.

The last year had been hard. Maintaining a relationship with Shane absent more than he was there, had certainly pushed her to her limits. Each time he went away, she found it harder to say goodbye.

"Okay, out I go!" Margery said, and slid her parka hood over her head, clutching the front ends of it tight over her middle. Her belly prevented her from zipping it up. She waddled out the door, and the bell overhead gave a frenzied jingle while another gust of frigid air and flying snow blasted in. Lila watched as she half ran to her car and slid in. Seconds later, the car disappeared down the street into a wall of white.

"Okay, I'm just about finished up with the book order I need to make and then I need to get to Hanniford's for a few essentials." Lila told Angela, who had unwrapped her multiple layers and secured them in the back office.

"Will you be okay to close up today?" She asked the girl and Angela nodded. "You're sure?"

"Absolutely. Don't worry, Boss. I got you covered."

"Okay. Maeve should be in soon. She asked for me to hold *Midnight at the Blackbird Cafe* for her. It's in its usual place."

Angela saluted and settled herself on the stool behind the cash register.

Lila couldn't help it; she was really looking forward to Shane's visit. He'd been gone five weeks this time, with a grueling assignment. He had said little about it, just that he was really looking forward to the two weeks off. She smiled at the thought of the surprise she had waiting for him. A trip to Sugarloaf, a full week in an Airbnb, in a *caboose* no less! She had been seconds away from sharing the link and showing him, ever since he told her about train-watching as a kid. She just knew he would love it. But she'd stopped. It was going to be a surprise. She couldn't wait to see his face when they arrived.

There will be skiing, sure, but also all the time in the world to curl up in the caboose, just the two of us.

The bell jingled and the icy blast of wind and snow hit. The thought of just how they would keep each other warm helped Lila brave the elements. She pulled her coat tighter around her as she skittered and slid through the snow to reach her car. She really hoped Angela wouldn't let her down or make it too difficult on Margery.

Although what I am going to do for full-time help once Margery's baby comes, I do not know. I really doubt that Angela will ever be dependable.

Shane had turned down her offer to pick him up at the airport. "I can catch an Uber. It's on Benton Security Services dime, anyway. No need to drive in the snow. Besides, I need to run an errand first."

The sun was already beginning to fade from the sky by the time she ran a couple of errands and pulled into the driveway. These days, the sun was gone by 4:30 and didn't reappear until seven in the morning. She hated winter for that very reason. Practically her entire day spent inside, and by the time it was over, it was already dark. Today, however, she welcomed the sunset and darkness. It meant that Shane would be here soon.

At a quarter to six, headlights illuminated the drive, and she rushed to the door to find Shane grinning at her, the thick snow already settling in a moist layer across his broad shoulders. His backpack was slung over one shoulder, his hands filled with grocery bags. She grinned as she spied a bouquet tucked under his arm.

He leaned in and captured her lips in a kiss.

"Are those for me?" She asked, taking the bags from him as he wrestled with his boots.

"Nah, I figured I'd give them to your roommate."

"Well, lucky me, I don't have a roommate." She also didn't have a vase yet, she kept forgetting to order one. The bouquet was exquisite, the roses were a lovely shade of lavender mixed with a spray of white baby's breath.

I really, really need to buy a vase.

Shane laughed as Lila reached for the tall metal cup that sat under her chrome Hamilton Beach milkshake mixer. It was that or a Contigo, and she only had the one.

"What? It works!" She busied herself with unwrapping the bouquet and adjusting the positioning of the flowers after she filled it up with water.

"I thought you were going to buy a vase."

"I keep meaning to, really I do."

Meanwhile, the stainless-steel milkshake cup was the perfect height. Lila finished futzing with the flowers and set it in the middle of the small dining room table. They looked good there. And it was a far better use for the milkshake cup. She still remembered the first time she had used it. She had tried to make a boozy shake with the mixer, gotten the measurements all wrong, and given herself the hangover of a lifetime on a vodka root beer float. At that point, the mixer, as cute as it looked there on the countertop, was relegated to household decor status. And because Shane always brought her flowers, and she had nothing else to put them in, even when he visited, the silly thing remained unused.

Shane's arms enveloped her from behind as he nuzzled her neck. His nose was ice cold, thanks to the wintry mix outside her warm, cozy house. She squirmed in his embrace.

"Two weeks. Alone. You and me."

She turned around, slipped her arms around his waist and kissed him deep, hungry. He responded in kind, his hands moving gently at first, then matching her with intensity. They moved from her hips to her back and then reached down, pulling her up, both hands firmly cupping her butt, her feet off the ground, her legs wrapping around his waist as his tongue melded with hers.

They had been apart more than they were together, but even after six months, the attraction hadn't slackened. She still felt a surge of desire every time he looked in her direction.

Shane walked forwards, holding her, his mouth devouring hers, until they crashed into the kitchen island. The bags full of groceries crinkled and shifted. He had done a decent amount of shopping. She could see that, although right now, her mind was only on one thing, and it wasn't food. She slipped a hand inside of his jeans, her fingers sliding along his flesh. His breathing changed, accelerated, and he sat her on the counter, swearing as something round and green went tumbling to the floor.

"I was going to fix dinner first." He reached for the fallen produce. Something that resembled a fat green onion teetered on the counter's edge, and he caught it before it fell.

Lila grabbed his shirtsleeve. "I love your cooking almost as much as I love other more energetic pursuits, but your priorities are all messed up, Shane Ellis." She pulled him back towards her. "Forget the lettuce."

"It's cabbage, actually..." He stopped talking as she pulled his mouth to hers and reached down to make sure the vegetable escape hadn't affected something far more vital.

Nope, his priorities are still right where they need to be.

He sucked in a breath as she undid the top button of his jeans and eased the zipper down. He set down the fat onion and returned to running his hands along her body. Roaming, exploring, possessing her in ways no man had ever done. Sex, hell, the lead-up to sex, was more thrilling than anyone she had ever been with. He reached up her skirt, his fingers questing. She shuddered as his fingers slid past the edge of her underwear and caressed her clit. A surge of dampness and she moaned against his mouth, pushing closer and closer until she risked slipping off of the edge of the counter. His erection tented his briefs, and he slipped his dick out of his bindings with one hand, the other continuing to caress her slick folds.

Lila wanted him inside her. Wanted to feel every bit of him fill her. She wrapped a hand around his silken shaft, teasing and tantalizing, listening to his breathing speed up, matching hers. The long weeks away from him had served only to build the sexual tension, and add fire to this moment here between them. Shane broke contact with her mouth and moved his lips to her neck, moving up to her earlobe where his teeth nipped her gently.

"Woman, you drive me insane. I was going to seduce you over a delectable dinner, dessert, and right now all I want to do is fuck you, right here, right now." He growled into her ear and nipped it again, harder this time.

Lila shivered, a wanton shiver she felt from the top of her head down to her toes.

She stroked him harder, slipped off the edge of the countertop, knowing he would catch her, hold her.

"You know me. I like to work up an appetite first."

A groan of frustration, lust, or perhaps both, was the only sound he made before he pushed his way inside her. A parade of groceries crashed to the floor, ignored by them both, as he thrust hard, and fast, into her. She could feel the tip of him slam into her cervix, his fingers from one hand dancing along her clit, sending waves of exquisite pleasure cresting through her as he pushed her back against the countertop.

Lila shoved a package away from the small of her back, moaned and wrapped her legs around his ass as he fucked her hard and fast. God, she had missed this! Shane ticked all the boxes for her, and the sex was simply out of this world.

Their two bodies moved as one now, both questing for the release, when the stars and planets aligned. She heard something else clatter to the floor, ignored it. She was so close. From the change in his breaths, so was he.

"Come in me now." Lila breathed, gasping in pleasure as she felt the orgasm flow through her, a wave cresting at its apex, and Shane cried out a millisecond later, groaning as he joined her. His body breaking and collapsing onto her as he rode the same wave with her.

Seconds, a moment passed. His hair tickled her bare chest. Lila sighed with pleasure. She barely remembered ripping her t-shirt off, or Shane's quick release of her bra. The oxytocin and dopamine rush were still circulating through her. She could feel it all the way through to the tips of her toes.

Shane groaned, nestled his face in her stomach, mumbled. "I love fucking you. I want to fuck you all night long, woman."

Lila smiled. "I'm good with that. As long as dinner is involved."

"I had a magnificent dinner planned. Veal scallopini with lemon and capers, potato and leek soup, and a crème brûlée for dessert."

On cue, her stomach rumbled, and he raised his head, quirked an eyebrow, and chuckled.

"I told you I wanted to work up an appetite. Well, now that I have..."

Shane's chuckle turned into a roar of laughter. He stood up, pulled his jeans back up, and straightened his clothes. Then he pulled her up against him, kissed her deeply, and set her back on the floor.

Lila reached for her t-shirt and bra, which was hanging off the corner of the butcher block next to the fat green onions. Before she could put them on, Shane pulled her into another hungry, lingering kiss.

"I cannot get enough of you, Lila. When I'm on assignment, all I can do is think about when I can see you again."

She smiled. "I feel the same way."

The corner of his mouth quirked up. "Are you sure you aren't just keeping me around for my cooking?"

Lila fastened her bra and slid her shirt back on. "Mm, a distinct possibility." She reached for the weird vegetable that was now on the floor. "This is the fattest green onion I have ever seen."

Shane snorted, "That's a leek, you uneducated heathen."

Their banter continued as he pulled out pans and pots and began working on dinner. An hour later, Lila groaned as she slipped the last spoonful of crème brûlée into her mouth. "This is almost better than sex." She caught Shane's look of dismay. "*Almost*, I said almost!"

Shane looked nonplussed, then arched an eyebrow, stood up from the table, and walked the two steps over to her. "I'll show you something far better than food, woman. It's nine inches long…"

"Eight." Lila interrupted.

"Nine. You caught me on an off day." He pulled her up to him and she could feel him growing hard. "As I was saying, I'm going to show you all nine inches of something better than food. And I'm going to do it slowly. You will beg me to finish you off." He growled in her ear.

Lila's breath caught in her throat as his mouth descended onto hers. She could taste the caramel and cream from the crème brûlée, and a hint of the lemony remnants of the veal. And, as if she hadn't already experienced one of the more memorable orgasms of her life, her body hummed with anticipation.

She reached for his hand and pulled him after her to the upstairs bedroom.

The next morning was just as satisfying. After a quickie, Lila slid from the bed, sated, and slipped into the shower. When she returned, Shane was gone from it. From the sound of it, he was busy in the kitchen again. A tantalizing aroma meandered its way up the stairs. Lila sniffed the air.

Mm. Bacon and maple syrup. I wonder if Shane knows how to make pecan pie?

She floated down the stairs, her long hair wrapped in a towel, and a thick, warm robe and slippers were the only clothing she needed.

He grinned as she entered the kitchen. "Hey Sexy, did you work up an appetite?"

"Always. It smells amazing, as usual."

"French toast with cinnamon and maple syrup. The bacon is cooking in the fridge." He swirled the pan. "The snowfall really added up. I figure the storm laid down four inches, maybe more, by the looks of it. And we have a two-hour drive in the best of conditions ahead of us. What time is check-in?"

Lila grinned. She couldn't wait to see his face when they arrived at the caboose Airbnb. "Three p.m. but she said we could come as early as two if we needed to."

"Perfect. We can eat breakfast in bed, make love until noon, shower, and leave."

Lila giggled. "Well, it sounds like the perfect start to our week-long skiing vacation!"

She leaned in to kiss him, but at that moment, his cell phone rang with a thumping melody. There was only one person it could be. Lila's heart sank as the tune yodeled, "Big, big, big boss."

Shane pulled away, dug the phone out of his jeans pocket and answered it. "Ellis here."

Lila couldn't hear what Jack Benton was saying. She didn't need to. The look on Shane's face was clear.

Are you kidding *me?*

She mouthed at Shane to tell his boss to find someone else.

"Yeah, I understand. Right. No, I'll be there. Yeah. Okay." He hung up the phone and stared at the French toast in the pan, avoiding meeting Lila's incredulous gaze.

"He did not tell you to come in. Tell me he didn't."

"Look, I have to go. It's a domestic battery situation. Wife of the chief of police. WitSec won't get involved and..."

"Tell him to find someone else!"

"There isn't anyone else. Everyone else is on assignment. He says it will only be for a week, and..."

"A week?!" Lila spat, furious and on the verge of tears. Her plans, all the plans she had made. The Airbnb she had rented. The dinner reservations at a nearby Italian restaurant, the ski package. They wouldn't be able to reschedule. There would be no one to watch the store in another few weeks other than Angela, and she was completely unreliable.

The happy, satisfied feeling she had gone to bed with, woken up with, with Shane by her side, it dissolved as if it hadn't ever really existed.

An hour later, Shane's phone dinged. He checked it. "The Uber is almost here."

Lila said nothing. She was too angry and heartbroken.

Damned if I'm going to make this easy on him, either. He just bends over for Benton. Lets him do whatever he wants, ask whatever he wants.

Shane had tried to explain. But Lila didn't want to hear it. She didn't care that there was no one else to do the job. Benton had promised Shane two weeks off. She didn't care about the reasons Shane felt he owed Jack Benton. After five years of dedicated service, he had damned well paid that debt, no matter the circumstances.

"Maybe you can get a refund on the Airbnb you rented?" His expression looked hopeful. Which merely infuriated her more.

Fuck the refund. Tell Jack to go suck an egg!

Lila settled for making a noncommittal, "Sure, whatever."

Shane shouldered his backpack. The Uber pulled up at the curb and he stared at it for a moment, then back at Lila.

"I really am sorry, Lila. If I had a choice, I'd tell him to find someone else, but I owe Jack. He needs me."

Lila closed her eyes and willed away the gathering tears.

Jack doesn't need you. I need you.

"Right." She opened them, and Shane's eyes bored into hers. Begging forgiveness and understanding. But she had neither to offer him.

He kissed her as the Uber honked impatiently. "I have to go now."

"Yeah, I know."

He stepped down onto the stoop and turned around at her again. "I'll make this up to you."

"Right." The effort to say anything felt as if she were chewing on sharp glass.

"Okay. I'll call you tonight."

She nodded, and he walked away. As he opened the door to the Uber, Lila couldn't take it anymore. She cupped her hands and called out, "Shane?"

Shane stopped and turned.

"The next time you talk to Jack Benton? You tell him I said to kiss... my... ass." She felt a small measure of satisfaction in watching Shane's eyebrows shoot up and his mouth fall open before she stomped back inside and slammed the door closed behind her.

She pressed her back against the door and let loose a string of profanity that would have shocked the townspeople, her employees, and likely even Shane. And with it came angry, hot tears of frustration.

It had taken her nearly three days to form the words and just say it. To tell him it was over. Whatever "it" was.

Long-distance relationships don't work. He picked his work over a relationship with me.

She had gathered her courage, called him, told him she couldn't do it anymore. He had said little. But really, what was there to say, anyway? It would not work. Not like this.

She missed Kaylee. She hadn't been able to talk to her friend for nearly two years. Kaylee would have told her to drop sexy pecan pie Shane Ellis like a rock. She would have taken her for sushi at Nara's and they would have gotten tipsy and gone dancing, just the two of them. But she was here, in Maine, living under an assumed name, and prohibited from contacting anyone. Angela was too young and unreliable to talk to. And Margery centered entirely on bringing a new human into the world and focusing on being a stay-at-home mom.

Lila had never felt more alone than she did now. Even when her mom had died, she could return to college, and Kaylee had been there. To listen, to hold her when she cried, and make her laugh when the time was right. This time, she was alone in her misery. She took the week off of work, if only because she didn't want to explain it to Margery or Angela. Later she could explain, when time had spooled out and the hurt and anger had diminished.

The groceries Shane had filled her fridge with eventually spoiled. Every day since he'd left, she would stand in the kitchen, refrigerator door open, and glare at the various packages. Angry, frustrated, and ultimately too depressed to even try to do anything with it all. After a week, she went to Hanniford's and purchased her regular heat and eat meals. They filled the freezer, and she stopped opening the fridge section except to grab milk for her cereal. By the third week, the smell was unbearable. She waited until the night before trash pickup and dumped the reeking mess into the Pay-As-You-Throw blue trash bags and taken to the curb while trying desperately not to breathe the stench in.

"Damn you, Shane Ellis. Kowtowing to your boss. Who cares if Jack Benton is a billionaire used to getting his way and to hell with anyone else's feelings?" She muttered angrily as she trudged back along the icy driveway. "Jack Benton can kiss my ass!"

Not Optimal

- Shane -

Her mouth moved under his, her tongue flicking, twining with his. Her body and hair, silky smooth, a tantalizing hint of vanilla and musk, moved against his. God, he wanted her, always her, and the thoughts of any other woman were half-measures, poor substitutions.

He moved from her mouth to her neck, just at the ear, and Lila writhed under him, her fingernails digging into his back. Her body was begging for more. The soft pants and moans had him hard. He slid down her body, his feet catching on the sheets. He tried to kick them away, once, twice.

And then his dream splintered into fragments. Shane woke instantly, alert in the dark night, and alone in the bed. Something had woken him, but what?

As with all of his assignments, Shane quickly came to identify every creak and groan of a safe house. Noises that meant nothing to the newest occupants. A certain squeak of floorboard, the smallest click of a doorknob turning in place. A change in air pressure that showed someone had opened an exterior door. Or someone in the hall outside of his bedroom.

He moved without sound. Slipping from his bed, clad in his boxers, his 9mm Ruger held in his right hand, easing the safety off. Shane knew better than most that one's fate can be measured in milliseconds. Whoever was entering his room wouldn't know the layout and likely wasn't expecting him to be awake. This was to his advantage. The heavy rain outside held no lightning, nothing to add anything but darkness to the already gloomy sky outside.

The doorknob gave itself away with a small, nearly imperceptible click. Whoever was outside in the hall was coming in. In the brief half-second between the doorknob turning, and the door quietly opening, he caught the scent, or rather the reek, of the girl's perfume, which preceded her entry.

The light in the hall illuminated just enough of the Ruger for Heather Bonatelli to give a yip of surprise. Dressed in a flimsy piece of lace and satin, her intent was clear. Had she hoped to climb into his bed? Likely. That's where it would have ended, however.

"Miss Bonatelli, I suggest you return to your bedroom."

"I..."

"Now, Miss Bonatelli."

The girl wilted, transforming from wannabe temptress to the sixteen-year-old girl that she was.

Voluptuous and attractive, sure. Jailbait. off-limits. And her father would kill me if I even think of touching her.

She turned away, her shoulders slumping.

And that would have been the end of it, had not the door at the far end of the hall not opened at that precise moment. In the days that followed, Shane would have time to think about how unlucky he was that Don "The Boss" Bonatelli took that moment in time to go in search of a midnight snack. Don saw his underage daughter walking from Shane's room, dressed as provocatively as the girls in one of his strip clubs. Considering that the amount of cloth covering the girl's body left nothing up to the imagination, and she was his only child, the roar of fury that erupted from Don's throat did not surprise Shane.

"Daddy! No!" Heather screeched in a panic. She reached for him, but he was past her and charging down the hallway toward Shane.

Well, shit.

The old man had three decades on Shane. And he was a client that Shane was supposed to protect. These facts flitted through Shane's mind in the few seconds it took for Don to close the distance and slam into Shane. His meaty ham hock hands slamming home with surprising accuracy. Shane danced back, the door of his room flying open and Don's body hurtled through the open doorway, uncontrolled, as the object of his fury moved nimbly back and swept the older man's legs out from under him.

The floor shook as Don fell, face first, with a loud grunt. This earned a shriek of dismay from Lucia Bonatelli, who was half-asleep, a dark face mask coating her entire face except for her Botox-plump lips and oblong circles for her eyes. Her hair, normally coiffed with care, was a nightmare of frizzy bedhead. She screamed again at the sight of Heather cowering near her door. A scream that turned to a snarl of anger and fury as she realized her daughter was wearing an outfit filched from her, and appeared to be coming from Shane's room. Shane watched as the older woman's eyes narrowed into angry slits, no doubt fueled by a rage that comes from one who feels another younger, nubile version of herself has upstaged her.

Shane groaned. Lucia had been eyeing him like he was a dessert she just had to taste for the past ten days. Anytime her husband Don was out of the room, she sidled up to Shane, batting her mascara-coated lashes in his direction. Now, she was jumping to the same conclusion her husband had, and she was better armed. Her hands clenched as she advanced toward him down the hall, snarling curses. Shane had watched her spend two full hours on the nails on the left hand alone the day before, filing them and painting them blood-red.

Don pushed himself up with a groan from the floor, a growl building in his broad, hairy chest. "You, sonofabitch!"

"Mr. Bonatelli, Mrs. Bonatelli, I need you to both calm down." Shane held out a hand and tried to monitor Lucia's advance as her husband recovered himself enough to rise again. "Miss Bonatelli was out in the hall. I told her to go to her room. Nothing else happened here tonight."

The words spewing from Lucia Bonatelli's mouth were unrepeatable. They called into question his legitimacy, his sexual tastes, and much more. Don Bonatelli was moving slowly, which was good for Shane, but also concerning. This was especially true when the man clutched his left arm and groaned. The light from the hall showed a sudden sheen of sweat across the older man's balding pate.

"I am going to ki..." He collapsed back to the ground, falling on his side before gravity took him onto his back. His pale, hairy, overly blubbered chest rising and falling as he gasped and choked.

Shane wasn't sure what the man planned to do, other than possibly die from cardiac arrest, and by that point Lucia Bonatelli had reached the doorway, still fixated on gouging holes in Shane's face, judging from the angle of her attack. She seemed unaware of the physical distress her husband was currently under, and Shane dodged as she raked her blood-red claws in his direction.

"Mrs. Bonatelli, stop!" He wrestled one hand, then another, raising his voice above her banshee screeches. The air was turning blue from her misuse of coarse language and now Heather, who had gone from cowering against the door to fully panicking at the sight of her father in the doorway, dove past her mother and Shane. Lucia Bonatelli was not the keenest observer. She seemed to think that Heather was returning to be molested further by the perverted bodyguard their family was currently at the mercy of, and flailed and fought, her teeth snapping as she tried every weapon at her disposal to free herself from Shane's grasp.

"Mom, stop! Stop! Daddy's having a heart attack!" Heather wailed at their feet and finally, after two more repetitions in increasing panic, Lucia relented, and turned instead, throwing herself to the ground as she alternated between screaming invectives and trying to hug her husband to death.

"Ma'am, if you could please let me..."

"Donny, wake up! Don't leave me here in this hellhole with this stupida guardia del corpo con un cazzo flosciol! Amore mio, amore mio, torna da me!"

"Mrs. Bonatelli, he needs CPR."

"Vaffanculo, idota! Amore mio! Cosa ti ha fatto questo mostro?"

Christ.

Don Bonatelli, first red-faced, then purple, and now a steady shade of grey, was fading fast. His eyes fixed. Heather was screaming, Lucia crying, with more Italian tripping from her lips. If looks could kill, Shane would writhe on the ground next to Don Bonatelli, his end in sight.

If I don't do something quick, this guy is going to die.

He reached for the girl's arm, shook her, and her scream stopped abruptly. Shane barked at Heather, "Call 9-1-1. Now!" The kid nodded and scrambled to her feet.

"Mrs. Bonatelli, get the fuck off of him *now*." He accompanied his words with a decisive shove, which sent the woman sprawling, her nightgown riding up over her wide hips, her rant momentarily suspended in the shock of being so rudely pushed aside.

Shane knelt by Don Bonatelli's side, laced his fingers together and began chest compressions. The corpulent man under his hands lay still, unmoving. He counted to ten, then administered the breaths, just as they had taught him. Jack, his boss, made it a point to send Shane and the other bodyguards to annual training for it. And for that, Shane was grateful. The training, which he had attended merely a month before, was still fresh in his mind.

His entire focus was on saving the life of the man in front of him. He returned to chest compressions, and Lucia glared at him and pulled her nightgown down over her thighs. Tears dripped down her cheeks as she mumbled what sounded like curses. It was all in Italian, and short of a few words that seemed similar enough to English, he wasn't getting much out of it other than "Die, fucker, die." He couldn't help wondering exactly who Lucia Bonatelli wanted to die. Shane or Lucia's husband?

"They want to know if he has a pulse." Heather's shaky voice interrupted as Shane administered the last of another set of breaths. He returned to chest compressions.

"Just tell them to hurry." He feared stopping for a second the compressions and breaths, but it was already wearing at him. The paramedics could check for a pulse when they got here. "Go unlock the door for them."

Moments later, the fire truck and ambulance arrived, and Shane moved out of their way. He felt wrung out, like a limp noodle as he watched them apply an AED. 3 Seconds later, Don "The Boss" Bonatelli's skin looked far less gray and his chest was rising and falling on its own. His eyes were closed, though, a line of drool escaping his mouth and crusting on the left side.

"Name?" The EMT asked.

"Don Smith." Shane replied, before Lucia or Heather could answer. "I'll bring his wife and daughter in the car."

"The hell you will," Lucia spat, "My Donny needs me." She scooted into the ambulance, her flimsy nightgown ratcheting up one side as she scooted to sit next to her husband's side, a death grip on his hand. She muttered curses under her breath, glaring at Shane.

The EMT looked at her and back at Shane. "Smith, huh?"

Shane nodded, "Yup."

The man's eyes traveled over to Heather, lingering there for a long second before nodding in return. "Okay, then. He's stable for now and we're taking him over to Mercy off of Hemlock Drive."

"See you there," Shane said, his hand on Tiffany's back. He had to get her off of the street. Neighbors were staring. The ambulance drove away, and he gave the kid a light push towards the hall. "Go get dressed and find some clothes for your mom, too."

He retrieved his phone from his room.

Jack is going to love this one.

Heather reappeared a few minutes later, suitably clothed, pale, and cowed. She held her mother's voluminous purse under one arm, and a stack of clothes and shoes close to her chest. Shane pocketed his phone. Arrangements were already being made for a change of guard and location once Don Bonatelli was stable enough to be moved. Among dozens of homes scattered across the country, Shane's boss, Jack Benton, also owned a hospital in Ohio, just a short flight away.

Who the hell owns a hospital, anyway? Shane shook his head at the thought.

"Well, that's not optimal." Jack's only response to Shane's description of the seduction gone wrong and debacle that followed brought a wry smile to Shane's lips.

The understatement of the year.

At least Jack didn't seem pissed. Not at the late hour, nor at Shane's handling of the situation. Which was a relief. He felt as if he had been walking on eggshells for a year now. Shane had promised Jack he would never sleep with a client again after Lila, and he'd meant it, but for a split second as he relayed the story, he'd wondered if Jack would believe him or not. He had, though. Jack had an uncanny way of sussing out the truth. Shane was pretty sure his boss could smell it; kind of like dogs could smell cancer.

He'd felt nothing but relief when Jack said he would send Luke out to take over. The Bonatelli family were a handful, and one he was happy to fob off on someone else.

Shane looked at Heather Bonatelli. Her mascara had left streaks down her rouged cheeks. She looked even younger than her sixteen years and she stared at the ground, unwilling to meet his eyes. "I'll tell Mama and Papa you did nothing."

"I already told them that."

One horny little teenager and his assignment shot to hell. He hadn't so much as looked at her. How had she made the leap to trying to jump in his bed?

"I'm sorry."

"Me too, kid, me too."

"I just..." she licked her lips and cast a quick nervous glance his way. She looked miserable. "I just, you know, all my friends they've all, you know, *done* it. And they think I'm, you know..." She bit her lip and scuffed one shoe along the ground.

Shit. Now I feel bad for her.

"Tiffany. You're never going to see those girls again. It doesn't matter what they think. The next school you go to, when all this shit is behind you and you've got a new name and a new place to live, you can make yourself into whoever you want to be. And they won't know any different. Keep that in mind. Okay?"

She glanced up and he could see the realization dawn in her eyes. Her back straightened, and she blinked. He could tell she was imagining what a future like that could look like.

"Come on, let's get you to the hospital."

1. "Stupid bodyguard with a limp dick! My love, my love, come back to me!"

2. "Fuck you, you idiot! My love! What has this monster done to you?"

3. Automated external defibrillator

Overheard

- Denise-

It had been an amazing day, and Denise couldn't wait to share it. Lionel always called her and invited her over, but this evening she would drop by and surprise him for once. She'd finished her practicum and passed her licensure exam with flying colors. Next step was to find a position!

She had practically floated down the steps from Miami Regional. She was so close, *so* close. Just a few weeks left to go until graduation and she would be a full-fledged professional nurse.

There had been no time to celebrate, however. Just enough time to grab an Enrollada de Pincana from Coloyo's and then hump it to the three blocks over to her shift at Happy Haven. There she'd filled in for Tonya, who normally worked the ice cream shop shift, where the residents would gather in dribs and drabs to order the ice cream cones.

She enjoyed slinging ice cream more than sitting at the front entry. When she posted at the front entry, she had to make sure none of the memory care residents tried to slip past. Their bracelets, coded to block access to the exits of the retirement village, automatically locked the doors. And while that was important for the residents' safety, the door locks often enabled at just the wrong time, and caused logjams at the front. Her job there was to guide the memory care patients back away from the doors without causing them to become upset. Sometimes they were combative, no matter how gentle and kind she was. Handing ice cream cones out was far easier logistically and interpersonally. Everyone smiled.

Denise had high hopes that they would consider her for the five nursing positions they had recently posted. Happy Haven's back half was undergoing a major expansion. In another month, the building would have twice as many openings for new residents.

The place was unique and centered on re-creating a small-town feel for all of its residents, many of whom were in the beginning to moderate stages of Alzheimer's. They accepted a range of residents. Some were perfectly capable of independent living. Others needed more help, and some needed a lot of help. Walking through the halls, or the courtyard, everyone looked happy, content. And more often than not, that was the atmosphere here. And it was certainly what had attracted Denise to staying on here in a more professional role once her studies were complete.

Just a few more weeks!

She handed Mrs. McKenzie a sugar cone with a scoop of strawberry ice cream and rainbow sprinkles on it. The old woman beamed at her, her mouth splitting into a cheerful grin. Mrs. McKenzie said little, thanks to frontotemporal dementia, and Denise brought the ice cream to her seat, so she didn't have to get up. She was unsteady on her feet, slow, but Mr. McKenzie stayed by her side. He smiled at her gratefully. The cherry-chocolate flavor was her favorite, but it was on back order.

"Thank you, Denise."

"Of course, Mr. McKenzie. Do you want your usual?"

"Yes, thank you."

A moment later, she set his cup of hot cocoa in front of him. He spared a glance for her, nodding thanks, but his gnarled hands were busy catching drips of ice cream from his wife's chin.

Denise handed him a stack of napkins and moved on to the next customer, three ladies in red hats cackling away in the corner.

The next few hours passed in a blur. The ice cream shop was a popular destination. Denise scraped the bottom of the sugar-free vanilla container, making sure Mrs. Bird had a full scoop. Like her last name, the woman was thin, petite, with dark eyes in a small face. Her hair was short, cropped close to her head. Mrs. Bird had diabetes; a piece of vital information transmitted by her bracelet. A piece of technology unique to each resident in the retirement village. In cases like the ice cream shop or the scattering of different restaurants and cafeteria, it transmitted a quick reminder of dietary restrictions when the resident walked in. This helped maintain a sense of independence and dignity for those who couldn't make the best of decisions any longer.

Yet another reason I love working here so much.

Cherie, the next girl on duty, waltzed in at half-past three. "Hey girl!" She was a year behind Denise in the same nursing program at Miami Regional. Her bright smile lit up the room and she glanced at the clock on the wall. "Ms. Eckles in HR asked me to come by a little early. She says you have an interview scheduled at four?"

Denise grinned in return, leaned in and whispered, "I think I've got a shot at one of the new nursing positions they're offering." Cherie hugged her.

"I'm rooting for you, girl. How did the licensure exam go?"

"Passed."

"Yes! I knew you would! Just like you'll ace the interview."

Denise hugged her back. "You are a gem!"

Moments later, she sat back straight, fully focused, as the interview began. She had met Oona, the Human Resources director, only in passing when she first interviewed at Happy Haven. Oona handled the medical personnel hires, while Lyda, the assistant director, handled the other positions.

Oona Valere had struck her as cold, and rather distant previously. It had unnerved her. Likely because she was so nervous and wanted the toe into Happy Haven so badly. As a teen, she had enjoyed volunteering at a nursing home and working for one now felt like a natural progression. Especially now that she had her degree. Now she was unnerved again, but in a much different way. Oona was practically purring as she looked over Denise's application and transcripts.

"I see you have scored at the top of your class there at Miami Regional. Impressive."

"Thank you, Ms. Valere. I've, uh, enjoyed my studies."

"Mr. Bush speaks highly of you." And there it was. The reason the Human Resources director was so friendly.

Oh my God, does she know I'm sleeping with him?

"Oh, he does?"

"Yes, he mentioned you by name, said you were just finishing up with your training at Miami Regional." The look on Oona Valere's face was rather inscrutable.

She has to be trying to figure it out. Our connection.

"I likely mentioned it. I see him often at my post in the front."

This was mostly true. After all, that is how they had first met.

Thankfully, it seemed to be enough to satisfy the director's curiosity. "Yes, of course. That makes sense. I gather that is why you began working with us?"

"Yes, ma'am. I volunteered at a nursing home as a teen. It, well, Happy Haven is changing the way we think of aging with dignity. I guess I just really wanted to be a part of that."

Oona smiled. The smile almost reached her eyes.

"That is good to hear, Ms. Fortuna. And yes, Happy Haven's goal is to have more forward-thinking individuals and caregivers who see how different we are, and what we can provide to our residents that no one else has." She tapped her pen over the papers arrayed before her and made a notation. "I think you will be an asset to Happy Haven, Ms. Fortuna. If you can wait for three more months, the new wing will open in August, and that is when we would need your nursing services. This is the starting amount. I expect approximately 15-30 hours of overtime each month may be required as well."

"I graduate next month, so, yes, that is more than acceptable for me, Ms. Valere." Denise's heart soared at the figure written on the page. It was five times the amount she was making. After years of struggle, scrimping, saving, and driving a car old enough to drink, she could see her fortune truly changing. And with a company she could truly enjoy working for. One that was honest and had its residents' best interests at heart.

I can't wait to tell Lionel!

Less than half an hour later, she stood inside of Lionel's glass and steel house, frozen. The exuberance that had driven her to drive to his house, uninvited, unexpected, suddenly draining from her. His voice, it was so different, so cold and business-like.

"No. Not at the Miami location. Too many eyes are on that one. Think backwater, provincial. The lower-income states with the politicians we can manipulate."

There was a pause. "Yes, have Lewis pull up dirt on all of them. We'll only do drug trials on select locations and residents. This is the initial test phase." Another pause. "No, they are still working out the kinks in dosage. We need test subjects with no family or friends. No one to complain if the subject has an adverse reaction."

Denise stood there outside of his home office, hand frozen in midair, about to push the door open. What was Lionel talking about? The tone of his voice sounded completely different from the kind and thoughtful lover who had asked about her family, her childhood.

"Right. Two drugs. We can do more in the lower-income areas." Another pause. "Death rate is right at thirty-eight percent for the Stultuzole, and the Augerezene stands at six percent in primate trials. The clients are fine with the numbers on the Stultuzole, but the Augerezene needs to be under three percent or less if we want to sell it. We test it on the adults, then move into the incarcerated population. I have several pools of test subjects ready and waiting for that stage of human trials."

Denise backed up, her mind whirling. Lionel was talking about drug trials on *humans*. And, considering he was CEO of Happy Haven Retirement Villages, it didn't take much of a leap to realize where those drug trials were happening.

She needed to leave *now*, before he realized she was here.

"Yes, yes, I understand. Rollout for both drug trials has already begun in Hammond and Durant."

Hammond, Louisiana? Durant, Oklahoma? Those were both the two newer Happy Haven Retirement Village locations. Oona Valere had asked her if she had any interest in working in either. Denise had told her no, of course. She loved living in Florida. Perhaps someday she would change her mind. Her roommate Taegan talked endlessly about becoming a traveling nurse. But Denise had her friends, a life here. Or she had.

Whatever I'm hearing. I'm not meant to hear. I need to go. NOW.

Her car. He hadn't heard her come in, but he would hear her trying to leave. The damn thing never started on cue. It took a couple of tries. She turned and eyed the front door she had come in through. She walked quietly, easy to do with tennis shoes. Denise walked up to the door, carefully opening it, only to hear Lionel end the call, his chair creaking as he stood up.

Shit.

She spun on her heel and let the door thump closed behind her. "Hello? Lionel? I have the best news!" Denise forced a broad grin on her face.

When he appeared at his study door, his face closed, tense, she nearly lost her nerve.

"What are you doing here, Denise?"

"I tried your cell, but it went to voice mail and I just couldn't wait to tell you the big news!"

"What news is that?" He asked, closing the distance between them. It unnerved her.

She smiled, likely a little manic in her desperate attempt to look normal. *Nothing to see here other than an excited girlfriend showing up unexpectedly.*

"I passed my licensure exam with flying colors and, even better, I interviewed today and got one of the nursing positions at Happy Haven!"

His face changed back to the gentle lover she remembered. "Congratulations, my dear! We should celebrate!" He hugged her to him and she stiffened in his arms. She wanted to run as far and as fast as she could from this place. She needed to sort this out in her head, maybe talk to one of her friends, and figure it all out first. Lionel seemed so kind, so thoughtful. Had she misheard? Misunderstood? He pulled away and looked down at her. Denise realized he was expecting some kind of response.

"I'm so sorry, I can't." Denise forced her shoulders into a hopefully carefree shrug. "I promised my roommates we would go out. They want to take me out for a celebratory dinner. Perhaps tomorrow?"

"Of course." His dark eyes bored into her, studying her.

"What is it?" Denise asked, doing her best to keep her voice steady.

"Nothing. Just proud of you and your hard work. You will make a fine nurse, Denise."

"Thank you."

She made her excuses and forced herself to stroll out of the door when all she really wanted to do was run. Her car started on the first attempt and Denise drove away, glancing in the rearview mirror as she did. Lionel stood there, unsmiling, watching her leave. Above him was a security camera. How had she never noticed that before?

Help is Hard to Find

- Lila -

Lila stared at the large ornate clock that hung over the front door of the bookstore. Angela was late, later than she had ever been, and Lila's stomach growled in distress. The booming thunder of the incoming summer storm had woken her in the wee hours of the morning. After that, she had fought to return to sleep as her mind immediately revved up and started cycling over the latest plot twist, or lack thereof, on dreaded book number two. The first book had just poured out of her. This one, however, was not that simple.

And thanks to not sleeping, she had then overslept. The sun was blinding as it shoved its way past the thin floral curtains and lit up the room. Cheery sunshine wasn't so nice when you were sleep-deprived. It had taken her a while to return to sleep as the wind and rain lashed the outside of the small rental house. Apparently, this had resulted in a power outage as well. The clock by her bed blinked a steady 12:00 in red, and Lila had cursed under her breath as she reached for her phone and read the time. Her phone's display told her she had less than fifteen minutes before it was time to open the store.

No time for a leisurely breakfast. Not even time for coffee or a quick shower. She had scrambled out of bed, tossed on clean clothes and ran out of the door with her Contigo in one hand and her purse in the other.

Mrs. Danbury had been there, like clockwork, at the door at two minutes past nine. A pleasant smile appeared on her face.

"Good morning, Felicia, I'll take two pork chops, please." Before Lila could answer, the old woman had waved a finger, "Cut thick, mind you. Murray hates thin chops."

Murray, long dead of cancer, had been quite particular about his cuts of meats. Lila had learned this and other odd details about the man from Mrs. Danbury, including that Murray never wore blue, preferred the boxers over briefs and was of the opinion that women, not just children, should be seen but not heard. Lila sighed, "Mrs. Danbury, I don't carry meats. Only books."

The old woman stood at the counter and stared at Lila, confused. "But Murray expects pork chops tonight. It's Wednesday!"

Lila nodded. There was no point in arguing. "I am so sorry, Mrs. Danbury, but we are fresh out of pork chops. However, there's someone else who can likely help with this." She placed a hand on the woman's frail, bony shoulder and guided her toward the glass door. She pointed with her other hand. "There is Hannaford's just down the street. I'll bet you anything they have pork chops."

Mrs. Danbury gazed out of the window glass. She bit down on her lower lip, a look of concern on her face.

"I don't know. Papa said I shouldn't cross a busy street, not with all the cars going past so quick." Her voice sounded younger, higher, less mature.

Okay, it's going to be one of those *days.*

Lila looked around, hoping beyond hope that Mrs. Danbury's grandson would show up soon. She could get the old woman across the street to Hannaford's, but Lila knew she would be back. After all, the building next door to the bookstore had once housed a bakery, and Murray, dead some twenty years or more, had been particular to a certain French bread the bakery, now a decade gone, had baked. She could see that, for now, the street outside was empty of cars. So was the sidewalk in either direction. The tourists weren't up yet, and no customers would show up for an hour, possibly two.

"I'll be happy to walk you across the street."

Mrs. Danbury's face lit up. "Oh, thank you. You are ever so kind!"

Lila scanned the street. No one else was out except the local stray, Sir Riley Brunswick, who everyone fed bits and scraps to. He sauntered down the sidewalk, sniffing the ground near one of the round public trash cans, and then lifted a leg to claim it as his. No sign of Angela. Lila suppressed another sigh. She was hopeless with managing employees and Angela seemed to sense that. She was perennially late, and the past two weeks had been especially bad now that she had fallen in love. Again.

Lila smiled at Mrs. Danbury and placed a hand on the older woman's bony shoulder. "Don't worry, I'll walk with you the entire way." She left the door unlocked. After all, the town was still half asleep, after all. The likelihood that anyone would walk into the bookstore and run off with a wheelbarrow full of books was small. Last night had been the annual Fourth of July celebration and the smell of sulphur still hung heavy in the air. The gathering storm had politely waited until the last of the fireworks lit up the sky before it unleashed a torrent of rain on everyone below. By then, Lila had been comfortably asleep in her bed. She'd watched the fireworks from her large window upstairs earlier and thought of the fireworks shows at home in Kansas City.

Home. Well, it used to be home. She couldn't return. Not for a year or two, possibly never. The lawyers in the WitSec program had hedged around that minor fact like pros. And Lila understood that once you were in, you never got to leave WitSec. At least, not as they continued to dig into the financial records of Kurgen Real Estate. The investigation had broadened and the chance that anything would go to trial was becoming a distant possibility with each month that passed.

"It's like cutting off the head of a hydra," her handler had explained. "This is deeper than we could have possibly imagined." And meanwhile, Lila's life was here. It wasn't a terrible life. Honestly, when she thought about it, living surrounded by books, and now writing her own books, well, it was a life she had dreamed of and wanted more than the data analyst job at Kurgen.

How many times did I hear that becoming a writer wouldn't pay?

They canceled her student loans and other debt as part of her inclusion in WitSec. Technically, they probably still existed, but she had a different last name now, a different social security card, and was in a small town in Maine where the likelihood of anyone from her past life ever running into her was infinitesimally small.

Mrs. Danbury tucked her hand into the crook of Lila's elbow and they walked down the street, crossing slowly at the crosswalk, moving at a leisurely pace. Lila's stomach grumbled again, and she was thankful that the old woman had provided an excuse for her to stop by Hanniford's and get something, anything, to eat.

Who knew how long it would take Angela to show up, after all? She'd mentioned yesterday that she was going out with Kenny, who ran the gift shop down the street. He was the third boy that Angela had fallen for since the school year ended and tourist season began in late May. Each time she did, her attendance worsened. Lila was beginning to believe it would be better to handle the bookstore herself and possibly shorten the hours so she could write in the early morning or in the evening after work.

"Such a lovely day," Mrs. Danbury's voice jostled Lila from her musings. "What month is it?"

Lila steered her around a pile of discarded fireworks tubes. "It's July, Mrs. Danbury. Did you watch the fireworks last night?"

Mrs. Danbury's answer was lost as Joel, her great-grandson, called from the far corner. "There you are, Gran!"

Lila could see from the teen's appearance that he had likely rolled out of bed, dressed and shoved his feet into shoes before he rushed out of the house in search of the old woman. He wore a rumpled shirt, and the buttons didn't align quite right. His tangled dark hair was flat on one side. She could see drool dried on the side of his mouth. He shot a nervous glance at Lila, barely making eye contact.

"I'm so sorry, Miss Brewer."

Even after living as Annie Brewer for more than a year now, Lila still had to remind herself forcefully that it was her name. "I thought I locked the door last night after the fireworks, but I guess I forgot." His eyes darted about, and he focused on his grandmother instead of looking at Lila. She suppressed a smile. She'd caught him staring at her several times over the past few months. Usually, they seemed to center on her breasts, but occasionally his gaze made it to her lips. Each time, he blushed from the bottom of his neck to the roots of his hair. She could see the red creeping up his neck and into his ears. The red made them stand out more than they already did.

"Not a problem, really, it wasn't. It's pretty quiet this time in the morning."

"Michael, darling, I need to get pork chops for your father." Mrs. Danbury was not to be deterred. "You know how he is, so set in his ways!"

"It's okay, Gran. I bought the pork chops last night. They're in the icebox waiting for your special recipe." The young man said.

Mrs. Danbury seemed to accept this and Joel flashed a rare smile towards Lila before ushering his great-grandmother away.

Lila watched them go. Her heart hurt for the two of them, especially Joel. Maeve, the town gossip, had told her that Joel was an orphan. First, his mother died of a drug overdose when he was barely out of diapers, and then his grandfather Michael, Mrs. Danbury's only son, had passed away from a heart attack when Joel was fifteen. After that, it had just been Joel and his great-grandmother alone in the house.

"Michael went and joined his dear wife Heather in heaven, God rest his soul. Heather passed on of leukemia when Joel's mother Natasha was just a little girl," Maeve had said, wiping at a nonexistent tear. "And that sweet young Joel has seen nothing but loss and heartache." Her nose had twitched, "And of course no one knows who his daddy is. It could be anyone, really. Natasha was, well, you know, kind of loose. All the boys in town knew about a certain little strawberry-shaped birthmark on her rear, if you know what I mean."

If there was a drawback to living in a smaller town like Brunswick, it was that gossip seemed alive and well. Lila hated to think about what Maeve might say about her. The Brunswick queen of gossip appeared to have dirt on everyone. Take the owner of Hanniford's, for example. He was a round, slightly balding man of fifty who, if Maeve was to be believed, enjoyed dressing in women's clothes. Once Hanniford's closed and the sun slipped below the horizon, Lyle Cobbler would retire for an evening of dress-up, complete with rather garish makeup. A harmless little secret that was exposed one evening when his toaster went up in flames and caught the kitchen curtains on fire, prompting a visit from the Brunswick Fire Department.

Lila hadn't been able to look at him since without imagining him dressed in stockings and an extra-large blue satin teddy from Frederick's of Hollywood. Maeve was rather detailed in her description. It was after a visit from Maeve that she missed the anonymity of city life the most. Small towns knew everything. She knew Maeve knew all about her love life, or lack thereof. In fact, Lila was sure of it. Hadn't Maeve mentioned, no less than three times, that Lila should go to O'Donoghue's for a bite and a pint, hinting that there was an active singles scene there.

Maybe Maeve is right. Maybe I need to get out and try dating. It's been six months, after all.

Six months of silence. Six months since she had told Shane not to visit anymore. Not after that last disaster. All of her plans, the special romantic escape she had planned, everything, just vaporized because he needed to work. After his boss had given him the time off, only to take it back and say he needed Jack for a job. Damn Jack Benton. If that was the life of a bodyguard, well, it wasn't a life she was comfortable with. Waiting around for weeks on end for him to show up, and then leave again? How many times did it have to happen before she got the message? Shane's work was his life, not her.

Mind-blowing sex? Check. Sexy as hell? Check. Amazing cook? Check. Pretty much everything I am looking for in a guy? Check. Except he is already married... to his work.

Still, she missed him. She found her thoughts drift to images of him, in her bed, in the shower, in the kitchen. He made the best omelets. Her stomach reminded her yet again that its current emptiness was completely unacceptable.

Nope, the only thing I need is food, not a dating life on top of running a bookstore and starting a writing career. Besides, why give Maeve more gossip? Her cousin runs O'Donoghue's. I'll bet she is in there all the time. Last thing I need is her speculating on my sex life, or telling everyone else how loose I am!

She watched as Joel and Mrs. Danbury disappeared around the corner. She debated whether she should head back to the bookstore. Her stomach twisted in complaint, and she wished she had eaten more than carrots and peanut butter while squeezing in her words for the day last night, even as her energy levels drooped. Angela had called in sick yesterday, and Lila had been on duty nonstop, from open to close, with only enough time to shove a reheated chicken drumstick down her throat in between customers. Today wasn't looking much better. At least yesterday she had woken on time, ate breakfast and packed leftovers in her lunch bag. Today, she had been in too much of a hurry.

With another quick glance up and down the street, she decided, then walked the last few steps to Hanniford's.

Stock up food for the day. Not just a donut or muffin, but lunch as well, and snacks. I'll bet anything that Angela is a no-show.

"Morning, Annie!" Andie waved at her as she walked in. Lila smiled and waved back. Andie was Lyle Cobbler's niece, and ran most of the operations of the small grocery store, stocking the shelves, running the register, cleaning the bathrooms. Lila sighed, wishing she could get lucky and get a girl like Andie to work for her. But the bookstore didn't make enough to pay more than minimum wage, thus she seemed stuck with kids like Angela. Still, she would ask Andie the next time the girl was over browsing the science fiction section if she was interested. At least Andie was interested in books. Angela found books "boring" and Lila couldn't even depend on her to re-shelve the books in alphabetical order.

Spending my days surrounded by books is pretty damn nice. But it would be nicer if I had a little help that I could rely on.

Lila moved through the aisles and collected enough in fruits and pre-made items to get her through the day, including a microwavable meal she could eat for dinner that evening. She was behind, and struggling with the current book project. And if Angela didn't show up for work, Lila would likely have zero time to work on it during the day. Another twenty minutes, maybe less, and the foot traffic would pick up. Then there would be shoppers there to keep her hopping.

"Find everything, okay?" Andie grinned at her.

"I did. Hey, the newest book in that *Gliese 581g* series you like just came in. *G581: Plague Tales*? Come by this afternoon and I'll have it for you." Lila answered. Andie squealed with excitement. The girl inhaled books, and her interests didn't stop at science fiction. She had been one of Lila's beta readers for her first book.

"Oh my God! Yes! I've been waiting for this! I'll be off at three, maybe four."

"Great, I'll see you then, Andie." She leaned close and winked at the girl, "And hey, if he keeps refusing to pay overtime, you can always come and work for me." She whispered.

Andie giggled. "I'd love that so much, but I'd probably spend my entire paycheck on books!"

"Employee discount is 30%!" Lila said and made her escape before Lyle caught her trying to swipe his best employee.

Outside, the heat was rising along with the sun, and she could see half a dozen people, mostly tourists, moving about. Time to get to work.

Leading with the Small Head

- Indalo -

Lionel watched Denise's car drive out of sight before he pulled up the security camera feed. He rewound to the time when her car had arrived. The time stamp showed 6:32 p.m. He watched her get out of it and walk toward the house. He then pulled up his call log. The call ended at 6:35. By then, according to the security feed, Denise had already been in the house for three minutes. He ground his teeth.

Damn shame. She would have made a fine nurse.

He would have to let Beta know. It was protocol in cases like this. It was past midnight there. She often stayed up late, however.

The phone rang once, twice, then clicked.

"I'm busy." The woman's voice was calm. "What could be so important?"

He wet his lips. "I have a situation here."

A small sigh of irritation sounded along with the rustle of bedsheets. He could hear her murmur to someone else. The door creaked open. He even heard the groan of wood under her feet, before she closed the door to her study behind her. He recognized the door as it closed. Nothing sounded quite like a 500-year-old oak door when it closed.

"I thought you were in Marrakesh."

"Change of plans, love, I took a quick detour to Bacharach."

He grimaced. The name of her detour was Wolfgang, age twenty-seven. He was part of an Olympic track team and lived in a cramped apartment a few blocks from the city center. She had brought him to the villa, to the bed they shared, instead of fucking him in his tiny, cramped apartment. His wife loved her creature comforts.

He heard the creak of a chair as she settled into the large armchair in the office. "Well, go on, what is it you need, Lionel?"

"A girl, she overheard something she shouldn't have, and she's in the wind."

Another sigh. "Couldn't keep your fun toy on the side and in the dark, could you?" He could hear the leather chair creak, imagined her leaning back in it. Was she naked? Or wearing a negligee? Lionel licked his lips. He wanted to do terrible, dark things to her. Make her scream with pleasure, and maybe a little pain.

"The problem here, dear Lionel, is that you are leading with the small head. It's why I should be Alpha and you should be Beta, not the other way round." She sighed again. "I'll contact Markus. He's reliable. Does good work. I'm assuming you want it clean? Since you were... close?"

He thought he had managed this dalliance more discreetly. Somehow, some way, she had known all about the girl. He stared at the security feed on his phone. Obviously, she had known. She had the same app on her phone. Lionel felt a snarl forming in his throat. He hated when she was one step ahead of him. As of late, that seemed to be a regular occurrence.

"I don't particularly care. If I remember right, Markus enjoys his work. Especially with fire."

She laughed. "Hm... interesting. Well, give me a minute here."

He could hear her fingers tapping on the keyboard. After a few seconds, the chair creaked again, and she spoke. "Consider it done. Tonight, if I don't miss my guess. I'll have Markus contact you for any extraneous details, as I already have most of the information necessary. Address, roommates, and more."

Of course, she did. They might have an open relationship, but she kept closer tabs on him than he did on her. Far closer. For his wife, everything was a chess move, and she knew well in advance who would win the game.

"I expect you do." He said nothing more on the subject, changing topics instead. "Shall we dine in Madrid next Tuesday?" The key to a successful marriage was keeping things exciting inside and out of the bedchamber. "I made reservations at DiverXO."

She practically purred. "DiverXO? I look forward to it."

If there was anything that Joyce enjoyed more than her muscled, yet vacuous boy toys, it was a Michelin star restaurant, and this one had earned *three*.

Still, he couldn't help but needle her. She wasn't the only one whose currency was information on who was fucking who.

"Oh, and darling? Be sure you don't bring any STDs back from Wolfgang." He hung up the phone without waiting for an answer. It was a cheap shot, and he knew it. What could he say? He was human. Open relationship or not, he didn't like the idea of sharing his wife with another man. Especially someone who ran in circles all day.

He made a note to have one of their men in Europe arrange for an accident. Just a small maiming. Perhaps a car accident that would cause a few broken bones. Or a mugging, yes, a mugging would be best. Make sure that dear Wolfgang found himself unable to run fast any longer.

His wife had played with her little boy toy long enough.

A Couple of Days

- Shane -

Shane's phone vibrated in his pocket as he sat in the hallway across from Don Bonatelli's room. Lucia glared at him, muttering epithets in Italian as she stalked inside, an iron grip on Heather's arm. The kid hadn't resisted or complained, just scuttled alongside her mother into the room. Minors weren't supposed to be there outside of visiting hours, but Lucia Bonatelli was a force no one seemed willing to tangle with, not even the dour by-the-books hospital security officer. He'd tried and Mrs. Bonatelli had shot him a look that would leave most fearing for their lives.

It might have gone differently if Shane hadn't interceded then. Explaining he was private security, a bodyguard, often caused more problems than it solved, but dropping Jack's name and his card usually helped defuse any potential problems. Jack's reach impressed Shane. Even here in the middle of nowhere flyover country.

He had settled himself in a chair outside of the room. It was mostly a window, anyway. He could see all the Bonatelli family from his vantage point. His phone buzzed again, and he slipped it out of his pocket. A text from Luke.

On my way. Flight lands at 1000 and I'll be there by 1100.

Shane checked his watch. It was 0800. Three hours to go, likely less. Luke Hall was a down-to-earth, flannel-wearing, outdoor type. When he wasn't working for Jack, he was usually up at a remote cabin he owned up in Alaska. Where Shane had street smarts from his formative years spent on city streets, Luke knew the woods, hunting, and other survival techniques. Jack Benton employed a wide range of talent, former soldiers, police, even those with survivalist training, and he insisted his men learn multiple disciplines. This meant that Shane had trained Luke in Bokator and Luke had given Shane a crash course in surviving the wilderness. It had not been without its hair-raising moments. The remote area had everything from grizzly to moose, and none of them were friendly.

He was tired, but sleep would wait. The chances that anyone knew they were here were minimal, and Lucia had stuck to the last name of Smith. They were already over 1,500 miles from New Jersey, where the name Bonatelli meant something, but one never knew for sure. Better to stay safe and keep his guard up. The girl trying to sneak into his room had unleashed all kinds of merry hell as it was. Shane wasn't one hundred percent sure that Jack believed him when he swore he hadn't encouraged the kid, but that was probably his guilty conscience talking.

I should have never slept with Lila. No, I should have quit my damn job and stayed with her.

The thought of her still stirred complex feelings inside of him. More than lust, although there was plenty of that. It had been six months, and he still dreamed of her. What did that say about him? Was it time to get out of this business? Do something different?

Being a bodyguard is all well and fine, but it isn't an end goal, Ellis, and you know it. But what else is there, really?

He wished he could stop thinking about Lila, but that just didn't seem possible. Not when his dreams remained filled with her, and his days felt empty. He knew exactly when it had all gone wrong. The look on her face when his two-week vacation was cut short. She had arranged for a week of activities, even booked a cabin and arranged for ski rentals at Sugarloaf. Everything had been in place. And then there'd been an emergency client, and Jack had needed him.

Shane had ended the call, looked up, and seen the look of hurt and disappointment on Lila's face. Once again, he had put his work first.

I owe Jack. He took a chance on me when no one else would. I'd be in prison if it weren't for him.

These choices, they all had drawbacks, consequences. They seemed to determine his life, limit it, even when he was trying to do the right thing, or at least the lesser wrong thing. Whether it was choosing to pull out of medical school to take care of his dying mother. Getting entangled with the sister of a head gangbanger of the Asian Boyz or trusting for a second that damned Dave Eggers.

Although if I hadn't had followed Dave Eggers, I'd still be in debt to my eyeballs and living in East L.A. eking out a living. And he might have killed Jack.

Conversely, his decision to choose a billionaire stranger over a childhood friend who sashayed down the wrong path had led him to a job that paid extremely well. It was worthwhile and meaningful more often than not. He might not be the doctor he had dreamed of being, or have a family, but in a few more years, those things could happen.

Not with Lila, though. I fucked that up.

He had boarded a plane, flown away. Off to protect some asshole that had pissed off the wrong person. He had called her. The phone rang and rang until voicemail turned on. "Hi, you've reached Lila, leave a message and maybe I'll return your call!" She sounded all bubbles and tease on the recording, but he knew if she wasn't answering, well, it was because she was angry. Their first argument, short as it was, revolved around her demand that he call Jack back and tell him to find someone else. "You should get a vacation every once in a while. One that he doesn't cut short!"

It hadn't been the first time Shane had disappointed her, but it sure as hell was the last. Two days later, after asking for time to think, his phone had rung.

"I just can't do this, Shane. I just... can't. After everything that has happened, I need..." she had stopped, her voice laden with emotion. "I need *normal*. If that even exists. If it is even something I have a right to expect in this insane world. I want you in my life. But not like this. It just can't work. I want to wake up in the morning and know you are lying there next to me. This can't work any other way."

The words he wanted to say deserted him in that moment. His tongue had felt thick, unwieldy, and he had struggled to respond at all. What was there to say, really? What could he really offer Lila?

Face it, Ellis. If she needs a bodyguard, you are her guy. If she needs a partner in life, well, you have a long way to go before you can give anyone that.

They spoke twice after that. Brief, awkward check-ins. In a moment of weakness a few months ago, he'd flown to Maine. Watched her move about the bookstore, while he felt like some damned stalker in a coffee shop across the street. She'd looked happy. Busy. No new guy in the picture yet, at least not from what he could see, but given time, that would change. A beautiful woman like that, well, a woman like her wouldn't stay single for long, even in a small town like Brunswick, Maine. Back on the job, he would catch himself thinking of her, imagining her meeting someone else, settling down, getting married, having kids.

She deserves happiness. She deserves more than a half-life, a half-assed "Hey babe, I'm here for two weeks, oh, sorry, make that two days. Gotta go save somebody now."

Doctors came and went. Occasionally, Heather scuttled out, avoiding looking his way, her cheeks red with embarrassment. A few minutes later, she'd return with a coffee or bag of donuts, scuttling past as if he didn't exist. Poor kid. He couldn't help feeling sorry for her. It wasn't likely that Lucia was going to let her forget it soon, either.

But it isn't my problem anymore now, is it?

As he was thinking this, a familiar face appeared at the end of the hall. Luke had on his trademark flannel shirt and jeans and a creased paper bag in the other. Shane rose from his seat and met him when he was a few paces from the door.

"Ellis."

"Hall."

Luke's green eyes took in the Bonatelli family. Lucia flashed a scathing glare at the two men, Heather briefly glanced over, red flushing her cheeks once again, and Don Bonatelli was peacefully sleeping. Shane hoped he got some decent rest in the hospital, because once they were back in a safe house, some place outside of the hospital in Ohio that Jack had arranged for them to be transferred to, he really doubted the guy would get a moment of peace from Lucia. From the grim expression on her face, he could see she disapproved of Luke.

This was likely for the best. She wouldn't try to seduce him, and Heather had likely learned her lesson from the disaster of the night before. If everyone was incredibly lucky, that girl wouldn't be trying to emulate her mother for a long while. Long enough for the WitSec program to take over once Bonatelli agreed to exchange testimony for a life in some Podunk nowhere town. He saw divorce looming on the horizon. But it wasn't his problem anymore, so there was that liberating fact.

"Brought you something for the flight back." Luke handed him the paper bag and a ring of keys. "Keys to the cabin and the truck. Take it easy around the last bend, will you? The runoff's made the going that way a little dicey. Jack says to check your email for the tickets."

"Will do."

Luke looked over at the Bonatelli's and whistled under his breath as Lucia glowered back at him. "Damn, she looks *pissed*."

"That's just her resting bitch face." Shane said, turning away, just in case Lucia Bonatelli could read lips.

Luke snorted. "I need you to take care of something while you're there."

Shane arched an eyebrow. "Oh? Besides that cord of wood you were hoping I'd chop for you?"

"I got something in a kennel on the back porch. Her name is Sue."

"I'm guessing this isn't a dog." Shane had seen Luke's affinity with wildlife. The last time he'd visited the log cabin Hall had built with his own hands, a three-legged skunk had walked up onto the porch, curled up on a cushion, and taken a nap as if it didn't have a care in the world. The smell had been... overwhelming.

"Black bear cub. About six months old. Mother was killed by poachers shooting out of season. I've got him on a mix of kitten formula and kibble. It'll be feeding time by the time you get back there."

Shane shook his head. "Of course it will." He laughed, then asked. "How's the skunk taking it?"

"Pepe is pissed. Took one look at that bear cub and huffed on out of there tout suite. Haven't seen him in three days."

"Well, I hate to say it, but this domestic situation is far more fraught than frontier land." Shane said, angling a thumb in the Bonatelli family's direction.

"Yeah, Jack filled me in. I think he's still pissed at you over the Benoit job."

Shane groaned. "I'll never live that down, will I?"

Luke grinned. "Probably not. Hey, if you get bored, the fence along the back forty is needing some repairs."

Shane flapped his hand at him and sniffed the bag. "Fry bread? From Tapeesa?" It smelled delicious.

"Of course." Luke grinned as Shane took a large bite. "I think she's really into you."

Pieces of fry bread flew out of his mouth as Shane choked. Tapeesa was a solid three bills and mother of nine children, ranging in age from eight years to the eldest son, who was in his early 20s.

Luke slapped him on the back. "She told me to tell you to come by. They're slaughtering a yak on Thursday night. Help 'em out and she'll send you home with some reindeer sausage and those tasty yak-a-dillas. Their herd is doing real well."

Shane was wondering if he was better off with the Bonatelli family. Luke was probably yanking his chain, but he had seen Luke's Inuit neighbor wink at him several times. He'd chalked it up to a cultural difference, but maybe it meant something far different.

It's a whole different world up there. Wildlife running amok, lascivious, middle-aged women, and a hell of a lot more work than I was hoping for while I get a few days off.

He looked over and saw Lucia glaring at him.

If looks could kill, damned if I wouldn't have the most excruciating death right now.

"Well, I guess I better get going. You'll probably be better off without me introducing you. They should be ready to transport later this afternoon to the Ohio hospital. Good luck, man."

"Hey, you too. And give Tapeesa a hug from me."

"Ha! Nice try, Hall. I'll leave that to you," Shane said as he walked away. After these past few weeks dealing with closed doors, and Lucia's oppressive perfume, he was looking forward to the fresh Alaskan air, even if it included wildlife husbandry, yak slaughter, and fence repair.

Torched

- Denise -

Minutes after arriving home, Tara's tear-stained face at the door pushed Denise's troubles to the back of her mind. Her best friend's left eye was already swelling and darkening. Her lip trembled and her mouth opened, but no sound came out, just more gut-wrenching sobs.

"Tara? Oh my God, sweetie, come inside now."

Laura and Taegan, both in the living room, looked first alarmed, then resigned, to see Tara. It wasn't the first time, and unfortunately, it wouldn't be the last. At least, Taegan had said it three weeks ago, when Tara had spent two days at the condo, nursing a black eye and swollen mouth from a tangle with her mercurial boyfriend.

"Eddie is a piece of shit, Tara. The sooner you dump his sorry ass, the better. Or you'll end up regretting it someday."

Tara vacillated wildly on this, unfortunately. At the moment, sore, and safe surrounded by strong women, she had agreed that yes, her boyfriend was a piece of shit. That had all changed two days later with the onslaught of chocolate, flowers, a card begging her to forgive him, and the biggest, dorkiest stuffed bear Denise had ever seen occupying their front stoop. Tara had gone back.

"Oh, let me guess." Taegan drawled, "Mr. Wonderful turned into a piece of shit again."

"Taegan, you aren't helping." Denise hissed as she helped Tara to the couch. Her friend collapsed in a sobbing, moist heap. Her long hair was limp, bedraggled. Outside, the quick and unexpected summer rain shower had all but disappeared. From the look of it, Tara had been out in the thick of it.

Walked the entire way, no doubt.

Laura was a touch more sympathetic. She got up, filled a plastic bag with ice and offered it to Tara, along with a small reassuring pat on the shoulder. "Here, sweetie, take this." She rolled her eyes at Denise and shook her head. It was clear to Denise that Laura knew, just as Denise did, how it would go. Tara would return to Eddie. Whether it was tomorrow or three days from now, it didn't matter. She'd go back.

Denise had volunteered at a women's shelter in her late teens as part of the community service required by her college program. She'd seen how the cycle continued over and over, until either a woman had finally had enough, or her partner killed her. She'd seen it, held hands with countless women, and seen them swear up and down they were done, just to return.

"I'm so done with him, Denise. I swear to God, I am." Tara sniffled, her voice warbled through the snot and tears. "He hit me because I didn't make the spaghetti the way he wanted it. I couldn't find the powdered Parmesan he likes at the store, just the fresh stuff, and I assumed, I mean, I'm so *stupid*, I thought it would be okay, y'know? I mean, it's *fresh*. Who doesn't like fresh Parmesan?"

"Piece of shit." Taegan said, softening. "Who the fuck likes that powdered crap when you can have fresh?"

Tara looked up at her, a grateful half-smile on her face. It lasted for half a second before it crumpled back into misery. "Then he hit me. Told me I was useless and incapable of following basic instructions."

"Girl, that man is a dick." Taegan said, plopping down on one side of Tara and wrapping a brightly tattooed arm around her.

"Who the hell likes powdered Parmesan?" Laura asked as she headed for the kitchen. "This is gonna take a bottle of wine and some of my famous straight-from-the-package gourmet ramen."

"Tell you what, we'll go kick him in the dick and then cover it with powdered Parmesan." Denise promised not to be outdone by her roommates.

Tara giggled at the last one.

With a tall glass of wine, the ice pack, and the trio's insistence she took part in several rounds of Cards Against Humanity, Tara's tears dried and she laughed along with the others. Denise wished for the umpteenth time that her best friend hadn't fallen madly in love with a complete dick and had instead moved in with her when she had first found the place two years earlier. Tara hadn't, though. And hours later, long after midnight, Tara had succumbed to a deep, wine-heavy slumber in Denise's double bed while Denise tossed and turned.

Perhaps it was the whole weird conversation she had overheard Lionel have, or that she knew with no doubt that Tara would return to Eddie *again* despite everything, or that her body just felt weird and *off* for some strange reason she couldn't quite identify - but finally Denise eased her way out of the double bed. Tara didn't wake as she moved about the room and gathered her shoes, purse, and keys.

Cookies and ice cream.

Life always felt better with a delicious Brookie cookie from Night Owl dipped in a pint of Haagen-Dazs. She would bring a Dirty Diana cookie back for Tara. They were her favorite. Denise peered at her phone. It was just past one. She had plenty of time to walk there, to the grocery store, and then even a quick jog along the beach. By the door to her bedroom, Denise paused.

I should wake her up. Have Tara come with me? We haven't been to Night Owl in forever.

It had been their thing, cookies and ice cream, still tipsy from a night out dancing and flirting with hot guys. But then Tara had met Eddie. And for a girl who liked her boy of the month, Tara had fallen hard for the *wrong* guy. Her friend was out cold. Snoring, even. Denise shook her head, pulled a sheet over Tara, and closed the door gently behind her. She slipped out of the front door and headed down the street.

Two hours later, she stood gaping in horror, lost among the crowd of onlookers. Her home was a burned ruin. While she had gorged herself on ice cream and cookies, dug her feet into the sand and stared up at the starlit night, her roommates, her *best friend*, had perished.

The flames were mostly gone, but the smoke still billowed. Denise stood there, shock holding her in place, lost in the crowd of spectators and gawkers. The police had established a perimeter and various uniformed men stood inside of it, far enough away that she had to strain to hear them. She couldn't hear all that they said. Just random bits of words.

"Blunt-force trauma."

"Arson."

"No survivors."

"Use of accelerant."

"Intentional."

Her mind cycled, taking the words in. Watched as the bodies, all three of them, came out. Covered, wrapped in body bags, she didn't know which was which, but she knew this. Tara, Laura, and Taegan were all dead. All of them.

Had Eddie done this? No. He was a complete shit, but he knew Tara would be back. It was a cycle they had played out over and over these past two years. Besides, Eddie didn't have the balls to kill Tara and two other girls. He was more of the small-minded bully.

Suddenly Denise couldn't breathe. The conversation she had overheard. The one that had made her uneasy, made the questions come up. Lionel. It had to be Lionel. It had to be. There had been something in his eyes. Something in the way he had asked if she had just come in. She'd lied then, in that moment. She'd smiled at him, told him she'd just come by to tell him the news, and that she had to go. A bullshit excuse. She thought she'd been convincing enough, but now she wasn't so sure. What if he hadn't bought it? What if he had called someone to make one foolish girl go the hell away?

From the back of the crowd came a wild, keening scream. Denise turned to see Tara's boyfriend, Eddie, staring at the house, his eyes black holes of panic and fear. "Tara! Tara!" He pushed forward, shoving several bystanders out of his way, edging closer to her. He didn't notice Denise until he was almost on top of her. "Denise? Oh God, thank God! Where's Tara?"

She tried to make her mouth work. She opened her mouth, closed it, and shook her head, staring back at the coroner's van where they were loading the first of the bodies. Eddie's hands were on her shoulders, shaking her, screaming, then pushing her away as he dove forward through the perimeter, bellowing Tara's name. She watched as the police converged on him, first trying to slow him down, and when he fought, subduing him. The last Denise saw of Eddie Vasquez was of his face, wordlessly screaming through the glass of a police car window at her as they drove him away.

The gawping bystanders stared at her with open curiosity. No one approached her. No one said anything to her, but she could hear their murmurs. Snatches of words, phrases. The rushing in her ears, the sounds of the water, the sirens and machines, all the other noise blocked out most of what her neighbors were saying.

The smell finally caused her to flee. The house had been old, one of the older ones in the area. But as they had brought the bodies out, there had been a different smell, one that turned her stomach, one that was part burned beef, mingled with the stench of burned hair, an almost metallic tinge, and, her stomach roiled, the taste of coagulated blood as an errant breeze struck at just the right moment. It smelled of horror. Of things unmentionable and unnamed. Denise lost all thought as she saw the last of the bodies pulled out of the smoking, shambling remnants of her home. She turned on her heel and ran. Her path was without direction, and it was pure luck that it took her toward her car. She had arrived later than her normal time that evening and missed out on the premium parking in front of the house that she usually managed. Laura had ribbed her about it when she first arrived home. It was a running competition between them.

Oh God. Laura.

Laura's car sat half-melted in the drive. The mint green finish of her Volkswagen Bug was blackened, the paint blistered. Denise fumbled for her keys, hearing them jingle as she dug into the Kate Spade purse Tara had given her for her last birthday. Her hands shook so hard, she felt like a resident at Happy Haven. It took three tries before she could hold them still long enough to get the key to unlock the door and slip inside of the car. The inside of the car was quiet, the air blessedly free of smoke, of that other terrible smell. She slipped inside, closed the door, and for reasons she didn't completely understand, locked the door.

To the left, toward the beach, the dark of night was giving way to dawn. The starlit black sky she had walked under just an hour ago was now gray, and she could see a glow appear at the edge of the horizon.

Tara. Taegan. Laura.

Whoever had done this. Had they thought Tara was her? Sleeping in her bed, and at the quickest of glances, same height, same hair. Her best friends in the entire world had been in that house.

And now they are all dead.

Still reeling, Denise felt her stomach roil again. She fumbled with the door lock and opened the door just in time, throwing up the cookie and ice cream along with the remains of the wine and ramen that Taegan had served up. The combination was revolting, soured with stomach acids. In a daze, she closed the door, reached for a napkin from the glove box, and wiped her mouth. Her keys lay in the seat beside her and she stared at them, thought of the smoking ruin behind her, and picked them up. Mechanically, she slipped on her seatbelt, turned the keys in the ignition, and maneuvered the battered car out of its position against the curve. Her thoughts were a maelstrom of grief, horror, and fear. She made her way to I-95 and then north. Denise did not know where she was going. No thought of what happened next. She just drove. To the east, the sun continued to rise.

In Transit

- Denise -

By the time Denise made it to just south of Jacksonville, it was past noon. The tank was nearly empty; the sun was high in the sky, and her throat parched.

Denise pulled into a Flying J. She filled the tank, then stepped inside of the station. Grabbing water, chips, and a cell phone charger.

I need to eat.

She could see an Arby's, but the thought of meat reminded her of the terrible smell and her stomach twisted again. She dodged a pack of gabbling teens dressed in beach gear and headed for the Cinnabon counter.

"WhatcanIgitcha?"

Denise blinked at the older woman behind the counter. "What?"

"What can I get ya?" the clerk said slower, her eyes scrutinizing her.

"Um, one of those, please." She pointed to the pastries warm on the display rack.

"Halfoffifyoubuytwo." The clerk said, then said again, slower, when Denise gaped at her. "Half off if you buy two."

Denise didn't answer. Just a nod. One. Two. Did it matter? Did anything matter? There was nothing left. Nothing but ash and that terrible smell still in her nose.

The cashier handed her a bag and receipt with her card and she headed outside into the hot Florida sun and swampy, humid heat when the image on a large tv screen overhead stopped her in her tracks. There were the smoking ruins of her house. A banner marched along the bottom of the screen: *Miami Fire Horror - Three Women Found Bludgeoned and Burned in Beach House. Boyfriend of Woman Arrested.*

Denise's hands shook.

They think Eddie did it?

She stood rooted to the spot, her eyes glued to the screen.

Eddie looked absolutely panicked. There's shit you can make up, pretend, and there's stuff that's genuine.

She forced her feet to move. To walk through the doors and outside. The moist heat surrounded her, sucking her energy, what little she had of it, and she sagged under the weight of it, her shoulders drooping. Inside of the car, once the engine was purring and the air conditioning flowing, Denise tried to order her thoughts.

What do I do now?

The down-to-earth part of her was trying to reason it all through. To make sense of it. Had it really been Eddie? If so, perhaps she should return home. Well, not home. Home was gone. But back to Miami, to the police, perhaps.

Eddie didn't act guilty. He looked positively terrified. Worried. Yes, Eddie was an abusive prick. But some part of him cared for Tara, had to, to act that way.

A honk sounded. A car, waiting for her to pull out. The driver held up his hands impatiently. Denise realized the parking lot was full, and she was just sitting in an idling car. She had to do something, had to go somewhere.

Decide, damn it. And make it now.

She pulled out of the parking space and the waiting car slid into her vacated place before she was ten feet away. Denise did not know where to go, but it seemed her hands did. They guided the car back to I-95 North. Headed away, up the east coast. Away from the fire, away from the terrible memories of just a few hours before.

She struggled with what to do next. Her friends were dead. Her home, and every possession she had in the world, burned to ash.

She thought of her mother, Janine. On the day of Denise's eighteenth birthday, Janine had given their landlord a thirty day notice. It wasn't completely without warning. She had long spoken of taking what little savings she had and heading for Europe. "I got pregnant a month into my gap year," she was fond of saying, "And that was that. My life of wandering was over. As soon as you are grown, darling, I'm spending the rest of my life as a gypsy."

That was just what Janine did. By the end of the month, she had sold or given away every possession she owned and bought a one-way ticket to Italy, leaving Denise to figure out what she wanted to do with her life in a tiny rented room that smelled like sour milk. The paper-thin walls broadcast every grumble, snipe or argument of the couple who she rented from. What little support system or security blanket Janine's presence had provided during Denise's formative years fell away. It had taken Denise a year or two of floundering, moving from one unsettling situation to another, couch surfing, and rundown rooms for rent before she stumbled into an interest in the medical field. She had worked in a hospital cafeteria, and that, combined with her excellent grades in high school, had eventually led to enrolling in a nursing program.

Janine checked in every so often. Denise had gotten a text from her mother a week or two ago. She had sent a picture of the bluest water Denise had ever seen and written, "Wish you were here. The Aegean sea is a thing of beauty. Don't forget, it's the cradle of civilization. The stories it could tell!"

Denise had stared at it, returning to it over and over. The words her mother had typed were irritating, like a tag on a shirt, poking at her, scratching.

She doesn't wish I was there. Not the slightest bit. She's happy to be done with the mother's role.

It still hurt a bit. Denise felt as if it had denied her something vital. She saw how her friends lived. Sure, plenty of them had both parents working outside of the home, but their parents still were involved and active parts in their lives. They attended soccer games, helped with bake sales, drove them to Girl Scouts. Her mother had never baked cupcakes, never played the domestic goddess. There had been few rules or boundaries, and Janine had never expected her to call her Mother. Men had come and gone. Janine was a butterfly, never content to settle down. Denise wanted something different. She wanted a career. Someday, she wanted to settle down, get married, and have kids. She wanted to walk into a house and know she owned it. Not some jerk who wouldn't bother to fix the dishwasher or replace the shingles that were falling off the roof.

Denise quickly learned to save every penny she could. Which wasn't much, honestly, but she knew she had at least a thousand dollars in the account. And that, along with a growing and undefined terror of returning to Miami, spurred her north. By the time she reached the outskirts of Philadelphia and visited an ATM, she had a hazy notion of what to do next. Perhaps it was the thought of her mother that made Denise remember a childhood trip to Maine. They had gone there to visit friends, well, friends of Janine's parents, and the people who had raised Janine during her early teens. To Denise's inexperienced eyes, the couple had been ancient. They were both in their late 70s, and Charles, or Uncle Chuck as Denise had known him as, ran a bookstore. His wife, Deidre, who Denise had called Aunt DeeDee, had run a knitting supply shop next door to it. It was the one, and only, time that Janine had tried to shirk her responsibilities as a mother. She had dropped six-year-old Denise off and disappeared for nine months, reappearing only after Deidre had grown too ill to work or care for a small child. It wasn't more than a year or two later that Deidre passed away from cancer and left Charles alone to care for the bookstore and their five-room cottage a few blocks away.

When Denise dreamed of a home, it was invariably of that house. She remembered the smell of the sea, the hot summer she spent playing on the beach, or skulking through the stacks of books and curling up in a corner to read. She wondered if Charles was alive still. Likely not. It had been nearly twenty years.

Still, she pointed the car north, drawn magnetically to the last place she had ever truly felt at peace. The memories of salt and fish and seagulls were still as fresh in her mind as if she had experienced them yesterday. Denise continued to drive, pulling into rest stops and sleeping in her car when sleep became necessary.

Suspect

- Miami Police Department -

"What have you got, Ames?" Jim Sievers asked, his hands desperate for something to do now that he'd been without cigarettes for four days. He reached for the stress ball his wife had given him and squeezed it.

Troy Ames was heavyset, balding, and the man wore a perpetual frown. This wasn't atypical, not in their line of work.

"Swears he didn't do it. Spent half the interview blubbering into a box of Kleenex." Ames answered, tipping back in his chair. The beleaguered piece of furniture groaned in protest.

"Huh." Jim leaned over and retrieved Eddie Lamar's rap sheet. "Domestic dispute. Stalking. Assault. Another domestic dispute. Protection order dismissed a week after issuance."

"Yeah, yeah, I know. The kid is a piece of shit. Loses his temper, hits women. You know, just the kind I tell my girls to avoid dating." Ames frowned deeper, shook his head.

"But?"

"But, what?"

"Aw, come on, Ames, out with it. You don't frown like that when you've nailed the bad guy dead to rights."

Ames snorted. A ghost of a smile flickered across his face. He sat forward abruptly; the chair groaning again. "Eddie doesn't have it in him. And he swears up and down his woman was in the building that burned."

"So?"

"So, that'd make four bodies, not three."

Jim shuffled through the folder on his desk. "We got a Taegan McMasters, age 23."

"Yeah, and a Laura McCoy, also age 23."

"And then a Denise Fortuna, age 22. Those are all the girls listed on the lease and it was a three-bedroom house. What's his girlfriend's name?"

"Tara Weatherby, age 22."

"So, how was this guy picked up?"

"He came in like a locomotive there at the scene. Hot as hell, half off his head, screaming for his girl Tara, and took a swing at an officer. They put him on ice and fingered him for the job. I just, I don't buy it, Jim."

"No chance that this Tara girl up and ran?" Jim asked.

Ames shrugged. "They're identifying the bodies now. Burned to a crisp all of them, but they were dead before that."

Jim raised an eyebrow. "Oh?"

"M.E.'s first look, off the record, is that someone walked inside, bashed the brains out of each of the girls while they slept, then used a can of gasoline to soak the carpet and set the place ablaze. Found the melted can."

"Blunt force trauma. Someone has to be powerfully angry to do something like that. And you don't think this Eddie Lamar did it?"

"He was blubbering like a pansy-assed baby. When I showed him pictures of the scene, he tossed his cookies. All over the damned interview room floor. Still smells in there. Lamar's definitely got anger issues, but murder? I don't see it, Jim."

"How soon until we get names on all the victims?"

"Any time now." Ames shot him a rare grin. "You're running later than usual, Sievers. I guess that means you're buying me lunch since I covered for your ass and said you were running down a lead when Sarge asked after you."

Jim nodded. "Taco Bile for lunch then."

"Oh, hell no, brother! You are getting me Taco Negro!"

Jim opened his mouth to argue, but the phone on their shared desk rang at that very moment.

Ames grabbed it. "Detective Ames speaking." He nodded, grunted, and scribbled on a notepad. "Right, thanks, man." He slid the paper over to Jim. "They identified the bodies. We got Taegan McMasters, Laura McCoy, and..."

"Tara Weatherby, Eddie Lamar's girl," Jim finished. "So where is Denise Fortuna?"

"That's the million dollar question, isn't it?" Ames tapped the pen on his desk and frowned. "Girl's roommates and friend bludgeoned to death and set on fire. You'd think she'd be in giving a statement to us at the very least. Maybe she was at her boyfriend's house?"

"Or is it something more?" Jim asked.

"Like what?"

"Shit, I don't know. It's Miami. She could've been running drugs or other dirty dealings. Hell, she could've done this to the girls herself."

"Blunt force trauma?" Ames turned to his computer and tapped a few keys. Denise's driver's license photo and details appeared. "This little girl? I don't see it, man."

"All I'm saying is we track it down, see where it leads. What do we know about this Denise, and the others?"

Ames returned to his computer, and Jim powered his laptop up as well. "You take those first two names. I'll look up the other two."

A half hour later, they had a clear yet perplexing picture. All four girls were medical students at Miami Regional University. All of them had squeaky clean records, except for Taegan, whose record showed they had collared her for underage drinking two years prior.

"They've rented this property for the past two years, no complaints or proceedings from the landlord." Ames mused. "No reason for them to be killed like this. Eddie Lamar is still looking like the prime suspect, but I'm telling you Sievers, it wasn't him. Boy hasn't got it in him. He's a small-minded bully. A control freak, sure, but not a murderer and arsonist."

"I believe you, man. But what else do we have? Some rando who just chooses this house and these girls? And if so, where is the Fortuna girl?"

"We have got to issue a bulletin. Put her name and face out there and get her to come in. Then we can sort this out," Ames said and ran his fingers back across his keyboard. "I'll put in the request to the Sarge, along with my interrogation of Lamar."

"Right. Well, hurry then. I didn't eat breakfast. I figure we can get an early start on lunch at Taco Bile."

"You mean Taco Negro, or I might let it slip to Sarge you overslept again."

Jim laughed. "Fine, fine, you old bastard. Taco Negro it is. Now get to typing."

Later that day, they released Eddie Lamar with a court summons for assaulting a police officer.

They issued a police bulletin on all local news websites and radio stations informing the public that the police considered Denise Fortuna a person of interest in the Miami Beach fire. It asked for information from anyone on her whereabouts.

Two rather dangerous individuals took notice of this bulletin. A man by the name of Markus, who was pissed off as all hell that they had given him insufficient information on his target, and Lionel Bush, who never enjoyed paying money to someone for a job left half-done. Neither were men to be trifled with.

Just for Now

Despite the beautiful weather, the morning had been rather quiet. That had changed in late morning, as tourists filled the sidewalks and made their way down the street. A gaggle of pre-teens were giggling over in the romance section. One, a mousy-looking girl with braces, had spots of color on her cheeks as one of her friends showed her a racy, bare-chested vampire looking to make a meal of the scantily clad woman in his arms. Another of the girls caught Lila watching, and whispered to her friends. They skulked away. Well, as much as a gaggle of girls like that can. Half strut, half awkward stumble, they fled for the section just beyond it that held a plethora of ghost stories that were more appropriate for their age.

Andie had slipped over on her lunch break and was running a finger along the spines of the new releases in the fantasy section, and a leggy brunette was currently perusing the magazines, her perfectly manicured fingers fluttering as they tried to choose between The Knot and Bride's Magazine. A rather large diamond solitaire ring on her left finger caught the sunlight that filtered in through the large floor to ceiling windows.

The bell at the top of the door jingled softly, and a young woman entered. She was a thin, mousy-haired slip of a girl. Lila watched her surreptitiously. She looked exhausted, but also her face had a familiar look on it. Lila had been running the bookstore long enough to recognize it. The look of someone who finds books a solace, and bookstores as a place of renewal and safety. She watched as the young woman moved to run her fingers along the women's fiction, then over to the poetry section, before stopping in front of the bulletin board. A draw for the teens, patrons posted everything from lost and found items to help wanted or services offered on it. It was how Lila had first hired Angela. The girl had seemed like a real go-getter at the onset. Until she fell in love. Now all she wanted to do was snuggle with her boyfriend and call in sick. Lila had fielded the fourth "I'm sick" call in a row yesterday, agreed to her showing up for a half day today and resolved to fire her later in the evening, after closing, if she didn't come through. A shot of despair rolled through her.

I hate firing her. But she's been gone more than she's been here. This is ridiculous.

"Good morning," Lila said, smiling at the young woman. "Is there anything I can help you find?"

The woman looked up, managed a small smile in return, and walked over. Now that she was closer, Lila could see she was actually closer to her mid-20s, likely the same age as Lila, or close enough.

"Oh, hi. Do you work here?" The young woman asked.

"Sure do."

"Do you know if, um, the bookstore is hiring at all?"

Lila looked her up and down. She looked normal, really, and maybe a little old for minimum wage work in a bookstore, but there was something about her. Something the woman was trying very hard to hide.

Fear.

Lila knew what it was like to be afraid.

"It is. It's minimum wage, though. If you are okay with that, I can get you an application. Are you new to the area?"

The young woman nodded. Conflicting emotions played across her face. The door chimed again, and the woman flinched in response, her eyes flitting to the door. Lila handed the application over, along with a pen. "Here, you can fill it out while I take care of this customer."

Half an hour later, and a dozen customers in and out, and the young woman returned. Lila had barely had a moment to breathe, but she had stolen a couple of glances over at the woman as she sat in an armchair and filled out the form. She had tucked her shoulder-length hair back behind her ears and was chewing on her lower lip nervously.

"You look like you could really use another clerk."

Lila's stomach growled audibly. She winced. "That obvious, huh?"

Her phone chimed, and she glanced at it. A text from Angela, claiming her *cat* was now sick, and she had to take it to a vet. The girl couldn't keep her stories straight to save her life. Last week, when she had called in, she told Lila that Pumpkin died that morning and she needed to bury the ancient creature. Now it had suddenly revived itself from the dead and desperately needed a vet? She'd call her tonight and tell her not to bother coming back. The girl would be happier working at one of the dozen restaurants along the pier. She'd find herself a well-heeled tourist boyfriend at the beginning of each week.

Like a Baskin-Robbins of boyfriends. A new flavor every week.

Lila studied the application, noting her recent employment at a Happy Haven Retirement Village. In Florida, no less. What in the world was the girl doing here in Maine? "So, Denise, I see you were in Florida until just recently?" She looked up and met Denise's gaze, waiting for her to speak.

"I, um, was in a relationship and it, um, it didn't work out. It's..." Denise stared at her shoes. "I just... I need to figure some stuff out. I'm a hard worker, and I've got retail experience. And while I never worked in a bookstore before, I really, *really* love books." She added it in a quick rush, as if afraid Lila would boot her out of the door.

There was something terribly wrong. Lila wasn't sure how she could tell, but she could, deep in her bones. The girl was scared, and she was hiding something. What, Lila wasn't sure, but it didn't feel like Denise was trying to mislead her, more that she was scared, truly, deeply afraid.

Lila felt her stomach growl again. She had woken up late again this morning, after having a burst of inspiration that had her typing away on her computer until nearly two in the morning. A sandwich from the deli counter at Hanniford's, one made with rare roast beef and swiss cheese with that spicy mustard, was what she was yearning for in that moment. Her mouth watered at the thought.

Her focus returned to Denise. The girl was frightened, and she looked rather sleep-deprived. From the application, Lila could see that, until two days ago, Denise lived, worked and attended nursing school in

Florida. Now she was here, some, what, 1,500 miles away from home? There was a story here. And likely someone who needed help.

She might just be here a day or two. Why not? It isn't as if I have anyone else to depend on. Besides, I want to know why she looks so damn scared.

"Can you start today?"

Denise's eyes widened in surprise. "Um, sure."

"How about this minute?"

Denise blinked. "Okay."

"Great." Lila dug into her pocket and pulled out a twenty-dollar bill. "I need you to run down to Hanniford's and buy us lunch. Tell Andie that Annie would like her regular sandwich. She'll know what I mean. Order yourself something, too. After we eat, I'll show you the ropes."

Denise's mouth opened and closed, and she stood there motionless for a half-second, the twenty-dollar bill in her hand. "Um, okay, I'll be right back." She slipped out the door of the bookstore and the bell gave a soft jingle as she did.

"She's not from around here." Maeve appeared before her, the latest beach read clutched in her hands. Lila blinked. Trust Maeve to walk in without Lila noticing and already want the lowdown on the new employee. If that's what Denise truly was.

Lila forced a bright smile on her face. "Why good afternoon, Maeve! How are you today?"

The busybody peered down the street, watching Denise slip inside of Hanniford's. The older woman gave a small harrumph of disapproval.

"Just this today, Maeve? I don't know if you saw it, but a new book by Shelby Van Pelt just came in. *Remarkably Bright Creatures*. It's supposed to be very good."

Maeve's gaze returned to Lila, and she frowned. "Did you actually hire that girl? Where's Angela?"

"Yes, Maeve, I hired her. And Angela isn't here, unfortunately."

Maeve snorted, "That girl has a flavor of the day boyfriend. Just as loose as..."

"That will be $16.49." Lila interrupted.

Maeve's frown deepened. She wasn't used to being interrupted or ignored. Lila suppressed a sigh. No doubt Maeve would note Lila's behavior as surly and the other denizens of the town warned away by the old cow. Lila tried to think of a compliment while the town gossip fished in her purse for cash. Maeve was one of a handful of holdouts. Most of Lila's transactions were with credit or debit cards.

"Your hair looks quite nice today, Maeve." The woman's surly expression wavered. If there was anything Maeve appreciated more than a juicy piece of gossip, it was someone noticing her appearance. Despite living in a small town, and there being really nothing to dress up for now that she was retired, Maeve inevitably appeared in classic outfits with nary a hair out of place, rings and jewelery just right, and her nails impeccably manicured.

"Oh, thank you, Annie. Here, and," she glanced over to the bookshelf at the new book by Shelby Van Pelt. "Be a dear and set that aside for me? I'll come by once I've finished this."

"Of course." Lila calculated it in her head. Maeve read at a pretty good clip in the winter. Summers, however, meant more social events. Bingo, book club, bridge. She figured she had at least three days of respite, perhaps four if she were lucky, until Maeve returned for her next book and the inevitable dose of gossip. She breathed a quiet sigh of relief as the woman left. Maeve wasn't malicious per se, just petty and intrusive more than anything else. The woman rubbed her wrong, though. And until Lila knew more about Denise, she didn't want Maeve getting her nose in either of their business.

Denise returned with two sandwiches and Lila's change. After hurried bites in between surges of customers, Lila showed Denise around the store and set her to shelve a new delivery of paperbacks and organizing the children's section that looked like a hurricane had just blown through. A standard day, really. There was a group of local mothers who often walked past on the way to the beach. Lila counted herself lucky that the children came through on the way to the beach, and not after. She cleaned up enough sand from the local tourists, after all. The rest of the afternoon passed quickly and Lila found time during a late afternoon lull to actually open her laptop and work briefly on her manuscript. She was finally at the part of the book where she felt the story taking shape, almost creating itself, and she felt more like a conduit than a sculptor. Which made her hope against hope that Denise might actually stay on for a while.

It would be really nice to focus on getting this manuscript done.

She looked up at the clock and realized it was already five minutes past closing. "Oh, wow. Time flies when you're having fun!" She smiled at Denise, who was working her way through organizing the romance section. "It's closing time!" She walked over to the front door and locked it, flipping the sign from open to closed.

"Are you a writer?" Denise asked, standing up and dusting her jeans off.

"I guess I am," Lila said, laughing at the puzzled expression on the woman's face. "It probably sounds silly, but I've written and self-published one book, and I'm working on a second one, and I never really thought about it until you asked." She shrugged. "I write in a vacuum. I don't talk to anyone about it because I'm writing under a pen name."

Denise smiled and raised an eyebrow suggestively. "Romance?"

"Of course." Lila answered. "Denise, I can't thank you enough for today and you starting right away."

Denise nodded, her smile fading slightly. "Sure. I mean, I was happy to help." Lila could see that Denise bit her fingernails to the quick. "Would you like for me to come back tomorrow?"

"Absolutely. Could you be here at nine? I could use you for a full nine-to-five shift if you were up to it." Lila threw up her hands. "I didn't even ask you what hours and days you're available for. And I also need to have you fill out some basic paperwork. A W-9 and all that jazz." She turned to dig under the front register. "Where are you staying, anyway? You left the home address blank."

When Denise didn't reply, Lila looked up. The woman stood there, twisting her hands, staring at her shoes.

"Denise?"

"I, uh, I've been playing it by ear. I was going to find a hotel room, but I walked in here first and well..."

Lila gaped at Denise with a mixture of shock and dismay. The town was small, with a strong tourist presence in the summer. Every beach house, cottage, and spare hotel room was likely booked already. Her new employee had nowhere to go, other than her car, for the night.

This, combined with the fear she could still see lurking beneath the surface, spurred her to action.

"Oh dear. You might have a really difficult time finding something tonight, what with all the tourists here right now."

Denise paled in response, biting her lip.

"I didn't think of that. Maybe the next town over?"

Lila shook her head. "Doubtful. The area is saturated, especially in July. Look, I have a room I sublet out of my rental house." She held up her hands at Denise's surprised stare. "I know we just met and all that. It comes furnished, and I had considered turning it into a shared room rental on Airbnb or VRBO for a little extra cash, but it's just been sitting there unoccupied. It's just for now, until you find a place of your own, or, you know, get back on your feet, but..."

"Thank you." Denise whispered, and Lila could see her fighting back tears. Her hands twisting.

"Yeah? Okay, well, my car's out front and I'm guessing that's yours down the way. I'll close up and you can just follow me to the house." Despite the tourist traffic during the day, most of the restaurants were on the opposite side of town, and the street was empty now, except for a glut of locals who were shopping at Hanniford's. Lila could see an older model Honda Civic with faded and chipped paint. Denise would never have been able to spend the night comfortably in that. Not to mention the local police were rather attentive at night. They would give her grief.

It was a short drive. Pretty much everything in Brunswick was a quick five-minute drive away, if that. As Lila pulled into the driveway of the house, and Denise parked beside her, Lila's thoughts strayed to Shane.

Mr. Pecan Pie Ellis would shit himself if he knew I had brought a practical stranger to the house. I wonder which one of his Code I'm breaking doing this?

She looked over at Denise as the young woman slung a messenger bag over her shoulder and looked like she was debating whether to get back in the car and drive far away from here.

"Come on in. I think I have some deli meat. We can make sandwiches for dinner."

Denise Fortuna was running scared. And she certainly knew what that was like. Lila was also determined to find out why. Not tonight, though. Tonight, her new employee needed food and a safe place to stay. She didn't wait for Denise to answer. She just turned on her heel and led the way to the front door.

Breaking News

Person of Interest Sought in Deadly Fire

Miami police are asking for the public's help in locating a Denise Fortuna in connection with the deadly fire on Friday that killed three young women in Little Haiti. The small home caught fire and was fully engulfed by the time Miami firefighters arrived on the scene two hours before dawn.

The fire appears intentional, according to police. One suspect, an Eddie Lamar, has a history of domestic abuse. Lamar is currently in police custody. The three victims may have already died prior to the fire.

Two of the victims were medical students at Miami Regional. As is the person of interest, Denise Fortuna, identified as a resident of the destroyed rental home.

They have identified the three victims as Taegan McMasters, Laura McCoy, and Tara Weatherby.

If you have any information on the whereabouts of Denise Fortuna, please call the Miami Police.

German Olympist Maimed in Violent Attack

Wolfgang Gestalt, a 27-year-old gold-medalist, was injured in a mugging yesterday in Bacharach, Germany. Residents of the small town are reeling at an uptick in violence in recent days. Both of Gestalt's legs were broken in the attack, and the German Olympic team manager, Friedrich Wolfson, stated that Gestalt also incurred serious head injuries. The attack occurred seconds after Gestalt stepped outside of his home yesterday evening. His attacker remains at large. He is currently in the hospital and expected to survive, but Herr Wolfson reported that the chance of Gestalt's full recovery is in question, as his legs received multiple fractures.

Gestalt has been a rising star in the German track team after rising to prominence during the last Olympics. Germany took home two Gold medals, and many speculated that Gestalt could rival Eliud Kipchoge in the men's marathon after recent sprint times beat Kipchoge's best time by nearly one minute. Now that future is in question, as the world waits to hear if Gestalt will recover.

Off to a Rough Start

The deck of cards lay before her, mocking her.

"Damn it."

Mary Shelley gazed up at her, the Boar card beside the Shelley card, an odd companion to be sure. According to the Literary Witches Oracle guidebook, the Mary Shelley card represented loss, the cycle of life, transitions and attachment. The Boar card, however, brought danger, aggression and masculinity.

"You are supposed to clarify things," she said aloud, "not make them more confusing."

A soft knock sounded at her door, and Lila jumped. It was dark, near midnight, and she had momentarily forgotten her new housemate.

"Annie?"

"Oh, hi. Come on in."

Denise pushed the door open, and it creaked loudly. She really needed to oil the hinges, and not just on this door, but all of them. Especially now that there was someone else in the house. She hadn't realized how loud the doors were, but every sound Denise made, every creak and groan, seemed to jostle her out of her focus. She had gone from writing a chapter a night to merely a few paragraphs in the past two days.

Maybe if I lay down area rugs over the wood. Perhaps that will help too.

"I was in the bathroom and heard a noise."

"Sorry, that was probably me talking to myself."

Lila looked up at Denise. She was beautiful, even with her hair a mess. Her face was pale, though, and there were still circles under her eyes. Her nails remained bitten to the quick. Despite the two of them spending not only all day at work with each other, but evenings too, Denise had remained very closed mouth about what had brought her all the way from Florida to Maine.

"I'm working on a new book and I just can't seem to figure out what's happening in it."

Denise gazed at the cards. "Are those tarot cards?"

Lila looked back at the deck in front of her. "Sort of." She pointed at a shelf to one side. It held a row of boxes. "Most of those are tarot, some oracle cards, like this deck here, and other things like the Archetypes there." She nodded at a round black box. "I use them sometimes for generating ideas or trying to figure out a direction to go." Lila touched the cards before her. "I have had little luck with Literary Witches, but I try them every so often."

"So, it tells you what to write next?" Denise asked, frowning.

Lila laughed. "No. Nothing quite like that. And often the cards just bring something random into the mix." She shrugged. "I'm not a huge believer, but every once in a while, the tarot surprises me." She frowned at the two cards. "These two, however, they just don't feel right. It's as if they match someone else, not me." Lila glanced up at Denise. "I probably sound like a loon, don't I?"

Denise stepped further into the room; her gaze fixed on the two cards. "Tell me more about these two cards."

"Um, okay, well, this card here is Mary Shelley."

"She wrote Frankenstein." Denise interrupted.

"Yeah, she did. She was just eighteen years old. Newly married to Percy Shelley. According to the guidebook, her card represents loss, the cycle of life, transitions and attachment, especially in parenthood. She bore four children, but only one survived to adulthood."

"And the other card?"

"The Boar? Well, that card represents danger, masculinity, and aggression." Lila gave a laugh. "Not anything I can use in my rom-com, to be sure." Her laugh cut short when she noticed Denise's expression. If it were possible for the girl to grow paler than she already was, Lila wasn't sure how. "Are you okay?" Denise was staring at the cards with an expression of horror. "Denise?"

"I, uh, I'd better get to bed." Denise fled through the doorway and down the hall to her bedroom. Her door shutting with a sharp click.

Lila wasn't sure what had just happened. Denise didn't strike her as conservative. Could she be uber-religious? Had Lila ended up inviting a bible-thumping ultra-conservative in her home? If so, tonight's reaction was the first sign Lila had seen of it.

Lila frowned, then stood up and stretched. Yawned. It was far too late to be fighting with her manuscript. Perhaps she could find some time tomorrow on break, or at lunch, to write more. She closed the door, turned off the lights, and stripped down to her bra and panties.

I need to buy pajamas. Can't exactly walk around the house in the nude any longer.

She closed her eyes and tried to sleep, but Denise's face, her look of horror, and the dark circles the woman still sported under her eyes continued to bother her. A mystery, really. And one she wanted to solve.

Denise had said little, but a few details had emerged over the past two days. For one, Denise had lived in Brunswick as a child, and the folks who had cared for her had owned the same bookstore Lila now ran. Denise had mentioned it the second day she worked there, as they opened it up in the morning.

She'd looked almost panicked afterward at Lila's surprised expression. "I just had fantastic memories from here. Uncle Chuck and Aunt DeeDee were so good to me. They weren't relatives, more friends of my grandparents. They raised my mom after my grandparents died in her early teens. Uncle Chuck ran the bookstore, and Aunt DeeDee had a knitting shop next door. I stayed with them for a summer, part of the fall and winter, before my mom came back and got me."

There sounded like there was a story there as well. But Denise had stopped with that, her words giving way to silence as she ran her fingers along the bookshelves, gently touching the book spines.

"Were you able to find them? Is that why you were there in the bookstore?"

Denise had shaken her head. "No, I knew they were gone. DeeDee passed away a year after I lived with them and it's been nearly twenty years. Uncle Chuck was in his late 70s when I lived here. I just, I don't know. I guess it was just the memories." She pointed to the southeast corner of the store where the non-fiction currently lived. "He had the children's section over there. A little cardboard castle with a puppet theater and beanbag chairs. I'd curl up there for hours with a pile of books. I had just learned to read the year before, and it really caught on while I was here."

After that tidbit of information, Denise had abruptly changed the subject and volunteered to work on shelving the two book orders that had come in the week before, patiently waiting in boxes in the back office.

I should just straight up ask her what is going on. I think by now, she'd trust me enough to answer with the truth.

Yesterday, near closing time, Denise had suggested they go to the grocery store and offered to buy groceries, since Lila refused to let her pay for any rent. After a disastrous attempt to make toast and eggs there at the house before they set off to work, Lila was pretty sure that Denise was catching on to what an awful cook she was. The small galley space still reeked. The toast had caught fire. And somehow, she had missed the broken eggshell in the scrambled eggs. The extra crunch was... off-putting.

When Lila hesitated to name a monthly figure for rent, Denise volunteered to do the cooking. "Look, I have to do something. I can't just live here rent-free and get paid for working at the bookstore. Let me handle the meals. It will save you money on eating out, and if you don't like my cooking, I'll look up average rental prices and we can talk about numbers then. What do you say?"

Lila had happily agreed to it, and tried to pay for all the groceries. The thought of someone cooking for her was damned appealing. She hadn't had a home-cooked meal since she had called it quits with Shane and as tasty as the sandwiches from Hanniford's were, when Denise started listing off the different meals she could make, Lila was more than happy to cover the cost of the groceries. Denise, however, insisted they split the cost of the groceries and by the second evening, the refrigerator was brimming with supplies.

Denise had deftly prepared a casserole with chicken and broccoli and a layer of gooey cheese with French fried onions. "It's the ultimate comfort food. My roommates and I all loved it and took turns making it." Her smile at Lila's compliments and return for a second helping faded as she uttered the words. Before Lila could ask after them, Denise bolted for the little half bath at the base of the stairs, next to the living room that led into the postage stamp of a backyard. Above, at the top of the stairs, were the two bedrooms and a full bathroom sandwiched in between.

"Are you okay?" Lila had asked when Denise returned, her face pale.

"Yeah, my stomach's just been upset the last couple of days. Probably from traveling." She had avoided looking Lila in the eyes, one arm tucked in and around herself, as if she needed a hug. "I think I'm going to head to bed a little early. Do you need me to clean up?"

"Are you kidding? I'm eating seconds. If there's any left, I think I can handle putting it away and cleaning the dishes. Go to bed, Denise, I can handle this, no problem." As the woman turned to walk away, Lila stopped her. "Oh, and Denise? Thank you. I haven't eaten this well in, well, in six months or more. I really appreciate it."

Denise's smile had returned to her pale face. "Happy to help, Annie. It's the least I can do."

Now, hours later, Lila turned on her other side, tired, ready for sleep, except that her thoughts were busy wondering about Denise. The third day had again been unremarkable. No major revelations, but Denise seemed to be a little more relaxed. The shadows beneath her eyes were a shade lighter. She had also been highly productive. The back office was neat as a pin now, and Lila had actually written for an hour or two during the early afternoon, after Denise returned from her lunch break.

The only thing that had been of Issue was Maeve. Of course, the old busybody had blasted her way through the latest book. This wasn't particularly surprising considering that Miss Nosy Parker was desperate to impart another piece of gossip, if only to see what Lila had to say.

She had come in late in the morning, just seconds before Denise had gone on lunch break. As soon as the door chime sounded and Denise disappeared out the door and down the block, Maeve was at the counter, tapping her blood-red fingernails on the counter. Lila felt her jaw clenching in response. She forced a smile to her face. "Ready for the Shelby Von Pelt book, Maeve?"

Maeve smiled and leaned close, "In a minute. I just wondered how your new employee is doing. Denise, right? Oona, down at the thrift shop, said she was shopping for clothes in the same outfit you hired her in the other day."

"Oh really? I hadn't noticed." Lila replied, trying to unclench her teeth. She had noticed, but had said nothing. From what she could tell, Denise had two sets of scrubs and the clothes she had on her back, plus an overly large t-shirt that read "Welcome to Florida" that still had the stiff straight-off-the-hanger creases in it.

She's scared. She has no clothes, no personal effects other than what she has purchased in the past day or two. Which means she's on the run. But from what?

"And furthermore. After that? She went across the street and bought underwear, socks, a hairbrush, even a toothbrush and toothpaste at the pharmacy."

Lila struggled to hold herself back from saying something sarcastic and biting. "Okay."

Maeve looked disappointed. "Well, I just thought you should know. After all, she's staying with you, isn't she? Dolores was driving past Pineview and said she saw a battered Honda Civic with Florida plates in your driveway."

And this is when I miss city life the most. Fucking annoying is what Maeve is.

"Let me get that book for you, Maeve." She bent down and located the book set aside under the register. "Ah, here it is." She felt a surge of relief. Two more customers had queued up behind Maeve, which meant she could shoo her away. With luck, the old biddy would get the hint and make her way out the door.

Find someone else to pick on. Why don't you?

Maeve had glared at the other customers and muttered under her breath as she left, chivvied along by Lila's bright, fake smile.

As Lila turned to the other side, yet again, the time on her digital clock read 2:04. If she didn't fall asleep soon, she was going to be dead on her feet the next morning. There was another rare midsummer storm heading their way. Which meant she needed to get to the bookstore early and set out buckets upstairs. A leak had developed, and the roofers were delayed. She had a two-week wait until they could patch the roof.

What, or who, is Denise on the run from? What had her so scared?

"Tomorrow. By hook or by crook, I need to get her to talk."

Lila flipped onto her back and said, "Alexa, play meditation music." A few minutes later, her eyelashes fluttered once, twice, and she fell into a deep sleep.

Tracker

- Indalo -

The phone vibrated in the seat next to Markus as he drove. Getting a terse call from Lionel had not been the start of his day that he had expected.

Everything had gone to plan there at the small rental house in Miami. Or so he thought. Only to find out some other girl had been in his target's bed. To be honest, he hadn't known which room belonged to Denise Fortuna, so he dispatched them all. Easy enough when it looked as if they had all been drinking until past midnight. His flashlight had picked up six empty wine bottles lined up in the tiny galley kitchen. The hammer in his hand had taken care of each girl, with little or no fuss. Only one had woken as he entered the room and she had been the last. No chance to scream before he was on her, swinging the hammer down. Then it had been a simple matter of dousing the house in gas and lighting the match.

The only challenge Markus had encountered had been the urge to stay and watch the pretty flames licking the sky as the fire slid through the house, consuming everything it touched.

He'd gone to bed satisfied at a job well done. The funds had cleared the next day.

Until Alpha called. Now I'm in Dutch with the head honcho.

After a few terse words from his employer, and hours of driving later, Markus was now on the broad coastal highway heading north. He had flashed a badge at the Flying J south of Jacksonville and struck gold. Sure enough, the Fortuna girl had been here. A pimply-faced assistant manager with shaky hands had pulled up the camera footage and a few minutes later he'd seen her on the footage. Definitely not dead.

The phone vibrated again and Markus snatched it up.

"Yes?"

The girl's voice on the other end was all too familiar. He'd spoken to Lucifer a handful of times before today.

"Just got a ping off of her debit card. It looks like she used it to get some fast food about an hour ago."

"Where?"

"Zaxby's at 1372 Airport Service Road."

"Think she's heading for the airport?" Markus asked, dread forming in his gut. If she got on a plane, who knew where she would end up? He needed to catch up with her. *Now.*

"Couldn't say, but I'll let you know when it pings again."

Markus sped up on the highway. He was at least two, maybe three, days behind Fortuna and needed to catch up. He would head for the airport.

An hour later, Markus pressed the buttons on his phone, snarling with frustration. A click and the girl's voice sounded bored.

"Lucifer speaking."

"You sent me to a fucking pet airport?" He hissed.

"I did no such thing. I gave you the address for Zaxby's, the site of the last debit card ping." Lucifer answered. "What you did with that information is not my problem."

His hand strayed to the handle of the hammer. The claw end, cleaned of every speck of hair and blood, was nestled deep within the car seat cushions. He fought to contain his rage. How he would love to sink it deep into the girl's head like he had the three young women at the rental house. He bit his tongue.

"I need more information."

"When I have it, I'll call you. She will need to stop at some point." Lucifer's voice was calm, indifferent. "Now, unless you needed something else..." The phone beeped as Markus slammed a finger down on the disconnect button.

The next ten days unspooled slowly. And for Markus, who prided himself on his quick turnaround times for targets, it was maddening. He didn't spend days following a target. He got in, got the job done, and back out. Lucifer's brief text informed him that Fortuna had withdrawn a significant amount of cash from an ATM on the second day, which wasn't surprising given that her face was plastered on news bulletins throughout Florida. But he figured she would have to come up for air soon.

When the next ping rolled in, it was a gas station in New York, and Markus felt a rush of pain as a tension headache rolled in. His target had made it to New York three days ago, on a Friday. Thanks to delays in bank reporting, Lucifer hadn't seen it come in until the close of Monday. Markus headed north. The next employee he saw was not as easy to impress with a badge.

"I think you gotta have a warrant or something before we hand over anything to the police. And that ain't a New York badge." The thin, greasy-haired man with acne and an odd facial tic said, then shuffled away from the bulletproof glass. Markus had tried threats, but the attendant looked unimpressed and returned to watching some wrestling match on his cracked cell phone, ignoring Markus until he left.

The rain and the wind from the approaching storm had driven him back inside of his car where he had glared through the rain pelting the windshield and cursed the attendant. Markus contemplated waiting until the man's shift ended, and then killing him, but the streets were busy and potential witnesses numbered in the dozens even now, in late evening. He didn't have time for this. He needed to find the girl and finish her. Markus didn't know what she had done to piss off Alpha, and he didn't particularly care. It wasn't in his job description.

A police car moved down the street slowly. He ignored it and contemplated what to do. If she was here, in New York, it would be even harder for him to track her. The city was vast. He picked up his phone and dialed Lucifer. He could hear the sounds of a battle in the background.

"Lucifer here."

"Does Fortuna have any connections in New York? Any friends? Anyone she would go to?"

Lucifer muted the sounds of the battle with a sharp click and he could hear additional rapid mouse clicks as she accessed the vast amount of illicit info at her fingertips. A few seconds of silence later, and she answered.

"I've got nothing. She's lived all over the U.S., but never in New York, only..."

"Only what?"

"Hold on." More clicks and rapid typing followed. "Brunswick, Maine."

"What's in Maine?"

"Probably nothing, but she lived there for around a year as a kid. I'm seeing school records from a Kate Furbish Elementary School. The only place on the east coast besides Florida that she's been. Other than that, it was flyover country and Georgia, Alabama, the Dakotas. I'm not saying she is in Maine," He could practically hear her shrug, "but that would be my guess at where to try next."

"Maine is over three hundred miles away."

Lucifer sounded bored. "Yeah? So?"

He hung up the phone.

Someday, she'll fuck up. And when she does, I hope they send me to take care of the uppity bitch.

He loved his job. There was something very special about taking a life - human or otherwise. To watch as the light in the eyes faded, and death erased everything a creature was from the world. Given his druthers, he preferred to take his time. What greater pleasure was there than seeing another person's pain?

His first try at ending the target had been rushed. The girls were in multiple rooms, so it had to be quick. He hadn't known which room was hers and time had been of the essence. He hadn't wanted her or the others she shared the house with sounding the alarm. It had left him feeling unfulfilled, dissatisfied. Worse, learning that he had missed the target had been humiliating. That had never happened before, and he was still smarting over it. He would make it better, however. When he found her, and he would, he would kill the girl slowly and savor every minute. Maybe he would keep a piece of her as a trophy.

For now, however, he had a decision to make. He sat there, the phone in his hand, and noticed the same police car drive by again. Slower this time. Had the attendant said something? Called someone? As soon as it eased past, around the corner, he started the car up, and cut in front of a truck, turned left at the next intersection, and entered Brunswick, Maine, into his GPS. He checked his watch. If he drove straight through, he would arrive before dawn. And if Lucifer steered him wrong, and the girl wasn't there, maybe he could lay the groundwork to have Lucifer replaced with someone far more capable.

The rain fell steadily as he made his way out of the Big Apple on the FDR and headed north again, along I-95. A massive wreck slowed his progress considerably. By the time he entered Connecticut, the rain had stopped. The clouds above hung low, blotting out the stars in this unsettled open land, which was a rarity on the over-populated East coast. A storm was brewing in the Atlantic, one threatening to become far more dangerous and violent. Markus drove on, the car eating the miles steadily. By three, however, he was feeling the missing hours of sleep far more than he preferred.

He pulled off the road when he saw the sign for a Rodeway Inn in Tolland. He'd get a night's rest, then move on in the morning. Maybe leave early, by five, before the sun rose. Markus set a ball cap on his head and headed into the motel office. A pimple-faced kid took his money and handed him a key without a word. The boy didn't look at his face or compare it with the driver's license, which Markus preferred. The likeness was close enough, but the previous owner of the license had died, rather suddenly, soon after obtaining the renewal. As far as the world at large was concerned, Andrew Talbot had simply disappeared, leaving his elderly mother and two ex-wives behind one fine summer's day two years ago. It would be another four years before Markus needed to worry about a finding someone else who looked like him, and hopefully one who had fewer family ties than dear Andrew had. It was easier that way.

Markus had conveniently parked near his room. And it was easier to leave the car where it was and avoid most of the downpour by staying underneath the overhang and following it to his room. The room was a standard no frills kind of place. As Markus tossed his damp backpack on the floor near the desk, his burner phone rang. It wasn't *his* number. Which meant it was likely *Beta*.

Shit.

He pressed the button and put the phone to his ear. "Yes?"

"What's your status?"

"I'm a four-hour drive from Brunswick, Maine."

"You aren't on the road." A statement, not a question.

"I needed to stop. It was slow going because of the storm. I will be there by morning."

Beta did not sound happy. "See that you are. I want this girl removed from play immediately."

"Yes, ma'am."

The phone beeped in response as she disconnected. Markus tossed it onto the bed, then stared at it, concern swirling. It was one thing for Alpha to be involved, and another for Beta to step forward. It meant he was well and truly fucked if he didn't get ahold of the girl and finish the job, once and for all.

Sleep, as much as he needed it, eluded him. Markus tossed and turned. The howl of the wind outside felt in tune with his own unease. He dreamed intermittently, his fingers unconsciously seeking the symbol inked in red on his wrist. Markus woke long before dawn and gave up on sleeping in disgust. He'd sleep when the mark was dead.

By the time he arrived in Brunswick, the sun had risen into the sky, but Markus couldn't see it. The dark clouds on the horizon warned of the impending storm. He'd heard all about it, the constant, repetitive stream of news as he drove, rain and wind lashing the world outside. Finally, tiring of the endless comparisons to Hurricane Carol that apparently had hit the region back in the 50s, he switched stations until he hit a classical station unperturbed by the storm heading their way. Through the downpour, he glanced around for a coffee shop and his eyes fell on a sign... Hanniford's. It didn't look like a cafe, more of a small grocer. He would stop there, get a sandwich and find out where he could find a coffee.

Street parking meant that it soaked him the second he stepped out of his car. The temperature had risen to a balmy 80 degrees, and the water falling from the sky felt warm instead of cold.

As if the sky were taking a great piss.

He hurried inside of the quaint grocery store and strode toward the delicatessen. Moments later, sandwich in hand, Markus waited at the register. Behind him stood a curious busybody who seemed to examine every inch of him.

If she doesn't stop staring at me, I'll throttle the old cow.

A young woman jogged up to the cash register, wiping her hands on a towel before shoving one end in her jeans. "Sorry to keep you waiting!" She rang Markus up. "That will be $7.25, sir." As she handed Markus his change, she smiled at the woman behind him. "Good morning, Maeve. How are you?"

There was a small alcove near the doors. Markus could see it held two small tables and chairs. He settled into one, his eyes focused on the food, ignoring the women. He would eat this and then see if he couldn't find the girl, make inquiries.

"Good morning, Andie. I came into town to get a new book, but the store isn't open yet. So I figured I would come and pick up a few things." The woman sniffed, glanced his way, and then away again. "Can you believe she hired that girl, the new one in town? Without so much as a by your leave, or asking if anyone could recommend anyone."

Andie said nothing. She just shrugged and rang up the older woman's groceries. "That'll be $24.18."

Maeve reached into her wallet and handed the younger woman a card. "I mean, I know Angela was just as flaky as could be, but I've known her since she was in diapers. Now another new girl breezes in, a complete stranger, and that Brewer gal immediately hires her. I can't say I care much about the way this town is changing. It's being invaded by outsiders."

"Oh Maeve, Denise is really nice. Just the other day, she saw Dale shoplifting and said something in time for Uncle Lyle to stop him. And it was a high-ticket item."

Markus' ears perked up. *Denise. From out of town? That couldn't be a coincidence.*

"Well, perhaps if she were focusing on her job, the bookstore would be open by now." Maeve snapped back, a disgruntled tone in her voice.

The girl sighed. "Have a good day, Maeve."

The older woman shook her head in disgust, glared at Markus as she walked past, and retrieved an umbrella from the floor next to the door. Another disgruntled "Hmph!" and she stepped outside, disappearing into the deluge. He watched as she marched across the street and down to the end, huddled under her umbrella for a long moment as she peered into the bookstore window, then straightened and walked off. The bookstore was dark, the front parking empty now that Maeve had gotten into her car and driven off.

A little B and E, a look through the office records, and I see what I can find.

He finished his sandwich, brushed the crumbs from his hands, tossed the remnants of the sandwich into the trash before he headed out, turning right instead of left. He would circle the block, see if there was a back door, and then apply one of the few non-violent skills he had learned in his teen years, lock-picking, to gain entry. It was one talent that had brought him to the attention of the Indalo two decades ago. If his target had made her way to Brunswick and was now working in a bookstore, he would soon find out. And following that, well, he would do what he did best.

It Wasn't Me

- Lila -

For an instant, between the gloom in her normally bright bedroom and a fading dream of Shane's slow, sensuous kisses, Lila was confused by the sound she was hearing. It was morning, although the sky outside was overcast and dark. Lila was shocked she had overslept. It wasn't as if it mattered that much. It was Sunday, after all. And she opened the store at noon on Sundays, even in summer. But normally she was awake at sunrise, or even earlier, now that it was warm out. The storm had changed that, apparently.

There was something about warm weather, spring and summer, that put a lightness in her step and energized her. Fall and winter always felt like death and spread over the land. A time to burrow deep and sleep. She wrote more in the summer. Which seemed ridiculous, really. She had bemoaned her situation to Margery once.

"There's nothing to do in the winter. It's the perfect time for writing. But am I writing? No! I just want to sleep all day and drink hot chocolate!"

The sound came again. This time, Lila was awake enough to recognize it. It was indisputably the sound of retching. It seemed her new roommate was unwell.

She slipped out of bed, reached for her deodorant and dressed. As Lila emerged from her room, Denise was exiting the bathroom, her skin pale, with the circles under her eyes even more pronounced.

"A touch of the stomach flu? Or my cooking?" She asked the young woman, fearing it might have been the latter, more than she was concerned about Denise spreading the flu to her. She was rarely ill.

Denise opened her mouth to answer, then just as quickly shut it. Her eyes panicked as she spun on her heel. She ran back inside the bathroom, and the door slammed behind her. More retching sounds.

"Yikes." Lila stared at the closed door for a moment and then headed downstairs. She would use the half bath down there and then fix some cereal. The last thing that her roommate needed was the smell of something cooking in the air.

Especially my cooking. I'll burn it to hell and back, anyway.

A few minutes later, sitting in the tiny kitchen, she flipped on the tv in the living room to the news. The weather would be on soon and she wanted to check on Hurricane Agnes, which had turned from a tropical storm into a far more serious hurricane yesterday. Hurricanes this far up the eastern seaboard were rare, but even this far north, they could actually be a problem. Lila had never been in a hurricane. The thought of it was rather exhilarating, honestly, although she was more worried about how to prepare for one. Did she need to put boards up on the windows? Would she need to leave if it headed towards them? Maeve had, of course, told her all about some family with beachfront property who stayed instead of leaving when they were warned to.

"Those poor children watched their father washed away in the floodwaters." Maeve had said the day before, crocodile tears glittering in her eyes. "Although, I'm not one to gossip, but their mother remarried less than a year later. To the husband's best friend, no less. It makes one wonder, it really does."

Lila shook her head. Maeve was a piece of work, she really was. She pointed the remote at the television, turned up the volume, and spooned cereal into her mouth.

"And next up we have our meteorologist, Anthony Parker, to weigh in on the prospects for some rather severe weather by the end of the week." A peppy blond in a sleek red dress chirped. "Anthony? What's the scoop on Hurricane Agnes?"

"Thanks Tiffany. Well, it looks like Agnes is continuing to gather in strength. She is now registering as a Category Two, with 97 mile per hour winds recorded this morning by the NOAA. And she is continuing to make her way north along the eastern coastline. Now, as you may already know, a Category Two storm can cause storm surges of six to eight feet, and endanger those in mobile homes, damage roofs, and cause flooding."

Denise appeared at the foot of the stairs. She walked into the kitchen, looking pale and wretched.

"So sorry."

Lila swallowed her mouthful. "Don't be. Hopefully, you will feel better now. I don't know about you, but once I throw up, I always feel better after." She pointed at her cereal. "Do you... want any?"

Denise shook her head and grimaced. "No, I think I'll just stick to water." She pulled a cup from the drain tray and filled it at the tap.

"Back to you, Tiffany." The meteorologist grinned, and the camera panned back to the blond bombshell in red.

"Thanks Anthony. Police are asking for help as the search continues for a person of interest in the mysterious fire and deaths of three young women in Miami, Florida, nearly two weeks ago. Miami police are asking for anyone who knows of the whereabouts of Denise Fortuna, age 25, a nursing student at Miami Regional and recently employee of Happy Haven Retirement Village, to please contact local authorities. The police do not consider Fortuna a suspect. Instead, they are concerned for her safety after a deadly fire broke out at the home she shared with two other roommates. Both roommates and a friend of Ms. Fortuna were in the house. Ms. Fortuna has not been seen since. The Miami County medical examiner's office released the autopsy reports on the three victims, showing they died of blunt force trauma *before* the flames broke out. Fire investigators declared it a crime scene after evidence of an accelerant was used, but police say the victims were already dead."

Lila sat, spoon in hand, gaping at the television in shock as they showed a photo of Denise, likely her student photo since she was wearing scrubs, on the television screen, before turning her gaze toward her new roommate.

The glass in Denise's hand fell with a crash to the ground. Glass splintering. If Lila had thought the girl looked pale before, it was nothing compared to now.

"Denise? What is going on?"

"I didn't hurt my friends. It wasn't me. They..." Whatever she had intended to say next was lost as she threw up violently all over the kitchen floor.

Suddenly, and not unsurprisingly, Lila's appetite vanished. She stood up, glanced at the television where the anchor was describing Denise's car and license plate. Then a litter of rolling, rollicking puppies took over the screen. She looked at Denise, who was holding onto the countertop, white-knuckles gripping the edge, still heaving.

"I'm... I'm sorry." She whispered, tears gathering in her eyes.

"Don't be," Lila said, letting the paper towels sop up the mess. She passed Denise a couple of them, and Denise wiped her mouth and then burst into tears. Lila skirted the mess and walked over to her, put her arm around her, and guided Denise to the table.

"Okay. Sit down. Just sit down and breathe, okay?"

A moment later, she had a box of Kleenex in hand, and another glass of water, along with a half pack of saltines. The saltines were likely stale, but Lila knew they would be the most that Denise could stomach, and from the way she was swaying, she needed something more than water in her stomach.

Denise sobbed for several minutes. Tears rolled down her cheeks. She gasped for breath, and her slight frame shook.

"I need... I need..."

Lila reached across the table. If Denise was putting on a show, it was one hell of one, and from Lila's perspective, she was for real, or one hell of an actress. She patted Denise's hand.

"Take your time. Just... breathe... okay?"

The younger woman nodded and burst into a fresh round of tears that lasted for several minutes. Lila hadn't known Denise long, but she seemed gentle. Lila couldn't imagine for an instant that it was Denise who had killed her roommates. That she had run, though, completely *left* the area. Now that was odd.

Lila remembered when the incident had occurred, just a day or two before Denise had walked into the bookstore. They had thought it was the three roommates, Lila was sure she remembered that much. But now it was apparently two of the roommates and a friend who didn't live there. At the first mention of it in the news, they had pointed the finger at a local man. Was he still a suspect? There was so much she didn't know.

No matter what, if I know now, so does Maeve. The old biddy lives and dies by the morning news. Which means we have hours, at most, before someone will be at our door.

Denise was calming. The sobs slowing. She wiped her eyes, blew her nose, and sipped the water. She let out a slow, shuddering sigh.

"I'm sorry."

Lila chose her words carefully. "Denise, you don't need to be sorry. But I think you need someone to talk to. If not me, then…"

"You. I know I can trust you. I mean, you took me in without question." Denise said, interrupting her. "I have told no one. I've been too scared. He's powerful. Rich."

Denise sucked in a breath and spoke then. The story spilled out of her in a flood, combined with more tears, and Lila sat there stunned, mouth hanging open. The silence hung between them.

"You don't believe me," Denise said softly, miserably. "And if you don't believe me, what good will going to the police do? It's hearsay."

Lila reached out and took the girl's hand. "I believe you, Denise. I do. Because I've been in a situation of my own. It wasn't exactly like yours, but still." She squeezed Denise's hand and then released it, frowning. "What concerns me is that everyone is seeing this broadcast. This is a small town and news spreads fast, especially with people like Maeve."

"I'm so…"

"Don't say it." Lila held up a warning finger. "Just don't."

She dug into her back pocket, pulled out her phone, and stared at it.

"What are you going to do?" Denise asked, her voice rising, her fear apparent.

"I'm going to get us help." Lila answered, frowning.

"Wait, I…" Denise rose, shakily, "I should just go. If I go now…"

"If you run, you look like you have something to hide," Lila said, looking up.

"The police will never believe me. I have no proof! And he's rich, powerful."

"I know. I'm not talking about going to the police. Look, I know someone who can help. Someone who can get you somewhere safe."

Denise stared at her. "What does that even mean? Nowhere is safe! They think I had something to do with it. A person of interest. That's as good as them saying I killed my friends. My *best* friends. I can't..." She sunk back down in her chair, hid her face in her hands.

"I need to make a call, Denise. But I promise you, I can help you. *He* can help you. I'd bet my life on it."

Denise stared at her with red-rimmed, puffy eyes. She dragged a Kleenex across her nose and sucked in a shuddering breath.

"Who?"

Lila grimaced. "The last person I want to call. Believe me." She typed in his number and listened as the phone rang three times before he answered.

The Last Person I Expected to Call

-Shane-

On the flight out, Shane had convinced himself that Luke was pulling his leg. Surely Tapeesa, who had buried her husband some eight or nine years earlier, wasn't setting her sights on him. He'd been visiting Luke's cabin in Alaska at least twice a year for the past three years. And with it, had come regular visits to Tapeesa's sprawling, ramshackle property. As Luke's nearest neighbor, and just a half mile down the road, Tapeesa and her family ran a 500-acre section that included a herd of yak, reindeer, goats and chickens. She was a short, stout Inuit woman. There were more kids on the property than were hers. Shane wasn't sure where they all came from, but you couldn't swing a stick and not hit one of them. They ran about, helping with the farm, playing games, drawing, and building. The last time he visited, there were at least two small houses and a boat, all in various stages of completion. Between chickens running loose, a half dozen cats and dogs, and the ever-wily escapee goat, it was absolute chaos there. The kids would follow Luke and Shane around like lemmings, eager to help, full of questions. And although Tapeesa always seemed to need some kind of help, Shane had enjoyed visiting. It was a world vastly different from the one he had grown up in with just his mother and no siblings.

He decided he would skip the yak slaughtering. Hell, maybe he would even put his feet up in the hammock that Luke had installed out back and relax, read a book.

Shane's plans, however, hadn't included one very pissed off skunk and a curious young bear. Nor had they included having to wash the bear cub inside the cabin in the bathtub, which meant the smell of skunk permeated every inch of the cabin the next day as Sue whined in the corner of his cage and sneezed repeatedly.

Damnitall, I've probably given him a cold.

It had turned out that Sue was a boy, not a girl. This had come as a surprise to Shane. Then again, trust Luke to not mention that minor fact. Shane had found a recipe for removing skunk smell on dogs online and figured it would work just as well for the bear cub. A mixture of dish soap with hydrogen peroxide and baking soda had done the trick, but Sue had squealed and fought the bath valiantly, splashing Shane until the front of his clothes were soaked through.

After he locked Sue into the wire kennel inside of the cabin where Pepe would be less offended by the bear cub's presence, Shane wrung out his clothes as best he could and ran them out on the clothesline to dry. Pepe, Luke's three-legged skunk, sniffed the drips and looked at Shane with curiosity. The cat food that Sue had scattered widely in his frenzy to escape the skunk spray had been devoured, and it seemed Pepe was hoping for more.

"Fine. Fine. I'll give you a little more." Shane grumbled, his eyes watering as he stood mere feet from the pungent creature.

"You know that talking to animals is the first sign of insanity." Shane turned to see Tapeesa's oldest, Hanta, standing a few feet away, a package tucked under his arm.

"And here I thought the Inuit talked to the animals." Shane countered.

The younger man snorted. "Ah, yes, Inuit talk big wampum to spirit animal." He rolled his eyes at Shane. "My mother sent me over with some reindeer sausage for your breakfast. She says to show up by noon."

So much for lazing out on the hammock with a book.

"Should I bring anything?" Shane asked, taking the package from Hanta. It was warm to the touch. The accompanying aroma of sausage and spices woke his stomach, despite the odoriferous presence of the skunk by his feet. Pepe ignored him, eating his cat food, stopping only to look toward the cabin door. Inside, Sue wailed his distress at being confined to the dog kennel.

"Nah, we got everything we need. See you there." He turned and left, disappearing into the forest.

Shane unwrapped the sausage, pulling off a chunk for the skunk at his feet. He tossed it a few feet out in the yard and Pepe looked up at him briefly, then did his funny three-legged hop walk out to where it had landed and chowed down.

"I better take the rest inside before you insist on more." Shane said. He walked inside and instantly Sue was on his back legs, his black button nose sniffing the air. "Well, shit, forgot about you." He slid a chunk through the metal bars and Sue pounced on it as if he were starving and hadn't eaten in days instead of a mere hour between eating his own food and attempting to take Pepe's.

"And we all know how that went, don't we?" Shane said to the cub, as the tiny cub devoured the chunk of meat. Sue had to weigh all of ten pounds at most. A mere fraction of the 400 pound behemoth he would grow up to be. As he was now, the wire kennel that Luke had wouldn't last longer than a month, possibly two, before the creature became large enough and strong enough to bend the wires. Luke would be back long before then, three weeks at the most.

The cub had practically inhaled the chunk he had given him. Shane looked at the package. Tapeesa had sent over six sausages, and between Pepe and Sue, he was now down to five. Shane reached for the fresh eggs that sat on the counter, cracked five of them into a skillet, and scrambled them. A few minutes later, he sat at the tiny dining table and divided the eggs and three sausage links between his plate and Sue's never-ending stomach. He had two sausages left to eat for breakfast tomorrow, or a snack tonight if he was feeling peckish.

Slight chance of that. Tapeesa's fry bread and the fresh yak-a-dillas will fill me to bursting.

He checked the time. There was enough for a brief nap on the hammock if he wanted, but when he stood to walk out, there was Pepe, on the hammock, belly full, making himself comfortable.

"I don't know how you do it, man, but damned if I'm going to spoon with a skunk." Shane said aloud, shaking his head. Pepe was friendly enough, but the smell was overwhelming. Caught in a trap, his front left leg had been too badly damaged by the time Luke had found him. He'd freed Pepe, nursed him back from the brink of death, and the creature had kept him company ever since. Shane had asked Luke once why he hadn't had the creature's glands removed, since he was more of a pet now than wild.

Luke had shrugged and said, "He was born wild. He should stay that way. The scent glands are his defense. I can't take away his freedom to run about, and if I did, it would change him in ways that the missing leg never could."

Still, it was a little more up close and personal than Shane felt like getting with Pepe. He leaned back on the bed, kicked off his shoes, and reached for a book. Despite the small size of the cabin, one that Luke had built himself, there was an entire wall dedicated to books. Luke was an omnivorous reader. He had everything from non-fiction to dystopian, history to sci-fi, and more. It seemed he had even organized them into separate genres. His gaze fell on the sci-fi section. He could see Asimov, Clarke, Herbert, Hogan, and more. One book caught his eye. A planet and spaceship on the front cover. "G581: The Departure. Huh." It looked well worn. As if Luke had read it more than once. He settled back and read, stopping only when Sue pawed at the cage door an hour later, obviously wanting to go outside. By then, Pepe had disappeared from the hammock, and from view, no doubt deep in the woods by now. He released Sue and watched the baby bear bound away toward the tree line and disappear. The cub would be back. He never went far, according to Luke, and it was nearly time to leave. A walk through the woods to Tapeesa's place would allow him to stretch his legs. The weather was excellent for it.

He could hear the kids long before he could see them. If it hadn't had been for their higher voices and the occasional shriek of laughter, he would have thought there was a war ahead. Instead, as he threaded his way through a large thicket of trees, which opened onto the western edge of Tapeesa's property, he could see some kind of water balloon fight going on. At least, it had started out as a water balloon fight, if the dots of color that littered the ground were any sign. Every kid was soaked to the bone. A handful had armed themselves with buckets of water, a couple of others were tussling over the garden hose, and he could see Kaya, Tonraq, and Meriwa still held several balloons each and were holding their own. Not bad for being the youngest and smallest of Tapeesa's offspring. Unlike their rather swarthy older brothers and sisters, the triplets were small-boned, almost willowy. It was such a stark difference from their elder siblings that if Shane were to guess; he was sure they were half-siblings to the rest. There were at least a half-dozen additional kids running about, possibly more, most of them screaming in a blend of Tlingit and English.

His arrival did not go unnoticed, however, and some kids had rather feral grins on their faces. Shane threw up his hands. "I'm a neutral party to this conflict! I'm Switzerland! You want help with some yak-killing. You best leave me out of your war!"

Hanta yelled in Tlingit and the handful of kids heading his way with chaos in their eyes slowed and turned away. Shane saluted him and headed for the barn where a small group of men and women had gathered. Tapeesa grinned at him broadly, then called out to the screaming children. Silence fell.

"Damn kids gonna scare the yaks with all that screaming. Make their meat taste off." She grumbled under her breath, then reached for his arm, pulled him down to her level and planted a smacking kiss on his forehead. "Good to see you, Ellis."

"Same. Thanks for the tasty reindeer sausage."

"Wait until you taste the yak-a-dillas. They taste better when the meat's fresh." She winked at him, handed him a sharp knife, said something in Tlingit to an older man a few feet away, then nudged Shane to join the group.

It had rather surprised Shane to find that yaks, unlike cattle, had little or no smell. They also didn't moo as much as they grunted. Despite the grunts, they still reminded him of hairy cows. He was relieved when the others took the lead, leading one yak far from the small group they had penned into the corral and handled the slaughter quickly and efficiently. After the beast was dead, they raised it up on hooks, drained the carcass, and got to work. Shane was pretty sure that after this, he would never eat meat again.

By the time he and the others finished dressing the five yaks, nearly five hours later, his empty stomach insisted that he absolutely could, and should, try one of the yak-a-dillas he had heard so much about. His muscles ached from helping to heave each thousand pound carcass into the air and then carefully remove the hide with a sharp knife. His clothes were bloody and caked in mud from one particularly energetic bull who was not going out without a fight. And despite looking as if he had played a grotesque part in a horror film, Shane sank down at the picnic table and dug into the yak-a-dillas stacked on his plate with gusto. They weren't strikingly different from shredded beef, and Tapeesa made a mean Pico de gallo to go with it. The other adults sunk into seats near him. The constant chatter in a Tlingit faded away as the adults tucked away stacks of the yak-a-dillas, Pico de gallo, and a pile of fry bread.

The sun was still high in the sky at seven, as Shane headed back to the cabin.

Tomorrow, I'm damned well sleeping in. I don't care what they want done, I'm saying "no."

They filled the sack in his hand with yak-a-dillas. A large grocery sack of them. Enough to slip plenty of the foil-wrapped delights into the freezer for Luke to chow down on.

He was tired, worn out from the hacking and slicing he had done. The only thing on his mind was Luke's Japanese-style soaking tub and a good night's rest. Sue met him along the way, giving a squeaky half-purr, half-rumble, as Shane tossed the beast two of the yak-a-dillas and closed the bear into his kennel.

An hour later, his eyes closed and his breathing slowing, the sound of his ringer ripped Shane from his sleep. "Christ, what now?" He reached for a towel, stepped out of the tub, and caught the phone before it went to voicemail.

"Ellis."

"Shane? It's Lila."

He could hear it in her voice. She sounded worried, maybe even afraid. "Lila? What's wrong?"

He listened as she explained the predicament. He asked a couple of questions. It was clear Lila's friend needed help.

"You were right to call. Head to the address I'm texting to you now. It should take you around four hours, maybe a little more, to get there." The phone chimed at the other end. "Take both cars, but switch the girl's plates with the set I left you in case of emergencies, and have her park it in the satellite airport parking. That'll slow things down, make you harder to track. Drive 1-2 miles over the speed limit. This attracts less attention than driving the speed limit or below. Don't stop for gas or anything else until you are well out of town. Park your car inside of the garage of the safe house. Stay put inside. The kitchen has basic supplies, and I'll be there by late afternoon with some more."

"Okay. Got it." Lila paused. "And Shane? Thank you."

Shane could hear another voice in the background ask, "Who *is* that?"

And in the half-second before Lila disconnected the call, he heard her reply, "The last person I ever expected to talk to again."

He stood there, staring at the phone in his hand. The call ended, the screen black. She didn't call him because she wanted him back. She called him because of what he did. The very thing that had driven them apart was forcing them together again.

"*You* were the last person I expected to call," Shane said in return, his words unheard by anyone save himself and a bear cub gently snoring in his kennel.

He scheduled the red-eye flight and checked the time. He had enough time to drive to the ferry and the airport with an hour or two to spare. As he drove, his thoughts circled from Lila's face to her body nestled against his.

She needs your help, that's all. Keep it professional, Ellis. Keep your dick in your pants.

The sun held its own near the horizon. By the time the plane took off, he could expect around a brief twilight that would darken only as the plane moved further south and then back to sunlight as he headed east.

Hours later, the traveling, his work dressing the yak meat, and more, caught up to him. He relaxed, leaned his seat back, and closed his eyes. Lila was waiting for him, and she needed his help. When he got to her, he'd keep it professional, like he should have done to begin with.

My Name is Lila

"I can't believe this is happening." Denise said. Lila had lost count of how many times her new friend had said it in the past hour.

Then again, Lila hadn't been sure that Denise wouldn't rabbit on her during the drive to the airport. She had followed Denise's car closely. The new plates she had dug out of the closet were from North Dakota and would definitely throw off anyone looking for them. Denise hadn't rabbited, which was good, and now they were well on their way to the address Shane texted her. It was a long drive, another two hours or more before they arrived, but Lila was confident they had left in time and there wasn't anyone following them.

Shane said he will be there this evening.

The thought of seeing him again, for the first time in six months, made her stomach give a nervous twist. Which then morphed into a memory of his hands on her and a wave of desire rushed through her.

No, no, no! You are not getting back in bed with that man, no matter how sexy he is!

"Annie?" Denise's voice brought Lila back to the present. "What's wrong?"

"Hm?"

"You were glaring just now. You just looked so, I don't know, so *angry*. I've gotten you involved in my mess. This is all my fault."

Lila spared a quick glance away from the road as Denise buried her face in her hands.

"Hey, come on now. You have done nothing wrong, Denise. Nothing at all. And I'm not mad at you, really, I'm not. I was just remembering something, that's all."

A few moments of silence passed before Denise sat up and asked.

"Is it Shane?"

"What?"

"Whoever had you looking like you wanted to punch someone in the throat? I figured it had to be this Shane guy because of the way you talked to him on the phone."

Lila gave a rueful laugh. "Yeah, Shane has a lot to do with why I was glaring. We dated for a while. It didn't work out. And I guess it's still a bit of a sore spot for me."

"And this is the guy we are meeting?"

Lila sighed. "Yeah."

"There's a story here, isn't there?"

"Yeah, there is. And it starts with me telling you that my name isn't Annie Brewer."

She snuck a look at Denise's face. The younger woman's eyes, still red-rimmed from crying, had widened.

"It's... not?"

A sign for Burger King appeared along the road and Lila's stomach growled for something, anything, past the cereal she had eaten hours ago.

"How do you feel about getting some fast food?" Lila asked, abruptly changing the subject. "My treat."

"Okay."

Silence returned for the two miles it took before the exit appeared. Lila turned off of the highway and made a left, following the signs for the Burger King.

"I'm just going to go through the drive-thru, okay?"

Denise nodded wordlessly.

They ordered two combo meals and Denise handed Lila her food, her own fingers picking at her fries, nibbling at one before shoving it *back in the* bag. Lila parked the car in the crowded parking lot and tore into her burger. The air felt heavy between them - full of questions. She had downed her third bite of a burger before Denise set her food down, turned toward her.

"I can't stand it anymore. Who are you? What's your real name? Are you on the run too?"

Lila sighed, finished chewing, and set the burger down.

"My name is Lila Benoit. I've been in WitSec, witness protection, for just over two and a half years now. And at the rate the FBI's investigation is going, I might never go back to my old life. In fact, I'd say it's highly unlikely."

Denise stared at her, eyes round. She swallowed convulsively. "And people in Witness Protection are supposed to keep a low profile, aren't they?"

Lila laughed, "Yeah, well..."

Denise buried her face in her hands. "I've brought this down on you. I'm so sorr..."

"Don't do that. Don't apologize. I knew the minute you walked into the bookstore that you needed help." Lila sighed, "I guess I just never expected things to go quite like this. I can't tell you much of why I'm in WitSec. Honestly, you have enough on your plate already. All I can say is that I saw something I shouldn't, and until they can find out who the puppeteers are, the real bad guys, then I'll have to stay in hiding."

They sat in silence for a while longer, finishing their food before Lila started the car and pulled back onto the highway. The sun was still high in the sky, but Lila glanced at the clock, feeling a sudden urgency.

"We need to hurry. I want to get there before dark."

Denise nodded and Lila pressed her foot down on the gas, driving faster now, feeling conflicted, and yet somehow eager to see Shane again. As they got closer to their destination, Lila could feel her nerves ramping up. She hadn't seen Shane in six months, not since he had broken her heart and left her alone and vulnerable. Despite this, she couldn't help but remember the way her body responded to him, the memory of his fingers trailing down her spine, and the way his body felt against hers. After two hours of driving, they pulled off the highway and onto a quiet rural road.

The address Shane had texted them led them to a secluded two-story cabin in the woods, surrounded by robust maple trees and the faint scent of jasmine in the air. The cabin looked new, the surrounding ground disturbed, rough, all indicative of new construction.

Lila parked the car in front of the garage and glanced at Denise.

"This is it," Lila said.

"Is anyone here?" Denise asked as they stepped out of the car. The sun was lowering in the sky, with plenty of light left, but the property looked empty.

"He mentioned getting here after sunset, so no, but there's a door code in the text he sent. Hold on." Lila thumbed through her phone until she found what she was looking for, typed the code in and heard the door lock click.

She turned the handle and opened the door to the cabin.

The interior was dimly lit, and the air smelled of cedar and fresh paint. Lila stepped inside and looked around. It had a rustic charm to it, with a spacious living room complete with a fireplace, a cozy-looking kitchen, and a steep wooden staircase leading up to the second floor, likely where the bedrooms were. The living room sported hardwood floors with wide, honey-colored planks and heavy wood beams ran across the ceiling. A mantel over the fireplace was pristine. The fireplace clearly had never been used. There was a marble island, and black granite countertops. The kitchen was equally spotless, with pots and pans hanging from the pot rack over the kitchen island, waiting to be used. Their footsteps echoed on the hardwood floors, and the sun streamed in through the windows, the room illuminated in a warm glow. A soft breeze rustled the leaves outside, and from far off, she could hear the birds chirping. Denise followed her inside, looking around nervously.

"Do you think he'll be here soon?" Denise asked, her voice barely above a whisper.

Lila shrugged, "I don't know. He didn't say. But I need to move the car into the garage and figure out the room situation upstairs."

After Lila drove the car into the adjoining garage, and they had brought their meager belongings into the house, the two women explored the rest of the house.

As they made their way up the stairs, Lila's thoughts strayed to Shane's imminent arrival. She couldn't help but feel her heart beat faster with anticipation. She hadn't seen Shane in so long, and she wasn't sure how she would feel when she did. Lila pushed the thought aside, reminding herself that this was about staying safe and hidden, not about rekindling an old flame.

The second floor had three spacious bedrooms that shared one bathroom. Lila took the middle bedroom, while Denise chose the one at the top of the stairs.

The crunch of wheels on gravel outside interrupted her thoughts. Lila stood up and walked over to the window, peering out through the blinds. A black SUV pulled up outside, and a figure climbed out, walking towards the cabin. It was Shane.

Lila felt her heart skip a beat as she watched him approach. He looked the same except for the scruff of beard. A five o'clock shadow that spoke of a day spent in travel. Where had he been? Had she pulled him from an assignment? She had to look at this as a business arrangement. Denise needed protection. *This isn't about Shane or me. It's about protecting Denise. Nothing more.*

"He's here."

Lila shoved the myriad of emotions she felt deep inside, walked down the stairs, and opened the door.

Reunion

-Shane-

Jack Benton's connections made travel easy. No cattle car seating on commercial flights, not with his varied financial holdings, including ownership, silent or otherwise, of several major airlines. Even when it wasn't work-related, Shane could simply call and schedule a flight wherever he wanted to go, first class. It was one perk of working for Benton Security Services.

He was the only one in first class. The back of the plane was perhaps half full, most of the others wore suits, and would get off at the first stop, New York, while he flew on to Bradley International, where a car was waiting for him.

The flight attendant was a familiar sight, although she wasn't usually on the red-eye. A willowy brunette, Dana had piercing green eyes and white teeth that she flashed in a megawatt-bright smile. Normally, she was on a regular daytime flight, not in the wee early morning hour shift. That was unusual. Over multiple trips, they had talked. She was his age, gorgeous and funny. She had given him her number four months ago. It had tempted him for a hot minute. But she had come along right after the break-up with Lila and he wasn't ready for anything, not even with the "no strings" that she scribbled on a napkin below her name and number.

"Shane Ellis, you are up early. Or is it a late night?" She asked, beaming.

"Hi Dana. Late night, I'm afraid. What are you doing on the red-eye?"

"Meeting my new boyfriend's family, actually. I'm attending his family reunion down in Texas with him."

"Sounds serious."

She giggled like a schoolgirl. "Yeah, it is. It took me by surprise. I didn't think I was cut out for anything long term. Not with my job. You know?"

Shit, yes, I know. My job screwed up my chances with Lila.

"I can certainly relate."

She nodded and then set a napkin down. "What can I get you?"

"Just a bottle of water, please. And a pillow. I think I'll try to catch some shuteye."

"Coming right up." She reached above him and turned off the light.

Shane allowed himself to relax. He tried not to think about what it would be like seeing Lila again. It had been six months, and still not a day went by that he didn't think about her, or worse, dream about her. His eyes closed, the sounds of other passengers trundling past with their suitcases lulling him to sleep. The plane taxiing to the runway barely registered, and he woke briefly as the plane left the ground and roared its way into the sky. When he opened his eyes hours later, there were only two more hours to go. He'd slept for nearly eight hours and felt refreshed, something that could not have happened were he stuck upright in the cattle car section of the plane.

He looked through the thick glass window at the bright blue sky. It was late morning by his estimate and the plane would land by 2:30, plenty of time to make the three-and-a-half-hour drive to the safe house. There had been closer airports, but Jack's reach, or that of the airlines he owned, while wide, did not go to every city in the country.

It was a pleasant drive. Plenty of scenic small towns along the way. Rural, with little changing in the past two hundred years. The picket fences and simple, well-built homes reminded him that some things lasted far longer than steel and concrete did on the west coast, especially in Los Angeles.

The safe house was new, and he had received access codes to it weeks ago when it came online. The photos he had seen of it shortly after they completed construction were nice, but it looked even better in reality. A sprawling, wood-shingle exterior with green-framed windows that let in light. They nestled it against a backdrop of forested land and set back from the road. Vaulted ceilings, wood-paneled walls, and three decent-sized bedrooms.

Custom-built, the windows were bulletproof and all doors, interior and exterior were steel-reinforced. A state-of-the-art security system was in place, as well as a panic room only accessible by fingerprint and retinal scan.

Ever since he had a near miss in his Los Angeles hills home, Jack made sure every one of his properties around the world, including the safe houses, were retrofitted, or built to order, to the new standards. Shane figured there was nothing quite like nearly being murdered in his own home to get serious about security. Shane suspected that Jack still felt bad about the Kansas City location not being updated at the time Shane and Lila were there two years ago. It had been further down on the list, and shortly after the shooting, Jack had it retrofitted.

Shane could see lights on inside. And movement. No great surprise, the driveway was long and winding, and he knew that Lila had followed safety protocols. Neither car was in sight and from the perimeter notifications he had received, she and this Denise Fortuna had arrived an hour ago. He had stopped for gas and bought some groceries. Fixings for dinner, and one of Lila's favorites, Chicken Piccata. Although he would have to make it with pasta, not the creamed polenta, and the country store had had no capers. Still, he was hoping an offering of a meal would smooth the way.

He had had most of a day to think of it, and he still couldn't figure out what to say, or do, to make things right between them. If it was even an option, which it didn't seem to be.

The last person I ever expected to talk to again.

It was on repeat in his head. She didn't want to give it another chance. How could she? She deserved better than a visit every few weeks or months. And the last one cut short by the call from Jack, demanding his return. She had only called him because she needed his help as a bodyguard, nothing more.

He could see the curtains move as he sat there in the car. She was waiting for him.

Waiting for me to come and do the only thing I'm good at. Stick to that, Ellis. Stick to your lane. Stop looking for more.

Shane sighed, shut the engine off, opened the door and stepped out from the car. His joints popped as he stretched, then reached for the bags of groceries and his go bag.

The door opened as he approached and Lila's beautiful face held a polite, perfunctory smile. "Thank you for this, Shane."

She took one bag from him and the door clicked shut behind them as he stepped inside.

All of his good intentions, the mental preparation he had made in the hours of travel, it all fell away. Just the sight of her was enough to undo six months of trying to convince himself that the two of them wouldn't work, couldn't. Shane wanted to reach out, pull her body against his, and kiss her. He wanted to feel her legs wrapped around his waist. He wanted tangled bedsheets, sweat, the scent of her hair.

Shane swallowed all of this down. Now was not the time. He set his bag on the entry floor, glanced at the young woman waiting nervously by the foot of the stairs, and did what he was supposed to do, what Lila needed from him, what she had asked of him.

"Of course. I'm Shane Ellis." He strode over to the young woman and extended his hand. "And you must be Denise."

"Y-yes." Denise said, her hand timid, limp in his.

"A pleasure to meet you. I've brought some fixings for dinner. Why don't I get started and after we eat, we can all talk about what comes next."

Undeniable

- Lila -

One day.
Two.
And now a third.

Damn it.

Lila could feel a hot flush creep over her. She'd tried to get over him. She was an educated, independent woman. So why was it whenever she was within ten feet of that arrogant muscled man, all she wanted to do was have him walk over, sling her over his shoulder like some damn cave man, and let him do wonderful, dirty things to her?

Get your mind out of the bedsheets, girl. The last thing you need is another roll in the hay with sexy, pecan pie Shane Ellis.

Shane cleared his throat. "Perhaps I should take over prepping the chicken."

Lila glared at him. "I know how to prep a chicken, Shane."

A ghost of a smile lifted the edge of his lips. "I know. It's just that..."

"What?"

"Well, you've been pounding that chicken with the mallet for five minutes now. At the rate you are going, it's going to be thinner than a tortilla." Lila glanced down at the chicken breast. She had pounded it flat.

He moved closer, his hand closing over hers. It was warm, and she felt a flush of desire slam into her.

If I feel like this when he simply puts a hand on me, how in the hell are we going to spend the next few days, or, heaven help me, weeks together?

"If you have some aggression to get out, might I suggest chopping some vegetables? Or would that be a bad idea to arm you with a knife?"

This close, she could smell him. It wasn't aftershave or cologne. Shane Ellis just smelled delectable. A mix of musk and sexy man reminded Lila of how long it had been.

Six months, three weeks, and two days, to be exact.

"Hand me a knife, then." Lila ground the words out.

He smiled, and removed his hand from hers, turned, and slipped a large knife into her free hand. She shuddered slightly, trying desperately to control her traitorous body and its runaway desire for the man next to her. She grabbed the head of broccoli and retreated to the far end of the kitchen island to work. It was close quarters, but she was better off creating space, any space, between her and Shane.

It's that or jump him and hump him like a sex-crazed dog.

"Are you cold?"

"What?" Lila responded, flustered.

"You shivered."

Why, oh why do even the simplest of words from him set me off? I just want to feel his hands wrap around my waist, cup my ass, slide me up against that wall, and...

"I'm fine." She said curtly. The knife sliced through the broccoli. Her knives at home were dull in comparison. This one sliced the broccoli as if it were nothing more than butter. She focused her intent on the broccoli, chopping away industriously at it, and trying desperately to avoid thinking of the man standing just a few feet away. Which wasn't so different from any of the hours, days, or weeks since she had told him they were over.

I can't stand it, the time apart. His job, his work, it isn't compatible with a relationship. This last year taught me that.

A mere moment passed before Shane was back at her side, his hand once again on hers.

For a man so invested in following The Code, he sure breaks the rules a lot.

"What now?" Lila barked, glaring up at him.

Why the hell did he have to be so tall, anyway?

"And now you have definitely ensured that any geriatric contingent of our group would have no problem consuming the meal."

"What?"

Lila followed his gaze down to the broccoli in front of her. She had devastated it, reduced the florets down to a fine mince. She had been so stuck in her own head that she hadn't even noticed.

"Oh."

She looked up at him, annoyed to see his lips twitch. Shane was clearly trying not to laugh.

The only thing the broccoli was good for now was, well, hell, she did not know. She had learned a handful of recipes from Shane. Mostly when he was in between assignments. They had either eaten out, or he had cooked while she wrote. The rest of their time together taken up with far more intimate, pleasurable pursuits. He pulled his hand away again and was at the refrigerator door.

He turned around, a small package in his hand. "Ah, this will work perfectly." He deposited a small square plastic-wrapped package in front of her.

"Wontons?" Lila read, "Like wonton soup?"

Shane had cooked her wonton soup the one time she came down with a miserable cold, thanks to a nasty virus making its way through town the past winter. It had been the next-to-last time he visited before she had broken it off.

"Actually, I'm thinking of fried wontons. It was one of my mom's comfort foods when I was growing up."

Lila blinked. Shane seldom spoke of his childhood. Both of their mothers had died of cancer, which seemed as if it would be something that they could speak candidly about, but Shane remained close-lipped about his life before he met Lila. He hadn't even really explained how he began working for Jack Benton as a bodyguard. *How did he describe it? A mistake that turned into an opportunity, one that he was lucky to get. Huh.*

It was yet another reason they couldn't work. She wanted to share everything, but Shane, well, he held a lot back. Why, she really didn't know. Whether it was a checkered past or a traumatic childhood, he wasn't willing to share. How could she think of the future with someone who avoided his past?

Shane tapped the top of the package. "Go ahead, open it up. And grab a ramekin and put some water in it."

"Ram-what?" Lila looked around the tiny kitchen.

Ram as in sheep? Why would I put water in sheep? Like, is that a cute name for sheep? Some sort of "love you, lambykins" kind of thing?

A white ceramic bowl appeared in front of her, his hand brushing hers. She felt another surge of lust and annoyance.

Oh. That's a ramekin?

She caught another grin from Shane. There and gone again, but his brown eyes twinkled with mischief.

It figures. He tells me to abide by the code and then does whatever the hell he wants. He's the one who keeps touching me!

The Code. Ugh. Cue the air quotes. As if The Code helped when the shit hit the fan last time.

It wasn't fair, though. Even as she thought it. She was the one who had opened the door to more danger. Using her phone had allowed the hitman to track her down there at the safe house.

Or maybe I'm jealous. Maybe he's interested in Denise now. Does protecting a woman make her somehow more attractive? Like some kind of macho man thing? Hell, maybe I'm still attracted to him. Of course I am, damn it, because why not be in a relationship with someone who simply cannot be here for me? I want him, but I want ice cream and junk food too. Just because I want something doesn't make it good for me.

His hand on her arm interrupted her thoughts again. "Are you okay?"

"Must you keep touching me?" The words popped out of her mouth before she could stop them. She glared up at him. He arched an eyebrow and his lips quirked into a trademark slow, sexy smile.

Standing there just as smug as can be.

"There should be a fifth rule." Lila added.

He blinked. "A fifth rule?"

"Of your stupid code. I think we need a rule that says, 'you shall not touch,'" Lila snapped. How in the world he expected her to stay calm with sexy pecan pie Shane Ellis standing so damned close, she did not know. It was impossible, the entire situation was impossible.

He laughed. Full throat guffaw. Lila could feel the heat rise in her cheeks.

"Jack would heartily approve of that rule."

He met her eyes, and Lila wasn't sure what she saw there. Was it desire? Frustration? Lust? Something more?

Shane opened his mouth, and Lila felt herself lean forward, wanting more than anything to hear what he would say next. Instead, his eyes flicked over her shoulder and past, to the doorway.

"Oh wow, I needed that. I really did," Denise said from the doorway, yawning as she stretched. "Did I get the best of the beds? It felt like I was sleeping on air." She blinked at the clock on the wall. "Is that clock right? Have I really been asleep for three hours?"

The moment between Lila and Shane was gone. Evaporated like mist. Whatever he started to say had disappeared into the ether.

It's better this way. After all, a couple of days and Jack will have someone else take over here. Shane will be gone and I can go back to my rental house and my bookstore, and Denise won't need my help anymore.

Still, the thought of saying goodbye to Shane left her with a cold, empty feeling in the pit of her stomach. For the hundredth time since she had called it off, whatever 'it' was between them, she felt the loneliness creep up and wrap itself around her heart.

We live far too different of lives to stay together. It won't work. It can't.

Lila smiled at her. "You definitely needed it. Do you mind helping Shane out? I think I'll go take a shower."

Denise nodded. "Oh yeah, for sure. I'd love to help."

Lila pointed to her spot in the kitchen and then marched upstairs to her en suite bathroom. She sighed, feeling conflicted. It was a relief to leave the kitchen. Being so close to him was harder than it should be. Why did he affect her so? Why did it have to be *his* touch that sent shivers through her body? Damn him. It felt as if her body didn't belong to her. It certainly did not obey her, not where Shane Ellis was concerned.

She thought about the differences between this safe house and the first one she had stayed in, trying to focus on anything else besides her ridiculous infatuation with the man downstairs.

The first safe house had been a study in contrasts - "the seventies have called and they want their flocked wallpaper back" had clashed with Victorian everything down to the dark, masterful Chesterfield sofa and chair that occupied the living room lined with wood parquet floors. This house was modern, yet with a rustic vibe. The toilet in the corner was also a bidet, and the controls on it seemed... *complicated*. She tugged her shirt over her head and reached into the shower, fiddling with it until she had one large showerhead, not all three, in action, before stripping off the rest of her clothes and stepping inside of it. The air conditioning kept the house cool, almost too cold, and Lila cranked the hot water up, fiddled with one of the other shower nozzles that dispensed a pulsating spray of heat into her lower back. This unfortunately reminded her of the hot tub at a wooded cabin deep in the forest. She'd gone away with Shane for a short two-day escape just as the fall was turning into winter. The nights had dipped below freezing, but the hot tub had been, well, hot. And in more ways than one. Thinking of that time with him, and the desires that ran through her body now, was stirring up so many emotions. Worse, her body was reacting to him. She felt as if she were no longer in control of it. Just being near him sent a curl of desire, heat, and more circulating through her.

I'm a hot mess around him. Maybe this was all a big mistake calling him. Perhaps I should have called Jack Benton directly, or stayed behind instead of coming with Denise.

The water pulsed into the small of her back. She reached for the shampoo and inhaled the scent of it. Sandalwood, musk, and peach floated into her nose. Shane baked a peach pie mid-summer when he had taken off for a long weekend last year. The shampoo brought the memory of it back, sharp. The taste of that pie, and the taste of it on his lips as he'd...

Get a hold of yourself, Lila!

But it was far too late. Now all she could think of were their stolen moments, scattered over the past year. Hands down, she had never, ever met a man who could satisfy her the way Shane had.

Mind-blowing sex, check.

Easy on the eyes, check.

Lila rinsed the last of the shampoo from her hair. Felt the suds slide down her body. Her hand strayed to that sensitive nub hidden in the now slick and sudsy folds. Overriding her better judgment, she allowed the memory of him standing before her, his mouth on hers. How he had pressed her against the cold tiles of the shower wall and worked his way down, ignoring the spray of the water by closing his eyes. His mouth sliding down to her breasts, taking one, then the other, gently nipping at them, before moving down her further, his hands sliding around to cup her ass and spread her legs apart just so.

Lila ran her finger along her clit, remembering how it had felt to feel his tongue questing, first gentle and barely there, to his mouth on her, his tongue slipping inside of her.

An orgasm ripped through her then, wringing a gasp of ecstasy from her lips. She felt the surge down to the tips of her toes as she stood there. A tremor rolled through her, the water cascading down over her head and pulsating into the small of her back, and then faded away. She came back to herself. A mixture of frustration and longing were all that remained in the aftermath.

This situation is impossible. I need to figure out what I want. And then I need to either leave and get on with my life, or...

Or what? Even she didn't know the answer to that.

Twenty minutes later, her hair damp, her body relaxed from the hot water, she returned to the common living area and breathed in the delicious aroma of dinner.

Denise was sitting on the couch, a troubled look on her face.

"What's wrong?" Lila asked, instantly concerned.

"It's my stomach. It just keeps acting up. The food was smelling so good and now..." Denise sat up suddenly, a look of panic on her face. She stood then and dashed past Lila, bolted into the half bath, and slammed the door. Lila could hear the faint sounds of retching.

She could feel Shane's presence behind her. Lila turned to face him. He frowned at the door, and then retching.

"Is she okay?"

They stood there listening as the toilet flushed and water ran in the sink.

Lila shrugged as her mind picked over the events of the past week. How many times had Denise been ill? This seemed excessive for a little stomach flu. A suspicion took root and grew. Lila opened her mouth to say something, but in that moment the door opened. Denise looked pale, distraught, her eyes filling with tears.

"Are you okay?" Lila asked. The girl looked like she needed a hug.

Denise shook her head. "I'm pretty sure I'm pregnant." And then she burst into tears.

What I Want

An hour later, Lila sat next to Denise, the pregnancy test Shane had brought back from the nearest convenience store sporting a plus sign on the table in front of them.

Dinner was a muted affair. Denise picked at her food, still pale, and managed only a few bites of the fried wontons before asking if there were any saltine crackers.

After the plates were cleared and Lila and Shane had cleaned the kitchen, Denise confirmed what they already suspected.

"It's his. It's Lionel's. I was on the pill and we, well, he, took no additional precautions past that. I thought the pill would be enough." She stared into the distance, one hand on her still-flat stomach.

Lila and Shane exchanged glances. This added a whole new level into an already complicated situation.

"Do you think he..." Lila paused, trying to find the words. "I mean..." Denise snorted. Shook her head.

"I'm so stupid. He's rich, he's powerful, and..." Denise laughed bitterly, "And I have this sneaking suspicion that he's married, so..." She looked down at her stomach, fingers brushing at an invisible crumb. "So, I guess I, or *we*, are on our own." A moment of silence passed. "I'm keeping it. I figured someday I'd have a kid, maybe two. Maybe get lucky, meet a doctor, settle down." She laughed again, then shrugged, tears welling up in her eyes. "Instead, I got knocked up by a rich and powerful man who wants me dead."

Shane spoke first. "We don't know that these events are connected, not for sure."

Denise stared at him. "I told you what I overheard. What I certainly was *not* supposed to hear. And the next thing I know, someone has murdered my three friends. All for what? Being in the wrong place at the wrong time? It's connected, believe me. He's done having his fun, and now I'm a liability." She looked down at her belly again and placed one hand over it protectively. "*We* are a liability."

Shane folded his arms in front of his check, frowning, deep in thought. "Denise, I need to talk to my boss, Jack. He can help you, and Jack has contacts and resources I don't. I need to check in and see what our people have learned about this Lionel Bush, anyway."

Denise nodded absently. Her hand twisted in the cloth of her t-shirt. Shane stood up.

"I'll just step into the garage. Give Jack an update."

Lila watched him go, then focused on Denise. They sat in silence for a couple of minutes. If Lila listened closely, she could hear Shane's voice in the garage as he talked to his boss. But she couldn't hear what he was saying.

"I think that I'm going to go to bed. I'm just, I um, need to be alone if that's okay." Denise said apologetically. "I've got a lot to think about, you know?"

"Of course." Lila hadn't known Denise long, but she could tell the younger woman was struggling.

How would I feel in her shoes? She must be terrified. No support system. No partner and on the run from the father of her child.

"Denise." The younger woman stood up and looked back at her. "I promise we will do whatever we need to do to protect you and your child. Shane, and Jack, and the others. It's what they do. And they do their jobs well."

Denise nodded. She walked over to the stairs, put a hand on the rail and turned back to look at Lila. "Thank you. I know I've made my mess your mess somehow and I'm sorry for that."

"Don't be. We'll figure this out. Get some rest, okay?"

Denise nodded and disappeared upstairs, her bedroom door at the top of the stairs closing behind her with a gentle click.

Shane walked back in from the garage a few minutes later, sliding his phone into his pocket. He glanced around for Denise.

"She's gone up to her room," Lila said. "I think she needs time to process everything."

Shane nodded, looking grim. "Liam's dug up plenty. He's been updating me along with Jack. I didn't want to say anything until I had a solid picture of the situation."

"What did Liam find?" Lila knew Liam was some teenage wunderkind that worked for Jack while attending college. Shane was fond of the kid and impressed with the young man's hacking skills. He had mentioned him often.

"It was more of what he found *around* Lionel Bush. Disappearances. Deaths. Former employees who refuse to talk or just disappear. Family of missing employees asking questions and then going silent themselves. Nothing concrete. Nothing we can bring to the police, or the FBI even and say definitively that he's committed a crime. He's smart, he's rich, connected to some questionable organizations, and he's..." Shane stopped, his mouth set in a grim line. "He's dangerous, Lila."

Lila felt a heavy dread forming in her chest. "Why do terrible people always get away with things? When do we get a chance to live without looking over our shoulder all the time?" Anger warred with the dread. Her situation wasn't any different. The powers behind Kurgen Real Estate, the hints of a secret crime syndicate, all of it. It had exploded her life, her chances at a normal existence. "I write under a pen name, have to remember to respond to 'Annie' when I'm in a crowd. I'm stuck in WitSec, waiting for a trial that might never happen. When do I get to live a normal life? And Denise? With a baby on the way? When does she get to feel safe?"

Shane reached out and pulled her against him. For the first few seconds, she felt hard, brittle, and so angry. She fought the temptation to lash out, to hit Shane. Her life had been upended. Denise and what she was going through was just yet another reminder of it.

"Hey." Shane said softly, "Breathe. Just... breathe."

This close to him, his body was warm, and the hot, moist air in the garage clung to his kin. His breath tickled the top of her head. He smelled of soap and the faintest hint of the lemongrass-scented shampoo the bathrooms were stocked with. His touch was reassuring, calming.

Lila felt her stress slipping away and replaced by something else, an attraction she wished she could fight, but had no genuine interest in doing so. Here in Shane's arms, no matter that they were in the middle of nowhere in some safe house, here she felt safe and... wanted.

What do I want from him? Another quick whirlwind of amazing food, sex, and then... what? I want him. I wish I didn't. I wish I was cool with just casual sex. That I could just...

Shane's voice interrupted her inner monologue. "Hey, where is your head at? I can feel you tensing up all over again."

His words tickled her ear and sent a wash of hedonistic desire down her spine. She didn't bother fighting it. She couldn't. It felt as if she and Shane were made for each other. The way their bodies moved together or the attraction they both felt. The sex. God, the mind-blowing sex.

She knew the choice was there. Step back, break the connection or move closer, consummate the desire thrumming there in the air, and coiling inside of both of them. She knew he wanted her just as much as she wanted him. It was there, unspoken, but real. And even as her mind gibbered questions of how they would make it work, what disaster this could bring, she melted into him, one hand on his chest, the other clenched in a fist. She gripped his t-shirt, pulled him down toward her, and tilted her head up to capture his mouth in hers.

His mouth crashed into hers. The months of being alone with only the memory of him, the frustration over his job, their lack of quality time together, it all melted away as their tongues entwined. As if they shared the same thoughts, Shane lifted her easily into his arms and strode toward the stairs, never breaking from the kiss. God, how she had missed this feeling. The feel of a man who could hold her, carry her up a flight of stairs without breaking a sweat. It felt as if she blinked twice and they were at his door, through it, and he set her on the edge of his bed, a hungry look in his eyes.

All the doubts, the hurt, the frustration - she pushed them aside. She wanted him and he wanted her, and really, what more was there than this moment, right now? Life can turn on its ear in a second, and everything you had or thought you wanted can be ripped away.

This is real, and this is what I want.

Shane nodded and Lila realized she had said it out loud. He knelt down in front of her, keeping eye contact as he slipped her t-shirt off, revealing the white lace bra underneath. His hand lit a fire inside her as he slid one, then the other bra strap down and bent to kiss, then gently nibble and suck at her breasts. Pleasure coursed through Lila and she leaned back on his bed, closed her eyes, and moaned. He continued his way down her body. His hand slid slowly, possessively, down her front, to the waist of her capris, past the waistband, plunging toward her hot depths. His mouth gave both pleasure and pain as he took first one breast than the other in his mouth, his tongue rolling over each sensitive nipple before nipping them lightly.

He slipped her pants off, and tossed them away, his hand already back against her mons, a finger slipping expertly inside the hot, slick folds. Lila moaned, clutched the bedding between her fingers, and fell back as Shane moved sensuously down her body, his mouth trailing kisses from her breasts down her breastbone, to her navel, and then slipping his fingers inside of her, his warm breath sent shivers across her skin.

The terrible and wonderful things his fingers and mouth were doing to her sent flashes of light across her closed eyes. It felt as if he had unleashed lightning in her bloodstream. Lila wanted to lose herself in the sensation.

"Come for me." Shane said, staring up at her, his tongue and mouth sparking a lightning storm inside of her. Then he did something with his fingers and there was no more thought, only sensation and light. Her body was on fire as an orgasm exploded through her.

Later, much later, after their bodies had come together in a frenzy of lovemaking, Shane curled his body around her. One arm underneath, curling over her possessively, his fingers stroking her skin. "Your skin feels like silk." He murmured in her ear. It tickled, but Lila was far too exhausted to wiggle away.

"What are we going to do about Denise?" she asked, yawning. Her body felt like a limp puddle after two mind-blowing orgasms.

"Jack will be here in the morning. He's got some ideas."

Oh great. Lila knew she should be thankful for Jack Benton. He had done plenty for her, and all with no payment. Although Shane had explained that the jobs he often took were the ones that paid for the other cases like hers, she still felt like she owed Jack Benton something. And she didn't like feeling indebted to anyone, not even a billionaire like Benton.

Besides, Benton is the reason Shane and I broke up. If Jack would have just honored Shane's time off, we...oh hell, who am I kidding? It was only a matter of time. I'm not made for long-distance relationships, or ones where I'm alone for weeks at a time. I know this.

As if sensing her displeasure, Shane said, "He's a good guy, Lila. One of the best I know."

Lila sighed. Damned if he couldn't read her mind.

"I know. And I'm *grateful*, really, I am. It's just..." Even now, they would not agree. She knew this. Shane felt he owed Benton, and maybe he did. All Lila knew was that she really didn't want to wait around for the bits and pieces that were left.

"It's just that you want more. You want me around, not off on assignment." Shane rumbled in her ear, finishing her sentence.

Lila flipped over, faced him. "Is that so wrong?"

"No, it absolutely isn't." He met her eyes, steady, unblinking. "And I'm trying to figure out how to make it all work. Maybe I can ask Jack to only give me work in the Northeast region, so I'm closer."

Lila felt the conflicting emotions bubble up. Shane was trying, at least, to make it different. But would it be that different? Close or far, it wasn't as if he could drive home every night. Gone, whether it was an hour's drive or half a continent, was still gone. She wanted to say it was enough, that they could make it work, but the nature of his work was the issue. Days, weeks, even months away on assignment. She'd never been a Tinder kind of girl. More of an eHarmony one. Once, back in Kansas City, she had signed up for it after Kaylee's persistent nagging. She'd met a couple of bland, run-of-the-mill guys, another weird one who gave off stalker-like vibes, before she'd connected a guy who met all her basic criteria. He also turned out to be in the military. She'd wrestled over it for a good part of a day, before turning down a second date. She wasn't interested in a military life. A friend in high school had grown up a military brat. She and Lila had been fast friends for the second half of ninth grade and then lost touch once the girl's father was assigned to a new post on the east coast.

And really, was this situation any different? Shane might as well be in the military. Days, weeks, months away from home and facing all kinds of situations and danger.

No thanks. I'd rather live alone.

"Lila?" Shane's voice intruded on her thoughts. "What are you thinking about?"

"Don't you want something different, Shane?"

"Different from what?"

"You know, different. You live out of a duffel bag. Your pistol and ammo take up more room in it than your socks do."

"I don't need much of anything." He said in response, his body tensing.

"What about us? Don't you want more for *us*? And don't you dare tell me how good Jack has been to you and how much he depends on you. He's a *billionaire*. He pays enough that he could buy whatever loyalty he needs five times over if you left. You know, you could go back to medical school, become the doctor you dreamed of being."

"Doctors are gone long hours, Lila. Even if I could get back into medical school, any internship would have me working 80 hours a week or more."

"At least you would come home every day! And you wouldn't have someone shooting at you," Lila snapped back, frustrated. She sat up abruptly. She knew where this was going.

What I want is a partner, someone to spend my days and nights with. And Shane will not be that for me. Not now, and maybe never.

She reached for her clothes. They were scattered across the room. A bra here, a pair of panties over there.

"Where are you going?"

"To my bed. This was a mistake." And before Shane could argue, she slid out of the door and closed it firmly behind her.

No Way to Prove It

Lila woke to the sunlight streaming in the window. It was a beautiful morning, at odds with her current frame of mind. Would anything she had said sway Shane? Could she even hope for him to show a spine to his boss?

He's not spineless. He's... devoted. But I wish he were a little less devoted. I really do.

She could hear sizzling sounds coming from the kitchen. The smell of coffee had wafted under her door, gently tempting her from her bed. No doubt it was Shane. The man was a wizard in the kitchen and in the bedroom. She groaned, pulling the sheet back over her face, wishing it was just the two of them in her rental house in Maine. Wishing she knew how she could make it work between her and Shane.

Today Jack Benton would be here. She hoped he had some miraculous solution for Denise's predicament. All Lila wanted to do was flee back to her bookstore and her life, single and lonely as it might be.

Two hours later, Jack Benton sat down across from Denise, who fidgeted and paced restlessly until Lila settled into a seat next to her.

"I wish I could tell you that the good guys always win." Jack said. "But that simply isn't the case." He tapped the folder on his lap. "My people dug up a lot. But none of it will stick. Not without more witnesses, a smoking gun, *something*. A judge will throw this out in an instant."

"What about evidence of medical testing?" Lila asked. "Surely someone could investigate that, find out if there have been any victims or deaths as a result?"

Jack shook his head. "We are looking into it, but honestly? Liam has found nothing so far. We'll keep trying, but until we have evidence, no one is going to believe it. The Happy Haven Retirement Villages are popping up everywhere, and they are revolutionizing senior care."

"My friends are dead. The police are hunting *me* and plastering *my* face all over the news and there's nothing I can do?" Denise said, her thin, strained. She pulled her legs up against her, wrapped her arms around herself, and rocked her body back and forth. "My life has been destroyed. My reputation, my future as a nurse. I can't go back to Florida, I can't even go back to Maine. I can't even be a nurse without documentation from my college. What in the hell do I do?"

Jack nodded and placed a business card on the coffee table, sliding it over until it sat within reach of Denise. She stared at it. "What's this?"

"I made a few calls before I left California. His name is Doc Diamond. He needs a nurse." Jack said.

"Who is this guy, really?" Denise asked, peering at the card.

"He's a well-qualified, brilliant doctor. I can tell you that. He got caught up in a family member's mess and the cops pinned a crime on him he didn't commit. He is offering you the full package, income, health insurance, paid leave, annual bonuses, and no questions asked. And we can make sure you have a new identity. Doc Diamond operates out of southern California, and he caters to those who don't want or need their medical needs leaked to the public. The rich, and others, not-so-rich, who are afraid of immigration."

Jack leaned forward. "This is only temporary, Denise. Consider it a stepping off point to your new life. One that establishes your employment history by giving you the necessary experience. In a few years, you can find something else in a smaller town. There are plenty throughout the west coast, but I have a couple in mind that I could get you a position in when one opens up."

"But... how?" Denise turned the card over in her hands, a frown on her face, "I mean, how can you make it look right, or authentic? Will it even hold up if I get pulled over? Or will I be in worse trouble?"

Jack smiled. His teeth were a brilliant white. "Money buys a lot of things, Denise. It buys silence. It buys zero questions, new identities, and plenty more. But don't worry, I use my powers for good."

She was still frowning. "And what will this cost me? I mean, I don't have money to pay you."

Jack shook his head. "I don't need payment. Or favors. Or for you to owe me. This is what I do." He templed his long, manicured fingers in front of him as if in supplication. "Some day, you will find someone to help, just as Lila helped you. You pay it forward however you can, when you can. I just hope that we can get enough on this Lionel Bush, and on Happy Haven for you to reclaim your life someday. For now, however, you can have a decent go at a different one. Is that acceptable?"

"I'll really be able to work as a nurse?"

"You will."

"Am I going to be working for the mob or gangsters?" She asked, apprehension clear from the frown on her face.

Jack smiled and shook his head. "No. Doc Diamond handles some celebrity cases, and a handful of those who might skirt the law, and I and others supplement his work with immigrants afraid to use the health care system, but it is a rare day Doc caters to organized crime. If he did, you could bow out of caring for any patient who made you uncomfortable. There is another nurse on his staff. He simply wanted to add a second. He mentioned it, and I thought immediately of you."

There was a moment of silence before Denise nodded slowly. "Okay. Yes, I would be interested."

"Excellent." Jack pulled out his phone and made a call. "Az? Tell Liam I'll need the full package. I'll fly back with her today. And reach out to Doc and tell him she can start next week. Yes. And the apartment in L.A. is vacant, right? Great. Set up access to that and a commuter car. Thanks." He pressed a button and slid the phone into his jacket pocket.

"I've included a place to stay. The apartment has two bedrooms and is in a secure building. There's parking as well and my assistant, Azule, is making all the arrangements for access to a no-frills, but reliable, car. The apartment and the car are payment-free for two years, enough time for you to get on your feet, have your child, establish credit under your new identity, and more. If you need something further, keep my card and simply reach out to me." He slid a plain card across the coffee table.

There was a long pause. Lila itched to say something about how it had been for her. Although WitSec, for what they were worth, had been involved, and it had been a completely unique experience, she knew how hard it was. You had to let go of the life you had lived and embrace another. At least Denise could use her education, something she trained for.

I wish I could have continued in data analysis, if only because it feels like I wasted years studying for it, only to end up in a completely different field. Still, I love the opportunities I have now.

Lila cast a glance in Shane's direction. He said little at breakfast other than to tell them that Jack Benton was on his way and would be there soon. It felt as if he'd been deliberately avoiding her. As if they were back to square one again. Even Denise, her mind full of her own problems, had noticed.

"What's with your hunky guy?" Denise had asked earlier, when Shane had slipped out of the door to walk around the property before Jack arrived.

"What makes you think he's mine?" Lila had asked in return, a surge of bitterness rising in her.

Denise had raised an eyebrow and snorted. "Maybe the way he looks at you like you are the only person in the world that matters? If I had a guy look at me like that, well, I wouldn't kick him out for eating crackers in bed if you know what I mean." She'd stopped and stared at Lila. "Oh my God, this is the sexy pecan pie guy from your novel, isn't it?"

"Yeah, well..." Lila had struggled with what to say, what to share.

"Write what you know?" Denise had giggled then, momentarily distracted from the morning sickness that had kept her from finishing the eggs and toast Shane had prepared.

Lila had laughed wryly and shrugged. "I guess so."

"Sex must be..."

"Epic with a side of 'now I'm leaving on assignment and I don't know when I'll be back,'" Lila finished, shoving her half-eaten breakfast away from her. She'd lost her appetite. "Also, 'you don't understand, I *owe* him my freedom, I can't just leave him in a lurch.'" She had added finger quotes in the air, her tone sounding bitter.

"Oh." Denise had practically wilted in her seat. "That…"

"Sucks. Yeah, I know." Lila had shrugged. "We got close again, had the same conversation, and now we are back where we started."

It was hard to even look at him. Part of her wanted to just rip off her clothes and fuck some sense into him, and the other part wanted him to look at her, realize how much he needed her and tell that silver fox, Jack Benton, to take his job and shove…

"Ms. Benoit." Speaking of silver foxes, Jack's gaze was now focused entirely on her.

"Um, what?"

Jack's mouth quirked to one side in amusement. "I asked how the bookstore and book writing is coming."

Coming? I have my characters coming all over the place.

"Um, fine, fine. Yeah. Uh, eager to get back to it."

"Well, Kaylee asked me to tell you she is looking forward to the next installment."

Lila gaped at him. "You are in contact with Kaylee?"

Jack's smiled deepened. "We reconnected when she reached out to me to get you protection. And, well, we've been together ever since."

Lila struggled to close her mouth. Her mind spun. *Kaylee and Jack? And here I had chalked him up as a billionaire playboy!*

She leaned toward him. "Is there a way, I mean, is it safe to call her? WitSec told me not to contact anyone from my past, and really, except for Kaylee, there wasn't anyone to contact. But if she's with you…"

Jack nodded, pulled a pen from his pocket, and jotted down a phone number. "I know she would love to hear from you. We all run with Purism Librem smartphones. They are untraceable." He slid his card across the table, a phone number written neatly at the bottom.

"Thank you. I'll call her soon." Excitement surged through her, replacing her disappointment and frustration with hope. Kaylee had always known exactly what to say or do with dating and relationships, and fashion, and more. Lila had missed her vivacious friend more than words could express. She missed late night pizza runs in the middle of study sessions, lunches at Nara when they were both working at Kurgen, and the First Fridays jaunts between Christopher Elbow Chocolates and Mean Mule Distillery. Kaylee embodied everything Lila missed of Kansas City, and her former life.

"Well," Jack said, clapping his hands together. "I think that wraps everything up. I'll escort Ms. Fortuna back to California."

"How will I get through airport security?" Denise asked, worry creasing her forehead.

"I have a private jet waiting for us in Laconia," Jack answered. He nodded at Shane. "You can head back to Alaska if you like, or elsewhere," his gaze strayed to Lila, "I don't have a new assignment for you yet."

Lila blinked. That was as close to a tacit approval of her and Shane's relationship as she had ever seen. Too bad it came months too late.

Jack turned back to Denise. "I'd like to leave soon. We have a long flight ahead of us and by midday, the queue for the runway can get rather long."

Denise nodded and stood. "I just need to gather my things and I can be ready in ten minutes."

Jack Benton smiled at her, nodded at Lila, and called after Denise as she walked up the stairs. "I'll be in the car waiting."

As Denise disappeared into her bedroom to pack, Lila stood as well. "Thank you, Jack, for everything." Somehow, knowing he was with Kaylee made him feel less like an adversary, and more like an ally. She still wished Shane would give his notice, choose a life with her instead, but knowing she could speak to her friend was an unexpected bonus.

Who knows, maybe Kaylee can help me figure this whole mess out. Or set me straight, hell maybe even tell me to dump Shane.

"Happy to help." Jack answered. He gazed up the stairs, then turned back to Lila. "I wish I had better answers for her, but connecting the fire and murders to Lionel Bush is impossible. Perhaps if they catch up with the one who actually did the deed, we can convince them to talk. Until then, well, the police will not see Ms. Fortuna as a victim in this situation. And worse, they cannot protect her."

Lila sighed and rubbed her face. "That sure sounds familiar."

Jack nodded. "If this were a movie, karma would catch up to the bad guys and rain down retribution on them. And believe me, I want to see that happen, Ms. Benoit, I do. You and Ms. Fortuna are being hunted by people who wish to do you harm, but we are also stalking our prey. If we can connect enough dots, we can bring them down. Give Liam time. He's working on it. So is Azule. Together, they make a rather formidable team."

Lila smiled at Jack's comment. Shane had mentioned both Liam and Azule often. Liam was still in his teens, but Shane described him as a converted black hat hacker. The kid had skills and had lived in Kansas City until he tracked Jack down and quickly made himself indispensable. Apparently, he was now living at Jack's estate and attending college while also handling anything computer-related. Then there was Azule, a competent, smart black woman a few years younger than Jack. She had grown up on the Benton estate while her parents worked for Jack's parents and began working for Jack once she had finished college. She was Jack's personal assistant, and ruled the office with an iron fist, according to Shane, who described her as "formidable."

It felt anti-climactic. Denise would get a new life, a new identity, although it differed considerably from Lila's experience. Denise was being sought by the police, hunted by a powerful man. Lila, at least, had been protected by WitSec, who she probably should update about all the goings on over the last few days. Especially with the hurricane hitting the entire North Atlantic seaboard, they might be a little concerned.

Or not. And talk about a case going nowhere. My case is going nowhere. Kind of like this off again, on again relationship with Shane.

"Well, it sounds like Denise is in excellent hands." She smiled to cover up the rush of depression that flooded her. "I guess I need to pack my bags as well. And get on the road if I want to make it back to Brunswick before nightfall. I have a bookstore to run." Lila said. She avoided looking at Shane, who had been sitting in an armchair a few feet away. She fixed her gaze on Jack. "Thank you again for this. I can't tell you how much I appreciate all that you are doing for Denise, and what you did for me as well."

She knew Jack Benton had been involved in setting up the bookstore for her, despite WitSec and the FBI being in charge of her case. Shane had admitted as much. Jack Benton had done a lot for her. And seeing him again reminded her of that. It gave her a new understanding of *why* Shane was so loyal. Jack protected people. He didn't make money on it, at least, not all the time. In fact, she suspected he probably operated Benton Security Services at a loss. It seemed that Jack continued to defy the stereotypical playboy billionaire image. Why, she wasn't sure.

I'll bet there is a story there, though.

It didn't make the situation between her and Shane any better – she still wanted a partner by her side, not this part-time thing they had – but at least she could see *why.*

"I'm happy I could help, Ms. Benoit." Jack answered.

Lila turned and headed for the stairs without looking at Shane. She could feel his eyes on her the entire way up the staircase. When she turned at the top and looked, his eyes met hers, his shoulders slumped. Her chest felt tight as she turned away and went into her room.

It took moments to pack, and another five to say goodbye to Denise, who teared up and hugged her.

"Thank you, Lila. I don't know what I would have done without your help."

Lila hugged her back. "You are going to be okay, Denise. And you will soon have a beautiful baby to keep your heart and hands full. I hope you will keep in touch."

The house will feel empty without Denise there.

Denise promised she would, hugged Lila again, and pulled away, wiping at the tears on her cheeks. As Lila turned to go, Denise put a hand on her shoulder, "I hope you work things out with pecan pie guy."

Lila laughed, gathered her bags, and headed downstairs.

Shane stood. "Let me walk you out."

Lila nodded and said, "Thank you again, Jack. And if you could let Kaylee know I'll try to call her while I'm on the road, I'd appreciate it."

"Will do." Jack answered as Shane picked up the heavier suitcase and slung Lila's duffel bag over his shoulder.

The door closed behind them. The heat of the summer day was just beginning to build.

"Lila, I feel like we left things unsaid last night."

"No, I don't think we did, Shane." She popped the back trunk lock and Shane slid both bags into it.

"Lila..."

"Shane. Let's just say goodbye, okay?" Lila didn't want to cry in front of him. She just wanted to smile and get out of here before the waterworks started. She'd cry on the road, call Kaylee, pour out her heart, and get past this. "I get it, I really do. What Jack does, the people he helps, that's important. It's meaningful. He's changing lives. And you are a part of that."

"Yes, but..."

"I'm going to go now." She could feel the tears threatening, and damned if she wanted to do it in front of Jack or Denise or even Shane. And before he could try to change her mind, she gave him a chaste kiss on the cheek, slipped into the driver's seat, and pulled out of the garage, leaving Shane standing there. She reversed, turned around in the wide driveway, and pulled away. She couldn't help thinking how forlorn he looked in the rearview as she drove away.

Where is She?

- Lila -

Returning home, or the equivalent thereof, after the last few days in the safe house, felt off, weirdly foreign, despite missing all of her belongings and familiar space. The hurricane had blasted through and left trees down; the electricity had been out, and from the smell coming from the fridge, it had been at least two days without power. She had been so distracted by Denise, and her reunion with Shane, that Lila hadn't realized how bad the storm had been until she arrived at the dark house.

On the door was a note, unsigned, telling her the bookstore had sustained damage. A broken window, possibly flooding. Lila groaned. She'd spent hours on the road driving home, had to prove she lived in the town in order before the guys in uniform at the edge of town would let her through the barricades, and now she would need to go to the bookstore and assess the damage.

I wish Shane was here.

She wrenched the car into drive and reached for her phone. The battery was red-lining, despite being plugged into the charger the entire drive home. She followed the cable to the plug, and it wiggled, loose, unconnected.

Well, shit. I ran it down while talking to Kaylee for so long. Damn it.

At that moment, it rang and she could see Shane's sexy mug staring up at her. Lila pressed the green button.

She tried to keep her voice noncommittal. They were done. She needed to get over it, get over him. "Hey."

"I tried calling earlier, but it kept going to voicemail. I was getting concerned."

"I was on the phone with my friend Kaylee."

"Oh." He paused, then asked, "Did you make it home yet?"

"I did. But now I have to run to the bookstore. There's damage from the storm. They left a note on my door."

"I can be there to help. I'm approaching some roadblock right now. When you didn't answer, I took a detour."

A four-hundred-mile detour? Really?

Lila sighed. "Really, it will be okay. I can handle it." She backed out of the driveway, neatly avoiding a fallen branch.

"Lila, I..."

"Look, Shane, there's really nothing more to say. You have your work, and I have a life here. What more is there to talk about?"

He fell silent. The only way she knew he was there was his breathing and the sounds of the occasional honk.

He really did take a detour. By now, he should be halfway back to Alaska! Then again, Jack had practically encouraged him to do so. As if he had a change of heart. Maybe Kaylee had said something to him. She'd certainly been supportive when they talked.

"Girl, it sounds like the two of you could really make something beautiful together." Those had been Kaylee's words after Lila poured her heart out. "But yeah, I have to agree, it would be impossible as a long-distance relationship. It was why I cut it off with Jack. He was in California; I was in college and then Kansas City. It was just too much." Her voice had softened then, "But seeing him again, Lila, in the middle of all the Kurgen shit that went down, I just... I don't want to ever be apart from him again."

"Lila, are you still there?" Shane asked, jostling her back to the present.

"Yep, just trying to drive around all the storm damage."

"So, what do you think?"

"About what?" Lila asked, momentarily confused.

"I asked if I could swing by the house, make you dinner."

Debris cluttered the intersection, and the signal lights were dark, lifeless. Thankfully, most of downtown Brunswick was closed thanks to the power outage. She waited for a truck to cross through the intersection and then turned right onto the side street behind the bookstore.

"There's no power." Lila answered.

"It's a gas stove. I can light it manually. Besides, I'd feel better if I just double-checked the house. Denise created a trail, cash withdrawals from the bank. If Lionel Bush hired a hit on her, he's got the same resources for tracking her down that we do, possibly more. Let me just look at the house, cook you something, and we could, you know, talk."

I can think of much more pleasurable activities than talking. Damn it. NO. No talking. Talking leads to... other things. Far more pleasurable to be sure, but what we need is to just... stop.

"I don't think that's a good idea." Lila said, hating how indecisive and weak her voice sounded. Damn Shane Ellis. He knew just what buttons to push.

I'm so damned predictable. Feed me wonderful food, turn those sexy brown eyes in my direction and my legs open like a...

"I just can't stop thinking about you. About us. I don't want this to be over."

In the background, she could hear someone shouting from another car. It had taken her an hour in line on the outskirts of town to get through. The hurricane had been a doozy from the looks of it. And most of the town had fled, and was only now returning. Tempers were flaring as the National Guard took its time looking up resident addresses and double-checking the occupants' identities.

She could also feel her will weakening. Hope threading through after talking with Kaylee and hearing in her friend's voice how in love she obviously was.

The silver fox and Kaylee. What a world. There had to be at least a decade between them, but if it works for Kaylee, and she is happy, who am I to judge?

And maybe, just maybe, she should give it one last chance. Lila drew in a lungful of breath, let it out, and relented.

"Okay."

"Yeah?" She could see his smile, hear it in his voice.

"Yeah. I've got some wood in the back of the bookstore. I'll get it up against the window, move some books..."

"I can be there in ten to help. I'm almost at the front of the line."

"See you soon," Lila said, and the phone beeped and went black. *Dead as a doornail. Damn it.*

She had circled the block. All the buildings were dark, the power was down throughout the town. Trees and debris still filled the streets. From the boards covering the other buildings, including Hannifords, it seemed the hurricane had mostly spared the businesses. The shrubbery and trees were the exception to this, and her bookstore, of course. She hadn't been here to add that spare wood to the front of the building in time. It was no wonder downtown was deserted. Most of the store owners were probably intent on cleanup at home. Lila spotted a parking space clear of debris at the front of the bookstore and pulled in and parked.

Her stomach churned in anticipation at seeing Shane again. It had only been a few hours, hours she had spent mostly on the phone, catching up with Kaylee. Still, a tiny thread of hope bloomed inside her.

He sounded so earnest. And he followed me four hours out of his way.

She turned off the engine, opened the door, and slid out of the car. There, near the front door, the glass was shattered, a long, battered tree branch lying half in, half out of the long glass show window. Several books, her thrillers and beachside cozies, lay sprawled willy-nilly underneath it, the covers and pages swollen with rain, the rest of the display case scattered in the wind. Lila sighed.

Really, it isn't as bad as I thought it would be. I think I got off lucky.

The door was unlocked. That raised Lila's eyebrows, but only for a moment, before she laughed out loud.

"I guess no one is as crazy for books as I am," she said out loud and pushed open the door. The bell jingled as the door scraped against broken glass.

The light of the day, already murky and hidden behind heavy cloud cover, was rapidly fading. She could make out the bookshelves and most of the main room, but the back office remained shrouded in darkness.

I could just wait for Shane. She eyed the dark outline of the closed office door. *Yeah, like a helpless ninny. No thanks. I can at least get the board out and ready for when he's here to help.*

She picked up the stack of damaged books and set them out of the way. Lyle, Hanniford's owner, had delivered the boards just days before the storm. It was one of the few things she appreciated about living in a small town. People looked out for each other, even newcomers like Lila. When she had looked confused at his offering, he had explained what they were for.

"So's your windows don't get blown out by the hurricane."

And she had planned on putting up the wood. Until that newscast and Denise's face plastered all over it. Three days, no, four, and it felt more like a month.

Suddenly, the thought of Shane on his way to the bookstore felt like a bad idea all over again.

I'll get the board up over the broken glass, clean up, and by the time he gets here, I'll just tell him to go. I can't keep doing this to myself, wanting what I can't have.

She picked her way past a pile of books, victims of the wind, all cozy mysteries, and headed for the back of the store. She knew right where it was, near the back wall next to a new shipment of children's books she had meant to ask Denise to shelve, but they had instead had to deal with a flurry of visitors intent on buying books to read during the upcoming storm. Lila opened the office door and stepped into the darkness. It smelled of paperbacks, books that were likely suffering in the humid heat left in the hurricane's wake. A small, barred window high on the wall was the only light source, and a rapidly fading one at that. There was some other, odd smell that hit Lila at around the same time as something slammed into the side of her, jabbering as it did, knocking her to the ground. Pain flared, pinpoints of electric pain, her muscles contracting without her consent, her mind momentarily knocked offline. Consciousness lost.

Someone dragging her by her hair, a sharp ache of agony from her scalp. She opened her mouth to scream and the man, it was a man, growled, "Scream and I'll kill you. Right here. Right now."

He crouched over her, a dark blocky figure that removed the light from the room. He pressed a hard object to her abdomen. It felt small, round, barrel-shaped. Lila's heart hammered in her chest.

"Where is she?"

"Wh...wh...who?" Lila stammered, desperate to buy time. How long would it take Shane to get through the roadblock? Could they even let him through? He wasn't a resident. She'd had to prove it, show her driver's license that listed her address. They might turn him away, even detain him if he argued.

"Denise Fortuna. Your employee. Your roommate. Do not play dumb with me." The man said. His breath stunk. It smelled of something familiar.

Shane. Oh God, Shane. I need you here. Now!

Even if they let him through, how long would it take him to get here? Five minutes? Maybe even ten?

When seconds count...

The man jabbed the gun harder against her skin. It jabbed painfully against the bottom of her left ribcage.

This close, I'll be dead, bled out, long gone, before anyone can get me to a hospital.

"Where... is... she?"

Lila's mind gibbered in fear. Her hand, lost in the shadows, closed on the Taser he had used to debilitate her. She slid it into her waistband.

If I tell him the truth, he'll kill me. If I lie, tell him she's at the house, he will kill me.

Somehow, she had to stay alive. She had to stay alive long enough for Shane to get there. Her mind spun.

"I can take you to her."

The gun jabbed her again, bruising, painful. "I want the address."

Give him an address and I'm dead.

Lila shook her head. "I... don't..." he jabbed her again. "I don't know the address. It was just... everyone was leaving, but Denise was sure you would find her, that you already knew what her car looked like, so we dumped her car at an airport, backtracked."

He reached up with his free hand, grabbed a handful of her hair, and twisted hard. Tears sprang to her eyes.

"We... we hid on the outskirts of town. I can... I can show you. Just please, please don't hurt me." She was sobbing now. It wasn't hard. She was terrified. Despite the moist heat, her limbs trembled, still reeling from the spasms.

He's got a gun and a Taser. Hit me with the Taser first. So where is the Taser?

"Get up."

Doritos. He smells of Cool Ranch Doritos.

The random fact popped into her brain. She stocked her desk drawer with the variety snack packs. Cool Ranch Doritos were ones she saved for last. Her favorite.

Fucker ate my Doritos!

She felt a flare of ridiculous and rather misplaced anger at the thought. But somehow, being angry was better than being scared. She had been so frightened that, if she had not run out of water miles ago, and stopped to use the restroom before coming to the bookstore, there would be an embarrassing puddle on the floor of her office right now. Angry felt more focused. Anger would keep her alive.

He yanked her to her feet by her hair. He was tall, a hair taller than Shane, and brutal. The darkness of the room and her prone position on the floor had kept his face hidden, but now, on her feet, she could see more details. This was a very dangerous man. There was no room for error, no way to fight, not with the gun held close against her body. Her head ached from where he had wrenched her hair, and she was sure he had pulled some of it out at the roots.

His bad breath, tinged with the hint of Cool Ranch Doritos, washed over her. "Try anything, and I'll fucking kill you."

Lila's stomach lurched in revulsion and terror. She thought of the man she had shot in the basement of Jack Benton's safe house. That had been simple. The hitman hadn't even known she was there. She had squeezed the trigger, half out of reflex, as he turned toward her. She knew she had been lucky, damned lucky. This situation was different. He was too close. She couldn't run and she didn't dare try to fight him. She was a fool to have even done what she had, grabbing that Taser. What if her shirt didn't cover it? What if he remembered he should have it?

He spun her around, shoved the barrel of the gun Into her side with one hand, and wrapped the other in her hair at the nape, twisting it painfully as he did.

"You parked out front. If there is anyone there, if you scream, fight, try to run, know I will kill you and anyone who gets in my way. Understand?"

"Y-yes." She hated how tiny and helpless her voice sounded. She wished she was brave, that she wasn't so damned scared right now.

They moved slowly out of the office, into the gloom of the bookstore, then out the front door. The bell jingled and Lila flinched at the sound of glass crunching under their feet.

"We'll take your car. Go to the passenger side."

There was no one in sight. A fact that Lila was both thankful and sorry for. The last thing she wanted was for anyone to be hurt, but right now, she was praying for a miracle.

Shane. Shane. Shane.

His name repeated in her head like a mantra, a supplication to the gods, perhaps. She didn't want to die, but this man, he would kill her. Of that, she had no question. He had been willing to beat to death three people, and set a house on fire, when only one woman had been on his list. That was enough of a reality check for her.

She stumbled, her legs going rubbery with fear as the man used the fist coiled in her hair to walk her forcibly to the passenger side of the car, open it, and climb inside as he climbed in behind her, forcing her into the driver's seat.

Her legs were twisting, struggling to get past the steering wheel and into the bucket seat of the tiny commuter car when the sound of tires screeching in the street and her attacker's momentary lapse of focus gave her the one opportunity she had to fight back. She pulled her one free leg back and slammed a foot into the man's chest. It sent him flying back out of the car and into the still-open door. The pistol barked one bullet out, sharp, loud, and Lila felt the heat of it tear through her side, a line of fire. The force of the bullet slammed her forward and her head cracked against the glass of the driver's side window, her body spasming, a fountain of pain washing over her.

A roar, then. Shane. His mouth contorted In rage, fear, as the sound of a gun clattering to the ground and a fist connecting with meat over and over ensued. Lila saw none of this. A rushing in her ears, the unbelievable pain in her side, and her aching skull were taking center stage in her now fading consciousness.

Tick, tock.

Wetness. Her entire middle felt like it was on fire. She touched the wetness, brought her hand up to her face and stared at it, her vision blurring.

Water? No. Blood.

The sound of a fist hitting meat had stopped. Gentle hands touching her. In the distance, sirens.

"Lila, stay with me, baby. Stay with me." Shane sounded so sincere, so... scared. The sirens grew closer. He pulled her out of the car, into his arms.

In her head, a familiar song played. She enjoyed playing it on repeat while writing.

We are here, and then we go.

"Easy come and easy go," Lila muttered.

"Shh, Baby. Hang on, I'm getting you help."

God, she was so *cold*. She could feel Shane's warmth, his hand pressing down on her side caused another dizzying burst of agony.

"I'm in the fire, but I'm still cold."

The sirens blasted through the air. Their lights split the gloom of the encroaching night. So bright. Voices, more voices, movement.

"Stay with me, Lila." Shane said. Did she hear his voice quaver?

"Police! Do not move!" A man shouted.

"I have a gunshot victim here, officer. Caucasian female. Age twenty-six. Pulse is [xx]. No other medical conditions." Shane's voice again. To anyone else, he would sound calm, but she could sense the urgency in his voice.

"The future's bright, lit up with nowhere to go."

"Lila? Lila!" Shane's voice faded. The lights, so bright, slipped away at the end of a long tunnel.

The world went black.

Time for a Change

- Shane -

Shane slid into the seat of the diner. Here, in the middle of Podunk nowhere, was where Jack has asked to meet. A strange destination, but then, the last few months had been strange overall. It wasn't something he could put into words, but it felt like something had changed for Jack in the last year, and especially in the last few months. His normal base of operations, the sprawling multimillion dollar home in the L.A. hills, where Shane had first come face to face with the man who would later become his boss, was now in various off the beaten path locations all over the country. And far more often, not meeting at all. A phone call from a new number, a quick text. In the six years that Shane had known Jack, the last year had deviated from the norm.

Perhaps that was why Jack had asked to speak with him. His gut twisted at the thought of the discussion ahead of him. Jack would have a new assignment for him, and he was going to have to turn it down.

Ever since the night in the bookstore, and the fear he had seen in Lila's eyes, he knew what the answer had to be. And it wasn't just that he owed Jack Benton for the opportunity, the life he had led for the past six years, it was his very freedom that he owed him as well. Jack had been within his rights to make sure Shane ended up in prison, but he hadn't. He had instead offered him a job, one that had paid him very well, and showed him a life he had only dreamed about.

It wasn't a straightforward thing to walk away from. He had been, until Lila Benoit entered into the picture, rather satisfied with his life. But now?

Now I can't stop thinking about the life I could have with her. One where I wouldn't just fit her in between assignments, but where I would wake up next to her every morning.

"If you were to change careers, what would you do?" Lila had asked him yesterday, her body spooned into his.

"Well, I hoped to be an oncologist. It would be nice to get back into medical school, I guess. I mean, if I even could. I had planned on either working in cancer research or treating patients."

"You could do it; you know. You are meant for more than this bodyguard work, Shane. I'll bet Jack Benton would even help you if you asked. He's got all kinds of connections."

Shane had shook his head. "I can't ask for that." He had felt her sigh. "What?"

"Men can be foolish, prideful creatures."

He had laughed. "I'll show you something I'm quite proud of."

The waitress appeared, coffeepot in hand, replacing the memory of their encore with a crooked, gap-toothed smile. She was older, edging into her fifties, and the deep lines on her face betrayed the evidence of a hard life. "Coffee, sweetheart? Something to eat?" Her eyes widened as Jack slid into the booth opposite Shane and smiled up at her. "Oh, well, hello there. Coffee? Pie? Me?"

"I'll take a coffee and your house special." Jack answered, ignoring the last offer. He smiled again and winked at her.

"Coming right up, darling. And anything for you?" She asked, turning back to Shane.

"Same for me, thanks."

"Okay, well, my name is Jane and you just holler if you need anything." She paused and gave Jack a come-hither look. "Anything at all." Then she sauntered away with an extra swing to her bony hips.

Shane suppressed a snort of laughter. Lila referred to him as the silver fox, and apparently, she wasn't far off.

Jack sipped from the black tar in his cup, winced, and set it down. "I'll stick to water."

Shane sipped from his own cup and had to agree. It rivaled Lila's attempts and producing something worse than nuclear waste. How anyone could screw up coffee so bad, he did not know, but the coffee could etch a hole in the Formica. He pushed it away.

"You asked to see me."

Jack tapped his nails on the table and leaned back. "How is she?"

"Lila? She's... healing."

"Liam kept me updated," Jack said, shaking his head in wonder. "How the bullet missed any major organs, despite the close range and being lodged inside, is a damned medical miracle."

"It was. Well, that and a Taser. The bullet would have caused organ damage if it hadn't been slowed when it hit the Taser. Once they pulled the pieces out and gave her a transfusion, she was in the clear. She's recovering well."

"I saw too that the police chalked it up to a burglary gone wrong, but the perp's prints matched some cold case on the west coast. The courts plan to extradite him to California after his sentencing here. He won't be out on the streets for a very long time." Jack added.

Shane's guts churned. Jack was making nice, asking after her, but now he was going to talk to him about another assignment, and Shane was going to have to tell him no. Despite going around and around it in his head, he still felt unready. Meeting Jack had changed everything. He knew he had savings enough to last the two of them for a year, possibly even three. He could live simple. Shane certainly had before he worked for Jack. Hell, he lived out of a duffel bag most of the time already. It wasn't his way of living that had him in knots, or even making ends meet in the future. It was the thought of leaving a guy who had sought him out, trusted him, and depended on him, in a lurch.

I can't keep doing this, though. Lila needs me, and I need her.

The memory of the panicked flight to the hospital filled his mind. When she had woken up from surgery, he had been there, holding her hand. He'd promised her he would never leave her side again. And he hadn't, not during her stay in the hospital or the weeks after. Not until now.

"It's good that you were there. You saved her life." Jack's eyes bored into Shane's and Shane looked away, clenched onto the coffee cup. The memory of those terrifying moments brought to the forefront of his mind. It had been four weeks now, and he still hated to leave her side, even for an instant. The heat from the hot coffee cup burned his skin and he let go, staring at the reddened flesh, remembering the blood on his hands.

Never again.

"I can't accept another assignment, Jack. I'm... uh, I'm done." The words came out easier than he thought they would.

"I know."

"I mean, not just now. I can't do this job anymore." Shane persisted.

"I know." Jack's tone was calm, matter of fact.

Shane jerked his head up, stared at his boss.

Jack smiled wryly. "Honestly? I'm surprised it has taken you this long to say it."

Shane blinked. "You knew?"

Jack shrugged. "I suspected. And after the bookstore, well, you didn't leave her side. That made it pretty clear what I needed to do."

Shane felt as if the floor was shifting under his feet. "What do you mean, what you needed to do?"

The waitress was back with two plates of greasy eggs, bacon, and a rather gray version of biscuits and gravy. It looked rather off-putting, but it smelled delicious. Jane smiled lasciviously at Jack while barely sparing a glance in Shane's direction.

"Here you go, you two. Can I get you anything else? Anything at all?" she asked, her eyes laser-focused on Jack.

"Thank you, Jane. I think we are good." Jack answered, a broad smile on his face for the aging waitress. Shane half-expected her to leap into Jack's lap. She looked hot to trot.

"Okay, well, you just give me a holler if you need anything." She slid a ticket onto the table and Shane could see she had written her name and what looked like a phone number before she walked away slowly, glancing back with something that looked like hunger and longing. Jack seemed oblivious.

The older man looked over the food and then slid the plate aside. He reached into his briefcase and pulled out a large legal envelope.

"Before I hired you, I had Azule provide a detailed history for you. Just as I would any potential employee." He slid the envelope over to Shane. "You have talents that are not being utilized. I knew when I hired you it wouldn't be forever, and I realize that, considering recent events, your future lies elsewhere."

Jack picked up the cup of coffee and tried sipping it again. While it might have cooled slightly, the taste had not improved if Jack's expression was any sign.

"Ugh, that really should come with a warning label."

"What are you saying, Jack?"

"I'm saying that there is no new assignment, Ellis. Well, there is, but it isn't one as a bodyguard. And honestly, it isn't for *you* so much as it is for *Lila*. I need someone to manage a property for me in Anchorage. I rarely visit. If I do, the guest room downstairs will suffice." Jack sipped his water and pointed at the envelope. "Go ahead, open it."

The envelope was stuffed full of paperwork. Here was a recommendation from a former teacher, no two, one of them a now retired cancer researcher who Shane had studied under. He scanned it, noticed a highlighted sentence, "best student I have ever seen in the medical program."

How had Azule found Dr. Botta? There were copies of his transcripts up to the time he had had to drop out to take care of his mother. An envelope, several other letters, and real estate brochure for a lavish wood home in Anchorage. Shane took a moment to stare at the house. It was beautiful, sprawling over and down the side of a hill. He could see a large pond, and the stunning views of the ocean close by. Edged by the forest, it looked private and spacious.

"I don't understand." Shane said, frowning.

"Keep reading." Jack picked up a fork and cut into the biscuits and gravy, scooping a bite into his mouth. His eyebrows raised in surprise and his fork dug out more.

Shane returned to the papers. A letter caught his attention. They addressed it to him, and the letterhead read University of Alaska Anchorage. His eyes shot up to Jack's.

"This is an acceptance letter. To their medical program. But how..."

Jack chewed, swallowed, and pointed back at the papers. "Keep reading."

Shane's eyes returned to the papers in front of him. It was a full-ride scholarship, all expenses paid. He moved to another letter, one addressed to Lila. This letter was offering her full use of the Anchorage house in the pictures, all utilities paid in exchange for her management of the residence, as well as a small monthly stipend.

"Any repairs will be covered as well." Jack added in between mouthfuls of food. "You should try the biscuits and gravy. They are really quite good."

"Jack, I... I don't know what to say."

"There's more. Keep going."

A separate envelope with his name on it, sealed, read "severance bonus" in Azule's meticulous script. Shane opened it and gaped at the amount. It was twice the amount he had set aside in savings, a stunning six-figure check.

Shane's mouth dropped open in shock. His eyes shot up to Jack.

"Really, try a bite of the biscuits and gravy." Jack scraped the last bite into his mouth and sighed with contentment. Then he reached into his pocket and pulled out his wallet, laying a crisp hundred-dollar bill on the table next to the tab. He extended his hand to Shane.

Shane took it, his mind struggling to keep up.

"Ellis, have Ms. Benoit call me and let me know if she doesn't want the job. Otherwise, I'll expect her to start next week. There's really not much to it, and hopefully will give her the time she needs to work on her novels. I do hope you will keep in touch. I look forward to hearing how you are doing in your studies and with Ms. Benoit."

Jack's grip was firm.

"It, this, I..." Shane struggled to put his whirling emotions into words. It felt as if his boss, well, now former boss, had stepped inside of his mind and read his thoughts. He had certainly done his research. Shane was being handed everything he could have ever possibly wanted or dreamed of.

Jack's voice softened. "Shane, it's time for you to claim your future. Make a difference in the world. Do it for your mother, and yourself, and all the rest of those who will benefit from your future work in cancer research. If you do this, that is all the payment I will ever need."

He slid out of the booth, stood, and clapped Shane on the shoulder. "Take care of yourself, Ellis." Then he turned and waved at the waitress and out the door, the bell ringing shrilly as he did.

Shane sat there in shock, staring at the papers before finally gathering them up carefully and placing them back in the envelope. He hadn't expected the meeting to go like it had, not at all.

Anchorage? College? Full ride? Holy shit.

He picked up his fork and tried the biscuits and gravy. Despite its grayish hue, Jack was right. It was damned good. Jane returned to fill his water, her lined face filled with disappointment. That changed the instant Shane pushed the hundred-dollar bill toward her and told her to keep the change.

The phone in his pocket buzzed, and he pulled it out and answered it.

He could hear the worry in Lila's voice. "Hey, how did it go? Where are you?"

"At a diner. Would you like me to bring you something?"

"Nah, just wondered how it went."

She hadn't pressured him or given him an ultimatum. But after everything that had happened, she didn't need to. He knew things had to be different. He could tell from her voice that she was waiting for him to tell her he was leaving again.

"Actually, it went really well. I have something to show you. I think it's going to blow your mind."

Anchorage

- Lila -

The Crow's Nest at the Hotel Captain Cook was pricey, but it was a celebration, after all. Lila's new book, *Burning Desire*, had blasted up the Amazon charts and was busy knocking off the competition and hitting new heights with each day. It had been hard to peel her eyes away from the sales charts as they ticked away, showing sale after sale after sale. There was work to do and the third book in the series wouldn't write itself.

Still, when Shane had insisted on taking her somewhere special to celebrate, she had been eager to go, even if it meant stepping out into the sub-zero temperatures.

The surprise had included a hotel suite with views of the city, and a gorgeous black dress and high heels. Sitting across from sexy pecan pie Shane Ellis, Lila felt as if she were walking on clouds. It had been over six months in this city and she still couldn't believe her luck. Their lives had changed completely. Now Lila's days were filled with writing and long walks in the woods. Shane remained buried in textbooks and back-to-back classes.

That Jack released Shane from his contract with a six-figure bonus made Lila's eyes bug out. But then he went even further, and secured Shane's entrance into the University of Alaska Anchorage, with a full-ride scholarship in their doctoral program.

The six-figure bonus, along with free housing, utilities, and her small stipend, would allow them to make ends meet while Shane finished his studies.

Certainly, Anchorage Alaska had never been high on Lila's list of destinations. Except for three short months each year, she was perpetually cold. This far north, the summers were short and intense. Now that it was winter, the hours of sunlight were a short-lived affair, dwindling to under six hours on the solstice, before slowly increasing again. By the mid-summer solstice, that would turn into 22 hours of sunlight. Right now, in early January, summer felt impossibly far away.

The city was beautiful, however, and so was the surrounding landscape. The house that Jack had asked her to be a caretaker of was a new build. It nestled on the edge of acres of private forest trails with a stunning view of the ocean. Here she felt safe. No hitman, no one who knew who Marie Trebuchet, romance author extraordinaire, truly was. And she liked that. It had certainly fed her popularity. Mystery author, no photographs, no book signings, just romantic thrillers that had women and men obsessively turning pages late into the night.

Lila had officially requested to be removed from Witness Protection after learning there would be no trial. A mysterious fire in the records room, and the deaths or disappearances of several key players there at Kurgen, had ensured that there would never be the closure she hoped for. And the shadowy organization hiding behind it? The one pulling the strings on the hitmen, the one that Jack had referred to as the Indalo? Quiet.

Jack had warned them that the shadowy figures who pulled the strings were at work on other things. Like a hydra, cut off one head, and the Indalo would grow two more.

Lila couldn't help but wonder if Jack had an ulterior motive in his desire to help Shane with his medical degree. Was he hoping Shane could shed more light on these supposed drugs that Happy Haven was giving to some of the unwitting residents? Watchdog agencies had been warned, but nothing had shown up, no sign that what Denise had overheard was actually true.

You don't kill someone if they are lying, however. You kill them to stop the truth from coming out.

"What are you thinking about?" Shane asked, his hand on hers. It was warm, and it enveloped her smaller, slender one. He stroked it gently, slowly, sensuous. Her body responded, heat flushing her cheeks and traveling down, down.

"I was a million miles away." She pulled her hand away. Reached for her glass and sipped the wine. It was sweet and bubbly, perfect. If he kept touching her hand like that, she might need to take him with her to the ladies, lock them in the stall, and demand he do dirty things to her.

"Thinking of your millions of readers already screaming for the next book?"

Lila shook her head. "I was thinking of, you know, Voldemort." Their own private codename for the Indalo. They had been using it for months, ever since helping Denise. As Jack had astutely pointed out, you never knew for sure when someone could be listening.

Shane groaned. "Lila."

"No, no, really. It's okay. I was also thinking that Anchorage isn't quite the frozen hellscape I imagined it would be." She pointed out the window, where thick snow was now falling, "Well, okay, maybe it's a frozen hellscape *now*, but it has its times of majestic beauty. It really does. And I'm with you, so..."

She lifted her glass again, sipped, and leaned forward conspiratorially. "Tell me, Mister Sexy Pecan Pie, are you having the pork chop with cipollini onion and hazelnuts, or the prime fillet with swiss chard and fondant potato?"

He matched her, raising an eyebrow and giving her a look that turned her insides to jello. "Neither. I think the Elk Osso Bucco with vegetable pave has my name on it." He leaned back, his eyes sliding down from her face to settle on the firm breasts that peeked out of her low-cut black dress. "And you, I don't see you going for the vegan grain bowl."

"God, no!"

He laughed. It was a long-running joke between them, after all. Lila had the appetite of a linebacker and the frame of a dancer.

"King crab legs?"

"Mm, tempting, but no. I think I'll have the ribeye with crushed fingerlings and broccolini."

"Of course you will."

The server returned with a plate of fresh oysters and plates, topped up their glasses, took their dinner order and departed. Lila slipped off her shoes and ran one bare foot up Shane's leg under the table.

"Oysters, huh?"

His face curved into a playful grin. "To cure frigidity."

"As if!" Lila's laugh drew attention for a moment before the other diners went back to their meals. She took that opportunity to move her toes up, up, up. His eyebrow arched, a slow grin spreading over his face.

Her phone pinged at that moment. She reached for it, even as Shane murmured some objection. "It could be Denise. The baby is due any day now."

She squealed with glee at the photos of a tiny baby swathed in blue. "Oh Shane, it *is* the baby! He was born two hours ago. Just look at him! He's perfect!"

Shane leaned forward to peer at the photo. "Cute little guy." He leaned back in his chair and gave her a contemplative look. The tiny furrow dimpled his brow.

"What?"

"Hm?"

She half-glared at him, tucking the phone back in her purse. "You have a look on your face."

A ghost of a smile as he asked, "What look?"

"I don't have baby fever. It's a myth, you know."

"Is it?"

"Yes. Just because I enjoy seeing a picture of Denise's baby does not mean my biological clock is ticking. I have a book to write."

A slow, sexy smile spread over his face. "Have an oyster." He reached for one himself, added a dash of hot sauce and swallowed it. He held out the plate, winking at her. "I've heard that women can be writers *and* mothers. And, believe it or not, I have burped babies and changed diapers before. I can cook and wash dishes. In a pinch, I can even fold laundry properly." If he were trying to convince her he would be the perfect father to her children, she was already there.

Lila gaped at him. "You just started medical school!"

"Yep, sure did." He reached for another oyster. "Damn, these are good."

"What are you saying, Shane Ellis?"

His face assumed an innocent expression. "What? About the oysters? Seriously, eat some before I devour them all."

"About..." Lila leaned close and Shane matched her, his lips brushing hers as their mouths met. "About having a baby." She whispered after he kissed her half-breathless.

"Eat the oyster."

She did. She stared into his beautiful brown eyes and felt the oyster slid down her throat. As it did, his hand slid up her leg, sending a wave of desire crashing through her.

"Now one more."

It felt like a challenge. Lila wondered if they truly had aphrodisiac properties as the second one slid down after the first. Or was it simply Shane and his sex appeal?

He undressed her with his eyes. "We have ten minutes until the main course comes out." He said, setting his napkin down, standing up, and reaching for her hand.

Lila felt a rush of giddiness overtake her. She took his hand and led Shane to the elegant restroom fifty feet away.

No one seemed to notice. The single occupant bathroom was spacious, a separate stall walled off from a sitting room, where a small couch sat positioned against one wall.

Shane locked the door, his hands roaming across her, his mouth sliding up her neck to the sensitive spot by her ear. Lila moaned in pleasure, her hands caressing him, feeling how hard he was for her. She pulled at his belt buckle, tugging it free and then gasping as his hand reached down to cup her ass and lift her effortlessly in the air, and against the wall, his body crushing her. There was pleasure and pain in it, and Lila moaned as he plundered her mouth with his, stealing her breath away.

The couch might have been nice, but they were not going there. She wrapped her fingers in his hair and pulled him closer, their tongues thrusting. She could taste sea salt and the tang of the hot sauce as he adjusted himself, pulled away any petty encumbrances, and thrust into her. Hot. Hard. Lila's gasp of pleasure muted by his tongue, twisting with hers. One shoe clattered to the floor, the other hung on out of pure spite as she wrapped her legs around him and felt him slide in and out of her. His hands dug into her ass, to the point of bruising, but she didn't care. All that mattered was the feel of them moving as one. His dick was deep inside her, thrusting in and out, their mouths fused. Tongues fucking as hard as their bodies were.

She could feel it coming. The orgasm rushing towards them like a freight train. Inevitable. Unstoppable. They came together. A collision of energy and matter that left them panting. Shane sagged, walked backwards with Lila still in his arms, and collapsed down onto the couch, still inside of her. His breaths came in short bursts, and Lila crumpled against him, the rush of endorphins overwhelming. If she stood up now, her legs would simply not work.

She thought of how they still needed to go back out into the restaurant and slid off of Shane.

"Oh my God." She groaned. "That was. Mm. Yeah." She nestled into the crook of his arm.

"Lila. I want you."

"Shane, you just had me. Give me a minute to recover."

He chuckled softly. "I want you in my bed. In my life. I want you standing there when I get my medical degree. When we buy our first house. I want you to have my children."

"You want to have children with me?"

"Yeah. I'm thinking five, maybe six."

"Oh, hell no," Lila said, scrambling up to stare at his face. "*You* go bear five or six kids. I'll sit here and eat popcorn and watch it go down. It'll be a medical miracle."

He laughed. "Fine. Four?"

"Three, tops. And that's my final answer."

"I can live with that. But we'll have to get married. My mom would have wanted me to make an honest woman out of you."

It was Lila's turn to snort. "I'm plenty honest. Thank you very much. But if you were to propose to me in a future moment and time when we haven't just had sex in a public restroom..."

"You might say yes?"

"I just might."

They lay there for a moment more. And then Lila's stomach rumbled. Shane laughed. "Come on. Your ribeye is waiting for you."

"Mm, sounds wonderful. I'm starving!" She sat up, arranging her dress back down around her. She turned to find him staring at her. "I look forward to taking that dress off completely later."

She gave him a coquettish smile, and they stepped out of the bathroom and returned to their table.

He wanted her. In his life, in his bed, bearing his child. Lila felt a rush of hope. She thought of Denise and her child, and of the news she had received just last week that Kaylee was expecting a child. The past two and a half years had been a whirlwind of change. Some moments had been terrifying, life-threatening. But with Shane by her side, everything felt possible.

The main course was absolutely delicious. Each bite felt like a symphony being played in her mouth. The ribeye was medium-rare, just the way she liked it, and they seasoned it to perfection. The fingerling potatoes were buttery and the broccolini a taste of fresh that lightened the heaviness of the meal.

Lila ate the steak slowly, savoring every bite.

Between Shane's cooking and meals like this, I have zero clue how I don't weigh two hundred pounds by now.

She closed her eyes and sat back, a dreamy smile on her face.

"How was everything?" The server asked, a wide smile on his face. It had been there ever since they returned from their escapade in the bathroom.

"Perfect." Shane answered, dabbing his mouth with a cloth napkin. "I think we are ready for the dessert you recommended."

Lila blinked. Had she heard the server mention dessert? If so, she certainly didn't remember.

"Of course, sir." He slipped away from the table before Lila could protest she was full and couldn't possibly fit a dessert in there as well. She wanted to *fit* into her little black dress, after all.

"Dessert? Really?"

Shane just smiled. "I've heard it isn't to be missed. Just one bite. I'll eat the rest if you don't want it." He reached over and took her hand, squeezing it gently before he released it, and stood as the server arrived, dessert balanced on a tray.

The server set down the dessert in front of Lila. It was a delicate crystal parfait glass filled with chocolate mousse with shaved chocolate and a large strawberry on top. Lila stared at it, confused by a tiny flash of light. The top of the strawberry had been removed and a small hole cut down into it. A multi-faceted sparkle at the center caught the candlelight. Lila's mouth fell open in shock. It was a ring. And not just any ring. A diamond engagement ring.

Shane wasn't standing any more. Instead, he knelt on one knee, his brown eyes nearly level with hers. He took her hand in his.

"Lila, these past few months have been the best I could have ever hoped for. I want to spend the rest of my life waking up next to you. Will you marry me?"

Lila's mouth worked, but no sound came out. Since she had woken up in the hospital, Shane had been by her side every single day. She realized now that he had planned this whole evening well in advance. All the months of back and forth, of heartache and hope, of danger and intrigue, it had all led to this moment, this man in her life.

I should say something.

The words had deserted her, though. Finally, she just nodded, happy tears spilling from her eyes.

Shane's lips stretched into a grin and he reached for the ring, gently lifting it from the strawberry and slipping it onto her left ring finger. It was stunning. The diamond was large, square, and set in an antique band, with white and gold filigreed leaves woven in and around it.

Shane pulled her into his arms, and his lips met hers in a passionate kiss. She tucked her face in the crook of his neck, self-conscious of her tears, as the wait staff and several diners applauded.

"I love you, Lila Benoit." Shane whispered.

"I love you too, Shane Ellis." Lila whispered in return.

"Was it too soon after sex in a bathroom?" He asked, still whispering.

Lila just hugged him and laughed.

Target Acquired

- Indalo -

Lucifer recognized the number on her phone and briefly considered not answering it. To say the person on the other end scared her wasn't entirely accurate. After all, she dealt with seriously dangerous people every day, day in, day out. It was the nature of the business, the terms she had accepted when she allowed them to ink her skin. It wasn't just a job, it was life, with the Indalo. Their gaze, their intent, wasn't directly on her, though. It was on people who were in the way of what they wanted. Lucifer did her job, looked up the information they asked for, gave it to them, and washed her hands of the consequences. Well, mostly she tried not to think of it.

How morally gray is that? Lucifer thought as she stared at the incoming call.

Zella Dean, however, was something far more than dangerous. Lucifer had met her once. A few seconds, a minute tops. That was all the in-person interaction she needed. A few months ago, a quick rap at the door, and Annabelle, her massive Great Dane, had woofed once. The dog fell silent, the hackles of her spine raised at the sight of the petite, dark-haired woman at the door. She hadn't growled at the woman, but she hadn't moved either. Not an inch from Lucifer's side, her blue-gray eyes focused on the visitor, her hackles raised in a hard ridge along her spine. The dog was spooked, and that never happened. If Annabelle sensed something off, then there was something terribly wrong with this petite beauty at her door. Lucifer had thrust the zip drive into Zella Dean's hands, doing her best not to show the fear coursing through her.

One glance at the woman's dark, death stare was enough to give her nightmares.

"This is everything I could find." Lucifer found her gaze straying away, then back to Zella. She was beautiful. Long, black hair that fell like a curtain along her back, her eyes a dark brown, with unblemished skin, red lips. No makeup, just natural beauty. Lucifer had found herself attracted for a brief second, despite preferring men. Zella had perfect breasts, an hourglass shape, and a kill count that exceeded most of the others. Beautiful, lethal, and from the reaction that Annabelle was giving off, probably the most dangerous human being Lucifer had ever encountered.

Another dart of the eyes back to Zella and Lucifer watched the woman bar her teeth in what might have been a smile, if it didn't feel more like a threat to her life. Any attraction fell away, changing into fear.

Annabelle whined. The sound of it had made Zella's smile grow wider, and Lucifer had felt the crazy radiating off of her. It had pulsed in the air. In the silence between them. In the distance, Lucifer heard the distant clickety-clack of a passing train, an ambulance siren a few blocks away, and the music from the bar at the far end of the street, the bass thumping. But there, in the space between them, an eerie silence. What the hell did this woman want from her, anyway? Lucifer had given her the information she had scraped together.

"Okay, well, I gotta get back to work."

"What's her name?" Zella had asked, her eyes fixed on Lucifer.

"Who?"

"The dog. What is your dog's name?"

Lucifer had fought the urge to slam the door in the woman's face. She couldn't describe it, other than a sense of dread, fear, and chaos in Zella's presence.

"It's um, Dante." Her stomach twisted, but the lie came smoothly out of her mouth. Lucifer didn't even know *why* she was lying. But the thought of Zella saying her dog's name made her want to hurl, or scream, or run gibbering in fear. Maybe all of it. And all at once.

Zella's mouth still held a smile, but there was nothing friendly at all about it. "Thank you, Lucifer. For this." She waggled the hand holding the zip drive in it. She looked down at Annabelle. "Dante. Huh." She shrugged and walked away and faded into the night.

Lucifer had stood there, peering into the darkness of the alleyway beyond for a minute more, Annabelle pressed against her leg, before finally closing the door. After that, she was too disturbed to do anything except lie in bed with her giant dog. Annabelle had twitched and jerked all night, her doggy dreams on overdrive.

That had been a year or more ago. Since then, Zella had called a handful of times. Always with the same questions, the same eerie, unsettling focus.

Tonight was no different. Lucifer paused the game, picked up her phone, and pressed the green button.

"Lucifer speaking."

"Lucifer. How is... Dante?" Zella paused as she said the name. She always did. And Lucifer couldn't help wondering if Zella knew she had lied.

Of all the stupid things to lie about. Maybe Nyra told her about Annabelle. She was the one who suggested the name, after all.

"Um, fine." Lucifer thought about the person she had been six years ago. Naïve. Stupid. Young. Nyra had been nice to her. Just a voice on the other end of a phone. And while she had known she was working for the black hats, she hadn't really known just how dark it got.

Damned if I didn't learn, though.

"I need you to run an address for me." Zella said after a second's pause.

The rabbit hole was deep. Full of bodies. They never talked about it, these voices on the phone. It was all information requests. And Lucifer had been curious. Too curious. She hadn't used the computer, provided to her by her employers. She hadn't even used the same ISP login. One day, shortly after a disconcerting phone call from Zella, a girl she had only heard of through Nyra, Lucifer had bought a phone, set up the protocols that all good hackers used to make her other inquiries as untraceable as those for the Indalo, and she had tracked what happened after she handed over an address to an Indalo operative. Hacking was nothing. It was the tip of the iceberg.

"Sure, go ahead." Lucifer replied, her voice steady, indifferent.

She typed the address that Zella rattled off. Dug into property records, tracked down the owners of record, dug in. It took seconds.

"It's a subsidiary. One that ties back to Benton."

"Excellent, thank you, Lucifer." Zella purred at the other end. Lucifer could hear the sounds of traffic in the background. A couple laughing. She suppressed a shiver. Lucifer wanted to yell at whoever was walking by, tell them to run like hell. She'd heard about a hit last year, shortly after Zella had visited her and retrieved the zip drive with a list of properties owned by Jack Benton. A family of five had died just for being in the wrong place at the wrong time. Zella had been in the middle of it, of course. Just being *near* Zella was trouble. There was a click and the phone call ended. At least Zella spared any getting to know you chitchat past asking after Annabelle. It would have been even more frightening for Lucifer if she had.

Hard to believe Zella is Nyra's baby sister. She's not like Nyra, not at all. Nyra had been an assassin, just like Zella. She had *trained* Zella. *Maybe I'm just a complete fool, buddying up with a killer and thinking we were friends.* She had been so new, so wet behind the ears back then.

Lucifer almost pitied Adrienne Cenac, or Kaylee Stromm, as she called herself these days. That she had survived a year of being hunted by Zella Dean was mind-boggling. Lucifer figured it had everything to do with Jack Benton's protective detail. Still, it wouldn't be long now. Kaylee Stromm and her rich billionaire boyfriend were running out of places to hide. One of these days, they would slip up, think they were safe, if only for a moment, and that is exactly when Zella Dean would strike. Lucifer stared at the black phone screen to the left of her keyboard.

Annabelle nudged her right hand, a moist nose pushing its way between the mouse and Lucifer's palm. Lucifer gently stroked the top of her dog's velvet soft head, distracted by the reality of her life.

I'm not just a hacker, I'm one of them. I'm a black hat.

And suddenly, days filled with video games and hacking challenges didn't feel as appealing as it once had.

In for a penny, in for a pound, as Gram would say. There isn't any way out. Not really. Lucifer was Indalo now. Whether she liked it or not.

Better Choices

A short story

THE BACK STORY OF HOW Shane Ellis came to work for Jack Benton. Heroes don't always start out on the right path...

Big Nick's

Shane lined up the shot. It was do or die, get it right, or lose the $20 that sat perched precariously on the corner of the pool table, a square of chalk holding it in place. The eight-ball was close to the corner pocket, but so was his opponent's nine-ball. He had to thread it close, not touch the nine-ball, just slip past with enough oomph to knock the eight-ball in while not following it with the cue-ball. He stared at it, bent down, and released a breath as his stick nudged the cue ball down the length of the table, whispering by the nine-ball. It connected with the eight-ball, sent it clicking into the pocket and advanced gently, inexorably, sitting on the edge of the pocket. Another millimeter, maybe two, and the out of towner who had been baiting him all evening would have collected the twenty.

Shane's luck held and the cluster of people around the table hollered, one of them clapping him on the back. "Ellis, you are on fire!"

Shane nodded, reached out and collected the twenty, shoving it into his pocket. Rent was due in another week, and his cupboards were looking bare. It would come in handy. His opponent shook his head and headed for the bar.

By the rack was a beat-up chalkboard with a list of names. It was Friday night, and there were plenty in line. "Carl's up next." Shane called out, "Is there a Carl here?"

"He's visiting the head. I'm next. I'll switch with him." A lanky man with a familiar face unfolded himself from one of the bar stools against the wall and stood up. He grinned at Shane.

Shane grinned, "Dave Eggers? What the hell are you doing here?" Despite living in California for the past ten years, his southern drawl still slipped through.

"Heard you ran the tables around here. Figured I'd see if you really are the shit." He bumped Shane's fist and punched his arm. "I thought you were gonna be some high faluting doctor, but here you are sharking these assholes out of their hard-earned money and drinking Bud Lite."

Shane shook his head. His dream of becoming a doctor had been driven by his drive to save his mother, some way, somehow. When she had died halfway through his third year at Stanford, those dreams had turned to dust, anyway. There was no way he could see watching the student loan debt ratchet up and spend most of his twenties becoming a doctor now. And for what? Mom was gone. The semester after her death had been a shit show and by the time he was halfway through the next, Shane could see the writing on the wall. Three years in college and over $80k in debt, and that had been with grants, a two part-time jobs and a scholarship. He'd dropped out, rented a tiny, cramped apartment, and started working a third job just to handle the student loan payments. It was a rather hand-to-mouth existence. Yet another reason for him to make some money on the side knocking balls around the pool table.

"Shit, driving an ambulance is close enough for me. Besides, weren't you going into business?" Shane gave Eggers a once-over. "Where's that three-piece suit and the fancy letters at the end of your name?"

Eggers grinned, "I'm in business, just ain't a business that needs a suit." He slipped the quarters into the slot and the balls released, rolling into the ball return with satisfying clicks. Dave arranged him in the rack, then leaned over the table, his eyes focused on sliding the rack into place on the worn out spot of felt. His fingers bunched against the edge, keeping the balls close, and gently lifted the rack out of the way. "College, hell, it just wasn't for me. You neither, by the look of it."

Shane said nothing, just focused on the triangle of balls in front of him and hit them with a solid whack to the cue ball. They flew across the table, the two-ball and the thirteen-ball both sinking into the far corners. The four-ball followed a few seconds later.

Eggers whistled, laid a crisp hundred-dollar bill down on the corner of the table, and grinned at Shane. "What d'ya say we raise the stakes a bit?"

Shane blinked. He had seen a flash of the roll of bills the man had in his pocket. A hundred dollars. Shit, he'd better win this round. Against his better judgment, he nodded and took aim at the six-ball. It slid past the eight-ball, bounced in the corner, and hovered there. Shane swore.

Eggers laughed as he balanced a stick in his hand, examining the length and heft of it in his hand before settling into the far corner, his eyes on a striped nine-ball.

A crowd gathered as the two men stalked around the perimeter of the pool table. They clawed their way, one ball at a time, toward the end prize, the black eight-ball and a hundred-dollar bill on the far corner. Each shot that ended with a ball in the pocket generated a shout of praise from the onlookers. They groaned in unison as Shane left the cue ball mired behind a wall of solid balls. Then whooped when Eggers jumped it out and hit a 13-ball into a side pocket. Every ball, every turn. It was close, damned close, and Shane was sweating over how he would have to fork over one hundred bucks if he lost to the other man.

And finally, after all but the eight-ball remained, Shane knew he had one chance, and one chance only. Do or die. Make a hundred bucks or eat ramen for the rest of the damned month. He took the shot, the cue ball bouncing the eight-ball off of the opposite wall, down the full length of the table and gently depositing it in the corner. Eggers whooped right along with the others, laughing as Shane slid the one hundred into his pocket.

"Shit, Suzie Sharpshooter, at least buy me a drink with that!"

Shane laughed and shook Eggers' hand. "Good game."

"Indeed, it was." He leaned closer. "Look, give the table to Carl and I'll buy you a drink. I got a business proposition for you."

Shane shrugged, "All right." He handed the stick to a woman who would have been a beauty ten years ago and smiled at her. He liked cougars. They knew exactly what they wanted and had no problems going after it. Women his age were still playing hard to get and bullshit mind games. "The table is all yours, darling," he said and winked at her. "Give Carl hell."

She smiled at him and winked in return. "I'll hold on to the table for you, Southern." She was a regular at the bar, and could hold her liquor and played a mean game of pool. She gave him the nickname Southern Comfort because of his drawl and propositioned him a week ago. Shane had regretted having to turn her down, but he didn't want to risk being late for his construction job the next morning. The money was good, and he needed all the hours he could get before the rainy season began. Maybe the offer was still open for tonight. He would hear what Eggers had to say and then head back her way.

Eggers chose a table far from the others. "Damned if I don't need some of them chili cheese fries they got here, too. Haven't eaten all day." He snapped his fingers at the barmaid and she took his order, "Give us four shots of Jägermeister along with that."

She nodded, winked at Eggers. "I'll be back with that in a jiffy." She walked away, her butt sashaying. The woman knew how to get tips.

Shane laughed, "Jäger? Didn't you have enough of that at the frat parties?"

"Hell, I was just getting started."

Shane looked Eggers over. They hadn't been close, but they had shared some entry-level classes during the first couple of semesters. They had also been in the same dorm, a few doors away from each other. Eggers was wearing a very expensive Rolex watch, from the looks of it. Shane knew little about them, but the thing was gold and had diamonds encrusted around the large dial.

"I guess life's treating you pretty well," Shane said, nodding his head at the watch.

Eggers grinned. "It ain't too shabby." His clothes were at odds with the watch, simple black jeans and a black t-shirt. "I hear you're working your tail off these days."

"I had been until the hospital started laying off a bunch of us." It had snuck up on him, caught him with barely a day's notice, and Shane's hours as an ambulance driver cut to three days a week. His other part-time job, cleaning the dojo, didn't pay squat, but he could train for free. "What have you got in mind?"

Eggers stared at him, and Shane felt like he was being assessed. "I'm looking for someone who is interested in making good, quick money and doesn't ask too many bullshit questions."

The barmaid came back with the drinks. She slid the shots and chili cheese fries into the space between the two men, her pink tongue moistening her lips before she asked, "You want me to start a tab for you?"

Eggers shoved another hundred-dollar bill out of his pocket and slid it towards her. "Sure, sweetheart, keep those Jägers coming whenever you see us go dry. All right?"

"You got it!" She chirped and slipped the bill into her cleavage. Dave grinned at her, his eyes on her ass as she sashayed away.

"Why have I not visited this bar before?" he mused as he tossed down a shot and grabbed at the fries. "There are some hot ones here!" He grunted in appreciation over the fries and shoved them closer to Shane.

"I need a little more info." Shane said, and Eggers nodded at him, his mouth full of fries. "Weapons?"

"No." Eggers said, "No weapons."

"Anyone gonna get hurt?"

"Nope."

"Why me?"

"I owe you one."

Shane drained one shot, stared at the man across from him, and shook his head. "No, you don't."

"You took the fall for that bullshit in Compton." Eggers drained his glass and then snapped his fingers at the barmaid standing two tables away. "How would you like $10k for a night's work?"

He laughed at Shane's expression, and the barmaid walked over and leaned in close. "Ready for another round, Hon?"

Eggers grinned at her, reaching out to run his hand down her leg. "Another four, and one for you."

She smiled coyly, cast a glance at a rotund man in the far corner who wore a perpetual glare on his face. "Can't, darlin', Nick'd can me for sure. No drinking on the job." She turned her body at an angle that Nick couldn't see and rested her hand on his sleeve. "But I'm off in thirty minutes, forty-five tops. Wanna party?" She invited both men with a sensual bat of eyelashes. Rather, it would have been sensual if Shane were into skinny chicks who obviously enjoyed a hefty dose of nose candy with their party.

Shane tried to hide his revulsion by stuffing his face with the last of the chili cheese fries. He studied the framed photos on the wall, avoiding eye contact. Her smile slipped for a minute, before re-focusing on Eggers.

Eggers grinned lasciviously at her. "Yeah, I'm up for a party, sweetheart," he pulled her halfway onto his lap and shoving another hundred-dollar bill into her cleavage. "But go get us those drinks. I gotta talk business with my home boy here." He smacked her ass as he helped her stand up.

"Whatever you say, darlin'." She sashayed away, casting a quick glance over at Nick. The fat man continued to glare in their direction. If it were possible for the man to glower more, Shane didn't know how.

He studied Eggers, who had leaned back to watch the barmaid's every move, practically licking his lips. Shane knew whatever the other man was into, it was illegal as hell. That didn't bother him. No matter how hard he worked, he never got ahead. Men like Eggers did, though. Fancy watches, cash, and a stash of coke back at his pad, without a doubt. Was it drug running? Debt enforcement? Or just plain old B&E? He was betting it was the latter.

"So you in?"

"Not until I know what I'm getting into."

Eggers barked out a laugh and downed another shot of Yager, licking his lips as he did. "You always were the careful one. That's what I like about you, Ellis."

"So, you gonna tell me what it is, or should I throw out guesses?"

"B and E, straight up, no danger."

Shane raised his eyebrows, a set look on his face. "No danger" was bullshit.

"Seriously, man, the places are always empty. It's part of the deal. Rich bitches on vacation in Europe. Or they're off to the South Pacific to work on their tans while we get nothing but rain and mud. Maybe a rich old coot going for treatments down in Central America so he can use his dick again. That kind of thing. In, out, no worries about the security alarms and no one to show up unexpectedly." He grinned like a cat. "I've been doing it for six months now. Another handful and I'll move to a whole new area, no muss, no fuss, and sure as shit, no trace of me. Hell, I wonder if they even notice I have robbed them."

"You work for some kind of alarm company? What's your way in that doesn't leave any trace?"

Eggers grinned wider. Some of the chili was stuck in his teeth and Shane could see they were graying in areas, a classic indicator of meth. The man didn't look jacked up right now, though. Still, it raised Shane's hackles. He'd never been a fan of meth, or any of the other heavy stuff. He'd seen what it had done to plenty of his classmates, chewing them up and spitting them out, ghosts of their former selves.

"It's a corporate secret, man. You gotta sign a NSA to learn that shit."

Shane held back from telling Eggers it was an NDA, a non-disclosure agreement, not a non-whatever the hell Eggers thought the 's' was supposed to stand for.

"I'll think about it."

Eggers' expression soured. "Yeah? Well, don't think too long about it. This ain't a marriage proposal and there are other fish in the sea."

"Don't get your panties in a twist. When do you want to do this?"

"Next Saturday. That's when the house is empty. Rich asshole's going to some conference in D.C. and the staff have the weekend off thanks to it being Memorial Day on Monday. A quick in and out, we even got us a shopping list and the codes to the safe."

"And no one gets hurt and there aren't weapons, right?"

"Didn't I already say that?" Eggers grinned again, "C'mon Ellis, this is a walk in the park. Easy in, easy out."

"For 10k?"

"For 10k." Eggers downed another shot. "You keep asking questions, though, and I'm knocking down the price. God damn, you are a pain in the ass."

"Let me sleep on it. Call me tomorrow."

"Whatever, man." Eggers said as Shane scrawled his phone number on a napkin and handed it over.

Worse Choices

Shane jiggled his key in the lock twice before it turned stiffly. One of these days, the whole damned contraption would freeze up and the key would break off inside of it. It was only a matter of time. The hallway smelled of vomit again and he was feeling lightheaded, having held his breath from the top of the stairs to his door, third on the right. Cat was inside of the door, meowing indignantly.

"Sorry, Cat, got tied up." He reached down to scratch the feline's ears, but Cat marched past him, his tail swishing, and promptly disappeared down the stairs. Apparently, Cat wasn't any more interested in breathing in air tinged with vomit, either. Shane watched him go, nearly gagging as he breathed in one last breath there in the hallway and firmly shut his door behind him. The Jäger rolled in his stomach.

He stood there for a minute and then growled in frustration. "Goddamn Kenny." Back out the door, trying desperately to breathe through his mouth as he marched to the door at the end of the hall. It was mostly closed, but not latched, and he walked inside. The stench hit him, and no amount of breathing through his mouth helped. The form on the floor looked like a mass of tattered bags with legs.

"Fuck, Kenny," Shane said, his stomach rolling now as he tried not to add to the mess on the floor, "lie on your side."

There was no response. He reached down and grabbed what he hoped was a shoulder and shook it hard. The figure moaned a little. "C'mon man. On your side, before you choke to death."

The bag with legs slowly contracted, bent, and groaned its way into laying on one side and gave a limp-fingered okay sign. At least, the fingers *tried* to curl in that direction. Kenny was too far gone to form words, and

Shane found a ratty couch cushion nearby. He wedged it behind Kenny so that he wouldn't roll onto his back and then backed away. Kenny's breaths were deep, lost in a heroin-induced dreamland.

A large cockroach skittered away as he tried to lock the door behind him. The lock was broken, and the mechanism twirled in place, a useless piece of metal set in a doorknob that rattled and slid inside of a too-large, ragged hole in a door that was warped and filthy. Shane cursed under his breath. He lived in a shithole.

He headed back to his apartment, catching a glance of Mrs. Langstroth. Despite the late hour, she was peering out the door from across the hallway from his apartment, her rheumy eyes suspicious. He nodded wearily, "Mrs. L."

Her face retracted, and the door banged shut, a parade of locks engaging one by one in quick succession. He sighed. Esther Langstroth had been heading down the road to dementia for longer than he had been in the building, but she still had her moments of clarity. This evening wasn't one of them. On clear nights, she knew who he was and foisted baked goods on him, insisting he needed fattening up. Over the past two years, those breads and cakes had become increasingly inedible. She would forget a key ingredient, add extra baking soda, or other foibles. In her worse moments, she had insisted he was a thief, a rapist, and part of the local gang, the Asian Boyz. He didn't have the heart to tell her he wasn't Chinese and, therefore, would be unwelcome in their ranks.

"Just making sure Kenny is all right, Mrs. L." He called to the locked door. She didn't answer, but he could hear her breathing through the thin, hollow-core door. He shook his head and returned to his apartment, smashing a cockroach that skittered in front of him with his shoe. "Die, fucker."

Mrs. Langstroth's shocked gasp was audible through the thin door.

"Sorry, ma'am, I wasn't talking to you. I was killing a cockroach." There was no response, not that he expected one. He opened the door to his apartment, cursing softly as he caught another cockroach heading towards his door, "Oh no, you don't." His boot slammed down again, grinding the body into the worn, filthy carpet. He shuddered slightly. Tiny insect or no, they creeped him out.

The apartment, now lit with a feeble, high efficiency, low-quality light, was stark and barren. A table with one chair, an armchair that had seen better days, and a futon in the corner. Near the one window, sitting on the floor in a saucer, were the mummified remains of what had been a poor excuse for a houseplant. The kitchenette in the far corner was neat and just as bare. Why he hadn't kept some of his mom's things, he couldn't really say. He had left most of it in the cramped apartment on the far side of town, too mentally worn out to bother getting any of it. And by the time he had answered her landlord's voicemails, it was all gone, off to landfill or donated or whatever they did in those situations. Shane was left with just two things in the wake of her passing - memories and debt.

He shook his head in frustration as he looked around the tiny room. He'd been such a fool, borrowing money to live on. And when he flunked out of school, surprise, surprise, they wanted their money back. No degree meant no extra money coming in. And no extra money meant no payments on the hefty student loan. After he went into default, there wasn't any chance of returning to college. Everything since then had just felt like an endless slide downhill.

Whatever Dave Eggers was up to, it was as illegal as fuck. And Eggers wasn't that bright, which meant it was a matter of time before he got caught.

Shane stripped off his boots and placed them neatly against the wall. His jeans were next, and he folded them and set them on top of the small dresser. The t-shirt landed in his laundry basket. He snapped off the light and lay in the dark, his mind spinning.

Ten thousand dollars would go a hell of a long way towards paying off the student loans and get him closer to moving out of this shitty hole in the wall. *Eggers is bad news though, and you know he is.*

The shots of Jäger were kicking in, and the room swam a little, a gentle spin that told him the booze had hit his cortex and was mucking up his reasoning skills. He reached for his cell phone. Part of him wanted to make the call and just tell Eggers to fuck off at the same time as he told him yes. Ten thousand dollars for one job. What the fuck were they trying to get into, then? *Who the fuck pays that much for a straight up B and E?* His mind spun down, tired after a long day and worked loose by the alcohol. As he lay there in the dark, his heartbeat slowing and sleep creeping up to meet him, a dream inserted itself.

As the clock ticked past midnight, his breathing evened. Shane slipped into a dream of an enormous house standing alone in the countryside with no other buildings in sight. Eggers by his side, carrying a machete, and Shane holding a shotgun. It unraveled, as most dreams do, into a chaotic jumble of unrealistic situations. By the end of the dream, he was carrying a massive pile of gold bricks in a sack on his back. All while arguing with Eggers about whether they should take the donkey they found locked in the safe with them.

Dojo Yo Mama

The bright rays of the sun warmed the room the next morning. It was his one day off, sort of, and Shane stretched and then winced at the throbbing pain in his skull. As he sat up, the Jäger sloshed about in his stomach rather alarmingly. That, and a full bladder, had him scrambling for the tiny bathroom in the corner. He groaned as he stood there, listing to one side, and pissed into the toilet.

I should have stuck to drinking beer.

He forced himself to eat breakfast. Four eggs, scrambled, and a slice of ham that looked like it was on its way out, a touch of green creeping through the fat on one side. He washed it all down with instant coffee, black, no sugar or cream.

Shane stared out of the filthy window at the street below. Kenny's mother was there, screaming at him. Shane had met her early last year, when she came around asking after Kenny. She looked nicely put together at that time. Still, there had been a small edge of desperation in her voice. Which could easily have been read as an honest concern for her son. Today, however, she looked like shit. Her hair was a tangled mass and the skin around both of her eyes looked bruised. She had lost weight. Before, she had been slim. Now she resembled a skeleton covered in skin.

Shane winced as he watched her slap her son's face, once, twice, hard. The crack of it was audible through the cheap glass window. Kenny looked raw, far more hungover from his opium-infused sleep than Shane was from his over-indulgence of Jäger. He considered going down there and trying to help, but as he mulled over what to say or do, Kenny handed her a small baggie and then skittered away like a beaten dog.

So it was like that, Shane thought, watching as she quickly stuffed the baggie into her pocket and wandered away in the opposite direction. *Junkie makes junkie.*

He felt like shit. Maybe he should skip today at the dojo. Master Pao would smell the booze, no matter how well he brushed his teeth, and then he would single him out for special training. The old man had a way of sussing out what a person had been up to, and making them re-think, and usually deeply regret, their shortsighted decisions. Shane's stomach gurgled sourly, working the food into the queue. It promised to make him pay later as the alcohol made its way through his body, poisoning everything it touched.

Master Pao's voice echoed in his head, "Your body is temple, you no poison it with alcohol and the drugs any more than with unhealthy foods."

The old man had been here long enough to watch the area where he lived and worked become filled with gangs and high unemployment. First, the Asian Boyz had taken most of Long Beach over. Their graffiti was only the beginning. They intimidated most of the business owners in the small strip mall where Master Pao's dojo had been located for the last fifteen years.

Master Pao, however, had remained free of their influence. The arrangement, while simple, had required violence. One old man against a handful of upstart young men, had ended quicker than it had started, with broken bones and two concussions, one unharmed, elderly dojo master, and a compromise. Ever since, Master Pao tolerated several of the Asian Boyz members within his dojo. He charged them twice as much for the classes. Some kids in the neighborhood got sponsored, and the dojo stayed free of illegal activities.. The three Prak brothers, all high-ranking among the gang, were all regulars at the dojo now.

Shane had found Master Pao's dojo just a few months after the situation came to blows. The uneasy truce had slowly warmed into a solid understanding between those who might have been natural enemies. Three days a week, he would stand next to the Prak brothers and practice the moves Master Pao taught without rancor or incident. The dojo, and anything within two hundred feet of it, was sacrosanct. Go more than that in any direction, and Shane knew better than to tangle with the Prak brothers. He kept his head down and maintained a cordial distance.

Shane walked over to where he kept his boots and one other pair of shoes, the soft-soled dojo shoes that Master Pao had insisted were required for all the students. The old man had intentionally misread the price, selling them to Shane for half of the cost. The old man had a sixth sense about these things. He could sense desperation. It was also why he had told Shane he needed him to clean the dojo each week.

"I give you class at half price. You clean every Saturday afternoon once class done." Pao had told him. Shane hadn't asked for a discount or a special deal, Pao had somehow just known. Each week, he wiped everything down, cleaned the bathrooms, ran a vacuum, took out the trash, and mopped the floor. He had progressed significantly in the past year. Where he used to get his ass handed to him by Pao, the Prak brothers, and even one of the Prak sisters, he could now hold his own against everyone except for Pao.

Hangover or not, Pao would expect him to clean up, so he needed to be there, anyway. His head thumped, and he dry-swallowed two aspirin, grabbed the soft-soled shoes and headed for the door.

It was easier to walk the four blocks than try to get his ancient Datsun to start up. Besides, the walk would help clear his head and get the toxins working through and out of his body faster. And it might appease Master Pao, who had a sixth sense about such things and would be full of disapproval.

He passed the five and dime. It had shut down last winter when the owners couldn't keep up with the extortion money. They folded, fleeing back to their extended family in Mexico rather than live to pay the Asian Boyz. Next to it, a hair salon that specialized in weaves and hair extensions was just opening their doors. The woman who ran it had a nice back door business that provided Kenny and plenty of others with their daily dose of heroin. She smiled at Shane as he walked by, and he nodded politely in return.

Pao sniffed in disapproval within seconds of Shane's arrival. "You smell of cheap alcohol and cigarettes." The old man said, frowning, "You stink up the dojo."

"My apologies, Master Pao," Shane said and bowed, his headache surging as the blood rushed to his head. He suppressed a groan.

The old man glared at him. "Better to apologize to self than Master Pao," and with that, he sniffed again and turned away.

The front door opened to admit Dara Prak, the one Prak sister that attended the dojo. The oldest Prak brother, Sarith, boasted that he had seven sisters. But only one was tough enough for Master Pao's dojo.

The corners of Dara's mouth twitched as she took in Master Pao's sour expression along with a whiff of the stench of Jäger still rolling off of Shane. She slipped off her street shoes and leaned close to Shane as she slipped on her soft dojo shoes. "Old Pao looks pissed. You reek, by the way."

"Yeah, thanks."

"He's gonna make me spar with you, 'cause Sarith would kick your ass right now. But I'm gonna kick it too, just so you know."

It had been a while since Dara had handed Shane his ass while sparring, but as shitty as he felt at the moment, he knew she was speaking the truth.

"Yeah? Just remember it's 'cause I've got a hangover. That's the only reason you have a chance."

She gave a small growl, then laughed. "I'm gonna enjoy kicking your ass today, Ellis."

"Bring it. I'll believe it when I see it."

Two hours later, as he limped down the length of the dojo, his head pounding and his ribs aching, Shane regretted ever meeting Dara Prak. He especially regretted the verbal sparring. This had directly led to the double roundhouse kick she had unleashed on him halfway through class. That was followed by a jump punch in the middle of his chest, which laid him out flat. Worse had been opening his eyes and seeing Dara standing over him, smirking, as she extended a hand to help him up.

Master Pao had taken a turn as well, and by the time class had ended, the mantra "I will not drink Jäger the night before class ever again," was firmly cemented in his brain. He had been an idiot.

He dragged the cleaning supplies out of the closet. Dara called over her shoulder, "See you Tuesday, Ellis."

"Bite me, Prak."

"Careful what you say, Ellis, she might just take you up on that." Sarith Prak laughed as he sauntered out of the front door.

Shane's stomach gurgled, threatening to revolt at the smell of the Pine Sol that Master Pao had him add to the mop bucket. He groaned quietly, but Master Pao heard it. "You better no throw up in my dojo."

"I won't. I won't. By the way, we need more paper towels."

He finished cleaning the bathroom, then swept and mopped. By the end, his headache had begun a slow retreat and his stomach grumbled loudly. Shane called out to Master Pao, "I'm all done, Master Pao, don't forget to get more paper towels. We're down to the last roll." The old man waved his hand at him dismissively and headed for his office in the back of the building without another word.

Shane winced, and then his stomach gave another growl.

I'll make it up to him next week.

The sun was blinding as he stepped outside of the dojo. He squinted, which made his head pound worse, and saw Dara leaning against the far corner of the building, smirking.

"I thought you left." He mumbled.

"I got nothing better to do." She shrugged. The dragon tattoo writhed on her shoulder in response. "Besides, you look like you could do with some hair of the dog." She cocked her head, "C'mon, I'll buy you a drink."

"I'd rather have a burger."

"What you need is my cousin's pho, fix you right up." She slid her arm around his. "It's the best pho around."

Her long hair tickled his arm, and he glanced around to see if he saw Sarith anywhere. He wasn't about to fuck with the head of the Asian Boyz gang, and that included Sarith's sister. She might be a bad ass in her own right, but Sarith might flat out murder him if he tapped that. "I dunno."

Dara laughed, "Sarith's gone. He had to head up north, to S.F., to deal with a... situation. He won't be back until Monday. So, come on, white boy, you're safe."

After considering the sad state of his refrigerator, and calculating the last time he had gotten laid, he went with her. An hour later, after filling his belly with the pho, which was the best he had ever tasted, his stomach had settled and his headache abated. To his surprise, he somehow walked back to his apartment with a bottle of Jack Daniels and Dara walking close by his side.

"I can't have you at my place," Dara said, running a sharp fingernail down his spine, "My sister would tell Sarith, and I'm pretty sure he'd try to kill you."

Shane's steps slowed. "You aren't giving me good vibes about this, you know."

Dara grinned lasciviously and stepped closer, her hands busy. "Believe me, you'll like it. A lot." She stood up on her toes, put her lips next to his ear, "I promise." She smelled of something exotic and unidentifiable and he couldn't help the all-body shiver he had in response. "Sarith doesn't need to know. Let's go to your place."

Shane pictured her face when she saw his crappy apartment. He kept it as clean as he could, but there was no way to make the cracked plaster and worn carpet look anything but cheap. Dara must have sensed his reticence, because she doubled her efforts.

"C'mon Ellis, don't back out on me now," her breath washed over him, a scent of Thai basil and spice, "I haven't gotten laid in weeks."

She didn't freak out when she saw several cockroaches dead on the ratty carpeted landing, smashed flat and slightly ground into the carpet. He opened the door to his apartment, and she slid past him, glancing around. "You make the Spartans look, well, spartan."

He blinked. "You're familiar with Sparta?"

"Don't sound so surprised." She sniffed. "Coming here from Cambodia sucked, but I learned English faster than any of my brothers or sisters. I'm majoring in History at UCLA."

Shane opened the lone cabinet in his kitchenette and removed two glasses. As he opened the refrigerator to retrieve a bottle of Coca-Cola,

Dara sat down on the side of the bed. She didn't bat an eye as she flicked a cockroach off of the sheets and crushed it beneath her booted heel.

"Tell me about it." Shane asked, handing her a cup with Jack and Coke and sat down next to her.

Dara snorted, "Tell you about what, white boy? The Cambodian refugee experience? Shit. Better to ask Sarith. He was older. I was, I dunno, maybe four when we came over. I barely remember the camps." She took a swig of her drink, "Well, on second thought, better not." She grinned at Shane wickedly. "He'd prefer to forget that time. He got his ass kicked regularly in the camps."

"I'm not asking your brother shit," Shane answered, taking a healthy swig of his drink. "The way he looks at me, I swear he'd sooner kill me than have me in the same room."

"Yeah, that's probably my fault." Her nails drew lazy circles on the denim of his jeans. They were long, a glossy red-black, encrusted with jewels, "He heard me tell my sister Akara that I thought you were hot, and he's been a little pissy ever since."

Shane felt his libido rise in response to her nails on his leg. That same libido took a nosedive at the thought of Sarith and the power of the Asian Boyz gang behind him, coming after him with full force. "You aren't doing much to talk me into this, Dara."

"Ah, come on, Ellis. Play with fire. The thrill, that's the fun part." She moved closer, her exotic scent preceding her, warm and sensual. Her fingernails were crawling up his arm, towards his neck, toying with his ear.

Shane swallowed another gulp of his drink, and Dara slid into his lap, straddling him. Her dark brown eyes stared into his and her mouth turned up on the left. She looked amused. She licked her lips then, a slow, intentional slip of the tongue that promised a trip to heaven, or, just as likely, hell. His jeans tightened, and he felt his heartbeat increase.

Danger has its appeal.

Danger was what this was. Hell, stupidity even. A word from her to Sarith and he would be better leaving the neighborhood.

More like the city, hell, the entire state.

He could already feel the whiskey working its way from his stomach into his body, worming its way to the decision-making centers of his brain.

Playing with fire here.

Dara was hot, smoking hot. Her body wasn't just shapely. It was toned. Athletic. She spent hours at the dojo, and he suspected she trained elsewhere besides the six hours a week she was at Pao's dojo. She dressed in a crop top that teasingly revealed a glimpse of a dragon curling around her side.

She smiled, and it was predatory. She knew what she wanted and was determined to get it. Shane leaned back against the wall and watched her slowly take her top off, a thin, spaghetti strap, black cotton bra underneath covering her tiny breasts. With a quick motion, the bra was gone, too. She pointed at her left breast. "You can start by putting your mouth here."

Shane obliged, his tongue tasting her flesh, his teeth tugging gently on her nipple. It tasted sweet to his questing tongue. Her hands were busy pulling at his jeans. He switched to the other breast. She stretched and swayed from side to side gently, one hand holding the back of his head, the other reaching down to free his cock from its confines.

Dara sighed with pleasure. She tightened her grasp, wrapping her long, slender fingers into the fine hairs at the nape of his neck. It forced his head back as she thrust her tongue into his mouth, swirling, nibbling with her sharp white teeth on the corner of his bottom lip. He could taste the sweet, heavy taste of the Jack and Coke on her tongue. Her other hand continued to stroke him. It felt a bit like heaven and hell as she ran her sharp nails up and down his shaft. Pleasure and pain curled together, became one.

He found his hands exploring her lithe body. He started at her slip hips, moved one hand up to thread his fingers through her dark hair. It was long and loose, cascading down her back and past the small of her back. He reached up into it, grabbed a handful of her hair, and pulled her head back. Breaking his mouth away from hers, he moved slowly, sensually down her neck. She gasped, and he tugged on her skin-tight pants which his free hand, one slipping into her crotch to run a finger along her sensitive nub. Dara moaned, arching her back in response.

A swift twist of her body, and Shane found himself on his back. Dara stood long enough to slide her pants off, a sliver of a red lace thong disappearing between her firm, tight ass. Before he could sit up, she had straddled him again, her nails scraping his ribs as she slipped his t-shirt off of his body. He eased his jeans down and his cock stood erect, hard, thrumming with desire. She licked the tips of her fingers and reached down to slip him inside of her, easing her tight, hot pussy onto his dick. She was tiny compared to some women he had been with, petite, but hard, her muscles tight.

He closed his eyes, the roll of desire coursing through him, felt her moving her hips, quick decisive thrusts that sent him deep inside of her. So deep, he could feel the tip of his penis slam into her cervix, a wall of muscle he could not penetrate. She lifted her hips away, then back again, and a piece of plaster from the cracked wall rained down, sprinkling them both with dust.

"Sorry about that."

She didn't pause, her hips continuing to thrust against him, pulling him into her hot wetness. "I've seen shittier places than this. Lived in 'em too." Her hands reached out and grabbed one of his nipples, twisting it in her sharp talons, "Look at me."

He yelped and opened his eyes, stared into Dara's black, dilated pupils. He could see a faint sheen of sweat on her skin as she continued to rotate her hips, slowly speeding up. She licked her fingers before she reached down and fingered her clit. "I'm close. Watch me come." A wicked smile formed on her lips. "And if you're good, I'll even let you join me."

There was no stopping this tide. He could feel the edges of it pull back, like the foam that retreats from the sandy beach just before the next wave crashes down over the rocks. As the wave rose, Shane's body rose with it. He broke and exploded inside Dara as she threw her head back and rode it with him.

Shane leaned back against the cracked plaster. His toes curled, his nerve endings filled with endorphins, sparking, twisting. He reveled in the delicious feel of the release and felt his breathing slow. Dara leaned back on her elbows. Her tawny skin shone with sweat. Her eyes were closed, a satisfied grin on her face.

She opened one eye. "Not bad, Ellis. You've got potential."

"Yeah, you too."

She cackled and slipped off of him. Her agile legs bent in an impossible position before she stood and walked into the bathroom, dressed only in a thong and high heels. Shane felt his dick harden again. Dara was smoking hot. She grabbed a towel from the rack and cleaned herself, tossed it to the floor, and slowly swayed back out into the main room. He could see that dragon wrapped around her body, its mouth opening around one nipple. She walked with confidence, no mincing about, no shyness. Not that he expected anything less, Dara was no fainting lily. She knew what she wanted and went after it. He stared down at his dick, which still stood at attention, and knew he was living proof of that.

Not that I didn't enjoy the hell out of that, but...

She bent over and slipped on her bra and crop top before wiggling back into her skin-tight pants. His dick was finally getting a clue that no more action was coming its way and Shane pulled up his pants, zipped his fly, and shifted. Between the workout at the dojo and the workout he had just had, combined with the fantastic pho in his belly, Shane felt relaxed, drained even. The endorphins had left him loose-limbed and somnolent.

Dara set one talon on his left nipple, drawing a circle around it. It left the skin red in a thin line. She smiled, slowly, with teeth, "I had fun. Let's do that again sometime."

Shane didn't answer, and she picked up the half-empty bottle of whiskey, uncapped it, and took a swig. "I think I'll keep this."

He laughed, "Go ahead. But remember what Master Pao says, 'Your body is a temple.'"

She laughed, took another swig and capped it and headed towards the door. "Damn straight, and the god this temple worships demands a sacrifice of spirits. I'll be seeing you, Ellis." She closed the door behind her and Shane bolted it after he heard her walk down the stairs and out the main entrance.

He stumbled as he walked back to the bed. Damn, but he was tired. Shane sprawled out on the bed, bouncing a little on the cheap mattress. His eyes slipped closed.

The House

Shane stood over the small table, which was nestled up to the window. How he had gotten there was as much a mystery until his cell phone rang again.

Dara was here and then I lay down and...

The phone rang again, and he picked it up. "Yeah?"

"Ellis, you sound like shit." Dave Eggers' voice crackled over the phone. It was overly loud to Shane's still half-asleep brain.

"Huh? No, I'm fine."

"So, you up for this job or not?"

The job. What job? Oh wait, that job.

His brain spun, struggling to wake up, to think. "I uh..."

"Jesus, Ellis, I'm not proposing marriage," Eggers sounded exasperated. "I'm offering you ten g's for a couple of hours out of your day. Are you interested or not?"

Shane thought of what ten thousand dollars could do, how much he could pay off with that money. It would take over two years for him to pay off that much debt at his current rate. Two years' worth of scrimping and saving and paying the sky-high interest rates for an hour or two of highly illegal activity.

As long as this doesn't go south, it's a straightforward decision.

"Yeah, yeah, I'll do it."

He could practically see Eggers grin over the phone. "Excellent! I'll pick you up next Thursday, around nine p.m."

"That'll work." He gave Eggers his address and hung up, still foggy with sleep. The sun was getting low in the sky, the rich colors of the sunset were emerging.

Screwing Dara, agreeing to doing a job with Eggers. I'm not just playing with fire, I'm playing Russian roulette.

The Thursday job was on Shane's mind often over the next five days. A handful of times, he had reached for his phone, ready to call Eggers and tell him to find someone else. But ten thousand dollars was a lot of money. A lot of money. Before he knew it, it was Thursday evening and Eggers pulled up to the curb in front of Shane's apartment building and honked. It was a black, sleek Ford Mustang, and Eggers revved the engine as Shane approached.

"What do ya think of my new wheels?" he called, his voice nearly inaudible above the roar of the engine. "Got an advance on tonight's job and figured it was time to get myself something nice. Besides, that barmaid Gina tossed her cookies right after I busted a nut in her. Goddamn disgusting, I got it detailed, and they used an entire can of deodorizing spray in it and it still smells like chili cheese fries and Jäger with a side of vomit."

Shane winced. "Ah, man, that sucks. But your wheels look sweet, so I guess it's a win, right?"

"Bitch did me a favor." Eggers chortled, leaned over and punched Shane in the shoulder. "Glad to have you with me on this one, man. Mark my words, it's gonna be a breeze! Easiest money you'll ever make." He slammed on the brakes at the intersection to avoid hitting a man dressed in rags and pushing a shopping cart. He threw up his hands as the man glared at him. The revving engine drowned any words or epithets he might have directed towards the two men in the car.

The old man, homeless by the look of it, took his time to cross. By the end, Eggers had inched the car forward to the edge of the crosswalk. The old man spat on the car and was off the street and onto the curb before Eggers could do more than give him the bird. He hit the accelerator and Shane it pushed into the bucket seat.

"Goddamn, just shoot me if I ever end up all decrepit and slow like that old fuck." Eggers snapped, tense. Shane felt a surge of foreboding. Eggers was on edge, more than normal. Was it blow? Meth? Whatever it was, it had him amped up.

This could go south real quick.

As they merged with traffic on Highway 110, Eggers drove aggressively, darting in and out of traffic, ignoring the car horns and shouting at the other drivers. He took an exit, moving onto Highway 10, heading west towards the beach.

"Where are we going?" Shane asked as Eggers cut off a semi and the driver lit up the inside of the Mustang with his high beams.

Eggers, distracted by the semi, hung out of the window to make sure the driver had a clear view of his middle finger. "Fuck you, asshole!" The car swerved, setting off other drivers and their horns. He turned to Shane, "What?"

"Where we are heading?" Shane asked again.

"Bel-Air, baby!" Eggers grinned. "Old money and a rich asshole who is out of town."

"So what are you after?" Second thoughts were invading Shane, setting his stomach on end with dread. Why had he agreed to this in the first place? How was Eggers so sure that the owner would be out of town and what if he wasn't?

Eggers gave him a sideways glance. "Don't you worry about it, man. This is easy money. I got the codes to get in, and confirmation of the guy's flight info. He's gone for three days. I'll be in and out in less than ten minutes. I just need you to keep a lookout, make sure no one drives by or nothing, and stay in the car. It'll be a breeze."

"No dogs? No staff?" Shane persisted, images of sharp-nosed Dobermans surrounding them showing their sharp canines.

"Nah, man. No dogs." Eggers laughed then, "Man, you shoulda seen me on this job two weeks ago. Two of those Doberman fuckers came at me. I kicked one in the head and had to bail into the car quick. I got out of there, but not before one of 'em took a chunk out of me." He raised his shirtsleeve and showed a healing scab on his right arm. "Still fuckin' hurts."

Traffic grew sparse as they turned onto Highway 405 and headed north into the hills. The homes they passed became fewer and farther between, but also increased in size. Tall walls, heavy gates, and shrubbery that hid the buildings became more commonplace. Shane saw tiny gatehouses appear, usually manned by security guards.

They turned off of 405, now moving along a winding, dimly lit road. Shane could see that the night sky, brightly lit by a full moon just moments before, had become overcast and dark to the west, the clouds moving fast. Soon they would completely blot out the light of the moon.

They slowed, taking another turn, and Shane was relieved that Eggers had slowed down and appeared more calm.

Definitely blow. I just hope he's going to be sane coming down from it.

Eggers had always partied harder than everyone else. It was no surprise he was still in that world. The car slowed, turned onto yet another dimly lit road and the sky darkened as the clouds blanketed the last of the sky, obscuring the moon's bright light. The wind had kicked up a notch and the trees overhead swayed and danced, their leaves fluttering. Shane had his window cracked and he could smell the rain approaching. A curl of lightning flickered through the clouds, promising a rare experience, a lightning storm in California of all places. Again, he felt a surge of anxiety rush through him. A storm, this job. It was no good. It felt as if fate was knocking on his door, and he wasn't listening.

The road forked, and they took the one to the left. A thick canopy of trees rose above the road, the right side a rocky cliff that extended up into the inky darkness, the left a chasm, a jumble of trees and scrub. It was remote and isolated, the perfect place for those who had money and wanted a solitary existence far from the melee of the city. One that was also a short drive back to civilization. The car slowed and Shane could see they were approaching the beginning of a private drive. Beyond it, a pair of heavy metal gates set in a stone fence which extended out of sight on either side.

"This is it," Eggers was keyed up. His fingers tapped out a quick rhythm on the steering wheel in excitement. He dug in his pocket, pulled a small card out, and slowly typed the numeric code into the keypad. The rain reached them then, a slow pitter-pat quickly increasing into a heavy downpour. Lightning flashed again, and Shane could hear the thunder grumble high above in the sky. The metal gate swung open, emitting a metallic groan. "Yes!" Eggers hissed and rolled up his window, fumbling for the window wipers as he sped through the gate and further along the private drive.

It was dark, a level of darkness that Shane rarely saw in the city. The flashes of light occasionally illuminated the sky. In the distance, the drive opened up, and they could see a large house, all the windows dark, obviously devoid of life. The rain resumed in a solid, relentless downpour. It obscured everything past the landscaping lights set low on the paths and the bulb that lit the front entry in a dim wash of yellow.

"Damn, the storm just couldn't have waited another hour, could it?" Eggers muttered and stared at the water washing down the windshield faster than the wipers. They rolled to a stop, the headlights illuminating the door. Shane peered through the gloom, looking for cameras but finding nothing.

That doesn't mean they aren't there, just that I don't see them.

"Right, well, shit. Wanna come in with me then?" Eggers reached between the seats and grabbed a small bag.

Shane fought down the wave of unease. This was a bad idea. He knew it was. But here he was, and the sooner they got in, the sooner they got out. Maybe it would be better to just go in with Eggers, monitor him, and then get the hell out of here.

One thing is for sure. I'm doing this one job and then I'm done. Hard work beats B&E any fucking day. You don't end up in jail for working two jobs. Breaking and entering is a completely different story.

"Yeah, sure." The anxiety was taking his dinner and tossing it around his stomach like a rollercoaster. The minute he stepped out of this car and into that house, he was in it. He swallowed down the indecision.

Ten grand takes my debt down by two years of busting my ass.

They opened their doors simultaneously and ran for the front door through the downpour. There was a wide overhang, which reduced it from a soaking shower to a fine spray, thanks to the wind. Shane huddled there, holding a flashlight that Eggers handed to him, and watched his friend pick the lock.

"You've picked up some skills, I see." The door swung open and Eggers grinned.

"You've got no idea what you can learn during a four month stretch at Lompoc." The door was wide, an enormous slab of carved wood. The lightning flashed and Shane could see a small village cut into the rich wood, with tall grass surrounding it.

An hour later, miles away...

Shane parked down the street from his apartment building, pulled off his shirt, and used it to run over any parts of the car he had touched. First the passenger seat and armrest, along with the wheel and all the handles. His breathing had evened, calmed, but he had little time. Hell, he'd hit Eggers hard and knocked him out, but he'd be awake by now and the rich dude, Benton, he would have called the police.

It was dark, and the rain still fell heavily. This meant there were fewer people out, something Shane was thankful for. It was windy, wet, and miserable. Still, Shane might have minutes before the cops came knocking. Time to get anything he wanted to keep and get the hell out of Dodge.

Where the hell am I going to go?

His mind spun, and he was far too busy looking for the bright police lights to notice the outer door of the apartment building was ajar and the hall light was out. A rushing sound and he had milliseconds to react in order to avoid the swift attack that came out of the darkness. He moved instinctively rather than with purpose. He was temporarily blinded anyway by the transition from the lighted street to the dark apartment building. But he felt rather than saw Sarith Prak coming towards him. Despite his quick reaction, the impact of Sarith's kick carried past Shane and slammed into the far wall with a tremendous crash. He could hear the other residents of the building shout in alarm. Upstairs, a light turned on, giving him a better view of Sarith leaping towards him again, murder in his dark eyes.

Great, someone's going to call the cops any second now.

The cops would take their time.

You could call in that someone was being murdered and it would be a solid twenty minutes before anyone arrived.

As he dodged another kick from Sarith, Shane thought about his luck so far.

Then again, I might have two minutes tops to get the hell out of here.

He took a deep breath and then lunged at Sarith, clocking him hard behind the ear. Sarith paused, then dropped like a stone.

Holy shit, that worked?!

He ran upstairs, taking the steps two at a time, and didn't bother to unlock the door. A solid shoulder thrust to it and the thin, cheap frame gave way with a crunch of wood. He scanned the room, grabbed a backpack and shoved a change of clothes in it, and slipped a photo of his mom out of its frame and into his pocket. He shoved his folder of documents, and the book a pretty librarian had given him years ago, into the backpack, and slung it over his shoulder. Outside, he could hear the police sirens approaching.

No time, no time.

He ran out in the hall, down to the back of the building and hit the emergency back door at a run, popping it open with his shoulder. There was a small landing outside of the door and then a metal ladder that descended to street level in the dark alley behind the building. Shane slipped on the wet rungs twice. Each time, he caught himself with a jerk on his already aching right arm and shoulder. He was relieved when his feet finally found the ground. Two police cars screeched to a halt in front of the apartment building. Shane ran through the tall grass, exiting out of the broken section of fence in the far corner before they could see him.

Shane could hear the officers shouting at Sarith, who had apparently been making his way back out of the front of the building. He was profoundly relieved their attention was fully on the gangbanger and not on him. It was too dangerous to drive away in Eggers' car. The car was maybe fifty feet away, but he needed to put space between the car, him, and Eggers. It wasn't safe to use it. He ran down the length of the alley, then intentionally slowed his pace to a ground-eating stride and turned away from where the officers had come from. It was too hot for him to get in his car either, especially with it parked in front of the apartment building.

Gotta get out of here. Greyhound station.

The rain soaked him as he headed for the nearest bus stop.

Digging

The police hadn't asked too many questions. And Jack hadn't offered any more details past pointing to the man unconscious on the floor. They hauled off the man, a Dave Eggers, according to the I.D. in his wallet, in handcuffs. The other man, his accomplice, had broken his nose, judging from the amount of blood on his shirt and Jack's marble floor, and his eyes were unfocused.

His partner hadn't held back.

Jack left the gun where it was. It had skittered across the floor as the two men fought. The second man, his partner in crime, had fought with precision and skill, obviously trained in martial arts.

He's familiar with Bokator if I don't miss my guess.

"Mr. Benton, do you need for us to call the paramedics to look at that head wound?" the police officer asked him as he closed his notebook and dug for a business card.

Jack reached up and wiped the blood that had gathered there. The wound was seeping and clotting. He was fine.

"I'm fine. I'll have my physician look at it later."

The officer raised an eyebrow. "After midnight?"

Jack smiled and shrugged. "He's on call."

"Must be nice," the officer muttered as he nodded to his partner. His partner had just finished placing the revolver from the floor in an evidence bag.

"Well, Mr. Benton, we will be in touch."

"Thank you, Officer."

As soon as the door closed, Jack turned on his heel and headed for his office. It was time to find out just who the second man was, and why he had turned on his partner.

After all, I owe my life to him.

Six hours later, his phone chimed, notifying him that the front gate was open. The sound jolted him from a light doze and he had forgotten about the wound on his forehead until Azule walked in the front door and gave a bloodcurdling shriek.

Jack winced, his head still hurt. He put up a hand as she dug into her enormous purse for a phone in a panic.

"I'm fine, really Az. It looks worse than it feels."

Azule paused, glared at him, "Have you called the doc yet?"

"No, but..."

"No, but nothing. We going, right now." She glanced again at his wound. "I'm gonna drive your car, though, Jack, I don't want you getting blood all over mine."

Jack held both his hands up. "Seriously, Az, I'm fine. A little headache, but nothing bad. I don't need to see a doctor."

"The hell you don't!" The woman puffed up her chest, "You are the best boss I ever had and I'll be damned if I'm gonna have to find some other boss after you die from a brain bleed. I got my aunt to care for, too. That's two people's on your conscience when you go into the great beyond!"

Jack stifled a laugh. *Trust Azule to make me getting hurt somehow about her.*

"The doc will be here in an hour or two, less if you do the honors. That's a quicker option than us driving there and waiting in the waiting room around sick people. Besides, I doubt we would survive you driving one of my sports cars."

Azule was bloody dangerous on the road. Barely a week went by when she didn't have another dent in her car, thanks to taking a corner too tight. She had come in last week hyperventilating after she had hit three squirrels and dented her fender on a tree, avoiding a fourth fluffy-tailed victim.

The woman harrumphed and, her mouth set in a firm line, marched to her office in the south wing, to make the call. A moment later, she reappeared. "He'll be here in twenty minutes," she said. "I told him there had been significant blood loss." She turned to go back to her office, stopped, and turned back around. "Weren't you supposed to be in D.C.? What are you doing here?"

"I got to the airport, learned the committee chairperson had canceled the meeting because of illness, and returned home."

"Uh huh, and how did you get that injury?"

"That was from the two men, well, one of them, who broke in here last night." He said it matter-of-factly, wincing again as Azule shrieked in response.

"What?!"

"Everything is fine, Az, I promise."

"Everything is *not* fine when bloodthirsty burglars are breaking in and trying to kill you!" Her eyes were bulging out of her head in alarm.

"Technically, I don't think they planned on killing me. I took them by surprise. They definitely did not expect me to be here."

"Well?"

"Well, what?" Jack asked, a hint of playful innocence in his voice, a smile creeping up at the edges.

She swatted at him. "Jack Benton, you tell me right now what happened last night. Or I swear I'm gonna go get my mama to come give you what for!"

He grinned at her, "I like your mother, Az. She's a fine woman."

Azule harrumphed again. Injury or not, Jack knew if he didn't tell her the entire story and stop teasing her, she would be in a snit for hours.

"Sit down, Az. You look like you are courting a coronary." When the woman didn't move, Jack sat down in one of the hall chairs. He sighed, rubbed his eyes. It wasn't as easy to stay up all night as it had been in his 20s. "Two men broke in at around 10:30 last night. I'm guessing they expected me to be out of town. And obviously, I was still here. One of them pulled a gun and the other guy disarmed him, kicked the shit out of him, knocked him out, and then took off."

Azule sat down muttering under her breath in a matching chair. "Fool white man, no security service. Lucky didn't get iced, and then where would I be? Out of luck, I'll tell you, all 'cause some rich folk got no common sense." The moss-green velvet armchair that creaked out a minor complaint.

He smiled at her. "Azule, I'm fine. And if it helps you to know, I've already planned for you in my will."

The woman glared at him, "As if money was the only thing that kept me coming back here." She shook her head. "Coulda been killed."

He shook his head, then winced. Moving it hurt, and if he were to admit it, he was glad she had called the doctor. It was turning into one hell of a headache.

"I need you to do some digging, Az, and find out who the second man was."

Her eyes lit up. "You gonna find the little shit, boss? Make him pay?" Azule was smarter than he was, but oh, how she loved her movies. And this little break-in fed her love of drama like a morphine drip.

"Something like that. Will you see what you can find out?" Giving Azule a pet project would keep her occupied, which meant less fussing over him.

The simpler tasks often bored Azule. She enjoyed the challenge of research, and her face lit up at his request. "I'll see what I can find out."

The gate alarm sounded and Jack pressed the button to let the doctor in. A few minutes later, Doc Diamond, the concierge physician that Jack kept on retainer, examined his head wound and checked his pupils.

"You have a slight concussion."

"I knew it!" Azule crowed, triumphant.

Jack sighed and sat still as he cleaned and disinfected the minor wound on his forehead. "Take it easy for a couple of days and let me know if your headache lasts longer than a day. Other than that, plenty of fluids, rest, and call if you have questions."

Azule continued to hover after the doctor left. She followed Jack as he walked from the entry towards the grand staircase, which led to the bedroom suites upstairs. "You know, Az, there is also the question of how the men knew I was going to be gone." He looked behind him and her steps had slowed. "While you are running down those two guys, will you also see if you can figure out how they might have known?"

He looked again and Azule had stopped midway up the stairs, her face perturbed. Azule wasn't the type to hide her emotions. Jack could see them clearly on her face as she mentally paged through her interactions over the past few days and possibly weeks. He was careful about that sort of thing, and he hadn't been at any recent social engagements, so no one should have known. Someone, though, somewhere, had said enough to the wrong person and his itinerary leaked. Setting Azule to work on that problem, especially since it pertained to someone she had potentially spoken to, was like setting a bloodhound to work.

Az is loyal, rabidly so, and she'll find the leak, guaranteed.

He finished climbing the stairs and watched her disappear into her office.

Excellent. I'll take two Tylenol, have a quick nap, and I'll bet there will be answers when I wake up.

By the time he woke up two hours later, the afternoon sun was pouring through the window. The warmth of it was like a drug, and he came awake slowly, fighting to wake up. His headache had eased, but every limb felt limp. The warmth of the sun had turned his arms to the consistency of noodles. Far from his sun-drenched room, he could hear Azule's voice. She didn't sound happy, not at all. Jack rolled out of bed, his left knee creaking, popping.

Damned knee, I'm too young for this.

It popped again with the first step he took, thankfully that seemed to straighten it out and the aching pain disappeared, at least for the time being. He had gone skiing in Vail last year, and each evening when he returned from the slopes it would have swollen so much he had difficulty removing his snow gear.

Charming Latia had helped with that, and other things.

He smiled at the memory as he headed downstairs and out to the small clubhouse beyond that, where his and Azule's offices were. Azule's voice barked in anger the closer he came to her office. Jack walked past it, and on into his. He hadn't eaten since last night and his stomach was registering its protests, despite his determination to get some work done before the weekend.

At least my headache is gone.

He rummaged through the mini-fridge and found leftover dolma, along with some pita bread, hummus and baba ghanoush. He set them on the counter and reached for a plate. Azule's voice raised, then quieted, and he waited for her to finish the call and seek him out. He reached into the pantry to open a container of Castelvetrano olives, their skins an almost neon green. He added a handful to the plate. Azule's distinctive stomp of anger encouraged him to reach for another plate, adding a large helping of baba ghanoush to it, and a small stack of pita bread. He pushed the plate towards her and smiled.

She was angry, her brown eyes snapping, her breathing coming in fast, angry huffs. Azule stared at the plate in confusion, then shook her head, grabbed a triangle of pita bread and dragged it through the baba ghanouj before shoving it in her mouth. Jack watched as she repeated it, clearing the plate of the food in hurried bites.

"Would you like some more?" He asked when the plate was clear.

"No," she snapped in return and reached for the leftovers, attacking the containers as if they had wronged her in some inexplicable way. She devoured another mountain of pita bread and baba ghanoush, then turned her attention to the olives. Jack suppressed a smile. He wondered if she even realized she used food to mediate her moods.

Jack waited. Azule would tell him what she had learned in her own time. As it was, he knew better than to step between her and food when her eyes were pinwheeling with anger. He almost felt sorry for whoever had screwed up and pissed her off so badly. After she scraped the second plate clean, the woman heaved an enormous sigh and stared at him critically, assessing him.

"How is your headache?"

He smiled, "Almost gone. The nap helped."

She nodded, idly running her finger along the edge of the plate, picking up the last little dabs of baba ghanoush. "It was Marley."

"Your cousin?"

"Yes." She met his eyes, still angry, a flush of red blooming on her brown cheeks, "He was over visiting his mama two weeks ago. I asked him if he could help this weekend because I was planning on a little mini-vacation while you were away and someone needs to watch Auntie Lorna. He knew your schedule because I, like a fool, mentioned it to Auntie and he overheard. The guy who approached him a few weeks back, he said he was skinny, tattoos and dark, short hair. But Marley, he sold you out. Hell, he sold me out for a lousy two hundred bucks."

She had just described the guy who had been holding the gun, the one arrested by the police. The other guy, who Jack had watched run off into the night after knocking his partner out, looked nothing like that.

So, who was the second guy? He had handled himself well, fighting efficiently. Just a few well-placed kicks and a punch to the nose had laid his partner out on the floor.

Jack had lied to the cops, letting them assume he was the one who had disabled the burglar, and never mentioning the second man at all. All because of a split second decision on the second man's part. Eggers had been first in the door, and as soon as he saw Jack, he'd pulled a gun. There hadn't been a discussion. Nothing. The second man had looked at Jack and back at Eggers, and just laid Eggers out with a few blows. Knocked him unconscious on the marble floor of the front entry.

Then he had looked back at Jack, his eyes wary, and said, "I'm sorry. This was a mistake." A moment later and he was gone, leaving the heavy front door standing open, the rain and wind misting the entry. Seconds after that, the car the two men had arrived in disappeared out of sight on the long drive. He'd left Eggers on the floor. The entire event was mystifying to Jack. Who was the second man, anyway?

Azule misinterpreted his silence as some sort of condemnation. "I should have known better, Jack. I never should have said anything to my aunt."

Her words jostled Jack out of his thoughts. "What? Don't worry about it, Az, no harm done."

She gaped at him. "No harm done? Jack, I..."

He smiled at her. "Examine the security footage and see what you can do as far as identifying the second man, the one who took off. I'd like to know exactly who he is." He turned away, then spun on his heel. "And Az? Keep it under wraps. I didn't tell the police about him."

He walked out of the kitchen as she sputtered in shock and called after him, "Oh no, boss, you are not adopting another stray!"

"Just find him, Az." He called over his shoulder.

On the Run

The Greyhound bus roared down the dark highway and it surprised Shane at how crowded it had been. The only seats left were one next to a drunk who was currently snoring and smelled as if he had pissed himself, and a young woman with a tiny baby. He chose the young woman. She eyed him apprehensively, relaxing a smidgen as he focused on the baby and smiled gently.

"How old is your baby?"

"She's six months, almost seven now." She whispered.

He smiled, "She's beautiful." He whispered in return.

Her lips curved up, "Thank you."

He settled back, reviewing the last week and the mammoth mistakes he had made. He had screwed around with the little sister of an incredibly dangerous gangbanger.

No, wait, go back to the beginning. Getting wasted with Eggers. That was my first fuck-up. And then going to the dojo the next day, hungover.

Right, and then screwing Dara.

And then, full of himself, having just gotten laid, and having not fucked his life up enough, he told Eggers to count him in. Eggers. Burglary. Breaking and entering.

What the fuck was I thinking?

His feelings must have showed on his face because the young woman looked nervous again.

"Sorry," he said, his voice a calm whisper, "Do you ever feel you've screwed up everything you've ever touched?"

A wry smile stole over her face. "Oh yeah. With this one, it feels like a daily occurrence."

Shane laughed softly and shook his head. "Par for the course, I guess. Where are you heading?"

Her lips pinched together. "As far as I can go on…" she paused and counted, "seventy-nine dollars and eleven cents."

Shane nodded. She was running.

"Did he hurt you?"

She stared at him for a moment, then pulled her hair away from her neck so he could see the dark mottling, an outline of fingers clear on her neck. The baby in her arms whimpered and wriggled in her arms, disturbed by her deep slumber. She let her hair fall back into position and stroked the baby's back. The baby's breathing settled then, and she quieted, a tiny bubble of spit appearing between her cherubic pink rosebud-shaped lips.

"It wasn't the first time, either." She said it as if she felt the need to defend herself, to legitimize her actions. "And I wouldn't leave Abby there with him. She needs me, and I did not know what he would do to her."

"Of course not. You did the right thing." Shane paused, and then added, "You did what you had to for the two of you. He lost the right to be a dad when he laid his hands on you."

The silence deepened then, and the bus roared on. In a few hours, the sun would come up. Shane wondered where in the hell he should go. He hadn't even looked at the end destination, just bought a ticket and sat down on a bus. They were heading north. The signs came infrequently now that they were far from L.A.

"Where are you running to?" Her voice was soft.

"How do you know I'm running?" he asked in return, unsure how to answer her.

"It takes one to know one, I guess."

She had him with that. He shrugged. "Actually, I don't have a clue. I picked the one that was leaving the soonest. Where is this bus going, anyway?"

She giggled, covering her mouth when she did it, as if smiling was a crime. "Seriously?"

"Yeah, seriously. I bought a ticket, but I can't remember where to, so..."

"So it's an adventure."

"Yeah, I guess. One born from sheer stupidity."

She stared at him, her mouth twisting as she evaluated him. "You don't look stupid. Not at all."

"Uh... thanks?"

"It's heading for Portland, and Spokane beyond that." She laughed softly as she answered his question.

"So, are you getting off at Portland?" he asked her.

She shook her head. "Like I said, I've only got seventy-nine dollars."

"And eleven cents," he added.

She laughed, "Yeah, those eleven cents make all the difference in the world."

He didn't stop for long to think about it. If this woman stopped in one of the smaller towns, she would be remembered easily, especially with a tiny baby in tow. If she got off in Portland, she could quickly lose herself in the crowd. Portland was large, sprawling, and home to over half a million people.

"Here," he handed her two twenty-dollar bills, "now you can make it to Portland."

She took the money, hesitating. "What do you want for it?"

"What do I...?" He paused then, looking at her, confused. "Nothing."

"Where are you going to go?" She asked, slipping the bills away in a pocket quickly, as if afraid he would change his mind.

He pulled out his ticket and stared at it. He had bought a ticket to Ukiah. "Um, looks like I'll be getting off at Ukiah." He felt stupid, panicked. He hadn't thought this through.

"Sorry, Buddy, but you'll have to get your ticket changed when the office opens at eight a.m."

Shane didn't fight it. One place was as good as another, if it meant he was far away from the Prak brothers, Eggers, and the cops. At least two of the three would just as soon see him dead, after all.

He was, however, surprised to see the young woman and her baby getting off of the bus as well a minute later.

"I've got a feeling about you," she said in response to his raised eyebrows. She handed him the two $20 bills back. "Mind if we stick together for a while? I'm Anne, by the way."

"Shane." He took the money and then shook her hand gently, whispering. The baby remained fast asleep in her arms, a bit of drool wetting a spot on the front of Anne's dress.

As they sat on a hard bench in front of the Greyhound station office, they swapped stories. Anne's story had been close to what he expected. She had married early, which angered her dad, who had disowned her. Her husband, who was over ten years older than her, kept her isolated her from others. He became increasingly controlling and eventually it turned to violence. She had made her escape one night after he passed out, knocked out by a double whammy of Flexeril and Dramamine that she had added to his beers.

Shane hesitated to tell Anne his story. She had gotten off the bus, taken a chance and tossed her lot in with him, and she deserved better. After all, he was nothing but a fool. He had turned his back on his slow but steady progress and pushed the self-destruct button. He wasn't any better than a common criminal.

He plowed through the story, leaving out nothing, and she stared at him.

"And right now you probably wish you had taken that forty bucks and let the driver toss me off the bus rather than get tangled up in my mess."

She gave a rueful half-laugh. "For all I know, I've killed my husband. He was sleeping really deep when I left. I was so scared, I didn't even dare keep his car. I ditched it at the Greyhound station."

"I was in pre-med before I had to drop out and take care of my mom. You just gave him one Flexeril and one Dramamine, right?" She nodded, and he continued, "He'll wake up in a few hours feeling more relaxed than he ever has before. At least, until he realizes you are gone." He patted her hand. "You have nothing to worry about."

The relief showed on Anne's face. "Thank God. He's an abusive asshole, but I don't want him dead." She looked at her baby's face, kissed her forehead gently. The baby stirred, opening one eye, before slipping back into dreamland. She stared into the distance. "I don't know what to do next."

"I know the feeling. Perhaps we can figure that out together," Shane said. Across the street, a donut shop was showing signs of life. Shane's growling stomach reminded him that the last time he had eaten was yesterday's ham and cheese sandwich at lunchtime. "C'mon, let's see if the bakery there is open."

When Opportunity Knocks

It wasn't as if they had planned it or even really discussed it. And after all the bad luck they had encountered, the next few weeks were full of good luck. Enough to give them hope before reality ripped it away again.

Stepping into the donut shop that morning in the pre-dawn hours had been the best damn luck Shane had seen in years. The owner, a wizened old man hobbling about, his left leg in a cast, looked up as they entered.

"We aren't open yet," he barked.

"Oh Louis, stop it. Yes, we're open, we're just..." An equally stooped and ancient woman stepped out of the back room. She held an enormous bowl full of yeasty dough in her hands. "... running behind a bit. Sit down, sit down, I'll have something done up in a jiffy. I've got coffee if you want some."

At that moment, Abby woke, her tiny hands pushing the blanket aside as she blinked in the harsh incandescent lights.

The older woman smiled broadly, cooing as she thrust the bowl of dough into Shane's hands, and reached for the baby, a hopeful question on her face. "Oh, she is beautiful!"

Anne smiled in return and handed Abby over, looking slightly relieved. She massaged her arms, and Shane realized she had been holding her baby for hours without a break.

He stood there, the bowl of dough in his hands, unsure of what to do. The old woman was too busy cradling the baby and peppering Anne with questions to spare a glance his way.

"Bring that over here," the old man said, and pointed to a stove with a large pot. "You mind working for your breakfast?"

Shane brought the dough over and shook his head. "Don't mind at all. If you talk me through it, I'll be happy to help."

Anne had sunk down in a booth, her entire body betraying her exhaustion. She leaned back, a weary smile on her face as she watched the old woman play with Abby.

"Oh, you two have made something truly beautiful here." The baby cooed in response to the old woman, reaching out a tiny hand to pet her lined face. "I'm Grace, by the way."

"We're not..." Shane said, and Louis interrupted him, gruffly pointing at the empty counter.

"Put the dough there. Just scrape it all out."

As Shane followed the old man's directions, Grace rocked the baby and kept a running commentary punctuated by kisses. Shane and Anne soon learned that Louis had broken his leg after slipping on the stairs the week before. Their lone employee had left unexpectedly to visit her ailing mother, leaving Louis and Grace to handle the store on their own.

"She'll probably need to stay there in Chicago until her mother recovers," the old woman had said, shaking her head. "Poor dear, she was so upset when she got the call. It was a rather severe stroke, and her mother is in the intensive care unit right now."

Grace glanced over at Anne, who looked wiped out. Her eyes kept fluttering open before slowly shutting again. "Jackie was down on her luck when she ended up at our door. I guess being here, across from the bus station, we see more than our fair share." She met Shane's eyes. He had finished rolling and cutting the first batch of doughnuts out and they were glistening with oil, ready for a coating of sugar or melted chocolate. "I'm guessing you could use a helping hand as well?"

Anne jerked awake, her face a study of exhaustion. "We can work. I mean, I can. I've had experience working in IHOP as a waitress." She sat up straighter, tucking several stray hairs behind her ears.

Grace laughed, "Honey, I don't doubt you, but right now, the only thing you should do is rest. We have a spare room above the shop. I'll show you where it is and you can get some rest while your man here helps us with the morning's work."

Anne protested, and Shane cut in. "Honey, why don't you rest? You need it." He shot Anne a look that he hoped she understood. If they thought he and Anne were a couple, fine. It made them a safer bet, and he and Anne would work something out.

She took his cue, nodded, and let Grace show her the way upstairs to the spare room while Shane prepared more donuts. The sun was barely over the horizon as a stream of customers continued in and out. Anne returned three hours later, looking refreshed.

She took Shane's place at the register. "Grace is taking care of Abby. Here, let me take over the register."

The days and weeks that followed fell into a steady rhythm. The spare room had two twin-sized beds. "It was our boys' room," Grace explained. "Neither of them wanted anything to do with running the shop or living in a small town," she said, smiling wryly. "Tom is in L.A., and Lou just settled in Portland."

Shane and Anne didn't really discuss it all. And they fell into the roles of husband and wife easily enough to pass general scrutiny. The employee they had replaced had sent word she would remain in Chicago. Her mother was out of the hospital now, but needed constant care.

"The job is yours if you want it, room and board as well." Grace offered. It wasn't much, but it was enough for now. The two of them had their reasons for hiding, and the donut shop was as good a place as most. The only concern was their proximity to the bus station. And in the end, it was what endangered all of them.

Better Choices

It had been more than a month now and Shane relaxed, looking forward to the simplicity of each day

He had finished with the prep work and the first customers would trickle in soon. Any minute now, Anne would finish nursing Abby and hand her over to Grace. Then she would come downstairs and take her place at the register.

They had grown closer, playing the role of husband and wife in public. The night before, at bedtime, he had entered the room without thinking, and caught Anne half-dressed. She hadn't jumped or covered herself. She had stared at him, and he at her, and he could feel the stirrings of something forming between them. A slow spark of attraction. They were sleeping in the same room, and Abby was a sweet baby. Shane found it easy to cuddle and hold her whenever Anne needed a break, or had her hands full.

Grace and Louis also lived above the shop in their own room. The two couples shared a living space and the one bathroom. It was rather like acquiring an instant family. Shane and Anne shared meals, chores, errands, and more with Louis and Grace. In the evening, they all gathered in the living room to play cards. And Grace, a rabid jigsaw enthusiast, had set to work on a jigsaw puzzle. Baby Abby tried her best to take swipes at the loose pieces, but was still too small to cause any real mischief. In a few more months, it would be a different story.

"My Lou walked early," Grace said. "Tom took his time." She smiled, happy to have a tiny one in the house. Both sons were in their 40s and seemed disinclined to provide their parents with grandchildren.

As the rays of the sun peeked over the horizon, Shane heard the door chime and looked up, a welcoming smile on his face. The first customer of the day was unfamiliar. He wasn't a local, at least not one that Shane had met.

There was a steady stream of locals who made it a point to stop in and load up on Louis' Famous Donuts, as the sign promised. And after a month, Shane knew most of them by name.

Three generations of the family had owned and operated it, but Louis would be the last owner and operator from the looks of it. Their oldest son, who both Louis and Grace referred to as Lou, which sounded a lot better than Louis IV and less like a monarch, was a venture capitalist. His brother worked for a large bank and handled real estate deals. Neither of them were interested in a tiny donut shop in a sleepy little town.

This man had a buzz cut of black hair and a five o'clock shadow and dark brown eyes. There was something about him that set off Shane's alarms. The other man gave him a curt nod and pointed to the glass case of donuts. "Give me two of the old-fashioned glaze." He leaned on the counter, tapping his fingers impatiently, and looked around, casting his gaze to the Greyhound station across the street.

"That'll be $1.89," Shane answered as he handed the man the donuts. The guy pushed over a twenty-dollar-bill and then reached into his pocket.

As Shane counted the change, the man cast another glance at the bus station across the street. "I'm looking for someone." He laid down another twenty and a photograph of him and Anne and what could only be Abby. She was tiny in the picture, only a few weeks old. "Maybe you've seen her?" Kirk had an obnoxious, shit-eating grin on his face in the picture and Anne had a huge fake smile plastered on. Her eyes, though, her eyes said it all. It was a plea for help that stared out of the photograph at him, caught forever in the space of a second. Who had taken the photo? It looked like a studio photo. He wondered if they had seen her desperation as well.

The bad feeling in Shane's gut grew, and he glanced at the clock. Anne would be down soon. Any minute now.

"Her name's Anne, Anne Withers. She would have had this baby girl with her. The baby's name is Abby." He paused, his eyes searching Shane's. "I'm wondering if you might have seen them." He smiled then, but there was no friendliness, nothing but emptiness and a shifting, coiling anger. Shane could see it now, all too clearly. "My wife. She got real depressed after our daughter was born. Took off just over a month ago. I'm trying to track her down, make sure they're both all right, y'know?" His lips stretched into the same shit-eating grin in the photo. It didn't reach his eyes. "I've been real worried about her."

Shane shrugged. "Eighteen dollars and eleven cents is your change." He handed the man the bag of donuts and looked down. He grabbed a nearby rag and began wiping the counter, praying Anne didn't walk in now. The building was old and he could hear every creak of the floor above. His heart rate increased. He strained his ears, listening for the telltale creak of the stairs that would announce Anne's imminent arrival. Would she hear Kirk Wither's voice in time?

The man stared at him. The twenty was still on the counter. "So, have you seen her?"

He could pull this off, he knew he could. He met the man's eyes. "Sorry, man, can't say I have."

The door jingled then, and Shane looked up, his eyes widening with shock at the man walking through the door.

Could my day possibly get worse?

Jack Benton wore jeans and a t-shirt, but everything about him spoke of wealth and power. If Anne's husband hadn't been so intent on questioning Shane, he would have stepped aside. As it was, his head snapped back for a double take of Jack, whose demeanor held a calm confidence. Shane's eyes tracked beyond Kirk Withers standing before him to Jack, who had taken a seat in a booth nearby. He glanced out of the front window. There was no cop car outside. Not yet, anyway.

Kirk Withers didn't take kindly to Shane's lack of response. Perhaps he was feeling ignored. He smiled, all teeth, and Shane could feel the man's anger rising. It was thick and dark, like a thunderstorm building behind a fake show of geniality. He wasn't buying it. Anne had opened up about how bad it had been. She had taken the slaps. Those had made way to blows, verbal and physical, and finally when he had shaken Abby once for crying too long, she knew it was time to go.

"It was past time, if I'm perfectly honest," she had said, looking at her fingers. "I would not let Abby grow up and see that or experience it. It wasn't right. I might not have been a perfect wife, but when he started taking it out on Abby, I just..."

"No one is perfect, Anne, and that's never an excuse for anyone to use you as a punching bag."

Remembering that conversation, and hearing a small creak on the stairs from the closed door behind him, it strengthened his resolve. He ignored Jack Benton's gaze from the other side of the room and focused again on the man in front of him.

He persisted, staring at Shane intently, jaw clenched, his pulse jumping in his neck. "Really? Can't say? Or won't say? Because you looked like you recognize her. Maybe you should look again."

He could feel Jack Benton's gaze alongside Kirk Withers. He made a show of peering at the photograph before answering, "Sorry, can't remember seeing them."

The door opened then, and his heart banged in his chest, his head turning in time with Kirk Withers. He nearly cried in relief. It wasn't Anne, thank God, but Louis, who had a broad smile plastered on his face. Considering how Louis barely smiled at customers, this spoke volumes to Shane. Anne must have heard Kirk's voice and returned upstairs, most likely in a panic. The old man never made an appearance downstairs before it was time to close mid-morning.

"Good morning!" He turned to stare at Kirk Withers, whose smile had vanished, replaced by what appeared to be his normal expression, a perpetually "angry at the world" scowl. The man's lip curled at the sight of the old man. "It looks as if you have your donuts, sir, so if you wouldn't mind, I believe there is a gentleman waiting to order."

Kirk glared at Louis and Shane before slowly turned and walked towards the door, glancing over his shoulder at Shane. It looked as if he were going to open his mouth and say something. At the door, he paused for a moment and glared as he walked out.

Louis' smile dropped, and he looked at Shane. "Was that who I think it was?" He asked softly, pitching his voice low so that it didn't carry.

Shane gaped for a moment. "You know?"

Louis snorted, "That you two aren't a couple? Son, I wasn't born yesterday. I've spent my life in this shop across from that there bus station. You think you and Anne are the first folks with trouble on their heels that we've seen?"

"I... I..." Shane didn't know what to say. He cast a glance over to Jack Benton, who was sitting at the table patiently waiting. He leaned back in the booth, body relaxed, watching Shane as if he had all the time in the world. How long had it been? Five weeks... six?

That dark, stormy night of bad choices and worse partners. There had been nothing on the news about it. Not surprising, not really. Jack Benton, who Shane had done a little digging into after the whole disastrous night, was a billionaire. A billionaire who liked his privacy and had power over plenty of key people. If he didn't want to be on the news, then you could be sure he wouldn't be.

Louis jerked his head in Jack Benton's direction. "And I'm guessing he's here for you. Am I right?"

Shane nodded, "Yeah, he is."

"Well, that's on you, Son. Damn shame, too, because you make some tasty donuts."

"I'm uh, I'm sorry, sir."

Louis tilted his head. "What for?"

"For bringing trouble to your door."

The old man snorted. "I've seen my share. Besides, I haven't seen Grace so happy as when she's holding that baby. So I'm not sorry at all, Son, and that's not something you need to carry, neither." He stared at Shane and set a gnarled hand on his arm. "Whatever you have done, it can't be that bad. I see good in you. I would never have let you stay if I didn't see that in both of you. So, you deal with it, and we'll make sure Anne and Abby are safe. Deal?"

"Yes, sir." Shane sucked in a breath, steeled himself, and walked out from behind the counter and over to Jack Benton. It was time to face the music. Enough running. He had to face what he had done and pay the price.

Jack Benton stared at him, a bemused and curious expression on his face. "I've had quite the adventure tracking you down, Mr. Ellis."

Shane winced. Some part of him had hoped that, somehow, it had simply been coincidence that Benton had found him here. He nodded then, trying to keep his cool, "Mr. Benton."

"Sit down, Ellis, I don't bite." Jack said, and Shane eased his way into a chair across from the man, fighting the urge to run from the donut shop and not stop running this time. Not for anything.

There was a small rustle of activity from Louis. Seconds later, both men had steaming cups of coffee set in front of them. Shane suppressed a smile. The old man was really something. Shane had underestimated him. All this time, and the old man had known the truth and said nothing.

Jack nodded to the old man. "Thank you." He nodded over to the glass case filled with donuts. "I hear that the glazed old-fashioned are the best in the county. Could I have one for here and a dozen to go?" He laid down a twenty-dollar bill on the table.

Louis nodded and busied himself with filling the order. As he did, several more regulars filed in, bleary-eyed, as they poured coffee from the carafe and placed their orders.

Shane returned Jack's stare, waiting for the older man to speak first. He didn't. After several minutes, the shop now filled with people eating, walking in and out, and talking, Shane finally couldn't stand it anymore.

"So, you found me."

Jack smiled, "Yes, I did."

"How?"

"I employ people who are incredibly loyal and good at their jobs. My assistant, Azule, handled your basic history. She learned you lost your mom a couple of years ago and ended up dropping out of college to care for her. And that you have been working at least two, sometimes three jobs, plus hustling pool on the side, to pay back what you owe."

"Master Pao said that except for a disheartening incident involving a hangover seven weeks ago, you are an apt pupil and decent with a mop."

He smiled. "I had an interesting discussion with a rather troubled young man named Kenny. He was itching for a fix, but I convinced him to try rehab instead and he's doing well there. Should be out in a couple more days and he is asking for you. He says you saved his life at least twice."

He frowned then. "I also had several discussions with a Mrs. Langstroth. She is a complicated woman. First, she claimed you were the gang leader of the Asian Boyz and had a rap sheet a mile long. She followed this up with a recitation of your more redeeming qualities. I understand you helped carry her groceries and fixed the lock on her door. And then I met a rather aggressive young woman, by the name of Dara. In addition to the lascivious glances she gave my car and my person, Dara asked me to pass on a message to you. She said she didn't hold you responsible for her brother's concussion or broken wrist. Apparently, this was because he started the fight. However, she did suggest you not come back to the area. Apparently, her brother has put a bounty on your head." Jack took a bite of the doughnut and rolled his eyes with pleasure. "Did you make these?"

Shane nodded.

"Excellent, truly."

"Um, thank you." Shane paused. "Can I ask you something?"

"Fire away." Jack replied.

"Did you point Kirk Withers here?"

Jack shook his head. "Nope. Not my style. Actually, *I* followed *him*. I already planned on coming by this place, but I wanted to see what you would do when he asked about his wife."

Shane stared at him. "He's an abusive prick. That guy will kill her if he gets a chance. I will not let that happen."

Jack nodded. "I expected nothing less of you, Ellis."

"I don't play games, Mr. Benton. I'm not a toy, and Anne deserves to be free and safe from that bastard."

"No games, I promise you." Jack said, leaning forward. "Are the two of you together?"

"What?" Shane stared at him, "No." He ran his hand through his hair. "Look. What do you want from me? You want me to turn myself in? I'll go with you right now, this minute. Just leave Anne and Abby out of this."

Jack shook his head. "I'm not the one you need to worry about. It's like you said, that guy? Kirk? He's the problem. He definitely will be back to ask more questions. Especially if he asks after Anne at the antiques store down the way. The shop girl there runs her mouth a mile a minute. And no, I don't want you to turn yourself in. I want to hire you."

Shane scoffed, "Yeah, right. For what? Robbing billionaires? Don't you have enough money?"

Jack smiled as he shook his head. "You don't get it, Ellis. I hire loyal, capable people to do jobs they were born to do. Take you, for example. You were born to save people. It's in your DNA. It's in every action you have taken your entire life, with one small anomaly. The one that brought you into my home six weeks ago."

"You took care of Kenny, Mrs. Langstroth, your mom, Anne and Abby Withers, even Louis and Grace. That's what I want to hire you to do - help people." He set down a card then. Plain white cardstock with simple black letters that read Benton Security Services. Shane picked it up and looked at it. It felt expensive, yet tasteful in its simplicity. "Come and work for me. It pays well and you will do something that comes naturally to you. Don't you think it's time to make better choices?"

"What... as a bodyguard? I know nothing about guns, or about security."

The older man nodded. "You'll learn."

Shane stole a glance at the door that led upstairs, and Jack nodded again. "She can't stay here, Ellis. That guy will be back. But I can help with that." He reached into his pocket and pulled out another card. It was identical to the first, except it read, "Benton Acquisitions."

"Sometimes enough is enough. Perhaps it is time for Louis and his wife to retire and live somewhere sunny and nice, like Florida. And perhaps they would like company. I can arrange for Anne and Abby to have new identities. I have holdings across the country and resources to employ Anne once we have her new identity in place. They will be safe. You can even keep in contact, if you like."

Shane gaped at him. "Why are you doing this?"

Jack Benton smiled at him. "You aren't the only one who gets to be the good guy. It's also what I do." He shrugged, "I guess you could say I collect good people." He leaned forward then, "So, do we have a deal?"

"You'll make sure Anne and Abby are safe, and Grace and Louis can retire?"

"Yes, you have my word."

Shane held out his hand. "Then you have mine as well."

The men shook hands.

Learning to Speak
A Short Story

Learning to Speak *takes place in the days following a tragic plane crash,* *one referenced in* Smoke and Steel, *Book 2 of the Benton Security Services series. Jack saves his sister and himself from the icy waters. His parents and the pilot of the plane are not as lucky.*

Jack's life changes, and he must take care of his younger siblings, including his non-verbal autistic brother, Malcolm.

It is in moments like these that shape the direction of our lives and give meaning to it. Pass through the crucible in order to become the person you were meant to be...

Love and Loss

Jack walked into his sister's hospital room on the heels of a group of medical professionals. Interns encircled the doctor in charge in his sister's hospital room. Jack tried to enter quietly, but he rapped his broken shoulder on the edge of the door, and his groan was audible.

"Ah, Mr. Benton." The doctor greeted him. "How is your left humerus treating you?" He gave a small laugh.

Cue the humorous jokes.

Jack had found that there was nothing humorous at all about a broken humerus. The fact was, it hurt like hell. The waves of pain from just the slight bump against the door frame seconds ago made everything seem wavy and fuzzy.

"It hurts. A lot."

"I'll bet it does. Especially when Mr. Benton here refused any pain meds, ladies, and gents." He smiled at the students clustered around him, his tone of derision clear. "How's that working out for you?"

Jack bit his tongue.

Ask for drugs and they look at me like I'm an addict. Avoid them and they think I'm trying to prove how tough I am. There's no winning here.

"Hanging in there, doc."

A look of pity flashed across the doctor's face before he turned away from Jack and addressed the others. "Here we have a 15-year-old adolescent female survivor of a small commuter plane crash. She suffered two broken ribs, a bruised spleen, head trauma, and has a heart arrhythmia..."

Jack tuned the rest out as he set his coffee cup down and eased his way into the chair by Allie's bedside. She would wake up soon. He was sure of it. Until then, he would stay in the hospital every minute. She deserved to have a familiar face waiting for her.

Three days later...

"Jack?"

His eyes snapped open. Allie was awake and obviously confused. She wiggled, weakly plucking at the IV in her arm.

"Allison. Whoa, hang on." He stood up, his upper arm flaring in agony as he did. His little sister looked confused, but she leaned back, wincing, her right hand reaching up to touch her ribs.

"Oh, ow. Ow!" She sucked in a breath and shifted back against the mattress. "Why does everything hurt? Where are we?"

"Barton Memorial, in Tahoe." Seeing her eyes open after four long days was exhilarating. But the smile dropped from his face seconds later.

She doesn't remember the crash. Which means she doesn't know Mom and Dad are gone.

"Tahoe?"

"Yeah. Look, let me just go get the nurse. They'll want to talk to you, examine you, now that you're awake."

He made it a few steps, and was almost to the door before she asked the dreaded question. "Jack? Where are Mom and Dad?"

"I, uh, let me just get the doctor, Allie. Hang on."

She was awake. And now the dread of what would have to come next coursed through him. He wasn't ready for this. He'd spent three days by her bedside, but he wasn't ready for this moment. Not at all.

My fault. My fault. My fault!

He was halfway through the door when he heard her whimper a single word. It sounded loud in the space.

"No."

Jack froze. Inside him, a war had broken out. He wanted to run. Find a bar. Slam some Vicodin and chase it with a scotch. Drink until all the sharp edges, the pain, was a distant memory that belonged to someone else. That was one faction. The other, the one made of steel, one that sounded a hell of a lot like his dad, was ordering him to turn around, to face the music.

You made this happen. You did. No one else. Partying with Jerry all night before the flight. You knew *he wasn't okay. Not enough sleep, alcohol, and who knew what else in his system. You knew how he was. The guy liked to party, same as you. And you let your parents and your baby sister get on a plane with him.*

Jerry Banks was dead. Jack couldn't blame the dead, not when the real fuck-up was standing right here, doing his best to flee.

Jack forced himself to look over, to meet Allie's eyes. She looked so small, so vulnerable there in the bed. She didn't look fifteen. The makeup had long washed from her face. She still looked battered and bruised from the impact of the water. She looked as she had at seven, when she had fallen while skateboarding and broken her wrist. Pale, bruised. That had been his fault as well. She had driven him nuts, following him everywhere. He'd told her to get on the skateboard as a joke, never thinking about the rough edge that he and all his friends knew to avoid. Seconds later, she'd sprawled on the ground, pale, cradling her right wrist in her hand.

He couldn't look away from her, couldn't move. She deserved the truth. As painful as it was. She had been closest to him, his window already shattered on impact. It had been all he could do to get her seatbelt and his off, to drag her out of the window and kick, kick, kick his way through the icy water to the life-giving oxygen above.

He slowly returned to her side, the pain of his shoulder a mere dull ache compared to the one spreading in his chest. He couldn't bring himself to say the words, so Allie said them for him.

"They're gone, aren't they?"

She blurred then, wavered, as if underwater all over again. It confused him until he felt the first tears slip down his cheeks. He couldn't make his mouth work. The words he had planned to say to Allie vanished from his mind. Instead, he nodded and reached for her with his one good arm, encircling her as gently as he could, and allowed himself, just this once, to mourn.

Hospitals Suck

Allie snatched at the bag Jack offered her with a small snarl.

"Good morning to you too, sis."

"Hospitals suck." She said, grimacing. "They keep poking and prodding me. I want to go home." As soon as she uttered the words, her face dropped.

Jack's bagel turned in his stomach, heavy as cement. The thought occurring to them both at the same time.

Is home even home without Mom and Dad?

"When are they going to release me? And what happens next?" Allie asked, sounding less like a grumpy teenager and more like a scared little girl.

It was all Jack had been thinking about since Allie had woken up. After extensive tests, including a trip through the MRI, the doctors had informed Jack that Allie was well on the way to recovery. Her ribs would take a while to heal, along with the bruised spleen. The doctors recommended follow-up care with a cardiologist on Allie's newly diagnosed heart arrhythmia. Other than that, he had just been told they could release her that afternoon.

"Today. This afternoon. I got us tickets back home."

"We're flying?" Her face blanched.

"Nope. Train. It'll get us down the coast all the way to L.A."

Allie's shoulders slumped in relief. Neither of them was ready to board a plane. Not after what they had been through.

"Thank you."

"It'll take a while. Around thirteen hours. We leave at six tonight, get to L.A. at seven something in the a.m. and we can get breakfast at Perch afterwards."

Allie shook her head. "I just want to go home." She picked at the blanket. "After that..." Her eyes turned back to his, her unspoken question hung heavy in the air.

"I'm not going back to college." Jack blurted. The thought of it, right now, seemed impossible. He couldn't leave Allison. He was all she had. Hell, they probably wouldn't even want him back. They had threatened him with academic suspension after half of his classes dropped precipitously in the past semester. The relief in her eyes was palpable.

"Jack, I..."

Jack reached out and took her hand. It felt so small inside of his. She was still just a kid, and she needed him. He couldn't replace Mom and Dad, but he had to be someone she could depend on. No more partying. No more drinking and carousing and immature bullshit. He'd fucked everything up. Now he had to pull the edges together, make it right, or at least as right as anything this messed up could be.

"I love you, Sis. You know that, right?"

She met his eyes, a solemn look on her face. "I know you do. But, I've been thinking abut a lot of things. Things that were... wrong at home."

"Wrong?"

Allie looked away, picked at the fabric of her hospital gown.

"Mom was unhappy. Ever since Dad sent Mal away."

Malcolm. Their baby brother. How long had it been since he saw Mal? Two years? Three? He'd be twelve now. The realization that Mal didn't know about the last week hit Jack like a brick. His baby brother had no clue his parents, *their* parents, were dead.

Would Mal even care?

Mom had always said that Mal felt everything, deeply, but you would never know by looking at him. Autism, the doctors had said. Non-verbal.

"He will never speak, never be normal, and certainly never be capable of taking part in the family business." That's what their father had said, the disappointment clear in his voice.

Mal, with his dark eyes and dark hair. His silence. Mal, who had never said a single word out loud. Who screamed if you tried to hug him? Dad had insisted he be sent to residential care shortly after his ninth birthday.

After the fire, it had been enough. Mom couldn't talk him out of it.

And it wasn't even Malcolm's fault. It was mine. I left the matches out. He'd seen me light them. He was only mimicking me. I should have known better.

"I want to go home, Jack. And I want you to get Malcolm out of that awful place and bring him home." Allie said, her voice quivering with emotion.

Jack looked at his little sister. Her bruised face held scabbed and healing wounds. Her movements were slow and painful thanks to the bruised ribs.

"You want Mal to come home?" He said, his voice steady. "Okay."

He didn't know how in the hell he was going to do it. But if Allie wanted Malcolm home, then he would do whatever he had to make it happen.

It's a Lot

The evaluation with a counselor was mandatory. The sharp-eyed, no-nonsense caseworker from Children's Division had not minced words.

"You wish to remove your brother from the institution he is currently in and assume custody of him? You also want to care for your younger sister. We need to be sure you are fit to care for them."

For once, his family's money held no sway. Not in the face of a nosy, bureaucratic machine.

He had submitted to her demands. He sat in an exceedingly plain office across from a man who spent an entire year earning what Jack's father would have made in a day, maybe less. The psychologist was middle-aged, balding, his tweed jacket cuff frayed.

"I see here that you have refused pain meds for your fractured humerus," the psychologist looked up from his notes. "My father-in-law had a fractured humerus. It was exceedingly painful."

Jack said nothing, just shrugged his uninjured arm. The pain from his arm still throbbed. It was distracting, the pain, yet somehow it was easier to feel pain than to be numb. Anyway, he didn't deserve the numbing gift of the painkillers. This was on him, his fault, his guilt, his mistake.

Jack and the psychologist sat in silence for a moment, then another, each staring at the other. "This will go better, quicker, if you could tell me what you are thinking about. How you feel right now, sitting here in my office."

Jack had sighed, the air rushing out of him, a great exodus of despair. "How do I feel? I let them down. My parents, Allie. Hell, even Malcolm."

"This is your," the psychologist consulted his notes, "Younger brother, is that correct?"

"Yeah. They diagnosed him with autism. My dad had him put in residential care three years ago, when he was nine. I haven't seen him much since."

"Would you like to?" the man asked, his pen held at the ready. "How did it make you feel to see him taken away?"

"I, uh," Jack struggled to put to words the complicated feelings surrounding having his baby brother placed in an institution. Not to mention how much he felt at fault for it.

"I wasn't as close to him as Allie was. The two of them, they had a connection. Mal was always calmer around Allie. But it really sucked. I missed him, even though by then I was in college."

"How often have you seen him since?" the man probed as he tapped his pen against his notebook.

"Once."

The man's eyebrows shot up. "Just once?" He leaned back, folded his hands over his chest. "And now you want to move him out of the place he has been in for over three years, a place where you visited him all of once, and back into the family home? Why?"

Jack shifted uncomfortably in his seat as he struggled to find the words. "It was... the place was, well, it was an institution. It was hard to see him there. My mom visited him every single week, my dad not so much."

The counselor shifted his questioning. "Tell me about your relationship with your dad."

The questions had gone on, seemingly endlessly. All Jack wanted to do was return to Allison's side, where he had stayed, day in, day out, as she slowly recovered. Jack hated to leave her, even for a few hours. He hovered so much since they had returned home that she was tired of him. She'd practically shoved him out of the door to go to the psych appointment that morning.

The meetings with the psychologist continued for several weeks. Jack endured the invasive questions. Finally, the psychologist relented and wrote the letter recommending Jack take custody of Allison and Malcolm.

They had the green light. Malcolm could come home.

Home

"You *promised*!" Allie looked pissed.

Jack held up his hands. "Allie, can we just wait one more week? We are both still recovering. We need to be... ready."

The last time Malcolm Benton had stepped inside of the L.A. house, he had been nine years old. Now he was twelve, on the cusp of adolescence, a full half-foot taller and stronger. Mom and Dad weren't here to help, although, when he thought of it that way, was probably a good thing, at least where their father was concerned.

The phone call, however, had set off all of Jack's alarms. Malcolm was prone to tantrums? He'd been destructive? Jack was struggling to imagine how this would all work while fending off a sister who had fire in her eyes.

"You *said* we could bring him home, Jack."

"I did, and we will. Would you just stop and listen for a damn second?"

Since returning to L.A. it had been one thing after another. First the funerals. They had struggled through them, helped by a handful of staff who had been with them for years. Then came the challenge of the business. Nadine Roberts, William Benton's longtime personal assistant, had tried to make it as easy as possible. But Benton Holdings was a massive company, something Jack was becoming more painfully aware of with each passing day. At first, he had thought it would fade, slacken. That the decisions, the approvals and paperwork directly resulted from his parents' passing and that things would settle. Instead, he found his days filled with decision-making he barely understood. His arm and ribs were still healing, but Allie's bruises had finally disappeared. Jack winced whenever he tried to use his left arm for anything. Dressing himself each morning left a film of sweat beading his face. He wanted Malcolm back, too. His baby brother had been odd, quiet, but there had been moments when Jack was sure the kid knew more, understood more, than what their father, William, saw.

"He's been violent, Mr. Benton." The director of Excelsior Mental Health had said over the phone. "Towards staff, other residents. I just want you to be prepared for what you might get into." He had explained that in cases like Mal's, the best treatment was often that of an institutional setting.

Allie folded her arms across her chest, wincing as she did it. She kept telling him she was fine, but Jack knew she wasn't. "I'm listening."

"The director there at Excelsior called me personally. He said Mal has had some violent outbursts."

"The director is a dick, Jack. He's just pissed his money-making prize pig is going away."

Jack couldn't disagree with that. He'd seen the monthly bill for Malcolm's care. It rivaled Nadine's annual salary.

"Allie..." Jack rubbed his eyes. A headache had started there earlier, likely from the two-foot-high pile of paperwork he had been working his way through. Not to mention the news from Nadine that she and Lucas had already given notice of retirement before the ill-fated family vacation. She then gently informed him she could extend that for three more months only.

"I would stay here, Jack, but Lucas has family in Florida, and we had scheduled our first cruise in late June." Her dark eyes had pleaded with him to understand.

"Seriously Jack, he's full of it. Mal wouldn't hurt a fly. If you had seen him, visited..." She turned away, stalked to the kitchen and began slamming cabinets. She was angry, sure he was going to break his promises to her. And could he blame her? When had he ever kept his word? She pulled out a knife and began to prepare a salad, angrily hacking away at a carrot.

The last thing she needs is a commitment-phobic jerk of an older brother.

What she needed, and what she had, well, "Allie. Please. Look, we'll go get him this weekend, okay?"

She stopped, her face brightening. "Really? This weekend?"

"Yeah. They want to send one of their staff home with him to help with the transition."

Her mouth flattened. "Who?"

"Um, a Leslie Jones?" He answered, squinting to read his own scribble.

"Nurse Ratchett? Oh hell, no!"

Jack rolled his eyes. The band around his head increased, tightening into a vise of pain. "Right, no in-home help. Got it. I'm going to go sign more documents. Who knows, maybe I'll sign one that gives up all of our wealth and fortune."

He turned to go back to the office, only to feel Allie's arms around him. "Thank you, Jack." She hugged him and his arm and ribs protested. He said nothing as the emotions, unnamed and complex, surged through him. He was a poor substitute for their parents. Allie deserved so much more.

Can I even be the brother that Malcolm needs?

This is Why

This lanky, haggard half man, half boy, was not Malcolm. He couldn't be. They sheared his hair close to his head, and he rocked incessantly. So much so that it took everything that Jack and Allie had to get him into the backseat of the car. His body was stiff, his limbs akimbo. And the incessant rocking was driving Jack insane. Allie pushed Jack away as he leaned in, trying his best to reach across and latch the belt.

"Just get in the car. I'll sit in the back with Mal."

She shut the passenger side door and sat in the back behind the driver. She reached over to fasten Mal's seatbelt..

Jack shoved the suitcase and clear plastic bag filled with prescriptions into the trunk, a myriad of emotions moving through him. His brother's eyes, the brief glimpse Jack had seen of them, were glassy and unfocused. He was drooling. Blotches of acne covered his face. And his shirt and pants, obviously new, the creases from the packages still clear, hung loose on his frame.

If he hadn't promised Allie he would try... hell, if she hadn't been standing beside him, he wondered if he would have brought their brother home. He felt completely unequipped for this.

The drive home felt interminable. Allie talked the whole way. As if, perhaps, to make up for her two brothers' silence. Jack didn't know what to say, and Mal, well, Malcolm had never spoken a word in his life.

They ordered Chinese for dinner. Again, Allie's idea.

"You always seemed to like the Broccoli Beef. Remember Mal?" Her voice, which had begun the day so chipper an excited, was now muted, almost pleading.

Upon arrival, Mal had allowed them to lead him to his old room at the lower level of the house. It had remained virtually unchanged, but Mal was unresponsive. He sat, unmoving on the bed, as Allie flitted about, talking, talking, talking. She always talked a blue streak when she was nervous.

Now they sat at the table. Mal stared at his plate, a small frown on his face, as if permanently perplexed. He'd eaten two bites, nothing more. Jack and Allie sat in their usual places, leaving the chairs normally occupied by Mom and Dad empty. Neither of them had known how to say what needed to be said. That Mom and Dad were gone. Dead. And that the three of them were all each other had.

Silence had descended. Allie had finally run out of things to say, it seemed.

"I suppose I should figure out this medication regimen they sent us home with." Jack said, breaking the silence.

"I already looked at them." Allie said. "They have him drugged to the gills, Jack." Her fingers clenched down on her chopsticks so hard, they were white, bloodless. "Some of them interact poorly with others. One of them is an anti-seizure medication."

"Mal has seizures?" Jack asked, instantly concerned.

"No Jack, he *doesn't*. They use it to sedate patients and control them." Allie practically spat. "Mom was real concerned the last time she visited. She told me she felt they were over-medicating him and now I can see why. Mom and Dad got into a huge argument shortly before you came home on break." She pointed at the bag of medicine. "Look at this. Six different medications! He wasn't on *any* medications until Dad insisted he go to that place. And that's not the worst of it."

Jack blinked. "Okay, so now is when I'm supposed to ask, 'What is the worst of it, Allie?'"

Allie stood up and whispered close to Mal's ear. He gave a small jerk of his head and pulled off his shirt, holding it balled up and close to his chest. Malcolm rocked faster, his distress obvious.

Jack sucked in a breath. Bruises mottled Malcolm's skin. Some were dark blue/black. Others seemed older, a mix of green and sickly yellow, fading from view. Jack could see one that looked distinctly like angry fingers wrapped around Mal's right arm. He saw tears spilling out of Allie's eyes as she pointed. "This is why we had to bring him home, Jack. They were abusing him. Mal belongs here, with us, with his family. No more drugs. No more institutions. And no more of those fucking doctors."

As Allison gently helped Malcolm put his shirt back on, Jack felt the fury rising inside of him. They had abused his baby brother in that institution. Worse than that, was that the people who were supposed to care for him, his family, had abandoned and locked him away there.

He stood up, grabbed the bag of prescriptions, marched over to the trash compactor, and shoved them inside.

"No more drugs, Mal. No more doctors or institutions. I promise."

His brother still rocked in place. But the rocking slowed, and Jack was sure he saw a single tear fall from his brother's eye. Jack knew Malcolm didn't like to be touched. He remembered that from the first nine years his brother had lived in the house. But he risked it, anyway. The lightest of touches, feather-light, as he said, "You are home, Mal. Mom and Dad, they're gone. They died in a plane crash three weeks ago. I'm sorry. I just want you to know that we are a family, the three of us. And families stick together. You are home, Mal. And home is where we want you to stay. With us."

The nod his brother gave was small, almost imperceptible. But Jack saw it. Malcolm was home, where he belonged.

A Challenging Alternative

Jack clutched his coffee cup and stared blearily at the stack of papers on his deck. He had tossed and turned last night, struggling to fall asleep. His dreams were at odds with his reality and he couldn't see a way around it. Despite the law degree not being his first choice, he wished he had finished. Just a few more months of work and he could have turned around his grades, finished his studies, even passed the bar. Returning to school was impossible, though. Especially with Allie and Mal to care for. Even with a half dozen staff on hand, his presence was required here. He couldn't go off to Stanford now. Maybe in a few more years, but certainly not now. There was a merger in process and lawyers insisting they needed him on the East Coast, as well as a dozen other pressing issues. He understood now just how much his father had handled in the day-to-day workings of the business. Jack struggled to keep up with it. The paper stacks had changed, shrunk in size, and he felt relief at the sight. Two months in, and Azule was taking on aspects of the business that her mother Nadine never had. Azule's Master's degree in Business Administration likely had something to do with it. With her advice, they had outsourced several tasks better suited to accountants and investment firms.

The daily grind of work that Benton Holdings required was slowly becoming manageable.

Azule bustled through his office door. "Good morning. I've scheduled some phone calls and meetings for you." She set a list of names and phone numbers down on the desk in front of him. Each of them had a time slot listed next to the name, except for one.

"Dean Mahoney?" Jack frowned, staring at the slip of paper.

"The dean there at…"

"My college. Yes, I know."

Azule raised an artfully sculpted eyebrow at him. "Not everyone gets a call from the Dean, you know."

Jack grimaced. He didn't want another one of his father's friends telling him what a great man his father was and how sorely he was missed. It just made him feel worse.

If I hadn't been out partying with Jerry…

"Right."

"I'll need that paperwork by early afternoon," Azule said, gesturing at the stack. "There are a couple of time-sensitive items in there."

Jack nodded, still staring at Dean Mahoney's phone number.

His stomach was growling two hours later, the mound of paperwork completed and two phone calls off the list. Dean Mahoney's name still sat there, waiting.

"You gonna call him, or just sit there staring at his number?" Azule asked bluntly, as she gathered the various piles of papers.

"He went to school with my father. Probably just wants to offer his condolences."

Azule's eyebrows shot up. "So…what, you're not going to call him back? That man is the dean of your college and a friend of Mr. Benton's. That should mean something to you."

Trust Az to give it to me straight. And when she says it like that…

"All right, fine, I'll call him." She gave him a small smile of victory and disappeared out the door.

Dean Mahoney picked up on the second ring. His professional tone turned personal as soon as Jack identified himself.

"Jack, it devastated me to hear about your father and mother. William and I went to school together and Renae was the kindest woman I know."

"Thank you, Dean. I really appreciate you reaching out to me."

"Listen, Son, I didn't want to intrude on you back when the college received your withdrawal. I know you have a lot on your plate. But I wanted to offer you an avenue to complete your studies here."

"Well, I appreciate that Dean, I really do, but I am responsible for my sister and my baby brother now, both still at home, and..."

"You won't need to leave home, Son. It would be remote learning. A pilot program."

Jack was silent. Could he hack it? With everything else happening, could he get his shit together and make it happen? Jack closed his eyes, imagining the look of pride on his father's face when Jack received his acceptance letter from Stanford. It had been years since he'd seen his dad look proud of anything he had done. And now, he would never see it again. A huge part of him wanted to finish what he had started. The study of law had been maddening at first, and yet, fascinating.

"You still there?" the Dean asked.

"Sorry, uh, yes. I..."

"If you need time to think about it..."

"I don't. I would really like that, sir. It would mean the world to me to finish my degree."

He imagined his father's smile as Dean Mahoney said, "Wonderful! I'm so glad we could find a solution that works for your family. I hope to see young Allison here in a few more years."

After a few moments of small talk, the dean told Jack to expect a packet. "It will give you all the details you need." Jack thanked him again, his mind reeling. He would get to finish his education. A second chance to make his father proud.

Weeks later, at breakfast, Jack barely noticed the food in front of him. He buried his nose in a textbook, his highlighter held at the ready.

"Jack, it's Saturday."

"Yeah, but I've got a big test on Monday."

"You're different, you know."

Jack looked up, frowning. His sister was smiling.

"Not in a bad way," Allie said. "More focused." She shrugged, "Grown up."

"I'm 24, I've been an adult for six years, Sis."

"You know what I mean. You aren't off partying all the time," Allie said, her hands busy peeling an apple, which she then placed on Malcolm's plate. "If you count up the hours spent doing that, and especially the time recovering from it, you can see how much of a difference it is."

She wasn't wrong. As it was, he was on track to take the bar exam in six more months at this rate. He didn't see himself building a law practice of his own. But he could see that it was something that would move him forward with building his own legacy in the Benton clan's fortune.

"Mom and Dad would be proud of you, Jack." Allie added softly.

Learning to Speak

The next morning, Jack found himself in the kitchen alone. Allie had been up late, talking with friends on her computer. As he opened the refrigerator door, something caught his eye. The word magnets his mother had covered the front of the refrigerator with had shifted.

Renae Benton had majored in literature in college, not long before a young, good-looking William Benton had swept her off her feet. Heir to a modest fortune, Jack's father had multiplied the fortune by a factor of ten by his second year post-college. And Renae had settled into being a wife and mother, and set aside her dreams of authorship. She had, however, found great joy in the magnetic words, leaving brief messages for Jack and Allison over the years, or composing quirky poems. They had left her last poem untouched, a reminder of happier times. Today, however, that had all changed.

Jack stared at the front of the refrigerator. The words, all of them, were now arranged alphabetically. They sat in perfectly aligned rows, with breaks between the starting letters. All words beginning with a, then b, and so on, aligned together for ease of access.

He suppressed a flash of annoyance at Allie's handiwork. The poem their mother composed was funny, and rather silly, but now it was gone. The last bit of Renae gone from the house except for the untouched master suite, where their parents' personal effects remained. Seeing the magnets rearranged reminded him he would have to take on the job of clearing their room at some point. He wasn't looking forward to it.

Three magnetic words stood separate from the alphabetized packs. A phrase of sorts.

more avocado please

He shook his head. Allie could have just added it to the grocery list, or gone online directly to order it for delivery.

Whatever. I'll add it to the shopping list.

He added the avocados to the grocery list, moved the magnetic letters back in place, and turned his attention to other things.

A day later, another note.

more avocado please

love chocolate need raisins

More? Christ, there were three avocados in the grocery delivery yesterday!

He added it to the list along with chocolate and raisins.

Raisins, huh? I thought Allie hated raisins.

By the time he emerged from the online test and a small mountain of paperwork the next day, the sun had slipped behind the mountains. Allison was digging around in the pantry.

"What the... ew!" She emerged holding a container of raisins. "Why did you order these, Jack? Raisins are so gross. It's bad enough you bought all that chocolate. I mean, seriously, I'm trying to get back into running and those things sitting there tempting me are *not* helping. And oh my god, how in the world are you eating so many avocados? I mean, seriously, do you know how much fat are in those things?"

"What are you talking about?" Jack asked. A knock sounded at the door and Jack could see through the glass that it was Azule. He waved her in.

"What, are you a closeted avocado eater, or something?" Allie asked, smirking, "I mean, I get it. I think you have eaten at least two pounds of fat in the past three days because those were monster-sized avocados they delivered. I'm just saying that, if you keep it up, you are going to need a larger size of clothes."

"I didn't eat any avocados!" Jack said, frowning at his sister.

"You missed these." Azule handed him a pen. "Two of them are contract renewals that expire at midnight. Sign all the marked pages, please."

Jack sighed and slumped into a chair at the table. Mal was quiet, as usual, in his corner spot at the far end, his chair pulled away from everyone to avoid any accidental touch. He had an empty plate in front of him, his gaze fixed on something out of sight on the table. Azule placed the stack of contracts down in front of Jack, folded her arms, and tapped her foot.

"Sign away, fearless leader. I'm already on overtime and I got a date tonight." Azule pointed at the documents and fluttered her long fingers.

"Yes, you did," Allie grouched at him. "You had to have eaten them. Who else could it be?"

Jack signed the first set of documents. He'd had a shit day. Cramming a major test into an already full Monday morning was not his idea of fun.

"Allison Renae Madrigal Benton, I did *not* eat those avocados!" He roared, causing Allie and Malcolm to both flinch. Even Azule, normally unruffled by anything he said or did, took a step back.

Malcolm pushed the plate away from him and Jack realized that the dark green plate *actually* had something on it. A pile of peeled avocado skins heaped on top of three large avocado seeds. Beside it, a small pile of the magnetic words from the fridge. Malcolm slid one word out, and Azule, who was closest, tilted her head to read it. She let out a bark of laughter, which caused Mal to flinch again.

"What does it say?" Allie asked, walking over to stare at the word. "It says... 'me.'" She blinked in confusion and stared at Mal. Their brother was staring at a space and point well beyond the others in the room. His eyes slid away anytime Jack or any of the others tried to make direct eye contact.

"Wait, Mal, *you* like avocado?"

The smallest nod came from Malcolm. Nearly imperceptible. Blink and you would miss it.

Azule let out a hoot of laughter. "And your father didn't even think you could read. Well, you showed him, didn't you, you brilliant boy!" She turned to Jack, "Where's your laptop?"

"By the door. What do you need it for?"

Azule gave him a pitying look and shook her head. "You white people take longer to process things, don't you? I'm going to get on Amazon and find every damned box of magnetic letters and words I can!"

By the end of the week, Azule presented Malcolm with a thick binder brimming with magnetic words and magnetic metal sheets to arrange them on. She grinned as he moved the pieces about, placing them alphabetically, just as he had the magnets on the refrigerator.

"Which ones did you order?" Allison asked Azule, a bemused look on her face as she watched her brother.

"All of them." Azule answered, a satisfied smile on her face. Mal's fingers flew back and forth, sorting, setting up individual letters and words.

Allison grinned over at Jack, who was fixing omelets. "Add avocado to Mal's."

Jack nodded, already cutting into a fat avocado with pebbled green, black skin.

Mal tapped a finger, looked up at Azule, his serious brown eyes meeting hers for a mere half-second. He looked down at his finger and tapped again. Azule leaned in and smiled broadly at the letters arranged on the metal plate.

thank you A Z

"You are more than welcome, Malcolm." She whispered. She wiped at her eyes. "My mama was so thrilled to hear you were back at home where you belonged." She waved a hand in Jack's direction. "Got enough for me to have one of those?"

Jack nodded and got to work making an omelet for Az. For the first time in a long time, things felt as if they were on the way up. Each morning, he found a reason to smile just by seeing Allison and Mal.

Jack couldn't help wondering how long his brother had been waiting to talk, to communicate. Mal certainly had it now. He had finally learned to speak. Their parents were gone, but had his siblings, and they had him. And for now? That was enough.

Author's Note

Thank you so much for reading this omnibus. I hope you enjoyed it and would like to read more! I have at least a dozen books planned for the Benton Security Services series. As I complete them, I will pack three at a time into an omnibus like this, along with at least two short stories.

That said, it might be a while until I have the next book in the Benton Security Services series ready. I am a cross-genre author, and my near future projects include sci-fi, non-fiction, and a new thriller book. Please visit my website, poke around, who knows what you might find! Here is the link: https://www.christineshuck.com/

I play around with some experimental journal format fiction, and you can find the Book of Z, my blog, and so much more there on my author website. I hope to see you there!

About the Author

FUELED BY HOMEMADE coffee ice cream, a lifelong love of words, and armed with strong female (and male) characters I cross genres like the Ghostbusters crossed the streams in pursuit of the question.

"What is the question?" you ask.

The question is simple. It asks, "What would you do, if..."

What would you do if you were fifteen years old and the world as you knew it fell apart? Would you run? Would you fight? Would you survive? – Meet Jess and her brother Chris in War's End[1].

What would you do if you had a chance to live your life over? Not just once, but twice? – Meet Dean Edmonds in Fate's Highway[2].

What would you do if everyone you loved was lost to a terrible virus and you faced the real possibility of the extinction of the human race in the dark void of space? – Meet Daniel Medry in G581: The Departure[3]

What would you do if hitmen were after you and you had no idea why? – Meet Lila and Shane in Hired Gun[4]

If I don't keep you turning pages late into the night, desperate to know what happens next, then I have failed at my job. I'm a Taurus and born in Missouri. That makes me bull-headed and stubborn to boot. I don't believe in failure or mistakes, only learning opportunities and clever conversation. There's not much I won't do to make you burn the

---

1.   https://books2read.com/u/bwYNpY

2.   https://books2read.com/u/bPJG5Y

3.   https://books2read.com/u/4jDgPl

4.   https://books2read.com/u/bP0dOj

midnight oil reading my words while you suffer sleep-deprivation the following day. It's my secret superpower.

Born in flyover country, I've also lived in Arizona and northern California. I am an eclectic mix of snark and oddball humor. My colorful metaphors would make a fishwife blush. I'm an incompetent gardener, a dreamer and doer, in love with old houses and shooting pool, and chief organizer of all thing's household and financial. Feed me tiramisu and I'm yours forever.

Follow me, find my books, and more by going to: https://linktr.ee/ christinedshuck

Don't miss out!

Visit the website below and you can sign up to receive emails whenever Christine D. Shuck publishes a new book. There's no charge and no obligation.

https://books2read.com/r/B-A-BOLF-EGOOC

BOOKS 2 READ

Connecting independent readers to independent writers.

Also by Christine D. Shuck

Benton Security Services
Hired Gun
Smoke and Steel
Broken Code
Benton Security Services Omnibus #1 - Books 1-3

Chronicles of Liv Rowan
Fate's Highway

Gliese 581g
G581: The Departure
G581: Mars
G581: Earth
G581 Plague Tales
G581: Zarmina's World

War's End
War's End: The Storm
War's End: A Brave New World
Tales of the Collapse
War's End Omnibus - Books 1-3

Watch for more at christineshuck.com.